CORINNE,

MADAME DE STAËL was born in Paris on 22 April 1766 as Anne-Louise-Germaine Necker, the daughter of Jacques Necker, who later became Louis XIV's finance minister. In 1786 she married Baron Eric de Staël-Holstein, the Swedish ambassador to France. Showing literary ability from an early age, she achieved fame both as a creative writer of fiction and drama and as an acute contributor to political, social, and literary thought. She was eminent as a theorist of Romanticism and also, surprisingly for a woman, as a political opponent of Napoleon, who exiled her, first from Paris and then from the whole of France. Induced by this to travel abroad, she visited Germany and Italy, and then wrote two major works, *Corinne, ou l'Italie* and *De l'Allemagne*. In her role as a political propagandist she collaborated with Benjamin Constant, her lover over a long period. She was a champion of women's rights, deploring 'domestic slavery' and showing in her own life that women could excel no less than men. This is one theme of *Corinne*, another being the clash of different cultures, a feature of her sociological thought. Her marriage to Baron de Staël was ended by separation in 1800 and he died two years later. In 1811 she began a quasi-marital association with John Rocca, a former army officer, twenty years her junior. They shared a thoroughly happy life and were formally married in 1816. Madame de Staël died in Paris on 14 July 1817.

SYLVIA RAPHAEL taught French language and literature at the universities of Glasgow and London, specializing in nineteenth-century literature. Her translations include a selection of Balzac's short stories and his *Eugénie Grandet* and *La Cousine Bette*, and also George Sand's *Indiana* and *Mauprat*. Sylvia Raphael died in 1996.

JOHN CLAIBORNE ISBELL is Assistant Professor of French at Indiana University. His publications include two critical editions of works by Madame de Staël.

OXFORD WORLD'S CLASSICS

*For over 100 years Oxford World's Classics have brought
readers closer to the world's great literature. Now with over 700
titles—from the 4,000-year-old myths of Mesopotamia to the
twentieth century's greatest novels—the series makes available
lesser-known as well as celebrated writing.*

*The pocket-sized hardbacks of the early years contained
introductions by Virginia Woolf, T. S. Eliot, Graham Greene,
and other literary figures which enriched the experience of reading.
Today the series is recognized for its fine scholarship and
reliability in texts that span world literature, drama and poetry,
religion, philosophy and politics. Each edition includes perceptive
commentary and essential background information to meet the
changing needs of readers.*

OXFORD WORLD'S CLASSICS

MADAME DE STAËL

Corinne, or Italy

Translated and Edited by
SYLVIA RAPHAEL

Introduction by
JOHN ISBELL

OXFORD
UNIVERSITY PRESS

OXFORD

UNIVERSITY PRESS

Great Clarendon Street, Oxford OX2 6DP

Oxford University Press is a department of the University of Oxford.
It furthers the University's objective of excellence in research, scholarship,
and education by publishing worldwide in

Oxford New York

Auckland Bangkok Buenos Aires Cape Town Chennai
Dar es Salaam Delhi Hong Kong Istanbul Karachi Kolkata
Kuala Lumpur Madrid Melbourne Mexico City Mumbai Nairobi
São Paulo Shanghai Taipei Tokyo Toronto

Oxford is a registered trade mark of Oxford University Press
in the UK and in certain other countries

Published in the United States
by Oxford University Press Inc., New York

Translation and Notes © The Executor of Sylvia Raphael 1998
Introduction and Bibliography © John Claiborne Isbell

The moral rights of the author have been asserted

Database right Oxford University Press (maker)

First published as an Oxford World's Classics paperback 1998
Reissued 2008

British Library Cataloguing in Publication Data

Data available

Library of Congress Cataloging in Publication Data

Staël, Madame de (Anne-Louise-Germaine), 1766–1817.
[Corinne. English]
Corinne, or Italy / Madame de Staël; translated by Sylvia
Raphael; introduction by John Isbell.
(Oxford world's classics)
Includes bibliographical references.
I. Raphael, Sylvia. II. Title. III. Series. IV. Series: Oxford
world's classics (Oxford University Press).
PQ2431.C7E5 1998 843'.6—dc21 98–10540

ISBN 978-0-19-955460-7

10

Printed and bound in Great Britain by Clays Ltd, Elcograf S.p.A.

CONTENTS

INTRODUCTION

GERMAINE DE STAËL, French Revolutionary activist and theorist of European Romanticism, was a thinker of unusual breadth and impact, living at a pivotal moment in world history. In women's history, her place may be unique. Four living authors were read throughout Romantic Europe: Staël, Scott, Byron, and Goethe. Staël also exercised a concrete political power of which Europe's other Romantics, except perhaps Chateaubriand, could only dream. Staël was born in 1766; in 1786, she married the Swedish ambassador and began her political activity, but she was already famous as the daughter of Louis XVI's chief minister Necker, hero of 1789. She influenced France throughout the Revolution, from 1788 to 1802, and Europe from 1812 to her death in 1817.[1] Her *Lettres sur Rousseau* in 1788 condemn women's 'domestic slavery'; in 1791, she co-wrote the report on women's education that made Mary Wollstonecraft dedicate *The Rights of Women* to Talleyrand.[2] Staël's first novel *Delphine* (1802), dedicated to 'silent France', brought on her ten years' exile by Bonaparte in 1803, splitting her political career but opening her to the world. Fleeing to Germany, she met Goethe, Schiller, and the Schlegels; she also met the leading men of Europe, from Wellington to Metternich and Tsar Alexander, even seeing Moscow a month before Napoleon saw it burn. Napoleon once blamed the Revolution on Staël's father; his Minister of Police blamed Napoleon's downfall in 1814 on Staël herself, as she linked Russia, Sweden, and England and pushed Bernadotte's candidature to the French throne. From 1788 to 1817, her long, lonely fight for freedom from exile is all the more amazing given her sex.

Corinne, or Italy: *composition and publication*

While in Weimar in 1803, Staël saw an opera based on La Motte-Fouqué's *Die Saalnixe* (*The Saal River Nymph*), which also inspired

---

[1] Simone Balayé, *Madame de Staël: Lumières et liberté* (Paris: Klincksieck, 1979), 62–91, 217–40, and John Isbell, 'Madame de Staël, Ministre de la Guerre? Les Discours de Narbonne devant l'Assemblée législative', *Annales historiques de la Révolution française* (1997/1), 93–104.

[2] *Madame de Staël: Écrits retrouvés*, ed. J. Isbell and S. Balayé, *Cahiers staëliens*, 46 (1994–5), 12–17.

Hans Christian Andersen's *The Little Mermaid*. Staël's journal and letters note the inspiration she found here for *Corinne*, and the opera's knight and river nymph leave traces in her realist novel of a second, magical story, a subtext which we could call *Romance d'Oswald le preux et de la fée Corinne* (*The Romance of Bold Oswald and the Fairy Corinne*).[3] Many Romantic texts exist in two versions, real and magical, which happen to fill the same pages; and much of this novel's love story is best understood in those terms. Staël then returned to Coppet on Lake Geneva, and found her father dead. Grief-stricken, she wrote a homage to him, and left for Italy in December 1804. At the Palazzo Borghese, her Roman journal notes 'a sibyl by Domenichino of the greatest beauty, her hair in a turban, her red mantle': a visual stimulus to anchor her new plot. She returned in June 1805, the year of Austerlitz and Trafalgar, to begin *Corinne or Italy*.[4]

In November 1806, hard at work on his own *Histoire des républiques italiennes*, Sismondi told Staël how good she was 'to admit me to the small council which will deliberate on the proofs'. Benjamin Constant, her partner for seventeen years, had just begun his masterpiece *Adolphe*, about a man too weak to leave the woman he has stopped loving, and their two great novels are certainly linked. We have 3,500 pages of Staël's three manuscripts, a refutation to those who believe she did not revise; the three sets of proofs she then requested are lost. Staël's publisher Nicolle paid 7,200 francs for her text, a sum that reflects her fame: he probably began typesetting as she revised the last manuscript, and *Corinne or Italy* came out on 1 May 1807, after her friend Bonstetten's *Voyage dans le Latium*.[5]

The twenty-part novel is set in Italy and Britain, 1794–1803, with a brief remembered liaison in Revolutionary France which echoes Laclos and oddly presages Wordsworth's *The Prelude*. Oswald, Lord Nelvil, comes to Rome from Scotland in 1794, after his father's death during Oswald's absence in France. Here, he meets Corinne, a raven-haired poetess of genius and beauty: the Roman people are crowning her at the Capitol, as they crowned Petrarch. Despite falling under

---

[3] Simone Balayé, *Les Carnets de voyage de Madame de Staël: Contribution à la genèse de ses œuvres* (Geneva: Droz, 1971), 97–8, with a letter to Hochet: 'I saw the other day a German play which gave me the idea of a novel I think charming.'

[4] Balayé, *Carnets*, 184.

[5] Staël, *Corinne ou l'Italie*, ed. S. Balayé (Paris: Folio, 1985), 603. See Georges Poulet, '*Corinne* et *Adolphe*: Deux romans conjugués', *RHLF* (July–Aug. 1978), 580–96.

her spell, Oswald hesitates, given Corinne's magical air and mysterious past, and the thought of his blonde bride-to-be Lucile in England. Corinne reveals, after much delay, the secret that she is herself half-English, and Lucile's half-sister: she left England, where she cannot breathe, after her own father's death, reinventing herself without any man's patronymic. Oswald returns to Scotland to prepare their marriage, succumbs to convention, and marries Lucile instead. He returns, after four years in the Indies, to an Italy now veiled itself by memory and loss, with his bride and their raven-haired daughter Juliet; he and Lucile drift increasingly apart; Corinne dies of grief, and Oswald survives to remember, alone and palely loitering like the hero in Keats's 'Belle Dame sans Merci'.

Bizarrely, Staël thought *Corinne or Italy* might get her back to Imperial Paris: she is indeed a master of the Enlightenment game of discreet allusion, but her politics is there for any alert ear, as she looks at Napoleon's conquered Europe and calls for its revolt. The text praises England, keeps a series of parallels to Nelson and Lady Hamilton in Oswald's and Corinne's story, and stresses troublesome details like the death of the Venetian Republic, handed by Napoleon to Austria in 1797.[6] Staël mentally restores to their original owners all the Italian paintings she herself saw in the Louvre, where Napoleon had collected them. She also told Sismondi that she consciously avoided 'any action, any word which might be a homage to power': her novel does not mention the French 'liberation' of Italy after 1796, in which Napoleon took particular pride.[7] The Emperor's shackled press was milder than it had been for *Delphine*, but he renewed her order of exile, and Constant was outraged enough by press reviews to publish a reply. 'A woman', wrote one critic, 'who distinguishes herself by qualities other than those of her sex contradicts the general order': Staël herself often colluded with such attempts to make of her public discourse a purely domestic debate, favouring a demure

---

[6] Staël, *Corinne ou l'Italie*, 604: *Notice* by Simone Balayé. Corinne and Lady Hamilton share public performance (improvisation and *attitudes*), the tarantella, the Britain/Italy divide, a dark past, the pursuit of the beloved in England, a love for Vesuvius, carping jealousy, abandonment, and death. Horatio Nelson and Oswald Nelvil share Britain, a chest wound (p. 132), people's praise, a military career, and the saving of an Italian port (Naples and Ancona).

[7] Staël, *Corinne ou l'Italie*, 604. Staël suddenly mentions this invasion just as *Corinne* ends: 'But Rome and Florence were already occupied by the French' (p. 369).

Romantic persona which is still visible today.[8] All Staël's works, after all, were weapons; and weapons have no business in the private sphere to which women authors were, in the nineteenth century, so thoroughly restricted. Elsewhere, Staël is more forthright: 'There were two nations out of fashion in Europe, Italy and Germany. I have set out to give them back the reputation of sincerity and wit.'[9] Compare *Blackwood's Edinburgh Magazine*, in December 1818: 'The sciences have always owed their origin to some great spirit. Smith created political economy; Linnaeus, botany; Lavoisier, chemistry; and Madame de Staël has, in like manner, created the art of analysing the spirit of nations and the springs which move them' (278). Staël's new 'science of nations' contributed to her success, as she praised the Italy which Metternich in 1847 would call a geographical concept.

Corinne or Italy saw thirty-two French editions in forty years, 1830–70: it stands among Romanticism's seminal texts, to use that now-antiquated word, a posthumous victory of sorts over Staël's rival and enemy Napoleon. The Bibliothèque nationale in Paris has two *Corinne* drames from the 1830s.[10] Corinne reappears in music from Rossini's *Viaggio a Reims*, which borrows her name, companions, and snatches of the novel's plot, to Bob Dylan's *Corinna Corinna*; in literature, from Balzac's *La Peau de chagrin*, with its 'obscene spectacles [. . .] to delight some Corinne', to an 1895 tale of slavery by the black author Mrs A. E. Johnson, entitled *Clarence and Corinne; or, God's Way*.[11] In art, Delacroix's *La Liberté guidant le peuple* has arguable structural debts to Gérard's *Corinne au Cap Misène*, a painting Stendhal praised in 1824: two mythic images of strong women leaders. *Corinne* prompted odes by Jane Taylor and Felicia Hemans; Hill's 1833 translation, with iambics by Letitia Landon for Corinne's improvisations, saw over twenty-five editions by 1900 with at least fifteen publishers, despite three rival versions.[12] There are traces of *Corinne*

[8] Simone Balayé, *Madame de Staël: Écrire, lutter, vivre* (Geneva: Droz, 1994), 245–78 and 251.

[9] To Gaudot, 20 Dec. 1808, in Mme de Staël, *Correspondance générale*, ed. B. Jasinski (Paris: Pauvert, Hachette, Klincksieck, 1960–), vi. 572.

[10] These *drames* figure in the Bibliothèque nationale's MS and print catalogues; the former's verse *drame* was performed at the Théâtre français, 23 Sept. 1830.

[11] Honoré de Balzac, *La Peau de chagrin* (Paris: Libraires de France, 1956), 30. Mrs A. E. Johnson, *Clarence and Corinne; or, God's Way* (Oxford: Oxford University Press, 1988).

[12] *National Union Catalog*, 'Staël-Holstein, Anne Louise Germaine de'. Jane Taylor, 'To Mad. de Staël', 1822; Felicia Hemans, 'Corinne at the Capitol', 1830. Letitia Landon's works do not reproduce her *Corinne* iambics; compare her 'The Improvisatrice'. *A History*

in *Little Women* and *Jane Eyre*. Clearly *Corinne* offered posterity a powerful symbol of *something*. The novel's sales in the 1830s were also double those of all Staël's other works, as if it gave a window on the rest: curiously, and rather romantically, Staël's recent feminist rediscovery has echoed this anomaly, with a gathering body of excellent work on *Corinne*, and somewhat less on Staël's other works.[13]

Corinne and her country

A century and a half later, one phenomenon stands out in sharp relief when assessing the book's powerful impact on its readers: the heroine's capacity to subsume her semi-eponymous novel. The act of naming illustrates this reduction: myths wear smooth with constant use, and the name Corinne, handy shorthand for 'suffering heroine' in the case of Mrs Johnson's tale of slavery, is simply a pretty name for a daughter in modern France, without reference to Staël. But children and heroines were not christened 'Italy', and we call the text *Corinne* when we discuss it: hence the oddity today of Constant's review of the novel, focused entirely on the figure of Oswald instead. Charlotte Hogsett brilliantly argues that Staël uses Europe's countries as allegorical veils to continue discussing women; whatever Staël's intentions, the story of *Corinne or Italy*'s reception makes that allegorical identification explicit. Staël may indeed have wanted just this triumph; but her triumph has a price. Corinne has led a mythic life independent of her creator and her text, much as Frankenstein's less fortunate creation has taken the doctor's name in popular mythology. This perceived symbiosis of novel and heroine raises four overriding questions: how and why does Staël encourage this symbiosis; what does she gain from it; and what does she lose?

How and why can perhaps be answered together and from a new perspective, with the new social contract running like a red thread

---

of Private Life, iv: *From the Fires of Revolution to the Great War*, ed. M. Perrot, tr. A. Goldhammer (Cambridge: Belknap, 1990), 283 notes a Corinne *tableau vivant* created by Gérard himself at Mme de Duras's salon. Stendhal praises Gérard's new *Corinne* at the Salon of 1824: Stendhal, *Du Romantisme dans les arts* (Paris: Hermann, 1966), 131–4, from the *Journal de Paris*, 9 Sept. 1824.

[13] This recent work is inspired by Simone Balayé and Madelyn Gutwirth in particular. In France, the novel was republished in 1979; a fine hardback translation in 1987, by Avriel Goldberger, reopened *Corinne* to English-speaking readers, and the critics are at work assessing *Corinne*'s impact on British and American literature and art.

through all Staël's works: with it, Staël combines two Protestant traditions in a fruitful synthesis, the philosophers' social contract theory
she found in Rousseau above all, and the bankers' theory of public
credit she found in her father Necker's Revolutionary career. It is
a contract of representation: from the nation's fertile soil arises the
inspired national genius or public hero, who represents the silent
millions by speaking with their voice. Corinne *is* Italy, the genius of
her nation, just as Washington or Bolívar spoke for America, and
Necker, Napoleon, Staël herself for France; hence Staël's dedication
to 'silent France' of her novel *Delphine*. Prescient and incisive, Staël
traces this contract of representation in art, politics, and economics,
at a watershed moment in world history: for the contract shapes our
modern world. It determines the salaries of our superstars; it takes
us to the polling booths; it gives us paper banknotes in return for the
nation's gold. Moreover, with this contract Staël goes two steps beyond
Rousseau: Rousseau's *Du contrat social* in 1762 calls representation a
false idol and demands Spartan direct democracy; thinkers since Staël
and Constant have linked that archaic impossibility to the Terror,
answering it with the simple distinction between positive and negative liberty which Isaiah Berlin still finds central to modern liberalism.[14]
But modern 'negative' liberty from state control, with the separate
spheres of ideology it implies, may suggest domestic slavery to a thinking woman, and Staël pillories it in *Corinne*. In these terms, Staël's
new social contract allows her to move back out from *oikos* to *polis*,
from house to city, without opening the door on Robespierre.[15]

From the yoked title onward—echoing Rousseau's *Émile ou de
l'éducation* or Voltaire's *Candide ou l'optimisme*—*Corinne or Italy* is
arguably Staël's most extended presentation of the symbiosis she seeks
between nation and public genius; the French word *nationalité* first
appears in this text (see p. 256), and we stand here at the birth of
modern nationalism. The Corinne–Italy link, which may seem self-
evident to readers, is in fact food for thought; associating Corinne with
England, for instance, might seem comical, but Corinne is half-English
too, and her Italian mother is unheard, unlike her English father. So

---

[14] Isaiah Berlin, 'Two Concepts of Liberty', in *Four Essays on Liberty* (Oxford: Oxford University Press, 1969), 118–72.

[15] John Isbell, 'Le Contrat social selon Benjamin Constant et Mme de Staël, ou la liberté a-t-elle un sexe?', *Cahiers de l'Association internationale d'études françaises* (May 1996), 439–56.

how does the text establish this link's self-evidence? Six devices stand out, so obvious as to be invisible. First, Corinne has chosen Italy as she never chose England, as Staël and Necker chose France and as a normal citizen cannot: it is Corinne's 'patrie d'élection' or motherland of choice. Second, the text stresses international polyphony, with characters representing Europe's nations and their traits: Erfeuil travels abroad and sees only France, thanks to his cultural 'great wall of China' (p. 119); Oswald and blonde Lucile are British, so darkhaired Corinne cannot be. Third, as the title suggests, Corinne is a *femme-pays*, conquered Italy's spokeswoman and advocate, spending 600 pages speaking for her silent nation as Pushkin or De Gaulle spoke for theirs: 'this beautiful land which nature seems to have adorned like a victim' (p. 54).[16] Fourth, the *populus* surrounds Corinne wherever she appears in public on Italian soil, from her native Rome to then-foreign Naples or Venice where her fame evidently precedes her; in an echo of Shakespeare's *Julius Caesar*, we hear the Roman crowd discussing her bloodless triumph before she even appears on stage. Fifth, the Corinne figure profits from the French Revolution's thorough reworking of an age-old tradition, using embodied women to represent abstract concepts, often grammatically feminine nouns like *la Liberté, la Révolution, la Vertu, la France, la Femme, l'Italie* (*Liberty, the Revolution, Virtue, France, Woman, Italy*). Corinne is all of these in some measure, and there is elegant work on this question; Corinne must die, for instance, because the Revolution and liberty died, in a text haunted by the dead which actually says 'there is no France any longer' (p. 208), just as Napoleon conquered Europe. Sixth, apart from some review of Corinne's public fame or of national heroes like Dante and Alfieri, *Corinne* enacts Staël's new nation–genius symbiosis as a self-evident truth. With that lack of analysis, Corinne's Italian identity is *naturalized* all the more.

How Staël's nation–genius symbiosis works is fairly new ground. Why she encourages this link in 1807 is more familiar: the novel is more than an appeal, it is propaganda, a weapon, directed like all weapons at shaping the future. *Corinne or Italy*'s battles are woven throughout Staël's career: battles with Napoleon above all, for the soul of conquered Italy, of liberty, the Revolution, and France itself—'there

---

[16] Marie-Claire Vallois, *Fictions féminines: Mme de Staël et les voix de la sibylle* (Stanford, Calif.: Anma Libri, 1987), 113, suggests the term *femme-pays*.

is no France any longer'; with Europe's post-Revolutionary dispensation, and its imprisonment of women in the domestic sphere—here curiously linked to England, not France; and with Staël's own private sorrows, from which this novel helps to free her. Such identical battles may encourage us to see Staël's fiction and non-fiction as one continuous text, and it can be liberating to treat her as the last of the *philosophes*, like Rousseau or Voltaire, using an eighteenth-century discourse which makes *Corinne* inexplicable in nineteenth-century discipline and genre terms. Many of *Corinne*'s devices recur throughout Staël's non-fiction, from her early political treatises to *De l'Allemagne* (*On Germany*) and her *Considerations on the French Revolution*, linking Germany and France to heroic figures like Goethe and Necker; and Staël's late non-fiction, with its expanded first-person voice, also brings her suffering heroine through fiction's mirror to draw on her myth's explosive energy, like Byron or Hugo. Are Staël's novels then just her brilliant ersatz for pure politics, her home-built weapon to fight Napoleon whenever her public voice was silenced? Or do Staël's novels and treatises allow her a dual voice, male and female, throughout her whole career, as Hogsett argues? Both these readings may in fact be true, but *Corinne's* specific qualities deserve closer examination.

Corinne or Italy's major contribution to Staël's nation–genius link lies perhaps in its openness to indeterminacy: the self-baptized Corinne is a floating signifier as her author can never be, and as only fiction can allow. Corinne's splendid indeterminacy allows Staël to fight all her different battles at one blow, just as it offered her *readers*, men and women both, a mythic figure they could read as they liked. Leopardi, for instance, and Margaret Fuller, 'the Yankee Corinna', were overwhelmed by two quite different Corinnes, inhabiting the same textual space; and this fact seems crucial in accounting for the novel's impact, as with so much of Staël's work.[17] Meanwhile, other allegorical gains are more precise. Certain tactical aspects of Staël's battles gain from personalizing her nation–genius link: first, Corinne's allegorical suffering both sidesteps Napoleon's political censors and embodies the nation's sorrows, whether Italy or France, while her niece Juliet survives her as a figure of hope and political rebirth; second, Corinne's

[17] Ellen Moers, 'Performing Heroism: The Myth of Corinne', in *Literary Women: The Great Writers* (Garden City, NY: Doubleday, 1976); John Isbell, 'The Italian Romantics and Madame de Staël: Art, Society and Nationhood', *Rivista di letterature moderne e comparate*, forthcoming.

nature lends beauty, dignity, and coherence of purpose to peoples and phenomena that lacked all three qualities in 1807; third, Corinne's very presence creates from Italy's conquered and divided lands the organic totality we associate with nationhood. Moreover, just as Corinne gives Italian lands a unity they conspicuously lacked, so Italy gives Corinne a mythic weight that Staël's earlier heroine Delphine for instance cannot hope to equal.

If these are above all the gains of Corinne as allegory, some gains are more literal. Almost nowhere else in literature before George Sand or George Eliot, and rarely thereafter, could women find a soul-sister with a public voice: by and large, Europe's Romantic heroines are domestic animals. In fact, almost nothing before *Corinne or Italy* had put *any* exceptional creative genius, man or woman, so gloriously centre stage: even Faust is no artist. Ossian and Rousseau hint at it, Byron completes the process; but Byron wrote *Childe Harold* in 1812, five years after *Corinne*. Did Staël then invent the Romantic hero, and do so in the feminine? Consider her superb pages on suffering and mediocrity. As with Byron and a host of imitators, Staël's fame lends credit for her readers to her heroine's prophetic genius, and the prestige of author and heroine are mutually reinforced. Staël's conscious elaboration of this personal myth, of her own star status, is a fascinating subject: strangers, friends, and Staël herself routinely called the author Corinne after 1807. Reusing that mythic status, in *Dix années d'exil* (*Ten Years' Exile*) and the *Considérations* for instance, Staël can then postulate herself and the usurper Napoleon as siblings, two rival voices for Revolutionary Europe struggling over its soul. Mme de Chastenay notes the saying in 1814 that there were three powers in Europe: England, Russia, and Mme de Staël.[10] Victor Hugo and others borrow this claim that their exiled artist's voice speaks for their silenced nation: *Wo ich bin ist die deutsche Kultur*, 'Where I am is German culture', announces Thomas Mann from exile.

Upon reflection, the gains of myth in art seem likely to outweigh its losses; but losses there are, and the two may be inseparable. Indeterminacy, to begin with: it is curious that the Romantic myth of Napoleon, launched in St Helena, shows clear affinities to *Corinne*'s myth of suffering genius, which nations who had read *Corinne* first

---

[18] In John Isbell, *The Birth of European Romanticism: Truth and Propaganda in Staël's De l'Allemagne* (Cambridge: Cambridge University Press, 1994), 100.

could then recover all the more easily, in a posthumous alliance that neither Staël nor Napoleon can prevent. Equally oddly, two other losses caused by Staël's nation–genius link in *Corinne* serve instead to reduce or eliminate the novel's polyphony for its readers: making Corinne herself less complex as a character, and deleting what stands around her in the text. The price is very high, for here lies the kernel of two centuries of *légende noire*, alleging that *Corinne* is univocal, and naïvely self-indulgent, women's work. Staël's aesthetic distance from her creation thus disappears.

Corinne as character

Let us begin with Corinne, who is rather more ambiguous, from her English father onward, than tradition suggests. The attributes of this 'most charming of foreign women' (p. 34) include a dark past, exotic present, and knowledge of art, history, and three languages at 26: if she is a magical being, is she muse, fairy bride, or succubus? Lucile must guess Oswald's thoughts, while Corinne knows them. In an endnote, Staël mentions Corinna, the poetess and muse who inspired Pindar, father of poetry; but Oswald is no Pindar.[19] Moreover, just as *Delphine* revisits an authorial self who died around 1794, so Corinne, if we listen carefully, shows more naive passion than her author and narrator, and though her myth may embody virtue, she is in fact guilty of several things. Echoing *Pamela*'s suspense erotics, and all Staël's heroines from the early Pauline to her own evil double Mme d'Arbigny, Corinne keeps Oswald by hiding her guilty past; she also misunderstands him, manipulates him through sacrifices, and talks of wanting marriage after having rejected it, as her author did with Constant; finally, after his marriage to her mute blonde sister Lucile, Corinne arranges a quasi-vampiric conclusion, secretly educating her raven-haired niece as her own *illegitimate* daughter, and asking—*only*, as she puts it—that Oswald should never feel emotion without thinking of Corinne beyond the grave: this is Poe's Ligeia in embryo,

---

[19] Compare Thomas Campion, 'When to her lute Corinna sings'; Vallois, *Fictions féminines*; Joan DeJean, *Fictions of Sapho, 1546–1937* (Chicago: University of Chicago Press, 1989); and Guibert, 'Zulmé: Morceau traduit du grec', ed. J. Isbell, *Cahiers staëliens*, 47 (1996), 1–15. The *Chansonnier des Grâces* of 1806 has a Euterpe which resembles Gérard's *Corinne*; and *Corinne*'s manuscripts contain Staël's verse translation of Dryden's *Alexander's Feast* (*Cahiers staëliens*, 46 (1995), 37–40).

where the dark-haired first wife returns from the dead to possess the narrator's new blonde bride.

Noting the bright spotlight Staël turns on Corinne and Oswald's demure public hideouts, or the word *jealous*, invisible for Corinne while much-repeated for Lucile, we might argue that Staël the author thus obeyed psychic pressures beyond her control. That *ad feminam* argument is routine; yet with a male author, one would begin by reading ambiguity as the product of art, and proof of that aesthetic distance between author and heroine which Staël has been called incapable of.[20] In these terms, we might observe that Staël bracketed *Corinne or Italy*'s publication in April 1807 with a two-part review, in the journal *Le Publiciste*, of her friend Bonstetten's epistemological analysis of the new Romantic imagination she embodied in *Corinne* as fiction: a critical discourse thus frames Staël's heroine.[21] Feminist jokes mark both this new aesthetic distance, and Staël's own growing strength of vision: back in 1802, other people's gossip and the heroine's irrevocable monastic vows caused *Delphine*'s catastrophe, and Staël now ironizes both devices in order to stress Corinne as a free agent. Corinne pointedly invites people she likes to come up and see her, over Oswald's priggish objections, and enters a Roman convent for a one-week visit, then walks back out a free woman into the streets of Rome.

The character Corinne tends also to subsume her surroundings. Even our routine deletion of half the title can only encourage claims like Starobinski's, hiding the fact that a generation used the novel as a guidebook, and the harmonic counterpoint between plot and description which Staël works hard to establish and which Balayé has retraced.[22] Corinne gazes, silent, into a moonlit Roman fountain, and Oswald's reflection appears; Lucile asks Oswald which he prefers, Domenichino's sibyl or Correggio's madonna (p. 386); Oswald's northern castle-prison mirrors his mind as Corinne's airy Roman studio

---

[20] Jean Starobinski, 'Suicide et mélancolie chez Mme de Staël', in *Madame de Staël et l'Europe* (Paris: Klincksieck, 1971), 242–52. This article had two elegant replies: Madelyn Gutwirth, *Madame de Staël, Novelist: The Emergence of the Artist as Woman* (Urbana: University of Illinois Press, 1978), 265, and Margaret Higonnet, 'Suicide as Self-Construction', in M. Gutwirth, A. Goldberger, and K. Szmurlo (eds.), *Germaine de Staël: Crossing the Borders* (New Brunswick, NJ: Rutgers University Press, 1991), 69–81.

[21] *Cahiers staëliens*, 46 (1995), 42–8: 'Bonstetten, *Recherches sur la Nature & les loix de l'Imagination.*'

[22] Balayé, *Écrire, lutter, vivre*, 91–136. A century later, *Corinne ou l'Italie* was still filed as a travel book in the Bibliothèque nationale: see Balayé, *Carnets*, 16 n. 8.

mirrors hers: throughout the novel, art and nature not only have meaning, they echo the life of the soul. Corinne's Italy is both real and a
hermetic space, from the opening scenes, where the ocean reflects the
sky, to Vesuvius where earth, fire, and air are in elemental dialogue,
retracing 'nature's universal harmony' (p. 146). These correspondences
—'The sounds imitate colours, the colours merge into harmony' (p. 29)
—fuse Saint-Martin and the German Romantics: Staël borrows from
Lessing's *Laokoön* and *How the Ancients Portrayed Death*, from Goethe,
Kant, and Schelling on architecture as frozen music (pp. 181, 59); her
endnotes quote Goethe in German, Humboldt, Winckelmann, and both
Schlegels. Antiquity too is almost as present as the Renaissance, in
this land of ruins: Staël quotes Propertius, Tibullus, and Pliny in Latin,
while two recognition scenes with Lucile, a sister at her father's tomb,
pay homage to Euripides. This rich texture marks a radical break with
two dominant novelistic traditions of the age, the short *récit* and the
epistolary novel, neither of which much stresses local colour or the
picturesque. *Corinne*'s bulk may even have helped to make Walter Scott
or Victor Hugo possible; certainly the book cries out to be put on film.

   Staël's author's endnotes offer some insight into this complexity.
German and Latin authors join Monti, Verri, Pindemonte, and
Alfieri, Staël's father Necker, her friends Talma, Sismondi, Mme
Récamier, and the Dane Friederike Brun; she cites the Romantic, or
neoclassical, painters David, Gérard, Guérin, Drouet, Rehberg, and
Wallis, from France, Germany, and England; she adds anecdotes about
Ancona, a child she met in Rome, or the Castel Sant'Angelo, sketch-
ing out her own Italian journey. Staël footnoted throughout her career,
allowing her an authorial voice reminiscent of Balzac's; but the effect
within a novel like *Corinne* is curious. First, it establishes Staël's first-
name familiarity with the great names of Europe: her national discourse is anchored in a circle of friends and a concert of nations.
Second, it outlines a striking, female authorial persona, stressing Staël's
learning and humour while further melting her into Corinne. Third,
like most framing devices, it opens a maze of arguments about nar-
rative realism: do Staël's endnote realia make Corinne's parallel universe more, or less real? Unusual for Staël's prose works in having
no preface, *Corinne* also has perhaps her only appendix, subtly shifting the erotics of the text and its harsh ending.

   Like the text's endnotes and its neglected German Romantic discourse, so the figure of Oswald illustrates our reliance on Corinne:

Benjamin Constant's focus on Oswald has a certain logic to it, when he reviews this novel which opens and closes with Oswald, not with Corinne as we might believe; and when his focus on Oswald surprises us, our surprise itself deserves a closer look. There is in fact strong evidence that this novel's shifting viewpoint stands closer to Oswald than to his female companion: we *hear* Corinne, while we share Oswald's mental reactions, and one reason Corinne seems so physically present is that we are looking at her, through his eyes. If this is so, then the force of Staël's new symbiosis was powerful enough to bury those markers for two centuries of readers; this despite Oswald's wound, echo of Tristan, his trial by fire at Ancona, and his other knightly attributes. We have, in a sense, a male Romantic *récit* in the *René-Adolphe* tradition, complete with a weak male narrator and dying heroine, but exploded from within by the heroine's vitality.[23]

In fact, Oswald speaks directly for a whole book of the novel; but our *ad hoc* reader's focus on the mythic figure of Corinne can leave a taste of monologue, which raises some delicate and intriguing questions: if Corinne is univocally the voice of her nation, then where are Montesquieu's checks and balances, and what becomes of the opposition? How is Staël's political stand then different from Robespierre's or Stalin's? Three answers occur. First, the sibyl's splendour lies in her alert receptivity to voices other than her own; and in Corinne's triumph at the Capitol, she is carried by others' hands. Second, Staël praises legislators and executors who abdicate after acting: Solon in Athens, Rousseau in Poland, Necker or George Washington.[24] Third, *Corinne*'s actual text is built around dialogue and polyphony—Oswald and Corinne, two Staël avatars, check and balance each other—and the *Considérations* in particular insist that nations need an opposition party. And yet, *Corinne*'s mythic symbiosis retains a life of its own. Nationalism was indeed born in hope of a new dawn for the oppressed, but the same is true of Victor Frankenstein's sad creation; time and again, the world's revolutionary nationalists, from Robespierre and Bolívar onward, have spoken for the people while in opposition, then arrived at power believing that this voice brooks no dissent.

---

[23] Compare Margaret Waller, *The Male Malady: Fictions of Impotence in the Male Romantic Novel* (New Brunswick, NJ: Rutgers University Press, 1993).

[24] I owe these two insights to Madelyn Gutwirth and Susan Tenenbaum respectively.

It seems, in short, that Staël saw a Faustian bargain in *Corinne or Italy*, took it, and paid the price; her triumphs and failures here thus stand or fall together. What Staël gained was mythic power; what she lost was the ability to control its fate. *Corinne*'s political impact in Europe and America, standing as it does at the birth of modern nationalism, is both real and unquantifiable—witness the word *nationalité*, part of the larger impact of Staël's ideas on national genius, reflected in *Blackwood*'s praise of her in 1818 as the creator of the science of nations. The novel's aesthetic impact on a century of readers, from Leopardi to Mrs A. E. Johnson, is both fascinating *per se* and somewhat easier to assess, an invitation to future study already made in 1825 by Stendhal, in a neglected remark from *Racine et Shakespeare*: 'I really see only *Corinne* which has acquired an imperishable glory without modelling itself on the ancients.'[25]

[25] Stendhal, *Racine et Shakespeare*, ed. Pierre Martino, 2 vols. (Paris: Champion, 1925), i. 74.

NOTE ON THE TEXT

A HISTORY of the text of *Corinne* is given in the scholarly edition of the work by Simone Balayé (Paris: Gallimard, 1985). *Corinne* was first published in Paris by H. Nicolle in May 1807 in 8vo format and was reprinted very soon afterwards in 12mo. The publisher considered the reprint as a second edition, although it is not expressly announced as such. Nicolle published a third edition, 'revised and corrected', in the same year, containing a number of corrections made by the author. He published a fourth edition in 1809, differing from the third only in the amendment of some 'accidentals' (specifically, punctuation and misprints). This implies that the changes were probably due to the printer, not the author. A fifth edition of 1812 and a sixth of 1817 each contains a few corrections with no indication of their source. The version of *Corinne* included in the *Œuvres complètes* of 1820, supervised by Madame de Staël's son Auguste, contains about 150 further corrections. It is not known whether he introduced them on his own initiative or was perhaps using notes left by his mother. Simone Balayé observes that he was ready to make extensive corrections of the works published posthumously, so that he might have felt free also, though to a lesser degree, to alter the works published in his mother's lifetime. Simone Balayé also observes that Madame de Staël tended not to bother about altering the text of her published works unless she had to. Madame Balayé accordingly decided to take the third edition as the most authentic text, since the corrections made in it are known to have been requested by Madame de Staël herself. For the present translation, Sylvia Raphael followed the expert judgement of Simone Balayé and used her reproduction of the third edition text.

Sylvia Raphael (my wife) completed the translation shortly before her unexpected death in October 1996. She had also made a start on the explanatory notes, having compiled a small number of them. I have written all the rest of the explanatory notes, translated the author's endnotes, and compiled the chronology. I have also made some adjustments to the translation of the text.

The author's notes are of two kinds. First there are brief footnotes on the pages of the text itself; they are indicated in the French edition by asterisks, but in this translation by daggers because asterisks are used, in the Oxford World's Classics series, to signal explanatory notes. The second kind of author's notes are endnotes, generally much longer than the footnotes; they are indicated, both in the French edition and in this translation, by arabic numerals.

D. D. Raphael

SELECT BIBLIOGRAPHY

General works on Staël

The most complete bibliography of Staël's works is F.-C. Lonchamp, *L'Œuvre imprimé de Madame Germaine de Staël* (Geneva: Cailler, 1949). See also the *Cahiers staëliens*, notably no. 46 (1995), *Madame de Staël: Écrits retrouvés*, with new Staël texts and a review of criticism; also Karyna Szmurlo, 'Madame de Staël', in David Baguley (ed.), *A Critical Bibliography of French Literature*, v. i: *The Nineteenth Century* (Syracuse, NY: Syracuse University Press, 1994), 51–69, strong on anglophone research, and the published acts of the six *Colloques de Coppet*. Add M. Gutwirth, A. Goldberger, and K. Szmurlo (eds.), *Germaine de Staël: Crossing the Borders* (New Brunswick, NJ: Rutgers University Press, 1991), two Italian colloquia, 1967–86, special issues of *RHLF* (1966) and *Europe* (1987), and the Bibliothèque nationale exhibition catalogue (1966). Pierre Kohler, *Madame de Staël et la Suisse* (Lausanne: Payot, 1916), and the Comtesse de Pange, *Mme de Staël et Auguste-Guillaume Schlegel* (Paris: Albert, 1938), are precious; as are Simone Balayé's *Madame de Staël: Lumières et liberté* (Paris: Klincksieck, 1979) and *Madame de Staël: Écrire, lutter, vivre* (Geneva: Droz, 1994). In English, see Madelyn Gutwirth, *Madame de Staël, Novelist: The Emergence of the Artist as Woman* (Urbana: University of Illinois Press, 1978), J. Christopher Herold, *Mistress to an Age: A Life of Madame de Staël* (New York: Bobbs-Merrill, 1958), and Charlotte Hogsett, *The Noise of Words and the Voice of Conscience: Germaine de Staël's Literary Existence* (Carbondale: Southern Illinois University Press, 1987). A monograph bibliography of criticism is now published: Pierre Dubé (ed.), *Bibliographie de la critique sur Madame de Staël* (Geneva: Droz, 1998)

Staël editions

Germaine de Staël, *Œuvres complètes*, 17 vols. (Paris: Treuttel & Würtz, 1820–1), is slowly yielding to critical editions: *De l'Allemagne* (Hachette, 1958–60), *Des circonstances actuelles* (Droz, 1979), *Delphine* (Droz, 1987–90), *Dix années d'exil* (Fayard, 1996), *De la littérature* (Garnier, 1997), *Écrits de jeunesse* [*Lettres sur Rousseau, Zulma*, the 1795 *Recueil*] (Desjonquères, 1997), the 1790s *Théâtre inédit* (Voltaire Foundation, 1998). Add the *Correspondance générale*, ed. B. Jasinski (Paris: Pauvert, Hachette, Klincksieck, 1960–), and Simone Balayé, *Les Carnets de voyage de Madame de Staël:*

Contribution à la genèse de ses œuvres (Geneva: Droz, 1971). *Corinne ou l'Italie*, ed. Simone Balayé (Paris: Folio, 1985), non-critical, alone uses the corrected third edition as copy-text.

Staël in translation

Corinne, or Italy, tr. Avriel Goldberger (New Brunswick, NJ: Rutgers University Press, 1987); *Delphine*, tr. Avriel Goldberger (DeKalb: Northern Illinois University Press, 1995); and three selections, *Germaine de Staël: On Politics, Literature and National Character*, tr. and ed. Morroe Berger (New York: Doubleday, 1964); *An Extraordinary Woman: Selected Writings of Germaine de Staël*, tr. Vivian Folkenflik (New York: Columbia University Press, 1987); Doris Kadish and Françoise Massardier-Kenney (eds.), *Translating Slavery: Gender and Race in French Women's Writing, 1783–1823* (Kent, Oh.: Kent State University Press, 1994).

Special studies of Corinne ou l'Italie

A few Balayé articles listed in Szmurlo's review, *supra*: 'Corinne et la ville italienne', 'Corinne ou le chant du cygne', 'Fonction romanesque de la musique dans *Corinne*', 'Pour une lecture politique de *Corinne*', 'Du sens romanesque de quelques œuvres d'art dans *Corinne*'. See also Joan DeJean, 'Staël's *Corinne*: The Novel's Other Dilemma', *Stanford French Review*, 11 (1987), 77–87; Geneviève Gennari, *Le Premier Voyage de Madame de Staël en Italie et la genèse de Corinne* (Paris: Boivin, 1940); Avriel Goldberger, 'Germaine de Staël's *Corinne*: Challenges to the Translator in the 1980s', *French Review* (Apr. 1990), 800–9; Maija Lehtonen, 'Le Fleuve du temps et le fleuve de l'enfer: Thèmes et images dans *Corinne*', *Neuphilologische Mitteilungen* (1967), 3–4: 225–42, 391–408; (1968), 1: 101–28; Nancy K. Miller, *Subject to Change: Rediscovering Feminist Writing* (New York: Columbia University Press, 1988); essays in Avriel Goldberger (ed.), *Woman as Mediatrix: Nineteenth-Century Women Writers* (Westport, Conn.: Greenwood Press, 1987); and Karyna Szurlo (ed.), *The Novel's Seductions: Corinne in Critical Inquiry* (Cranbury, NJ: Bucknell University Press, 1998).

Further reading in Oxford World's Classics

George Eliot, *Middlemarch*, ed. David Carroll, with an introduction by Felicia Bonaparte; Mme de Lafayette, *The Princesse de Clèves*, trans. and ed. Terence Cave; Petrarch, *Selections from the Canzoniere and Other Works*, trans. and ed. Mark Musa; Stendhal, *The Charterhouse of Parma*, trans. Margaret Mauldon, ed. Roger Pearson; and Mary Wollstonecraft, *Mary and The Wrongs of Woman*, ed. Gary Kelly, and *A Vindication of the Rights of Woman and A Vindication of the Rights of Men*, ed. Janet Todd.

A CHRONOLOGY OF
MADAME DE STAËL

1766   Birth on 22 April of Anne-Louise-Germaine Necker in Paris. Her
        father was Jacques Necker, the Genevan banker whom Louis XVI
        appointed in 1776 director of the royal treasury, a title changed
        in 1777 to director-general of the finances. Her mother, Suzanne
        née Curchod, also Swiss, established a salon that attracted many
        distinguished persons, both men and women.

1786   In an arranged marriage of convenience, Mademoiselle Necker
        is wedded to the Swedish ambassador to France, Baron Eric de
        Staël-Holstein, and institutes her own salon. Writes *Sophie ou les
        sentiments secrets*, a romantic drama.

1787   Gives birth to a daughter, Gustavine, who, however, dies in
        infancy.

1788   Publication of *Lettres sur les ouvrages et le caractère de J.-J. Rous-
        seau*, which draws inspiration from Montesquieu as well as Rous-
        seau. Beginning of liaison with Louis, Comte de Narbonne.

1789   Witnesses in Paris the beginning of the French Revolution.

1790   Gives birth to a son, Auguste. Writes *Éloge de Monsieur de Guibert*
        and a tragedy, *Jane Grey*.

1792   Helps escape from Paris of Narbonne and other friends threat-
        ened by the excesses of the Revolution. She herself narrowly avoids
        death in a riot and retreats to the family residence at Coppet, near
        Geneva. Gives birth to a second son, Albert.

1793   Makes brief visit to England, where Narbonne had taken refuge.
        Falls in love with a Swedish exile, Count Adolph Ribbing. Pub-
        lication of *Réflexions sur le procès de la reine*.

1794   Her mother dies. Publication of *Zulma*, a novel, and *Réflexions
        sur la paix*. Liaison with Narbonne broken off. Meets Benjamin
        Constant.

1795   Returns briefly to Paris, accompanied by Constant. Publication
        of *Recueil de morceaux détachés*, including *Essai sur les fictions*. A
        further work, *Réflexions sur la paix intérieure*, is printed but not
        published.

1796   Ends liaison with Ribbing. Publication of *De l'influence des passions*.

1797   Founds, with Constant and others, the Constitutional Club.
        Gives birth to a daughter, Albertine. Meets Napoleon, whom

she admires for his accomplishments; she hopes he will realize republican ideals.

1798   Writes but does not publish *Des circonstances actuelles pour terminer la Révolution*.

1799   Comes back to Paris, where she resides for two years. Helps Constant to be nominated a member of the Tribunate, where his speeches rouse the ire of Napoleon against both of them.

1800   Publication of *De la littérature*, which is attacked by Chateaubriand. Marriage to Baron de Staël is formally ended by legal separation.

1802   Constant is expelled from the Tribunate. Baron de Staël dies. Publication of *Delphine*, a sociological novel which, like *De la littérature*, arouses fierce criticism. Napoleon forbids Madame de Staël to approach within forty leagues of Paris.

1803   Napoleon's decree is repeated.

1803–4 She visits Germany in the company of Constant; meets Goethe and Schiller in Weimar.

1804   Meets August Wilhelm von Schlegel in Berlin and persuades him to come to Coppet to act as tutor to her children. Her father dies; she publishes *Manuscrits de M. Necker*, preceded by a memoir written by herself.

1804–5 Visits Italy with her children and Schlegel.

1807   Publication of *Corinne*, with immediate resounding success.

1807–8 Visits Vienna.

1810   *De l'Allemagne* printed but suppressed by Napoleon on the alleged ground that it is anti-French; he orders that she be exiled from France.

1811   Meets John Rocca, a young Genevan, twenty years her junior, who had served as an officer in Napoleon's army; they exchange a secret promise of marriage. She writes but does not publish *Sapho* (a drama) and *Réflexions sur le suicide*.

1812   Gives birth to a son, Louis-Alphonse Rocca. Manages to leave Coppet with Rocca and Schlegel, gets to Vienna, and then visits Russia and Sweden.

1813   Publication of *Réflexions sur le suicide*. She visits London. Her son Albert is killed in a duel. *De l'Allemagne* is republished in London.

1814   She returns briefly to Paris after the abdication of Napoleon.

1815   Supports, but without enthusiasm, the restored monarchy.

1815–16 Visits Italy.

1816   *De l'esprit des traductions* is published in Milan. Her daughter Albertine marries Victor, Duc de Broglie, whose mother owed her life to Madame de Staël. She herself marries Rocca in secret.

1817   Dies on 14 July in Paris.

1818   Rocca dies. Publication of *Considérations sur la Révolution française*.

1820   Publication of *Œuvres complètes*.

1821   Publication of *Dix années d'exil, Essais dramatiques*, and *Œuvres inédites*.

CORINNE

or Italy

Udrallo il bel paese,
Ch' Apennin parte, e'l mar circonda; et l'Alpe.

PETRARCH

[Her name] will resound in the fair land
parted by the Apennines and bounded by the sea and the Alps.

CONTENTS

CONTENTS

BOOK I
OSWALD

CHAPTER I

OSWALD, LORD NELVIL, peer of Scotland, set out from Edinburgh to go to Italy during the winter of 1794 to 1795. He had a distinguished, handsome face, was highly intelligent, bore a great name, and had independent means. A deep sorrow had, however, affected his health, and his doctors, fearing that his lungs had been damaged, had advised him to go south. He followed their advice, although he took little interest in the preservation of his life. He hoped, at least, to find some distraction in the variety of things he was going to see. The most poignant grief of all, the loss of a father, was the cause of his illness. Painful circumstances, remorse inspired by scruples of conscience, intensified his grief, enhanced by phantoms of his imagination. When one is suffering, it is easy to be convinced of one's own guilt, and intense sorrows carry the pain into conscience itself.

At the age of twenty-five, he was disenchanted with life, his opinion was formed about everything, and his wounded feelings no longer entertained illusions of affection. No one was more obliging or devoted to his friends when he could be of service to them, but nothing gave him pleasure, not even the good he did. He would continually and readily sacrifice his own preferences to those of his friends, but generosity alone could not explain the complete renunciation of all self-interest, and it had often to be ascribed to the kind of melancholy which prevented him from taking an interest in his own fate. Those who did not care about him appreciated this trait and thought it attractive and charming, but those who loved him felt that he was concerned for the happiness of others like a man who had no hope of happiness for himself, and they were almost saddened by the happiness he gave them without their being able to give him any in return.

Yet he had an emotional, acutely sensitive temperament, which combined every feature that could move others and himself, but misfortune and repentance had made him afraid of destiny and he thought he could disarm it by making no demands on it. In devoting himself strictly to his duty and in renouncing keen pleasures, he hoped to find a guarantee against heart-rending sorrows. He had been frightened by his past experiences, and nothing in this world seemed worth the risk of incurring such sorrows. But if you have the capacity to feel them, what kind of life can shield you from them?

Lord Nelvil imagined he could leave Scotland with no regrets since he had no pleasure in remaining there, but that is not the way the gloomy imaginations of sensitive souls are made; he did not appreciate the bonds which tied him to the places that gave him most pain, to his father's dwelling. In that dwelling there were rooms and places he could not approach without a shudder, and yet when he decided to go away from them he felt himself to be even more isolated. A kind of atrophy took possession of his heart; he no longer had the power to shed tears when he was suffering; he could no longer revive the little local incidents which moved him deeply; there was no longer anything alive about his memories; he no longer had any link with the objects around him; he did not think less about the man whose loss he was mourning, but he found it more difficult to recall his presence.

Sometimes, too, he would reproach himself with deserting the places where his father had lived—'Who knows whether the shades of the dead can follow those they love everywhere?' he would say to himself. 'Perhaps they are allowed to wander only near the places where their ashes are laid to rest; perhaps at this moment my father too is missing me but he lacks the strength to recall me from such a great distance! Alas! When he was alive, a combination of abnormal events must have convinced him that I had betrayed his affection, that I had rebelled against my native land, against his paternal wishes, and against all that is sacred on earth.' These memories gave Lord Nelvil such unbearable pain that not only could he not confide them to anyone but he was afraid of probing them fully himself. It is so easy to do oneself irreparable harm with one's own thoughts!

It is more painful to leave one's native land when one has to cross the sea to go away from it. Everything about a journey which starts with a sea-passage is momentous. It is as if an abyss is opening up behind you and the return journey might never be possible. Moreover, the sight of the sea always makes a profound impression; it is the reflection of the infinite, to which our thoughts are continually attracted and in which they continually get lost. Oswald, leaning on the helm, his eyes fixed on the waves, was outwardly calm, for his pride combined with his shyness hardly ever let him show what he felt, even to his friends, but inwardly he was agitated by painful feelings. He recalled the time in his youth when the sight of the sea made him want to swim through the water and measure his strength against it. 'Why give myself unremittingly to reflection?' he would say to himself. 'There is so much pleasure in an active life, in the strenuous exercises which make us feel the energy of existence! Then death itself seems only an event, perhaps glorious, at least a sudden one, which has not been preceded by failing faculties. But the death which comes without being courageously sought, the death which comes in the darkness of night and carries off what you hold most dear, which despises your regrets, wards off your arm, and confronts you pitilessly with the eternal laws of time and nature, such a death inspires a kind of contempt for human fate, for the impotence of grief, for all the fruitless efforts which are going to be broken against the inevitable.'

Such were the feelings which tortured Oswald, but the outstanding characteristic of his unfortunate situation was the vivacity of youth joined to the thoughts of another age. He identified himself with the ideas that must have occupied his father's mind in the last period of his life, and he transported the ardour of his twenty-five years into the melancholy reflections of old age. He was weary of everything and yet he regretted happiness as if he still had illusions. This contrast, entirely opposed to the will of nature, which puts consistency and gradualness in the natural order of things, cast disarray into the depths of Oswald's soul, but his behaviour to the outside world was always gentle and even-tempered, and his sadness, far from making him irritable, gave him even more humility and kindness towards others.

Two or three times during the crossing from Harwich to Emden the sea threatened to become stormy. Lord Nelvil gave advice to the sailors, reassured the passengers, and when, taking the pilot's place for a moment, he helped to man the ship, in everything he did there was a skill and a strength which must not be put down only to bodily suppleness and agility, for the heart is involved in everything.

When the moment of separation came, the whole ship's company gathered around Oswald to take leave of him. They all thanked him for the countless little services he had done them during the crossing and which he could no longer remember. Once it was a child he had looked after for a long time; more often it was an old man whom he had supported when the wind rocked the vessel. Perhaps they had never come across such a lack of self-concern. His day was spent without his taking a moment for himself; he gave it up to others out of melancholy or kind-heartedness. As they left him, the sailors said almost all at the same time: *Dear Sir, may you be more happy!* Yet Oswald had not once expressed his grief, and the men of another class who had made the crossing with him had not said a word to him about it. But people of the lower classes, in whom their superiors rarely confide, are used to ascertaining feelings by means other than language; they pity you when you suffer although they do not know the cause of your sorrows, and their spontaneous pity is unmixed with blame or advice.

CHAPTER II

WHATEVER people may say, travelling is one of the saddest pleasures in life. When you feel comfortable in some foreign town, it is because you are beginning to belong to it; but to cross unknown countries, to hear people speak a language you barely understand, to see human faces that have no connection either with your past or your future, means loneliness and isolation without peace or dignity. The eagerness, the haste to arrive at a place where no one is waiting for you, the excitement aroused by mere curiosity, inspires you with little self-esteem until the moment when new objects become a little old and create a few pleasant bonds of feeling and habit around you.

So Oswald's sadness was increased twofold as he crossed Germany to go to Italy. Because of the war France and the neighbouring territory had to be avoided at that time; the armies which made the roads impassable had also to be kept at a distance. Lord Nelvil found it quite unbearable to have to think about the material details of the journey and make a new decision every day and almost every moment. Far from improving, his health forced him to stop frequently when he would have liked to hurry on to his destination, or at least to set off. He was spitting blood, and he took as little care of himself as possible, for he thought he was guilty and blamed himself too severely. He wanted to go on living only to defend his country. 'Has not our fatherland some paternal rights over us?' he would say to himself. 'But one must be able to serve it usefully; I must not offer it the feeble existence I am dragging out, going to ask the sun for some

life-giving properties to fight against my ills. Only a father would
receive one in such a state and love one all the more because one has
been abandoned by nature or by fate.'

Lord Nelvil had persuaded himself that the continual variety of the
sights that met his eyes would turn his mind away a little from its
usual ideas, but at first he was far from experiencing this happy outcome. After a great misfortune, one must become re-acquainted with
everything around one, become used to faces that one sees again, to
the house where one lives, to the daily habits that one must re-assume.
Every one of these efforts is a painful shock, and nothing multiplies
them like a journey.

Lord Nelvil's only pleasure was to ride through the Tyrol mountains on a Scottish horse he had brought with him and which, as is
usual with the horses of that country, galloped up the heights. He
avoided the main roads and went along the steepest paths. To start
with, the astonished peasants cried out with terror when they saw
him on the edge of abysses; then they clapped their hands as they
admired his skill, his agility, and his courage. Oswald quite enjoyed
the feeling of danger; it relieves the weight of grief and reconciles one
for a moment with the life one has regained and which it is so easy
to lose.

CHAPTER III

IN the town of Innsbruck, before going into Italy, at the house of a
businessman where he had stopped for a while, Oswald heard the story
of a French émigré called Count d'Erfeuil; this greatly interested Lord
Nelvil and gave him a very good opinion of the Count. He had borne
the loss of a very great fortune with complete equanimity. By his
talent for music he had supported himself and an old uncle, whom
he had cared for till his death; he had constantly refused to accept the
financial assistance that people had hastened to offer him; he had displayed the most outstanding valour, French valour, during the war
and the steadiest cheerfulness during reverses. He wanted to go to
Rome to seek out a relative from whom he was to inherit, and he
wanted a companion, or rather a friend, to make the journey more
pleasantly in his company.

Lord Nelvil's most painful memories were connected with France;
nevertheless he was exempt from the prejudices which separate the

two nations, because his greatest friend had been a Frenchman, and in this friend he had found the most admirable combination of all the virtues of the heart. So he spoke to the businessman who told him Count d'Erfeuil's story, offering to accompany that unfortunate young nobleman to Italy. After an hour, the businessman came and told Lord Nelvil that his proposal was gratefully accepted. Oswald was happy to render this service, but it cost him a lot to give up his solitude, and his shyness made him suffer from finding himself suddenly in the constant company of a man he did not know.

Count d'Erfeuil paid Lord Nelvil a visit to thank him. He had elegant manners, a ready courtesy, and good taste. Right from the start he was completely at ease. On seeing him, one was surprised at all he had suffered, for he endured his lot with a courage that went as far as seeming to forget about it, and in his conversation there was an unconcern that was truly admirable when he was talking of his own misfortunes but less admirable, it must be admitted, when it was extended to other subjects.

'I am very obliged to you, my Lord, for taking me out of Germany, where I was being bored to death,' said Count d'Erfeuil. 'Yet, you are generally liked and esteemed here,' said Lord Nelvil. 'I have friends here, whom I sincerely regret, for in this country you meet only the nicest people in the world,' replied Count d'Erfeuil. 'But I do not know a word of German, and you will agree that it would take rather a long time and be a little wearisome for me to learn it. Since I had the misfortune of losing my uncle, I do not know what to do with my time. When I had to look after him, that filled my day; at the present time the twenty-four hours weigh heavily on me.' 'The considerate way you behaved towards your uncle creates a very high opinion of you, Sir,' said Lord Nelvil. 'I only did my duty,' replied Count d'Erfeuil. 'The poor man had heaped kindnesses upon me during my childhood. I would never have left him had he lived to be a hundred! But it is fortunate for him that he is dead. It would be fortunate for me too,' he added with a laugh, 'for I have not much to hope for in this world. During the war I did my best to get killed, but since fate spared me I must live as best I can.' 'I shall be pleased that I came here if you like living in Rome, and if . . .' answered Lord Nelvil. 'Oh, well,' Count d'Erfeuil interrupted, 'I shall like living anywhere; when one is young and cheerful everything works out well. It is not books or reflection which are responsible for my philosophy, but a knowledge of the world and misfortunes. And you can see clearly, my Lord, that I was right to count on chance since it has procured for me the opportunity of travelling with you.' As he finished making these remarks, Count d'Erfeuil made a very gracious bow to Lord Nelvil, agreed on the departure time for the following day, and took his leave.

Count d'Erfeuil and Lord Nelvil set off the next day. After the initial courtesies, Oswald did not say a word for several hours, but noticing that this silence wearied his companion, he asked him if he was looking forward to going to Italy. 'Well, I know what to think of that country; I don't at all expect to enjoy myself there,' Count d'Erfeuil replied. 'One of my friends who spent six months there told me that there was not a province in France that did not have better theatre or pleasanter company than Rome; but in what used to be the capital of the world, I am sure to find some French people to talk to and that is all I want.' 'Have you not been tempted to learn Italian?' interrupted Oswald. 'No, not at all,' Count d'Erfeuil replied. 'That did not enter into my plan of study.' And as he said this he assumed so serious a look that you would have thought there were important reasons behind his resolve.

'If you really want to know, as nations, I like only the English and the French,' continued Count d'Erfeuil. 'One must be proud like them, or brilliant like us. All the others are only imitators.' Oswald made no reply and some moments later Count d'Erfeuil resumed the conversation with pleasant wit and humour. He played with words and sentences very ingeniously but he talked neither about the things around them nor his personal feelings. His conversation came, as it were, neither from without nor within. It was in between reflection and imagination, and dealt only with social relationships.

He mentioned twenty names of people to Lord Nelvil, some French, some English, to enquire if he knew them and, in doing so, told some amusing anecdotes very charmingly. But on listening to him, one would have said that the only conversation befitting a man of taste was, if one may say so, high society gossip.

Lord Nelvil thought for some time about Count d'Erfeuil's character, about this curious mixture of courage and frivolity, about his contempt of danger, which would be so great if it had cost more effort, and so heroic if it did not come from the same source which made him incapable of deep affections. 'An Englishman,' Oswald said to himself, 'would be overwhelmed with sadness in similar circumstances. What is the cause of this Frenchman's strength? What, too, is the source of his restlessness? Does Count d'Erfeuil really understand the art of living? When I think I am superior, am I only sick? Is his frivolous existence better suited to the pace of life than mine? Ought reflection to be avoided like an enemy, instead of being the object of whole-hearted devotion?' Oswald would have tried in vain to resolve these doubts. Nobody can depart from the intellectual sphere which has been allotted to him, and virtues are even more insurmountable than faults.

Count d'Erfeuil paid no attention at all to Italy and made it almost impossible for Lord Nelvil to take an interest in it, for he continually turned Oswald's attention away from the attitude of mind which allows one to admire a beautiful country and to appreciate its picturesque charm. Oswald listened as carefully as he could to the sound of the wind and the murmur of the waves, for all the voices of nature did his soul more good than society gossip related at the foothills of the Alps, among ruins, and by the seashore.

Oswald's consuming melancholy would have put fewer obstacles in the way of his appreciation of Italy than did this cheerfulness of Count d'Erfeuil. The regrets of a sensitive soul can be combined with the contemplation of nature and appreciation of the arts, but frivolity, of whatever kind, deprives one's attention of its power, thought of its originality, and feeling of its depth. One of the strange results of this frivolity was to make Lord Nelvil very withdrawn in his relationship with Count d'Erfeuil. Embarrassment is nearly always felt by the more serious-minded character. Witty frivolity dominates the reflective mind, and the man who says he is happy seems wiser than the man who suffers.

Count d'Erfeuil was gentle, obliging, easygoing, serious only on the question of his *amour propre*, and deserving to be liked as he liked others, that is to say as a good companion in pleasures and dangers, but he understood nothing about sharing sorrows. He was irritated by Oswald's melancholy, and out of good-heartedness as well as inclination he would have liked to dispel it. 'What do you lack?' he would often say to him. 'You are young and rich, and you could be in good health if you wanted to, for you are ill only because you are sad. *I* have lost my fortune, my role in life, I do not know what will become of me, and yet I enjoy life as if I had all the prosperity in the world.' 'Your courage is as unusual as it is honourable, but the reverses you

have experienced hurt less than the sorrows of the heart,' replied Lord
Nelvil. 'The sorrows of the heart,' cried Count d'Erfeuil, 'they are
the most cruel of all; that's true . . . But . . . but . . . one must get over
them, for a sensible man should banish from his heart everything which
can be no use to others or to himself. Are we not on this earth, first
to be useful, and then to be happy after that. My dear Nelvil, let's
go no further than that.'

In the ordinary meaning of the word, what Count d'Erfeuil said
was reasonable, for in many respects he was what is called level-headed.
It is characters who feel deeply rather than frivolous ones who are
capable of folly. But Lord Nelvil's trust was far from being aroused
by the Count's attitude, and Oswald would have liked to be able to
assure Count d'Erfeuil that he was the happiest of men so as to avoid
the pain his consolations gave him.

Count d'Erfeuil, however, became greatly attached to Lord Nelvil.
Oswald's resignation and simplicity, his modesty and his pride aroused
in the Count an esteem which he could not help feeling. He was concerned about Oswald's external calm; he racked his brains in an effort
to remember all the most serious things he had heard elderly relatives say in his childhood, so as to try them out on Lord Nelvil, and,
quite amazed at not overcoming Oswald's apparent coldness, he would
say to himself, 'But am I not kind, frank, and brave? Am I not agreeable in company? So what can I lack that would enable me to make
an impression on this man? And is there not perhaps some misunder-
standing between us which arises from the fact that he does not know
French well enough?'

CHAPTER IV

AN unexpected incident greatly enhanced the feeling of respect
which Count d'Erfeuil, almost involuntarily, already had for his
travelling companion. Lord Nelvil's health had obliged him to stop
at Ancona for a few days. The mountains and the sea give the town
a very fine situation, and the many Greeks who sit in the oriental manner, working outside the shops, together with the varied dress of the
Levantines one sees in the streets, make Ancona look unusual and interesting. Civilization continually tends to make all men look alike and
almost really be alike; but one's mind and imagination delight in the
differences which characterize nations. Men resemble each other only

by pretence or calculation, yet everything natural is varied. So differences in dress are a small pleasure, at least to look at; they seem to predict a new way of feeling and thinking.

Greek, Catholic, and Jewish forms of worship exist peacefully, side by side, in the town of Ancona. There is a great difference between the ceremonies of these different religions, but the same feelings are lifted up to Heaven in their different rites, the same cry of pain, the same need for help.

The Catholic church is on a hilltop and dominates the town, overlooking the sea. The sound of the waves is often mingled with the priests' chanting. The inside of the church is overloaded with a host of decorations in rather bad taste. But if you stop at the portico, you have the pleasure of combining the purest feeling of the heart, religion, with the sight of the magnificent sea on which man can never leave his mark. Man has worked on the land, has cut through the mountains with roads, has restricted rivers into canals so that they can carry his goods, but if, for a moment, ships plough through the waves, the sea reappears as it was on the first day of creation.

Lord Nelvil had fixed his departure for Rome for the next day when, during the night, he heard terrible screams in the town. He hurried out of his inn to find out the reason for them and saw a blaze coming from the harbour and climbing up from house to house to the high part of the town. In the distance the flames were mirrored in the sea; the wind, fanning them, also ruffled their image in the water, and in a thousand ways the mounting waves reflected the blood-red flashes of a lurid fire.

As the people of Ancona had no pumps in working order, they rushed to give help with the strength of their arms.[1] Through the screams one could hear the clang of the chains of the galley slaves employed to save the town which had been their prison. Terror was expressed in the dazed looks of the different Levantine peoples whom trade attracts to Ancona. The merchants, seeing their shops go up in flames, lost all presence of mind. Concern for their wealth is as disturbing to the common run of men as the fear of death and does not inspire the upsurge of spiritual power and the enthusiasm which make us resourceful.

Sailors' cries are always rather doleful and lingering; terror makes them even more frightening. The sailors of the Adriatic coast wear very unusual red and brown jackets, and from out of these garments emerged expressive Italian faces which portrayed fear in a thousand ways. Some of the townspeople, lying flat in the streets, covered their heads with their coats as if all that was left for them to do was not to see their disaster; others threw themselves into the flames without the least hope of escape. Fury and blind resignation could be seen in turn but nowhere was the cool-headedness which doubles capabilities and strengths.

Oswald remembered that there were two English ships in the harbour which had pumps on board in good working order. He hurried to the Captain and went by boat with him to fetch the pumps. The townspeople who saw him go into the launch shouted, *That's fine for you foreigners to leave our unfortunate town.* 'We are coming back,' said Oswald. They did not believe him. He came back, however, set up one of the pumps opposite the first house which was burning in the harbour, and the other opposite the one which was burning in the middle of the street. Count d'Erfeuil risked his life unconcernedly, bravely, and cheerfully; the English sailors and Lord Nelvil's servants all came to his aid, for the people of Ancona did not move, barely understanding what these foreigners were trying to do, and having no faith in their success.

Bells were ringing on all sides, priests were forming processions, women were weeping as they knelt before statuettes of saints at street corners, but no one thought of the natural help that God has given to man to defend himself. But when the townspeople saw the happy outcome of Oswald's activity, when they saw that the flames were dying down and their houses would be saved, they went from amazement to enthusiasm. They crowded round Lord Nelvil and kissed his hands so eagerly that he was compelled to become angry in order to push back anything which might delay the rapid series of orders and movements required to save the town. Everybody had lined up under his command, because in trivial as well as in serious matters, as soon as danger arises, courage takes its place; as soon as people are afraid, they cease to be jealous.

Through the general din, however, Oswald made out some screams, more horrible than all the others, coming from the other end of the town. He asked where these screams were coming from and he was told they originated in the Jewish quarter. It was the practice of the police officer to close the gates to the quarter at night, and as the fire was progressing in that direction the Jews could not escape. Oswald shuddered at this thought and requested that the quarter should be opened immediately, but several poorer-class women who heard him threw themselves at his feet to beg him to do nothing of the kind. *Don't you see, you good angel*, they said, *that it's certainly because of the presence of the Jews that we have had this fire. It is they who bring us misfortune, and if you set them free all the water of the sea will not put out the flames.* And they begged Oswald to let the Jews burn, as eloquently and sweetly as if they had been asking for an act of mercy. They were not wicked women but their superstitious imaginations were keenly affected by a great misfortune. Oswald could barely contain his indignation when he heard these strange requests.

He sent four English sailors with axes to break down the gates which held back these unfortunate people. They immediately spilled out into the town, running to their wares in the midst of the flames, with the greed for wealth that seems sinister when it leads to defiance of death. It is as if, in the present state of society, man has almost no appreciation of the gift of life alone.

At the top of the town there remained only one house so surrounded by flames that it was impossible to extinguish them and still more impossible to go through them. The Ancona townspeople had shown so little concern about this house that the English sailors thought it was uninhabited and had withdrawn their pumps towards the harbour. Even Oswald, bewildered by the screams of those around him who were shouting to him to help them, had paid it no attention. The blaze had reached that part of the town later but it had advanced very quickly. Lord Nelvil asked about this house so insistently that a man replied at last that it was the lunatic asylum. Oswald was quite appalled at the thought. He turned round and saw his sailors were no longer near him. Count d'Erfeuil was not there either and it would have been useless to turn to the Ancona townspeople; they were all busy saving their wares or having them saved and thought it ridiculous to take risks for people not one of whom was not hopelessly mad. *It is a blessing from heaven, for them and for their relatives*, they said, *if they die like that without its being anyone's fault.*

As people around Oswald were talking in this way, he was striding towards the asylum, and the crowd, while finding fault with him, followed with a feeling of involuntary, embarrassed enthusiasm. When Oswald came near the house, at the only window not surrounded by the flames he saw lunatics watching the progress of the fire and laughing with the heart-rending laugh which suggests either ignorance of all life's ills or so much deep-seated sorrow that no form of death can any longer terrify. At this sight an indescribable shudder gripped Oswald. In the most frightful moments of his desperate grief he had felt his reason almost giving way, and from that time the sight of madness always filled him with the most heart-rending pity. He grabbed a ladder standing near him, leaned it against the wall, climbed up in the midst of the flames, and through the window went into the room where all the unfortunates left in the asylum were assembled.

Their madness was mild enough for them all to be allowed to move about freely in the house, except for one who was in chains in the very room where the flames were making a breach in the door but had not yet consumed the floor. Oswald's appearance amongst these miserable creatures, all degraded by illness and suffering, had such an effect of surprise and delight that at first he commanded their unresisting obedience. He commanded them to go down the ladder ahead of him, one after the other; it could be consumed by the flames at any moment. The first of these unfortunates obeyed without a word; Lord Nelvil's tone and expression had entirely conquered him. Another wanted to resist, not suspecting the danger he incurred from every moment of delay and not thinking of the danger to which he was exposing Oswald by detaining him longer. The townspeople, appreciating the full horror of the situation, shouted to Lord Nelvil to come down and to leave these madmen to extricate themselves as best they could, but the liberator listened to no one till he had completed his generous undertaking.

Of the six unfortunates who were in the asylum, five had already been saved; only the sixth, who was in chains, remained. Oswald undid his irons and wanted to make him use the same means of escape as his companions, but he was a poor young man totally bereft of reason and, finding himself free after two years of chains, he rushed about the room in wild delight. This delight turned into rage when Oswald wanted to make him go out through the window. Then, seeing that the flames were advancing still further into the house and that it was impossible to persuade the madman to save himself, Lord Nelvil took him in his arms, in spite of the unfortunate creature's struggles as he resisted his benefactor. Oswald was so blinded by smoke that he carried the madman away without seeing where he was putting his feet. He jumped down the last rungs at random and committed the still protesting unfortunate to the care of some townsfolk, making them promise to look after him.

Oswald, stimulated by the risk he had just run, his hair in disarray, looking proud but gentle, inspired the watching crowd with almost fanatical admiration. The women, especially, expressed their feelings in the imaginative language with which nearly all Italians are gifted and which often lends nobility to the speech of ordinary people. They flung themselves on their knees in front of him and cried, *You must certainly be Saint Michael, the patron saint of our town. Spread your wings, but do not leave us; go up there to the top of the cathedral tower so that the whole town can see you and pray to you.—My child is sick, cure him,* said one.—*Tell me where my husband is; he has been away for several years,* said another. Oswald looked for a means of escape. Count d'Erfeuil appeared and shook his hand, saying, 'Dear Nelvil, but you must share things with your friends; it is wrong to incur all the risks yourself.' 'Get me out of here,' Oswald said to him quietly. A moment of darkness gave them the opportunity to escape and they both hurried off to get post horses.

At first Lord Nelvil felt a little quiet satisfaction arising from the good deed he had just performed, but with whom could he enjoy it, now that his best friend was no longer alive? Such is the misfortune of orphans! Happy events as well as sorrows make them feel the loneliness of their hearts. How, indeed, can we ever replace the innate affection, the inherited community of feeling, the friendship arranged by Heaven between father and child? One can still love, but to be wholeheartedly committed to another is a happiness one can never again recover.

CHAPTER V

OSWALD travelled through the Ancona Marches and the Papal States as far as Rome, without noticing or taking an interest in anything. This was because of his melancholy disposition, but he also had a certain natural indolence from which he was aroused only by strong passions. His appreciation of art had not yet been developed. He had lived only in France, where social life is everything, and in London, where political interests absorb nearly all others. His imagination, concentrated on his woes, did not yet enjoy the wonders of nature or the masterpieces of art.

Count d'Erfeuil went through every town, guidebook in hand. At one and the same time, he had the double pleasure of wasting his time seeing everything and of asserting that he had seen nothing worth admiring when one knew France. Count d'Erfeuil's lack of enthusiasm discouraged Oswald, who, moreover, was prejudiced against Italy and the Italians. He had not yet got to the heart of the mystery of that people or country, a mystery which has to be understood by the imagination rather than by the critical intellect which is particularly developed through English education.

The Italians are much more outstanding for what they have been and by what they might be than by what they are now. The wasteland surrounding the city of Rome, a land weary of glory, which seems to despise being productive, is only an uncultivated, neglected area to anyone who judges it by standards of utility. Oswald, accustomed from childhood to a love of order and public prosperity, was, at first, unfavourably impressed as he crossed the deserted lands that herald the approach of the city which was once queen of the world. He blamed the indolence of the inhabitants and their leaders. Lord Nelvil judged Italy as an enlightened administrator, Count d'Erfeuil as a man of the world. So the one because of reason, and the other because of frivolity, did not experience the impression which the Roman Campagna makes on the imaginations of those who are steeped in the memories and sorrows, in the natural beauties and the celebrated misfortunes, which imbue this land with an indefinable charm.

Count d'Erfeuil made amusing laments on the environs of Rome, 'What! No country houses, no carriages, nothing which suggests the proximity of a big city!' he said. 'Oh, my goodness, isn't it dreary!' As they drew near to Rome, the postillions cried delightedly, *Look, look, that's the dome of Saint Peter's!* The Neapolitans point out Vesuvius in the same way and coastal dwellers take pride similarly in the seashore. 'You'd think you were looking at the dome of the Invalides,' cried Count d'Erfeuil. The comparison, more patriotic than accurate, destroyed the effect that this magnificent wonder of human creativity might have had on Oswald. They entered Rome, not on a fine day, not on a fine night, but on a dark evening, in dreary weather which makes everything dull and indistinct. They crossed the Tiber without noticing it; they entered Rome by the Porta del Popolo which leads straight into the Corso, the main street of the modern city but the least distinctive part of Rome because it is more like other European cities.

Crowds were strolling in the streets; groups were clustering around puppets and mountebanks on the square where the column of Antoninus* stands. All Oswald's attention was caught by the objects nearest to him. The name of Rome did not yet arouse a chord in his heart; he felt only the deep isolation that afflicts the soul when you enter a foreign town, when you see the crowd of people who do not know of your existence and who share none of your concerns. These reflections, so sad for all men, are even more so for the English, who are used to living in their own community and find it difficult to get used to the ways of other peoples. In Rome, that vast caravanserai, everything is foreign, even the Romans, who seem to live there not like owners, *but like pilgrims resting beside the ruins*.[2] Oswald, depressed by painful feelings, shut himself up in his room and did not go out to see the town. He was far from thinking that the land he was entering with such feelings of depression and sadness would soon be the source of so many new ideas and pleasures.

BOOK II
CORINNE AT THE CAPITOL

CHAPTER I

OSWALD awoke in Rome. Brilliant sunshine, Italian sunshine, met his eyes as soon as he opened them, and his heart was filled with loving gratitude for the heaven which seemed to reveal itself in these beautiful rays. He heard the bells ringing from the many churches in the town; bursts of cannon fire from different places proclaimed some important occasion. On asking the reason for this, he was told that that very morning, at the Capitol, the most famous woman in Italy, Corinne, poetess, writer, and improviser, and one of the most beautiful women in Rome, was to be crowned. He asked a few questions about the ceremony, consecrated by the names of Petrarch and Tasso,* and all the replies he received keenly aroused his curiosity.

There was certainly nothing more contrary to the customs and opinions of the English than this publicity given to the fortunes of a woman, but the enthusiasm which all imaginative talent arouses in the Italians infects foreign visitors, at least momentarily. They even forget their native prejudices when they are among people who express their feelings so vividly. The common people of Rome are familiar with the arts, and discuss sculpture with good taste. Pictures, monuments, antiques, and a certain level of literary merit, are for them a national interest.

Oswald went out to go to the public square. There he heard people talk about Corinne, about her talent and her genius. The streets she was to pass through had been decorated. The ordinary people, who usually foregather only to see the wealthy or powerful go by, were almost clamouring to see someone distinguished only by her mental powers. In their present state, the only glory permitted to the Italians is that of the arts. They appreciate this kind of genius with a keenness which would give birth to many great men if acclaim alone could produce them, if strength of purpose, great interests, and an independent existence were not essential food for thought.

Oswald strolled about the streets of Rome while awaiting Corinne's arrival. People were talking about her all the time; they were telling of yet another of her qualities which heralded the combination of all the talents that capture the imagination. One said that she had the most moving voice in Italy, another that no one performed tragedy like her, yet another that she danced like a nymph and that her drawings were as charming as they were original. Everyone said that such beautiful verses had never been written or improvised before and that at times the grace and at times the eloquence of her ordinary conversation captivated the minds of all around her. People argued about which Italian town she had been born in, but the Romans stoutly maintained that one had to be born in Rome to speak such pure Italian. No one knew her surname. Her first work had appeared five years earlier and bore only the name of Corinne. No one knew where she had lived or what she had been doing before then; she was now about twenty-six. This combination of mystery and publicity, this woman that everyone was talking about and whose real name no one knew, seemed to Lord Nelvil one of the wonders of the strange country he had come to see. In England he would have judged such a woman very severely, but he did not apply any of the social conventions to Italy. Corinne's coronation aroused in him the kind of expectant interest he would have taken in one of Ariosto's* tales.

Beautiful, striking music preceded the arrival of the triumphal procession. Any kind of event heralded by music always arouses excitement. Many of the Roman nobility and a few foreigners walked in front of the chariot bearing Corinne. *That's the string of her admirers*, said one Roman. *Yes*, replied another, *she receives homage from everyone, but she gives special preference to no one. She is rich and independent; they even think, and she certainly looks it, that she is a woman of noble birth who wants to remain incognito. Whatever the truth may be*, continued a third, *she is a goddess surrounded by clouds*. Oswald looked at the man who was speaking in this way. Everything about him indicated that he belonged to the lowliest rank of society, but in the South, people naturally express themselves in the most poetic language; it is as if they breathe it in from the atmosphere and are inspired by the sun.

At last the four white horses drawing Corinne's chariot made their way into the midst of the crowd. Corinne was sitting on the chariot, built in the style of ancient Rome, and white-robed girls walked alongside her. Everywhere she went people lavishly threw perfumes into the air; everyone looked out of their windows to see her and the outsides of the windows were decorated with pots of flowers and scarlet hangings; everyone shouted, *Long live Corinne! Long live genius! Long live beauty!* There was universal enthusiasm but Lord Nelvil did not yet share it. Although he had already told himself that if he were to have an opinion about all this he must set aside English reserve and French jesting, he did not share the festive attitude of the crowd when at last he caught sight of Corinne.

She was dressed like Domenichino's Sibyl.* An Indian turban was wound round her head, and intertwined with her beautiful black hair. Her dress was white with a blue stole fastened beneath her breast, but her attire, though very striking, did not differ so much from accepted styles as to be deemed affected. Her demeanour on the chariot was noble and modest; it was obvious that she was pleased to be admired, but a feeling of shyness was mingled with her happiness and seemed to ask pardon for her triumph. The expression on her countenance, in her eyes, and in her smile aroused interest in her, and the first sight of her inclined Lord Nelvil in her favour even before he was conquered by any stronger feeling. Her arms were dazzlingly beautiful; her tall, slightly plump figure, in the style of a Greek statue, gave a keen impression of youth and happiness; her eyes had something of an inspired look. In her way of greeting people and thanking them for the applause she was receiving, there was a kind of naturalness which enhanced the effect of her extraordinary situation. At one and the same time she gave the impression of a priestess of Apollo who approaches the sun-god's temple, and of a woman who is completely natural in the ordinary relationships of life. In short, all her movements had a charm which aroused interest and curiosity, wonder and affection.

The nearer she came to the Capitol, that place so rich in memories, the more the crowd admired her. The beautiful sky, the wildly enthusiastic Romans, and above all Corinne, fired Oswald's imagination. In his own country he had often seen statesmen borne in triumph by the people, but it was the first time he had witnessed honour done to a woman, to a woman renowned only for the gifts of genius. Her triumphal chariot had cost no one tears, and no regrets or fears restrained admiration for the finest gifts of nature, imagination, feeling, and reflection.

Oswald was so lost in his thoughts, so absorbed by new ideas, that he did not notice the famous, ancient places through which Corinne's chariot passed. It was at the foot of the staircase leading to the Capitol that her chariot came to a halt, and immediately all Corinne's friends rushed to hand her down. She chose Prince Castel-Forte, the Roman nobleman most highly esteemed for his intellect and character, a choice universally approved. She went up the steps of the Capitol, whose imposing majesty seemed to give a kindly welcome to the light tread of a woman. The moment Corinne arrived, there was a fresh blast of music, the guns roared, and the triumphant Sibyl entered the palace which had been prepared to receive her.

At the far end of the hall where she was received were the senator who was to crown her and the conservators of the Senate. On one side were all the cardinals and the most eminent women in the land, on the other the men of letters of the Roman Academy. At the opposite end, the hall was filled by a part of the huge crowd that had followed Corinne. The chair intended for her was on a step below the senator's. According to custom, before sitting on it, Corinne had to go down on one knee on the first step, in the presence of the august assembly. She did this with such nobility and modesty, with such charm and dignity, that at that moment Lord Nelvil felt his eyes fill with tears. He was himself surprised at his emotion, but in the midst of all this splendour and success it seemed to him that Corinne's eyes had sought the protection of a man friend, a protection no woman, however superior she may be, can ever dispense with. And he thought it would be pleasing to be the support of a woman who would feel the need for such support only because of her sensitivity.

As soon as Corinne was seated, the poets of Rome began to read the sonnets and odes they had composed in her honour. All of them lauded her to the skies, but the praise they gave her made no distinction between her and any other woman of genius. Their verses were a pleasant combination of imagery and mythological allusions which, from Sappho's* day to our own, might have been addressed throughout the centuries to all women renowned for their literary talents.

Lord Nelvil was already suffering from this way of praising Corinne. He felt already that, just by looking at her, he would have produced right away a more true, accurate, and detailed portrait, a portrait which would have fitted no one but Corinne.

CHAPTER II

PRINCE CASTEL-FORTE began to speak and what he said about Corinne attracted the attention of the whole gathering. He was a man of fifty, whose speech and bearing were restrained and dignified. His age, and the assurance that Lord Nelvil had been given that the Prince was no more than Corinne's friend, aroused Oswald's unalloyed interest in his portrait of her. Without these safeguards, Oswald would already have felt capable of feeling vaguely jealous.

Prince Castel-Forte read some passages of prose which were unpretentious but nevertheless particularly suited to an account of Corinne. He began by pointing out the special merit of her works. He said that this merit consisted partly in the extensive study she had made of foreign literatures; she knew how to combine to the highest degree the imagination, the descriptions, the brilliant life of the South with the observations of the human heart which seems to be the province of countries where the outside world arouses less interest.

He extolled Corinne's charm and gaiety, a gaiety in no way linked to mockery but only to liveliness of mind and originality of imagination. He tried to praise her sensibility but it was easy to see that a personal regret entered into his words. He lamented the difficulty a superior woman finds in meeting the one who corresponds to her imagined ideal, an ideal endowed with all the gifts that heart and genius could wish for. He took pleasure, however, in describing the passionate sensibility which inspired Corinne's poetry and her skill in understanding the emotional links between the beauties of nature and the most deep-seated impressions of the soul. He pointed out the originality of Corinne's language, a language which has its source in her character and way of feeling, and has a kind of natural, involuntary charm, in no way spoilt by any trace of affectation.

He spoke of her eloquence as a powerful force that was the more bound to move her listeners the more they themselves were intelligent and sensitive. 'Corinne is undoubtedly the most famous woman in our land,' he said, 'and yet only her friends can describe her; for the soul's qualities always have to be felt when they are genuine. Fame as well as obscurity can prevent their recognition if some fellow-feeling does not help us to appreciate them.' He dwelt on her talent for improvisation, which bore no resemblance to anything normally given that name in Italy. 'It must be attributed,' he continued, 'not only to her fertile mind, but to the deep emotion aroused in her by all generous thoughts. She cannot utter a word about them that is not stimulated and inspired by that inexhaustible source of emotions and ideas, enthusiasm.' Prince Castel-Forte conveyed also the charm of a style that is always pure, always harmonious. 'Corinne's poetry is an intellectual melody which alone can express the charm of the most fleeting and subtle impressions,' he added.

He lauded Corinne's conversation and one felt that he had savoured its delights. 'Imagination and simplicity, sound judgement and rapturous emotion, strength and gentleness, are combined in one person in order to vary all the pleasures of the mind at every moment,' he said. 'This charming line from Petrarch suits her well:

Il parlar che nell'anima si sente;[†]

and I think she has something of the much vaunted graciousness and oriental charm which the ancients ascribed to Cleopatra.

'The places we have visited together,' added Prince Castel-Forte, 'the music we have heard together, the pictures she has shown me, the books she has helped me to understand, make up the world of my imagination. In all these things there is a spark of her life. If I had to exist far away from her, I should at least want to surround myself with them in the certainty that nowhere else would I find again that trace of fire, in short, that trace of herself, which she has left on them. Yes,' he continued (and at that moment his eyes happened to fall on Oswald), 'look at Corinne, if you can spend your life with her, if this double existence that she will give you can be made secure for a long time; but do not look at her if you are condemned to leave her. As long as you live, you would seek in vain that creative spirit which shared and multiplied your feelings and your thoughts; you would never find it again.'

Oswald winced at these words. He looked steadily at Corinne, who was listening to them with an emotion not aroused by vanity but connected with more attractive and more affecting feelings. Prince Castel-Forte resumed his eulogy which he had been obliged to interrupt because of a momentary emotion. He spoke of Corinne's gifts

---

† The language which is felt from the bottom of the heart.

for painting, music, oratory, and dancing. He said that in all these gifts Corinne was always herself, not restricting herself to a particular style or particular rules, but expressing in a variety of ways the same powerful imagination, the same fascination of the arts in their various forms.

'I do not flatter myself that I have been able to portray someone of whom one cannot have any idea without hearing her,' concluded the Prince. 'But for us in Rome, her presence is like one of the bounties of our brilliant sky and of our inspiring countryside. Corinne is the bond that unites her friends; she is the motive, the force, that animates our lives; we count on her kindness; we are proud of her genius. We say to foreigners: "Look at her, she is the image of our beautiful Italy; she is what we would be but for the ignorance, the envy, the discord, and the indolence to which our fate has condemned us." We delight in gazing at her as an admirable product of our climate and of our arts, as an offshoot of the past, as a harbinger of the future. And when foreigners talk ill of this land which gave birth to the great minds that have enlightened Europe, when they have no pity for our failings which arise from our misfortunes, we say to them: "Look at Corinne." Yes, we would follow her in her footsteps, we would be men as she is a woman, if men could, like women, make a world for themselves in their own hearts, and if the fire of our genius, compelled to be dependent on social relationships and external circumstances, could be fully set alight by the torch of poetry alone.'

As Prince Castel-Forte stopped speaking, applause broke out on all sides, and although, at the end of his speech, he indirectly blamed the present condition of Italians, all the important state dignitaries approved of it; for it is so true that in Italy one finds the breadth of outlook which does not lead to a change in institutions but allows superior minds to be forgiven inactive opposition to current prejudices.

Prince Castel-Forte had a very high reputation in Rome. He spoke with unusual wisdom, and that was a remarkable talent in a country where people behave more intelligently than they speak. He lacked the business skill which often distinguishes Italians, but he enjoyed thinking and was not afraid of the effort of reflection. The fortunate inhabitants of the South sometimes refuse to make this effort and flatter themselves that they can discover everything through the imagination, just as their fertile land produces fruit without being cultivated, with the help only of beneficent nature.

CHAPTER III

WHEN Prince Castel-Forte had finished speaking, Corinne stood up. She thanked him with a little bow which was so noble and so gracious that one could feel both her modesty and her natural pleasure in being praised as she wanted to be. It was customary for the poet crowned at the Capitol to recite some verses before his laurel wreath was placed on his head. Corinne had her lyre, her chosen instrument, brought to her; it closely resembled a harp but it had a more antique shape and simpler sound. As she was tuning it, she was initially overcome by a great feeling of shyness and it was in a trembling voice that she asked for the subject that had been set for her. *The glory and happiness of Italy!* was the unanimous cry of all around her. 'Why yes,' she said, repeating it, already stirred, already sustained by her talent, *The glory and happiness of Italy!* And inspired by love of her country, she raised her voice in verses full of a charm which can be only imperfectly rendered in prose.

CORINNE'S IMPROVISATION AT THE CAPITOL

'Italy, empire of the Sun; Italy, mistress of the world; cradle of literature; I salute you. How many times has the human race been under your sway, sustained by your arms, your arts, and your skies!

'A god left Olympus to seek refuge in Ausonia.* The appearance of the land gave rise to the dream of the virtues of the Golden Age, and man seemed too happy there to be thought sinning.

'Through her genius Rome conquered the universe and through freedom she became queen. The Roman character was stamped on the world, but in destroying Italy the barbarian invasion darkened the whole universe.

'Italy emerged again with the divine treasures which the fugitive Greeks brought into her heart. Heaven revealed to her its laws. Her daring children discovered a new hemisphere; she became queen again through the sceptre of thought, but this sceptre wreathed in laurels aroused only ingratitude.

'Imagination restored to her the world she had lost. Painters and poets created for her a land, an Olympus, hells and heavens, and no European Prometheus stole the fire which inspired her and was better protected by her genius than by the pagans' god.

'Why am I at the Capitol? Why is my humble brow about to receive the crown Petrarch bore and which hangs on Tasso's grave-side cypress? Why? . . . if it be not, my fellow citizens, that you love glory enough to worship devotion to it as much as attainment of it.

'If, then, you love that glory which often selects its victims from the victors it has crowned, think with pride of those centuries which saw the renaissance of the arts. Dante, the Homer of modern times, the sacred poet of our hidden mysteries, the heroic thinker, plunged his genius into the Styx to approach hell, and his soul was as deep as the abysses he has described.

'Italy, at the height of its power, lives again to the full in Dante's work. Animated by the spirit of the Republic, a warrior as well as a poet, he fans the flames of action amongst the dead, and his shades are more vibrantly alive than those living today.

'Memories of earth still pursue them; their aimless passions claw at their hearts; they agonize over the past, which to them seems more irrevocable than their eternal future.

'It is as if, banished from his own country, Dante has transported his consuming sorrows to imaginary places. His shades continually ask for news about the living, just as the poet himself enquires about his native land and hell appears to him in the shape of exile.

'In his eyes everything dons the garb of Florence. The dead of antiquity, whom he conjures up, seem to be reborn as Tuscan as he. It is not his intellectual limitations but his emotional power which brings the universe into the circle of his thoughts.

'A mystical chain of circles and spheres leads him from hell to purgatory, from purgatory to paradise. A faithful recorder of his vision, he floods the darkest regions with light, and the world he creates in his three-part poem is complete, lively, and gleaming as a new planet glimpsed in the firmament.

'At his voice the whole earth is transformed into poetry. Laws, ideas, phenomena, seem a new Olympus of new divinities, but this mythology of the imagination fades away, like paganism, at the sight of paradise, that ocean of light, sparkling with stars and beams of light, with virtue and love.

'The magical words of our greatest poet are a prism of the universe; they reflect, decompose, and recombine all its wonders. The sounds imitate colours, the colours merge into harmony. The rhyme, rich or strange, swift or lingering, is inspired by poetic insight, that supreme beauty of art and triumph of genius which discovers in nature all secrets close to the human heart.

'Dante hoped his poem would put at an end his exile. He counted on fame as his mediator, but he died before he could be acclaimed by his native land. Transient human life is often worn out in reverses, and if glory triumphs, if one finally lands on a happier shore, the grave opens up behind the harbour and a many-faceted destiny often heralds the end of life by the return of good fortune.

'Such too was the fate of the unfortunate Tasso, whom your admiration, Romans, was to console for much injustice. He was handsome, sensitive, and chivalrous, dreaming of great deeds, experiencing the love celebrated in his songs, and drew nigh to these walls like his heroes in Jerusalem with respect and gratitude. But the day before that chosen for his coronation, death claimed him for her terrible celebration. Heaven is jealous of the earth and calls her darlings away from the deceptive banks of time.

'In an age more proud and free than Tasso's, Petrarch, like Dante, was the courageous poet of Italian independence. In other lands all that is known of him is his love, but here more austere memories honour his name for ever and his native land inspired him better than Laura* herself.

'In his night-time vigils he made ancient times live again and, far from being an obstacle to profound study, the creative power of his imagination, by laying the future before him, revealed to him the secrets of past ages. He learned from experience that knowledge is a great help for invention, and his genius was all the more original because, like the eternal forces, it knew how to be a witness of all times.

'Our pure air, our smiling skies, inspired Ariosto. He was the rainbow who appeared after our long wars. Brilliant and varied like this harbinger of fine weather, he seemed to frolic with life on familiar terms, and his gentle, light-hearted cheerfulness is not man's mockery but nature's smile.

'Michelangelo, Raphael, Pergolesi, Galileo, and you intrepid travellers, eager to explore new lands although nature could present you with none more beautiful than your own: join your glory, too, to that of the poets. Artists, scholars, philosophers, like them you are children of the sunshine, which in turn develops imagination, stimulates thought, arouses courage, and lulls into happiness, seeming to promise everything or sending everything into oblivion.

'Know you the land where bloom the orange trees* whose fruit is lovingly nourished by heaven's rays? Have you heard the melodious sounds which celebrate the gentle night? Have you breathed in the luxurious perfumes of the air, already so pure and sweet? Reply, visitors from other lands, is nature so beautiful and beneficent in your countries?

'Elsewhere, when social disasters afflict a land, people must feel deserted by the divine powers, but here we always feel protected by Heaven; we see that it is concerned for man and has deigned to treat him as a noble being.

'It is not only with vines and ears of wheat that our countryside is adorned, but, as at a monarch's celebration, it lavishly scatters an abundance of flowers and useless plants which, meant to give pleasure, do not stoop to be useful.

'The subtle pleasures fostered by nature are enjoyed by a nation worthy of appreciating them. It is satisfied with the simplest dishes, it is not intoxicated by the fountains of wine which are abundantly provided. It delights in its sunshine, in its arts, in its buildings, and in its countryside which is both ancient and youthful as the spring. Not for it are the refined pleasures of a brilliant society, nor the coarse pleasures of a greedy populace.

'Here sense impressions mingle with ideas, all life is drawn from the same spring, and the soul like the air extends to the boundaries of earth and heaven. Here the genius feels at home, because here reverie is so sweet. If he is restless it soothes him, if he regrets some unattained goal it presents him with a thousand golden visions. If men oppress him nature is there to welcome him.

'Thus she always heals, and her helping hand cures all wounds. Here one finds consolation even for the sorrows of the heart by admiring a bountiful God and fathoming the secret of his love. The transitory misfortunes of our ephemeral life are lost in the fertile, majestic bosom of the immortal universe.'

For some moments Corinne was interrupted by the most enthusiastic applause. Oswald alone did not join in the rapturous clamour around him. He had bowed his head onto his hands when Corinne said, *Here one finds consolation even for the sorrows of the heart*, and after that he had not looked up. Corinne noticed him and soon, by his features, by the colour of his hair, by his dress, by his tall stature, in short by his whole demeanour, she realized he was an Englishman. She was struck by his mourning dress and his sad expression. Then his gaze, fixing on her, seemed to reproach her gently. She understood the thoughts which filled his mind and felt impelled to respond to them by speaking less confidently of happiness and by devoting a few verses to death during a celebration. So, to this end, she picked up her lyre again and, imposing silence on the whole assembly with the moving, lingering sounds she drew from her instrument, she began again with these words.

'Yet there is grief which our consoling sky cannot wipe away, but in what other place of abode can sorrow convey to the soul a nobler and more soothing impression than in this land?

'Elsewhere the living barely find space for their hectic activity and ardent desires; here ruins, deserts, uninhabited palaces, leave a vast space for the shades of the departed. Is Rome not now the land of tombs?

'The Colosseum, the obelisks, all the wonders which are collected here from the depths of Egypt and Greece, from the most distant centuries, from Romulus right up to Leo X,* as if greatness attracted greatness, and as if one place had to contain everything man could shield from the ravages of time, all these wonders are in honour of the dead. Our idle way of life is barely noticed; the silence of the living pays homage to the dead. They endure and we pass on.

'They alone are honoured; they alone are still renowned. The obscurity of our destinies enhances the splendour of our ancestors; our present lives leave only the past still standing, and not a stir is aroused by our memories. All our masterpieces are the works of those no longer alive, and genius itself is amongst the illustrious dead.

'Perhaps one of Rome's secret charms is the reconciliation of the imagination with this long slumber. One is resigned to it for oneself, and suffers less from it on behalf of those one loves. The peoples of the South picture death in less sombre colours than the inhabitants of the North. The sun, like glory, warms even the tomb.

'Under this beautiful sky and beside so many funeral urns, timorous minds are less haunted by the chill and solitude of the grave. We imagine a host of shades awaits us, and from our lonely city to the city of the underworld the passage seems quite smooth.

'So the sharpness of pain is dulled, not because the heart is indifferent or the soul withered, but because a more perfect harmony, a more fragrant air, pervade existence. One is less afraid of abandoning oneself to nature, to that nature of whom the Creator has said, "the lilies of the field, they toil not neither do they spin, and yet what royal robes can equal the splendour with which I have clothed these flowers!" '*

Oswald was so delighted with these final stanzas that he expressed his admiration by the most rapturous applause, and this time the acclaim of the Italians themselves did not equal his. Indeed, it was to him rather than to the Romans that Corinne had addressed her second improvisation.

Most Italians read verse in a kind of monotonous chant called *cantilena* that destroys all feeling.[3] The impression is the same, however different the words, since the tone, which is even more affecting than the words, almost never varies. But Corinne declaimed in a variety of tones which did not destroy the sustained charm of the harmony. It was as if she were playing different airs on a celestial instrument.

The sound of Corinne's moving, sensitive voice, singing in the stately, resonant Italian language, produced an entirely new impression on Oswald. English prosody is regular and muted. Its natural beauties are all melancholy; clouds have formed its colours and the sound of waves its harmony. But when Italian words, sparkling like a festive day, ringing out like the sound of victorious trumpets, which has been likened to scarlet amongst the colours, when these words, still marked by the happiness spread in all hearts by a beautiful climate, are uttered with feeling, their softened brilliance, their concentrated power, give rise to an emotion as keen as it is unexpected. Nature's purpose seems faulty, her beneficence of no avail, her offerings rejected, and the expression of grief in the midst of so many delights is more surprising and deeply moving than sorrow expressed in the northern tongues it seems to have inspired.

CHAPTER IV

THE senator took up the crown of myrtle and laurel he was to place on Corinne's head. She removed the turban entwined round her forehead, and all her jet black hair tumbled down in curls onto her shoulders. Bareheaded she stepped forward with a look of pleasure and gratitude she did not seek to conceal. She knelt down a second time in order to be crowned, but this time she seemed less anxious and trembling. She had just spoken, she had just filled her soul with the noblest thoughts; enthusiasm had won the day over bashfulness.

No more a timorous woman, she was an inspired priestess joyfully dedicating herself to the worship of genius.

When the crown was placed on Corinne's head, all the instruments rang out and played those triumphal airs that so powerfully and sublimely uplift the soul. The roll of the kettle-drums and the flourish of the trumpets moved Corinne yet again; her eyes filled with tears, she sat down for a moment and hid her face in her handkerchief. Oswald, keenly touched, stepped out from the crowd and moved forward a little to speak to her, but an insurmountable embarrassment held him back. Corinne looked at him for a while, taking care, nevertheless, not to let him notice that she was paying attention to him. But when Prince Castel-Forte took her hand to escort her from the Capitol to her chariot, she let herself be led absent-mindedly and, under various pretexts, looked back several times to see Oswald again.

He followed her and, as she was descending the stairs escorted by her retinue, she looked back to catch one more sight of him; the movement made her crown fall off. Oswald hastened to pick it up and, as he handed it back to her, said in Italian a few words, whose meaning was that humble mortals laid at the feet of the gods the crowns they dared not place upon their heads.[4] Corinne thanked Lord Nelvil in English with that pure national accent, that pure island accent, which can hardly ever be imitated on the continent. How great was Oswald's surprise when he heard her! At first he was rooted to the spot; then, feeling giddy, he leaned against one of the basalt lions which are at the foot of the Capitol stairs. Corinne looked at him again, keenly struck by his emotion, but she was swept on towards her chariot and the whole crowd had disappeared long before Oswald had regained his strength and presence of mind.

Until that moment Corinne had delighted him as the most charming of foreign women, as one of the wonders of the country where he wanted to travel; but her English accent brought back all the memories of his native land, naturalizing all her charms. Was she an Englishwoman? Had she spent several years of her life in England? He could not tell. But study alone could not possibly have taught her to speak so well. Corinne and Lord Nelvil must have lived in the same country. Who knows if their families had not been acquainted with each other? He might even have seen her in his childhood! Often there is in the heart a vague, innate image of what we love which might lead us to think that we recognize something we are seeing for the first time.

Oswald was very prejudiced against Italian women. He thought they were passionate but fickle, incapable of experiencing deep, permanent affection. Corinne's words at the Capitol had already given him quite a different idea. How would it be, then, if he could simultaneously find memories of his native land and, through the imagination, receive a new life, if he could be reborn for the future without breaking with the past!

In the midst of his reveries, Oswald found he was at the Sant'Angelo Bridge, which leads to the Castle of the same name, or rather to Hadrian's tomb which has been turned into a fortress. The silence of the spot, the pale waters of the Tiber, the moonbeams lighting up the statues on the bridge turning them into white ghosts watching impassively the flow of the river and the passage of time, now no longer of interest to them—all this brought Lord Nelvil back to his usual thoughts. He touched his breast and felt his father's portrait which he always kept there. He took it out to study it, and the happy moment he had just experienced, together with its cause, reminded him only too well of the feeling which had, in the past, made him so guilty towards his father. This thought renewed his remorse.

'Undying memory of my life,' he cried, 'friend, so wounded and yet so generous! Could I have believed it possible the feeling of pleasure would so soon be able to gain entry into my soul? It is not you, the best and kindest of men, who reproach me for it. You want me to be happy, you want that in spite of my faults. But at least if you speak from the high heavens, may I not misunderstand your words as I misunderstood them on earth!'

BOOK III
CORINNE

CHAPTER I

COUNT D'ERFEUIL had been present at the ceremony on the Capitol and, coming the next day to see Lord Nelvil, said, 'My dear Oswald, would you like me to take you to Corinne's this evening?' 'What,' interrupted Lord Nelvil eagerly, 'do you know her?' 'No,' replied Count d'Erfeuil, 'but people as famous as that are always flattered if anyone wants to see them, and I wrote to her this morning to ask permission to call on her this evening with you.' 'I should have preferred not to be named like that without being asked,' replied Oswald, blushing. 'Be grateful to me', Count d'Erfeuil went on, 'for having spared you some tedious formalities. Instead of going to an ambassador, who would have taken you to a cardinal's, who would have taken you to some lady's house, who would have brought you to Corinne's, I introduce you, you introduce me, and we shall both be very well received.'

'I am less confident than you, and probably rightly so,' replied Lord Nelvil. 'I am afraid Corinne will be displeased with this abrupt request.' 'Not at all, I assure you,' said Count d'Erfeuil. 'She is too sensible for that and her reply is very courteous.' 'What, she answered you,' replied Lord Nelvil. 'And so what did she say, my dear Count?' 'Oh, you say "my dear Count,"' said M. d'Erfeuil with a laugh. 'So you calm down when you know Corinne has answered me. But still, *I am fond of you and forgive you everything.* I shall confess to you modestly that in my note I had mentioned myself more than you, but in her reply, it seemed to me she mentioned you first. But I am never jealous of my friends.' 'Indeed,' replied Lord Nelvil, 'I think neither of us can flatter himself that Corinne finds him attractive, and as far as I am concerned, all I want is to enjoy occasionally the company of such a remarkable person. We shall meet this evening then, since that is how you have arranged it.' 'So you will come with me?' said Count d'Erfeuil. 'Well, yes,' replied Lord Nelvil, obviously embarrassed. 'Then why,' continued Count d'Erfeuil, 'why did you complain so much of what I did? You end up where I began, but you had to be left the honour of being more reserved than I, provided, however, that you lost nothing by it. Corinne is really a delightful person; she is intelligent and charming. I did not fully understand what she was saying because she was speaking in Italian, but to look at her, I would wager she knows French very well. We shall form an opinion about that this evening. She leads a strange life. She is rich, young, and free, and with no one able to find out definitely whether or not she has any lovers. Yet it does seem certain that, at the moment, she gives no preference to anyone. Moreover, it is possible that in this country she has not met a man worthy of her,' he added. 'That would not surprise me.'

Count d'Erfeuil continued talking in this vein for some time longer without being interrupted by Lord Nelvil. There was nothing exactly improper in what he said, but he kept on offending Oswald's sensitive feelings by speaking too loudly or too frivolously about a matter of interest to him. There is a kind of tact which even intelligence and social experience cannot teach, and the heart is often wounded by the most unfailing courtesy.

Lord Nelvil was very restless the whole day as he thought about the evening's visit, but, as far as he could, he put aside the reflections which troubled him and tried to persuade himself that a feeling could give pleasure and yet not determine his lot in life. False security! For the soul derives no pleasure from what it itself knows to be transient.

Lord Nelvil and Count d'Erfeuil arrived at Corinne's house; it was in the Trastevere district, a little beyond the Castel Sant'Angelo. The view of the Tiber enhanced the beauty of the house, and its interior was elegantly decorated in the most perfect taste. The drawing room was adorned with plaster copies of Italy's finest statues, Niobe,* Laocoön,* the Medici Venus,* and the dying gladiator;* but in Corinne's personal sitting room could be seen musical instruments, books, and furniture which was simple but comfortable and arranged only to bring her friends into a small circle to facilitate conversation. Corinne was not yet there when Oswald arrived. As he waited for her, he walked up and down in her rooms, and in every detail he noticed an agreeable mixture of everything that is most pleasing in the three nations, French, English, and Italian, the taste for social life, the love of literature, and the appreciation of the arts.

At last Corinne appeared. She was dressed without any affectation, but still in a picturesque style. In her hair she was wearing antique cameos, and round her neck a string of coral. Her courtesy was dignified and easy. As she mingled freely with her friends one could recognize the divinity of the Capitol, although she behaved simply and naturally in every way. She greeted Count d'Erfeuil first, but was looking at Oswald, and then, as if she had regretted this kind of duplicity, she came towards him. When she called him Lord Nelvil, his name seemed to have a strange effect on her and she repeated it twice in a voice filled with emotion as if it recalled touching memories.

At last she said a few gracious words in Italian to Lord Nelvil, in appreciation of his previous evening's kindness in picking up her crown. In his reply Oswald tried to express the admiration she had aroused in him and gently complained that she did not speak to him in English. 'Am I more of a foreigner to you today than I was yesterday?' 'By no means,' replied Corinne, 'but when, like me, you have spoken two or three different languages for several years, you are moved to use one or the other according to the feelings you want to express.' 'English,' said Oswald, 'must surely be your native language, the one you speak to your friends, the one . . .' 'I am Italian,' Corinne interrupted. 'Forgive me, my Lord, I think I see in you the national pride which is so often characteristic of your compatriots. In this country we are more modest; we are neither self-satisfied like the French, nor proud of ourselves like the English. All we ask of foreigners is a little indulgence, and as, for a long time, we have been denied the lot of being a nation, we are often greatly at fault, as individuals, in lacking the dignity which is not permitted to us as a people. But when you know the Italians, you will see that in their character they have a few traces of ancient greatness, a few scanty, half-obliterated traces which might, however, reappear in happier times. I shall speak English to you occasionally, but not always. Italian is dear to me. I have suffered much to live in Italy,' she said with a sigh.

Count d'Erfeuil chided Corinne in a friendly way for completely forgetting him in expressing herself in languages he did not understand. 'Lovely Corinne,' he said, 'for pity's sake, speak French. You are truly worthy of it.' Corinne smiled at this compliment and began to speak fluently in a very pure French, but with an English accent. Lord Nelvil and Count d'Erfeuil were both equally surprised. Count d'Erfeuil, however, who thought he could say anything provided it was said gracefully, and who imagined that discourtesy lay in the manner and not in the matter, asked Corinne directly the reason for this peculiarity. At first she was a little put out by his unexpected questioning; then, recovering her composure, she said to Count d'Erfeuil, 'Evidently, Monsieur, I learned French from an Englishman.' He renewed his questioning with a laugh. Corinne became still more embarrassed and said at last, 'During the four years I have been settled in Rome, none of my friends, none of those who, I am sure, take a great interest in me, have questioned me about the course of my life. Right from the start they have realized that it was painful to me to speak of it.' These words put an end to Count d'Erfeuil's questions, but Corinne was afraid she had hurt his feelings. Since he seemed very close to Lord Nelvil, without trying to explain to herself why, she feared even more that he would speak unfavourably of her to his friend, and she again took some pains to please him.

Just then Prince Castel-Forte arrived with several of his and Corinne's Roman friends. They were likeable, cheerful people with friendly manners and so easily animated by the conversation of others that it was a keen pleasure to speak with them, so greatly did they appreciate what was worth appreciating. Italians are so indolent that in company, and often on any occasion, they do not display all the wit they have. Most of them do not even cultivate privately the intellectual faculties with which nature has endowed them. But they rapturously enjoy what comes to them with no effort.

Corinne's wit was full of gaiety. She noticed the ridiculous with a Frenchwoman's shrewdness and portrayed it with an Italian's imagination, but kindness pervaded all she said. There was no malice or unfriendliness in anything she said, for in everything it is coldness which is wounding, and imagination, on the contrary, is nearly always good-natured.

Oswald thought Corinne altogether charming, and in a way quite new to him. An important, terrible incident in his life was connected with a very witty, delightful Frenchwoman, but Corinne was not in the least like her. Corinne's conversation was a mixture of every kind of mental activity, enthusiasm for the arts and knowledge of the world, subtle ideas and deep feeling. In short, all the charms of liveliness and verve were to be seen in it and yet, for all that, her thoughts were never unfinished, nor her reflections ill-considered. Oswald was simultaneously surprised and charmed, uneasy and carried away. He did not understand how all Corinne's attributes could be combined in one person. He wondered if the link between so many opposing qualities was inconsistency or superiority, if it was because she felt everything or because she forgot everything in turn, that she went in this way, almost instantly, from melancholy to gaiety, from depth to charm, from conversation quite remarkable both in knowledge and ideas, to the coquetry of a woman who seeks to please and wants to captivate. Yet this coquetry was so completely dignified that it inspired as much respect as the strictest reserve.

Prince Castel-Forte was very taken up with Corinne, and all the Italians in her social circle showed their feelings for her by the most delicate and assiduous attentions and compliments. The devotion with which they usually surrounded her spread a kind of festive air on all the days of her life. Corinne was happy to be loved, but happy as one is to live in a mild climate, to hear harmonious sounds, in short to receive only pleasant impressions. The deep, serious emotion of love was not portrayed in her face, where extremely lively, mobile features expressed everything. Oswald looked at her in silence. Corinne was animated by his presence, which made her want to be agreeable. But sometimes she paused at the most brilliant moments of her conversation, surprised at Oswald's outward calm, not knowing whether he approved of her or secretly blamed her, or whether his English ideas would allow him to applaud this kind of success in a woman.

Oswald was too entranced by Corinne's charms to remember at that moment his former opinions on the obscurity appropriate to women, but he wondered if it were possible to be loved by her, if it were possible for so many beams of light to be concentrated on oneself alone. In short he was both dazzled and uneasy, and although she had very courteously invited him to come and see her again, as he had a kind of terror at the feeling which was sweeping over him, he let a whole day go by without calling on her.

Sometimes he compared this new feeling with the fatal error of his early youth, but then swiftly rejected such a comparison; for it was artfulness, moreover a perfidious artfulness, which had conquered him, while he could not question Corinne's sincerity. Did she owe her charm to magic or to poetic inspiration? Was she Armida* or Sappho? Could a genius gifted with such brilliant wings ever be captured? It was impossible to say, but at least he felt it was not society but rather heaven itself which had formed this extraordinary being and that her mind was as incapable of imitation as her character was of pretence. 'Oh, father,' wondered Oswald, 'if you had known Corinne, what would you have thought of her?'

CHAPTER II

In the morning, as was his wont, Count d'Erfeuil came to Lord Nelvil's. He reproached him for not being at Corinne's the previous evening, saying, 'You would have been very pleased if you had come.' 'Oh, why?' replied Oswald. 'Because yesterday I became certain that she is very interested in you.' 'Frivolous yet again!' interrupted Lord Nelvil. 'Do you still not know that I neither can nor wish to be so?' 'Do you call frivolity the speed with which I make my observations?' said Count d'Erfeuil. 'Am I less right because I am right more quickly? You were all made to live in the happy time of the patriarchs, when men lived for five centuries. I warn you, our lives have been cut short by at least four.' 'All right,' answered Oswald. 'And what did you find out from these rapid observations?' 'That Corinne is in love with you. Yesterday I went to see her. She certainly received me very well, but her eyes were fixed on the door to see if you were following me. For a moment she tried to talk of other things but, as she is a very lively, natural person, she asked me at last quite simply why you had not come with me. I said it was your fault; you won't mind. I said you are a gloomy, odd individual, but I shall spare you all the praise I lavished upon you.

'"He is sad," Corinne said. "He has surely lost someone who was dear to him. For whom is he wearing mourning?" "For his father, Madame," I told her, "although it is more than a year now since he lost him, but as it is natural for us all to survive our parents, I imagine that there is some other hidden reason for his long, deep-seated melancholy." "Oh," replied Corinne, "I am far from thinking that sorrows which seem to have the same cause are the same for all men. Your friend's father and your friend himself are perhaps not of the common run of men and I am greatly tempted to think so." Her voice was very gentle, my dear Oswald, as she said these last words.' 'Are those the only proofs of her interest that you have to tell me?' asked Oswald. 'In fact, in my opinion, it is quite enough to be sure of being loved,' replied Count d'Erfeuil, 'but since you want something better, you will have something better. I have reserved the most convincing proof for the end. Prince Castel-Forte came in and told the whole story of what you had done in Ancona, without knowing he was speaking about you. He told it with great verve and imagination, as far as I can tell, thanks to the two Italian lessons I have had. But there are so many French words in foreign languages that we understand nearly all of them even without knowing them. In any case Corinne's expression would have explained to me what I did not understand. The turmoil in her heart could so easily be seen on her face! She held her breath for fear of losing a single word. When she asked if anyone knew the Englishman's name, such was her anxiety that it was very easy to judge how great was her fear that a name other than yours would be mentioned.

'Prince Castel-Forte said he did not know who the Englishman was, but Corinne, turning round towards me, cried, "Isn't it true, Monsieur, that it was Lord Nelvil?" "Yes, Madame," I replied, "it was." Corinne then burst into tears. During the whole account she had not wept; so what was there in the hero's name even more moving than the story?' 'She wept!' exclaimed Lord Nelvil. 'Oh, why was I not there?' Then, suddenly stopping, he lowered his eyes and his manly face expressed the most sensitive shyness. He hastened to speak again in the fear that Count d'Erfeuil would disturb his secret joy if he noticed it. 'If the Ancona incident deserves to be related, the honour belongs to you too, my dear Count,' said Oswald. 'People certainly spoke of a pleasant Frenchman who was there with you, my Lord,' replied the Count with a laugh, 'but nobody but me paid attention to that digression in the tale. Beautiful Corinne prefers you; she no doubt thinks you are the more faithful of the two of us. Perhaps you will not be; you may even cause her more distress than I would have done, but women like sorrow, provided it is very romantic; so you suit her.' Count d'Erfeuil's every word made Lord Nelvil suffer, but what should he say to him? The Count never argued, he never listened carefully enough to change his mind; once his words had been uttered, he took no further interest in them, and the best thing to do was to forget them, if one could, as quickly as he himself did.

CHAPTER III

In the evening Oswald arrived at Corinne's with quite new feelings; he thought he might be expected. What delight in the first glimmer of understanding with a loved one! Before memory comes to share with hope, before words have expressed feelings, before eloquent language has been able to describe emotions, in these first moments there is an indefinable mystery of the imagination, more fleeting than happiness itself, but even more heavenly.

When Oswald went into Corinne's room, he felt more nervous than ever; he thought he was perhaps expected. He saw she was alone and this almost upset him; he would have preferred to observe her for a long time surrounded by people. He would have liked to be assured in some way of Corinne's preference before being suddenly engaged in a conversation which might cool her feelings towards him if, as he was sure, he showed he was embarrassed and his embarrassment made him cold.

Whether Corinne noticed this trait of Oswald's character, or whether a similar trait made her want to stimulate conversation to dispel the constraint, she quickly asked Lord Nelvil if he had seen any of the monuments in Rome. 'No,' replied Oswald. 'What did you do yesterday then?' asked Corinne with a smile. 'I spent yesterday in my own rooms,' said Oswald. 'Since I have been in Rome, I have seen only you, Madame, or I have been alone.' Corinne wanted to speak to him about what he had done in Ancona and she began with the words, 'Yesterday, I learned . . .' Then she stopped, and said, 'I shall talk about that when more people come.' Lord Nelvil had a dignified manner which made Corinne feel embarrassed, and in reminding him of his noble behaviour, she was, moreover, afraid of showing too much emotion. She thought she would be more composed when they were no longer alone together. Oswald was deeply touched by Corinne's reserve and the frankness with which, without further thought, she revealed the reasons for this reserve. But the more agitated he was, the less could he express what he felt.

So he suddenly got up and went towards the window. Then he felt that Corinne would not be able to understand his move, and more disconcerted than ever, he came back to his seat without a word. Corinne had more self-assurance in conversation than Oswald, but she shared his embarrassment, and in an effort to save face she fingered the harp beside her and struck a few random chords. These harmonious sounds heightened Oswald's emotion and seemed to make him a little bolder. He had already dared to look at Corinne. Oh, who could look at her without being struck by the divine inspiration in her eyes? And, at the same moment, reassured by the kindly expression which softened the flash of her glance, Oswald was perhaps about to speak, when Prince Castel-Forte came in.

He was not altogether pleased to see Lord Nelvil alone with Corinne, but he was used to hiding his feelings. This habit, which, in Italians, is often combined with very strong emotions, stemmed in him from indolence and gentleness. He was resigned to not taking first place in Corinne's affections; he was no longer young. He had a high intelligence, a great appreciation of the arts, an imagination as lively as was required to vary life without disturbing it, and such a need to spend all his evenings with Corinne that, if she had been married, he would have begged her husband to let him come and see her every day as usual. On this condition he would not have been very unhappy to see her bound to another. In Italy the sorrows of love are not complicated by the distress of vanity, so that you meet either men with such passionate feelings that they stab their rivals out of jealousy, or men modest enough to be willing to take second place with a woman whose conversation they like. But you will find hardly any who, from fear of being thought spurned, would refuse to retain any relationship they enjoyed. In this country society has almost no power over *amour propre*.

When Count d'Erfeuil and the friends who came every evening to Corinne's had assembled, the conversation turned on the talent for improvisation so gloriously displayed by Corinne at the Capitol, and they came round to asking her what she thought about it herself. 'It is so rare to find someone capable of both enthusiasm and analysis, gifted as an artist but able to observe herself, that we must beg her to reveal as best she can the secrets of her genius,' said Prince Castel-Forte. 'The talent for improvisation is not more unusual in the languages of the South than political oratory or brilliant, lively conversation is in other languages,' replied Corinne. 'I shall go as far as to say that unfortunately it is easier in our country to improvise verses than to speak well in prose. Poetic language is so different from prose that, from the very first lines, attention is commanded by the expressions themselves, which, as it were, distance the poet from the audience. It is not only to the gentleness of Italian, but more to the strong, pronounced resonance of its sounds, that the supremacy of poetry with us must be attributed. Italian has a musical charm so that there is pleasure in the sound of words almost independent of the ideas; moreover, these words have nearly always something picturesque about them, their sound reflects their meaning. You can feel that this melodious, highly coloured language was formed with the fine arts around it, beneath a beautiful sky. So it is easier in Italy than anywhere else to charm without any deep thoughts or novel images. Poetry, like all the arts, captivates the senses as well as the mind. But I am bold enough to say that I have never improvised unless inspired by genuine emotion or by an idea that I thought new, so I hope I relied less than others on our enchanting language. It can render a prelude blindly, as it were, and still give keen pleasure by the charm of rhythm and harmony.'

'So you think the talent for improvisation has a bad effect on our literature; I used to think so too, before hearing you, but you have made me change my opinion completely,' interrupted one of Corinne's friends. 'I said,' replied Corinne, 'that, as a result of this facility, of this abundance of literature, there is a great deal of mediocre poetry, but I am very pleased this productivity exists in Italy, just as I like seeing our countryside covered with thousands of superfluous crops. This generosity of nature fills me with pride. Above all I like ordinary people's improvisations; they reveal their imaginations, which, hidden everywhere else, are developed only in our country. They give something poetic to the lowest ranks of society and spare us the distaste one cannot help feeling for any kind of vulgarity. When our Sicilians address pleasing compliments in their charming language to travellers they take in their boats, and say in verse a long, gracious farewell to them, it is as if the pure breath of sea and sky acts on the human imagination like the wind on Aeolian harps,* and poetry, like the harmonies, is the echo of nature. One more thing makes me value our talent for improvisation; it is that this talent would be almost impossible in a society prone to mockery. For poets to take this risk, the good nature of the South is necessary—if I may say so—or rather of a country where people like to enjoy themselves without taking pleasure in criticizing what amuses them. A mocking smile would be enough to take away the presence of mind necessary for an unpremeditated and uninterrupted composition; the audience must be aroused along with you and their applause must inspire you.'

'But you, Madame, but you,' Oswald said at last, having kept silent till then without ceasing to look at Corinne for a moment. 'Which of your poems do you prefer? The works of reflection or the works of sudden inspiration?' 'My Lord,' replied Corinne, with a look showing both a great deal of interest and the even more delicate feeling of respectful attention, 'I should make you the judge, but if you ask me to consider what I myself think, I shall say that for me improvisation is like a lively conversation. I don't let myself be bound by any particular subject, I go along with the impression that my listeners' interest makes on me, and it is to my friends that I owe the greatest part of my talent in this field. Sometimes the passionate interest aroused in me by a conversation on the great, noble questions about man's moral being, his destiny, his objective, his duties, his affections, raises me above my powers, enables me to discover in nature, in my own heart, bold truths, expressions full of life, which solitary reflection would not have produced. At such a time I think I experience a supernatural enthusiasm and I have the definite feeling that the voice within me is of greater worth than myself. It often happens that I depart from poetic rhythms and express my thought in prose; sometimes I quote the finest verses of the different languages I know. They are mine, those divine verses which imbue my soul. Sometimes, too, with chords and simple, national melodies, I complete on my lyre feelings and thoughts I cannot express in words. Finally, I feel I am a poet, not only when a happy choice of rhymes or harmonious words, when a happy combination of images, dazzles the audience, but when my soul is uplifted, when from on high it despises selfishness and baseness, in short, when a great deed would be easier for me. It is then that my verses are better. I am a poet when I admire, when I despise, when I hate, not out of personal feelings, not for my own sake, but for the dignity of humankind and the glory of the world.'

Then Corinne realized that she had been carried away by the conversation. This made her blush a little and, turning towards Lord Nelvil, she said, 'You see, I cannot approach any subject which moves me without experiencing the kind of excitement which is the source of ideal beauty in the arts, of religion in solitary hearts, of generosity in heroes, of disinterestedness in men. Forgive me, my Lord, although a woman like that is hardly likely to be approved of in your country.' 'Who could be like you,' replied Lord Nelvil, 'and can one make laws for someone who is unique?'

Count d'Erfeuil was thoroughly delighted, although he had not understood everything Corinne said. But her gestures, the sound of her voice, her manner of speaking, entranced him and it was the first time a charm that was not French had affected him. But in fact, Corinne's great success in Rome gave him some guidance as to what he ought to think of her, and in admiring her, he did not lose his good habit of letting himself be directed by other people's views.

As he was leaving with Lord Nelvil, he said, 'My dear Oswald, admit that I deserve some credit for not trying to curry favour with such a charming lady.' 'But it seems to me that people say generally that she is not easy to please,' replied Lord Nelvil. 'They say so,' answered Count d'Erfeuil, 'but I find it difficult to believe. An independent woman on her own, who leads almost an artist's life, should not be difficult to win.' This idea hurt Lord Nelvil. Whether he did not notice this, or whether he wanted to follow the train of his own thoughts, Count d'Erfeuil went on in this vein.

'Yet if I wanted to believe in a woman's virtue,' he said, 'I would as gladly believe in Corinne's as in any other woman's. She has, to be sure, a look a thousand times more expressive, and arguments far more lively, than would be needed in your country, and even in mine, to make us doubt a woman's austerity. But she has such a superior mind, such deep learning, such delicate tact, that ordinary rules for judging women cannot be applied to her. Indeed, would you believe that I find her impressive in spite of her disposition and her free-and-easy conversation. Yesterday, while respecting her interest in you, I wanted to venture a few words on my own behalf. I used words which can be taken any way you like; if they are listened to, well and good; if they are not listened to, still well and good; but Corinne looked at me coldly in a way that quite embarrassed me. Yet it is unusual to be nervous with an Italian woman, an artist, a poet, in short everything which ought to put one at ease.' 'Her name is unknown,' replied Lord Nelvil, 'but her manners make one think it must be distinguished.' 'Oh, in novels it is usual to conceal the finest things,' said Count d'Erfeuil, 'but in the real world we tell everything that is to our credit, and even a little more than everything.' 'Yes,' Oswald interrupted, 'in some social circles, where people think only of the impression they make on each other, but where there is an inner life, circumstances may be mysterious just as feelings may be concealed. Only the man who would like to marry Corinne could know . . .' 'Marry Corinne,' interrupted Count d'Erfeuil, bursting out laughing. 'Oh, that idea would never have occurred to me! Believe me, my dear Nelvil, if you want to do something foolish, do something that is not irreparable. But for marriage, you must consider only the conventions. I may seem frivolous to you, yet I wager that in the ordering of my life I shall be more sensible than you.' 'I think so too,' replied Lord Nelvil, and he did not add another word.

Indeed, could he tell Count d'Erfeuil that frivolity often contains much selfishness, and this selfishness can never lead to errors of feeling, errors in which one nearly always sacrifices oneself to others? Frivolous men are often capable of becoming very skilful in the management of their own interests, for in everything that is called politics, in private life as well as in public, people are more successful because of the qualities they do not have than because of those they have. Lack of enthusiasm, lack of firm opinions, and lack of sensitivity are a kind of negative wealth. If you add to these a little wit, they allow life in society properly speaking, that is to say fortune and rank, to be quite well achieved and maintained. Nevertheless Count d'Erfeuil's joking remarks had hurt Lord Nelvil. He disapproved of them but he was upset as he recalled them.

BOOK IV
ROME

CHAPTER I

For two weeks Lord Nelvil devoted himself completely to Corinne. He left his rooms only to go to visit her, he saw nothing, he sought nothing, but her, and without ever telling her of his feelings he enabled her to enjoy them at every moment of the day. She was used to the lively flattering compliments of the Italians, but Oswald's dignified manner, his apparent coldness, and his sensitivity, revealed in spite of himself, exercised a much greater power over her imagination. Never did he tell of a generous deed, never did he speak of a misfortune, without his eyes being filled with tears, but he always tried to conceal his emotion. He aroused in Corinne a feeling of respect that she had not experienced for a long time. No intelligence, however distinguished, could surprise her, but nobility and dignity of character affected her profoundly. With these qualities Lord Nelvil combined elevated language and an elegance in the smallest actions of life which contrasted with the carelessness and informality of most of the great Roman noblemen.

Although Oswald's tastes were in some respects quite different from Corinne's, they understood each other marvellously. Lord Nelvil was extremely skilful in guessing Corinne's reactions, and at the slightest change in his expression she detected what was going on in him. Used as she was to the passionate outbursts of Italians, this shy, yet proud devotion, this feeling constantly proved but never expressed, spread an altogether new interest over her life. She felt as if immersed in a purer, gentler atmosphere, and every moment of the day gave her a feeling of happiness which she loved to savour without trying to explain it.

One morning, Prince Castel-Forte came to see her. He was sad and she asked him why. 'That Scotsman is going to take your affection from us,' he said, 'and who knows if he won't take you far away.' Corinne was silent for a few moments and then she replied, 'I swear to you that he has not told me he loves me.' 'Nevertheless you think he does,' replied Prince Castel-Forte. 'He talks to you about his life, and his very silence is a skilful way of arousing your interest. What, indeed, can he say to you that you have not already heard? What praise has not already been bestowed on you? What compliments are you not accustomed to? But there is something restrained and unrevealed in Lord Nelvil's character which will never allow you to judge him in quite the same way as you judge us. You are the easiest person in the world to know, but it is precisely because you willingly show your-self as you are that you like reserve and mystery, and they have power over you. The unknown, whatever it may be, influences you more than all the feelings expressed to you.' Corinne smiled. 'Do you think, then, my dear Prince, that I have an ungrateful heart and a capricious imag-ination?' she said. 'But I think Lord Nelvil possesses and gives evi-dence of such remarkable qualities that I cannot flatter myself that I discovered them.' 'I agree he is a proud, generous, intelligent man, even sensitive and, above all, melancholy, but, unless I am mistaken, his tastes are quite unlike yours,' replied Prince Castel-Forte. 'You will not realize this as long as he is under the spell of your presence, but your power over him would not be maintained if he were far from you. Obstacles would weary him; his sorrows have drained his soul and that is bound to impair the strength of his resolve. You know, moreover, how much the English in general are slaves to the customs and habits of their country.'

At these words, Corinne fell silent and sighed. Painful thoughts about the events of her early life went through her mind, but in the evening she saw Oswald again more attentive to her than ever, and all that remained in her mind of her conversation with Prince Castel-Forte was the desire to keep Lord Nelvil in Italy by making him appre-ciate the beauties of every kind with which that land is endowed. It was with this in mind that she wrote him the following letter. The freedom of the Roman way of life excused this step and, although she could be reproached with too open and impulsive a character, Corinne, especially, knew how to maintain a great deal of dignity in independence and modesty in liveliness.

Corinne to Lord Nelvil

15 December 1794

'I do not know, my Lord, if you think I have too much self-confidence or if you will do justice to the motives which may excuse such confidence. Yesterday I heard you say you had not yet driven round Rome, that you have not seen either our artistic masterpieces or the ancient ruins that teach us history through the imagination and feelings. So I have had the idea of venturing to suggest myself as a guide to these journeys through the centuries.

'Rome could no doubt easily offer many scholars whose profound learning might be of much greater service to you, but if I can succeed in making you enjoy your stay in this city, to which I have always felt so powerfully attracted, your own studies will complete what my sketchy outline will have begun.

'Many foreigners come to Rome, as they would go to London, as they would go to Paris, in search of the amusements of a big city, and if people dared admit they were bored in Rome I think most of them would. But it is also true that a charm can be found here of which one never tires. Will you forgive me, my Lord, for wishing you to be acquainted with this charm?

'To be sure, here all the political interests of the world must be forgotten, but when these interests are not linked to duties or sacred feelings, they chill the heart. What in other places are called social pleasures must also be given up, but these pleasures nearly always wither the imagination. In Rome one can enjoy a life that is both solitary and lively, freely developing all that Heaven has placed within us. I repeat, my Lord, forgive me this love for my country, which makes me want to make it loved by a man such as you, and do not judge with English severity the gestures of goodwill that an Italian woman feels able to make without losing anything in her own eyes or in yours.

                                                                'CORINNE'

It was in vain that Oswald would have liked to hide from himself that the receipt of this letter made him extremely happy. He had a confused glimpse of an enjoyable, happy future. Imagination, love, enthusiasm, everything divine in man's soul, seemed to him to be combined in the delightful plan of seeing Rome with Corinne. This time he did not stop to think; this time he went out immediately to go and see Corinne, and on the way he looked at the sky, he felt the fine weather, and bore life lightly. His sorrows and fears were lost in clouds of hope; his heart, long oppressed with sadness, was beating and quivering with joy. He was greatly afraid that such a happy frame of mind could not last, but the very idea that it was fleeting made this fevered happiness stronger and more forceful.

'You have come!' Corinne said when she saw Lord Nelvil come in. 'Oh, thank you!' And she held out her hand to him. Oswald took it and with eager affection pressed his lips upon it; at that moment he did not feel the crippling shyness that was often mingled with his pleasantest impressions and sometimes gave him bitter, painful feelings with the people of whom he was most fond. Since they had separated, close friendship had developed between Oswald and Corinne, and Corinne's letter had confirmed it. They were both pleased and were affectionately grateful to each other.

'This morning, then, I shall show you the Pantheon* and Saint Peter's. I had had some hope that you would agree to drive round Rome with me, so my horses are ready,' she said with a smile. 'I expected you; you have come. Everything is in order; let us go.' 'Amazing person,' said Oswald. 'Who are you then? Where did you acquire so many different charms which would appear to be mutually exclusive, sensitivity, gaiety, depth, grace, lack of constraint, modesty? Are you an illusion? Do you bring supernatural happiness to the life of the man who crosses your path?' 'Oh, if I have the power to do you some good, you must not think that I shall ever give it up,' replied Corinne. 'Beware,' answered Oswald, grasping Corinne's hand with emotion, 'beware of the good you want to do me. For nearly two years an iron hand has gripped my heart; if your sweet presence has given me some respite, if, near you, I can breathe, what will become of me when I must go back to my fate?' 'Let us leave it to time, let us leave it to chance, to decide if the impression I made on you in one day will last more than a day,' interrupted Corinne. 'If our hearts understand each other, our mutual affection will not be ephemeral. Whatever the outcome, let us go and admire together everything that can elevate our minds and hearts. In this way we shall still be able to enjoy some moments of happiness.' As she finished speaking Corinne went out to the carriage, and Lord Nelvil, surprised by her reply, followed her. It seemed to him that she admitted the possibility of a superficial feeling, of a temporary attraction. In fact he thought there was a hint of frivolity in her way of speaking and it hurt him.

Without a word, he took his seat in Corinne's carriage. Guessing his thoughts, she said, 'I do not think the heart is so made that one always feels either no love at all or the most unconquerable passion. There are incipient feelings which a deeper examination can dispel. We delude ourselves, we undeceive ourselves, and the very enthusiasm to which we are liable may also make disenchantment more speedy.' 'You have thought deeply about feelings, Madame,' said Oswald bitterly. Corinne blushed at this remark and was silent for a few moments. Then, starting to speak again with quite a striking mixture of frankness and dignity, she said, 'I do not think any sensitive woman has ever reached the age of twenty-six without experiencing the illusion of love, but if never having been happy, if never having met the person who could deserve all her heart's affection, entitle her to some interest, I have a right to yours.' These words, and the tone in which Corinne uttered them, dissipated a little the cloud which had arisen in Lord Nelvil's heart. Nevertheless, he said to himself, 'She is the most entrancing of women, but she is an Italian and she has not the innocent heart, unknown to itself, which, I am sure, belongs to the young Englishwoman whom my father intended for me.'

This young Englishwoman was called Lucile Edgermond, the daughter of Lord Nelvil's father's best friend. She was still too young, however, when Oswald left England, for him to be able to marry her or even to foresee with any certainty what she would be like one day.

CHAPTER II

OSWALD and Corinne went first of all to the Pantheon, which today is called *Santa Maria Rotonda*. Catholicism has inherited from paganism everywhere in Italy, but the Pantheon is the only ancient temple in Rome which has been preserved intact, the only one in which can be seen in its entirety the beauty of classical architecture and the particular nature of ancient worship. Oswald and Corinne stopped in the Pantheon square to admire the temple's portico and the columns supporting it.

Corinne remarked to Lord Nelvil that the Pantheon was built in such a way that it seemed much bigger than it really was. 'Saint Peter's church makes quite a different impression,' she said. 'At first you will think it is less vast than it is. The illusion which is so favourable to the Pantheon comes, I am told, from the greater space between the columns and the free passage of air around them; but it comes, above all, from the almost total lack of ornamental detail, while

Saint Peter's is overloaded with it. In the same way classical poetry depicted only the broad outlines and left it to the listener's thoughts to fill in the gaps and develop the themes. In every genre, we moderns say too much.

'This temple,' continued Corinne, 'was dedicated by Augustus' favourite, Agrippa,* to his friend, or rather to his master. His master, however, had the modesty to refuse the dedication of the temple and Agrippa was obliged to dedicate it to all the gods of Olympus to replace the earthly god, power. On top of the Pantheon was a bronze chariot, on which were placed the statues of Augustus and Agrippa. On either side of the portico, the same statues reappeared in another form, and on the main façade of the temple one can still read: *Agrippa consecrated it.* Augustus gave his name to his era, because he made it a period of the human spirit. His contemporaries' masterpieces in different genres form, as it were, the rays of his halo. He knew how to honour skilfully writers of genius and so his glory in posterity was all the greater.

'Let us go into the temple,' said Corinne. 'You see, it remains open to the sky, almost as it was in the past. It is said that the light which came from above was the symbol of the divinity superior to all divinities. The pagans always liked symbolic images. Indeed such language seems more appropriate than words to religion. Rain often falls on these marble precincts, but the sun's rays, too, often cast light upon prayer. What serenity! What a festive air pervades this building! The pagans deified life and the Christians deified death. That is the spirit of the two religions. But our Roman Catholicism is less sombre than was that of the North. You will notice that, when we are at Saint Peter's. Inside the sanctuary of the Pantheon are the busts of our most famous artists. They decorate the niches where the gods of the ancients had been placed. As we have hardly ever had political independence in Italy since the destruction of the Roman Empire, neither statesmen nor great military leaders are to be found here. Our only glory is the genius of the imagination. But do you not think, my Lord, that a people which, in this way, honours the talents it has would deserve a nobler fate?' 'I judge nations severely,' replied Oswald. 'I always think they deserve their lot, whatever it may be.' 'That is hard,' answered Corinne. 'Through living in Italy, perhaps you will come to feel an affection for this beautiful land which nature seems to have adorned like a victim. But remember at least that the fondest hope of us artists, of us lovers of fame, is to win a place here. I have already booked mine,' she said, showing him a niche that was still empty. 'Oswald, who knows if you will not come back to this same place when my bust will be in place there? Then . . .' Oswald interrupted her brusquely, saying, 'You who are resplendent with youth and beauty, how can you talk like this to one whom misfortune and suffering are already inclining to the grave?' 'Oh, in one moment the storm can break flowers that still hold their heads high,' replied Corinne. 'Oswald, dear Oswald,' she added, 'why should you not be happy, why? . . .' 'Never question me,' answered Lord Nelvil. 'You have your secrets; I have mine. Let us mutually respect each other's silence. No, you do not know what emotion I would feel if I had to recount my misfortunes!' Corinne fell silent and, as she left the temple, her steps were slower and her expression more reflective.

She stopped under the portico. 'In that place,' she said to Lord Nelvil, 'there used to be an outstandingly beautiful porphyry urn, now removed to Saint John Lateran;* it contained Agrippa's ashes, which were placed at the base of the statue he had erected to himself. The ancients took such care to soften the idea of destruction that they knew how to remove anything about it that was mournful or frightening. Moreover their tombs were so magnificent that the contrast between the nothingness of death and the splendours of life was made to feel smaller. It is also true that, as they had a much less keen hope of another world than the Christians had, the pagans tried to contend with death for the memory which we place without fear in the bosom of the Eternal.'

Oswald sighed and remained silent. Melancholy thoughts are very attractive so long as one has not oneself been deeply unhappy, but when grief in all its harshness has gripped the soul, one can no longer hear without a shudder words which formerly aroused only more or less pleasant reveries.

CHAPTER III

To go to Saint Peter's one goes over the Sant'Angelo Bridge, and Corinne and Lord Nelvil crossed it on foot. 'It was on this bridge,' said Oswald, 'that, as I came back from the Capitol, I first thought about you at length.' 'I did not expect that my coronation at the Capitol would bring me a friend,' replied Corinne. 'But yet, in seeking fame,

I always hoped it would make me loved. What use would it be, at least to women, without that hope?' 'Let us stay here a little while,' said Oswald. 'What memory from any age can be as precious to my heart as this place which reminds me of the first day I saw you?' 'Unless I am mistaken, it seems to me that people become dearer to each other when, together, they admire monuments whose true greatness speaks to the soul,' replied Corinne. 'The buildings of Rome are neither cold nor dumb; genius created them, memorable events consecrate them. Perhaps, Oswald, we must love, above all, a character like yours, to enjoy sharing with him appreciation of all that is noble and beautiful in the universe.' 'Yes,' replied Lord Nelvil, 'but as I look at you, as I listen to you, I need no other marvels.' Corinne thanked him with a most charming smile.

On the way to Saint Peter's, they stopped in front of the Castel Sant'Angelo. 'This building has a very original exterior,' said Corinne. 'Hadrian's tomb, turned into a fortress by the Goths, bears the mark of its first and its second purpose. It was built for death and is surrounded by an impenetrable wall, but the living have added something hostile with the external fortifications which form a contrast to the silence and noble uselessness of a funeral monument. On the top you can see a bronze angel with his naked sword,[5] and inside cruel prisons are carved out of the rock. All the events of Roman history from Hadrian to our own day are linked to this monument. Belisarius* defended himself here against the Goths and, almost as much a barbarian as his attackers, he hurled the beautiful statues which ornamented the inside of the building against the enemy. Crescentius,* Arnault de Brescia,* Nicolas Rienzi,*[6] those friends of Roman liberty, who so often took memories for hopes, defended themselves for a long time in an emperor's tomb. I love these stones which are linked to so many glorious deeds. I love this luxury for the master of the world, a magnificent tomb. There is something great about the man who, though he enjoys all earthly pleasures and pomp, is not afraid to think a long time ahead about his death. Moral ideas, disinterested feelings, fill the soul as soon as it goes, in any way, beyond the limits of life.

'It is from here that one should glimpse Saint Peter's,' continued Corinne. 'And the columns which lead up to it ought to extend as far as this. That was Michelangelo's magnificent plan; he hoped at least that it would be completed after him, but the men of our day

no longer think of posterity. Once enthusiasm has been ridiculed, everything is destroyed, except money and power.' 'It is you who will revive
that feeling,' cried Lord Nelvil. 'Who ever experienced the happiness
I enjoy? Rome shown by you, Rome interpreted by imagination and
genius, *Rome, a world given life by feeling, without which the world itself
is a desert.*[7] Oh, Corinne, what will follow these days that are happier
than my fate and heart allow?' Corinne replied gently, 'All sincere affections come from heaven, Oswald. Why would it not protect what it
inspires? It is for heaven to dispose of us.'

Then Saint Peter's came into view, the tallest building man has
ever erected, for even the Egyptian pyramids are not so high. 'Perhaps I ought to have shown the most beautiful of our buildings last,'
said Corinne, 'but that is not my plan. If you want to stimulate appreciation of art, I think you have to begin with things that inspire a deep,
keen admiration. Once you have had this feeling, it reveals, as it were,
a new realm of ideas, and so makes you better able to love and judge
everything that, even if it is of a lesser order, still recalls your first
impression. This gradual process, this carefully moderated way of
preparing great effects, is not to my taste. You do not reach the sublime by degrees; the distance between it and the merely beautiful is
infinite.' Oswald felt an extraordinary emotion when they reached the
front of Saint Peter's. It was the first time a work of man had affected
him like a work of nature. It is the only work of art in our world today
which has the kind of greatness that is characteristic of the direct works
of creation. Corinne enjoyed Oswald's amazement. 'I have chosen
a day when the sun is shining in all its brilliance, to show you this
monument,' she said. 'I am reserving for you a more intimate, a more
religious pleasure, that of looking at it by moonlight. But first of
all I had to show you the most brilliant of spectacles, human genius
ornamented by nature's splendour.'

Saint Peter's Square is surrounded by columns that seem slender
at a distance but massive at close range. The ground which rises gradually to the portico of the church adds to its effect. In the middle of
the square is an obelisk, eighty feet high, which barely seems tall beside
the dome of Saint Peter's. In the very shape of obelisks there is something pleasing to the imagination. Their summits disappear into the
skies and seem to carry a great human idea up to heaven. This monument, which came from Egypt to decorate Caligula's* baths and which
Sixtus V* later had transported to the foot of Saint Peter's temple,

this contemporary of so many ages which had been powerless against it, inspires a feeling of respect. Man feels he is so ephemeral that he is always moved in the presence of the unchanging. Some way from each side of the obelisk are two fountains, whose waters spurt up continually, cascading down again in abundance through the air. The murmur of water, usually heard in the heart of the country, gives rise to quite a new sensation in such an area, but the sensation is in harmony with that aroused by the sight of a majestic temple.

Painting and sculpture, as they usually imitate the human form or some object which exists in nature, arouse in our souls perfectly clear, definite ideas; but a beautiful architectural monument has, as it were, no specific meaning, and in gazing at it one is gripped by the aimless, unthinking reverie which leads one's thoughts such a long way. The sound of the water befits these vague, deep impressions. It is regular, just like the building.

Eternal movement and eternal rest[†]

are thus drawn close together. It is above all in this spot that time is powerless, for it no more dries up these gushing springs than it makes these motionless stones collapse. The jets of water which shoot up in columns are so light and hazy that on a fine day sunbeams make most beautifully coloured little rainbows.

'Pause a moment here,' said Corinne to Lord Nelvil when he was already under the portico of the church. 'Pause before raising the curtain which covers the temple door. Does not your heart beat as you approach the sanctuary? And, at the moment of entry, do you not feel all that the expectation of a solemn event would arouse?' Corinne herself raised the curtain and held it to let Lord Nelvil pass. Her attitude was so graceful that Oswald's first glance was to look at her in this position. For some moments he took pleasure in looking only at her. He went forward into the temple, however, and the impression he received under the enormous vaults was so deep and religious that even the feeling of love no longer sufficed to fill his heart. He walked slowly beside Corinne; both were silent. There, everything commands silence; the slightest sound reverberates so far that, in this almost eternal dwelling, no words seem worthy of such repetition! Prayer alone, the accent of sorrow, however faint its voice, is profoundly

† Line of verse by M. de Fontanes.*

moving in this immense space. And when, under the vast domes, we hear from afar the approach of an old man dragging his trembling steps on the beautiful marble, watered by so many tears, we feel that man is impressive because of the very infirmity of his nature, which submits his divine soul to so much suffering; we feel, too, that the religion of pain, Christianity, contains the true secret of the passage of man on earth.

Corinne interrupted Oswald's reverie, saying, 'You have seen Gothic churches in England and Germany. You must have noticed that they are much gloomier than this church. There was something mystical about the Catholicism of northern peoples. Ours appeals to the imagination through external objects. When he saw the dome of the Pantheon, Michelangelo said, "I shall place it in the sky." And in fact Saint Peter's is a temple on top of a church. There is a kind of alliance between the ancient religions and Christianity in the effect which the interior of this building has on the imagination. I often come here to restore to my soul the serenity that it sometimes loses. The sight of such a monument is like a permanent, continuous music waiting to benefit you when you draw near. And we must certainly count, amongst our nation's claims to glory, the patience, courage, and unselfishness of the church leaders who devoted one hundred and fifty years, so much money and work, to the completion of a building which those who erected it could never claim to enjoy.[8] It is a service rendered even to public morality to present the nation with a monument that is the symbol of so many noble, generous ideas.' 'Yes,' replied Oswald, 'here the arts have the greatness, the imagination, of genius. But the dignity of man himself, how is it defended here? What institutions, what weakness, in most Italian governments! And although they are so weak, how they enslave minds!' 'Other peoples have endured the yoke like us,' interrupted Corinne, 'but they lack the imagination which makes us dream of another fate.

'Servi siam si, ma servi ognor frementi.

We are slaves, but slaves who are still quivering, said Alfieri,* the proudest of our modern writers. There is so much feeling in our arts that perhaps one day our character will equal our genius.

'Look at those statues on the tombs, those mosaics, patient, faithful copies of our great masterpieces,' continued Corinne. 'I never study

Saint Peter's in detail because I do not like finding the multiplicity
of beauties which slightly disturbs the impression of the whole. But
what then is a monument in which the masterpieces of the human
spirit themselves seem superfluous ornaments? This temple is like a
world apart. You can find refuge here from the cold and the heat. It
has its own seasons, its perpetual springtime, which the external atmosphere never alters. A subterranean church was built beneath the courtyard of this temple; Popes and several rulers of foreign lands are buried
there, Christina* after her abdication, the Stuarts* after the overthrow
of their dynasty. For a long time Rome has been the refuge of the
world's exiles. Is not Rome herself dethroned? The sight of her consoles kings who, like her, have been despoiled.

> Cadono le città, cadono i regni,
> Et l'uom, d'esser mortal, par che si sdegni!*

Cities fall, empires disappear, and man resents his mortality!

'Stand here,' Corinne said to Lord Nelvil, 'near the altar, directly
beneath the dome. Through the iron grating you will see the church
of the dead beneath our feet, but when you raise your eyes you will
barely be able to see the top of the vault. Even seen from below, the
dome arouses a feeling of terror. Abysses seem to be suspended over
one's head. Everything beyond certain proportions inspires in man,
in that limited being, an unconquerable terror. What we know is as
inexplicable as the unknown, but we have studied, as it were, the obscur-
ities we are used to, while new mysteries terrify us and upset our minds.

'The whole church is decorated with ancient marble and these stones
know more than we do about past ages. Here is the statue of Jupiter,
turned into a Saint Peter by putting a halo on its head. The overall
impression made by this temple is perfectly characteristic of the mixture of sombre dogma and brilliant ceremony, the basic sadness in
the ideas, but the easygoing liveliness of the South in their applica-
tion, strict intentions but very gentle interpretations, Christian the-
ology but pagan imagery, in short the most admirable combination
of brilliance and majesty that man can give his worship of the divine.

'Decorated with artistic marvels, the tombs do not present death
in a fearsome light. It is not quite like the ancients, who carved dances
and games on the sarcophagi, but thoughts are deflected from the contemplation of a coffin by masterpieces of genius. They remind us of

immortality on the very altar of death. The imagination, stimulated by the admiration they inspire, does not, as in the North, feel silence and cold, the immutable guardians of sepulchres.' 'We probably want sadness to surround death,' said Oswald, 'and even before Christianity enlightened us, our ancient mythology, our Ossian,* places only regrets and funeral chants beside the grave. Here, you want to forget and enjoy life. I am not sure if I would like your beautiful sky to do me that kind of good.' 'But do not think,' Corinne replied, 'that we have flighty characters and frivolous minds. It is only vanity that makes people frivolous. Indolence can give some intervals of sleep or forgetfulness in life but it neither wears out nor withers the heart, and unfortunately for us, we can emerge from that state by means of deeper and more terrible passions than those of more habitually active souls.'

As she finished speaking, Corinne and Lord Nelvil were coming to the church door. 'One last look at this vast sanctuary,' she said to Lord Nelvil. 'See how puny man is in the presence of religion, even though we can do no more than study its material symbol! See what permanence, what durability, mortals can give their works while they pass on so quickly and survive only through genius! This temple is an image of the infinite; there is no limit to the feelings it inspires, to the ideas it recalls, to the enormous number of years it brings to mind, whether of the past or future, and on leaving its precincts one seems to pass from heavenly thoughts to worldly interests, from religious eternity to the ephemeral realm of time.'

When they were outside the church, Corinne pointed out to Lord Nelvil that the bas-reliefs on the doors represented Ovid's *Metamorphoses*.* 'Pagan imagery does not scandalize the Romans when it is hallowed by art,' she said. 'The wonders of genius always convey a religious feeling to the soul and we pay homage to Christian worship through all the masterpieces that other forms of worship have inspired.' Oswald smiled at this explanation. 'Believe me, my Lord,' continued Corinne, 'there is a great deal of sincere faith in the feelings of nations with very lively imaginations. But we shall meet tomorrow. If you like, I shall take you to the Capitol. I have, I hope, still several expeditions to suggest. When they are completed, will you leave? Will you . . .' She stopped, afraid she had already said too much. 'No, Corinne,' replied Oswald. 'No, I shall not give up the ray of happiness that some guardian angel may have shone on me from the heights of heaven.'

CHAPTER IV

WHEN Oswald and Corinne set out the next day, they were confident and at ease. They were friends who were travelling together.
They began to say *we*. Oh, how touching it is when lovers say *we*. What
a declaration it contains, shyly and yet eagerly expressed! 'So, we are
going to the Capitol,' said Corinne. 'Yes, we are going there,' replied
Oswald, and his voice was so sweet and tender that it said everything
with those simple words. 'The top of the Capitol as it is today is the
place from which we can easily have a view of the seven hills,' said
Corinne. 'Then we shall explore all of them, one after the other. There
is not one of them which does not preserve some traces of history.'

To start with, Corinne and Lord Nelvil followed what was formerly
called the sacred way or the triumphal way. 'Did your chariot follow
that route?' Oswald asked Corinne. 'Yes,' she answered. 'The ancient
dust must have been amazed to bear such a chariot. But since the
Roman Republic, the footprints of so much wickedness have been left
on this road that the respectful feeling it used to inspire is greatly
reduced.' Then Corinne had them driven to the foot of the stairs of
the present-day Capitol. The entrance to the old Capitol was through
the Forum. 'I wish these stairs were the same as those Scipio* climbed
when, refuting slander by his glorious deeds, he went into the temple
to give thanks to the gods for the victories he had won. But these new
stairs, this new Capitol, was built on the ruins of the old to receive the
peaceable magistrate who, quite on his own, bears the prestigious name
of Roman senator, formerly respected by the whole universe. Here,
we now only have names, but their musical sounds, their ancient dignity, arouse a kind of unease, a rather pleasant feeling, a mixture of
pleasure and regret. The other day I asked a poor woman I met where
she lived. *At the Tarpeian Rock** she replied, and these words, even
devoid of the ideas which used to be connected with them, still have
an effect on the imagination.'

Oswald and Corinne stopped to examine the two basalt lions which
can be seen at the foot of the Capitol stairs.[9] They come from Egypt;
Egyptian sculptors had much greater genius in catching animal than
human faces. These Capitol lions are nobly peaceable and their kind
of expression is the true image of tranquillity in strength.

A guisa di leon, quando si posa.

DANTE

Like the lion when at rest.

Not far from these lions you can see a mutilated Roman statue, put there by modern Romans who did not realize that in this way they were presenting the most perfect symbol of their present-day Rome. This statue has neither head nor feet, but what remains of the torso and drapery still retains some of their ancient beauty. At the top of the stairs are two colossi which are thought to represent Castor and Pollux, then Marius'* trophies, then two military columns which were used for measuring the Roman universe, and the equestrian statue of Marcus Aurelius,* beautiful and calm in the midst of these different mementoes. So everything is there, the heroic age represented by the Dioscuri,* the Republic by the lions, the civil wars by Marius, and the great days of the emperors by Marcus Aurelius.

As you go towards the modern Capitol you can see, on the right and on the left, two churches built on the ruins of the temples of Jupiter Feretrius* and Jupiter Capitolinus.* In front of the entrance is a fountain presided over by two rivers, the Nile and the Tiber, together with Romulus' she-wolf.* The name of the Tiber is not spoken like that of rivers which are not renowned. One of the pleasures of Rome is to say, *Take me along the banks of the Tiber: let us cross the Tiber.* It is as if by speaking those words you are evoking history and bringing the dead back to life. On your right, as you go to the Capitol by way of the Forum, are the Mamertine prisons.* These prisons were built first by Ancus Martius* and were used in his day for ordinary criminals. But Servius Tullius* had much crueller ones built underground for political prisoners, as if these criminals did not deserve most consideration since there may be good faith in their errors. Jugurtha* and Catiline's* accomplices perished in these prisons. It is said, too, that Saint Peter and Saint Paul were confined there. On the other side of the Capitol is the Tarpeian Rock; today at the foot of the Rock stands a hospital called the *Hospital of Consolation.* It is as if the strict spirit of antiquity and the gentleness of Christianity are thus brought together in Rome across the centuries and are presented to the eye as well as to the mind.

When Oswald and Corinne had reached the top of the Capitol tower, Corinne pointed out the seven hills, the city of Rome bounded first by Mount Palatine, then by Servius Tullius' walls enclosing the seven hills, and finally by Aurelian's* walls, which still today surround the greater part of Rome. Corinne recalled the lines of Tibullus and Propertius* which celebrate the small beginnings from which emerged the mistress of the world.[10] For some time, Mount Palatine on its own

was all of Rome, but later on the emperors' palace filled the space
which had been enough for a nation. A poet of Nero's day* wrote
this epigram on the subject.† *Rome will soon be no more than a palace.
Leave for Veii, Romans, unless the palace already fills even Veii.*

The seven hills are much less high than they used to be when they
deserved the name of *steep mountains.* Modern Rome is forty feet above
the level of ancient Rome. The valleys that separate the hills have nearly
all been filled in by time and ruined buildings. But, what is stranger
still, a heap of potsherds has formed two new hills.‡ This progress
or rather these remnants of civilization, putting mountains and
valleys on the same level, morally as well as physically obliterating all
the beautiful inequalities produced by nature, is almost an image of
modern times.

Three other hills,†† not included in the seven famous ones, give the
city of Rome a certain picturesqueness which makes it perhaps the
only town that, by itself and within its own walls, offers the most magnificent viewpoints. There is such a remarkable mixture of ruins and
buildings, of countryside and wasteland, that one can look at Rome in
every direction and always see a striking picture on the opposite side.

Oswald could not weary of contemplating the remnants of ancient
Rome from the heights of the Capitol where Corinne had taken him.
The reading of history, the reflections it arouses, have less effect on
our soul than these ruins mingled with new dwellings. The eyes are
all powerful over the soul; after seeing the Roman ruins, we believe
in the ancient Romans as if we had lived in their day. Intellectual
memories are acquired by study. Memories of the imagination stem
from a more immediate, more profound impression, which gives life
to our thoughts and makes us, as it were, witnesses of what we have
learned. We are undoubtedly irritated by all the modern buildings
which are mixed up with the ancient remains. But a portico standing beside a humble roof, columns between which little church windows have been inserted, a tomb used as a shelter for a whole peasant
family, produce an indescribable mixture of great and simple ideas,
an indescribable pleasure of discovery which inspires a perpetual interest. Everything is ordinary, everything is prosaic, from the outside in

---

†   Roma domus fiet: Veios migrate, Quirites;
      Si non et Veios occupat ista domus.
‡   Monte Citorio and Monte Testaccio.
†† The Janiculum, Monte Vaticano, and Monte Mario.

most of our European cities, but Rome, more frequently than any other, offers the melancholy sight of poverty and degradation. But suddenly a broken column, a half-destroyed bas-relief, stones linked together in the indestructible manner of the ancient architects, remind you that there is in man an eternal power, a divine spark, and that you must never weary of kindling it in yourself and of reviving it in others.

The Forum, so restricted an area which has seen so many surprising things, is striking proof of man's moral greatness. When, in Rome's latter days, the universe was subjected to inglorious masters, there are whole centuries about which history can barely preserve a few facts. But this Forum, a small area, the centre of a town, then of a very limited space, whose inhabitants used to fight around it for its territory, this Forum, has it not interested geniuses of all ages by the memories it revives? Honour then, eternal honour, to courageous, free peoples, since they thus enthral the gaze of posterity!

Corinne observed to Lord Nelvil that in Rome very few ruins of the Republican era can be found. The aqueducts, the canals built underground for the flow of water, were the only luxury of the Republic and of the kings who preceded it. Useful buildings, tombs erected in memory of its great men, and a few surviving brick temples are all that remain to us from the Republic. It was only after the conquest of Sicily that, for the first time, the Romans used marble for their monuments. But it is enough to see the places where great deeds took place to feel an indefinable emotion. It is to this disposition of the soul that the religious power of pilgrimages must be attributed. Even when divested of their great men and their monuments, countries famous in many different ways have great power over the imagination. What was striking to behold no longer exists, but the charm of memory has remained.

You can no longer see in the Forum any trace of the famous rostrum from which oratory governed the Roman people. There are still three columns of a temple built by Augustus in honour of Jupiter Tonans when lightning struck near by without harming him, and a triumphal arch erected by the Senate in honour of Septimius Severus* as a reward for his heroic deeds. The names of his two sons, Caracalla* and Geta, were inscribed on the pediment of the arch, but when Caracalla murdered his brother, Septimius had his name removed and you can still see the marks of the obliterated letters. Further on is a temple to Faustina, a monument to the blind weakness of

Marcus Aurelius,* and a temple to Venus, which in the Republican
era was consecrated to Pallas.* A little further on still are the ruins
of a temple dedicated to the sun and the moon; it was built by the
Emperor Hadrian, who, jealous of the celebrated Greek architect
Apollodorus, had him put to death for criticizing the proportions of
his building.

On the other side of the square you can see the ruins of monuments dedicated to nobler and purer memories. There are columns
of a temple thought to be in honour of Jupiter Stator, the Jupiter who
prevented the Romans from ever fleeing before their enemies; one
column, remnant of a temple to Jupiter the Guardian, is said to stand
not far from the abyss into which Curtius plunged,* and there are
columns of a temple which some say was erected to Concord, others
say to Victory. Do victorious peoples perhaps confuse these two ideas
and think there can only be real peace when they have conquered the
universe? At the far side of the Palatine hill is a beautiful triumphal
arch dedicated to Titus for the conquest of Jerusalem. People say the
Jews of Rome never pass under this arch and point out a little path
they use to avoid it. For the honour of the Jews it is to be hoped this
story is true; long memories befit long misfortunes.

Not far from there is Constantine's arch, ornamented by some bas-
reliefs taken from Trajan's* forum by the Christians, who wanted
to beautify the monument in honour of the *founder of peace*; that is
the name they gave to Constantine. At that period, the arts were already
on the decline and they plundered the past to honour new exploits.
These triumphal gateways that can still be seen in Rome perpetuated, as far as men can, the honours rendered to great deeds. On their
topmost points was a place intended for flute and trumpet players,
so that the conqueror, as he passed by, would be carried away by music
and praise at the same time, and thus, in one moment, savour all the
most exalted emotions.

Opposite these triumphal arches are the ruins of the Temple of Peace
built by Vespasian.* There was so much bronze and gold ornamentation inside that, when it was consumed by fire, burning metal poured
like lava into the Forum. Lastly, the Colosseum, the most beautiful
ruin in Rome, is at the end of the glorious enclosure where all history is on show. This magnificent building, of which only the stones,
stripped of the gold and marble, survive, was used as an arena for the
gladiators who fought wild animals. It was in this way that the Roman

people was entertained and deceived by strong emotions when natural feelings could no longer take wing. Entry to the Colosseum
was by two doors; one was for the victors, the other for carrying away
the dead.[†] Strange contempt for humankind to turn in advance the
life or death of a man into the simple pastime of a show! Titus, the
best of the emperors, dedicated the Colosseum to the Roman people,
and these remarkable ruins contain in themselves such magnificent
touches of genius that one is tempted to delude oneself about true
greatness and accord to artistic masterpieces the admiration due only
to monuments dedicated to great-hearted institutions.

Oswald did not allow himself to share Corinne's admiration. As
he looked at the four galleries, the four structures, rising one above
the other, at the mixture of pomp and decay which simultaneously
arouses respect and pity, he could see only the masters' luxury and
the slaves' blood; he felt prejudiced against the arts which are not concerned with aims but lavish their talents on any objects that are assigned
to them. Corinne tried to counter this frame of mind. 'Do not take
the severity of your principles of justice and morality into the contemplation of Italy's monuments,' she said to Lord Nelvil. 'As I
have told you, they mostly recall the splendour, the elegance, and the
taste of classical forms, rather than the glorious era of Roman virtue.
But do you not find some traces of the moral greatness of the early
periods in the enormous luxury of the monuments which came after
them? The very degradation of the Roman people is impressive. In
mourning freedom they have covered the world with marvels, and the
genius for ideal beauty tries to console man for the real, true dignity
he has lost. Look at these enormous baths open to everyone who wants
to savour oriental pleasures, these circuses intended for elephants
who come to fight tigers, the aqueducts which suddenly changed the
arenas into a lake, in which galleys took turns to fight, in which
crocodiles appeared where once lions had been displayed. That was
the luxury of the Romans when they based their pride on luxury! These
obelisks brought from Egypt and stolen from darkest Africa to decorate Roman tombs; these statues, of which there used to be an abundance in Rome, can only be considered the useless and sumptuous pomp
of Asian despots. They represent the genius of Rome, conqueror of
the world, to which the arts have given an external form. There is

---

[†] Sana vivaria, sandapilaria.*

something supernatural in this magnificence, and its origin and purpose are forgotten in its poetic splendour.'

Corinne's eloquence aroused Oswald's admiration, without convincing him. He was looking for a moral feeling everywhere, and all
the magic of the arts could never satisfy him. Corinne then remembered that in this same arena persecuted Christians had died, victims
of their steadfastness; she pointed out to Lord Nelvil the altars erected
in honour of their ashes, and the Stations of the Cross which the
penitents followed at the foot of the most magnificent ruins of human
grandeur, and asked him if the martyrs' dust did not touch his heart.
'Yes,' he cried, 'I have a profound admiration for the strength of feeling and will against pain and death. Any kind of sacrifice is more splendid, more difficult, than any impulse of feeling or thought. Exalted
imagination can produce miracles of genius, but it is only in devoting oneself to one's opinion or feelings that one is truly virtuous. It is
only then that a heavenly power overcomes the mortal man in us.'
These noble, pure words upset Corinne, however. She looked at Lord
Nelvil, then lowered her eyes; and although at that moment he took
her hand and pressed it to his heart, she trembled at the thought that
such a man might sacrifice himself and others to the worship of opinions, principles, or duties that he had chosen.

CHAPTER V

AFTER the expedition to the Capitol and the Forum, Corinne and
Lord Nelvil spent two days visiting the seven hills. In former times
the Romans had a festival in their honour. These hills, enclosed
within the precincts of Rome, are one of its original beauties and it
is not difficult to understand how, in their love for their native land,
Romans delighted in celebrating this unusual feature.

As they had seen the Capitoline hill the day before, Oswald and
Corinne began their tour with the Palatine hill. The palace of the
Caesars, called *the golden palace*, used to occupy it completely. Now,
only the ruins of the palace remain on the hill. Augustus, Tiberius,
Caligula, and Nero built its four sides, but stones, completely cov-
ered all over by proliferating plants, are all that remains of it today.
Nature has regained its empire over the works of man and the beauty
of the flowers is a consolation for the ruin of the palaces. Luxury in

the eras of the kings and of the Republic consisted entirely of public buildings; private houses were very small and very simple. Cicero, Hortensius,* the Gracchi,* lived on the Palatine hill, which, in the days of Rome's decadence, had barely enough space for the home of one man. In later centuries, the nation was no more than an anonymous crowd, referred to only by its master's reign. There is no point in searching in these places for the two laurel bushes planted in front of Augustus' door, the laurel of war and the laurel of the arts cultivated by peace; both have disappeared.

Some rooms of Livia's* baths still remain on the Palatine hill. They show where precious stones used to be lavished on ceilings like an ordinary decoration, and you can see there paintings whose colours are still perfectly intact; the very fragility of the colours adds to our amazement at seeing them preserved and brings the past close to us. If it is true that Livia shortened Augustus' life, it was in one of these rooms that the crime was plotted, and the eyes of the sovereign of the world, betrayed in his profoundest affections, may have dwelt on one of these pictures whose elegant flowers still survive. In his old age, what did he think of life and its pomp? Did he remember his proscriptions or his glory? Did he fear or hope for a world to come? And the last thought which reveals everything to man, the last thought of a master of the universe, does it still wander beneath these arches?[11]

More than any other, the Aventine hill shows traces of the earliest days of Roman history. Exactly opposite the palace built by Tiberius you can see the remains of the Temple of Liberty built by the Gracchi's father. At the foot of the Aventine hill was the temple dedicated to Manly Fortune by Servius Tullius to thank the gods for his becoming a king though born a slave. Outside the walls of Rome are also the ruins of a temple which was dedicated to Womanly Fortune when Veturia* stopped Coriolanus.* Opposite the Aventine hill is the Janiculum,* where Porsena* placed his army. It was opposite this hill that Horatius Cocles* had the bridge leading to Rome destroyed behind him. The foundations of the bridge still exist. On the river banks there is a triumphal arch built of brick, as simple as the deed it recalls was great. It is said that this arch was built in honour of Horatius Cocles. In the middle of the Tiber you can glimpse an island made out of sheaves of wheat gathered in Tarquin's fields and exposed on the river for a long time because the Roman people, believing that an evil fate was connected with them, did not want to take them. It would be difficult nowadays to inflict on any kind of wealth curses so effective that nobody would be willing to grab it.

It was on the Aventine hill that the temples of Patrician Chastity and Plebeian Chastity were placed. At the foot of this hill you can see the Temple of Vesta* that still survives almost intact, although often threatened by the Tiber's floods.[†] Not far from there are the remains of a debtors' prison, where the well-known act of filial piety* occurred. It was also in this same place that Porsena's prisoners, Cloelia* and her companions, swam across the Tiber to join the Romans. The Aventine hill gives the soul a rest from all the painful memories recalled by the other hills and it looks as beautiful as the memories it revives. The name of beautiful shore (*pulchrum littus*) had been given to the river bank at the foot of this hill. It was there that Roman orators strolled as they left the Forum. It was there that Caesar and Pompey used to meet as ordinary citizens and try to win over Cicero, whose independent oratory mattered more to them at that time than even the power of their armies.

Poetry came to beautify this region even more. Virgil placed Cacus' cave* on the Aventine hill, and the Romans, so great by their history, are great too by the heroic tales with which the poets have glorified their legendary origin. Lastly, coming back from the Aventine hill, you can see Nicolas Rienzi's house; he tried, in vain, to make ancient times live again in modern times, and the memory of this, insignificant though it is compared with the others, still gives rise to long reflection. The Caelian hill is remarkable because there you can see the remains of the camps of the Praetorians and of the foreign soldiers. In the ruins of the building erected to house these soldiers, the following inscription has been found: *To the holy guardian spirit of the foreign camps*. Holy, indeed, for those whose power it upheld! What remains of these ancient barracks gives rise to the opinion that they were built in the style of cloisters, or rather that cloisters were built in their style.

The Esquiline hill is called the *Poets'* hill because, as Maecenas'* palace was there, Horace, Propertius, and Tibullus also had their dwellings there. Not far away are the ruins of the Baths of Titus and Trajan. Raphael is thought to have modelled his arabesques on the frescos of Titus' baths. It is there too that the Laocoön was discovered. Cool

---

[†] Vidimus flavum Tiberim, etc.*

water is so pleasantly refreshing in hot countries that people liked combining every luxury and all the pleasures of the imagination in the
places where they bathed. The Romans exhibited masterpieces of painting and sculpture there. They looked at them by lamplight, for the
structure of the buildings seems to indicate that daylight was never
let in and that this was how people chose to protect themselves from
the burning rays of the southern sun. It is, no doubt, because of the
effect of the sun's rays that the ancients called them Apollo's darts.
From the extreme precautions taken by the ancients against the heat
you could think that in those days the climate was even more burn-
ingly hot than in modern times. In the Baths of Caracalla were placed
the Farnese Hercules, Flora, and the Dirce group.* Near Ostia, Apollo
Belvedere* was found in Nero's baths. Is it conceivable that Nero did
not have some generous emotions when he looked at that noble figure?

The only traces in Rome of buildings devoted to public entertainment are the baths and circuses. Marcellus'* theatre is the only one
of which there are any surviving ruins. Pliny relates that three hundred and sixty marble columns and three thousand statues were seen
in a theatre that was to last only a few days. Sometimes the Romans
constructed such solid buildings that they withstood earthquakes,
sometimes they liked to devote enormous work projects to buildings
that they themselves destroyed when the festivities were over; thus
did they trifle with time in all its forms. Moreover, the Romans, unlike
the Greeks, did not have a passion for dramatic performances; only
Greek works and artists made the arts flourish in Rome, and Roman
grandeur was expressed by the colossal magnificence of architecture rather than by masterpieces of the imagination. This enormous
luxury, these marvels of wealth, have a great quality of dignity: it was
no longer liberty, but it was still power. The buildings erected for
public baths were called 'provinces'; in them all the different prod-
ucts and organizations that can be found in a whole country were
brought together. The Circus (called *Circus Maximus*), whose ruins
can still be seen, was so near the Caesars' palaces that Nero could give
the signal for the start of the games from his palace window. The Circus
was large enough to contain three hundred thousand people. Almost
the whole nation was entertained at the same time. These enormous
festivities could be considered a kind of popular institution which
brought all men together for pleasure, as once they had been brought
together for glory.

The Quirinal hill and the Viminal hill are so near each other that it is difficult to make out which is which. It was there that Sallust* and Pompey had houses, and it is there too that the Pope has now fixed his residence. You cannot take a step in Rome without bringing together the present and the past and the different pasts between them. But you learn to take the events of your own day calmly when you see the ever-changing vicissitudes of human history. You are almost ashamed to be worried in the presence of so many centuries which have all overturned the work of their predecessors.

Beside the seven hills, or on their slopes or summits, you can see a multitude of church towers, obelisks, Trajan's column, the column of Antoninus Pius, the Conti tower* from where it is claimed that Nero watched Rome burn, and the dome of Saint Peter's which is even more dominating than everything else that dominates. The air seems to be filled with all these buildings which reach up to the sky, and a city in the air seems to hover majestically over the city on the ground.

As they came back into Rome, Corinne led Oswald under the Porticus of Octavia,* a woman who loved so well and suffered so much. Then they crossed *the wicked woman's path*, where the infamous Tullia* trampled her father's body under her horses' hooves. From afar they could see the temple built by Agrippina in honour of Claudius* whom she had poisoned; and finally they went past Augustus' tomb, where the inner space is used today as an area for animal fights.

'I have rushed you through some of the landmarks of ancient history,' Corinne said to Lord Nelvil, 'but you will understand the pleasure to be found in these researches, which are both scholarly and poetical, and appeal to the imagination as well as to the mind. In Rome there are many distinguished men whose only occupation is to discover new connections between history and the ruins.' 'I do not know of any other study which would hold my interest more, if I felt calm enough to devote myself to it,' replied Lord Nelvil. 'This kind of study is much more interesting than what is acquired in books. It is as if you bring back to life what you discover, and the past reappears from beneath the dust that buried it.' 'Undoubtedly,' said Corinne, 'and the passion for antiquity is not a pointless predisposition in its favour. We live in a century when self-interest seems the only motive for all men's actions, but what sympathy, what emotion, what enthusiasm, can ever result from self-interest? It is pleasanter to dream of those days of devotion, sacrifice, and heroism, but they have existed and have left honourable traces in the world.'

CHAPTER VI

SECRETLY Corinne felt sure she had won Oswald's heart, but as she knew his reserve and strict code of conduct, she had not dared reveal all the interest he aroused in her, although her character inclined her not to conceal her feelings. She may also have thought that, even when they talked of matters unrelated to their feelings, the tone of their voices betrayed their mutual affection and that a secret confession of love was depicted in their looks and in the melancholy, veiled language which penetrates so deeply into the soul.

One morning when Corinne was getting ready to continue her expeditions with Oswald, she received an almost formal note from him, telling her that his poor state of health was keeping him at home for several days. Corinne's heart was gripped by a painful anxiety. At first she thought he was dangerously ill, but Count d'Erfeuil, whom she saw in the evening, told her it was one of the attacks of depression to which Oswald was very prone and during which he did not want to talk to anyone. 'When he is in that state,' Count d'Erfeuil then said, 'even I do not see him.' Corinne was a little unhappy about this *even I* but she took good care not to show her feelings to the only man who could give her news of Lord Nelvil. She questioned him, assuming that such an apparently frivolous man would tell her all he knew. But whether he wanted to hide by an air of mystery that Oswald had confided nothing to him, or whether he thought it more honourable to refuse her request, he suddenly opposed an imperturbable silence to Corinne's burning curiosity. She, who had always had ascendancy over everyone she had talked to, could not understand why her powers of persuasion had no effect on Count d'Erfeuil. Did she not know that *amour propre* is the most inflexible motive in the world?

What could Corinne then do to find out the state of Oswald's heart? Write to him? One has to be so restrained when writing, and Corinne was attractive above all because she was uninhibited and natural. Three days passed during which she did not see Lord Nelvil and she was tortured by terrible anxiety. 'What have I done to alienate him?' she wondered. 'I did not tell him I loved him; I did not make that mistake, so terrible in England but so pardonable in Italy. Has he guessed? But why should that lower his opinion of me?' Oswald had stayed away from Corinne only because he felt too keenly attracted by her charm. Although he had not given his word that he would marry Lucile Edgermond, he knew his father had intended her to be his wife and he wanted to comply with his father's wishes. Finally Corinne was not known by her real name and for some years had lived far too independent a life. Lord Nelvil thought that such a marriage would not have obtained his father's approval and he felt strongly that that was not the way to atone for the wrongs he had done him. These were his reasons for keeping away from Corinne. He had formed the plan to write to her when he left Rome, and that condemned him to carry out this resolution. But as he did not feel strong enough to do so, he simply did not go to see her and after the second day even this sacrifice seemed too painful.

The thought had occurred to Corinne that she would never see Oswald again and that he would go away without saying goodbye to her. Every moment she expected to have news of his departure and this fear so inflamed her feelings that she was suddenly gripped by passion, by that vulture's claw which ruins happiness and independence. Since Lord Nelvil did not come she could not stay at home, and so she sometimes wandered around in the gardens of Rome, hoping to meet him. She could better bear the hours she spent wandering about with the possibility that she might catch sight of him. Corinne's ardent imagination was the source of her talent, but unfortunately for her, her imagination was linked to her natural sensitivity and often caused her great pain.

On the evening of the fourth day of this cruel separation there was a lovely moon, and Rome is very beautiful during the silence of the night when it seems inhabited only by its illustrious ghosts. On her way back from visiting a woman friend, Corinne, dejected and sorrowful, got out of her carriage and rested for a few moments by the Trevi Fountain, in front of the abundant stream of water which cascades down the centre of Rome and seems, as it were, the life of this calm spot. When the waterfall stops flowing for a few days, it is as if Rome were struck with amazement. In other towns, you need to hear the din of carriages, but in Rome it is the murmur of this enormous fountain which seems the necessary background to the daydreaming life you lead there. Corinne's image could be seen in the water, which is so pure that for several centuries it has borne the name of *virgin water*.* Oswald, having stopped at the same place a few moments later, caught sight of her charming face reflected in the water. He was gripped by such intense emotion that at first he did not know if his imagination was bringing Corinne's shade before him as it had done so often with his father's. He bent down over the fountain to see better and his own features were then reflected beside Corinne's. She recognized him, uttered a cry, rushed quickly towards him, and gripped his arm as if she feared he would escape again. But hardly had she given way to this impetuous gesture than, remembering Lord Nelvil's character, she blushed at having shown her feelings so blatantly, and letting go the hand that was holding on to Oswald, she covered her face with the other one to hide her tears.

'Corinne,' said Oswald, 'dear Corinne, so has my absence made you unhappy?' 'Oh, yes,' she replied, 'and you knew that very well. So why did you hurt me? Have I deserved to suffer at your hand?' 'No,' cried Lord Nelvil, 'certainly not. But if I do not consider myself free, if I feel that in my heart I have only anxieties and regrets, why should I associate you with the torment of my feelings and apprehensions? Why . . .' 'It is too late,' interrupted Corinne, 'it is too late. Grief is already in my heart; spare me.' 'You, grieving?' replied Oswald. 'In the middle of such a brilliant career, of so much success, with such a keen imagination?' 'Stop,' said Corinne. 'You do not know me. Of all my gifts, the most powerful is my gift for suffering. I was born for happiness; my character is trusting, my imagination is lively, but pain arouses in me an indefinable impetuosity which can disturb my reason and cause my death. I repeat it again, spare me. Cheerfulness and a lively temperament only help me superficially; but within my heart there are depths of sadness from which I can defend myself only by shielding myself from love.'

Corinne uttered these words with an expression that deeply moved Oswald. 'I shall come and see you tomorrow morning,' he replied. 'You can count on that, Corinne.' 'Do you swear it to me?' she asked, trying in vain to conceal her anxiety. 'Yes, I swear it,' cried Lord Nelvil, as he disappeared.

BOOK V
TOMBS, CHURCHES, AND PALACES

CHAPTER I

WHEN they saw each other the next day, Oswald and Corinne were embarrassed. Corinne no longer had confidence in the love she inspired. Oswald was displeased with himself; he knew there was a kind of weakness in his character which sometimes made him annoyed with his own feelings as with a tyranny. Both of them tried not to speak of their mutual affection. 'Today,' said Corinne, 'I am suggesting an excursion which is rather solemn but will certainly interest you. Let us go and see the tombs; let us go and see the last resting-places of those who lived amongst the monuments whose ruins we have gazed upon.' 'Yes,' replied Oswald. 'You have guessed what suits the present state of my feelings.' He uttered these words in such a melancholy tone that Corinne fell silent for a few moments, not daring to try to speak to him. But her desire to bring Oswald some relief from his sorrows by arousing his keen interest in everything they saw together made her take heart again and she said, 'You know, my Lord, that the sight of the tombs, far from discouraging the living, was thought by the ancient Romans to inspire a new emulation, and so these tombs were sited on public roads; young people were thus reminded of famous men and silently invited to imitate them.' 'Oh,' said Oswald with a sigh. 'How I envy all those whose sorrows are not mingled with remorse!' 'You, remorse!' cried Corinne. 'You! Oh, I am sure that in you it is just one more virtue, a scrupulous feeling, a heightened sensibility.' 'Corinne, Corinne, do not touch on that subject,' interrupted Oswald. 'In your happy country sombre thoughts disappear in the brightness of the skies, but grief which has burrowed right to the depths of our soul shatters our whole life for ever.' 'You misjudge me,' replied Corinne. 'I have already told you. Although my personality is naturally made for the keen enjoyment of happiness, I would suffer more than you if . . .' She broke off and changed the subject. 'All I desire, my Lord, is to distract you from your painful thoughts for a while,' she continued. 'I hope for nothing more.' Lord

Nelvil was touched by her gentle reply and, seeing a melancholy expression in Corinne's eyes, naturally so full of interest and enthusiasm, he reproached himself for saddening someone born for eager, happy emotions, and tried to bring her back to them. But Corinne's anxiety about Oswald's plans and the possibility of his departure completely upset her usual calm.

She led Lord Nelvil beyond the city gates, along the route of the remains of the old Appian Way. In the countryside outside Rome, these remains are marked to right and left by tombs whose ruins are visible for several miles beyond the walls as far as the eye can see. The Romans did not allow burial of the dead inside the city; only emperors' tombs were permitted there. An ordinary citizen, however, by the name of Publius Biblius, was granted this privilege as a reward for his humble virtues. Indeed, contemporaries are more willing to honour such virtues than any others.

To go to the Appian Way, you go through Saint Sebastian's gate, which used to be called *Capena*. Cicero says that as you go out by this gate the first tombs you see are those of the Metellus, the Scipio, and the Servilius families. The tomb of the Scipio family was found at this very place and later transferred to the Vatican. It is almost a sacrilege to remove the ashes and interfere with the ruins; imagination is more closely connected with morality than one thinks, and it must not be offended. Amongst so many tombs that strike the eye, names are placed at random and you cannot be sure whose they are; but this very uncertainty arouses an emotion which does not let you look with indifference at any of these monuments. Some of them have peasants' homes fitted up inside them, for the Romans devoted a large area and quite spacious buildings to the funeral urns of their friends or of their distinguished fellow citizens. They did not have that arid principle of utility which fertilizes a few more scraps of land but renders barren the vast domain of feeling and thought.

Some distance from the Appian Way can be seen a temple erected by the Republic to Honour and Virtue, another to the god who made Hannibal retrace his steps, and Egeria's* fountain where Numa went to consult the deity of upright men, conscience examined in solitude. Around these tombs it seems that only traces of virtues still survive. No monument from the centuries of crime is to be found beside the resting places of these illustrious dead; they are surrounded by an honourable area where the noblest memories may reign undisturbed.

There is something unusually remarkable about the appearance of the countryside round Rome. It is undoubtedly wasteland, for there are no tress or dwellings. But the ground is covered with natural plants, which are continually renewed by their vigorous growth. These parasitical plants insinuate themselves into the tombs, decorate the ruins, and seem to be there only to honour the dead. It is as if nature, in her pride, has spurned all the works of man since the Cincinnati* ceased to drive the plough which furrowed her bosom; she produces plants at random without allowing the living to make use of her abundance. These uncultivated stretches of land must irritate agriculturalists, administrators, and all those who speculate on the land and want to exploit it for man's needs, but imaginative souls, concerned as much with death as with life, enjoy contemplating this Roman countryside where the present day has left no mark, this earth which cherishes its dead and lovingly covers them with useless flowers, with useless plants which trail along the ground and never grow tall enough to detach themselves from the ashes they seem to caress.

Oswald agreed that here one ought to enjoy calm more than anywhere else. The soul suffers less from the images brought to mind by grief; it is as if you were still sharing the charms of the air, of the sun, of the greenery, with those who are no more. Corinne noticed the impression made on Lord Nelvil, and this gave her some hope. She did not expect to console Oswald; she would not even have wanted to erase from his heart the legitimate grief due to the loss of his father. But in the very feeling of sorrow there is something gentle and soothing that we must try to make known to those who have as yet experienced only its bitterness. That is the only good we can do them. 'Let us stop here opposite this tomb,' said Corinne. 'It is the only one which still remains almost intact; it is not the grave of a famous Roman, but of Caecilia Metella,* a young girl whose father had this monument erected.' 'Happy, happy are the children who die in their fathers' arms,' said Oswald; 'they encounter death in the bosom of him who gave them life. Death itself then loses its sting for them.' 'Yes,' replied Corinne with feeling. 'Happy are those who are not orphans. Look, they have carved arms on this tomb, although it is a woman's. But heroes' daughters may have their fathers' trophies on their tombs. The union between valour and innocence is indeed beautiful. There is an elegy by Propertius which depicts better than any other ancient text the dignity of women among the Romans; it was purer and more impressive even than the brilliant position of women during the age of chivalry. Cornelia,* who died young, bids farewell to her husband and comforts him in the most touching terms, and in almost every word you can feel all that is sacred and worthy of respect in family ties. The noble pride of a blameless life is depicted in that majestic Latin poetry, a poetry noble and rigorous like the masters of the world. *Yes*, said Cornelia, *no stain has marred my life from marriage to the funeral pyre; my life has been pure between the two flaming torches.*[12] What admirable language!' cried Corinne. 'What a sublime image! And how enviable is the lot of a woman who has thus been able to preserve the most perfect unity in her destiny and carries only one memory to the grave. That is enough for a life.'

As she finished speaking, Corinne's eyes filled with tears, and a painful feeling, a cruel suspicion, gripped Oswald's heart. 'Corinne,' he cried, 'Corinne, has your sensitive soul nothing to reproach itself with? If I were free to make my own choice, if I could offer myself to you, would I not have rivals from the past? Could I be proud of my choice? Would a cruel jealousy not disturb my happiness?' 'I am free and I love you as I have never loved,' replied Corinne. 'What more do you want? Must you make me confess that before knowing you my imagination may have deceived me about the feeling someone inspired in me? And is there not in man's heart a divine pity for the errors that feeling, or at least the illusion of feeling, would have made me commit?' As she finished speaking, a modest blush suffused her face. Oswald trembled but said nothing. In Corinne's eyes there was a repentant, shy expression which prevented him from judging her strictly, and it seemed to him that a ray of light shone down on her from heaven to give her absolution. He took her hand, pressed it against his heart, and knelt before her, saying nothing, promising nothing, but with a loving look which allowed every hope.

'Do as I suggest,' Corinne said to Lord Nelvil. 'Let us not make any plans for the years ahead. The happiest times in life are still those granted to us by a benevolent chance. Is it really here, is it really among the graves, that we should believe so much in the future?' 'No,' cried Lord Nelvil. 'I do not believe in a future which would separate us. These four days of separation have made me too well aware that now I live only through you.' Corinne made no reply to these gentle words, but she gathered them reverently into her heart. She was still afraid that, by prolonging the conversation about the only feeling which filled her heart, she would stimulate Oswald to declare his plans before he became so used to a longer association with her that a separation would be impossible. Often she even intentionally directed his attention towards other subjects, like the Sultana of the *Arabian Nights* who, by thousands of different tales, tried to arouse the interest of the man she loved so as to put off the decision about her fate until the moment when the charming inventions of her mind would win the day.

CHAPTER II

NOT far from the Appian Way, Oswald and Corinne were shown the *Columbaria*, where slaves were reunited with their masters, and in the same tomb you can see everyone who lived under the protection of one man or one woman. Livia's women, for instance, those women who, dedicated long ago to the care of her beauty, fought for her against time and contended with the years for some of her charms, are placed beside her in little urns. It is as if you can see a gathering of obscure dead around one of the illustrious dead, who is as silent as her followers. A little distance away from there you can glimpse a field where Vestals* unfaithful to their vows were buried alive, an unusual case of fanaticism in a naturally tolerant religion.

'I shall not take you to the Catacombs,' Corinne said to Lord Nelvil, 'although by a strange chance they are beneath the Appian Way, so that graves rest upon graves. But there is something so grim and so terrible about this refuge of the persecuted Christians that I cannot bring myself to go back there. It is not the touching melancholy that is inspired by open spaces; it is the prison cell next to the sepulchre; it is the torture of life beside the horrors of death. One is undoubtedly filled with admiration for the men who, by their zealous enthusiasm, were able to endure this subterranean life and so cut themselves off entirely from the sun and nature, but one's soul is so uncomfortable in this spot that no benefit can be obtained from it. Man is part of creation; he must find his moral well-being in the universe as a whole, in the usual order of destiny. Certain fearful, violent exceptions may astonish the mind, but they terrify the imagination so much that the usual state of the soul can derive no benefit from them. Instead, let us go and see Cestius' pyramid,'* continued Corinne. 'Protestants who die here are all buried around this pyramid and it is a gentle haven, tolerant and liberal.' 'Yes,' replied Oswald. 'It is there that several of my compatriots found their last resting place. Let us go there. Perhaps in this way, at least, I shall never leave you.' At these words, Corinne shuddered and her hand trembled as she leaned on Lord Nelvil's arm. 'I am better, much better, since knowing you,' he continued. And Corinne's face was again lit up by the gentle, tender happiness that was her usual expression.

Cestius presided over the Roman games; his name is not to be found in history, but he is famous for his tomb. The huge pyramid enclosing him guards his death against the oblivion into which his life sank without trace. Aurelian, fearing this pyramid would be used as a fortress for attacking Rome, had it enclosed by walls which still stand, not as useless ruins but as the present-day boundary of modern Rome. The shape of the pyramids is said to imitate the flame which rises over a stake. What is certain is that this mysterious shape attracts the eye and gives a picturesqueness to all the views of which it forms a part. Opposite the pyramid is the Monte Testaccio; beneath it are very cool grottoes where banquets are held during the summer. In Rome banquets are not at all disturbed by the sight of tombs. The pines and the cypress you can glimpse at intervals in the smiling Italian countryside also arouse solemn memories, and the contrast produces the same effect as these lines of Horace in the middle of a poem devoted to all the enjoyments of the earth.

Moriture, Delli,

Linquenda tellus, et domus, et placens
Uxor,†

The ancients always felt that there is a sensual pleasure in the idea of death. Love and festive occasions bring it to mind and a keen emotion of joy seems enhanced by the very idea of the brevity of life.

Corinne and Lord Nelvil came back from their visit to the tombs along the banks of the Tiber. In the past it was covered with ships and there were palaces along its banks; in the past even its floods were looked on as omens. It was the prophetic river, Rome's guardian divinity.[13] Now it is so isolated, its waters seem so pale, that it is as if it were flowing amongst the shades of the dead. The most beautiful artistic monuments, the most wonderful statues, have been thrown into the

† Dellius, you must die . . .
  You must leave the earth and your home, and your beloved wife.

Tiber and are hidden beneath its waters. Who knows if someone will not divert it from its bed one day to look for them? But when you think that the masterpieces of human genius are perhaps there in front of us, and that a keener eye would see them through the waters, you experience an indescribable emotion which, in many guises, is continually revived in Rome and makes your thoughts find companionship in physical objects which everywhere else are dumb.

CHAPTER III

RAPHAEL said that modern Rome was built almost entirely with the debris of ancient Rome, and you certainly cannot take a step without being struck by some remains of antiquity. You can catch sight of what Pliny* called the *eternal walls* beneath the work of the last centuries. Rome's buildings nearly all bear the stamp of history; it is as if you could see the aspects of the different ages in them. From the Etruscans to our own day, from these peoples, older than the Romans themselves, whose workmanship is as solid and whose designs are as bizarre as those of the Egyptians, from these peoples to the cavalier Bernini,* the artist whose mannered style was like the style of the seventeenth-century Italian poets, you can study the human spirit in Rome in the different qualities of the arts, the buildings, and the ruins. Through their works the Middle Ages and the brilliant century of the Medici reappear before our eyes, and this study of the past in objects we can see gives us insight into the genius of other times. It is thought that Rome used to have a mysterious name, known only to a few of the initiated; it seems that it is still necessary to be let into the secret of this city. It is not simply a collection of dwellings; it is the history of the world, represented by different symbols and portrayed in different forms.

Corinne and Lord Nelvil agreed that first they would go and see together the buildings of modern Rome and they would reserve for another time its admirable collections of pictures and statues. Without realizing it, Corinne may have wanted to put off as long as possible what one simply must see in Rome, for who has ever left the city without looking at the Apollo Belvedere and Raphael's pictures? However slight it was, this guarantee that Oswald would not go yet was pleasing to her imagination. Can you be proud of wanting to hold on to what you love for a reason other than feeling, you will ask. I do not know, but the more you love the less you trust the feeling you inspire; whatever reason guarantees the presence of the beloved, we are always delighted to accept it. In a certain kind of pride there is often a lot of vanity, and if there is any real advantage in generally admired charms like Corinne's, it is that they allow pride to be felt more in the feeling you experience than in the one you inspire.

Corinne and Lord Nelvil began their expeditions again by visiting the most remarkable of the many churches in Rome. They are all adorned by splendours of the past, but there is something gloomy and strange about these beautiful marbles, these festive ornaments carried off from pagan temples. There were so many porphyry and granite columns in Rome that they were used lavishly with almost no value being set on them. In Saint John Lateran, a church famous for the councils held there, there are so many marble columns that several of them have been covered with plaster to make pilasters, so great was the indifference caused by the abundance of these riches.

Some of these columns were in Hadrian's tomb; others at the Capitol still bear on their capitals figures of the geese* that saved the Roman people. These columns support Gothic decorations and some have Arab-style ornamentation. Agrippa's urn harbours a Pope's ashes, for the dead themselves have given way to other dead, and the tombs have changed owners almost as much as the dwellings of the living.

Near Saint John Lateran is the holy staircase, which, they say, was moved from Jerusalem to Rome. You can climb it only on your knees. Caesar himself, and Claudius too, climbed the stairs leading to Jupiter Capitolinus' temple on their knees. Beside Saint John Lateran is the baptistery where Constantine was said to have been baptized. In the middle of the square you can see an obelisk that may be the oldest monument in the world. An obelisk contemporary with the Trojan war! An obelisk the barbarian Cambyses* still respected enough to halt the burning of a town in its honour! An obelisk for which a king pledged the life of his only son!* Miraculously the Romans had it brought from the depths of Egypt to Italy. They altered the course of the Nile so that it would seek out the obelisk and transport it to the sea. This obelisk is still covered with the hieroglyphics which have kept their secret for so many centuries and defied the most learned research up to the present day. The Indians, the Egyptians, the antiquity of antiquity might be revealed to us through these signs. Rome's marvellous charm lies not only in the actual beauty of its monuments but also in the interest they arouse by stimulating thought, and this kind of interest increases daily with each new piece of research.

One of the most peculiar churches in Rome is Saint Paul's. Its exterior looks like a badly built barn, but the interior is decorated by eighty columns made of such beautiful marble and of such a perfect shape that you would think they belong to an Athenian temple described by Pausanias.* Cicero said, *We are surrounded by the remains of history*. If he said that then, what do we say now?

The columns, statues, and bas-reliefs of ancient Rome are scattered so lavishly in the churches of the modern city that there is one (Saint Agnes) where bas-reliefs upside down are used as steps of a staircase without anyone taking the trouble to find out what they portray. What an amazing sight ancient Rome would offer now if the columns, the marbles, and the statues had been left exactly where they had been found! Almost the entire ancient city would still be standing, but would the men of our own day dare walk in it?

The palaces of the great lords of Rome are huge and their architecture is often very beautiful and always impressive, but inside the decorations are rarely in good taste and there is no conception of the elegant apartments which the perfected pleasures of social life have produced elsewhere. These vast dwellings of the Roman princes are deserted and silent. The lazy inhabitants of their superb palaces withdraw to a few unnoticed little rooms and let strangers walk through their magnificent galleries where the finest pictures of the age of Leo X are collected. These Roman lords are as far removed now from the ostentatious luxury of their ancestors as these ancestors themselves were from the austere virtues of the Romans of the Republic. The country houses convey even more the idea of the owners' solitude and indifference to the most splendid dwelling places in the world. You can walk about in these huge gardens without suspecting that they have an owner. Grass grows in the pathways, and in these same neglected paths the trees are artistically pruned in the style that used to be prevalent in France, a curious idiosyncrasy, this neglect of the essential and predilection for the useless! But in Rome and in most other Italian cities you are often surprised at the Italians' taste for mannered ornamentation, though they have the noble simplicity of ancient times before their eyes. They like what glitters rather than what is elegant or useful. In every way they have the advantages and disadvantages of not usually living in society. Their luxury is for the imagination rather than for enjoyment. Isolated as they are, they cannot dread the mocking wit which in Rome rarely makes its way into family secrets; and when you see the contrast between the inside and the outside of the palaces, you are often inclined to say that most of the great Italian lords organize their homes to dazzle the passers-by but not to receive friends.

After visiting the churches and the palaces, Corinne took Oswald to the Villa Mellini, a lonely garden with no other ornament than magnificent trees. From there you can see in the distance the chain of the Apennines. The transparency of the air gives colour to these mountains, brings them near, and outlines them in a peculiarly picturesque way. Oswald and Corinne remained in this spot for some time, savouring the charm of the sky and the peace of nature. You can have no conception of that strange peace when you have not lived in southern countries. On a hot day you do not feel the slightest breath of wind. The most slender blades of grass are perfectly motionless. Even the animals share the indolence induced by the fine weather. At midday you cannot hear the buzzing of the flies, nor the chirp of the crickets, nor the song of the birds. No one tires himself with useless, fleeting activity; everything sleeps till the moment when storms or passions reawaken the violence of nature, which impetuously emerges from its deep repose.

In Roman gardens there are a great many evergreen trees, which add further to the illusion already created by the mild winter climate. Unusually graceful fir trees, wide and bushy towards the top and standing close together, form a kind of plain in mid-air; the effect is charming if you go up high enough to see it. The lower trees stand in the shade of this arch of greenery. There are only two palm trees in Rome and both are in monastery gardens; one of them, set on a little hill, is a useful landmark, and there is always a feeling of pleasure when, from the different points of view in Rome, you rediscover this representative of Africa, this image of a South even more scorching than Italy which arouses so many new ideas and sensations.

'Do you not think that nature in Italy makes you daydream more than anywhere else?' Corinne said as she and Oswald gazed at the surrounding countryside. 'It is as if it were in a closer relationship with man here, and the Creator uses it as a means of communication between his creatures and himself.' 'Probably, I think so,' replied Oswald. 'But who knows if it is not the deep tenderness you inspire in my heart which makes me sensitive to everything I see. You reveal to me the thoughts and emotions which external objects can arouse. I used to live only in my heart, you have awakened my imagination. But this magic of the universe you are teaching me to know will never offer me anything more beautiful than your look, more touching than your voice.' 'May this feeling I inspire in you today last as long as my life,' said Corinne, 'or at least may my life last no longer than your feeling!'

Oswald and Corinne concluded their tour of Rome at the Villa Borghese. Of all the Roman gardens and palaces where the splendours of nature and art are gathered together, that is the one arranged with the most taste and brilliance. Trees of all kinds and magnificent stretches of water can be seen there. An incredible collection of statues, vases, and ancient stone coffins mingle with the freshness of young nature in the South. The mythology of the ancients seems brought to life again there. There are naiads on the banks of streams, nymphs in woods worthy of them, tombs in Elysian shade. The statue of Aesculapius* is in the middle of an island; that of Venus seems to emerge from the shadows. Ovid and Virgil could be walking in this lovely spot and think they were still in the Augustan age. The masterpieces of sculpture contained in the palace give it a magnificence eternally new. From a distance, through the trees you can catch sight of the town of Rome and Saint Peter's, and the countryside and long archways, remains of the aqueducts which carried the mountain streams to ancient Rome. Everything is there to stimulate thought, imagination, and reverie. The purest sensations mingle with the pleasures of the soul and give the idea of perfect happiness; but when you ask why no one lives in this delightful place, you are told in reply that the bad air (*la cattiva aria*) keeps people from living there in the summer.

You could say that this bad air is besieging Rome. Each year it takes a few steps further forward and people are forced to abandon the most charming residences to its rule. The lack of trees in the countryside round the town is probably one of the causes of the unhealthy air, and perhaps that is why the ancient Romans dedicated the woods to goddesses; they wanted to make the people respect them. Now, innumerable forests have been cut down. In our day could there be places sacred enough not to be laid waste by greed? The bad air is the scourge of the inhabitants of Rome and threatens to depopulate the town completely, but perhaps it adds still more to the effect made by the magnificent gardens that one sees in the precincts of Rome. There is no external indication of this malign influence; you breathe an air that seems pure and is very pleasant; the earth is smiling and fertile; in the evening a delicious coolness gives you a respite from the burning heat of the day; but all that is death!

'I love this mysterious, invisible danger, this danger which lurks beneath the most pleasing impressions,' Oswald said to Corinne. 'If, as I believe, death is only a call to a happier existence, why should not the scent of flowers, the shade of beautiful trees, be given the task of announcing it to us? Undoubtedly the government must take care to preserve human life in every way, but nature has secrets that only the imagination can penetrate, and I easily understand why inhabitants and visitors are not put off Rome by the kind of danger they run there during the most beautiful seasons of the year.'

BOOK VI
ITALIAN CUSTOMS AND CHARACTER

CHAPTER I

OSWALD'S indecisive nature, enhanced by his misfortunes, inclined him to be afraid of all irrevocable decisions. In his uncertainty he had not even dared to ask Corinne the secret of her name and fate, and yet his love for her grew stronger every day. He could not look at her without being moved; in company he could hardly bear to leave her side, even for a moment; she did not say a word that did not affect him; she had not a moment of sorrow or joy which was not mirrored in his own expression. But while admiring and loving Corinne, he recalled how little such a woman was in keeping with the English way of life, how different she was from his father's idea of a suitable wife for him, and what he said to Corinne was affected by the anxiety and constraint these thoughts aroused in him.

Corinne was only too well aware of this, but it would have cost her so much to break with Lord Nelvil that she herself avoided any decisive explanation between them, and as she was rather improvident by nature she was happy with the present such as it was, although it was impossible for her to know what the outcome would be.

She had cut herself off completely from society to devote herself to her feeling for Oswald. But finally, hurt by his silence about their future, she decided to accept an invitation to a ball where her company was greatly desired. Nothing matters less in Rome than people's coming and going in society as it suits them; it is the country where one is the least concerned with what elsewhere is called *gossip*. Everyone does what he likes without anyone asking questions, unless some obstacle to love or ambition is found in others. The Romans are no more concerned with the behaviour of their compatriots than with that of the visitors who come and go in their town, a meeting place for Europeans. When Lord Nelvil learned that Corinne was going to the ball, he was a little annoyed. For some time he thought he could see in her a melancholy temperament in sympathy with his own. Suddenly she seemed to him keenly interested in dancing, a talent she excelled in, and her imagination seemed stimulated by the prospect of a party. Corinne was not a frivolous person, but each day she felt more dominated by her love for Oswald and she wanted to try and weaken its power. She knew from experience that reflection and sacrifices have less sway over passionate natures than diversions, and she thought that the sensible thing to do was not to conquer oneself according to the rules but as best one can.

In reply to Lord Nelvil's reproaches for her decision, she said, 'But I must know if there is anything other than you in the world which might fill my life, if what I used to enjoy cannot still give me pleasure and if the feeling you arouse in me is to absorb every other interest and every other thought.' 'Do you want to stop loving me then?' replied Oswald. 'No,' answered Corinne. 'But only in domestic life can it be pleasant to feel dominated in this way by a single affection. Yet I need my talents, my wit, and my imagination to sustain the brilliant life I have adopted, and it does me harm, much harm, to love as I love you.' 'So you would not sacrifice for me this homage, this fame . . .' said Oswald. 'What does it matter to you,' said Corinne, 'to know if I would sacrifice them for you? Since we are not destined for each other, we must not destroy for ever the kind of happiness I must content myself with.' Lord Nelvil made no reply, because, to express his feelings, he also had to say what plan these feelings inspired in him, and his heart did not yet know. So, with a sigh he said nothing and followed Corinne to the ball even though he found it very painful to go.

It was the first time since his great misfortune that he had come to a large gathering and the din of a party aroused such a feeling of sadness in him that he stayed a long time in an ante-room, his head in his hands, and not even trying to see Corinne dance. He listened to the dance music which, like all music, makes one dream though it seems intended only for gladness. Count d'Erfeuil arrived, quite delighted with a ball, with a party, with a large company which at last reminded him a little of France. 'I did what I could to find some interest in those ruins so much talked about in Rome,' he said to Lord Nelvil. 'I see nothing beautiful in all that. It is just a prejudice to admire those thorn-covered ruins. I shall give my opinion when I go back to Paris, for it is time to put an end to Italy's prestige. There is not a monument intact in Europe today which is not worth more than those stumps of columns, than those bas-reliefs blackened by time that can be appreciated only with a lot of scholarly knowledge. A pleasure that has to be gained by so much study does not seem to me very great in itself, for to be delighted by the sights of Paris no one needs to grow pale over books.' Lord Nelvil made no answer. Count d'Erfeuil again asked him what impression Rome had made on him. 'The middle of a ball', said Oswald, 'is not the right time to talk seriously, and you know I cannot talk in any other way.' 'All right,' replied Count d'Erfeuil. 'I am more cheerful than you, I agree, but who knows if I am not wiser? Believe me, there is a lot of philosophy in my apparent frivolity; that's how you should take life.' 'Perhaps you are right,' replied Oswald. 'But it is because of your temperament, and not because you have thought about the matter, that you are like that, and that is why your style of life suits only you.'

Count d'Erfeuil heard Corinne's name mentioned in the ballroom, so he went in to find out what it was all about. Lord Nelvil went as far as the door and saw Prince d'Amalfi, a very handsome Neapolitan, ask Corinne to be his partner in the *Tarantella*, a graceful and original dance from Naples. Corinne's friends also asked her to do so. She agreed without being asked twice; that rather surprised Count d'Erfeuil, accustomed as he was to the refusals which usually precede acceptance. But in Italy that kind of charming behaviour is unknown and people simply think they please society more by eagerly doing what is asked. Corinne would have invented this natural behaviour if it had not already been the custom. Her ball gown was light and elegant; her hair was gathered into a silken net in the Italian style and her eyes expressed a keen pleasure which made her more desirable than ever. Stirred and struggling against himself, Oswald was annoyed at being fascinated by charms he should be complaining of, since, far from trying to please him, it was almost to escape from his influence that Corinne was making herself so captivating. But who can resist the attractions of gracefulness? Even if it were disdainful, it would still be all powerful, and that was certainly not Corinne's nature. She caught sight of Lord Nelvil and blushed; as she looked at him, there was an entrancing sweetness in her eyes.

As he danced, Prince d'Amalfi accompanied himself with castanets. Before starting, Corinne gracefully waved to the assembled company with her two hands and, turning lightly round, took the tambourine Prince d'Amalfi was holding out to her. Shaking her tambourine in the air she began to dance, and in all her movements there was a graceful litheness, a modesty mingled with sensual delight, giving some idea of the power exercised by the temple dancing girls over the Indian imagination. They are, as it were, poets in their dancing, expressing so many different feelings by their ritual steps and the charming tableaux they present to the eye. Corinne knew so well all the poses depicted by the ancient painters and sculptors that, with a slight movement of the arms, placing her tambourine now above her head, now in front of her with one hand while the other ran along the bells with incredible skill, she brought to mind the dancing girls of Herculaneum* and aroused, one after another, a host of new ideas for drawing and painting.[14]

It was not at all like French dancing, so remarkable for its elegant and difficult steps; it was a talent much more closely linked to imagination and feeling. The character of the music is expressed in turn by the precision and gentleness of the movements. As she danced, Corinne made the spectators experience her own feelings, as if she had been improvising, or playing the lyre, or drawing portraits. Everything was language for her; as they looked at her, the musicians made greater efforts to make their art fully appreciated, and at the same time an indefinable passionate joy, and imaginative sensitivity, stimulated all the spectators of this magical dance, transporting them into an ideal existence which was out of this world.

There is a moment in this Neapolitan dance when the woman kneels, while the man dances around her not as a master but as a conqueror. How charming and dignified Corinne was at that moment! How queenly she was as she knelt! And when she got up, playing her instrument, her cymbal high in the air, she appeared animated by an enthusiasm for life, youth, and beauty which seemed to give an assurance that to be happy she needed no one else. Alas, that was not the case, but Oswald feared it was so and sighed as he admired Corinne, as if every one of her successes had separated him from her. At the end of the dance, it is the man's turn to fall on his knees and it is the woman who dances around him. At that moment, Corinne surpassed herself, if that were possible. Her steps were so light, as she traced the same circle two or three times, that her feet, clad in light buskins, flew, swift as lightning, over the floor, and when, shaking her tambourine, she raised one of her hands and with the other signed to Prince d'Amalfi to get up, all the men were tempted to kneel like him, all except Lord Nelvil, who moved a few steps backwards, and Count d'Erfeuil, who walked a few steps forwards to congratulate Corinne. As for the Italians who were there, they were not thinking of drawing attention to themselves by their enthusiasm; they abandoned themselves to it because they felt it. They are not sufficiently used to society and the vanity it arouses to be concerned about the effect they produce; they never let themselves be distracted from their pleasure by vanity, nor from their goal by applause.

Corinne was delighted with her success and, thanking everyone with unaffected charm, she good-naturedly allowed her pleasure to show. But what concerned her most of all was her desire to make her way through the crowd to reach the door Oswald was leaning against. She reached it at last and paused for a moment, expecting him to say a word. 'Corinne,' he said, trying to conceal his emotion, his fascination, and his suffering. 'Corinne, what great homage, what great success! But amongst all these admirers and enthusiasts, is there a brave, reliable friend? Is there a lifelong protector? And should the empty uproar of applause be enough for a heart like yours?'

CHAPTER II

THE crowd prevented Corinne from replying to Lord Nelvil. People were going for supper and every *cavaliere servente** hastened to sit down beside his lady. A lady visitor came in and could not find a seat; no one, except Lord Nelvil and Count d'Erfeuil, offered her his own. It was not out of discourtesy, nor selfishness, that no Roman had got up. But the great Roman nobleman's idea of honour and duty is not to leave his lady's side even for a moment. Some who could not find seats stood behind their ladies, ready to attend to their slightest needs. The ladies spoke only to their escorts; gentlemen visitors wandered in vain around the circle; no one had anything to say to them. Women in Italy do not know what coquetry is, what in love is only satisfied pride. They want to please only the man they love; there is no seduction of the mind before that of the heart and eyes; the most sudden beginnings are sometimes followed by sincere devotion and even by a long faithful attachment. In Italy, infidelity is more severely blamed in a man than in a woman. Three or four men with different functions follow the same lady, who, sometimes without even taking the trouble to mention their names to her host, takes them with her; one is the favourite, another is the man who aspires to be so, the third is

called the sufferer (*il patito*). He is completely scorned; but he is allowed
to play the part of ardent admirer; and all these rivals live peacefully
together. Only the lower classes have still retained the custom of using
daggers. In this country, there is a strange mixture of simplicity and
corruption, of deceit and truth, of good nature and vengeance, of weakness and strength, which can be explained by careful observation. The
fact that nothing is done out of vanity explains the good qualities,
and the bad ones develop because a great deal is done out of self-
interest, be it concerned with love, ambition, or wealth.

Distinctions of rank are not usually deemed important in Italy. This
is not because of any philosophical considerations, but because Italians'
easygoing natures and their informality make them less liable to aristocratic prejudices; since society does not set itself up as a judge of
anything, it allows everything.

After supper, everyone began to gamble. Some women played games
of chance, others very silently played whist, and not a word was uttered
in the room which, but a short while ago, had been so noisy. Southern peoples often go from great excitement to complete repose. Idleness
together with the most tireless activity is yet another of the contrasts
in their characters. In everything they are people you must be wary
of judging at first sight, for the most contradictory virtues and vices
are to be found in them. If at one moment you see them acting pru-
dently, it is possible that in another they may turn out to be the most
daring of men. If they are idle, it is perhaps because they are resting
after doing something or are preparing to act again. In a word, they
lose no spiritual strength in society, but gather it all up within them
for crucial situations.

At the Roman gathering Oswald and Corinne went to, some men
were losing enormous sums gambling, without it being at all noticeable in their faces; but these very same men would have had the liveli-
est expressions and the most animated gestures if they had been relating
some unimportant facts. But when passions reach a certain degree of
violence, they are afraid of witnesses and almost always are veiled in
silence and immobility.

Lord Nelvil was still bitterly resentful of what he had seen at the
ball. He thought that the Italians and their lively way of expressing
enthusiasm had, momentarily at least, turned Corinne's interest away
from him. This caused him great unhappiness, but his pride coun-
selled him to hide it or to express it only by showing scorn for the

voices that were flattering his brilliant friend. He was invited to join in the gambling but he refused. So did Corinne, and she beckoned to him to come and sit beside her. Oswald was afraid of compromising Corinne by spending the evening alone with her in full view of the whole company. 'Do not worry,' she said. 'No one will bother about us. It is normal here to do only what one wants to do in company; there is no settled convention, no special consideration required. Courtesy and goodwill suffice and no one expects people to inconvenience themselves for each other. Liberty such as you understand it in England certainly does not exist in this country, but people enjoy complete social independence.' 'That is to say,' replied Oswald, 'that people have no respect for morals.' 'At least,' interrupted Corinne, 'there is no hypocrisy. M. de La Rochefoucauld* said: *The least failing of a woman of loose morals is to have loose morals.* Indeed, whatever their failings, Italian women do not resort to lies, and if marriage is not sufficiently respected, it is with the agreement of both husband and wife.'

'It is not sincerity but indifference to public opinion that is the reason for this kind of frankness,' replied Oswald. 'When I came here I had a letter of recommendation to a princess. I gave it to my local servant to take to her; he said, *Monsieur, this letter will be of no use to you at the moment, for the princess is not seeing anyone, she is* INNAMORATA. And this state of being INNAMORATA was announced like any other situation in life; moreover the publicity is not excused by any exceptional passion, for several attachments, all equally well known, follow each other. Women are so open about it all that they admit their affairs with less embarrassment than our women would have in talking about their husbands. It is easy to believe there is no deep feeling or sensitivity in such shameless fickleness. So, in this country where people think only of love, there is not a single novel because love develops so rapidly and publicly that it does not lend itself to any kind of development, and to give a true picture of people's behaviour, you would have to start and finish on the same page. Forgive me, Corinne,' exclaimed Lord Nelvil, noticing the distress he caused her. 'You are Italian and my knowledge of that ought to make me less outspoken. But one of the reasons for your incomparable grace is that it combines all the charms characteristic of different countries. I do not know in which country you were brought up, but you certainly have not spent all your life in Italy; perhaps it was even in England . . .

Oh, Corinne, if that were so, how could you have left that haven of modesty and sensitivity to come here, where not only virtue but even love is so little understood? People breathe it in the atmosphere, but does it enter into the heart? The poetry in which love plays such a great part is full of charm and imagination; it is embellished by brilliant, vivid, colourful, and sensual imagery, but where will you find the melancholy, tender feeling which pervades our poetry? What could you compare to the scene of Belvidera and her husband in Otway?* to Romco in Shakespeare? Finally, above all, to Thompson's* admirable verses in his song of spring, when he depicts in such noble and touching language happiness and love in marriage? Is there a marriage like that in Italy? And can love exist where there is no domestic happiness? Is it not this happiness which is the objective of the heart's passion, as possession is the aim of the passion of the senses? Are not all young, beautiful women alike, if qualities of heart and mind do not fix one's preference? And what do these qualities make us wish for? Marriage, that is to say, complete partnership of feelings and thoughts. Illegitimate love, when, unfortunately, it exists in our country, is still a reflection of marriage, if I may put it that way. People look in it for the intimate happiness they have not been able to enjoy at home, and infidelity itself is more moral in England than marriage in Italy.'

These harsh words wounded Corinne deeply. Getting up immediately, her eyes full of tears, she left the room and suddenly went home. Oswald was in despair at having offended Corinne, but his irritation at her success at the ball could be seen in the words that had just escaped him. He followed her home but she refused to speak to him. He returned the next day but again to no avail; her door was closed. It was not like Corinne to persist in refusing to see Lord Nelvil, but she had been grievously upset by the opinion he had expressed on Italian women, and it was because of that very opinion that she made it a rule to hide, if she could, the feeling which was carrying her away.

For his part Oswald thought that Corinne was not behaving in this situation with her natural straightforwardness, and his displeasure at what had happened at the ball became even stronger; it aroused his inclination to fight against the feeling he dreaded. His principles were strict, and the mystery which surrounded the past of the woman he loved pained him greatly. He thought Corinne's ways were charming but sometimes stimulated a little too much by a dominating desire to please. He found her speech and bearing noble and reserved, but her opinions too lenient. In a word, Oswald was a man captivated and swept away but retaining within himself an opponent who was fighting against his feelings. Such a situation often provokes bitterness. You are annoyed with yourself and with others. You suffer but have a kind of need to suffer still more, or at least to provoke a violent explanation which would bring about the complete victory of one or other of the two feelings which are rending the heart.

It was in this frame of mind that Lord Nelvil wrote to Corinne. His letter was bitter and inappropriate. He knew it, but conflicting emotions drove him to send it. His struggles made him so unhappy that, whatever the cost, he wanted anything which would put an end to them.

A rumour he did not believe, but which Count d'Erfeuil had come to relate, may have led him to use even sharper language. They were saying in Rome that Corinne would marry Prince d'Amalfi. Oswald knew quite well that she did not love the Prince and was bound to think that the ball was the sole reason for this news. But he persuaded himself that she had received Amalfi at her home on the morning of the day when he had not himself been able to gain admission. Too proud to express a feeling of jealousy, he satisfied his secret annoyance by denigrating the nation which, to his great distress, he saw Corinne preferred.

CHAPTER III

Oswald's letter to Corinne

24 January 1795

'YOU refuse to see me. You are offended by our conversation of the day before yesterday. Presumably you propose in future to admit to your home only your compatriots; apparently you wish to atone for the wrong you did in receiving a man from another nation. Far from repenting, however, of speaking to you sincerely about Italian women, you whom in my fantasies I wanted to think of as English, I shall dare to reiterate even more strongly that you will find neither happiness nor dignity if you wish to choose a husband from the society around you. Among the Italians I do not know one who might be worthy of you; there is not one whose connection would do you honour, whatever title he bestowed on you. In Italy, the men are worth much less than the women, for they have the women's faults as well as their own. Will you convince me that they are capable of love, these dwellers in the South who take such care to avoid trouble and are so determined to pursue happiness? Did you not see last month, at the theatre, a man who had lost his wife the week before, and a wife he said he loved—you told me so yourself? Here people want to get rid both of the dead and of the idea of death as soon as possible. The funeral ceremonies are performed by the priests, just as the attentions of love are carried out by the *cavaliere servente*. The rites and customs are all prescribed in advance; grief and passionate love have no part to play. Lastly, and this above all destroys love, men inspire no kind of respect in women, who are not at all grateful to them for their submissiveness, because the men have no strength of character and no serious occupation in life. For nature and the social order to be revealed in all their beauty, man must be the protector and the woman the protected. But the protector must adore the weakness he defends and respect the impotent divinity who, like the Roman household gods, brings happiness to his home. One is inclined to think that in this country women are the sultan and men the harem.

'Men's characters have the gentleness and flexibility of women's. An Italian proverb says: *He who knows not how to feign, knows not how to live*. Is that not a woman's proverb? And indeed, in a country where there are no military careers nor free institutions, how would a man be able to acquire dignity and strength? So they turn all their minds to being clever; they play life like a game of chess, in which success is everything. All that remains to them of memories of antiquity is grandiloquent language and external splendour. But beneath this superficial grandeur you often see the most vulgar tastes and the most miserable neglect of domestic life. Is that the nation you should prefer to all others, Corinne? Is that the one whose noisy applause is so necessary to you that you feel every other fate is silent beside these resounding *bravos*? Who could hope to make you happy by snatching you away from this hubbub? You are a person one cannot imagine, with deep feelings but frivolous tastes; your proud soul makes you independent and yet you are enslaved by the need for distractions; you are capable of loving one man alone, but you need them all. You are a sorceress who alternately makes people anxious and reassures them, who appears sublime and suddenly disappears from the sphere where you

are alone to mingle with the crowd. Corinne, Corinne, I cannot but
fear you as I love you!

'OSWALD'

When Corinne read this letter she was offended by the bitter prejudice Oswald expressed against her nation. She had, however, the
happiness of realizing that he was annoyed by the ball and by her refusal to receive him after the conversation at supper. This reflection
slightly mitigated the painful impression his letter had made on her.
She hesitated for a while, or at least she thought she hesitated, about
the way she should behave towards him. Her feelings urged her to
see him again, but she found it very painful that he could imagine
she wanted to marry him, although their fortunes were at least equal
and by revealing her name she could show it was in no way inferior
to Lord Nelvil's. Nevertheless, the unusual and independent way of
life she had adopted was bound to make her disinclined to marry, and
she would certainly have rejected the idea if her feelings had not made
her blind to all she would have to suffer in marrying an Englishman
and renouncing Italy.

You can abandon pride in all affairs of the heart. But as soon as
conventions or worldly interests are presented as obstacles in any way,
as soon as you can suppose that the loved one would make any kind
of sacrifice in being united to you, it is no longer possible to show
him your feelings as far as that is concerned. Nevertheless, as she could
not make up her mind to break with Oswald, Corinne wanted to convince herself that henceforth she would be able to see him and conceal the love she felt for him. So it was with this in mind that in her
letter she restricted herself to replying only to his unjust accusations
against the Italian nation, and to reasoning with him about this
matter as if it were the only one that interested her. Perhaps the
best way for a woman of superior mind to regain her self-control and
dignity is to retreat into the haven of intellectual activity.

Corinne to Lord Nelvil

25 January 1795

'If your letter affected only me, my Lord, I would not try to justify
myself. It is so easy to know my character that anyone who does not
understand me on his own would understand me no better from
the explanation I would give. Believe me, the virtuous reserve of

Englishwomen and the graceful artfulness of Frenchwomen often serve
to conceal half of what is going on in their hearts. What you chose
to attribute to sorcery in me is an unrestrained temperament which
sometimes exhibits opposing feelings and divergent thoughts without endeavouring to make them agree with each other, for such agreement, when it exists, is nearly always artificial and most sincere
characters are inconsequential. It is not of myself, however, that I want
to speak, but of the unfortunate nation which you attack so cruelly.
Could it be my affection for my friends which has aroused this bitter resentment in you? You know me too well to be jealous of them,
and I am not proud enough to believe that such a feeling would make
you unjust to the extent that you are. What you say about the Italians
is what all foreigners say, what must strike them at first sight. But
you must probe more deeply to judge this country, which at different periods has been so great. How comes it then that this nation was
the most military of all under the Romans, the most jealous of its liberty in the medieval republics, and in the sixteenth century the most
famous for literature, science, and the arts? Has it not sought distinction
in every way? And if now it is no longer distinguished, why would
you not blame its political situation, since in other circumstances it
has shown itself to be so different from what it is now?

'I do not know if I am deceiving myself but the failings of the Italians
only arouse in me a feeling of pity for their fate. In every age, foreigners have conquered and torn apart this beautiful country, the goal
of their permanent ambition; and yet foreigners bitterly reproach this
nation with the failings of nations that have been conquered and torn
apart! Europe has received the arts and the sciences from the Italians,
and now that it has turned their own gifts against them it still often
disputes the last glory that is allowed to nations without military power
or political liberty, the glory of the sciences and the arts.

'It is so true that governments make the character of nations that
in this same Italy you can see remarkable differences in behaviour
between the different states of which it is composed. The Pied-
montese, who used to form a national entity on their own, are more
militarily minded than the rest of Italy; the Florentines, who have
known liberty or liberal-minded princes, are enlightened and gentle;
the Venetians and the Genoese have shown a capacity for political
thought because they have a republican aristocracy; the Milanese are
more sincere, because the northern nations have for a long time been

bringing them that quality; the Neapolitans could easily become bellicose, because for several centuries they have been united under a government which is very imperfect but is at least their own. The Roman nobility, having nothing to do either militarily or politically, is bound to be ignorant and lazy, but the minds of the churchmen, who have a career and an occupation, are much more developed than those of the nobles. As the papal government does not admit of any distinctions of birth, there is, as a result, a kind of liberality, not in ideas, but in habits, which makes Rome a very pleasant place in which to live for all who no longer have the ambition or the possibility of playing a role in the world.

'The peoples of the South are more easily moulded by their institutions than are the peoples of the North. Their indolence soon becomes resignation, and nature offers them so many delights that they are easily consoled for the advantages society refuses them. There is certainly a lot of corruption in Italy, and yet civilization there is much less polished than in other countries. Despite their intellectual subtlety, you could find something almost primitive about this people; their subtlety is like a hunter's in the art of surprising his prey. Indolent peoples easily become cunning; they are used to being gentle and so, when necessary, learn to hide even their anger. It is always by their normal behaviour that they manage to conceal an unusual incident.

'Italians are sincere and loyal in personal relationships. Self-interest and ambition influence them greatly, but not pride or vanity; distinctions of rank make very little impression on them. There is no society life, no salon, no fashion, no little daily means of making an impression by paying attention to details. They have no such usual sources of deceit and envy. When they deceive their enemies and their rivals, it is because they consider themselves at war with them, but in peace they are unaffected and sincere. It is this very sincerity which is the cause of the scandal you complain of. Women hear constant talk of love, live amongst the allurements and examples of love, do not hide their feelings, and bring a kind of innocence, as it were, even into their coquetry; nor do they dread ridicule, particularly the kind that society can inflict. Some are so ignorant that they do not know how to write, and publicly admit it. They answer a morning note with a reply from their lawyer (*il paglietto*) on large paper in a legal style. But, on the other hand, amongst educated women you will see some who teach in the academies and give public lectures, wearing black sashes; and if you were inclined to laugh at that, people would reply: *Is there any harm in knowing Greek? Is there any harm in working for a living? So why are you laughing at something so simple?*

'Lastly, my Lord, may I touch on a more sensitive subject? Shall I try to show you why the men are often so little interested in military matters? They readily put their lives at stake for love and hatred, and dagger blows exchanged in that cause neither astonish nor intimidate anyone. They do not fear death when natural passions require them to brave it. But, it must be admitted, they prefer life to political interests, which barely touch them because they have no fatherland. Often, too, chivalric honour has little sway over a nation in which public opinion and the society that makes it do not exist. When all public authorities are so disorganized, it is quite natural that women should acquire a great ascendancy over men, and perhaps they have too much to make respect and admiration for men possible for them. Nevertheless, men's behaviour towards women is extremely sensitive and devoted. In England, domestic virtues constitute the glory and happiness of women, but if there are countries where love continues to exist outside the sacred bonds of marriage, Italy is the one, of all those countries, in which women's happiness is best fostered. There men have made a morality for immoral relationships, but at least they have been fair and generous in sharing obligations. When they break the bonds of love, they consider themselves more blameworthy than women because women have made more sacrifices and lost more. They think that, before the tribunal of the heart, the most guilty are those who do the most harm. When men do wrong, it is out of hardness; when women do wrong, it is out of weakness. Society which is both strict and corrupt, that is to say, pitiless for faults when they bring misfortunes, must be more severe for women, but in a country where there is no society, natural kindness has more influence.

'I would agree that thoughts of reputation and dignity are much less powerful and even less well known in Italy than elsewhere. The reason for this is that there is no society or public opinion, but in spite of all that has been said about the perfidiousness of the Italians, I maintain that Italy is one of the countries in the world where the most good nature is to be found. That good nature is so great in everything pertaining to vanity that, although foreigners have said worse things about Italy than about any other country, there is none where they are received more cordially. Italians are reproached with being too inclined to flattery but it must be admitted that most of the time it is not from calculation, but only from the desire to please, that they use many charming expressions, inspired by a genuine goodwill; and these expressions are not belied by their normal behaviour. Yet, would they be faithful to friendship in extraordinary circumstances if, for its sake, they had to face danger and adversity? A few, I agree, very few, would be capable of doing so, but it is not only to Italy that that remark is applicable.

'Italians are as indolent as orientals in their daily lives, but no men are more persistent or active once their passions are aroused. And these very same women, too, whom you see as indolent as harem odalisques, are suddenly capable of very devoted deeds. There are mysteries in the character and imagination of Italians, and you will find in them, in turn, unexpected marks of generosity and friendship or dark and fearsome proofs of hatred and vengeance. Here there is no rivalry to achieve anything. Life is nothing more than a dream-filled sleep under a beautiful sky. But give these men an objective, and you will see them learn and understand everything. It is the same with the women. Why should they educate themselves when most men would not understand them? In cultivating their minds, they would isolate their hearts. But these same women would very quickly become worthy of a superior man if that superior man was the object of their affections. Everything is asleep here, but in a country where the great interests are dormant, rest and indifference are more noble than futile activity about little things.

'Literature itself ceases to flourish where ideas are not renewed by the strong and varied activity of life. Yet in what country more than in Italy have people shown admiration for literature and art? History teaches us that Popes, princes, and peoples have rendered the most striking homage in all ages to distinguished painters, poets, and writers.[15] I admit, my Lord, that this enthusiasm for talent is one of the main reasons for my attachment to this country. You do not find here the blasé imagination, the discouraging mentality, or the tyrannical mediocrity which elsewhere are able to torment or stifle natural genius so effectively. An idea, a feeling, a felicitous expression, ignite a spark, as it were, amongst the listeners. Precisely because talent occupies the highest rank here, it arouses a great deal of envy. Pergolesi* was murdered for his *Stabat*; Giorgione* armed himself with a breastplate when he was obliged to paint in a public place. But the violent jealousy which talent inspires in us is aroused by power elsewhere. This jealousy does not degrade its object; this jealousy can hate, proscribe, and kill, and though it is always mixed with the fanaticism of admiration, while persecuting genius, it still stimulates it. Finally, when you can see so much life in such a narrow sphere, in the midst of so many obstacles and restrictions of every kind, it seems to me that you cannot help taking a great interest in this people, which greedily breathes in the little air that imagination allows to infiltrate through the barriers enclosing it.

'I shall not deny that those barriers are such that in Italy men rarely acquire the dignity and pride characteristic of free, military nations. If you like, my Lord, I shall even admit that the character of those nations might arouse more enthusiasm and love in women. But might it not also be possible that a brave, noble, strictly moral man could combine all the qualities which inspire love without possessing those which promise happiness?

'CORINNE'

CHAPTER IV

FOR a second time Corinne's letter made Oswald repent of having thought of breaking away from her. The spirited dignity and the commanding gentleness with which she had refuted the harsh words he had allowed himself touched him and filled him with admiration. So great, so simple, so true a superiority seemed to him above all ordinary rules. He certainly still felt that Corinne was not the weak, shy, woman, unsure of everything but her feelings and duties, whom, in his imagination, he had chosen for his life's companion. The memory of Lucile, as he had seen her at the age of twelve, was more in accord with this idea, but could one make any comparison with Corinne? Could the usual laws and rules be applied to someone who in herself combined so many different qualities linked by genius and sensitivity? Corinne was a natural miracle, and was not the miracle working on Oswald's behalf when he could take pride in interesting such a woman? But what was her name, what her destiny, what would her plans be, if he declared his intention of marrying her? Everything was still unclear and, although Oswald's enthusiasm for Corinne convinced him that he had decided to marry her, the thought that Corinne's life had not been quite above reproach, and that his father would certainly have disapproved of such a marriage, often thoroughly upset him again and made him extremely troubled.

He was not as prostrate with grief as in the days when he did not know Corinne, but neither did he feel the kind of calm which can exist even in the midst of repentance, when one's whole life is devoted to the expiation of a great fault. Formerly he was not afraid of giving himself up to his memories, however bitter they were; now he was afraid of those long, deep, reveries which would have made him aware of what was happening in the depths of this heart. He was, however, getting ready to visit Corinne to thank her for her letter and to obtain her forgiveness for the one he had written when he saw Mr Edgermond, a relative of young Lucile, come into his room.

He was a worthy English gentleman, who had lived most of his life in Wales, where he owned a property. He had the principles and the prejudices which, in every country, are used to maintain things as they are, and it is a benefit when these things are as good as human reason allows. Men like Mr Edgermond, that is to say, partisans of the established order, although firmly and even obstinately attached to their customs and way of looking at things, ought to be considered as enlightened and reasonable.

Lord Nelvil started when he heard Mr Edgermond announced in his apartment. It seemed to him that all his memories were presenting themselves at the same time. But presently it occurred to him that Lady Edgermond, Lucile's mother, had sent her relative to reproach him, thus trying to restrict his independence. This thought restored all his determination and he received Mr Edgermond extremely coldly. He was all the more wrong to receive him in this way, as Mr Edgermond had nothing at all in mind concerning Lord Nelvil. He was travelling in Italy for his health, taking a lot of exercise, hunting, and drinking to the health of King George and Old England. He was the finest gentleman in the world, and he even had more wit and education than his way of life would have led one to believe. Above all he was English, not only as he ought to be but also as one would have preferred him not to be. Everywhere he followed the customs of his own country, living only with Englishmen and never mixing with foreigners, not out of contempt, but out of a kind of reluctance to speak foreign languages, and a shyness, even at the age of fifty, which made it difficult for him to make new acquaintances.

'I am delighted to see you,' he said to Lord Nelvil. 'I am going to Naples in a fortnight. Will you be there? I hope so, for I have not long to stay in Italy. My regiment is due to set sail soon.' 'Your regiment,' repeated Lord Nelvil, and he blushed, as if he had forgotten that he had a year's leave as his regiment was not due to be called up any earlier. But he blushed to think that Corinne might perhaps make him forget even his duty. 'Your own regiment', continued Mr Edgermond, 'will not be called up for a while yet, so get your health back here without worrying. Before leaving, I saw my young cousin whom you are interested in. She is more charming than ever, and when you return in a year's time I am sure she will be the most beautiful woman in England!' Lord Nelvil said nothing and Mr Edgermond too fell silent. Laconically but pleasantly, they exchanged a few more remarks and Mr Edgermond was about to leave when he turned round and said, 'By the way, my Lord. You can do me a favour. I am told you know the celebrated Corinne, and although, usually, I do not like meeting new people, I am very curious to know what she is like.' 'I shall ask permission from Corinne to bring you to her home, since you would like to go,' replied Oswald. 'Do please arrange for me to see her on a day when she will improvise, sing, or dance for us.' 'Corinne does not show off her talents like that to strangers. She is a woman who is your and my equal in every respect.' 'Forgive my mistake,' replied Mr Edgermond; 'since she is known only by the name of Corinne, and at the age of twenty-six she lives quite alone without anyone else of her family, I thought that she supported herself by her talents and would be glad to take the opportunity of making them known.' 'Her fortune is quite independent,' replied Lord Nelvil sharply, 'and her heart even more so.' Mr Edgermond immediately stopped talking about Corinne and was sorry he had mentioned her when he saw that Oswald was interested in her. The English are the most discreet and considerate men in the world in everything connected with sincere affections.

Mr Edgermond went away. Lord Nelvil, left alone, could not help exclaiming in his emotion, 'I must marry Corinne, I must be her protector so that, in future, no one can make any mistake about her. I shall give her the little I can give, a rank, a name, while she will lavish on me all the joys that she alone in the world can bestow.' It was in this frame of mind that he hurried to go to Corinne's, and never did he enter her house with a sweeter feeling of hope and love. But in a natural feeling of shyness and to put himself at ease, he began the conversation by speaking of unimportant things, and amongst them was the request to bring Mr Edgermond to see her. At the mention of his name, Corinne was visibly upset and, in a voice filled with emotion, refused Oswald's request. He was completely taken aback and said, 'I thought that, in a house where you receive so many people, the fact that he is my friend would not be a reason for excluding him.' 'Do not be offended, my Lord,' replied Corinne. 'Believe me, I must have very powerful reasons for not agreeing to what you want.' 'And will you tell me those reasons?' asked Oswald. 'Impossible,' cried Corinne, 'impossible!' 'And so,' said Oswald . . . but as the violence of his emotion rendered him speechless, he made to go. Then Corinne, in tears, said to him in English: 'In God's name, unless you want to break my heart, do not go.'

Oswald was deeply moved by Corinne's words and her tone of voice, and he sat down again some distance away from her, his head resting against an alabaster vase which lit up her room. Then suddenly he said, 'Cruel woman, you see that I love you, you see that twenty times a day I am ready to offer you my hand and my life, and you do not want to tell me who you are! Tell me, Corinne, tell me,' he repeated, putting out his hand to her with the most touching expression of feeling. 'Oswald,' cried Corinne, 'Oswald, you do not know how you are hurting me. If I were crazy enough to tell you everything, if I were, you would no longer love me.' 'Good God,' he replied, 'then what have you to disclose?' 'Nothing which makes me unworthy of you; but chance events, differences between our tastes and opinions which once existed, which would no longer exist. Do not insist that I make myself known to you. One day perhaps, one day, if you love me enough, if . . . Oh, I do not know what I am saying,' continued Corinne, 'but do not desert me before hearing me. Promise me in the name of your father who lives in heaven.' 'Do not pronounce that name,' cried Lord Nelvil. 'Do you know if he unites us or separates us? Do you believe he would consent to our union? If you believe he would, swear it to me and I shall no longer be anxious and torn apart. One day I shall tell you what my sad life has been, but for the moment, see what state I am in, what a state you put me in.' And, indeed, his brow was bathed in a cold sweat, his face was pale, and his lips trembled as, with difficulty, he articulated these last words. Corinne sat down beside him and, holding his hands in hers, gently restored his composure. 'My dear Oswald,' she said, 'ask Mr Edgermond if he has ever been in Northumberland, or at least, if he has, it has only been in the last five years. Only in that case can you bring him here.' At these words Oswald looked intently at Corinne. She cast down her eyes and said nothing. Lord Nelvil answered, 'I shall do as you command,' and he left.

Back in his own apartment, he exhausted himself in making conjectures about Corinne's secrets. It seemed clear to him that she had spent a lot of time in England and that her name and family must be known there. But what was the reason for her concealing them, but why had she left England if she had been settled there? These different questions worried Oswald greatly. He was convinced that nothing bad could be discovered in Corinne's life, but he was afraid of a combination of circumstances which might make her guilty in the eyes of others; and what he dreaded most for her was the disapproval of England. He felt strong enough to defy the disapproval of any other country, but the memory of his father was so closely linked in his thoughts with his native land that the two feelings enhanced each other. Oswald learned from Mr Edgermond that he had been in Northumberland for the first time the previous year and promised to take him that very evening to Corinne's house. He arrived first, to warn her of Mr Edgermond's preconceived ideas about her, and asked her to make him realize by her cold, reserved behaviour how mistaken he was.

'If you will allow me,' replied Corinne, 'I shall behave towards him as I do towards everybody. If he wants to hear me, I shall improvise for him. In short, I shall be my usual self, but I think, nevertheless, that he will perceive my inner worth just as well in my natural behaviour as if I assumed an affected constraint.' 'Yes, Corinne,' replied Oswald. 'Yes, you are right. Oh, how wrong would be the man who would want to change in any way your wonderful disposition!' At that moment, Mr Edgermond and the rest of the company arrived. At the beginning of the evening, Lord Nelvil, sitting beside Corinne, and showing an interest suggestive of both the protector and the man in love, said everything that could bring out her merits. He showed her a respect intended less for his own satisfaction than to command the consideration of others, but he was soon delighted to find that all his worries were groundless. Corinne won over Mr Edgermond completely. She won him over, not only by her wit and charm, but by inspiring in him the feeling of respect that sincere characters always arouse in honest characters. So when he dared to ask her to let him hear her on a subject of her choice, he asked for that favour with as much respect as eagerness. She agreed without a moment's hesitation, and thus could show that the worth of this favour was quite separate from the difficulty of obtaining it. But she was so anxious to please a compatriot of Oswald's, a man who, by the esteem in which he was deservedly held, could, in speaking of her, influence Lord Nelvil's opinion, that she was suddenly overcome by a shyness that was quite new to her. She wanted to begin but emotion deprived her of speech. Oswald was upset that she did not display all her superiority to an Englishman. He lowered his eyes and his embarrassment was so obvious that Corinne, concerned only with the effect she was producing on him, continued to lose the presence of mind required for the talent of improvising. Finally, feeling that she was hesitating, that the words were coming to her from memory and not from feeling, and so she was depicting neither what she was thinking nor what she was really experiencing, she suddenly stopped and said to Mr Edgermond, 'Forgive me if shyness robs me of my talent today. My friends know it is the first time that I have not done myself justice in this way, but it may not be the last,' she added with a sigh.

Oswald was deeply moved by Corinne's touching weakness. Till then he had always seen imagination and genius triumph over her affections, and restore her spirits when she was most depressed. This time, her feelings had entirely prevailed over her mind, but Oswald had so identified himself with Corinne's glory that he suffered from her distress instead of enjoying it. As he was certain, however, that another day she would shine with her natural brilliance, he gave himself up with no regrets to the sweet emotions aroused by what he had just seen, and the image of his loved one reigned more than ever in his heart.

BOOK VII
ITALIAN LITERATURE

CHAPTER I

LORD NELVIL was very anxious for Mr Edgermond to enjoy Corinne's conversation, which was just as good as her improvised verses. The following day, the same company was gathered at her house, and to encourage her to speak, he brought the conversation round to Italian literature. He provoked her natural liveliness by affirming that England possessed a greater number of true poets, superior in their mental energy and sensitivity to all those of whom Italy could boast. 'To start with,' replied Corinne, 'for the most part, foreigners know only our poets of the first rank, Dante, Petrarch, Ariosto, Guarini,* Tasso, and Metastasio.* But we have several others, such as Chiabrera, Guidi, Filicaia, Parini, etc., without counting Sannazzaro, Poliziano,* and others who have written with genius in Latin. All of them combine harmony with a vivid style; with more or less talent all of them know how to introduce the wonders of art and nature into the picture they paint with words. I agree, in our poets there is not the deep melancholy and knowledge of the human heart which is typical of yours, but does not that kind of superiority belong more to philosophical writers than to poets? The sparkling melody of Italian is more suited to the brilliance of external objects than to reflection. Our language is better suited to depicting rage than sadness, because thoughtful feelings require more metaphysical language, while the desire for vengeance stirs the imagination and turns grief outwards. The best and most elegant translation of Ossian is by Cesarotti,* but to the reader it seems as if the words in themselves have a festive air contrasting with the melancholy thoughts they call to mind. One lets oneself be charmed by our gentle words, *limpid stream, smiling countryside, cool shade*, as one would be by the murmuring waters and varied colours. What more do you ask of poetry? Why ask a nightingale the meaning of his song? He can explain it only by starting to sing again; we can understand it only by letting ourselves go to the impression it makes. The metre of the lines, the harmonious rhymes, those sudden endings of two short syllables whose sounds indeed slide as their name (*Sdruccioli*) indicates, sometimes imitate a light dancing step; sometimes more solemn tones recall the sound of the storm or the clash of arms. In short, our poetry is a marvel of the imagination and one must look in it only for all forms of the pleasures imagination provides.'

'You certainly explain as well as possible the beauties and the defects of your poetry,' replied Lord Nelvil. 'But when these defects are found in prose, without the beauties, how can you defend them? What is merely vague in poetry becomes empty in prose, and that host of banalities that your poets know how to make attractive with their melody and images emerges as cold in the tedious liveliness of prose. Today, most of your prose writers use a language so inflated, so long-winded, so filled with superlatives, that they all seem to be writing to order, with stock expressions, for a conventional temperament. They seem to have no idea that writing is an expression of one's character and thought. For them, literary style is an artificial fabric, a mosaic of recollected patterns, something, in a way, foreign to their souls, which is made with the pen just as a mechanism is made with the fingers. They possess to the highest degree the secret of developing, commenting on, inflating an idea, of frothing up a feeling, if I may put it that way. They do it to such an extent that one would be tempted to say to these writers, as the African woman did to a French lady who was wearing a large hoop under a long dress: *Madame, is all that yourself?* Indeed, where is the real person beneath all this pompous verbosity? One sincere expression would make his empty glamour disappear.'

'First of all you forget Machiavelli and Boccaccio,' interrupted Corinne sharply, 'then Gravina, Filangieri, and in modern times, too, Cesarotti, Verri, Bettinelli,* and so many others as well, who know how to write and think.[16] But I agree with you that, being deprived of their independence over the last few centuries by unfortunate circumstances, Italians have lost all interest in truth, and often even the possibility of expressing it. The result has been the habit of enjoying words without daring to touch on ideas. Since people were sure they could not influence anything by their writings, they wrote only to show their wit, which is the surest way to end up quite quickly without even wit; for by directing our efforts towards something noble and useful, we conceive most of our ideas. When prose writers can have no influence at all on the well-being of a nation, when they write only to shine, in short when the journey is its own objective, they fall back in a thousand detours but go no further forward. Italians, it is true, are afraid of new thoughts, but they dread them because of laziness and not because of slavish imitation of other writers. There is a great deal of originality in their characters, their humour, and their imagination but, as they do not take the trouble to think, their generalizations are banal. Even their eloquence, which is so lively when they speak, is very artificial when they write; it is as if they become cold as they work. Moreover, the peoples of the South are inhibited by prose and depict their true feelings only in verse. It is not the same with French literature,' said Corinne, turning to Count d'Erfeuil. 'Your prose writers are often more eloquent and even more poetic than your poets.' 'It is true that we have the real classical authorities in this medium,' replied Count d'Erfeuil. 'Bossuet, La Bruyère, Montesquieu, and Buffon cannot be outdone, especially the first two; they belong to the century of Louis XIV,* which cannot be praised too much and whose perfect models should be imitated as much as possible. This is advice which foreigners ought to be eager to follow as well as ourselves.' 'I have difficulty in believing that it would be desirable for the whole world to lose all national colour, all originality of feeling and thought,' answered Corinne, 'and I shall venture to say, Count, that even in your country the literary orthodoxy, if I may use that expression, which opposes every felicitous innovation, must in the long run make your literature very sterile. Genius is essentially creative; it bears the stamp of the individual who possesses it. Nature, which did not want to make two leaves alike, has made human souls even more diverse, and imitation is a kind of death, since it deprives everyone of his natural individuality.'

'Would you want us, beautiful foreign lady, to admit to our country Teutonic barbarism, Young's* *Nights* from England, *Concetti** from Italy and Spain?' asked Count d'Erfeuil. 'What would become of the taste and elegance of French style after such a mixture?' Prince Castel-Forte, who had not yet spoken, said, 'It seems to me we all need each other. To those who know how to appreciate it, the literature of every country reveals a new sphere of ideas. Charles V* himself said that *a man who knows four languages is worth four men*. If that great political genius held this opinion about material affairs, how much more is that not true for literature? Foreigners all know French, so they have a wider point of view than that of the French who do not know foreign languages. Why do they not take the trouble more often to learn them? They would keep their distinguishing characteristics and, in this way, would discover sometimes what they may lack.'

CHAPTER II

'AT least you will acknowledge that there is one respect in which we have nothing to learn from anyone,' replied Count d'Erfeuil. 'Our drama is definitely the best in Europe, for I do not think the English themselves would think of putting Shakespeare up against us.' 'I beg your pardon,' interrupted Mr Edgermond. 'They do think of it.' And, having said his piece, he lapsed into silence again. 'In that case, I have nothing to say,' continued Count d'Erfeuil with a charmingly disdainful smile. 'Everyone can think what he likes. But I persist in believing that one can state without presumption that we are the leaders in dramatic art. As for the Italians, if I may speak frankly, they do not even suspect that there is a dramatic art in the world. The music is everything with them, and the play is nothing. If the second act of a play has better music than the first, they begin with the second act. If two first acts of two different plays have better music, they play these two acts on the same day and put between them an act of a prose comedy. This usually contains the best moral in the world, but a moral completely made up of maxims which our ancestors have already sent off to other lands as too antiquated for them. Your famous musicians do as they please with your poets. One declares he cannot sing unless the word *felicità* is in his aria; the tenor demands *tomba*, and the third singer can only do vocal flourishes on the word *catene*. The poor poet has to fit these different tastes to the dramatic situation as best he can. And that is not everything. There are virtuosi who do not want to walk straight onto the stage; they must make their entry on a cloud, or come down from the top of a palace staircase to make a more effective entrance. When he has sung the aria, however touching or violent the situation may be, the actor must bow to show his thanks for the applause he receives. The other day, at *Semiramis*, after Ninus' ghost had sung his aria, the actor who played the part made a big bow to the pit, wearing his ghost's costume; that greatly diminished the fright caused by the apparition.

'In Italy people are used to looking on the theatre as a great assembly hall where they listen only to the arias and the ballet. I am right to say *people listen only to the ballet*, for it is only when it is going to begin that the audience in the pit imposes silence. What's more, this ballet is a masterpiece of bad taste. Apart from the freaks who are true caricatures of the dance, I do not know what can be amusing in these ballets, unless it is their absurdity. I saw Genghis Khan made into a ballet; he was all covered in ermine, all clothed in fine feelings, for he was giving up his crown to the child of the king he had conquered and, standing on one foot, was raising him up on high—a novel way of setting a monarch on the throne. I have also seen Curtius' sacrifice, a three-act ballet with all the divertissements. Curtius, dressed as an Arcadian shepherd, danced with his beloved for a long time before mounting a real horse in the middle of the theatre and plunging into a gulf of fire made of yellow satin and gilded paper, which made it look more like the centre-piece of a dessert table than an abyss. And I have also seen a complete summary of Roman history as a ballet, from Romulus to Caesar.'

'All you say is true,' replied Prince Castel-Forte gently, 'but you have spoken only about music and dancing, and that is not considered as dramatic art in any country.' 'It is much worse,' interrupted Count d'Erfeuil, 'when they perform tragedies or plays which are not called *plays with a happy ending*. They bring together more horrors in five acts than the imagination could possibly conceive. In one of the plays of this kind, the lover kills his mistress's brother as early as the second act; in the third he blows out the brains of his mistress herself on the stage; the fourth is filled with the funeral; in the interval between the fourth and fifth acts, the actor who plays the lover comes to announce to the audience, in the calmest possible way, the harlequinade that will be played the following day, and he reappears on stage in the fifth act to kill himself with a pistol. The tragic actors are perfectly suited to the lifelessness and exaggeration of the plays. They commit all these terrible deeds extremely calmly. When an actor gets excited, people say he flings himself about like a preacher, for indeed there is much more action in the pulpit than on the stage, and it is fortunate that these actors are so calm in pathetic situations, for, as there is nothing interesting in the play or in the situation, the more noise they made the more ridiculous they would be. It would not be so bad if this ridiculous stuff were cheerful, but it is only dull. There is no more comedy in Italy than tragedy; in that area too we are the first. The only genre which really belongs to Italy is the harlequinade;

a scoundrelly, gluttonous, and cowardly valet, an old, deceived, miserly, or love-sick guardian, that's the whole subject of these plays. You will agree, not much effort is required to think that up, and *Tartuffe* and the *Misanthrope** imply a little more genius.'

Count d'Erfeuil's attack rather annoyed the Italians who were listening to him; they laughed at it, however, and Count d'Erfeuil much preferred to display wit rather than good nature in his conversation. His natural kindness influenced his deeds, but his vanity influenced his words. Prince Castel-Forte and all the Italians who were there were eager to refute Count d'Erfeuil, but as they thought their cause would be better defended by Corinne than by anyone else, and as they were not much concerned with the pleasure of shining in conversation, they begged Corinne to reply and contented themselves only with citing the well-known names of Maffei, Metastasio, Goldoni, Alfieri, and Monti.* First of all Corinne agreed that the Italians had no theatre, but she wanted to prove that circumstances and not lack of talent were the reason. Comedy which depends on the observation of manners can exist only in a country where people normally live in the midst of a numerous and brilliant society. In Italy there are only violent passions or idle pleasures, and violent passions produce such highly coloured crimes and vices that they make all distinctions of character disappear. But what can be called ideal comedy, that is to say, comedy which stems from the imagination and can be relevant to all times and in all countries, was invented in Italy. The characters of Harlequin, Brighella, Pantaloon, etc. are found in every play with the same personalities. In every situation, they have masks and not faces; that is to say, their features are those of a certain type of people and not of a particular individual. Certainly, since modern authors of harlequinades find all the roles given in advance, like the pieces in a game of chess, they cannot take the credit for inventing them, but they were first invented in Italy. So these whimsical characters, who amuse all children, and people whom imagination turns into children, must be considered a creation of the Italians and that gives them rights to the art of comedy.

The observation of the human heart is an inexhaustible source for literature, but the nations which are more suited to poetry than to reflection indulge more in the intoxication of joy than in philosophical irony. There is something sad at the heart of humour based on the knowledge of men. Real harmless gaiety is the kind which is purely imaginative. It is not that Italians do not study skilfully the men they deal with, and do not discover with more subtlety than anyone the most secret thoughts, but they use this talent to guide their behaviour and do not usually make a literary use of it. Perhaps they even would not like to generalize their discoveries or publicize their insights. In their characters there is something cautious and secretive, which perhaps advises them not to bring into the open what they use to guide themselves in private relationships, and not to reveal fictions that may be useful in the circumstances of real life.

Far from hiding anything, however, Machiavelli revealed all the secrets of a criminal theory of politics and, through him, you can see the Italians' terrifying capacity for knowing the human heart. But such depths do not belong to the province of comedy, and only through the leisure activities of an actual society can people learn how to portray men on the comic stage. Goldoni, who lived in Venice, the Italian town which has most society life, already puts into his plays more subtle observations than are usually found in the other authors. Nevertheless his comedies are stereotyped. You see a recurrence of the same situations, because there is little variety in the characters. His numerous plays seem modelled on the generality of plays and not on life. The true character of Italian humour is not mocking, it is imaginative; it is not the portrayal of manners, but poetic exaggeration. It is Ariosto and not Molière who can entertain Italy.

The works of Gozzi,* Goldoni's rival, contain much more originality; they are much less like comedies according to the rules. He chose to devote himself entirely to the Italian genius, portraying fairy tales, and mingling slapstick comedy and harlequinades with the wonders of poetry; he decided not to imitate nature at all but to indulge in humorous fantasies as well as in the illusions of fairyland, and in every way to carry the mind beyond the limits of what happens in the world. He was prodigiously successful in his day and he is, perhaps, the comic author best suited to the Italian imagination. But to know for certain what comedy and tragedy could be like in Italy, there would have to be a theatre and actors somewhere. The multitude of little towns which all want to have a theatre disperses the few resources that might be available. The division into states, normally so favourable to liberty and happiness, is harmful to Italy. It would need a centre of enlightenment and power to resist the prejudices which devour it. Elswhere governmental authority often represses individual initiative. In Italy such an authority would be to the good if it fought against the ignorance of separate states and of men isolated from each other, if, by promoting rivalry, it fought against the indolence natural to the climate, in short, if it gave life to the whole of this nation which is satisfied with a dream.

These different ideas, as well as several others, were wittily developed by Corinne. She also very well understood both the art of making quick remarks in light chat which dwells on nothing, and the business of pleasing others by showing each person to advantage in turn. In conversation, however, she often indulged in the kind of talent which made her a famous improviser. Several times she asked Prince Castel-Forte to come to her aid by making known his own opinions on the same subject, but she spoke so well that all her listeners enjoyed listening to her and tolerated no interruption. Mr Edgermond particularly could not have enough of seeing and hearing Corinne; he scarcely dared express the feeling of admiration she aroused in him and he uttered a few words under his breath in her praise, hoping she would understand them without his having to say them to her. He wanted so much, however, to know her thoughts about tragedy that, in spite of his shyness, he ventured to say a few words to her on the subject.

'Madame,' he said, 'what seems to me to be above all lacking in Italian literature is tragedy. It seems to me there is less distance between children and men than there is between your tragedies and ours, for though children are unstable and their feelings superficial, they are sincere, while the seriousness of your tragedies has something affected and exaggerated about it which, for me, destroys all emotion. Is that not so, Lord Nelvil?' continued Mr Edgermond as, in turning towards Oswald, he looked for support, quite astonished that he had dared speak in front of so many people.

'I entirely agree with you,' replied Oswald. 'Metastasio, who is praised as the poet of love, portrays that passion in the same way in every country and in all situations. The arias are certainly admirable, sometimes to be applauded for their grace and harmony, sometimes for their supreme lyrical beauties, but especially when they are removed from the plays in which they are placed. For us, however, who have Shakespeare, the poet who has best understood human history and passions, the two pairs of lovers, who share between them nearly all Metastasio's plays, are unbearable. They are called now Achilles, now Tircis, now Brutus, now Corilas, and all sing in the same way of the sorrows and martyrdom of love, barely touching the soul superficially and depicting insipidly the most violent feeling that can stir the human heart. It is with the greatest respect for the character of Alfieri that I shall allow myself a few reflections on his plays. Their aim is so noble, the feelings expressed by the author fit his personal behaviour so well, that his tragedies must always be praised as deeds even when they would be criticized in certain respects as literary works. But it seems to me that his tragedies are all the same in their strength, as Metastasio is in his gentleness. In Alfieri's plays there is such a profusion of energy and magnanimity, or such an exaggeration of crime and violence, that it is impossible to recognize in them the true nature of men. They are never as wicked or as generous as he depicts them. Most of the scenes are devised to contrast vice and virtue, but these oppositions are not presented with the gradations of truth. If, in real life, tyrants put up with the remarks made to their faces by the oppressed in Alfieri's tragedies, one would be almost tempted to pity the tyrants. The play *Octavia* is one of those in which the lack of plausibility is most striking. Seneca continually makes moralizing speeches to Nero, as if the Emperor were the most patient of men, and Seneca himself the most valiant. In the tragedy, the master of the world agrees to let himself be insulted and to fly into a rage in every scene, for the pleasure of the audience, as if it did not depend on him to make an end of it all with one word. The dialogues do indeed give an opportunity for some fine replies from Seneca and one would be pleased to find the noble thoughts he expresses in a speech or a literary work. But is that how to convey the concept of tyranny? That is not depicting it in its terrifying aspect, it is simply making it the subject for verbal fencing. But if Shakespeare had represented Nero surrounded by trembling men who scarcely dare to reply to the most harmless question, with the Emperor himself hiding his agitation and trying to appear calm, and Seneca beside him working hard to excuse Agrippina's murder, would not the terror have been a thousand times greater? And for one reflection made by the author, would not a thousand have arisen in the minds of the audience by the very absence of rhetoric and the verisimilitude of the scenes?'

Oswald could have gone on talking longer still without being interrupted by Corinne. She enjoyed so much both the sound of his voice and the noble style of his language that she would have liked to prolong this pleasure for hours. She found it hard to detach her eyes from him even when he had finished speaking. She turned slowly towards the rest of the company, who were asking her impatiently what she thought of Italian tragedy, and looking back towards Lord Nelvil, she said, 'My Lord, I agree with you on nearly everything, so it's not to argue against you that I am replying, but to indicate a few exceptions to your remarks, which are perhaps too generalized. It is true that Metastasio is more a lyric poet than a dramatist, and that he depicts love more as one of the arts which embellish life and not as the most intimate and hidden source of our joys or our sorrows. In general, although our poetry has been devoted to the expression of love, I shall venture to say that we have greater depth and sensitivity in the portrayal of all the other passions. Through writing amorous verses, we have developed a conventional language for love poetry in our country; it is not, however, their experiences but their reading that inspires the poets. Love, as it exists in Italy, bears no resemblance to love as our writers portray it. I know of only one novel, Boccaccio's *Fiammetta*, in which one can form an idea of that passion described in truly national colours. Our poets make the feeling more subtle and extreme, but what really characterizes the Italian nature is a swift, deep impression, expressed more by silent, passionate deeds than clever language. On the whole our literature expresses little of our character and manners. We are too modest a nation, I might even say almost too humble, to venture to have our own tragedies, derived from our own history, or at least characteristic of our own feelings.[17]

'By a strange chance, Alfieri was, as it were, transplanted from antiquity to modern times. He was born to act, but he could only write. His style and his tragedies are affected by this constraint. He wanted to achieve a political objective by means of literature. This objective was, no doubt, the noblest of all, but that is irrelevant; nothing mars works of the imagination more than to have an objective. Alfieri was impatient to live in a nation in which one met very learned scholars and very enlightened people, but its writers and readers were mostly uninterested in anything serious and enjoyed only stories, tales, and madrigals; so he wanted to give his tragedies as serious a character as possible. He cut out the confidants, the unexpected surprises, everything but the interest of the dialogue. It seemed as though he wanted to make the Italians do penance for their liveliness and their natural imagination. He was, nevertheless, much admired, because there was

a real greatness in his character and in his soul, and because the inhabitants of Rome applaud above all the praise given to the deeds and
feelings of the ancient Romans, as if they were still involved in them.
They appreciate energy and independence as they do the beautiful
pictures in their art galleries. But it is no less true that Alfieri has not
created what one could call an Italian theatre, that is to say, tragedies
where one can find a merit peculiar to Italy. What is more, he has
not shown the particular characteristics of the countries and periods
he portrays. His *Conspiracy of the Pazzi*, *Virginia*, and *Philip the Second*
are admirable because of their noble, powerful ideas, but one always
sees on them the stamp of Alfieri's nature and personality and not
that of the nations and periods he presents on the stage. Although
the French mind and Alfieri's bear no resemblance to each other, they
are alike in this, that both give their own characteristics to all the subjects they treat.'

When he heard the French mind mentioned, Count d'Erfeuil took
his turn to speak. 'It would be impossible for us to put up with the
inconsistencies of the Greeks or the monstrosities of Shakespeare on
the stage,' he said. 'French taste is too pure for that. Our theatre is
a model of refinement and elegance; that is what makes it outstanding, and to introduce any foreign element into it would be to plunge
us into barbarism.' 'You might as well build the great wall of China
round yourselves,' said Corinne with a smile. 'There are, to be sure,
uncommon beauties in your tragic authors; but new ones might be
developed if you would occasionally allow something different from
the French to be shown on stage. But our Italian dramatic genius would
lose a great deal by being forced into rules which we did not have the
privilege of claiming as our own and whose constraints would be
imposed on us. The imagination, character, and customs of a nation
must shape its theatre. Italians are passionately fond of the fine arts,
music, painting, and even pantomime, in fact everything which strikes
the senses. How then could they be satisfied with an austerely eloquent dialogue as their only pleasure in the theatre? Alfieri, with all
his genius, tried in vain to restrict them in that way, but he himself
felt that his system was too rigid.[18]

'In my view, Maffei's *Merope*, Alfieri's *Saul*, Monti's *Aristodemus*,
and above all Dante's poem (although he never wrote a tragedy) give
a good idea of what dramatic art could be in Italy. In Maffei's *Merope*,
the action is very simple but it contains brilliant poetry, clothed in

the most apt imagery. But why should poetry be banned from dramatic works? In Italy, the language of verse is so magnificent that it would be more mistaken here than anywhere else to renounce its beauties. Alfieri, who, when he chose to, excelled in all genres, made a superb use of lyric poetry in his *Saul*, and one might with advantage introduce into it music itself, not to mix song and speech, but to calm Saul's mad fits with David's harp. We have such delightful music that our pleasure in it can make us lazy about intellectual pleasures. So far from separating them, we must try to combine them, not by making heroes sing—that would destroy all the dignity of the play—but either by introducing choruses, as the ancient Greeks did, or musical effects which are linked to the situation naturally, as happens so often in life. Far from diminishing the pleasures of the imagination in the Italian theatre, it seems to me that, on the contrary, they should be enhanced and multiplied in every way. The keen liking of Italians for music and for spectacular ballets is an indication of the power of their imaginations and of the necessity of always appealing to them, even when serious subjects are treated; they should not be portrayed as even more harsh than they really are, as Alfieri has done.

'The nation thinks it is in duty bound to applaud what is austere and serious, but it soon reverts to its natural tastes. It might like tragedy if it were embellished by the charm and variety of the different kinds of poetry and of all the dramatic devices which the English and the Spanish appreciate.

'There is some of the frightening pathos of Dante in Monti's *Aristodemus*, and this tragedy is rightly one of the most admired. Dante, that great master of so many genres, had the kind of tragic genius which could have been extremely successful in Italy if it could somehow have been adapted to the stage; for that poet knows how to portray for our eyes what takes place in the depths of the soul, and his imagination makes one feel and see sorrow. If Dante had written tragedies, they would have impressed children as much as grown men, the crowd as much as refined minds. Dramatic literature ought to be popular; it is, as it were, a public event, and the whole nation ought to judge it.'

'When Dante was alive the Italians played a great political role in Europe and in their own country,' said Oswald. 'Perhaps it is impossible for you to have a national tragic theatre nowadays. Important situations in real life must arouse the feelings expressed on the stage to enable such a theatre to exist. Of all literary masterpieces there are none so intimately linked to a whole people as a tragedy. The audience contributes almost as much to it as the authors. Dramatic genius is formed from the public state of mind, history, government, customs, in short from everything which enters into each day's thinking and shapes the moral being, as the air one breathes nourishes physical life. Yet the Spanish, with whom your climate and religion ought to make you linked, have much more genius for drama than you. Full of their history, their chivalry, and their religious faith, those plays are original and lively, but their success in this genre goes back to the glorious period of their history. So how could something which has never existed, a tragic theatre, be founded now in Italy?'

'Unfortunately, you are perhaps right, my Lord,' replied Corinne. 'Nevertheless, I still have great hopes for us from the natural ability of the Italian mind to soar, from their personal desire to excel, even when there are no favourable external circumstances; but above all we lack tragic actors. Affected language inevitably leads to declamatory, artificial diction. There is, however, no language in which a great actor can show as much talent as in ours, for the musical sound adds a new charm to the sincerity of the tone. There is a continual music which blends with the expression of feelings without detracting in any way from its power.' 'If you want to convince us of the truth of what you are saying, you must prove it,' interrupted Prince Castel-Forte. 'Yes, give us the inexpressible pleasure of seeing you act in tragedy. You must grant foreigners you think worthy of it the rare enjoyment of becoming acquainted with a talent that you alone in Italy possess, or rather you alone in the whole world, because it bears the stamp of your whole soul.'

Secretly, Corinne longed to act in tragedy before Lord Nelvil, and so show herself off to great advantage; but not daring to agree without his approval, her eyes asked him for it. He understood her request and, as he was both touched by the shyness which had kept her from improvising the previous day, and anxious for Mr Edgermond's appreciation of her, he joined in her friends' entreaties. So Corinne hesitated no longer. 'Well, then,' she said, turning to Prince Castel-Forte, 'if you agree, we shall carry out the plan I made a long time ago, of acting my translation of *Romeo and Juliet*.' 'Shakespeare's *Romeo and Juliet*?' exclaimed Mr Edgermond. 'So you know English?' 'Yes,' replied Corinne. 'And you like Shakespeare?' continued Mr Edgermond.

'Like a friend,' she replied, 'for he knows all the secrets of grief.' 'And you will act him in Italian!' exclaimed Mr Edgermond. 'And you will hear it too, my dear Nelvil. Oh, how fortunate you are!' Then, immediately regretting his indiscretion, he blushed. But the blush aroused by tact and kindness is touching at any age. 'How fortunate we shall be to see such a performance,' he added with embarrassment.

CHAPTER III

WITHIN a few days, everything was arranged, the parts were cast, and the evening was chosen for the performance in a palace belonging to a friend of Corinne's, a female relative of Prince Castel-Forte. As this new success came nearer, Oswald's feelings were a mixture of apprehension and pleasure; he was enjoying the performance in advance, but he was also jealous in advance, not of any one particular man, but of the public who would be spectators of the talents of the woman he loved. He would have liked to be the only one to know how witty and charming she was; he would have liked Corinne to be as shy and reserved as an Englishwoman and to reveal her eloquence and genius to him alone. However distinguished a man may be, he never appreciates the superiority of a woman without mixed feelings. If he loves her, his heart is troubled; if he does not love her, his pride is offended. When he was with Corinne, Oswald was more intoxicated than happy and the admiration she inspired increased his love without making his plans any more definite. He saw her as a remarkable phenomenon, reappearing before him each day, but the very delight and surprise she aroused in him seemed to preclude the hope of a calm, peaceful life. Yet Corinne was the gentlest of women and very easy to live with. She was lovable for her ordinary virtues, quite apart from her brilliance; but the thought kept recurring to him that she combined too many talents; she was too remarkable in every way. Whatever advantages Lord Nelvil was gifted with, he thought he was not her equal, and this idea made him fear for the permanence of their mutual affection. It was in vain that, out of love, Corinne made herself his slave; the master, often troubled by this queen in chains, did not enjoy his power in peace.

A few hours before the performance, Lord Nelvil accompanied Corinne to Princess Castel-Forte's palace, where the theatre was ready. It was a beautiful, sunny day and Rome with its surrounding countryside could be seen from one of the staircase windows. Oswald made Corinne pause for a moment, saying, 'You see this beautiful weather; it is for you; it is to light up your success.' 'Oh, if that were so,' she replied, 'it is you who would bring me luck; it is to you that I would owe Heaven's protection.' 'Would the sweet, pure feelings aroused by the beauty of nature here be enough to make you happy?' asked Oswald. 'The air that we breathe here, the reverie aroused by the countryside, are a far cry from the noisy hall which is going to resound with your name.' 'Oswald,' said Corinne, 'if I win applause, it is because you will hear it that I shall be affected by it. And if I show some talent, will it not be my feeling for you that inspires it? Poetry, love, religion, in fact everything connected with strong feeling, is in harmony with nature. When I look at the azure sky and give myself up to the feeling it arouses in me, I understand Juliet's feelings better; I am more worthy of Romeo.' 'Yes, you are worthy of him, heavenly being,' exclaimed Lord Nelvil. 'Yes, it is an emotional weakness, this jealousy of your talents, this need to live alone in the universe with you. Go, receive the homage of society, but let that loving look, which is even more divine than your genius, be only for me.' Then they parted and Lord Nelvil took his seat in the hall and waited for the pleasure of seeing Corinne appear.

Romeo and Juliet is an Italian subject. The scene takes place in Verona. People there still point out the lovers' tomb. Shakespeare wrote the play with the full power of the southern imagination, an imagination which is triumphant in happiness and yet goes so easily from that happiness to despair, and from despair to death. Its emotions are quickly aroused, but they can never be obliterated. In a violent climate, it is the power of nature, not the whims of feeling, that hastens the development of the passions. The soil is not thin, although vegetation grows quickly, and Shakespeare, better than any other foreign writer, understood Italy's national character, the fertile mind which invents a thousand different ways of expressing the same feeling, and the oriental eloquence which uses images from the whole of nature to depict what takes place in the heart. It is not, as in Ossian, just one shade, just one sound, which responds to the heart's most sensitive string. Yet the variety of colours Shakespeare uses in *Romeo and Juliet* does not make his style cold and artificial; it is the ray of light, divided up, reflected, and varied, that produces these colours, and one can always feel the light and fire from which they stem. In this work,

there is the sap of life, a brilliance of language which is characteristic of the country and its inhabitants. The play of *Romeo and Juliet*,
translated into Italian, seems to return to its native tongue.

Juliet appears for the first time at a ball in the Capulets' house, which
Romeo, son of their mortal enemies, the Montagues, has surreptitiously
entered. Corinne was wearing a ball gown that was charming and yet
in keeping with the dress of the period. Her hair was decorated with
an artistic combination of flowers and precious stones. At first she
struck the audience as a person they had not seen before; then they
recognized her voice and face, but her face was transformed into that
of a goddess, expressing only poetry. At her appearance, applause from
the whole audience resounded through the hall. Her eyes immediately found Oswald and dwelt on him. A sparkle of joy and sweet,
lively hope lit up her face. Hearts beat with fear and pleasure at the
sight of her; it was felt that so much happiness could not last on earth.
Was it for Corinne that this foreboding was to come true?

When Romeo drew near to whisper to her of her grace and beauty
in lines of verse, so brilliant in English, so magnificent in the Italian
translation, the audience, delighted at being interpreted in this way,
all ecstatically identified with Romeo and the sudden passion which
gripped him; that passion, kindled by the first glance, seemed to all
the spectators quite probable. From that moment, Oswald became
uneasy. It seemed to him that everything was about to be revealed,
that Corinne was about to be proclaimed an angel amongst women,
that people were going to question him about his feelings for her, to
dispute his claim to her and snatch her from him. An indescribable,
dazzling cloud passed before his eyes, he was afraid of not being able
to see any more, he was afraid of fainting, and he retired behind
a pillar for a few moments. Corinne, worried, was looking for him
anxiously and declaimed the line:

'Too early seen unknown and known too late!'

in such a heartfelt tone that Oswald trembled when he heard it, because
it seemed to him that Corinne was applying it to their personal
situation.

With unflagging admiration he watched her gracious gestures, her
dignified movements, her face which showed what words could not
convey and revealed the secrets of the heart that, though unspoken,
control our lives. The tone of voice, the look, the slightest movement,

of an actor who is genuinely moved and inspired continually reveal the human heart, and the artistic ideal is always coupled with these revelations of human nature. So all the heart's feelings and all the soul's changing emotions are experienced through the imagination without losing anything of their truth.

In the second act, Juliet appears on the balcony looking onto the garden, to converse with Romeo. Of all Corinne's ornaments only the flowers remained, and a little later the flowers, too, were to disappear. The lighting of the theatre, dimmed to represent night, shed a softer, more touching light on Corinne's face. The sound of her voice was more melodious than during the brilliance of a ball. Her hand, raised up towards the stars, seemed to invoke the only witnesses worthy of hearing her, and when she repeated *Romeo, Romeo,* Oswald, although he was sure that it was him she was thinking of, felt jealous of the delightful sounds which made the air resound with a name other than his own. Oswald was opposite the balcony and, as the actor playing Romeo was a little hidden by the darkness, all Corinne's glances could fall on Oswald when she spoke these enchanting lines:

> 'In truth, fair Montague, I am too fond;
> And therefore thou may'st think my haviour light:
> But trust me, gentleman, I'll prove more true,
> Than those that have more cunning to be strange.
>
> . . . .
>
> . . . therefore pardon me.'

At these words: 'pardon me! pardon me for loving! pardon me for letting you know that I love!' there was such a loving prayer in Corinne's look, so much respect for her lover, so much pride in her choice, when she said, 'Noble Romeo! Fair Montague!' that Oswald felt as proud as he was happy. He raised his head that he had bowed in his emotion and believed he was king of the world, since he reigned over a heart which contained all life's treasures.

Seeing the effect she was having on Oswald, Corinne was stimulated more than ever by the heartfelt emotion that alone can produce miracles, and when, at daybreak, Juliet thinks she hears the lark singing, the sign for Romeo to go, Corinne's voice had a supernatural charm. It had expressed love, and yet one could hear in it the mystery of religion, memories of heaven, an omen of return there, a quite heavenly grief like that of a soul exiled onto earth but soon to be recalled to its divine home. Oh, how happy was Corinne on the day when, before her chosen friend, she played a noble part in a beautiful tragedy! How many years, how many lives, would be colourless compared to such a day!

If Lord Nelvil had been able to act the part of Romeo with Corinne, the pleasure she savoured would not have been so unalloyed. She would have wanted to set aside the lines of the greatest poets to speak according to her own heart. An insurmountable feeling of shyness might have constrained her talent; she might not have dared look at Oswald, for fear of betraying herself. In short, truth carried to this point would have destroyed the prestige of art. But how sweet it was to know that the man she loved was there when she experienced the exalted feeling that only poetry can convey, when she felt all the delight of the emotions without the distressing agony of reality, when the love she was expressing was neither personal nor abstract, and she seemed to be saying to Lord Nelvil, 'See what love I am capable of!'

It is impossible to be satisfied with oneself in one's own situation. Passionate love and shyness carry away or restrain one in turn, inspire too much bitterness or too much submission. But to reveal oneself as perfect without being affected, to be both calm and sensitive when too often sensitivity destroys calm, in short to live for one moment in the sweetest of the heart's dreams, that was Corinne's most unalloyed enjoyment in acting tragedy. To this pleasure she added that of all the success and all the applause she received, and her look laid them at Oswald's feet, at the feet of the being whose approval by itself was worth more than fame. Oh, at least for one moment, Corinne knew happiness. For one moment, at the cost of her peace of mind, she experienced those delights of the soul that, till then, she had longed for in vain and that she was to mourn for ever.

In the third act Juliet secretly becomes Romeo's wife. In the fourth, since her parents want to force her to marry another man, she decides to take the sleeping draught a monk gives her and which is to give her the appearance of death. All Corinne's movements, her agitated step, the changed tone of her voice, her expression alternately lively and depressed, portrayed the cruel struggle between fear and love, the terrible images which obsessed her at the idea of being carried alive into her ancestral tomb, and yet the strong emotion of passionate love which made so young a heart conquer such a natural dread. Oswald felt an almost irresistible need to fly to her rescue. Once she raised her eyes towards heaven with a fervour which expressed intensely her need of that divine protection from which no human being has ever been able to liberate himself. Another time, Lord Nelvil thought she was stretching out her arms to him to summon him to her aid, and, in a crazy outburst of passionate love, he got up. Then he sat down again, brought to his senses by the surprised looks of the people around him, but his emotion became so strong that he could hide it no longer.

In the fifth act Romeo, thinking Juliet is lifeless, lifts her from the tomb before she awakes and presses her, unconscious, against his heart. Corinne was dressed in white, her black hair all dishevelled, her head gracefully inclined towards Romeo, but yet she had an appearance of death so touching and so sad that Oswald felt shattered simultaneously by the most contradictory emotions. He could not bear to see Corinne in the arms of another. He shuddered as he looked at the woman he loved thus bereft of life and, like Romeo, he felt the cruel mixture of despair and love, death and ardour, which make this scene the most heart-rending in the theatre. And at last, when Juliet awakes from the tomb, after Romeo has taken his own life at the foot of it and when her first words in her coffin under the burial vault's funereal arches are not inspired by the terror they must arouse, when she exclaims,

'Where is my lord? Where is my Romeo?'

Lord Nelvil's moans answered her cries, and he came to himself when Mr Edgermond dragged him from the hall.

Once the play was over, Corinne felt exhausted with emotion and fatigue. Oswald was the first to enter her room and saw her alone with her attendants, still dressed as Juliet and, like her, half lifeless in their arms. In his great disarray, he could not distinguish between truth and fiction, and throwing himself at Corinne's feet, said these words of Romeo in English,

'Eyes, look your last! arms, take your last embrace.'

Corinne, still beside herself, cried, 'Good God! What are you saying? Would you want to leave me, would you?' 'No, no,' Oswald interrupted, 'No, I swear . . .' At this moment the crowd of Corinne's friends and admirers forced their way through the door to see her. She looked at Oswald, anxiously waiting for what he was about to say,

but for the whole evening they could not speak to each other as they
were not left alone for a moment.

Never before in Italy had tragedy made such an impression. The
Romans, enraptured, praised to the skies the translation, the play, and
the actress. They said that was the tragedy really suited to the Italians, portraying their manners, making the most of their beautiful language by a style in turn eloquent and lyrical, inspired and natural.
Corinne accepted the praise sweetly and good-naturedly, but her heart
continued to hang on Oswald's words *I swear* . . . which had been interrupted by the arrival of the company; what he had been going to say
might indeed contain the secret of her fate.

BOOK VIII
STATUES AND PICTURES

CHAPTER I

AFTER the day that had just passed, Oswald could not close his eyes all night. He had never been more ready to sacrifice everything to Corinne. He did not even want to ask her her secret, or at least, before knowing it, he was willing to make the solemn pledge to devote his life to her. For a few hours, his mind was entirely free of uncertainty and he delighted in composing in his head the letter he would write the next day which would seal his fate. But this confident happiness, this calm resolve, did not last long. His thoughts soon brought him back to the past. He remembered that he had been in love before; much less, it is true, than he loved Corinne, and the woman of his first choice could not be compared to her. But still it was this feeling that had led him on to thoughtless behaviour, to behaviour that had broken his father's heart. 'Oh!' he cried. 'Who knows if today, too, he would not be afraid that his son would forget his native land and his obligations to it?'

'Oh, you, the best friend I shall ever have on earth,' he said, addressing his father's portrait, 'I can no longer hear your voice, but by your look, which cannot speak but still has such power over my heart, tell me what I should do in order to give you in heaven some satisfaction with your son. But yet do not forget mortal beings' ardent desire for happiness; be indulgent in your heavenly abode as you were on earth. I shall become better if I am happy for a time, if I live with this angelic being, if I have the honour to protect, to save, such a woman.' 'Save her?' he repeated suddenly, 'and from what? from a life she enjoys, from a life of homage, of success, of independence?' This thought, which was his own, frightened him as if it were inspired by his father.

In conflicts of feeling, who has not often experienced some kind of secret superstition which makes us take our thoughts for a premonition and our suffering for a warning from heaven? Oh what a struggle goes on in hearts susceptible to both passionate love and conscience!

Oswald, in cruel distress, paced to and fro in his room, stopping now and again to look at the gentle, beautiful Italian moon. The appearance of nature teaches resignation but has no effect on uncertainty. Day broke while he was in this state, and when Count d'Erfeuil and Mr Edgermond came into his room they were worried about his health, for the night's anxieties had changed him so much! Count d'Erfeuil was the first to break the silence that had settled between them. 'We must agree that last night's performance was charming. Corinne is wonderful. I lost half of what she said, but I guessed everything from her tone of voice and her expression. What a pity that it is a rich person who has such a talent. For, if she were poor, free as she is, she could go on the stage; and an actress like her would be the glory of Italy.'

This speech pained Oswald but he did not know how to show his feelings. For an odd feature of Count d'Erfeuil was that there was no proper reason for being annoyed by what he said, even when one was upset by it. There are sensitive souls who know how to spare each other's feelings. *Amour propre*, so susceptible itself, is hardly ever aware of other people's susceptibility.

Mr Edgermond praised Corinne in the most appropriate and flattering terms. Oswald replied in English, so as to draw the conversation about Corinne away from Count d'Erfeuil's objectionable words of praise. Then Count d'Erfeuil said, 'I seem to be in the way; I am going to Corinne's. She will be very pleased to hear my comments on her acting yesterday evening. I have a little advice to give her about details, but details make a big difference to the total effect and she is truly such a remarkable woman that nothing should be neglected to make her achieve perfection. And then,' he said, leaning over towards Lord Nelvil's ear, 'I want to encourage her to act in tragedy more often; it is a sure way of getting herself married to some distinguished foreigner who will come this way. You and I, dear Oswald, will not fall for the idea; we are too used to charming women for them to make us do anything foolish. But a German prince, a Spanish grandee, who knows?' At these words, Oswald got up, beside himself, and it is impossible to know what would have happened if Count d'Erfeuil had noticed his movement. He had been so pleased, however, with his last comment that he had gone away quietly, on tiptoe, not suspecting that he had offended Lord Nelvil. If he had known, although he was as fond of him as he could be of anyone, he would certainly have stayed. Count d'Erfeuil's splendid courage was more responsible than his vanity for deluding him about his failings. As he was very touchy about everything concerned with honour, he did not conceive that he could be deficient in anything connected with sensitivity. Rightly believing that he was likeable and brave, he congratulated himself on his lot and did not suspect there was anything more profound in life.

None of Oswald's agitated feelings had escaped Mr Edgermond's notice, and when Count d'Erfeuil had gone, he said, 'My dear Oswald, I am leaving, I am going to Naples.' 'And why so soon?' asked Lord Nelvil. 'Because it is not good for me here,' Mr Edgermond went on. 'I am fifty years old, and yet I am not sure that I would not become crazy about Corinne.' 'And if you were to, what would happen to you?' interrupted Oswald. 'A woman like that is not made to live in Wales,' replied Mr Edgermond. 'Believe me, my dear Oswald, only English women are suited to England. It is not my place to give you advice and I do not need to assure you that I shall not say a word about what I have seen, but however lovable Corinne is, I think, like Thomas Walpole,* *What would you do with that at home?* And, as you know, home is everything in our country, everything for the women at least. Can you imagine your beautiful Italian staying at home while you are out hunting or going to Parliament, and leaving you at dessert to go and make tea when you leave the table? Dear Oswald, our women have domestic virtues that you will not find anywhere else. Men in Italy have nothing to do but please women, and so the more they are lovable the better. But in our country, where men have an active career, women must be in the shade and it would be a pity to put Corinne there. I should want to put her on the English throne and not under my humble roof. I knew your mother, my Lord, whom your worthy father missed so much. She was someone exactly like my young cousin, and that is how I should like a woman to be if I were still of an age to choose and to be loved. Goodbye, my dear friend. Do not bear me a grudge for what I have just said, for no one admires Corinne more than I do, and perhaps, if I were your age, I should not be able to give up the hope of her love.' As he finished speaking, he took Lord Nelvil's hand, shook it cordially, and went away, without Oswald saying a word in reply. But Mr Edgermond understood why he was silent and, satisfied with Oswald's handshake which had responded to his, he left, glad to finish a conversation he found painful.

Only one word of all he said touched Oswald's heart; that was the memory of his mother and of his father's deep attachment to her. He had lost her when he was still only fourteen, but with deep respect he recalled both her virtues and the reserved, shy nature of those virtues. 'Fool that I am,' he cried when he was alone. 'I wanted to know what the wife my father intended for me was like. And don't I know, since I can recall the image of my mother whom he loved so much? So what more do I want? And why deceive myself in pretending not to know what he would think now if I could still consult him?' It was, however, terrible for Oswald to go back to Corinne's house after what had happened the previous day without saying anything which would confirm the feelings he had shown towards her. His worry and his suffering became so intense that they brought the recurrence of an injury that he thought cured. The healed blood vessel in his chest reopened. While his frightened servants called for help in every direction, he wished secretly that the termination of his life would put an end to his sorrows. 'If I could die after seeing Corinne again,' he thought, 'after she had called me her Romeo!' And tears stole down his cheeks, the first that another sorrow had drawn from him since his father's death.

He wrote to Corinne about the mishap that kept him at home and finished his letter with a few melancholy words. Corinne began the same day with very deceptive presentiments. She was enjoying the impression she had made on Oswald and, believing herself to be loved, she was happy, for she did not know clearly what she wanted. A thousand things made her apprehensive at the idea of marrying Lord Nelvil, and as she was a more emotional than prudent person, dominated by the present but not much concerned about the future, the day which was to bring her so many sorrows had risen for her as the purest and serenest day of her life.

When she received Oswald's note, she was gripped by a cruel anxiety. She thought he was in great danger and set off instantly on foot, crossing the *corso** at the time when the whole town is out walking there, and going into Oswald's house in full view of nearly all Roman society. She had not given herself time to think and she had walked so fast that, on reaching Oswald's room, she was out of breath and could not say a single word. Lord Nelvil understood everything she had risked to see him and, as he exaggerated the consequences of her action, which in England would have ruined a woman's reputation completely and particularly that of an unmarried woman, he felt gripped by generosity, love, and gratitude, and, weak as he was, he pressed Corinne to his heart, crying, 'Beloved friend! No, I shall not desert you when you are compromised by your feeling for me, when I must repair . . .' Corinne understood his thoughts and interrupted him. Gently freeing herself from his embrace, she asked him about his condition, which had improved, and then said, 'You are mistaken, my Lord. I have done nothing in coming to see you which most Roman women would not have done in my place. I heard you were ill; you are a stranger here; I am the only person you know and it is my duty to look after you. The established conventions are all very well when it is only oneself that has to be sacrificed to them, but ought they not to give way to the sincerely deep feelings aroused by the danger or the pain of a friend? So what would be the lot of a woman if these same social conventions allowed her to love but forbade only the irresistible feeling which makes her fly to the help of her beloved? But, my Lord, I repeat, do not fear that I compromised myself by coming here. In Rome, because of my age and talents, I have the freedom of a married woman. I do not conceal from my friends that I have come to your house. I do not know if they blame me for loving you, but they will certainly not blame me for being devoted to you when I love you.'

When he heard these unselfconscious, sincere words, Oswald experienced a mixture of different feelings. He was touched by Corinne's tactful reply, but he was almost annoyed that his first thought was not correct. He would have liked her to have committed a serious error in the eyes of society, so that that very error would make it his duty to marry her and thus put an end to his indecision. He thought with annoyance of the freedom of Italian manners, which prolonged his anxiety by allowing a great deal of happiness without imposing any obligation on him. He would have liked honour to command him to do what he wanted to do. These painful thoughts produced more dangerous bleeding. Corinne, desperately anxious, was able to lavish on him the most soothing and charming care.

Towards evening Oswald seemed worse, and Corinne, kneeling beside his bed, supported his head in her arms, though she herself was more upset than he was. He often looked at her with a feeling of happiness through his suffering. 'Corinne,' he said in a low voice, 'read to me from this notebook in which my father has written his thoughts, his reflections on death. Do not think I believe myself to be in danger,' he said when he saw Corinne's fear, 'but I always read his consolations when I am ill; it is as if I can still hear them from his own mouth. And then, my beloved friend, I want to enable you to know what kind of man my father was, so that you will understand better both my grief and his influence over me, and everything that I want to confide to you one day.' Corinne took the notebook, which Oswald always kept by him, and, in a trembling voice, she read a few pages.

'Righteous men, beloved of the Lord, you will speak of death without fear, since for you it will be only a change of dwelling and the one you will leave is perhaps the least of all. O countless worlds, which to our eyes fill the infinity of space! Unknown communities of God's creatures, scattered throughout the firmament and placed under its dome! May our praise be joined to yours! We do not know your state, we do not know your first, your second, your last share in the generosity of the Supreme Being, but when we speak of death and life, of time past and time to come, we reach, we touch on, the interests of all intelligent and sensitive beings, whatever the places and distances that separate them. Families of peoples, families of nations, gatherings of worlds, you say with us: Glory to the master of the heavens, to the king of nature, to the God of the universe; glory, homage, to him who can at will transform sterility into fruitfulness, shadow into reality, and death itself into eternal life.

'Oh! The end of the righteous man is no doubt the death to be desired, but few of us, few of our ancestors, have witnessed it. Where is he, the man who would come without fear before the eyes of the Eternal one? Where is he, the man who has loved God single-mindedly, who has served him ever since his youth and who, on reaching old age, finds no cause for anxiety in his memories? Where is he, the man whose every deed is virtuous and who has no thought of praise or the rewards of public opinion? Where is he, that man so rare amongst men, that being so worthy of serving as an example to us all? Where is he? Where is he? Oh, if he exists in our midst, may he be surrounded by our respect; and ask, you will do well to ask, to be present at his death as at the finest of sights. Arm yourselves only with courage so as to observe him closely on the bed of terror from which he will not rise again. He foresees it, he is sure of it, but his look is serene and his brow seems surrounded by a heavenly halo. He says with the apostle,* *I know in whom I have believed*, and as his strength ebbs away, his features still express this confidence. Already he envisages his new abode; but without forgetting the one he is about to leave, he already belongs to his Creator and to his God, without thrusting far from him the feelings that have embellished his life.

'According to the laws of nature, it is a faithful wife who should be the first of his family to follow him. He consoles her, he wipes away her tears; he says he will meet her in that joyful dwelling place he cannot imagine without her. He recalls to her the happy days they spent together, not in order to rend the heart of a sensitive friend, but to increase their mutual confidence in heavenly goodness. He further reminds the companion of his lot of the tender love he always had for her, not in order to arouse sorrow that he would like to allay, but to enjoy the sweet thought that two lives have clung to the same twig and that, through their union, they will become perhaps a defence, a further guarantee in that uncertain future where a Supreme Being's pity is the last refuge of our thoughts. Alas! Can one form an exact idea of all the emotions which pierce a loving heart at the moment when the feelings and concerns which have filled the prime of his life are going to vanish for ever? Oh! You who are to survive this being, similar to yourself, whom Heaven had given you as a support and whose looks bid you a frightening farewell, you will not refuse to place your hand on a failing heart, so that a final beat will still speak to you when every other language will no longer exist. And would we blame you, faithful friends, if you had wished your ashes to be mingled and your mortal remains to be reunited in the same sanctuary? God of goodness, waken them together, or if only one of them deserves that favour, if only one of them is to be of the number of the elect, may the other be told the news; may the other see the angels' light at the moment when the fate of the happy is announced, so that he may still have a moment's joy before falling back into eternal night.

'Oh! Perhaps we lose our way when we try to describe the last days of the sensitive man, of the man who sees death approaching with great strides, who sees it ready to separate him from all his dear ones.

'He revives, regains strength for a moment, so that his last words serve as a lesson to his children. He says to them, "Do not be afraid to be present at your father's, your old friend's, last moments. It is by a law of nature that he leaves before you this earth where he came first. He will show you courage, and yet it grieves him to leave you.

He would probably have wished to help you longer with his experience and to take a few more steps with you through the perils that beset your youth. *But life has no defence when one must go down to the grave.* You will go alone, alone in a world from which I am going to disappear. May you gather abundantly the benefits Providence has scattered in it. But never forget that this world itself is a temporary home and another more lasting one summons you. Perhaps we shall see each other again and somewhere, in the sight of God, I shall offer up my prayers and tears as a sacrifice on your behalf. Love religion, which is so full of hope; love religion, this final treaty of alliance between fathers and children, between death and life . . . Come near to me! May I see you once more, may the blessing of a servant of God be upon you . . ." He dies . . . Oh! Heavenly angels, receive his soul, and leave us on earth the memory of his deeds, the memory of his thoughts, the memory of his hopes.'[19]

Oswald's and Corinne's emotion often interrupted this reading. In the end they were forced to stop. Corinne was afraid that Oswald was weeping too much. She was very upset at seeing the state he was in but did not notice that she herself was as troubled as he was. 'Yes,' said Oswald, giving her his hand, 'yes, dear beloved, your tears have mingled with mine. With me you mourn the guardian angel whose last embrace I still feel, whose noble look I still see. Perhaps it is you he has chosen to console me; perhaps . . .' 'No, no,' cried Corinne, 'no, he did not think I was worthy of that.' 'What are you saying?' interrupted Oswald. Corinne was afraid she had revealed something she wanted to hide, and repeated the words that had just escaped her, saying only, 'He would not think me worthy of that!' The change dissipated the unease that the first wording had aroused in Oswald's heart and, unafraid, he continued talking to Corinne about his father.

The doctors arrived and reassured her a little, but they absolutely forbade Lord Nelvil to speak until the blood vessel which had burst in his chest had healed. Six whole days went by during which Corinne did not leave Oswald; she prevented him from uttering a single word, gently imposing silence on him as soon as he wanted to speak. She found ways of varying the hours by reading, by music, and sometimes by a conversation of which she bore the whole burden, endeavouring to stimulate herself and to maintain interest in serious as well as in amusing subjects. All this grace and charm concealed her inner anxiety, which had to be kept from Lord Nelvil; not for a moment,

however, was she distracted from it. She noticed what Oswald was
suffering even before he did himself, and his courage in concealing
it never deceived Corinne. She always found something that would
do him good and hastened to bring him relief, trying only to fix his
attention as little as possible on the care she was giving him. Yet when
Oswald turned pale, Corinne's lips lost their colour too and her hands
trembled as she helped him. But she soon made an effort to pull herself together and she smiled although her eyes were filled with tears.
From time to time she pressed Oswald's hand to her heart as if she
wanted to give him her own life. At last her care was successful and
Oswald recovered.

'Corinne,' he said, when she allowed him to speak, 'why did my
friend Mr Edgermond not witness the days you have just spent with
me? He would have seen that you are no less good than you are remarkable. He would have seen that, with you, domestic life is made up of
continual delights and that you differ from other women only in adding
to all the virtues the glamour of all the charms. No, this is too much;
I must cease the struggle which is rending me apart, this struggle which
has just led me to the edge of the grave. Corinne, you will hear me,
you will know all my secrets, you who conceal your own from me,
and you will decide our fate.' 'Our fate,' replied Corinne, 'if you feel
as I do, is not to leave each other. But will you believe me when I
tell you that up to now, at least, I did not dare to want to be your
wife. My feeling is quite a new one for me. My ideas on life, my plans
for the future, are completely upset by this feeling, which troubles
and enslaves me more each day. But I do not know if we can, if we
ought, to join together in marriage.' 'Corinne,' replied Oswald, 'would
you despise me for my hesitation? Would you attribute it to petty considerations? Have you not guessed that the painfully deep remorse,
which for nearly two years has pursued and tortured me, was the only
possible cause of my uncertainty?'

'I understood,' replied Corinne. 'If I had suspected that you had
a motive alien to the heart's affections, you would not be the man
I love. But life, I know, does not consist wholly of love. Habits,
memories, circumstances create some kind of web around us that even
passionate love cannot destroy. Even if it were broken for a moment,
it would grow again, and the ivy would get the better of the oak. My
dear Oswald, let us not give to each period of our lives more than it
requires. What I need at the moment is for you not to leave me. I am

constantly tormented by the fear of your sudden departure. You are
a foreigner in this country; no tie keeps you here. If you leave, everything will be over; all that would be left to me of you would be my
grief. Nature, the arts, the poetry I feel with you, alas! only with you,
all that would no longer speak to my soul. When I awake I do nothing but tremble; I do not know, when I see the beautiful daylight, if
I am not deceived by its gleaming rays, if you are still there, you, the
light of my life. Oswald, deliver me from this fear and I shall see nothing beyond that delightful security.' 'You know', Oswald replied, 'that
no Englishman ever renounced his native land, that I might be recalled
by war, that . . .' 'Oh, good God,' cried Corinne. 'Do you want to
prepare me? . . .' And all her limbs trembled as if the most frightful
danger were drawing nigh. 'Well, if that is the case, take me with you
as your wife, as your slave . . .' But she suddenly recovered her composure, saying . . . 'Oswald, you will never leave without telling me
first, never, isn't that so? Indeed, there is not a country in the world
where a criminal is led to execution without being granted a few hours
in which to collect his thoughts. You will not inform me by letter;
you will come yourself to tell me; you will give me due warning; you
will hear what I have to say before you leave me.' 'But in that case,
would I be able to? . . .' 'What! Do you hesitate to grant my request?'
cried Corinne. 'No,' replied Oswald. 'I do not hesitate since you want
me to tell you before I go. Well, I swear that if I have to leave, I shall
let you know and that moment will decide our lives.' 'Yes,' said
Corinne, 'it will decide them.' And she went away.

CHAPTER II

DURING the days following Oswald's illness Corinne carefully
avoided everything that could bring about an explanation between
them. She wanted to make her friend's life as easy as possible but she
did not yet want to tell him the story of her past. Everything she had
noticed in their conversations had made her only too certain of the
impression he would receive when he learned who she was and what
she had sacrificed; nothing frightened her more than this impression
which might detach him from her.

So she returned to the gentle skill which she normally used to prevent Oswald from succumbing to his emotional anxieties, and again
wanted to stimulate his mind and imagination by the marvellous art

treasures he had not yet seen, and so delay the moment when their fate would become clearer and be decided. Such a situation would be unbearable with any feeling other than love, but love gives such delightful hours, it conveys such a charm to each minute, that although it needs a limitless future, it is intoxicated with the present and accepts each day as a century of happiness or grief, so filled is that day with a multitude of emotions and ideas. Oh, it is certainly through love that eternity can be understood; it confuses all thoughts about time; it destroys the ideas of beginning and end; one thinks one has always been in love with the person one loves, so difficult is it to conceive that one could live without him. The more frightful the separation, the less probable it seems; like death, it becomes a dread one speaks about more than one believes in, a future that seems impossible even though one knows it to be inevitable.

Among the innocent devices to vary Oswald's entertainments, Corinne had kept the statues and pictures in reserve. So one day, when Lord Nelvil had recovered, she suggested to him that they should go together to see the most beautiful sculptures and paintings that Rome had to offer. 'It is a shame', she said with a smile, 'that you know neither our statues nor our pictures, and tomorrow we must start to go round our museums and galleries.' 'Since you want to,' replied Lord Nelvil, 'I agree. But, to tell the truth, Corinne, you do not need these external activities to make me stay with you. On the contrary, when I look away from you for anything at all, I am making a sacrifice to please you.'

First they went to the Vatican gallery, that palace of statues where one sees the human form exalted by paganism, as the soul's feelings are exalted today by Christianity. Corinne pointed out to Lord Nelvil the silent rooms where likenesses of the gods and heroes are assembled, where the most perfect beauty, in eternal repose, seems to admire itself. As one contemplates those admirable features and physiques, there is revealed an indescribable divine intention for man, expressed by the noble face that God has deigned to bestow upon him. In this contemplation, the soul is uplifted to hopes filled with enthusiasm and virtue, for beauty is one in the universe, and whatever form it assumes, it always arouses a religious feeling in the hearts of mankind. What poetry lies in those faces where the most sublime expression is fixed for ever, where the greatest thoughts are clothed in an image worthy of them!

Sometimes a sculptor of the ancient world would make only one statue in his life; it was the story of his whole life. He would perfect it each day; if he loved, if he was loved, if he received from nature or the arts a new impression, he would embellish his hero's features with his memories and feelings. In our modern times, in our cold, oppressive society, grief is our noblest emotion, and in our day, he who has not suffered will have neither felt nor thought. But in ancient times, there was something more noble than grief; it was heroic composure, it was the feeling of one's own strength, which could develop freely in free institutions. The most beautiful Greek statues have rarely conveyed anything but the idea of rest. The Laocoön and Niobe are the only ones that portray violent grief, but they both recall the vengeance of heaven and not passions born in the human heart. The moral being of the ancients had such a healthy constitution, air circulated so freely in their broad chests, and the political system was so well in tune with their mental powers, that there were hardly ever any maladjusted souls as there are today. That maladjusted state leads to the discovery of many subtle ideas but does not provide the arts, and particularly sculpture, with the simple affections, the basic feelings, that alone can be expressed in everlasting marble.

Scarcely any traces of melancholy can be found in their statues. A head of Apollo in the Giustiniani palace, another of the dying Alexander, are the only ones in which there are suggestions of meditation or suffering, but they both appear to belong to the time when Greece was enslaved. From then on, there was no longer amongst the ancients the pride or the calmness of spirit which produced the masterpieces of sculpture and poetry composed in the same frame of mind.

Thought without external nourishment turns in on itself, analyses, works on, digs into, inner feelings, but it no longer has the creative strength which depends on happiness and the ample strength which only happiness can give. Among the ancients, even the sarcophagi arouse only warlike or cheerful ideas. In the large number to be found in the Vatican gallery, you can see battles and games portrayed in bas-reliefs on the tombs. The memory of life's activity was the finest homage that was thought should be rendered to the dead. Nothing weakened, nothing diminished its strength. Encouragement and emulation were the mainsprings of the arts as of politics; there was room for all the virtues as for all the talents. Ordinary people took pride in knowing how to admire, and the cult of genius was served even by those who could not hope to aspire to its achievements.

Unlike Christianity, the Greek religion was not the consolation of the unhappy, the wealth of the poor, the future for the dying. It wanted fame and triumph; it formed, as it were, man's apotheosis. In this worship of the perishable, beauty itself was religious dogma. If artists were called on to depict base or fierce passions, they spared the shame to the human form by joining to it some of the features of animals as in fauns and centaurs. And to give beauty its more sublime nature, they combined, turn and turn about, in the statues of men and women, in the warlike Minerva and in the Apollo Musagetes,* the charms of the two sexes, strength with gentleness, gentleness with strength, a happy mixture of two opposing qualities, without which neither would be perfect.

As she continued her comments, Corinne kept Oswald a little time in front of the sleeping statues placed on tombs which show the art of sculpture in its pleasantest aspect. She pointed out to him that every time the statues are supposed to portray an action, the arrested movement produces a kind of surprise that is sometimes painful. But statues in sleep, or only in a pose of complete rest, present an image of eternal calm that harmonizes marvellously with the general effect of the South on mankind. There, it seems, the arts are peaceful spectators of nature, and genius itself, which in the North disturbs the soul, under a fine sky is but one more harmony.

Oswald and Corinne went on into the room where there is a collection of sculptured images of animals and reptiles, but, by chance, the statue of Tiberius* is in the middle of this court. It was not a planned juxtaposition. These marble statues have arranged themselves around their master on their own. Another room contains the sad, stern monuments of the Egyptians, of that people whose statues resemble mummies more than men, and which through its silent, stiff, and servile institutions seems to have assimilated life to death as much as it could. The Egyptians excelled much more in the art of imitating animals than men; it was the realm of the soul which seems to have been inaccessible to them.

Next come the porticoes of the gallery, where new masterpieces can be seen at every step. Vases, altars, ornaments of every kind, surround the Apollos, the Laocoön, and the Muses. It is there that one learns to appreciate Homer and Sophocles; it is there that a knowledge of antiquity, impossible to acquire elsewhere, is revealed to the soul. It is useless to rely on the reading of history to understand the spirit of peoples. Our ideas are stimulated much more by what we see than by what we read, and visible objects arouse a strong emotion which gives to the study of the past the interest and life we find in the observation of contemporary men and events.

Among the splendid porticoes, harbouring so many wonders, are permanently flowing fountains, which gently tell us of the hours that passed in the same way two thousand years ago, when the creators of these masterpieces were still alive. But the most melancholy feeling one has in the Vatican museum is in looking at the remnants of statues collected there, Hercules' torso, heads separated from bodies, one of Jupiter's feet which suggests a bigger and more perfect statue than all those we know. It is as if we were seeing the battlefield where time fought against genius, and these mutilated limbs bear witness to its victory and our loss.

After leaving the Vatican, Corinne took Oswald to the colossi of Monte Cavallo. These two statues are said to represent Castor and Pollux. Each of these two heroes controls a spirited, rearing horse with a single hand. Like all the works of the ancients, these colossal figures give an admirable idea of the physical power of human nature. But this power has a noble quality no longer existing in our society, where most physical exercises are left to the lower classes. It is not the animal strength of human nature, if one may put it that way, which is noticeable in these masterpieces. Among the ancients, who lived perpetually in the midst of war and a war almost of man–to–man fighting, there seems to have been a more intimate union between physical and moral qualities. Before a completely intellectual religion had placed man's power in his soul, strength of body and generosity of soul, dignity of features and pride of character, the height of the statue and the authority of command, were inseparable ideas. The human form, which was also the form of the gods, seemed symbolic, and the sinewy colossus of Hercules and all the classical forms of that type do not represent the ordinary details of daily life but the omnipotent will, the divine will, underlying the symbol of a supernatural physical strength.

Corinne and Lord Nelvil concluded their day by going to see the studio of Canova,* the greatest modern sculptor. As it was late, they were shown round by torchlight, but statues gain a lot by being seen like this. That was the opinion of the ancients, since they often put them in their baths where daylight could not enter. By torchlight, the more pronounced darkness dims the uniform dazzling whiteness of the marble, and the statues seem pale forms with more touching qualities of gracefulness and life. In Canova's studio there was a wonderful statue intended for a tomb. It represented the spirit of grief, leaning against a lion, the symbol of strength. When she looked at this statue, Corinne thought she found some resemblance to Oswald, and the artist himself was struck by it too. Lord Nelvil turned aside so as not to attract attention of that kind but he whispered to his friend, 'Corinne, I was condemned to that everlasting grief when I met you; but you have changed my life, and sometimes hope and always an excitement mingled with delight fills my heart, which was to have known only regrets.'

CHAPTER III

AT that time the masterpieces of painting were all assembled in Rome, and its riches in this field surpassed all those in the rest of the world. Only one point of debate could exist on the effect produced by these masterpieces. Did the kind of subjects chosen by the great Italian artists give scope for all the variety and originality of passions and characters which painting can express? Oswald and Corinne had different opinions on this matter, but their disagreement, like all those existing between them, had to do with the differences between nations, climates, and religions. Corinne maintained that religious subjects were the most suitable for painting. She said sculpture was the art of paganism as painting was that of Christianity, and in these arts, as in poetry, were found the qualities which distinguish ancient and modern literature. The pictures of Michelangelo, the painter of the Bible, of Raphael, the painter of the Gospels, suggest as much depth and sensitivity as can be found in Shakespeare and Racine. Sculpture could show the spectator only a vigorous, simple existence, while painting indicates the mysteries of reflection and resignation, and gives voice to the immortal soul through transient colour. Corinne also maintained that events of history or taken from poems were rarely pictorial. Painters from bygone ages had the custom of writing the words people were to say on balloons coming from their mouths, and these are often necessary for the comprehension of such pictures. But religious subjects are immediately understood by everyone and attention is not diverted from the work of art by the effort to guess what it represents.

Corinne thought that, in general, modern painters often expressed themselves theatrically, that they bore the stamp of their period, and that, unlike Andrea Mantegna,* Perugino,* and Leonardo da Vinci, they no longer knew the uniform lifestyle and natural demeanour which still retain something of the calm of the ancients. But to this calm is joined the depth of feeling characteristic of Christianity. All faces are turned towards the main subject, although the artist had not thought of grouping them in that pose or of working at the effect they might produce. Corinne said that in the imaginative arts, as in everything else, this confidence is the mark of genius and that to work for success is nearly always to destroy strong feeling. She claimed that there is rhetoric in painting as in poetry, and that all painters who did not know how to portray character strove after accessory ornamentation and combined all the prestige of an outstanding subject with rich costumes and striking poses, while a simple virgin holding her child in her arms, an old man listening attentively to the Bolsena Mass, a man leaning on his stick in the school of Athens, Saint Cecilia* raising her eyes to heaven, by the mere expression of the eyes and face aroused much deeper feelings. More of these natural beauties are discovered every day, but in pictures painted for effect, the first glance is always the most striking.[20]

To these reflections Corinne added a comment which confirmed them further. It was that, as the religious feelings of the Greeks and Romans, and every aspect of their sensibility, could not be the same as ours, it is impossible for us to create as they did, to invent, as it were, on their territory. Study enables us to imitate them, but how could genius soar to its full extent in a labour requiring so much memory and erudition? It is not the same with subjects belonging to our own history and religion. Painters can themselves be personally inspired by them; they feel what they paint, they paint what they have seen. They use life to imagine life, but by transporting themselves into antiquity they have to invent according to books and statues. Finally Corinne thought religious pictures did the soul good in a way nothing else did, and they assumed in the artist a holy enthusiasm which is indistinguishable from genius, animates it, and alone can support it against life's disappointments and men's injustices.

In some respects Oswald's impressions were different. First of all, he was almost scandalized to see the figure of the Divinity himself with human features as Michelangelo had painted him. He believed thought dared not give him form and that, in the depths of one's soul, one could barely find an idea spiritual enough, ethereal enough, to reach the height of the Supreme Being. As for subjects taken from Scripture, it seemed to him that the expression and the imagery in this kind of picture left much to be desired. Like Corinne, he believed that, as religious meditation is the most deep-seated feeling man can experience, it is the one that for painters is the source of the great mysteries of look and facial expression. But as religion represses all emotions of the heart that do not arise directly from it, there can be little variety in saints' and martyrs' faces. The feeling of humility, deemed so noble by Heaven, diminishes the strength of earthly passions and is bound to make most religious subjects monotonous. When Michelangelo, with his formidable talent, intended to paint these subjects, he almost altered their spirit by giving his prophets a powerful, terrifying expression which turns them into Jupiters rather than saints. Often, like Dante, he too uses pagan imagery and mingles mythology with Christianity. One of the most remarkable circumstances about the establishment of Christianity is the lowly state of the Disciples who preached it, the servitude and the poverty of the Jewish people, long entrusted with the promises foretelling Christ. This contrast between the lowliness of the means and the greatness of the outcome is morally very fine, but in painting, which can show only the means, Christian subjects are bound to be less striking than those taken from heroic, legendary times. Among the arts, music alone can be purely religious. Painting could not be satisfied with such a dreamy and vague means of expression as that of sound. It is true that the happy combination of colours with light and shade produces, as it were, a musical effect, but as painting represents life, the expression of the passions in all their strength and diversity is demanded of it. Certainly, from the historical facts one has to choose those which are so well known that no study is required to understand them, for the effect produced by pictures must be immediate and swift, like all pleasures given by the arts. But when historical facts are as well known as religious subjects, they have the advantage of the variety of the situations and feelings they reproduce.

Lord Nelvil thought, too, that in pictures preference should be given to tragic scenes or to the most touching poetic fictions so that all the pleasures of the imagination and the heart might be combined. Corinne argued against this opinion, however attractive it might be.

She was convinced that the encroachment of one art upon another was harmful to them both. Sculpture loses its own special advantages when it tries to reproduce the groups found in paintings; so does painting when it tries to achieve dramatic expression. The arts are limited in their means, although unlimited in their effects. Genius makes no attempt to fight against the essential nature of things; on the contrary, its superiority consists in being aware of it. 'My dear Oswald,' said Corinne, 'you do not like the arts in themselves, but only because of their relationship to the heart or the mind. You are moved only by what recalls your heart's suffering. Music and poetry suit your temperament, while the arts which appeal to the eye, although they may represent the ideal, please and interest us only when our hearts are at peace and our imaginations completely free. Nor do we need the cheerful animation of society to appreciate them, but only the serenity aroused by a beautiful day and a beautiful climate. In the arts that represent external objects, we must feel nature's universal harmony, but when our soul is troubled we no longer have that harmony within ourselves; unhappiness has destroyed it.' 'I do not know whether, in the visual arts, I seek only what can recall the heart's suffering,' replied Oswald, 'but at least I am well aware that I cannot bear to see in them the portrayal of physical suffering. My strongest objection to Christian subjects in painting', he continued, 'is the painful feeling aroused by the depiction of blood, wounds, and torture, even though the victims are inspired by the noblest enthusiasms. Philoctetes* is perhaps the only tragic subject in which physical ills may be allowed. But those cruel ills are surrounded by so many poetic situations! They are caused by Hercules' arrows; Aesculapius' son is to cure them. Indeed, this wound is almost inseparable from the moral resentment it creates in the person afflicted, and cannot arouse any feeling of disgust. But in Raphael's superb picture of the Transfiguration, the possessed boy's face is an unpleasant image, with none of the dignity of the arts. They ought to reveal to us the charm of grief and the melancholy of prosperity; they ought to portray the ideal of human destiny in every individual situation. Nothing torments the imagination more than bleeding words or nervous convulsions. In such pictures it is impossible not to look for, and at the same time not to fear, the exact imitation of reality. What pleasure would we derive from art which consists solely of this imitation? From the moment it aspires only to resemble nature, such art is either more horrible or less beautiful than nature itself.'

'You are right, my Lord, in wanting to remove painful imagery from Christian subjects,' said Corinne. 'It is not essential to them. But you must admit that genius and the soul's genius can triumph over everything. Look at Domenichino's *Last Communion of Saint Jerome*. The body of the venerable dying man is livid and emaciated; it is death that is rising up. But eternal life is in the expression of his eyes and all the earth's woes are there only to vanish before the pure brilliance of a religious feeling. Yet, dear Oswald,' continued Corinne, 'although I do not agree with you on everything, I want to show you that we still share some tastes. I have tried to carry out your wishes in the picture gallery that has been arranged by artist friends of mine and includes some of my own sketches. There you will see the weaknesses and the strengths of your preferred subjects for painting. The gallery is in my country house at Tivoli. The weather is good enough to go and see it. Should we go tomorrow?' And as she waited for Oswald's agreement, he said, 'My friend, can you have any doubt about my answer? Have I any other happiness in the world, any other thought, but you? I have detached my life perhaps too much from every occupation and from every interest, and it is filled only by the happiness of hearing and seeing you.'

CHAPTER IV

THE next day, then, they set off for Tivoli. Oswald himself drove the four horses that pulled their carriage and enjoyed the speed of the drive. Speed seems to enhance the sense of being alive and this feeling, beside one's beloved, is delightful. He drove with the greatest caution, for fear that the slightest accident might befall Corinne, taking the protective care which forms the sweetest bond between a man and a woman. Unlike most women, Corinne was not easily frightened by the possible dangers of the road, but she was so happy to see Oswald's solicitude that she almost wanted to be afraid so that he would reassure her.

As will be seen from what follows, it was the unexpected contrasts, lending his whole demeanour a special charm, that gave Lord Nelvil such a great ascendancy over his friend's heart. Everyone admired his intelligence and his charming looks, but he was bound to appeal particularly to someone who, containing in herself an unusual combination of fidelity and instability, enjoyed impressions that were at the same time varied and unchanging. He was never concerned with

anything but Corinne; this very concern, however, continually assumed
different forms. At times he was reserved, at times he expressed himself without constraint; at times he was gentle and tender, at times
he was morose and bitter, and though this proved the depth of his
feelings, it mingled worry with trust and constantly gave rise to a new
emotion. Internally ill at ease, Oswald tried to control himself, but,
absorbed in trying to understand him, the woman he loved found a
constant interest in the enigma he presented. It was as if Oswald's
very failings were designed to set off his attractions. However distinguished a man might be, if his character did not contain contra-
dictions or inner struggles, he would not have captivated Corinne's
imagination in this way. She had a kind of fear of Oswald which
enslaved her to him. He reigned over her heart by a good and evil
power, by his good points and by the anxiety that these ill-assorted
good points could arouse. Moreover, there was no security in the happiness Lord Nelvil gave, and perhaps Corinne's rapturous passion
must be explained by this very lack; perhaps she could love so much
only a man she was afraid of losing. A superior mind, a sensitivity as
fervent as it was discerning, might weary of everything except a truly
exceptional man, whose constantly agitated soul seemed, like the sky
itself, now serene, now covered with clouds. Oswald, always sincere,
always deeply passionate, was nevertheless often ready to give up the
woman he loved because, being long accustomed to sorrow, he believed that only remorse and suffering were to be found in excessive
affections of the heart.

On their way to Tivoli, Lord Nelvil and Corinne passed the ruins
of Hadrian's palace with its enormous surrounding garden. In this
garden were assembled the most exceptional works, the most remarkable masterpieces of the countries conquered by the Romans. A few
scattered stones which are called *Egypt, India, and Asia* can still be
seen there today. Further on was the refuge where Zenobia,* Queen
of Palmyra, ended her days. In adversity she did not maintain the
grandeur of her fate; unlike a man, she was not able to die for glory,
nor, like a woman, die rather than betray her friend.

At last they reached Tivoli, which was the home of so many famous
men; Brutus,* Augustus, Maecenas, Catullus, but especially Horace,
for it is his verse which has made this place famous. Corinne's house
was built above Teverone's noisy waterfall. On the hilltop, opposite
her garden, was the Sibyl's temple. The ancients had a good idea in

putting temples on high places. They dominated the countryside as religious ideas dominated all other thoughts. They inspired more enthusiasm for nature by proclaiming its divine source and the eternal gratitude of successive generations to that source. From whatever angle one looked at it, the countryside formed a picture together with the temple which was there as the centre or the ornament of everything. Ruins diffuse an unusual charm over the Italian countryside. Unlike modern buildings, they do not remind us of man's work and presence; they merge with the trees, with nature; they seem to accord with the lonely mountain stream, an image of time which has made them what they are. If they recall no memories, if they bear no stamp of any remarkable event, the most beautiful countries are devoid of interest in comparison with historic lands. What place could be better suited to Corinne's Italian home than that consecrated to the Sibyl, to the memory of a woman stimulated by divine inspiration? Corinne's house was delightful. It was decorated with the elegance of modern taste, and yet in it could be felt the charm of an imagination which enjoys the beauty of antiquity. Noticeable here was an unusual understanding of happiness, in the highest meaning of the word, that is to say, placing it in everything that ennobles the soul, stimulates thought, and animates talent.

As he walked about with Corinne, Oswald noticed that the wind blew with a melodious sound, which seemed to come from the sway of the flowers and the rustle of the trees, lending a voice to nature. Corinne told him it was the sound caused by the wind in the Aeolian harps which she had put in some garden grottoes so as to fill the air with sounds as well as scents. In this delightful residence, Oswald was inspired by the purest feeling. 'Till today I felt remorse at being happy with you, but now I tell myself that it was my father who sent you to me so that I should suffer no longer on this earth. It was him I offended, yet it was he whose prayers in heaven have obtained my pardon. Corinne,' he cried, kneeling before her, 'I am forgiven. The sweet innocent tranquillity reigning in my soul gives me that feeling. You can join your lot to mine, without fear; this will no longer bring disaster.' 'Well,' said Corinne, 'let us enjoy a little while longer the emotional peace that has been granted to us. Let us not tamper with destiny. It is so frightening when one tries to interfere with it, trying to obtain more than it gives. Oh, my friend, let us change nothing since we are happy!'

Lord Nelvil was hurt by Corinne's reply. He thought she ought to understand that he was ready to tell her everything, to promise her everything, if she confided her story to him, there and then; this way of continuing to avoid doing so hurt and saddened him. Oswald did not realize that a feeling of delicacy prevented Corinne from taking advantage of his emotion to bind him with a vow. Perhaps, too, it is in the nature of a deep, true love to dread a solemn moment, however longed for, and only tremblingly to exchange hope even for happiness. Far from having the same opinion, Oswald was convinced that Corinne, while she loved him, wanted to retain her independence and that she carefully put off anything which could bring about an indissoluble union. This thought irritated him painfully and, assuming immediately a cold, constrained look, he followed Corinne into her picture gallery without saying a word. She quickly realized the impression she had made on him, but since she knew his pride, she did not dare tell him she had noticed it. However, as she showed him her pictures and spoke of general ideas, she had a vague hope of soothing him, and this gave her voice a more touching charm even when she was talking on indifferent subjects.

Her collection was made up of historical pictures, pictures on poetic and religious subjects, and landscapes. There were none which contained a very large number of human figures. That kind of painting no doubt presents great difficulties, but it gives less pleasure. Its beauties are too confused or too detailed, and unity of interest, the principle of life in the arts, as in everything, is of necessity broken up. The first historical picture portrayed Brutus* seated at the foot of the statue of Rome in deep meditation. In the background, slaves carry away his two lifeless sons, whom he himself has condemned to death, and on the other side of the picture the mother and sisters give way to despair; fortunately women are exempt from the courage which entails the sacrifice of the heart's affections. The statue of Rome, placed beside Brutus, is a fine idea; it is that which tells the whole story. Yet, without an explanation, how could one know that it was Brutus the Elder, who has just sent his sons to execution? It is impossible, nevertheless, to show the nature of the event more clearly than in this picture. In the distance can be seen Rome, still simple, without great buildings, unadorned, but very great as a fatherland since it inspires such a sacrifice. 'No doubt, when I told you it was Brutus, your whole soul was attracted to this picture,' Corinne said to Lord Nelvil. 'But you might have seen it without realizing its subject. And this uncertainty which nearly always exists in historical pictures, does it not mingle the strain of a riddle with enjoyment of the arts, which ought to be so easy and so clear?

'I chose this subject because it recalls the most terrible deed that love of one's native land has inspired. The counterpart to this picture is Marius spared by the Cimbrian* who cannot bring himself to kill such a great man. Marius' face is imposing; the Cimbrian's dress and facial expression are very picturesque. It was Rome's second period, when there were no longer any laws but when genius still had a great influence on events. After that came the period when talents and renown attracted only misfortune and insults. The third picture shows Belisarius bearing on his shoulders the young guide who died begging alms for him. That is how Belisarius, blind and a beggar, was rewarded by his master, and in the world he conquered his only task is to bear to the grave the sad remains of the poor child who, alone, had not deserted him. Belisarius' face is wonderful and, since the artists of old, scarcely any so fine has been painted. The artist's imagination, like a poet's, has combined every kind of misfortune, but perhaps even too many to arouse pity. But who tells us it is Belisarius? Must not the artist be faithful to history to recall it? And if he is, is the picture quite suitable for art? After these pictures which, in Brutus, portray virtue that is like crime, in Marius, glory as a cause of misfortune, in Belisarius, services repaid by the foulest persecution, in short, all the woes of the human lot portrayed each one on its own way by historical events, I have put two pictures of the old school. They bring a little relief to the depressed soul by recalling the religion which consoled the enslaved and ravaged universe, the religion which brought life to the depths of the heart, when everything outside was only oppression and silence. The first one is by Albani;* he painted the Christ child asleep on the cross. See what gentleness, what calm, is in that face! What pure ideas it brings to mind! How it makes us feel that celestial love has nothing to fear from pain or death! Titian painted the second picture; it is of Jesus Christ collapsing under the weight of the cross. His mother is coming to meet him. She kneels down when she sees him. How wonderful a mother's respect for her son's misfortunes and divine virtues! What a look in Christ's eyes! What divine resignation and yet what suffering, and through his suffering what sympathy with the human heart! This is undoubtedly the finest of my pictures. This is the one to which I continually return, without ever being able to exhaust the emotion it arouses. What come next', Corinne went on, 'are the dramatic pictures drawn from four great poets. Join me, my Lord, in judging the effect they produce. The first shows Aeneas in the Elysian Fields when he wants to approach Dido. The indignant ghost moves away and congratulates herself on not bearing any longer in her breast the heart that would still throb with love at the sight of the guilty man. The misty colour of the ghosts and the pale countryside which surrounds them afford a contrast with the appearance of life in Aeneas and the Sibyl who is his guide. But that kind of effect is the artist's performance, and the poet's description is inevitably far superior to what can be done in paint. I shall say the same of the picture that we see here, the dying Clorinda and Tancred. The extreme pity that it can evoke comes from recalling the beautiful lines of Tasso when Clorinda forgives her enemy who adores her and has just stabbed her in the breast. When painting is devoted to subjects treated by great poets, it is necessarily subordinated to poetry, for the words of the poets leave an impression which blots out everything else, and the situations which they have chosen derive their strongest force, almost always, from their eloquent expression of the development of the passions, whereas most of the effects of painting arise from calm beauty, simple expression, a noble attitude, in short a moment of repose worthy of being indefinitely prolonged without ever leading the eye to grow tired of it.

'Your terrifying Shakespeare, my Lord,' continued Corinne, 'has provided the subject of the third dramatic picture. It is Macbeth, the invincible Macbeth. About to fight Macduff, whose wife and children he has had put to death, he learns that the witches' prophecy has been fulfilled; Birnam Wood seems to be marching on Dunsinane and he is fighting a man born after the death of his own mother. Macbeth is conquered by fate, but not by his opponent. He wields his sword in desperation, knowing he is going to die but wanting to test whether human strength can overcome destiny. There is certainly a fine expression of uncontrolled rage, of agitation and energy, in that face. But how many beautiful poetic qualities have had to be sacrificed? Is it possible to paint Macbeth pushed into crime by the prestigious rewards of ambition presented to him in the shape of witchcraft? How can his terror be expressed, a terror which, however, goes along with intrepid courage? Can one portray the kind of superstition which torments him? This belief devoid of dignity, this doom of hell that weighs on him, his contempt for life, his horror of death? The human countenance is undoubtedly a very great mystery, but fixed in a picture, it can barely express the depth of a single feeling. Indeed, contrasts, struggles, events belong to dramatic art. It is difficult for painting to convey the succession of events; in that art there is neither time nor movement.

'Racine's *Phèdre* has provided the subject of the fourth picture,' said Corinne, pointing it out to Lord Nelvil. 'In the full flower of his youth and beauty, Hippolytus is refuting the treacherous accusations of his stepmother. The hero Theseus has his arm round his guilty wife, whom he is still protecting. On Phaedra's face there is a terrifying, chilling, strained look, and her remorseless nurse encourages her in her crime. In this picture Hippolytus is perhaps more handsome even than in Racine; he is more like Meleager* of old, because no love for Aricia interferes with the impression of his noble but untamed virtue. But is it possible to assume that Phaedra could maintain her lie in the presence of Hippolytus, that she could see him innocent and persecuted, and not fall at his feet? In his absence a woman spurned may falsely accuse the man she loves, but when she sees him there is only love in her heart. After Phaedra slandered Hippolytus, the poet never put her on stage with him again; the painter had to do so in order to bring together, as he did, all the beauties of the contrasts. But is that not a proof that there is always such a difference between poetic subjects and subjects suitable for painting that it is better for poets to write about pictures than for artists to paint pictures about poems? Imagination should always precede thought; the history of the human mind is proof of that.'

While Corinne was talking about her pictures to Lord Nelvil, she had stopped several times, but he said not a word which revealed his wounded heart; only every time she expressed a thought showing sensitivity, he sighed and turned his head away, so that she should not see how easily he was moved in his present frame of mind. Corinne, worried by his silence, sat down, covering her face with her hands. Lord Nelvil walked quickly up and down the room for a time; then he came up to Corinne and that was the moment for him to complain and express his feelings. But a feeling of quite unconquerable pride in his character suppressed his tender emotion, and he turned back to the pictures as if he was expecting Corinne to continue showing them to him. She had great hopes of the effect of the last one of all and, in her turn, making an effort to appear calm, she got up saying, 'My Lord, I still have three landscapes to show you. Two suggest interesting ideas. I am not very fond of country scenes, which as painted idylls are merely insipid, unless they allude to mythology or history. What is best in this genre seems to me to be Salvator Rosa's* style, which, as you see in this painting, depicts mountain streams and trees without a single living being, without even the flight of a bird suggesting the idea of life. The absence of man in the midst of nature gives rise to deep reflection. What could the land be that is deserted like this? A pointless work but yet one still very beautiful; the puzzled feeling it arouses could only be addressed to God.

'Finally, here are two pictures in which I think history and poetry are happily linked to the landscape.[21] One depicts the moment when the consuls invite Cincinnatus to leave his plough for the command of the Roman armies. In this landscape you can see the luxuriant South, its abundant vegetation, its burning sky, the smiling face of nature which is seen again even in the appearance of the plants. The other picture, which forms a contrast to that one, is Cairbar's son* asleep on his father's tomb. For three days and nights he has been waiting for the bard who is to honour the memory of the dead. The bard can be glimpsed in the distance, coming down the mountain. The father's ghost hovers over the clouds; the countryside is covered with hoar frost; the trees, though bare, are shaken by the winds, and their dead branches and withered leaves still follow the direction of the storm.'

Till then, Oswald had retained his resentment at what had happened in the garden, but when he saw this picture, his father's memory and the Scottish mountains were recalled to his mind and his eyes filled with tears. Corinne took her harp and, in front of the picture, she began to sing the Scottish songs whose simple tunes seemed to accompany the sound of the wind moaning in the valleys. She sang of a warrior's farewells as he left his country and his beloved, and the phrase *no more*,* one of the most melodious and touching in the English language, was uttered with great emotion by Corinne. Oswald could not resist the feeling which overwhelmed him, and they both unrestrainedly gave way to their tears. 'Oh,' cried Lord Nelvil, 'that native land which is my own, does it say nothing to your heart? Would you follow me to those retreats peopled by my memories? Would you be the worthy companion of my life, as you are its charm and its delight?'

'I think so,' replied Corinne, 'I think so, since I love you.' 'In pity's and love's name, hide nothing more from me,' said Oswald. 'You want my story,' interrupted Corinne. 'I agree to tell it. My promise is given. I attach only one condition; that is that you will not ask me to do so before the approaching season of our religious festivals. At the moment when I am going to decide my fate, do I not need the support of Heaven even more?' 'Come, come!' cried Lord Nelvil. 'If this fate depends on me, Corinne, it is no longer in doubt.' 'Do you think so?' she replied. 'I am not so confident. But in any case, I beg you, have the indulgence I desire for my weakness.' Oswald sighed without granting or refusing the requested delay. 'Let us go back to the town,' said Corinne. 'How can I keep anything from you in this solitude? But if what I have to tell you will separate you from me, must it be so soon . . . ? Let us go, Oswald. You will come back here, whatever happens. My ashes will rest here.' Oswald, moved and anxious, obeyed Corinne. He returned with her and, on the way, they hardly spoke to each other. From time to time they would look at each other with an affection which said everything. Yet there was a feeling of melancholy in the depths of their hearts when they arrived at Rome.

BOOK IX
THE PEOPLE'S FESTIVAL AND MUSIC

CHAPTER I

IT was the day of the most boisterous festival of the year at the end of the carnival, when the Roman people are seized with a kind of feverish desire for merrymaking, a craze for amusement not to be found elsewhere. The whole town puts on a disguise; at the windows there are hardly any spectators without masks to look at those who are wearing them. The amusement begins on a fixed day at a particular time, and public or private events rarely prevent anyone from enjoying themselves at this time.

It is at the carnival that one forms an opinion of the imaginative range of the ordinary people. The Italian language is full of charm even when they speak it. Alfieri used to say that he would go to the public marketplace in Florence to learn good Italian. Rome has the same advantage, and these two towns are perhaps the only ones in the world where the ordinary people speak so well that the pleasure of wit can be encountered at every street corner.

The kind of amusement that sparkles in the authors of harlequinades and opera buffa is very commonly to be found even among the uneducated. During the carnival period, when exaggeration and caricature are allowed, extremely comical scenes take place between the masqueraders.

A grotesque solemnity often contrasts with the liveliness of Italians and it could be said that their bizarre clothes inspire them with an unnatural dignity. At other times, in their disguises, they reveal such an unusual knowledge of mythology that you would think the old legends were still popular in Rome. More often they make fun of the different classes of society with telling, original jokes. The nation seems to be a thousand times more distinguished in its games than in its history. The Italian language lends itself to all the nuances of fun with an ease which requires only a slight inflection of the voice, a slightly different ending, to increase or diminish, to ennoble or make a travesty of the meaning of words. It is especially delightful in the mouths of children. The innocence of that age and the natural mischievousness of the language make a very striking contrast.[22] Finally it could be said that it is a language which goes by itself, is expressive without anyone's interference, and always seems wittier than the person speaking it.

There is neither luxury nor good taste in the carnival festivities. A kind of universal irrepressibility makes them seem like bacchanalia of the imagination, but of the imagination only; for generally the Romans are very abstemious and even rather solemn, except on the final days of the carnival. One can make all kinds of unexpected discoveries about the character of Italians and this is what contributes to their reputation for cunning. There is no doubt that people habitually dissemble in this country, which has endured so many different yokes, but one must not always attribute to deceit the swift change from one type of behaviour to another. It is often caused by an easily kindled imagination. Peoples that are only rational or witty can easily be understood and are predictable, but everything concerned with the imagination is unexpected. It skips the transitions; it can be wounded by a trifle, but sometimes it is indifferent to what should move it most. In short, everything takes place within the imagination itself, and one cannot judge of its reactions from what arouses them.

For example, one cannot understand the pleasure taken by great Roman lords in going for carriage drives up and down the *corso* for hours on end, whether on carnival days or other days of the year. Nothing interferes with this habit. Also, among the masqueraders there are men wearing extremely ridiculous costumes, who walk about in the most irritating way and who, sad Harlequins and taciturn Punchinellos, do not say a word the whole evening; but they have satisfied their carnival consciences, as it were, in neglecting nothing in search of amusement.

There is a kind of mask that is found uniquely in Rome. They are masks imitating the faces of ancient statues, and from a distance they give the impression of perfect beauty. Women often lose a great deal when they take them off. But yet this immobile imitation of life, these strolling wax faces, however pretty they may be, inspire a sort of fear. On the last days of the carnival the great lords show off rather luxurious carriages, but the pleasure of the festival lies in the crowd and the commotion. It is like a remembrance of the Saturnalia.* All classes in Rome mingle together; the most solemn magistrates drive assiduously and almost officially in their carriages among the masqueraders; all the windows are decorated; the whole town is in the streets. It is truly a people's festival. The people's pleasure does not lie in the spectacles or banquets provided for them, nor in the splendours which they see. They neither eat nor drink to excess. They enjoy merely being set free and mingling with the great lords, who in their turn find their pleasure in being amongst the people. It is above all the refinement and subtlety of their amusements, as well as the elegance and superiority of their upbringing, which create a barrier between the different classes. In Italy, however, ranking of this sort is not very distinctly marked and the country is more outstanding for the natural talent and imagination of all than for the cultivated minds of the upper classes. So during the carnival there is a complete mingling of ranks, customs, and minds, and the witticisms and sugared almonds showered indiscriminately on all passing carriages mix up together all human beings, jumble up the whole nation as if there were no longer any social order.

Corinne and Lord Nelvil, both of them musing and thoughtful, arrived in the midst of this uproar. At first they were dazed by it, for when the soul is completely lost in its own thoughts, nothing seems stranger than the bustle of noisy merrymaking. They stopped at the Piazza del Popolo to go up into the amphitheatre near the obelisk, from where one can see the horse race. Just as they got out of their carriage, Count d'Erfeuil espied them and took Oswald aside to speak to him.

'It is not right to show yourself in public like this, coming back from the country alone with Corinne,' he said. 'You will compromise her and then what will you do?' 'I do not think I am compromising Corinne by showing the affection she inspires in me,' replied Lord Nelvil. 'But if that were so, I would be only too happy for my life's devotion . . .' 'Oh, as for being happy,' interrupted Count d'Erfeuil, 'I do not think so in the least. One is happy only if one behaves conventionally. Whatever you do, society has great power over happiness, and one must never do what it disapproves of.' 'Then we would always live according to what society says about us,' replied Oswald, 'and we would never be guided by our own thoughts and feelings. If that were the case, if we ought continually to be imitating each other, what would be the use of a soul and a mind for each of us? Providence could have spared itself that luxury.' 'That is very well expressed,' answered Count d'Erfeuil; 'it is a good philosophical point, but one is ruined by that sort of maxim, and when love has gone, public censure remains. I seem frivolous to you, but I shall do nothing which might incur society's disapproval. You can allow yourself little liberties, amusing pranks, which proclaim an independence in your way of looking at things, provided there is none in the way you do things. For when it comes to serious matters . . .' 'But love and happiness are serious matters,' replied Lord Nelvil. 'No, no,' interrupted Count d'Erfeuil, 'that is not what I mean. I mean certain established conventions which must not be flouted if you do not want to be thought strange, to be a man . . . in short, you understand me, to be a man who is not like others.' Lord Nelvil smiled and, without ill humour or taking offence, he teased Count d'Erfeuil about his frivolous severity. He was delighted to feel that for the first time, on a subject which touched his emotions so deeply, Count d'Erfeuil had not had the slightest influence on him. From afar, Corinne had realized what was taking place, but Lord Nelvil's smile put her heart at rest again. Moreover, Count d'Erfeuil's remarks, far from upsetting Oswald or his friend, aroused in them feelings more suited to the festivities.

They were getting ready for the horse race. Lord Nelvil expected to see a race like the English ones, but he was surprised that little Barbary horses were to run against each other by themselves, without riders. Romans are particularly attracted to this spectacle. Just as it is about to begin, the whole crowd lines up on both sides of the street. The Piazza del Popolo, which was filled with people, is empty in a moment. Everyone climbs up onto the amphitheatres that surround the obelisks, and an immense multitude of heads and black eyes are turned towards the gate from where the horses are to rush forward.

They arrive with no bridle or saddle; their backs are covered only with gleaming cloths, and they are led by very well-dressed grooms who are passionately interested in their success. The horses are placed behind the gate and are excessively eager to go through it. They are being constantly restrained; they rear, neigh, and stamp as if they were impatient for a glory they will win on their own without human control. The horses' impatience and the grooms' shouts make the moment when the gate falls truly dramatic. The horses set off, the grooms shout *Make way, make way!* with delirious excitement. Gesticulating and shouting, they accompany their horses for as long as they can see them.

The horses are jealous of each other like men. The pavement throws out sparks under their hooves, their manes fly, and the desire to win the prize is such that, at the finish, some fall dead from the speed of the race. One is amazed to find these free horses so roused by personal passions; it is frightening, as if thought had assumed animal form. The crowd breaks up when the horses have passed by, and follows them in an uproar. They reach the Palazzo di Venezia, which is the finishing point. And you should hear the shouts of the grooms whose horses have won. The winner of the first prize flung himself on his knees in front of his horse, thanking it and recommending it to Saint Anthony, the animals' patron, with an enthusiasm that was as serious to the groom as it was amusing to the onlookers.[23]

Usually the races finish at the end of the day. Then another kind of amusement begins; it is far less picturesque but also very noisy. The windows are lit up. The guards desert their posts so that they too can participate in the universal merrymaking. Everyone then takes up a little torch called a *moccolo* and they try to put out each other's lights, repeating the word *ammazzare* (kill), with terrible eagerness, CHE LA BELLA PRINCIPESSA SIA AMMAZZATA! CHE IL SIGNORE ABBATE SIA AMMAZZATO! (*May the beautiful princess be killed! May the lord abbot be killed!*) they shout from one end of the street to the other.[24] Since, at this time, horses and carriages are prohibited, the crowd feels safe and rushes about in all directions. In the end there is no other pleasure than uproar and giddiness. Yet the night moves on; gradually the noise stops; it is followed by the deepest silence, and all that remains of the evening is a confused recollection which, by turning everyone's life into a dream, has made ordinary people forget their labours, scholars their studies, and the great lords their idleness.

CHAPTER II

SINCE his misfortune Oswald had not yet had the heart to listen to music. He dreaded the enchanting harmonies which are a pleasure to the melancholy but cause genuine pain when we are burdened by real sorrows. Music revives memories that we were trying to still. When Corinne sang, Oswald would listen to her words; he would look at the expression on her face; he would think only about her. But if, in the streets in the evening, several voices joined together to sing the lovely songs of the great masters, as often happens in Italy, initially he would try to stay and listen to them; but then he would go away because an emotion, at once keen and vague, would bring back all his grief. However, in the theatre at Rome, a splendid concert, bringing together the finest singers, was due to take place. Corinne urged Lord Nelvil to go with her and he agreed, hoping that the presence of the woman he loved would soothe any feelings he might have.

Corinne was recognized straight away when she entered her box and, the memory of the Capitol adding to the interest she usually aroused, the hall resounded with applause at her arrival. On all sides people shouted *long live Corinne*, and even the musicians, galvanized by the general emotion, began to play victory fanfares, for triumph, of whatever kind, always reminds man of war and combat. Corinne was greatly moved by this universal demonstration of admiration and goodwill. The music, the applause, the *bravos*, and the indefinable impression always produced by a great crowd of people expressing the same feeling, touched her deeply. She tried to control her emotions, but her eyes filled with tears and the beating of her heart made her gown rise with her heaving breast. Oswald felt jealous and, coming close up to her, said, 'You must not tear yourself away from such success, Madame; it is as worthwhile as love, since it makes your heart beat so.' As he finished speaking and without waiting for her reply, he went and sat down at the far end of the box. She was sorely troubled by what he had just said, and immediately he destroyed all the pleasure she had taken in her success and had been happy for him to witness.

The concert began. Those who have not heard Italian singing can have no idea of the music. In Italy, voices have a gentle sweetness that recalls both the scent of flowers and the purity of the sky. Nature has destined this music for this climate; the one is like a reflection of the other. The world is the work of a single mind expressing itself in a thousand different ways. For centuries, Italians have loved music rapturously. In his poem *Purgatory* Dante meets one of the best singers of his day. He asks him for one of his delightful songs and, as they listen, the entranced souls forget their situation till their warder calls them back. Christians as well as pagans have extended the power of music after death. Of all the arts it is the one that acts most directly on the soul. The others lead it to some idea or other; music alone is addressed to the fundamental source of life and completely changes the inmost feelings. What has been said about divine grace suddenly transforming hearts can, humanly speaking, be applied to the power of melody, and among the intimations of life to come, those originating in music are not to be dismissed.

Even the cheerfulness so greatly stimulated by *buffa* music is not a commonplace cheerfulness with no appeal to the imagination. At the heart of the pleasure given by such music there are poetic feelings, pleasant daydreams which spoken jests could never inspire. Music is such a transient pleasure, you have such a strong feeling that it is slipping away even as you are experiencing it, that a melancholy feeling is mingled with the cheerfulness it arouses. But also, when it expresses grief it still arouses a pleasant feeling. Your heart beats faster as you listen. The satisfaction aroused by the regularity of the beat, in recalling the swift passage of time, arouses the need to make full use of it. You are no longer surrounded by emptiness and silence; your life is full; your blood flows swiftly; within you there is the feeling aroused by an active existence and you no longer have to fear the obstacles in its way, outside yourself.

Music redoubles our perception of our souls' abilities. On hearing it we feel capable of the noblest efforts. It is music that enables us to approach death with enthusiasm. Fortunately, it is powerless to express any base feeling, any deceit, any lie. In the language of music, misfortune itself is without bitterness, without heart-rending pain, without ill-humour. Music gently lifts the weight that nearly always burdens the hearts of those capable of serious, deep affection, a weight causing such enduring pain that it sometimes mingles with our very feeling of existence. When listening to pure, delightful sounds we are about to grasp the Creator's secret, to penetrate life's mystery. No words can express this feeling, for words trail behind original feelings like prose translators behind the steps of the poets. Only a look can give some idea of it, the look of a loved one fixed on you for a long time and gradually penetrating your soul so deeply that in the end you have to lower your eyes to retreat from such great happiness. The rays of another life would thus consume the mortal being who would want to gaze at it.

The wonderful correctness of two voices in perfect harmony, in the duets of the great Italian masters, produces a delightfully touching emotion, one which, however, cannot be prolonged without a kind of pain. It is a sense of well-being too great for human nature, for the soul then vibrates like an instrument in an accord with others which would be broken by too perfect a harmony. During the first part of the concert Oswald had obstinately remained at a distance from Corinne, but when the duet began, almost in a whisper, accompanied by wind instruments making gentle sounds even purer than the voice itself, Corinne, covering her face with her handkerchief, was completely overcome by emotion. She wept without suffering, she loved without any fear. The image of Oswald was doubtless present in her heart, but the noblest enthusiasm was mingled with his image, and crowds of confused thoughts wandered in her soul; she would have to control them to make them clear. It is said that a prophet travelled through seven different regions of the heavens in one minute. He who had such an idea of all that can be contained in a moment had surely heard the harmonies of beautiful music in the company of the one he loved. Oswald felt its power; gradually his resentment abated. Corinne's emotion explained everything, justified everything. Quietly he came near to Corinne and she heard him breathing beside her at the most enchanting moment of this heavenly music. It was too much; the most moving tragedy would not have aroused so much agitation in her heart as the profound feeling of deep emotion that they both experienced simultaneously and that was exalted more and more at every new sound. The words of the singer are of no importance in such emotion. A few words about love and death barely guide one's thoughts, but more often the vagueness of the music lends itself to all the emotions of the soul, and everyone thinks that, in the melody as in the pure, tranquil star of the night, he finds again the image of what he desires on earth.

'Let us go,' Corinne said to Lord Nelvil. 'I feel faint.' 'What is the matter?' Oswald asked anxiously. 'You are turning pale; come out with me into the fresh air, come.' And they left together. Supported by Oswald's arm, Corinne felt her strength return as she leaned on him. They drew near to a balcony together and Corinne, deeply moved, said to her friend, 'Dear Oswald, I am going to leave you for eight days.' 'What do you mean?' he interrupted. 'Every year,' she replied, 'as Holy Week draws near, I spend some time in a convent to prepare myself for the solemn observance of Easter.' Oswald made no opposition to her plan. He knew that at this period most Roman ladies follow very strict practices, but for all that, they do not seriously concern themselves with religion during the rest of the year. He remembered, however, that Corinne professed a different religion from his own and that they could not pray together. 'Why are you not of the same religion, of the same country, as I am?' he cried. And, having expressed this wish, he stopped. 'Do not our hearts and minds belong to the same land?' replied Corinne. 'That is true,' answered Oswald, 'but none the less I am painfully aware of all that separates us.' And he was so upset by the thought of the eight days' absence that, since Corinne's friends had come to join them, he did not say a single word for the rest of the evening.

CHAPTER III

EARLY the next day, worried by what she had said, Oswald went to Corinne's house. Her maid came to meet him and handed him a note from her mistress; it told him that she had retreated to the convent that very morning and would not see him again till after Good Friday. She admitted that on the previous day she had not had the heart to tell him she was going away the next day. Oswald was surprised as if struck by a sudden blow. This house, where he had always seen Corinne and which had become so lonely, made an extremely painful impression on him. In it he saw her harp, her books, her drawings, everything that usually surrounded her, but she was no longer there. Oswald was gripped by a painful shudder. Remembering his father's room, he was forced to sit down, for his legs were giving way.

'So it is possible that this is how I would hear of her death!' he cried. 'That keen mind, that lively heart, that face radiant with life and the bloom of youth, might be struck by lightning, and youth's grave would be as silent as old men's! Oh, what an illusion is happiness! What a moment snatched from relentless time that always hovers over its prey! Corinne! Corinne! You should not have left me. It was your charm that prevented me from thinking. My thoughts were all confused, dazzled as I was by the happy moments I spent with you. Now, here I am alone, now I come to myself again, and all my wounds will reopen.' And he called Corinne with a kind of despair which was not attributable to her short absence but to the habitual anguish in his heart that Corinne had the power to relieve. The maid came back. She had heard Oswald's laments and, touched by his missing her mistress so much, she said, 'My Lord, I want to console you by betraying one of my mistress's secrets; I hope she will forgive me. Come to her bedroom; you will see your portrait there.' 'My portrait!' he cried. 'She painted it from memory,' Theresina replied (that was the name of Corinne's maid). 'For a week she got up at five o'clock in the morning so as to finish it before going to her convent.'

Oswald looked at the portrait, which was a very good likeness and beautifully painted. This testimony to the impression he had made on Corinne filled him with the most delightful emotion. Opposite the portrait was a charming picture representing the Virgin and in front of it was Corinne's prayer stool. This curious mixture of love and religion is to be found in the homes of most Italian women in much more extraordinary situations than in Corinne's bedroom; for, free as she was, the memory of Oswald was connected in her heart with the purest hopes and feelings. Nevertheless, to put a picture of the man she loved opposite a symbol of the divinity, and to prepare for a week's retreat into a convent by a week painting his picture, was a general characteristic of Italian women rather than peculiar to Corinne. Their kind of religious devotion presupposes more imagination and sensitivity than sincere feeling or strict principles, and nothing was more alien to Oswald's ideas about the way to understand and feel religion. But could he have blamed Corinne at the very moment when he was receiving such touching proof of her love?

Greatly moved, he looked round the room that he was entering for the first time. At Corinne's bedside he saw the portrait of an elderly man, but his face did not look Italian. Two bracelets were linked together beside the portrait, one made of dark hair and the other wonderfully fair. But—and this seemed very strange to Lord Nelvil—the blond hair was exactly like Lucile Edgermond's, which he had carefully noticed three years ago, because of its unusual beauty. Oswald looked at the bracelets but said nothing, for it would have been beneath his dignity to question Theresina about her mistress. But Theresina, thinking she could guess what was worrying Oswald and wanting to remove all his jealous suspicions, was quick to tell him that during the eleven years she had been with Corinne, she had always seen these bracelets with her and knew they were made of the hair of her father, mother, and sister. 'You have been with Corinne for eleven years,' said Lord Nelvil, 'so you know . . .' And then, blushing, he suddenly interrupted himself, ashamed of the question he was about to ask, and hurriedly left the house so that he would not say another word.

As he went away, he turned round several times to see Corinne's windows once more, but when he had lost sight of her dwelling he felt a sadness that was new to him, a sadness caused by loneliness. In the evening he made an effort to go to a Roman society gathering. He was seeking distraction, for to find daydreaming attractive, in happiness as in sorrow, one must be at peace with oneself.

Lord Nelvil soon found the gathering unbearable. He realized even more what charm and interest Corinne shed on society when he noticed what a gap was left by her absence. He tried to speak to a few women; they replied with the insipid conventional phrases used to express neither their feelings nor their opinions truthfully, if indeed, they have anything of the sort to hide. He approached several groups of men, who, to judge from their gestures and voices, seemed to be talking heatedly about something important, but he heard them discussing the pettiest material interests in the most commonplace way. Then he sat down to study at leisure the pointless and groundless animation which is to be found in most large gatherings. Yet in Italy mediocrity is quite good-natured; it has little vanity or jealousy and it has much goodwill towards superior minds. And although it may be wearing and burdensome, at least it is hardly ever wounding in its pretensions.

Yet it was these same gatherings that Oswald had found so interesting a few days earlier. The slight obstacle that high society had put in the way of his conversation with Corinne, the care she had taken to come back to him as soon as she had been sufficiently polite to the others, the agreement existing between them about the comments suggested to them by society, Corinne's pleasure in talking in Oswald's presence, in addressing indirectly to him comments whose meaning only he understood, all this gave such variety to the conversation that Oswald recalled happy, entertaining, pleasant moments which had made him think the gatherings themselves were amusing. 'Oh!' he said, going away, 'here, as in every place in the world, it is she alone who gives life. Let me at least go to the most deserted places until she returns. I shall miss her less painfully when there is nothing around me resembling pleasure.'

BOOK X
HOLY WEEK

CHAPTER I

OSWALD spent the following day in the gardens of several monasteries. First he went to the Carthusian monastery, stopping for a moment before going in to look at two Egyptian lions not far from the door. These lions have a remarkable expression of strength and repose. There is something in their looks which belongs neither to animal nor man. They are like a force of nature and on seeing them one can understand how the pagan gods could be represented in that form.

The Carthusian monastery is built on the remains of Diocletian's baths and the adjacent church is decorated with the granite columns found standing there. The resident monks point them out eagerly. Their only concern with the outside world is their interest in the ruins. For men who are capable of it, the Carthusian way of life presupposes either an extremely limited mind or the noblest and most unremitting exaltation of religious feeling. The regular succession of unvaried days calls to mind the well-known line:

> Time sleeps motionless on ruined worlds.*

It seems that life there serves only to contemplate death. In such an unchanging existence an active mind would be the cruellest torture. In the middle of the monastery stand four cypress trees. The dark, silent trees, not easily stirred even by the wind, bring no movement to this dwelling. Near the cypresses there is a fountain; a little water flows from it but the jet is so slow and weak that it is scarcely audible. One might say that it is the water-clock suited to this lonely place, where time makes so little noise. Sometimes the pale moonlight reaches this place; its absence and return are events in its monotonous life.

Yet war and all its activity would barely satisfy these same men if that were their usual way of life. The different components of human destiny on earth form an inexhaustible subject for reflection. Within the soul a thousand chance events take place, a thousand habits are formed, making each individual a world with its history. To know another being completely would be a lifetime's study. So what is meant by 'knowing' men? To govern them may be possible, but only God can understand them.

From the Carthusian monastery Oswald went to the Bonaventura monastery, built on the ruins of Nero's palace. There, where so many crimes were committed without remorse, poor monks, tormented by scruples of conscience, inflict cruel tortures on themselves for the slightest failings. *We only hope that at the moment of death our sins will not exceed our penances*, said one of the monks. As Lord Nelvil entered the convent he stumbled against a trap door and asked what it was for. *We are buried through that*, said one of the youngest monks, already stricken with the illness caused by foul air. As southern peoples greatly fear death, it is surprising to find institutions among them which bring it to mind to this extent; it is natural, however, to like entertaining the very idea that one dreads. There is a kind of intoxication of sadness which benefits the soul by filling it entirely.

A young child's ancient sarcophagus serves as fountain to this monastery. The beautiful palm tree, Rome's pride, is the only tree in the monks' garden, but they pay no attention to external objects. Their discipline is too harsh to allow their minds any kind of liberty. Their eyes are cast down, their step is slow, they no longer exercise their wills about anything. They have abandoned control over themselves, so greatly does this power *wear out its sad owner*! The place did not, however, have a powerful effect on Oswald's soul. The imagination rebels against such a manifest intention of reminding us of death in all its forms. When we are reminded of death unexpectedly, when it is nature that speaks of it and not man, we receive a much deeper impression.

When, at sunset, Oswald went into the garden of *San Giovanni e Paolo*, sweet, gentle feelings filled his heart. The monks of this monastery are subjected to less strict practices and their garden dominates all the ruins of ancient Rome. From there you can see the Colosseum, the Forum, all the triumphal arches still standing, the obelisks and the columns. What a lovely site for such a retreat! The hermits are consoled for being nothing when they gaze at the monuments erected by those who are no more. Oswald walked for a long time in the shady monastery garden, something very rare in Italy. For a moment, these beautiful trees interrupt the view of Rome as if to redouble the emotion we feel when we see it again. It was the time of evening when all the bells of Rome can be heard ringing the *Ave Maria*:

> . . . squilla di lontano
> Che paia il giorno pianger che si muore.

DANTE

and the sound of bells, in the distance, seems to pity the dying day. The evening prayer is used to tell the time. In Italy they say: *I shall see you an hour before, an hour after the Ave Maria*; and thus religion marks the periods of the day or night. Oswald then enjoyed the wonderful sight of the sun descending slowly towards evening among the ruins and, for a moment, appearing to decline like the works of man. Oswald felt all his usual thoughts revive within him. Corinne herself had too many charms, promised too much happiness, to fill his mind at this moment. He sought his father's shade among the celestial shades that had welcomed him. It seemed to him that, by dint of love, his vision would bring to life the clouds he was contemplating, and enable him to make them assume the sublime, touching shape of his immortal friend. Indeed, he hoped his prayers would bring from heaven some indefinable, pure, beneficial breath that would be like a father's blessing.

CHAPTER II

THE desire to know and study Italy's religion prompted Lord Nelvil to look for an opportunity to hear some of the preachers who make their voices heard in the Roman churches during Lent. He was counting the days that were to reunite him to Corinne, and as long as she was absent he did not want to see anything connected with the arts, anything whose charm stemmed from the imagination. He could not bear the pleasurable emotion given by masterpieces when he was not with Corinne; he forgave himself happiness only when it came from her. Poetry, painting, music, everything that embellishes life with vague hopes, pained him everywhere unless she was with him.

It is in the evening, with the lights almost out, that the Roman preachers can be heard in the churches during Holy Week. All the women are then dressed in black, in memory of the death of Jesus Christ, and there is something very moving in this anniversary of mourning, so often renewed for so many centuries. It is, therefore, with genuine emotion that one enters these beautiful churches where the tombs dispose one so well to prayer; but nearly always the preacher dispels that emotion in a few moments.

His pulpit is a fairly long platform which he paces up and down from one end to the other with as much excitement as regularity. He never fails to start off at the beginning of a sentence and to return at the end, like the pendulum of a clock, and yet he makes so many gestures, he looks so passionate, that one would think he would be capable of forgetting everything. But, if one may say so, it is an organized frenzy, such as one often sees in Italy, where the liveliness of outward movements often indicates only a superficial emotion. A crucifix hangs at the end of the pulpit. The preacher takes it down, kisses it, presses it to his heart, and then, with great composure, when the pathetic period is over, puts it back in its place. There is another device which the run of preachers often use to produce an effect; it is the square cap they wear on their heads. They take it off and put it on again with incredible speed. One of them attacked Voltaire and particularly Rousseau for the period's irreligion. He threw his cap into the centre of the pulpit and gave it the task of representing Jean-Jacques. In that role he harangued it, saying: *Well, Genevan philosopher, what have you to say against my arguments?* Then he would be silent for a few moments, as if waiting for an answer, and as the cap would say nothing in reply, he would put it back on his head and would finish the conversation with the words: *Now that you are convinced, let us say no more about it.*

These strange scenes are often repeated among Roman preachers, for in that field, real talent is very rare. Religion is respected in Italy as an all-powerful law. It captivates the imagination by its practices and ceremonies, but in the pulpit much more is said about dogma than morality, and religious ideas never reach the depths of the human heart. Like many other branches of literature, pulpit oratory is thus completely given over to commonplaces which depict and express nothing. A new thought would cause almost a kind of consternation in these minds, at once so passionate and so lazy that to calm themselves down they need uniformity, which they like because it is restful. In sermons there is a kind of pattern for ideas and phrases. Some nearly always follow others, and this order would be upset if the preacher, speaking according to his own ideas, looked into his own soul for what he should say. Christian philosophy, one that looks for an accord with human nature, is as little known to Italian preachers as any other philosophy. They are so used to routine in this kind of subject that to think about religion would scandalize them almost as much as to think against it.

Worship of the Virgin is particularly dear to the Italians and to all the southern nations. In some way it seems linked to what is purest and most sensitive in affection for women. But the same formulae of exaggerated rhetoric are found again and again in everything the preachers say on this subject, and the way their gestures and language continually turn the most serious subject into a farce is inconceivable. In the august function of the pulpit in Italy, there is hardly ever to be found a sincere note or natural language.

Oswald, wearying of the most tiring monotony of all, that of affected vehemence, wanted to go to the Colosseum to hear the Carthusian monk who was to preach in the open air, at one of the altars in the arena which mark out what are called *the Stations of the Cross*. What finer subject for eloquence than the sight of this monument, than this arena, where martyrs took the place of gladiators! But you must not expect anything about that from the poor Carthusian, who knows nothing of human history but his own life. Nevertheless, you manage not to listen to his bad sermon, you are moved by the different people around him. Most of the audience come from the Camaldulian fraternity.* During religious exercises they wear a kind of grey robe which entirely covers the head and the whole body, leaving only two little openings for the eyes; that is how ghosts might be portrayed. Concealed like this beneath their clothes, these men prostrate themselves, faces right down to the ground, and beat their breasts. When the preacher falls on his knees, crying *mercy and pity!* the surrounding populace also fall on their knees and repeat the same cry, which becomes lost under the old porticoes of the Colosseum. It is impossible not to feel a deeply religious emotion. Suffering's appeal to goodness, earth's to heaven, moves the soul in its inmost sanctuary. Oswald quivered when all those present knelt down. He remained standing so as not to participate in a form of worship not his own, but it pained him not to associate himself publicly with any mortal beings, whoever they might be, who prostrate themselves before God. Alas! Is there, indeed, any invocation to heavenly pity not equally fitting to all men?

People had been struck by Lord Nelvil's handsome face and foreign ways but were not scandalized by his not kneeling. No one is more tolerant than the Romans; they are used to people coming to their city only to see and observe. And whether out of pride or indolence, they do not try to force their opinions on anyone. What is even more extraordinary is that during Holy Week there are many who flagellate themselves in penance, and while they are wielding the whip the church door is open, others come in, it makes no difference to them. They are people who do not bother about others; they do nothing to be looked at and do not refrain from doing anything because others are looking at them. They go steadily towards their goal or their pleasure, without suspecting that there is such a feeling as vanity which has no pleasure or goal except the need to be praised.

CHAPTER III

THE Holy Week ceremonies in Rome have often been talked about. All foreigners come on purpose during Lent to enjoy this spectacle, and as the music in the Sistine Chapel and the illumination of Saint Peter's are unique beauties of their kind, it is natural that they should arouse keen curiosity. But the expectation is not satisfied as much by the ceremonies themselves. The supper of the twelve Disciples, served by the Pope, his washing of their feet, indeed the different customs of that solemn period, all bring moving thoughts to mind, but a thousand unavoidable circumstances often mar the interest and dignity of the spectacle. Not all those who take part in it are equally meditative, equally filled with pious thoughts. These often repeated ceremonies have become a kind of mechanical exercise for most of those who take part in them, and the young priests hurry through the services of the great festivals with unimpressive speed and skill. The feeling of the vague, the unknown, and the mysterious, so befitting to religion, is completely destroyed by the kind of attention one cannot help paying to the way each one performs his functions. The greed of some of them for the food they are offered, and the indifference of others to the genuflexions they multiply or the prayers they recite, often deprive the festival of its solemnity.

The old costumes which are still worn by ecclesiastics go badly with modern hair fashion. The Greek bishop with his long beard is the one whose attire seems the most worthy of respect. The old practices, too, such as that of curtseying like women, instead of bowing as men do nowadays, make no significant impression. In short, the whole ceremony is discordant; the ancient and modern are mixed together with no care being taken to strike the imagination and, above all, to avoid distracting it. A form of worship, brilliant and majestic in its external forms, is certainly well fitted to fill the soul with the most exalted feelings, but care must be taken lest the ceremonies degenerate into a performance with each one playing his part opposite the other, learning what he has to do, at what moment he has to do it, when he has to pray, stop praying, kneel down, or get up. The regularity of court ceremonies introduced into a place of worship impedes the free impulse of the soul which alone gives man the hope of drawing near to the divinity.

These failings are quite usually noticed by foreigners, but most Romans never weary of the ceremonies and every year enjoy them anew. A peculiar feature of the Italians is that their instability does not incline them to inconstancy and their liveliness does not make them feel the need of variety. In everything they are patient and persevering. Their imaginations embellish what they have; it fills their lives rather than making them restless. They find everything more magnificent, more imposing, more beautiful than it really is, and while elsewhere vanity makes people appear blasé, Italian vanity, or rather their inner warmth and vivacity, makes them find pleasure in the feeling of admiration.

From everything the Romans had told him, Lord Nelvil expected to be more affected by the ceremonies of Holy Week. He missed the noble, simple festival days of Anglican worship. He returned to his apartment with a painful impression, for nothing is sadder than not to be moved by what ought to move us. We think our soul has dried up, we fear we have lost the power of enthusiasm, without which the faculty of thinking would serve only to give a distaste for life.

CHAPTER IV

SOON, however, Good Friday restored to Lord Nelvil all the religious emotions that he regretted not having felt on the previous days. Corinne's retreat was about to come to an end; he was looking forward to the happiness of seeing her again. The sweet hopes of feeling harmonize with piety; only artificial society life can turn us away from them completely. Oswald went to the Sistine Chapel to hear the famous *Miserere** lauded throughout all Europe. It was still daylight when he arrived and he saw Michelangelo's celebrated paintings which depict the Last Judgement with all the terrifying power of the subject and of the talent which portrayed it. Michelangelo had steeped himself in Dante's work, and the painter like the poet depicts mythological beings in the presence of Jesus Christ; but he nearly always assigns the evil element to paganism and represents the pagan fables in the shape of demons. On the chapel's vaulted ceiling you can see the Prophets and the Sibyls summoned by the Christians to bear witness.[†] They are surrounded by a crowd of angels, and the whole ceiling, painted in this way, seems to bring heaven closer to us, but heaven is gloomy and frightening. Daylight scarcely filters through the stained-glass windows, which cast shadows rather than light on the pictures; already so imposing, the figures Michelangelo painted are magnified still more; there is something funereal about the scent of the incense which fills the air, and all our sensations prepare us for the deepest of all, the one that music is to produce.

While Oswald was absorbed in the thoughts aroused by all the objects around him, he saw Corinne enter the women's gallery behind the grille which separates them from the men. He had not hoped to see her yet; she was dressed in black, pale from fasting, and trembling so much at the sight of Oswald that she had to lean on the railing in order to keep walking. At that moment the *Miserere* began.

Perfectly trained in this pure, ancient music, the voices emanate from a gallery where the vaulted ceiling begins to curve. The singers are invisible; the music seems to hover in the air; every moment the declining daylight makes the chapel still darker; it was not the sensual, passionate music that Oswald and Corinne had heard the previous week; it was wholly religious music, counselling renunciation of the earth. Corinne fell to her knees in front of the grille and remained wrapped in the deepest meditation; even Oswald disappeared from her view. It seemed to her it was in such a moment of exaltation that one would want to die if there were no pain in the separation of the soul from the body, if an angel suddenly came and on its wings carried away feeling and thought, those divine sparks which would return

[†] Teste David cum Sibylla.*

to their source. Death would then be, as it were, only a spontaneous act of the heart, a more fervent, better answered prayer.

The *Miserere*, that is to say *have pity on us*, is a psalm composed of verses sung, turn and turn about, in very different styles. In turn a heavenly music can be heard, and the following verse, in recitative, is murmured in a muffled and almost harsh tone. It is as if it were the answer of hard characters to sensitive hearts, the reality of life which comes to blight and thrust aside the wishes of generous souls. When the choir resumes, hope is reborn, but when the recited verse starts again, a cold sensation grips anew. It is not caused by terror but by the discouragement of enthusiasm. Finally, the last section, more noble and touching still than all the others, leaves a sweet, pure feeling in the depths of the soul. God grants us this same feeling before we die.

The lights are extinguished; night approaches; the figures of the Prophets and Sibyls seem like ghosts wrapped in the twilight. The silence is profound; speech would be unbearably painful in that emotional state when everything is inward and private. When the last sound dies away, everyone departs slowly and silently, as if afraid to return to the ordinary interests of this world.

Corinne followed the procession going into Saint Peter's, which then is lit only by an illuminated cross. This sign of grief, shining alone in the majestic darkness of the enormous building, is an extremely beautiful image of Christianity in the midst of the gloom of life. A pale light is projected from afar onto the statues decorating the tombs. The living, who can be seen in crowds beneath the arches, look like pygmies in comparison with these effigies of the dead. Around the cross and illuminated by it there is an area where the Pope and all the cardinals behind him are prostrated. They stay there nearly half an hour in the deepest silence, and it is impossible not to be moved by the sight. We do not know what they are praying for; we cannot hear their private laments. But they are old; they are ahead of us on the road to the grave. When we, in our turn, pass on to that terrible vanguard, may God grant us the favour of giving our old age sufficient dignity to make the close of life the first days of immortality!

Corinne too, the young, beautiful Corinne, was kneeling behind the priestly procession and the gentle light which lit up her face made her complexion look pale without dimming the brightness of her eyes. Oswald gazed at her looking so, as at a charming picture and as an adored being. When she had said her prayer she got up. Lord Nelvil, respecting the religious meditation in which she was absorbed, did not yet dare go up to her, but, transported with happiness, she approached him first, her emotion pervading all she did. With eager cheerfulness she welcomed people who came up to her at Saint Peter's, which was suddenly turned into a public promenade, where people arranged to meet to discuss their business or their pleasures.

Oswald was surprised at the instability of temperament which allowed such different feelings to follow each other so quickly and, although Corinne's joy made him happy, he was surprised to find in her no trace of the day's emotions. He could not understand how, on such a solemn day, people allowed this beautiful church to be the Roman café where people met each other for pleasure. As he looked at Corinne among her friends, talking vivaciously, regardless of her surroundings, he became mistrustful of the frivolity of which she might be capable. Immediately noticing this, she suddenly left the company and took his arm saying, 'I have never discussed my religious feelings with you. Allow me to do so today so that I can perhaps dispel the doubts that I saw arise in your mind.'

CHAPTER V

'MY dear Oswald,' Corinne continued, 'the difference in our religions is responsible for the secret blame that you could not help letting me see. Your religion is harsh and solemn, ours is lively and affectionate. People usually think Catholicism is stricter than Protestantism, and that may be true in countries where there has been strife between the two religions. But in Italy we have not had these religious quarrels, while in England you have experienced a great deal. A consequence of this difference is that in Italy Catholicism has become gentle and lenient, but in England, in order to destroy Catholicism, the Reformation armed itself with the strictest principles and morality. Like the ancient religions, ours stimulates the arts, inspires the poets, is, as it were, a part of all life's pleasures, while yours, being established in a country where reason is more dominant than imagination, has assumed a character of moral austerity from which it will never depart. Ours speaks in the name of love, yours in the name of duty. Your principles are liberal, our dogmas are absolute. Yet in practice, our orthodox despotism makes allowances for individual circumstances, while your religious freedom has its laws observed without any exceptions. It is true that our Catholicism imposes very severe penance on those who enter the monastic state. That state, freely chosen, is a mysterious relationship between man and God, but in Italian laity religion is usually a source of touching emotions. Love, hope, and faith are the principal virtues of this religion, and all of them proclaim and give happiness. Far from forbidding the pure feeling of gladness at any time, our priests tell us that it expresses our gratitude to the Creator for his gifts. What they require of us is the observance of practices which prove our respect for our religion and our desire to please God; it is charity for the unfortunate and repentance for our weaknesses. But they do not refuse to give us absolution when we ask for it fervently, and here, more than elsewhere, the heart's affections arouse an indulgent pity. Did not Jesus Christ say to Mary Magdalene, *She will be forgiven much because she loved much.** These words were uttered beneath a sky as beautiful as our own and this same sky beseeches God's pity for us.'

'Corinne,' Lord Nelvil replied, 'how can I argue against such soothing words which my heart needs so badly? But I shall do so all the same, because it is not only for one day that I love Corinne, and I hope for a long, happy, virtuous future with her. The purest religion is the one which makes the sacrifice of our passions and the performance of our duties a continual homage to the Supreme Being. Man's morality is his worship of God. To ascribe to the Creator, in his relationship with the created being, an intention unconnected with his spiritual improvement is to degrade our idea of that Creator. Fatherhood, the noble image of an all-benevolent master, asks nothing of children that does not make them better or happier. How then can one imagine that God would require from man something that would be unrelated to man? Look, too, at what confusion in the minds of your people comes from their habit of attaching more importance to religious ritual than to morality. You know that it is after Holy Week that the greatest number of murders are committed. People think they are, as it were, in funds because of Lent, and spend the riches of their penance in murders. We have seen criminals, still dripping with the blood of their murdered victims, having scruples about eating meat on Fridays, and ignorant people who have been persuaded that the greatest crimes lie in disobeying the rituals commanded by the Church, and who wear out their consciences on the matter, thinking

God is like worldly governments, who place submission to their power above all other virtues. These are courtiers' attitudes substituted for the respect inspired by the Creator as the source and reward of a scrupulous and sensitive life. Composed entirely of external manifestations, Italian Catholicism relieves the soul of meditation and thoughtfulness. When the show is over, feeling subsides, duty is fulfilled, and people are not, as in our country, lost in thoughts and feelings aroused by the strict examination of their behaviour and their hearts.'

'You are severe, dear Oswald,' replied Corinne. 'It is not the first time I have noticed it. If religion consisted only in strict moral observance, what more would it have than philosophy or reason? And what religious feelings would develop in us if our principal aim was to stifle the heart's feelings? The Stoics knew almost as much as we do about duties and strict behaviour, but it is Christianity alone which brought the religious fervour that is linked to all the soul's affections; it is the power to love and pity; it is the worship of feeling and compassion which so encourages the soul to soar towards heaven! What is the meaning of the parable of the Prodigal Son? Is it not that love, genuine love, is preferable to the most exact accomplishment of all duties? That boy had left his father's house but his brother stayed there. He immersed himself in all the worldly pleasures but his brother did not stray for a moment from the order of domestic life. But the prodigal returned, but he wept, but he loved, and his father made a feast for his return. Oh, no doubt the mysteries of our nature, to love, to go on loving, are what has been left to us of our celestial heritage. Even our virtues are too often intertwined with our lives to enable us always to understand what is good, what is better, and what secret feeling directs us and leads us astray. I ask my God to teach me to worship him and I feel the effect of my prayers by the tears I shed. But to sustain this frame of mind, religious rituals are more necessary than you think; they are an established link with God; they are daily actions with no connection to any of life's interests, and aimed only at the invisible world. External objects are also very helpful to religion. The soul falls back on itself if the arts, great monuments, harmonious song, do not help to bring new life to that poetic genius which is also religious genius.

'When he prays, when he suffers and places his hopes in heaven, at that moment the most ordinary man has something within him which would be expressed in the language of Milton, of Homer, or of Tasso if education had taught him to clothe his thoughts in words. There are only two distinct classes of men on earth, those who have strong feelings and those who despise them. All other differences are made by society. The former have no words to express their feelings. The latter know what must be said to conceal the emptiness of their hearts. But the spring which gushes from the very rock at heaven's voice, that spring is true talent, true religion, genuine love.

'The pomp of our worship, the pictures in which the eyes of kneeling saints express continual prayer, the statues placed on tombs as if to awaken one day with the dead, the churches with their high arches, have a close connection with religious ideas. I love the glittering homage rendered by men to what promises them neither fortune nor power, to what punishes or rewards them only through a feeling in the heart. At such times I feel prouder of my being; I recognize something disinterested in man, and even if the religious splendour is excessive, I love this lavishness of earthly riches for the sake of another life, of time for the sake of eternity; enough things are done for tomorrow, enough care is taken for the management of human affairs. Oh, how I love what is useless, useless if life is only painful labour for a miserable profit. But if we are on this earth on our way towards heaven, what is there better to do than to lift up our souls so that they may sense the infinite, the invisible, and the eternal amid all the limits that surround them?

'Jesus Christ allowed a weak and perhaps repentant woman to sprinkle his feet with the most delicious perfumes. He repulsed those who advised him to reserve these perfumes for something more profitable. *Let her be*, he said, *for I am not with you for long.** Alas! Everything good and sublime on this earth is not with us for long. Age, infirmity, and death will soon dry up the drop of dew that falls from heaven and comes to rest only on flowers. Dear Oswald, let us then mingle everything, love, religion, genius, with sunshine, perfume, music, and poetry. Atheism exists only in coldness, selfishness, and baseness. Jesus Christ said, *When two or three are gathered together in my name, I shall be in the midst of them.** But what does it mean, oh God, to be gathered together in your name if it is not to enjoy the sublime gifts of the beautiful nature you have created, to do homage to you for it, to thank you for it, and above all to thank you for it when another heart you have created responds completely to our own?'

At that moment a heavenly inspiration animated Corinne's countenance. Oswald could barely restrain himself from falling on his knees
in front of her in the middle of the church, and for a long time he
was silent so as to savour the pleasure of recalling her words and of
finding them yet again in her eyes. At last, however, he wanted to
reply; he did not want to desert the cause he held dear. 'Corinne,' he
then said, 'allow your friend still a few more words. His soul is by
no means arid. No, Corinne, not in the least, believe it is not. But if
I love austerity in principles and actions it is because it adds depth
and duration to feeling. If I love reason in religion, that is, if I reject
both contradictory dogmas and human means of impressing men, it
is because I see the divine in reason as well as in strong feeling. If I
cannot bear man to be deprived of any of his faculties, it is because
all of them are not too many to know a truth, because the existence
of God and the immortality of the soul are revealed by thought as
well as by strong feeling. What can be added to these sublime ideas,
to their union with virtue? What can be added to them that is not
beneath them? I venture to say that the poetic enthusiasm which makes
you so attractive is not the healthiest way of being devout. Corinne,
how could this frame of mind prepare us for the innumerable sacrifices duty demands of us? When human destiny, present and future,
was presented to the mind only through the clouds, revelation came
only from impulses of the soul. But for us, for whom Christianity
has made it clear and certain, feeling can be our reward, but it ought
not to be our only guide. You describe the existence of the blessed,
and not of mortals. Religious life is a battle and not a hymn. If we
were not condemned in this world to curb the evil inclinations of
others and of ourselves, there would indeed be no other distinction
to make between cold souls and impassioned souls. But man is a
rougher and more formidable creature than your heart depicts; both
reason in religion and authority in duty are a necessary brake to his
arrogant misdemeanours.

'Whatever you may think about external ceremonies and the many
practices of your religion, believe me, dear friend, contemplation of
the universe and its author will always be the pre-eminent rite; it is
the one that will fill the imagination, without examination finding anything futile or absurd about it. Dogmas which offend my reason also
cool my feelings. The world, such as it is, is certainly a mystery that
we can neither deny nor understand, so the man who would refuse to

believe everything he cannot explain would be quite crazy. But what is
contradictory is always man's creation. Such as God has given it to us,
the mystery is beyond the mind's comprehension but not in opposition to it. A German philosopher* said, *I know but two fine things in the
universe, the starry heaven above our heads and the feeling of duty in our
hearts.* Indeed, all the wonders of creation are combined in these words.

'Before knowing you, Corinne, I would have thought that, far from
making the heart cold, a simple, strict religion could alone concen-
trate the affections and make them last. I have seen the strictest and
purest behaviour develop an inexhaustible affection in a man. I have
seen him retain, right into old age, a purity of soul that stormy passions and the errors engendered by them would have been bound
to tarnish. Repentance is undoubtedly good and I, more than anyone, need to believe it is efficacious, but repeated repentance wearies
the soul; it is a feeling that is effective only once. It is redemption
which is brought about in the depth of our soul and this great sacrifice
cannot be repeated. When human weakness becomes used to it, it loses
the strength to love, for strength is essential in order to love, at least
steadfastly.

'I would make the same kind of objections to the magnificent ritual which you say has such a keen effect on the imagination. I think
imagination is modest and retiring like the heart. In the Cévennes
at nightfall, I saw a Protestant minister preaching, deep in the
mountains. He invoked the graves of the Frenchmen, banished and
outlawed by their brothers, whose ashes had been brought to this place.
He promised their friends that they would find them again in a
better world. He told them that a virtuous life was a guarantee of
happiness, saying, *Do good to men so that God may heal the wound of
sorrow in your hearts.* He was amazed at the inflexibility, at the harshness, of a man who lives only for one day, towards a man who also
lives only for one day, and he seized on the terrible idea of death,
which the living have imagined, but which they will never exhaust.
In short, he proclaimed nothing that was not moving and true; his
words were completely in harmony with nature. The mountain stream
that could be heard in the distance, the stars' twinkling light, seemed
to express the same thought in a different form. The magnificence
of nature was there, the only magnificence which celebrates without
offending misfortune. And all this impressive simplicity moved the
soul more deeply than brilliant ceremonies.'

Two days after this conversation, on Easter Sunday, Corinne and Lord Nelvil were together in Saint Peter's Square, at the time when the Pope comes out onto the church's highest balcony and asks heaven for the blessing it is going to spread over the earth. When he pronounces the words 'to the city and to the world' (*urbi et orbi*), all the assembled people fall to their knees and, through their emotion at that moment, Corinne and Lord Nelvil felt that all forms of worship are alike. Religious feeling binds men closely together when vanity and fanaticism do not make it an object of jealousy and hatred. Praying together, in whatever language, according to whatever rite, is the most moving fraternity of hope and sympathy that man can develop on this earth.

CHAPTER VI

EASTER Sunday had passed, but Corinne did not talk of carrying out her promise to confide her story to Lord Nelvil. One day, hurt by her silence, he said in her presence that the beauties of Naples were greatly praised and he wanted to go there. Corinne, who understood immediately what was going on in his heart, suggested making the journey with him. She imagined she could postpone the confession he required of her by giving him this proof of love which ought to satisfy him. Moreover she thought that if he took her with him, it was no doubt because he intended to devote his life to her. So she awaited his reply anxiously and her almost pleading eyes asked him for a favourable reply. Oswald could not resist them. At first he was surprised at the offer and at the artlessness with which Corinne made it. For a while, he hesitated to accept it, but when he saw his friend's distress, her heaving breast, and her tearful eyes, he agreed to go with her, without realizing the importance of such a decision. Corinne was ecstatically happy, for, at that moment, her heart trusted Oswald's feelings completely.

The day was settled and the delightful prospect of travelling together banished every other idea. They enjoyed arranging the details of the journey and there was not one detail which was not a source of pleasure. What a happy frame of mind in which all life's arrangements have a special charm, because they are linked to some hope of the heart! Only too soon the moment comes when every hour of existence, as well as existence in its entirety, is tiring, when every morning requires a labour to make awakening bearable and to take us through the day till the evening.

Just as Lord Nelvil was leaving Corinne's house to get everything ready for their departure, Count d'Erfeuil arrived, and learned from her the plan they had just drawn up together. 'What, are you really thinking of setting off with Lord Nelvil without being married to him, or without his promising to do so? And what will become of you if he leaves you?' 'What would become of me in all situations of my life, if he ceased to love me, the most unhappy person in the world?' 'Yes, but if you have done nothing to compromise yourself, you will retain your reputation entirely.' 'Me, retain my reputation when the deepest feeling in my life would be blighted! When my heart would be broken!' cried Corinne. 'The outside world would not know, and by concealing it you would lose nothing in public opinion.' 'And why consider public opinion,' replied Corinne, 'if it is not to have yet one more attraction in the eyes of one's beloved?' 'You stop loving,' answered Count d'Erfeuil, 'but you do not stop living in society and needing it.' 'Oh! If I could think that the day will come when Oswald's affection would not be everything for me in this world, if I could think that, I would already have stopped loving him. What then is love, if it foresees, if it calculates the moment it will no longer exist? If there is anything religious in this feeling, it is because it makes all other interests disappear and, like piety, takes pleasure in complete self-sacrifice.'

'What are you saying?' replied the Count. 'Can an intelligent person like you fill her head with such nonsense? It is an advantage for us men that women think like you, for then we have much more influence over them. But your superiority must not be wasted; it must be of some use to you.' 'Use to me?' said Corinne. 'Oh, I owe it a lot if it makes me better appreciate all that is generous and touching in Lord Nelvil's character.'

'Lord Nelvil is a man like any other,' replied Count d'Erfeuil. 'He will go back to his own country, and he will pursue his career; in short he will be sensible. And you imprudently risk your reputation by going to Naples with him.' 'I do not know Lord Nelvil's intentions,' said Corinne, 'and perhaps I would have done better to think about them before loving him. But now, what does one more sacrifice matter? Does not my life still depend on his feeling for me? On the contrary, I find a certain pleasure in leaving myself no resource; there never is any when the heart is wounded. Nevertheless society may sometimes believe you have one left, and I like to think that even in this respect my unhappiness would be complete if Lord Nelvil were to leave me.' 'But does he know to what extent you are compromising yourself for him?' continued Count d'Erfeuil. 'I took great care to conceal it from him,' replied Corinne, 'and as he is not well acquainted with this country's customs, I may have exaggerated a little the freedom they give. I ask for your word that you will not say anything to him about the matter. I want him to be free and to remain free in his relationship with me. He cannot make me happy by any kind of sacrifice. The feeling which makes me happy is the flower of life, and if it were to wither, neither kindness nor tact could revive it. So, my dear Count, I beg you not to interfere with my destiny. Nothing you know about the heart's affections can be right for me. What you say is wise, well reasoned, very applicable to ordinary people and situations. But, in all innocence, you would hurt me terribly if you wanted to judge my character according to the usual broad categories, for which there are ready-made maxims. I suffer, I enjoy, I feel, in my own way, and if you wanted to have an influence on my happiness, you would have to observe me alone.'

Count d'Erfeuil's vanity was a little hurt at the uselessness of his advice and at the great mark of love that Corinne was giving to Lord Nelvil. The Count knew very well that she did not love him and he also knew that she loved Oswald. But he found it unpleasant that this was all declared so openly. In a man's success with a woman there is always something displeasing even to his best friends. 'I see I can do nothing about it,' said Count d'Erfeuil, 'but when you are very unhappy you will remember me. Meanwhile, I am going to leave Rome, since neither you nor Lord Nelvil will be here any longer. I would be too bored in your absence. I shall certainly see you both again in Scotland or in Italy, for till I find something better to do, I have acquired a taste for travel. Forgive my advice, charming Corinne, and believe in my constant devotion.' Corinne thanked him and was quite sorry to part from him. She had met him and Oswald at the same time and the memory of this formed bonds between them which she did not like to see broken. She behaved as she had told Count d'Erfeuil she would. For a moment, a few anxieties marred Lord Nelvil's pleasure in agreeing to the proposed journey. He was afraid the departure for Naples might harm Corinne, and before leaving, he wanted to learn her secret so as to be quite sure they were not separated by some invincible obstacle. But she maintained that she would tell her story only in Naples and gently deluded him about what people might say about her decision. Oswald lent himself to this illusion. In a vacillating, weak character, love half deceives, reason half enlightens, and it is the immediate emotion that decides which of the two halves will be the whole. Lord Nelvil's mind was exceptionally broad and discerning, but he was a good judge of himself only about the past. He had only a blurred vision of his current situation. He was liable to enthusiasm, remorse, and shyness all at once, and these contrasts did not allow him self-knowledge till the outcome had settled his inner struggle.

When Corinne's friends, and especially Prince Castel-Forte, learned of her plan, they were greatly distressed. Above all, Prince Castel-Forte was so upset by it that he decided to join her before long. There was certainly no vanity in following on after a preferred lover, but what he could not bear was the terrible void left by his friend's absence. He had not one friend whom he did not meet at Corinne's, and he never went to any house but hers. The society gathered around her would disperse when she was no longer there; it would be impossible to reassemble what remained. Prince Castel-Forte was not much used to living in his family home; although he was very witty, study wearied him, and so the whole day would have been unbearably burdensome if, morning and evening, he had not visited Corinne. She was leaving; he did not know what to do with himself, and vowed secretly to go to her side as an undemanding friend, a permanent consolation in misfortune; and that friend may be quite sure his time will come.

Corinne felt a little melancholy in breaking all her habits in this way. For some years she had adopted a style of life in Rome that she liked. She was the centre of all the famous artists and enlightened men; a complete independence of ideas and habits made her life very attractive; what was going to become of her now? If she was destined to the happiness of having Oswald for a husband, he was bound to take her to England, and what would people think of her there? How would she be able to keep to the strict rules of a way of life so different from the kind she had been leading for six years? But these thoughts only crossed her mind, and slight traces of them were brushed aside by her feeling for Oswald. She saw him, she heard him, and counted the hours only by his absence or presence. Who can quarrel with happiness? Who does not welcome it when it comes? Corinne, above all, was without foresight; neither fear nor hope was made for her. Her faith in the future was blurred, and in this respect her imagination served her neither well nor ill.

On the morning of her departure, Prince Castel-Forte came to see her, saying with tears in his eyes, 'Will you never come back to Rome?' 'Oh, my goodness, yes,' she replied. 'We shall be back in a month.' 'But if you marry Lord Nelvil, you will have to leave Italy.' 'Leave Italy!' said Corinne with a sigh. 'This country, where your language is spoken, where you are so well understood and so greatly admired,' continued Prince Castel-Forte. 'And your friends, Corinne, and your friends! Where will you be loved as you are here? Where will you find the imagination and the arts you love? Does one feeling alone then suffice for life? Is not love of country composed of language, customs, and manners? It is this love which gives exiles their terrible sorrow.' 'Oh, what are you telling me?' cried Corinne. 'Have I not experienced it? Is it not that sorrow which has decided on my fate?' Sadly she looked round her room, at the statues which adorned it, then at the Tiber which flowed beneath her windows and at the sky whose beauty seemed to invite her to stay. But at that moment Oswald was crossing the Sant'Angelo Bridge on horseback. He was coming with lightning speed. 'There he is!' cried Corinne. She had scarcely uttered these words when he was already there. She ran to meet him. Impatient to set off, they both hurried to get into the carriage. Corinne, however, bade a kindly goodbye to Prince Castel-Forte, though her pleasant words were lost in the air, in the midst of the postilions' shouts, of the horses' neighing, and of all the noise of departure, sometimes sad, sometimes elating, according to the fear or hope inspired by destiny's new chances.

BOOK XI
NAPLES AND THE HERMITAGE
OF SAN SALVATORE

CHAPTER I

OSWALD was proud of carrying off his conquest. This time, he, who nearly always spoilt his enjoyment by reflections and regrets, no longer felt the pain of uncertainty. It was not that he had made up his mind, but he did not worry about doing so, and he let himself be guided by events, greatly hoping that he would be led by them to what he wanted. They crossed the Alban countryside, the place where people still point out what is believed to be the tomb of the Horatii and the Curiatii.*25 They went past Lake Nemi and the sacred woods surrounding it. It is said that Hippolytus was brought back to life by Diana in these parts. She did not let horses come near* and by this prohibition she perpetuated her young favourite's memory. In this way, at almost every step, poetry and history are brought to mind, and the charming sites that recall them soothe all that is melancholy in the past and seem to keep it eternally young.

Next Oswald and Corinne crossed the Pontine Marshes, a fertile but, at the same time, pestilential countryside. Not a single dwelling is to be seen there although nature seems fertile. A few sick men harness your horses and advise you not to fall asleep as you cross the marshes, for sleep there is the veritable harbinger of death. Buffaloes with low, fierce faces pull the ploughs which unwise farmers still sometimes drive across the deadly land, and brilliant sunshine lights up the sad sight. The unhealthy, marshy places of the north are easily identified by their frightening appearance, but in the more fatal regions of the south, with nature retaining its deceptive serenity, travellers are deluded. If it is true that it is very dangerous to fall asleep when crossing the Pontine Marshes, the overpowering inclination to fall asleep, brought on by the heat, it still another of the treacherous feelings which the place arouses. Lord Nelvil watched over Corinne all the time. Sometimes she would lean her head against Theresina, who was travelling with them, sometimes she would close her eyes, conquered by the languid air. Absolutely terrified, Oswald would quickly wake her and, although not naturally talkative, he made and sustained new subjects of conversation inexhaustibly, in order to prevent her from succumbing for a moment to the fatal sleep. Oh, must we not forgive women feeling heart-rending regrets for the days when they were loved, when their lives were so essential to the life of another, when they felt supported and protected at every moment? What loneliness is bound to follow those delightful days! And how fortunate are those who are gently led from love to friendship without their lives being torn apart by a cruel moment!

After the anxious journey across the Pontine Marshes, Oswald and Corinne arrived at last at Terracina, a town by the sea at the Naples border. It is there that the South really starts; it is there that, in all its splendour, it welcomes travellers. The land of Naples, *that happy countryside*, is, as it were, separated from the rest of Europe both by the surrounding sea and by the dangerous territory that has to be crossed in order to reach it. It is as if nature, reserving for itself the secret of this delightful place, wanted to make it perilous to approach. Rome is not yet the South; you have a foretaste of its delights but its entrancing quality really begins only in the area of Naples. Not far from Terracina is the promontory chosen by the poets for Circe's* dwelling, and behind Terracina rises Mount Anxur, where Theodoric, King of the Goths, had built one of the fortresses with which the northern warriors covered the land. There are very few traces of the barbarians' invasion of Italy; or at least, where these traces consist of ruins, they are inseparable from the effects of time. The northern peoples have not given Italy the warlike appearance preserved in Germany. Apparently the soft earth of Ausonia could not retain the fortifications and citadels which bristle up in northern countries. A Gothic building or a feudal castle can only rarely still be found in the South, and memories of ancient Romans reign alone across the centuries, in spite of the peoples who have conquered them.

The whole mountain dominating Terracina is covered with orange and lemon trees, which perfume the air delightfully. In our climate nothing is like the southern perfume of the lemon trees in the open countryside. It has almost the same effect on the imagination as melodious music; it makes you poetically inclined, stimulates talent, and intoxicates it with nature. The aloes, the broad-leafed cacti that you encounter at every step, have a special appearance which recalls what one knows of the terrifying vegetation of Africa. These plants arouse a kind of fear; they seem to belong to a violent, overbearing nature. The country's whole appearance is foreign. You feel as if you are in another world, in a world known to you only through the descriptions of the ancient poets who, in their portrayals, show both so much imagination and so much precision. Children had so much confidence in nature's bounty that, as Corinne's carriage entered Terracina, they threw into it a huge quantity of flowers which they gathered from the roadside and looked for in the mountains. The carts which brought back the harvest from the fields were decorated every day with garlands of roses, and sometimes the children put flowers round the cut corn, for under this beautiful sky even the people's imagination becomes poetic. Alongside these happy scenes the sea, whose waves were breaking furiously, could be seen and heard. It was not a storm which whipped them up but the rocks, the obstacle which regularly resisted the waves and provoked the ocean's majesty.

> E non udite ancor risuona
> Il roco ed alto fremito marino?*

And do you not still hear how the harsh, shuddering deep sea resounds?

That aimless motion, that purposeless force, eternally renewed, whose cause and end we can never know, attracts us to the shore where this great sight meets our eyes. We feel, as it were, a compulsion mingled with terror to draw near to the waves and deaden our thoughts with their uproar.

Towards evening, everything became calm. Corinne and Lord Nelvil strolled through the countryside slowly, with great pleasure. Crushing the flowers with each step, they released the scents they contained. The nightingales settled more readily on the bushes bearing roses. Thus the purest song combined with the sweetest scents. All the charms of nature were attracted to each other, but what is, above all, inexpressibly delightful is the sweetness of the air you breathe. When you look at a beautiful landscape in the North, you are sensitive to the climate, and this always mars a little the pleasure you might feel. Those little sensations of cold and damp, which more or less distract your attention from what you see, are like a false note in a concert, but when you come near to Naples, you experience such perfect well-being, such great kindliness towards you on the part of nature, that nothing spoils the pleasant feelings it brings you. In our northern climates all man's links are with society. In hot countries, nature relates us to external objects, and feelings expand gently outwards. It is not that the South does not have its melancholy aspects; in what places does man's destiny not give that feeling? But in that melancholy there is neither anxiety nor regret. Elsewhere, it is life such as it is which is not enough to satisfy all the heart's capacities; here, the heart's capacities are not enough to satisfy life, and the superabundant feelings inspire a dreamy indolence which, on experiencing it, you scarcely realize.

During the night, fireflies appeared in the air. It was as if the mountain was glittering and the burning earth was letting some of its flames escape. The fireflies flew through the trees, sometimes alighting on the leaves, while the wind rocked these little stars, varying their wavering light in a thousand ways. In the sand, too, gleaming everywhere, were a great number of ferruginous stones. It was as if the fiery earth still retained in its bosom traces of the sun, whose last rays had just ceased to give it warmth. In this nature, there is, at one and the same time, life and repose, which fully satisfy all the different aspirations of existence.

Corinne gave herself up to the evening's charm, becoming completely and delightedly absorbed in it; Oswald could not hide his emotion. Several times he pressed Corinne to his heart, several times he moved away, then came back, then moved away again, so as to respect the woman who was to be his life's companion. Corinne was not thinking of dangers which might have alarmed her, for so great was her esteem for Oswald that, if he had asked for the total gift of herself, she would not have doubted that this request was the solemn pledge of marriage. But she was very pleased that he triumphed over himself and honoured her by this sacrifice, and in her heart was the complete love and happiness that does not allow of one more desire. Oswald was far from feeling such calm. Corinne's charm had set him on fire. Once he violently clasped her knees and seemed to have lost all control over his passion, but Corinne looked at him so gently and with so much fear, she seemed to recognize his power so fully by asking him not to abuse it, that her humble defence more than any other aroused his respect.

Then they noticed in the sea the reflection of a torch that the hand of an unknown man on the shore was carrying as he made his way to a nearby house. 'He is going to see the woman he loves,' said Oswald. 'Yes,' replied Corinne. 'And for me,' continued Oswald, 'today's happiness is coming to an end.' Corinne's eyes, at that moment raised to heaven, filled with tears. Oswald was afraid he had offended her, and knelt before her to beg pardon for the love that was carrying him away. 'No,' said Corinne, giving him her hand and asking him to return with her. 'No, Oswald, I am certain you will respect the woman you love. You know that a simple request from you would be all-powerful; so it is you who answer for me; it is you who would refuse me for ever as your wife if you made me unworthy of you.' 'Ah well!' replied Oswald. 'Since you believe in the cruel power of your will over my heart, then why, Corinne, are you sad?' 'Alas,' she replied, 'I was thinking that these moments I have been spending with you now were the happiest in my life, and as I lifted my eyes to heaven in gratitude, I did not know by what chance a childish suspicion was revived in my heart. A cloud covered the moon as I was gazing at it and the sight of this cloud was fatal. I have always thought that heaven had a feeling now paternal, now angry, and I tell you, Oswald, this evening it condemned our love.' 'Dear friend,' replied Lord Nelvil, 'the only omens in man's life are his good or bad deeds, and this evening, have I not sacrificed my most ardent desires to a virtuous feeling?' 'Well, so much the better, if you are not included in this prophecy,' replied Corinne. 'Indeed, it is possible that the stormy sky has threatened only me.'

CHAPTER II

THEY arrived at Naples, by day, in the midst of that huge population, at once so lively and so idle. First they crossed the Via Toledo, seeing the Lazzaroni* lying on the pavement or withdrawn into wicker baskets which they use as dwellings day and night. There is something very original about the uncivilized state existing there side by side with civilization. Among these men there are some who do not even know their own names and go to confession to admit sins anonymously since they cannot say what the name of the sinner is. In Naples there is a subterranean grotto where thousands of Lazzaroni spend their lives, emerging only at midday to see the sun; they sleep the rest of the day while their wives spin. In climates where food and clothing are so readily available, a very independent and active government is required to set an adequate example to the nation, as it is so easy for people to exist physically in Naples that they can do without the kind of industry required elsewhere to earn a living. Laziness and ignorance, combined with the volcanic air you breathe in the place, are bound to produce ferocity when passions are aroused, but the people here are no more vicious than others. They have imagination which could motivate disinterested behaviour, and through this imagination they could be led to goodness if their political and religious institutions were good.

You can see Calabrians set out to cultivate the land with a violinist at their head and dancing from time to time to take a rest from walking. Every year, near Naples, there is a festival dedicated to the *Madonna* of the grotto, where girls dance to the sound of the tambourine and the castanets, and it is not unusual for them to put in their marriage contracts the condition that every year their husbands must take them to this festival. At the Naples theatre you can see an eighty-year-old actor, who for sixty years has been making the Neapolitans laugh in their national comic role of Punchinello. Can you imagine what immortality of the soul will be like for a man who fills his long life in this way? The people of Naples have no other idea of happiness than pleasure, but the love of pleasure is still better than arid selfishness.

It is true that these people, more than any others in the world, love money. If, in the street, you ask a man of the people your way, he holds out his hand after pointing the way, for they are lazier with words than gestures. But their taste for money is not methodical or calculated; they spend it as soon as they get it. If money were introduced among savages, they would ask for it like that. The greatest lack in this nation is the sense of dignity. They perform kind and generous deeds out of good-heartedness rather than on principle, for all their theorizing is worthless, and in this country, public opinion has no power. But when men or women escape this moral anarchy, their behaviour is more remarkable in itself and more worthy of admiration since nothing in their outward circumstances encourages virtue. They pluck it entirely from their own souls. Neither laws nor customs reward or punish them. The virtuous person is all the more heroic in that he is not more respected or sought after because of his virtue.

Apart from a few honourable exceptions, the upper classes are much like the lower. Their minds are hardly more cultivated, and society manners are the only outward differences. But in the midst of this ignorance, there is such a fund of natural intelligence and aptitude for everything that one cannot foresee what a nation like this would become if all the government's strength were directed towards enlightenment and morality. Since there is little education in Naples, up till now more originality of character than of mind is to be found there. But this country's outstanding men, such as the Abbé Galiani, Caraccioli,* etc., are said to have possessed to the highest degree humour and thoughtfulness, rare powers of the mind, and a combination without which pedantry or frivolity prevents you from knowing true values.

In some respects the common people of Naples are not at all civilized, but they are not boorish in the manner of other peoples. Their very coarseness strikes the imagination. The African shore which is on the other side of the sea can almost be felt already, and in the wild shouts that can be heard on all sides there is something indefinably Numidian. The tanned faces, the garments made of a few scraps of red or purple cloth, whose rich colour attracts the eye, the ragged clothes artistically arranged by this artistic people, give a kind of picturesque quality to the rabble, whereas in other places it shows only the miseries of civilization. In Naples a certain taste for ornament and decorations is often found side by side with the absolute lack of what is necessary or convenient. The shops are pleasantly decorated with flowers and fruit. Some have a festive look, which is linked neither to plenty nor to public happiness but solely to the liveliness of the imagination; people want above all to delight the eyes. The mild climate allows every kind of worker to work in the street. Tailors make suits there, caterers their meals, and domestic tasks, also performed out of doors, multiply activity in a thousand ways. Songs, dances, and noisy games are quite a good accompaniment to this spectacle and there is no country where you can appreciate more clearly the difference between amusement and happiness. Finally, you leave the heart of the city to go to the quays, from which you can see both the sea and Vesuvius, and then you forget all you know about mankind.

Oswald and Corinne reached Naples while Vesuvius was still erupting. By day it was only a black smoke which could be confused with the clouds, but in the evening, as they went out on the balcony of their lodging, they experienced a completely unexpected emotion. This river of fire goes down towards the sea, with its waves of flame, like the waves of the ocean, revealing the quick, continual succession of tireless motion. It is as if nature, in assuming different aspects, nevertheless still retains some traces of a single, originating idea. The phenomenon of Vesuvius makes the heart really beat. Usually we are so familiar with external objects that we barely notice their existence, and we hardly ever have a new emotion about them in our prosaic countries. But suddenly the amazement which the universe ought to arouse is renewed at the sight of an unknown wonder of creation. Our whole being is moved by nature's power, from which society's arrangements have so long distracted us; we feel that the world's greatest mysteries do not lie in man and that an independent force threatens or protects him according to unfathomable laws. Oswald and Corinne decided to climb Vesuvius, and the possible peril of the undertaking lent an additional charm to a plan they were to carry out together.

CHAPTER III

THERE was in the port of Naples at that time an English man-of-war, where a religious service was held every Sunday. The captain and Naples's English community suggested to Lord Nelvil that he should come the following day. At first he agreed to go without thinking whether he would take Corinne and how he would introduce her to his compatriots. Anxiety about this tortured him all night. The following day, as he was walking near the harbour with Corinne and was about to advise her not to go on the ship, an English launch, manned by ten sailors dressed in white and wearing black velvet caps embroidered with silver leopards, came into view. A young officer landed, greeted Corinne by the name of Lady Nelvil, and suggested that she should embark on the boat to go to the big ship. At the name of Lady Nelvil, Corinne was embarrassed, blushed, and lowered her eyes. Oswald seemed to hesitate a moment; then suddenly, taking her hand, said in English, 'Come, my dear.' And she followed him.

The sound of the waves and the silence of the sailors, who with admirable discipline made not an unnecessary movement nor said an unnecessary word, but swiftly steered the ship over the sea they had traversed so many times, gave rise to daydreams. Corinne, moreover, did not dare question Lord Nelvil about what had just happened. She was trying to guess his plan, not realizing (as was most probably the case, however) that he did not have one and was letting himself drift according to each new situation. For a moment she imagined he was leading her to divine service to make her his wife there, but at that moment the thought frightened her rather than made her happy; she felt as if she were leaving Italy and returning to England, where she had suffered greatly. That country's strict manners and customs came back to her mind, and even love could not triumph completely over her anxious memories. Yet, in other circumstances, how much will these thoughts surprise her, however fleeting they may have been! How much will she abjure them!

Corinne boarded the ship, whose interior was maintained with the utmost care and cleanliness. The only sound was the captain's voice, which was taken up and repeated from one deck to the other by command and obedience. The subordination, the seriousness, the regularity, the silence, noticeable on this ship was the image of a free but strict social order, in contrast to the town of Naples, so lively, so passionate, so tumultuous. Oswald was concerned with Corinne and her impressions, but sometimes, too, he was distracted from her by the pleasure of being in his native land. And indeed, for the English, are not ships and the sea a second native land? Oswald strolled about with the English who were on board, to have news of England and to talk about his country and politics. Meanwhile, Corinne was with the Englishwomen who had come from Naples to be present at divine service. They were surrounded by their children, beautiful as the day, but shy like their mothers, and not a word was spoken in the presence of a new acquaintance. This silent constraint made Corinne quite sad; she lifted her eyes towards beautiful Naples, towards its shores lined with flowers, towards its animated life, and she sighed. Fortunately for her, Oswald did not notice the sigh; on the contrary, when he saw her sitting amongst the Englishwomen, her black eyelashes lowered like their fair ones, and conforming in every way to their manners, he experienced a great feeling of joy. It is in vain that an Englishman momentarily likes foreign ways; his heart always returns to the first impressions of his life. If you question Englishmen sailing on a ship at the other end of the world and ask them where they are going, they will reply: 'home,' if it is to England that they are returning. Their wishes, their feelings, however far they are from their homeland, are always turned towards it.

Everyone went down between the first two decks to listen to divine service, and Corinne soon realized that her idea was without foundation and that Lord Nelvil did not have the solemn plan she had at first supposed. Then she reproached herself for having been afraid of it and felt anew the embarrassement of her situation, for everyone present had no doubt that she was Lord Nelvil's wife, yet she had not the strength to say a word which might affirm or refute the idea. Oswald too was suffering cruelly, but mingled with a thousand outstanding virtues there was much weakness and indecisiveness in his character. The man who has these failings is unaware of them and, in his eyes, they assume a new form in every situation. At times it is prudence, sensitivity, or tact which puts off the moment of decision; he never realizes it is the same failing which presents the same kind of problem in all circumstances.

Corinne, however, despite the painful thoughts occupying her mind, was deeply impressed by the sight she witnessed. Indeed, nothing touches the soul more than divine service on a ship, and the noble simplicity of Protestant worship seems particularly suited to one's feelings at such a time. A young man performed the chaplain's duties. He preached in a firm, gentle voice and his face had the sternness of a youthful pure soul. This sternness contains an idea of strength, which befits religion preached in the midst of the perils of war. At specific moments, the Anglican minister said prayers whose last words were repeated with him by the congregation. Their mingled yet gentle voices came at intervals to revive interest and emotion. The sailors, the officers, and the captain knelt down several times, especially at the words 'Lord have mercy upon us.' The captain's sword, that could be seen dragging beside him while he was on his knees, recalled the noble union of humility before God and intrepid courage before men that makes warriors' religious faith so moving. And while all these good people prayed to the God of armies, the sea could be glimpsed through the portholes, and sometimes the gentle sound of the waves, calm just then, seemed to say: 'Your prayers are heard.' The chaplain finished the service with the English sailors' special prayer. They said, *May God grant us the favour of defending abroad our happy constitution and of finding domestic happiness again in our homes on our return!* What fine sentiments are combined in these simple words! The preliminary and continuous study required by the navy, the austere life on board ship, make it a kind of military monastery in the midst of the waters, and the regularity of the most serious operations is interrupted only by perils and death. In spite of their warlike habits, sailors speak very gently and show unusual compassion for women and children when there are any on board. These feelings are all the more touching in that one knows how calmly sailors face the terrible dangers of war and sea; there is something supernatural about man's presence in their midst.

Corinne and Lord Nelvil again boarded the boat that was to take them back to land. They saw again the town of Naples, built like an amphitheatre as if to be present more comfortably at Nature's festival, and as Corinne set foot on the shore she could not repress a feeling of joy. If Lord Nelvil had suspected this feeling, he would have been keenly hurt, perhaps with reason. And yet he would have been unjust to Corinne, for she loved him passionately, in spite of the painful impression made by memories of a country where cruel circumstances had made her unhappy. Her imagination was volatile; there was a potential for love in her heart, but talent, and especially talent in a woman, creates a tendency to boredom, a need for diversion not entirely dissipated by the deepest passion. The vision of a monotonous life, even in the midst of happiness, frightens a mind which needs variety. It is when there is little wind in the sails that one can always hug the coast, but the imagination wanders although the feelings are faithful. At least that is how it is until the moment when misfortune makes all these inconsequential things disappear and leaves only a single thought, arouses only one pain.

Oswald attributed Corinne's reverie entirely to her continuing embarrassment at the position in which she must have found herself when she heard herself called Lady Nelvil. Keenly reproaching himself for failing to rescue her from it, he was afraid she might suspect him of frivolity. So, in order to have at last the explanation he was longing for, he began by offering to confide to her his own story. 'I shall speak first,' he said, 'and then you will confide in me.' 'Yes, of course, I must,' Corinne replied, trembling. 'Well, is that what you want? What day? What time? When you have spoken, I shall tell you everything.' 'How painfully upset you are!' said Oswald. 'What then, will you always be so afraid of your friend, so mistrustful of his heart?' 'No, I have to tell you,' continued Corinne. 'I have written it all down. Tomorrow, if you like . . .' 'Tomorrow we are to go to Vesuvius together,' said Lord Nelvil. 'I want to gaze at that amazing marvel with you, to learn from you how to admire it and, if I have the strength, to tell you during the journey itself. I must confide before you do; my heart has decided.' 'Well, yes,' replied Corinne. 'You still give me tomorrow, then. Thank you for that day. Oh, who knows if you will still feel the same towards me when I have opened my heart to you, who knows? And how can I not shudder at this doubt?'

CHAPTER IV

THE ruins of Pompeii are on the same side of the bay as Vesuvius, and it was with these ruins that Corinne and Lord Nelvil began their expedition. They were both silent, for the decisive moment of their fate was drawing near, and the vague hope they had been enjoying for so long, and which so well befits the indolence and reverie inspired by the Italian climate, was to be replaced at last by an actual destiny. Together they saw Pompeii, antiquity's most peculiar ruin. In Rome, it is mostly the remains of ancient monuments that are to be found, and these monuments recall only the political history of past centuries; in Pompeii, however, it is the private lives of the people of ancient times which are set before you just as they were. The volcanic eruption which covered this town with ashes has preserved it from the ravages of time. Buildings exposed to the air would never have survived like this and the buried memorial of the past has been found again in its entirety. The paintings, the bronzes, were still in their pristine beauty and everything that can be used for domestic purposes is preserved in a frightening way. The amphorae are still prepared for the following day's banquet; the flour that was going to be kneaded is still there; the remains of a woman are still adorned with the jewels she wore on the festive day disturbed by the volcanic eruption, but her desiccated arms no longer fill out the bracelet of precious stones that still encircles them. Nowhere else can be seen so striking a picture of the sudden interruption of life. Wheeltracks are visibly marked on the paving slabs in the streets, and the stones on the rims of wells bear traces of the ropes that gradually made grooves in them. On the walls of a guard-house can still be seen the badly shaped letters and roughly sketched figures drawn by soldiers to while away the time, while this time was advancing to engulf them.

When you stand at the centre of the crossroads, on every side you can see almost in its entirety the still surviving part of the town; it is as if you are waiting for someone, as if the master is about to arrive, and the very semblance of life in this place makes you even more sad at feeling its eternal silence. It is with pieces of petrified lava that most of these houses have been built, and they have been buried beneath other pieces of lava. So there are ruins upon ruins and tombs upon tombs. This history of the world where periods are counted from ruin to ruin, this human life whose trail is followed by the gleam of the volcanic eruptions that have consumed it, fills the heart with profound melancholy. What a long time men have existed! What a long time they have lived, suffered, and perished! Where can their feelings and thoughts be found again? Is the air you breathe amongst these ruins still marked with their traces or are they forever deposited in heaven where immortality reigns? A few burnt manuscript pages found at Herculaneum and Pompeii, which people at Portici are trying to unroll, are all that is left to enable us to learn about the unfortunate victims consumed by earth's thunderbolt, the volcano. But as you pass by those ashes which art manages to bring back to life, you are afraid to breathe, in case a breath carries away the dust perhaps still imprinted with noble ideas.

Public buildings even in this town of Pompeii, one of the smaller Italian towns, are still quite fine. The luxury of the ancient peoples was nearly always directed to something of public interest. Their private houses are very small and you do not see any search for splendour in them, but you notice a keen taste for the arts. Almost all the interior was decorated with very agreeable paintings and with pavings of artistically worked mosaics. On many of these pavings you find written the word 'greetings' (*salve*). It was placed on the threshold and was certainly not mere politeness but rather an invocation to hospitality. The badly lit bedrooms are exceptionally narrow, with no windows looking onto the street and nearly all looking onto a portico that, like the marble courtyard it surrounds, is inside the house. In the middle of this courtyard is a simply decorated cistern. This kind of dwelling indicates clearly that the ancient peoples nearly always lived in the open air and that was where they received their friends. Nothing gives a pleasanter and more agreeable idea of existence than this climate which unites man intimately with nature. It would seem that, with such habits, the character of social intercourse must be different from that in countries where the severe cold forces people to shut themselves up in their houses. You can understand Plato's dialogues better when you see these porticoes, under which the peoples of the ancient world strolled up and down for half the day. They were continually animated by the sight of a beautiful sky. The social order as they conceived it was no arid combination of calculation and power, but a happy unity of institutions which stimulated the faculties, developed the soul, and gave man the aim of perfecting himself and his fellow men.

Antiquity arouses insatiable curiosity. The scholars who are concerned only to gather a collection of names which they call history are undoubtedly devoid of any imagination. But to delve into the past, to question the human heart across the centuries, to grasp a fact through one word, and the character and customs of a nation from one deed, in short to go back to the most far-off times, to try to imagine how the world, in its first youth, appeared to the eyes of men, and how at that time they bore the gift of life which civilization has made so complicated today, that requires a sustained effort of the imagination, which penetrates and discovers the finest secrets that meditation and study can reveal to us. Oswald was particularly attracted to that kind of interest and occupation, and he often told Corinne that if he had not had noble interests to serve in his own country, he would have found life bearable only in places where historical monuments take the place of present-day existence. Glory must at least be regretted when it is no longer attainable. It is forgetfulness alone that degrades the soul, which can take refuge in the past when barren circumstances deprive actions of their purpose.

As they left Pompeii and went back to Portici, Corinne and Lord Nelvil were soon surrounded by the native inhabitants shouting at them to come and see *the mountain*, as they call Vesuvius. Does it need to be named? For the Neapolitans it is glory and fatherland; their region is made outstanding by this marvel. Oswald insisted that Corinne should be carried on a kind of palanquin to the San Salvatore hermitage, which is halfway up the mountain and where travellers rest before undertaking the ascent to the summit. He rode on horseback beside her to supervise the bearers, and the more his heart was filled with the generous thoughts aroused by nature and history, the more he adored Corinne.

The countryside at the foot of Vesuvius is the most fertile and best cultivated to be found in the Kingdom of Naples, that is to say in the European country most favoured by heaven. The famous vine whose wine is called *Lacryma Christi* is to be found here, but right beside it are lands devastated by lava. It is as if nature has made a final effort in the area beside the volcano and has adorned herself with her finest gifts before perishing. Turning round as you go higher, you can see

Naples and the wonderful surrounding countryside. The sun's rays make the sea glitter like precious stones, but all creation's splendour dies away gradually up to the area of ash and smoke which heralds the proximity of the volcano. The ferruginous lava streams of previous years leave the traces of their broad, black furrows on the ground, and all around them is barren. At a certain height, birds no longer fly, at another, plants become very scarce, then even insects find nothing to live on in this devastated nature. Finally every living thing disappears, you enter the empire of death, with only the ashes of this pulverized earth rolling away beneath your unsteady feet.

> Ne greggi ne armenti
> Guida bifolco mai, guida pastore.*

Never do shepherds or herdsmen lead their flocks or their cattle to that place.

A hermit lives there on the border between life and death. A tree, vegetation's last farewell, stands before his door. It is in the shade of its pale foliage that travellers usually await night's arrival to continue on their way, for, by day, the fires of Vesuvius are to be seen only as a cloud of smoke, and the lava, so blazing by night, seems dark in the sunlight. The transformation itself is a fine sight, renewing every evening the surprise that a permanent appearance might weaken. The impression of the place, its profound solitude, gave Lord Nelvil more strength to reveal his secret feelings, and as he wanted to encourage Corinne to confide in him, he agreed to speak to her. Deeply moved he said to her, 'You want to read to the bottom of your unhappy friend's heart; well, I shall confess everything to you. My wounds are going to reopen; I can feel that, but in the presence of unchanging nature, must one then be so afraid of the sufferings that are borne away by time?'

BOOK XII
LORD NELVIL'S STORY

CHAPTER I

'I WAS brought up in my father's house with an affection and kindness that I have come to admire much more since I have known men. I have had no deeper love than that for my father, and yet it seems to me that if I had known, as I do today, how unique his character was in the world, my affection would have been even more keen and more devoted. I remember a thousand incidents in his life which seemed quite simple to me because my father thought them so, and which move me painfully today when I know their worth. The reproaches we inflict on ourselves concerning a person who was dear to us but who is no more give an idea of what eternal punishment might be if divine mercy did not come to the aid of such grief.

'I was happy and calm living with my father, but I wanted to travel before enlisting in the army. In my country, a very fine civilian career is open to good orators, but I was, and still am even now, so extremely shy that I would have found it very painful to speak in public, and so I preferred the military condition. I preferred to risk certain danger rather than possible humiliation. In every respect my *amour proper* is more susceptible than ambitious and I have always found that men present themselves like ghosts to the imagination when they blame you, but like pygmies when they praise you. I wanted to go to France, where the Revolution had just broken out, a revolution which, in spite of the great age of humanity, claimed to begin the history of the world anew. My father had retained some prejudices against Paris, which he had visited towards the end of Louis XV's reign; he was unable to believe that cliques could be turned into a nation, pretension into virtue, and vanity into enthusiasm. Nevertheless he agreed to the journey I wanted because he was afraid of making any demands on me. He hesitated in a way to exercise his paternal authority when duty did not order him to do so. He was always afraid that his authority would interfere with the truth, with the purity of affection, which depends on what is most free and involuntary in our nature, and above all he needed to be loved. So, at the beginning of 1791 when I had reached the age of twenty-one, he allowed me to go to France for six months and I left to become acquainted with that nation, which is so near to us and yet so different in its institutions and the consequent way of life.

'I thought I would never like that country. I held against it the prejudices aroused in us by English pride and seriousness. I was afraid of ridicule against all devoted attachment to feelings and thoughts; I detested their art of deflating all emotion and of robbing all lovers of their illusions. The basis of that highly vaunted gaiety seemed to me quite sad, since it brought death to my most cherished feelings. At that time I did not know any truly distinguished Frenchmen, and they combine very charming manners with the noblest virtues. I was amazed at the simplicity and freedom which prevailed in Parisian society. The most important issues were discussed seriously but without pedantry. It seemed as if conversation had inherited the most profound ideas and all the world had a revolution only to make Paris society more pleasant. I met well-educated, highly talented men, who were stimulated by the wish to please even more than by the need to be useful; they sought a salon's approval even after success at the speaker's rostrum, and lived in the company of women to be applauded rather than loved.

'In Paris, everything concerned with outward happiness was extremely well organized. There were no difficulties in the details of life, which was fundamentally selfish but never superficially so, and there were activities and interests that took up each of your days without much to show for them, yet without your feeling weighed down. People had a quickness of mind which enabled them to point out and understand in a word what elsewhere would require a long exposition, and they had a capacity for imitation which might indeed be inimical to any true independence of thought but which brought to conversation harmony and friendliness not to be found elsewhere. In short, there was an easy way of leading one's life, of bringing it variety, of removing from it all serious thought, without depriving it of intellectual attraction. To all these distractions you must add theatres, foreigners, and the news of the day, and you will have some idea of the most sociable city in the world. I am almost surprised to be pronouncing its name in this hermitage in the middle of a desert, at the other extreme of the impressions aroused by the most lively population in the world, but I had to describe to you my stay in Paris and the effect it had on me.

'You, Corinne, who have known me so gloomy and dispirited now, would you believe that I let myself be seduced by that intellectual whirlwind? Even if I were not to have time for reflection, I was glad not to be bored for a moment, and even though my ability to love was diminished, I was glad to stifle my capacity for suffering. If I can judge by myself, it seems to me that a serious-minded, sensitive man can be wearied by the very intensity and depth of his impressions. He always returns to his own nature, but what takes him out of it, at least for a while, does him good. It is by raising me above myself, Corinne, that you dispel my natural melancholy; it was by diminishing my real worth that a woman I shall tell you about shortly, dulled my inner sadness. Yet, although I had developed a taste for Parisian life, it would not have satisfied me for long, if I had not acquired the friendship of a man who was a perfect example of the French character in his old-fashioned loyalty, and of the French intellect in his modern culture.

'I shall not tell you the real names of the people I am going to speak about, my dear, and when you hear the rest of the story you will understand why I have to conceal them from you. Count Raimond belonged to the most famous family in France. In his soul was all the chivalrous pride of his ancestors, and his reason embraced the new philosophical ideas when they required him to make personal sacrifices. He had not been actively involved in the Revolution, but he loved the virtues of each party, courage and gratitude in some, the love of liberty in others. Everything that was disinterested pleased him. The cause of all the oppressed seemed to him just, and the generosity of his character was further enhanced by his very great carelessness of his own life. He was not exactly unhappy, but there was such a contrast between his soul and society as it usually is that the daily pain it caused him made him detach himself from his own nature. I was fortunate enough to arouse Count Raimond's interest. He wanted to overcome my natural reserve and to conquer it; he took pains to give our friendship a truly romantic aspect and he brooked no obstacle either to rendering a great service or to giving a small pleasure. He wanted to settle in England for half the year so as not to leave me, and I had great difficulty in preventing him from not sharing with me all he possessed.

' "I have only one sister," he told me, "married to a very rich old man, and I am free to do as I please with my money. Moreover, the Revolution will take a turn for the worse and I might well be killed, so help me to enjoy what I have by looking on it as yours." Alas! Generous Raimond foresaw his destiny only too well. When one is capable of self-knowledge, one is rarely mistaken about one's fate, and very often forebodings are merely self-judgements not yet fully admitted. Noble, sincere, and even imprudent, Raimond revealed his whole soul. For me a character like that was a new pleasure. In my country, the treasures of the soul are not easily revealed and we have acquired the habit of being wary of everything that is made visible. But my friend's exuberant kindness gave me pleasure, both certain and enjoyable, and I had no doubt at all about his virtues, although from the first moment they were all revealed. I did not feel at all shy in my relationship with him and, what was even more important, he put me at ease with myself. Such was the likeable Frenchman for whom I felt the perfect friendship, the brotherly affection of a comrade-at-arms that one is capable of only when young, before knowing the feeling of rivalry, before irrevocably planned careers furrow and divide the field of the future.

'One day Count Raimond said, "My sister is a widow, and I admit that I am not at all sad about that. I did not like her marriage; she had accepted the hand of the old man who has just died, at a time when neither of us had any money, for I inherited mine only recently. Nevertheless, at the time, I had opposed this marriage as much as I could have done. I do not like people to do anything for pecuniary reasons, and still less the most solemn act of their lives. But in fact she behaved admirably towards the husband she did not love; in society's eyes, there was nothing to be said against that. Now she is free, she is coming back to live with me. You will see her. She is very nice when you have known her for a while, and you English like making discoveries. I personally prefer to see the whole character in a face right away. But though your ways, Oswald, have never upset me, I find my sister's a little disturbing."

'The next day Madame d'Arbigny, Count Raimond's sister, arrived, and the same evening I was introduced to her. Her features were like her brother's and she had a similar tone of voice, but the expression in her eyes was more reserved and subtle. Moreover, her face was very pleasing, her figure most graceful, and there was perfect elegance in all her movements. She did not utter an inappropriate word, she was never inconsiderate, yet her courtesy was never overdone. She flattered your vanity very skilfully and showed she liked you without ever compromising herself, for in everything to do with feelings she always expressed herself as if she wanted to conceal from others what was going on in her heart. I was captivated by this apparent resemblance in her manner to that of the women of my own country. It did indeed occur to me that Madame d'Arbigny revealed too often what she claimed to want to conceal, and that chance did not provide so many opportunities for involuntary tender emotion as arose around her, but this thought barely crossed my mind and my feelings in Madame d'Arbigny's company were usually sweet and new.

'I had never before been flattered by anyone. In my country, love and the rapture it arouses are deeply felt, but the art of insinuating yourself into someone's heart by flattery is little known. Besides, I had just left the university, and till then no one in England had paid any attention to me. Madame d'Arbigny picked up every word I said and she paid attention to me unremittingly. I do not think she fully realized my potentialities but she made me aware of myself by a thousand detailed remarks whose shrewdness amazed me. Sometimes I felt her language was a little artificial, that she was speaking too well and too sweetly, and that her sentences were too carefully constructed. But her resemblance to her brother, the most sincere of men, banished these doubts from my mind and contributed to my feeling attracted to her.

'One day I told Count Raimond about the effect this resemblance had on me. He thanked me, but after a moment's thought said, "Yet my sister and I are quite unlike in character." After these words he said no more, but on recalling them as well as many other circumstances, I was convinced, later on, that he did not want me to marry his sister. I cannot doubt that such was her intention even then, although this was not as obvious as it became later on. We spent our lives together, and often pleasantly, always calmly, the days slipped by. Since then, on reflection, I have realized that she usually agreed with me. Whenever I began a sentence, she would finish it or, anticipating what I was going to say, she would be quick to agree with it. Yet despite this perfect amiability of manner, she exercised a despotic control over my actions. I was completely dominated by her way of saying, *Surely that is what you will do, surely you will not take such a step*. It seemed to me that if I did not live up to her expectations, I would lose all her esteem, which she often showed by very flattering remarks.

'Yet, believe me, Corinne, for I thought so even before knowing you, the feeling Madame d'Arbigny aroused in me was not love. I did not tell her I loved her. I did not know if such a daughter-in-law would be acceptable to my father. It never entered his head that I would marry a Frenchwoman and I did not want to do anything without his consent. I think my silence did not please Madame d'Arbigny, for sometimes she showed irritation, which she always put down to sadness and explained by touching motives, although at times, when she was off her guard, she had a very harsh expression. However, I ascribed these moody moments to our relationship, which I too found unsatisfactory, for it is painful to love a little without loving wholeheartedly.

'Neither Count Raimond nor I spoke about his sister. It was the first constraint to exist between us, but several times Madame d'Arbigny had urged me not to talk about her to her brother, and when I expressed surprise at this request, she said, "I do not know if you are like me, but I cannot endure a third person, even my close friend, interfering with my feelings for any one else. I like secrecy about all my affections." I found this explanation adequate and I conformed to her wishes. Then I received a letter from my father, recalling me to Scotland. The six months fixed for my stay in France had elapsed and, as that country's troubles were getting worse than ever, he did not think it fitting for a foreigner to stay there any longer. At first his letter greatly distressed me. Nevertheless I felt how right my father was. I wanted very much to see him, but I liked my life in Paris with Count Raimond and his sister so much that I could not tear myself away from it without bitter grief. I went immediately to Madame d'Arbigny and showed her my letter, and while she was reading it I was so overcome by my grief that I did not even see what impression it made on her. I only heard her say a few words, urging me to delay my departure and to write to my father saying I was ill, in short to "hedge" with regard to his wishes. I remember that was the expression she used. I was going to reply, and I would have said truthfully that I had decided to leave the next day, when Count Raimond came in. Knowing what we were talking about, he declared categorically that I ought to obey my father and there was no reason for hesitation. I was surprised by this quick decision. I expected him to beg me to stay. I wanted to resist my own regrets but I did not think my triumph would be so easy, and for a moment I misinterpreted my friend's feelings. He realized this and took my hand, saying, "In three months I shall be in England, so why should I keep you in France? I have my reasons for doing nothing about that," he added quietly. But his sister heard him and hastened to say that indeed it was prudent to avoid the dangers that an Englishman might run in France in the middle of the Revolution. I am now quite sure that was not what Count Raimond was referring to, but he neither denied nor confirmed his sister's explanation. I was leaving; he did not think it necessary to say anything more about the matter.

' "If I could be useful to my country I would stay," he went on, "but as you see, there is no France any longer. The ideas and feelings that made me love it no longer exist. I shall still miss my country but I shall find my native land again when I breathe the same air as you." How moved I was by the touching expression of such a true friendship! How much stronger at that moment was my affection for Raimond than my feeling for his sister! She quickly noticed this and that very evening I saw her in a new light. Visitors came and she performed her duties as a hostess admirably; she talked about my departure quite naturally and in general gave the impression that for her it was the most ordinary occurrence. I had already noticed on several occasions that she valued reputation so highly that she never let anyone see the feelings which she revealed to me. But this time it was too much and I was so hurt by her indifference that I decided to leave before the rest of the company and not to stay alone with her for a single moment. She saw that I went up to her brother to ask him to say goodbye to me the next morning before I left. Then she came up to me and, in a voice loud enough for everyone to hear her, she said she had a letter to give me for one of her friends in England, but in a low voice she added very quickly, "It is only my brother you are sorry to leave; you talk only to him and you want to break my heart by going away like this!" Then she immediately went back to her circle of friends and sat down. I was upset by her remarks and I was going to remain, as she wanted, when Count Raimond took me by the arm and led me to his room.

'When everyone had gone we heard repeated bell-ringings from Madame d'Arbigny's room. Count Raimond paid no attention to them, but I forced him to be concerned and we sent to enquire what was the matter. The answer came that Madame d'Arbigny was feeling unwell. I was acutely affected. I wanted to see her again, to go back to her once more, but Count Raimond resolutely prevented me from doing so. "Let us dispense with these emotions," he said. "Women always recover better when they are alone." I could not understand this harshness towards his sister, in such strong contrast with my friend's constant kindness, and I left him the next day with a kind of constraint which made our farewells less affectionate. Oh, if I had only realized the great tact which prevented him from agreeing to my being ensnared by his sister when he did not think she would make me happy! If, above all, I had foreseen what events were going to separate us for ever, my farewells would have satisfied both his heart and mine.'

CHAPTER II

FOR some moments Oswald stopped speaking. Corinne, afraid to delay the moment when he would begin to speak again, listened so eagerly that she too was silent. 'I would be happy,' he continued, 'if my relationship with Madame d'Arbigny had then come to an end and if I had not set foot again on French soil! But fate, perhaps that is to say my weak character, has poisoned my life for ever, yes for ever, my love, even when I am with you.

'I spent nearly a year in Scotland at my father's side and our affection became closer every day. I made my way into the sanctuary of that heavenly soul, and in the friendship uniting me to him I found those affinities of the blood whose mysterious bonds stem from our innermost being. I received very affectionate letters from Raimond. He told me of his difficulties in taking his money out of the country in order to join me, but he was still persevering in his plan. I was still very fond of him, but what friend could I compare to my father? My respect for him did not prevent me from confiding in him. I had faith in my father's words as in an oracle, and the indecisiveness which, unfortunately, is in my character always ended as soon as he had spoken. *Heaven has formed us to love what is worthy of veneration*, an English writer said. My father did not know, he could not know, how much I loved him, and my disastrous behaviour must have made him dubious.

'Yet he took pity on me. As he lay dying he pitied the grief I would feel at losing him. Oh, Corinne! As I go on with my sad tale, keep up my courage; I need it.' 'My love,' said Corinne, 'take some comfort from revealing so noble and sensitive a soul to the person who most in the world admires and cherishes you.'

'He sent me to London on business,' continued Lord Nelvil, 'and without a single tremor warning me of my misfortune, I left him never to see him again. In our last conversations he was more lovable than ever. It is as if righteous souls, like flowers, give off more scent towards the evening. He kissed me with tears in his eyes. He would often tell me that at his age everything was solemn, but I believed in his life as in my own. Our souls understood each other so well; he was so young in his capacity for love that I did not think of him as old. Trust, like fear, is inexplicable in strong affections. This time my father accompanied me to the door of his house, the house which I have seen abandoned and ravaged like my sad heart.

'I had been in London barely a week when I received Madame d'Arbigny's fatal letter, every word of which I have remembered. "Yesterday, the tenth of August," she said, "my brother was slaughtered at the Tuileries defending his King. As his sister, I am outlawed and forced to hide to escape my persecutors. Count Raimond had taken all my fortune as well as his own to send it to England. Have you received it yet? Or do you know to whom he entrusted it to hand over to you? I have only a line from him written from the palace itself just as the attack was about to begin, and all it says is to apply to you to learn everything. If you can come here to take me away, perhaps you would save my life, for the English can still travel freely in France, but I myself cannot get a passport; my brother's name makes me suspect. If Raimond's unhappy sister interests you enough for you to come and fetch her, you can learn of my hiding-place in Paris from my relative, M. de Maltigues. But if, in your generosity, you intend to help me, do not lose a moment in doing so, for they say war between our two countries may break out any day."

'Imagine the effect this letter had on me. My friend slaughtered, his sister in despair, and, according to her, their fortune in my hands, although I had heard absolutely nothing about that. Add to these circumstances the danger Madame d'Arbigny was in, and her idea that I could be of use to her by going to fetch her. I did not think it possible to hesitate, and I set off immediately, sending my father a messenger, who took him the letter I had just received and my promise that I would be back in a fortnight. By a really cruel chance, the man I sent fell ill on the way, and a second letter, which I wrote to my father from Dover, reached him before the first. So he learned of my departure before knowing its purpose, and when the explanation arrived he had conceived an anxiety about the matter which was never dispelled.

'I reached Paris in three days. I learned there that Madame d'Arbigny had taken refuge in a provincial town sixty miles away, and I continued on my way to join her. On seeing each other again we both felt deeply moved. In her misfortune she was much more likeable than before, because her manners were much less constrained and artificial. We shed tears together for her noble brother and the public disasters! I inquired anxiously about her fortune. She told me she had heard nothing about it, but a few days later I learned that the banker to whom Count Raimond had entrusted it had returned it to her. But what was odd was that I heard this, in the town where we were, from a businessman who told me so by chance and assured me that Madame d'Arbigny must never really have been worried about it. I could not understand this at all, so, to ask Madame d'Arbigny what it all meant, I went to her house. There I found one of her relatives, M. de Maltigues, who, calmly and with remarkable alacrity, told me he had just arrived from Paris to bring Madame d'Arbigny the news of the return of the banker, who, she thought, had gone to England, and whom she had not heard of for a month. Madame d'Arbigny confirmed what he said and I believed her, remembering, however, that she always found pretexts for not showing me the note she claimed her brother had sent her and which she had mentioned in her letter. I learned later that she had tricked me into being concerned about her fortune.

'It was true, at least, that she was rich and that she had no mercenary motive in wanting to marry me. But Madame d'Arbigny's great failing was to undertake something for emotional reasons, using wiles where love would have been enough, and dissembling all the time when she would have done better simply to show what she felt. For at that time she loved me as much as one can love when one plans one's actions, almost one's thoughts, and conducts affairs of the heart as if they were political intrigues.

'Madame d'Arbigny's sadness added additional charm to her appearance and gave her a touching expression which I very much liked. I had told her firmly that I would not marry without my father's consent but I could not help expressing the rapture her alluring appearance aroused in me. But as it was in her plans to ensnare me at any price, I thought I could detect that she was not unalterably resolved to repel my desires, and now that I recall what happened between us, it seemed to me that she hesitated for reasons that had nothing to do with love and that her apparent struggles were inner debates. I was alone with her all day and, in spite of the resolutions which I felt propriety demanded, I could not resist being swept away, and Madame d'Arbigny imposed all duties on me in granting all rights. She showed more grief and remorse than perhaps she really felt, binding me closely to her lot by her very repentance. I wanted to take her with me to England to make my father acquainted with her and to urge him to agree to my marriage with her. But she refused to leave France unless I was her husband. She may have been right about that, but as I always knew I could not decide to marry her without my father's consent, she adopted the wrong means both not to leave and to retain me in spite of the duties which were recalling me to England.

'When war was declared* between our two countries, I wanted even more keenly to leave France, and the obstacles that Madame d'Arbigny raised against my departure multiplied. Sometimes she could not obtain a passport, sometimes she asserted that if I wanted to leave alone, her remaining in France after I had gone would compromise her because she would be suspected of corresponding with me. This gentle, reasonable woman occasionally gave way to fits of despair, which entirely shattered my soul. She used her attractive looks and charming mind to please me and her grief to intimidate me.

'Women are perhaps wrong to dominate by means of tears and thus enslave strength to their weakness. But when they are not afraid to use this means, they nearly always succeed, at least for a time. Feeling is no doubt weakened by the very rule that is usurped over it, and the power of tears, if it is used too often, cools the imagination. But in France at that time there were a thousand opportunities for reviving interest and pity. Madame d'Arbigny's health, too, seemed to be more delicate every day, and for women illness is yet another means of domination. Those who, unlike you, Corinne, have not a justified confidence in their minds and hearts, or those who are not, like our Englishwomen, so proud and so shy that pretence is impossible for them, have recourse to artfulness to arouse affection. And then the best you can expect of them is that a genuine feeling is the cause of their deceit.

'Unknown to me, a third person was involved in my relationship with Madame d'Arbigny. That was M. de Maltigues. He was attracted to her; he wanted nothing better than to marry her. But a studied immorality made him indifferent to everything. He liked intrigue as a game even when its objective did not interest him, and he supported Madame d'Arbigny in her wish to marry me, ready to thwart this plan if the opportunity to further his own presented itself. He was a man for whom I had a peculiar aversion. At the age of barely thirty, his manners and appearance were unusually distant. In England, where we are accused of being cold, I have seen nothing comparable to his solemn demeanour when he entered a room. I would never have taken him for a Frenchman if he had not had a taste for cracking jokes and a need to speak that was strange in a man who seemed blasé about everything and deliberately made use of that characteristic. He claimed he was born very sensitive and very enthusiastic, but that what he had learned of men during the French Revolution had disabused him of all that. He said he had realized that the only good in this world is money or power, or both, and that usually friendships had to be considered as means to be used or discarded according to circumstances. He was quite clever in putting this opinion into practice. His only mistake was to talk about it. But though, unlike the French of the past, he had no desire to please, he retained the need to impress by his conversation, and that made him very imprudent. In that he was very different from Madame d'Arbigny, who, while wanting to achieve her aim, unlike M. de Maltigues never gave herself away in trying to shine by immorality itself. What was strange about these two people was that the more lively one hid her secret well and the cold man could not keep quiet.

'This M. de Maltigues, such as he was, had a strange ascendancy over Madame d'Arbigny. He read her thoughts or else she confided everything to him. Perhaps, from time to time, this usually deceitful woman needed to be imprudent as if to breathe. It is certain, at least, that whenever M. de Maltigues looked at her severely, she would always tremble. If he looked displeased, she would get up to take him aside. If he went away annoyed, she would nearly always shut herself up in her room immediately to write to him. I ascribed M. de Maltigues's power over Madame d'Arbigny to his having known her since childhood and having managed her affairs ever since he had been her nearest relative. But her main motive for this strange consideration was her plan, which I learned only too late, to marry him if I left her, for on no account did she want to be considered an abandoned woman. Such a reason ought to make you think she did not love me, and yet her feelings were her only reason for preferring me. But all her life she had combined selfish motives with strong feelings, and artificial social pretensions with natural affections. She would weep because she was moved, but also because that is the way to arouse sympathy. She was happy to be loved, because she was in love, but also because that gives one an honourable position in society. She had good feelings when she was all alone, but they gave her no pleasure unless they were favourable to her self-esteem or her wishes. She was someone moulded by and for high society and she had the art of improving on the genuine, which is often encountered in countries where the desire to make an impact through one's feelings is more keen than the feelings themselves.

'For a long time I had had no news of my father because the war had interrupted our correspondence. At last, by a chance opportunity, a letter reached me. In the name of my duty and of his affection he begged me to leave. At the same time he stated quite categorically that if I married Madame d'Arbigny I would cause him mortal grief and he asked me at least to return to England a free man and not to make up my mind till I had heard him. I replied immediately, giving my word of honour that I would not marry without his consent and assuring him that I would soon return to him. Madame d'Arbigny used entreaties, then despair, to retain me, but at last, seeing that she was not succeeding, I think she resorted to cunning. But, at that time, how could I have suspected that?

'One morning she arrived pale and dishevelled at my lodgings, and fell into my arms, begging me to protect her. She seemed to be dying of fright. Through her expressions of terror, I could barely make out that the order had come for her arrest as the sister of Count Raimond

and that I had to find her a refuge where she could hide from her
pursuers. Even at this period, women had perished and all fears seemed
justified. I took her to the home of a businessman who was devoted
to me. I hid her there, I thought I had saved her life, and only M.
de Maltigues and I knew the secret of her hiding-place. How could
I not be keenly concerned in the fate of a woman in this situation?
How could I leave a proscribed person? At which hour of which day
can one say, "You counted on my support and I am withdrawing it
from you"? Yet I was continually haunted by the memory of my father
and on several occasions I tried to obtain Madame d'Arbigny's permission to depart alone. But she threatened to give herself up to her
would-be murderers if I left her, and twice she went out in broad daylight in a terrible state which filled me with grief and fear. I followed
her into the street, begging her in vain to come back. Fortunately,
whether by chance or design, on each occasion we met M. de Maltigues
and he brought her back, making her realize the imprudence of her
behaviour. I then resigned myself to remaining and wrote to my father
justifying my behaviour as best as I could. But I was ashamed of being
in France in the middle of the terrible events that were taking place
and when my country was at war with the French.

'M. de Maltigues often made fun of my scruples. But, intelligent
as he was, he did not foresee or did not take the trouble to notice the
effect of his jokes, for they aroused in me all the feelings he wished
to kill. Madame d'Arbigny certainly noticed the impression made on
me, but she had no control over M. de Maltigues, who often decided
capriciously when his self-interest was not involved. To arouse my
affection she had recourse to her genuine, excessive grief. She made
use of her poor health as much to attract as to move me, for she was
never more attractive than when she was fainting at my feet. She knew
how to enhance her beauty like all the rest of her pleasing qualities,
and her charming appearance itself was cleverly combined with her
emotions to captivate.

'So I lived in perpetual anxiety and uncertainty, trembling whenever I received a letter from my father, but even more unhappy
when I did not. I was retained in France by the attraction I felt for
Madame d'Arbigny, and above all by the fear of her despair, for she
was an odd mixture, usually a very gentle person in normal life, very
even-tempered, often even very lively, but when she made a scene
she was very violent. She wanted to bind me to her through happiness

and fear, and so she always transformed her natural gifts into means to an end. One day, in September 1793, when I had already been in France for more than a year, I received a letter of few words from my father, but these words were so melancholy and grieving, Corinne, that you must spare me the pain of repeating them to you; they would hurt me too much. My father was already ill, but he did not tell me; his tact and pride prevented him. His letter expressed so much grief, however, both at my absence and at the possibility of my marriage to Madame d'Arbigny, that I still cannot conceive how, when I read it, I did not foresee the misfortune threatening me. Nevertheless I was sufficiently moved to hesitate no longer and I went to Madame d'Arbigny's retreat, completely decided to take leave of her. She was soon aware that my mind was made up and, after some thought, she suddenly got up, saying, "Before you go, you must know a secret that I was ashamed to confess to you. If you desert me, you will be not only the cause of my death, but the fruit of my shame and of my guilty love will perish in my womb together with me." Nothing can express my emotion; this new and sacred duty gripped my whole soul and I was subservient to Madame d'Arbigny like the most devoted slave.

'I would have married her, as she wished, had there not been at that time very great obstacles to an Englishman getting married in France, as he had to declare his name to the civil authorities. So I put off our marriage till the time when we would be able to go to England together, and I resolved not to leave Madame d'Arbigny till then. At first she calmed down when she no longer feared the danger of my departure, but soon she began to complain again and to appear now wounded and now unhappy that I did not overcome all difficulties in marrying her. I would have ended up by giving in to her wishes. I had fallen into a very deep melancholy; I spent whole days in my room without being able to go out; I was prey to an idea that I never admitted to myself and that continually tormented me. I had a presentiment of my father's illness, but I did not want to believe my presentiment, which I took for a weakness. In a strange way, a result of the fear Madame d'Arbigny's grief aroused in me, I fought against my duty as if it were a passion, and what could have been thought of as a passion tormented me like a duty. Madame d'Arbigny wrote to me continually, urging me to visit her. I went, but when I saw her I did not speak to her about her condition because I did not want to recall what gave her rights over me. It seems to me now that she too spoke less about it than she ought to have done, but at that time I was suffering too much to notice anything.

'I had stayed at home for three days, devoured by remorse, writing twenty letters to my father and tearing them all up, when at last, one day, M. de Maltigues came in. He rarely came to see me because we did not like each other, but he had been deputed by Madame d'Arbigny to tear me away from my solitude; as you will see, however, he was not much interested in the success of his errand. As he came in, he noticed my tear-stained face before I had time to hide it. "What is the use of all this pain, my dear man?" he said. "Leave my cousin or marry her. Both courses of action are equally good, since they put an end to the matter." "There are situations in life in which, even though one makes a sacrifice, one still does not know how to fulfil all one's duties," I replied. "The fact is that you do not need to make a sacrifice," answered M. de Maltigues. "For my part, I do not know of any situation in which that is necessary. With ability one can extricate oneself from anything. Skill is the queen of the world." "It is not skill I envy," I said, "but I repeat, that in resigning myself to unhappiness, I would at least not want to cause pain to someone I love." "Believe me," said M. de Maltigues. "Do not mix up feelings with the difficult work called living; that makes it even more complicated. They are a sickness of the soul. I have an attack sometimes, just like anyone else, but when I have one, I tell myself that it will pass and I always keep my word to myself." "But," I replied, trying like him to speak in general terms, for I neither could nor would confide in him, "even if I could set feelings aside, honour and virtue would still remain, and they are often opposed to our desires of all kinds." "Honour," said M. de Maltigues, "by honour, do you mean fighting when you are insulted? In that respect, there is no doubt. But in every other connection, what interest would you have in letting yourself be shackled by a thousand futile scruples?" "What interest?" I interrupted. "It seems to me that is not the right word." "Speaking seriously," continued M. de Maltigues, "there are few words with such a clear meaning. I know very well that in former times people used to say: *An honourable misfortune, a glorious defeat*. But nowadays when everyone is persecuted, rogues as well as those commonly called good people, the only difference in this world is between the birds caught in the net and those which have escaped." "I think there is another difference," I replied, "prosperity despised and reverses honoured by the respect of good men." "Find them for me then," answered M. de Maltigues, "these good men who console you for your sorrows by their courageous esteem. On the contrary, it seems to me that most so-called virtuous people make excuses for you if you are happy and love you if you are powerful. It is no doubt very fine on your part to feel unable to act against the wishes of a father, who by now ought no longer to be interfering in your affairs, but in any case that is no reason for wasting your life here. As for me, whatever happens to me, I want at all costs to spare my friends the pain of seeing me suffer, and myself the sight of long, consoling faces." I interrupted sharply, saying, "I thought the aim of a good man's life was not happiness, which is of use only to himself, but virtue, which is of use to others." "Virtue, virtue . . ." said M. de Maltigues, hesitating a little, then finally making up his mind, "that is the common people's language, which the augurs* cannot speak among themselves without laughing. There are good souls who are still moved by certain sounds and certain harmonious words; it is for them that we have the instrument played. But all that poetry called conscience, devotion, enthusiasm, was invented to console those who were not able to succeed in the world; it is like the *de profundis* which is sung for the dead. The living, when they prosper, are not at all concerned to receive that kind of homage."

'I was so annoyed by these words that I could not stop myself saying haughtily, "If I had any rights over Madame d'Arbigny's household, Monsieur, I should be angry if she received a man who allowed himself to think and talk in such a way." "In that matter, you can decide what you like when the time comes, but if my cousin takes my advice, she will not marry a man who seems so unhappy at the possibility of being her husband. As she can tell you, I have for a long time been reproaching her for her weakness and for all the means she uses to achieve an aim which is not worth the trouble." At these words, made even more insulting by their tone, I made a sign to M. de Maltigues to go out with me, and I must say that, on the way, he continued to develop his system with the greatest coolness in the world and, though he might die in a few moments, he said not a pious or sensitive word. "If I had listened to all the foolish remarks made by you young men," he said, "do you not think that what is happening in my country would have cured me? When have you seen any point in being scrupulous like you?" "I agree with you," I said, "that, at present in your country, it is a little less use than elsewhere, but in time, or beyond time, everything has its reward." "Yes," replied M. de Maltigues, "in bringing heaven into your calculations." "And why not?" I asked him. "Perhaps one of us may know what the situation is." "If it is I who am to die," he went on with a laugh, "I am quite sure that I shall know nothing about it, and if it is you, you will not come back to enlighten me." On the way I thought that if I were killed by M. de Maltigues, I had taken no precautionary measures to let my father know my fate, or to give Madame d'Arbigny a share of my fortune, to which I thought she had rights. As I was making these reflections, we passed by M. de Maltigues's house and I asked his permission to go in and write two letters, and when we continued on our way out of the town, I gave them to him, speaking of Madame d'Arbigny with great concern and commending her to his protection as a reliable friend. He was touched by this proof of trust, for it must be said to the glory of virtue, that the men who profess immorality most openly are very flattered if, by chance, they are given a token of esteem. Our situation, too, was serious enough for M. de Maltigues perhaps to be moved by it, but as he would not want that to be noticed for anything in the world, he said jokingly what I think was inspired by a more serious feeling.

'"You are a decent fellow, my dear Nelvil, so I want to do something generous for you. They say that brings happiness and, indeed, generosity is such a childish virtue that it must be rewarded in heaven rather than on earth. But before I do anything for you, our conditions must be settled. Whatever I say to you, we shall fight anyway." I agreed very contemptuously with these remarks for I found the precautionary speech oratorical, or at least useless. M. de Maltigues continued dryly and off-handedly. "Madame d'Arbigny does not suit you; your characters have nothing in common. Besides, your father would be extremely upset if you contracted this marriage and you would be extremely upset at distressing him. So, if I live, it is better for me to marry Madame d'Arbigny and, if you kill me, it would still be better for her to marry someone else; for my cousin is a very sensible lady who, even when she is in love, always takes sensible precautions against the eventuality that she will be loved no longer. You will learn all that from her letters. I leave them to you and you will find them in my writing-desk. Here is the key. I have been close to my cousin ever since she was born and you know that, although she is very secretive, she does not hide any of her secrets from me. She thinks I say only what I want to. It is true that I am not carried away by anything, but in addition I do not attach much importance to anything and think that we men owe it to ourselves not to keep silent where women are concerned. So if I die it is for the sake of Madame d'Arbigny's pretty face, and though I am ready to die for her with good grace, I am not very grateful to her for the situation she has put me in by her double intrigue. Besides," he added, "it is not definite that you will kill me." And since we were outside the town, he drew his sword, prepared to fight.

'He had spoken with unusual animation, and I was left dumbfounded by what he had told me. Without upsetting him, the approach of danger nevertheless made him more animated and I could not make out if he was revealing the truth or making up a lie to avenge himself. Nevertheless, in this uncertainty, I was very sparing of his life. He was less skilful than I in bodily exercises and I could have plunged my sword into his heart ten times; but I contented myself with wounding him in the arm and disarming him. He appeared appreciative of my behaviour, and as I took him home I reminded him of our conversation immediately before our duel. Then he said, "I am annoyed that I betrayed my cousin's confidence. Danger is like wine; it goes to the head. But anyway, I am not altogether sorry, for you would not have been entirely happy with Madame d'Arbigny; she is too much of a schemer for you. Yet I don't mind, for although I think she is charming and I like her wit very much, she will not make me do anything to my own disadvantage. We shall be of great help to each other in everything, because marriage will make our interests mutual. But you, who are a romantic, would have been deceived by her. As you had it in your power to kill me, I owe you my life, so I cannot refuse to show you the letters I had promised you after my death. Read them, leave for England, and do not be too worried about Madame d'Arbigny's grief. She will weep because she loves you. But she will console herself because she is a woman reasonable enough not to want to be unhappy and, above all, not to appear to be so. In three months' time she will be Madame de Maltigues." Everything he told me was true; the letters he showed me proved it. I was convinced that Madame d'Arbigny was not in the condition she had blushingly pretended to confess in order to make me marry her, and that in this respect she had shamefully deceived me. She was undoubtedly in love with me since she said so and told M. de Maltigues himself in her letters. She flattered him skilfully, however, giving him great hope and, to attract him, revealed a very different character from the one she had always shown me. Consequently I could not doubt that she was being considerate to him with the intention of marrying him if our marriage did not take place. Such, Corinne, was the woman who has for ever cost me the peace of my heart and conscience!

'Before I left, I wrote to her, and I never saw her again. Since then I learned that she had married M. de Maltigues, as he had predicted. But I was far from expecting then the misfortune awaiting me. I thought I would obtain my father's forgiveness. I was sure that when I told him how badly I had been deceived, he would love me more because he would know I was more to be pitied. After nearly a month's journey, travelling day and night through Germany, I reached England, with complete confidence in my father's inexhaustible kindness. Corinne, as I disembarked, I saw an item in a newspaper saying my father was no more! Twenty months have passed since that moment, but it is always before my eyes like a ghost pursuing me. The letters forming the words *Lord Nelvil has just died*, those letters were blazing; the fire of the volcano there in front of us is less terrifying than they were. And that is not everything. I learned he had died deeply distressed by my stay in France, afraid that I was giving up my military career, would marry a woman of whom he had no very good opinion, and, settling in a country at war with my own, would lose entirely my reputation in England. Who knows if these painful thoughts did not shorten his life? Corinne, Corinne, am I not a murderer, am I not, tell me?' 'No,' she exclaimed. 'No, you are only unfortunate. It is goodness, it is generosity, which have carried you away. I respect you as much as I love you. Judge yourself by my heart. Take it for your conscience. You are distraught with grief. Believe one who loves you dearly. Oh, love, as I feel it, is by no means an illusion. I admire and worship you because you are the best and most sensitive of men.' 'Corinne,' said Oswald, 'I do not deserve this homage. But perhaps I am not so guilty. Before dying my father forgave me. In one of his last writings addressed to me, I found gentle words. A letter of mine, justifying me a little, had reached him. But the harm was done, and the grief caused by me had broken his heart.

'When I returned to his house, and his old servants surrounded me, I brushed aside their condolences. I accused myself in front of them and, as if I still had time to make up for what I had done, I prostrated myself on his grave, swearing I would never marry without my father's consent. Alas! What was I promising him, who was no more? What then was the meaning of my delirious words? I ought to think of them, at least, as a pledge to do nothing of which he would have disapproved in his lifetime. Corinne, my dear, why do these words worry you? My father could ask me to give up a deceitful woman, whose skill alone was responsible for the inclination she aroused in me, but the most sincere, spontaneous, and generous person, the one for whom I first felt love, the kind of love which purifies the soul rather than leads it astray, why would heavenly beings want to separate me from her?

'When I went into my father's room, I saw his coat, armchair, and sword, which were still there as they used to be. Still there! But his seat was vacant and my cries called him in vain. This manuscript, this collection of his thoughts, is all that answers me. You know a few parts of it already,' said Oswald, giving it to Corinne. 'I always carry it with me. Read what he wrote about children's duties to their parents. Read it, Corinne. Your sweet voice will perhaps help me to remember his words.' Corinne obeyed Oswald's behest and read the following.

'Oh! How little it takes to make a father or mother, advanced in years, diffident about themselves; they readily think they are in the way on earth. What use do they think they are to you, who no longer ask their advice? You live completely in the present. You are confined within it by a dominant passion, and everything unconnected to this moment seems to you old and out of date. In short, you are so much involved with your own person, both in heart and mind, that you think you make a historic moment on your own. You are thus unaware of the eternal resemblance between times and men, and the authority of experience seems a fiction to you or a meaningless guarantee intended only for the benefit of old men and the final enjoyment of their self-respect. What an error is yours! The world, this vast theatre, does not change actors. It is always man who comes on stage. But man does not renew himself. He becomes different, yet all his forms depend on a few principal passions, all of which have been explored for a long time. So it is rarely that, in the little arrangements of private life, experience, the knowledge of the past, does not provide very useful lessons.

'So honour to fathers and mothers, honour to them, honour and respect, if only for their past reign, for the time of which they alone were masters and which will never return, if only for the sake of those years lost for ever, but whose majestic imprint they wear on their brows.

'There is your duty, presumptuous children, who seem impatient to travel alone along the road of life. They will go away, those parents who are so long in making way for you, you cannot doubt that. That father who still speaks in a slightly severe tone which hurts you, that mother whose old age imposes cares on you which you find a nuisance, they will depart. Those attentive supervisors of your childhood, those lively protectors of your youth, they will depart. They will depart and you will look in vain for better friends. They will depart, and as soon as they are no more they will appear before you in a new guise, for time, which ages people we see before us, rejuvenates them for us when death has made them disappear. Time then endows them with an unfamiliar brilliance. We see them in the picture of eternity, where age no longer exists as progression no longer takes place. If they have left a memory of their virtues on earth, in our imaginations we would adorn them with a heavenly ray, we would follow them with our eyes to the sojourn of the elect, we would behold them in those happy, glorious dwellings. And near the bright colours with which we would depict their saintly halo, we would be wiped out in the very midst of our heyday, in the very midst of the triumphs which most dazzle us.'[26]

'Corinne,' cried Lord Nelvil in heart-rending grief, 'do you think it was against me he wrote these eloquent complaints?' 'No, no,' replied Corinne. 'You know he loved you dearly, he believed in your affection, and I have it from you yourself that these reflections were written a long time before you had done the wrong for which you reproach yourself.' Corinne looked over the collection of thoughts she still had in her hand and continued, 'Listen rather to these reflections on indulgence, which are written a few pages further on.

' "We go stumbling through life, surrounded by snares; our senses let us be seduced by deceptive lures; our imagination leads us astray with false gleams of light, and our reason itself receives every day from experience the degree of illumination it lacked and the confidence it needed. So many dangers allied to such great weakness, so many diverse interests with limited foresight, such slight ability, in sum so many unknowns and so short a life, all these circumstances, all these aspects of our nature, are they not an indication of the high place we ought to accord to indulgence in the order of social virtues? . . . Alas, where is the man with no weaknesses? Where is the man who has nothing with which to reproach himself? Where is the man who can look back on his life without a single feeling of remorse or knowing any regret? He alone who has never examined himself, who has never dwelt in the solitude of his conscience, is a stranger to the perturbations of a timorous soul."[27]

'These are the words your father speaks to you from high heaven,' continued Corinne. 'These are the ones for you.' 'That is true,' said Oswald. 'Yes, you are the consoling angel; you do me good. But if I had been able to see him for a moment before he died, if he had learned from me that I was not unworthy of him, if he had told me he believed it, I would not be troubled by remorse as the most criminal of men. I would not be behaving in this indecisive way, a troubled soul who cannot promise to give happiness to anyone. Do not accuse me of weakness, for courage is powerless against conscience. Conscience is the source of courage, so how can it triumph against it? Even now, in the advancing darkness, I think I see in these clouds the shafts of lightning threatening me. Corinne! Corinne! Reassure your unhappy friend or leave me lying on this ground, which will perhaps open up at my cries and let me enter into the abode of the dead.'

BOOK XIII
VESUVIUS AND THE NAPLES COUNTRYSIDE

CHAPTER I

LORD NELVIL remained exhausted for a long time after the cruel account which had deeply shaken his whole soul. Corinne tried gently to bring him back to himself. The river of fire which was flowing down from Vesuvius, made visible at last by the night, had a keen effect on Oswald's troubled imagination. Corinne took advantage of this impression to snatch him away from his distressing memories and hurried to take him with her along the blazing lava's shore of ashes.

The ground they crossed before reaching it gave way beneath their feet and seemed to push them back from a territory inimical to all living things. In this place nature has no longer any relationship with man. He can no longer believe himself to be the dominating power; nature escapes from her tyrant by dying. The torrent is a funereal colour; when it burns the vines or the trees, however, you can see a clear bright flame coming from it. But the lava itself is dark, like the picture of hell in one's imagination. It flows slowly like black sand by day and red by night. When it comes near you can hear a little noise of sparks, all the more frightening because it is slight, and cunning seems to combine with strength. Thus the royal tiger arrives secretly with measured tread. The lava advances, without hurrying but without losing a moment. If it encounters a high wall, or any kind of building that stands in its path, it stops, piles up its black, bituminous torrents in front of the obstacle, and finally buries it beneath its burning waves. Its progress is not so swift that people cannot flee before it, but, like time, it overtakes the unwary and the old, who, seeing its lumbering, silent approach, imagine they can escape from it easily. Its glare is so fiery that for the first time the earth is reflected in the sky, giving it the appearance of continual lightning; in turn the sky is repeated in the sea and nature is set ablaze by this triple image of fire.

The wind can be heard and is made visible by the whirlwinds of flame in the chasm from which the lava comes. We are afraid of what is happening in the heart of the earth and we feel that strange furious forces make it tremble beneath our steps. The rocks surrounding the source of the lava are covered with sulphur and bitumen, whose colours have an infernal quality. A livid green, a brownish yellow, a dark red, make as it were a discord for the eyes and a torture to one's sight, as one's hearing would be rent by the piercing sounds of witches when at night they call to the moon from the earth.

Everything surrounding the volcano reminds one of hell, and the poets' descriptions are no doubt borrowed from these places. It is there that one can understand how men have believed in the existence of an evil genius which contradicted the intentions of Providence. In gazing at such a place, people must have wondered whether benevolence alone presided over the phenomena of creation or whether some hidden principle forced nature, like man, into ferocity. 'Corinne,' cried Lord Nelvil, 'does pain stem from these infernal shores? Does the angel of death take off on its flight from this summit? If I did not see your heavenly look, I would lose here even the memory of the divine works that adorn the world, and yet this sight of hell, frightful as it is, frightens me less than the heart's remorse. All dangers can be faced, but how can a person who is no more deliver us from our self-reproach for the wrongs we have done him? Never! Never! Oh, Corinne, what a word of iron and fire! Tortures invented by dreams of suffering, the endlessly turning wheel, the water which recedes as soon as one tries to come near it, the stones which fall down again as one lifts them, are only weak images to express that terrible thought, the impossible and the irreparable.'

A profound silence reigned around Oswald and Corinne. Even their guides had withdrawn to a distance, and as, near the crater, there is neither animal nor insect nor plant, nothing could be heard but the hissing of the restless flame. Nevertheless, one sound from the town reached this spot. It was the tolling of the bells which could be heard ringing out through the air. Perhaps they were signalling a death, perhaps they were announcing a birth. No matter, they aroused a gentle emotion in the travellers. 'Dear Oswald,' said Corinne, 'let us leave this desert, let us go down again towards the living; my soul is uneasy here. By drawing us near to heaven, all other mountains seem to raise us above earthly life, but here I feel only anxiety and fear. I seem to

see nature treated like a criminal and, like a depraved being, condemned
to feel no more its Creator's benevolent breath. This is certainly not
the abode of the righteous. Let us go.'

Heavy rain was falling as Corinne and Lord Nelvil went down again
to the plain. Every minute, their torches almost went out. Lazzaroni
accompanied them, uttering continual cries which might terrify anyone who did not know that this was their usual behaviour. But these
men are sometimes aroused by an excessive vitality and they do not
know what to do with it, because they combine to the same degree
laziness and violence. Their expressions, more pronounced than their
characters, seem to indicate a kind of vitality in which the mind and
the heart play no part. Oswald, worried in case the rain would be
harmful to Corinne, and the light would fail them, in short that she
would be exposed to some danger, was concerned only for her, and
this affectionate concern gradually made his soul recover from the state
he had been put into by what he had confided to her. They found
their carriage again at the foot of the mountain. They did not stop at
the ruins of Herculaneum, which has, as it were, been buried again
so as not to destroy the town of Portici which is built on that ancient
town. They reached Naples about midnight and, as she left him,
Corinne promised Lord Nelvil to hand him the story of her life the
next day.

CHAPTER II

INDEED, the next morning Corinne decided to make the effort she
had promised, but although the knowledge she had gained of Oswald's
character made her doubly anxious, she left her room, carrying what
she had written, trembling but nevertheless determined to give it to
him. She entered the public room of the inn where they were both
staying. Oswald was there and had just received letters from England. One of these letters was on the mantelpiece and Corinne was
so struck by the handwriting that, extremely troubled, she asked who
had sent it. 'It is from Lady Edgermond,' replied Oswald. 'Are you
in correspondence with her?' interrupted Corinne. 'Lord Edgermond was my father's friend,' answered Oswald, 'and since chance
has made me speak to you about her, I shall not conceal from you
that my father had thought it would be appropriate for me to marry

his friend's daughter, Lucile Edgermond, one day.' 'Oh, my God!' cried Corinne and, almost fainting, she fell onto a chair.

'What is the cause of this painful emotion?' asked Lord Nelvil. 'What can you fear from me, who idolize you? If, as he died, my father had asked me to marry Lucile, I would, no doubt, not think myself free and I would have kept away from your irresistible charm, but he only advised me to marry her. He wrote to me himself, that he could not have an opinion about Lucile since she was only a child. I myself have seen her only once, when she was barely twelve years old. I made no commitment to her mother before I left. My indecisive, anxious behaviour that you may have noticed was a result only of this desire of my father. Before I knew you I wanted to be able to fulfil it, fleeting as it was, as a kind of expiation to him, as a way of prolonging after his death the sovereignty of his will over my resolutions. But you have overcome this feeling, you have overcome my whole being, and I need only to be forgiven what must have seemed to you weakness and indecision. Corinne, one never recovers completely from the kind of grief I experienced. It withers hope and arouses a painful, sorrowful feeling of timidity. Fate has treated me so badly that even when it offers the greatest good, I still do not trust it. But, my dear, these anxieties have gone; I am yours for ever, yours. I tell myself that if my father had known you he would have chosen you for my life's companion, it is you . . .' 'Stop,' cried Corinne, bursting into tears, 'don't speak to me like this, I beg you.'

'Why would you object to the pleasure I find in uniting you in my thoughts with my father's memory, in this mingling in my heart all that is dear and sacred to me?' asked Lord Nelvil. 'You cannot,' interrupted Corinne. 'Oswald, I know only too well that you cannot.' 'Good heavens,' replied Lord Nelvil. 'What have you to tell me? Give me the manuscript which is to contain the story of your life, give it me.' 'You shall have it,' answered Corinne. 'But I beg you for eight days' grace, only eight days; what I have heard this morning obliges me to put in a few more details.' 'How is that?' asked Oswald. 'What connection have you? . . .' 'Do not insist on my replying to you,' interrupted Corinne. 'You will soon know everything, and perhaps that will be the end, the terrible end of my happiness. But before that moment comes, I want us to see together the smiling countryside round Naples with feelings still serene, with hearts still receptive to the charms of its natural beauty. I want to sanctify the most solemn period of my life in some way in this beautiful region. You must retain a last memory of me as I was, as I would have been always, if my heart had protected itself from loving you.' 'Oh, Corinne,' said Oswald, 'what do you want to tell me with these distressing words? It is impossible for you to tell me anything that might cool my affection and my admiration. So why prolong for another week this anxiety, this mystery, which seems to raise a barrier between us?' 'Dear Oswald, that is what I want,' replied Corinne. 'Forgive me my last act of power. Soon you alone will decide for both of us. I shall await my fate from your mouth without complaint, if it is cruel, for I have no feelings or ties on earth which condemn me to survive your love.' With these final words she went out; Oswald wanted to follow her but she pushed him away gently with her hand.

CHAPTER III

CORINNE had decided to give a party for Lord Nelvil in the course of the eight days' delay she had requested, but the idea of a party was for her combined with the most melancholy thoughts. As she studied Oswald's character, she could not but be anxious about the impression he would receive from what she had to say to him. Corinne had to be judged as a poet, as an artist, if she were to be forgiven the sacrifice of her rank, of her family, of her country, of her name, to enthusiasm for talent and the arts. Doubtless Lord Nelvil had all the intellect required to admire imagination and genius, but he thought that the relationships of social life ought to be more important than anything, and that the priority for women and even for men was not the exercise of the faculties of the mind but the performance of each person's particular duties. The cruel remorse he had experienced for having strayed from the path he had worked out for himself had strengthened even further his innately strict moral principles. English ways, the customs and opinions of a country where the most scrupulous respect for duty, as for the law, is so readily to be found, held him in quite tight bonds in many respects. And the low spirits stemming from deep sadness arouse love for what is in the natural order and taken for granted, not requiring a new decision or one contrary to the circumstances which fate has indicated to us.

Oswald's love for Corinne had modified his whole way of feeling. But love never entirely eclipses the character, and Corinne perceived his character through the passion that triumphed over it. And perhaps Lord Nelvil's charm was due largely to this opposition between his temperament and his feeling, an opposition which gave an added value to all the expressions of his affection. But, for Corinne, the decisive moment was approaching when the fleeting anxieties that she had continually pushed aside, and that had mingled only a slight vague anxiety with the happiness she was enjoying, were bound to decide on her life. Her soul, born for happiness, used to the varying feelings of talent and poetry, was surprised at the bitterness and steadiness of grief. Then a shudder, which women who are long resigned to suffering never experience, troubled her whole being.

In the midst of the cruellest anxiety, however, she was secretly preparing a brilliant day which she still wanted to spend with Oswald. Her imagination and her feelings were thus romantically combined. She invited the English who were at Naples, and some Neapolitan men and women whom she liked. On the morning of the day she had chosen to be both a festive occasion as well as the day before a confession which might destroy her happiness for ever, a strange agitation enlivened her features, giving them a quite new expression. Casual onlookers might take that very lively expression for happiness, but her quick, anxious movements, her eyes which did not rest on anything, were more than enough proof to Lord Nelvil of what was taking place in her heart. In vain he tried to calm her by the most tender protestations of affection. 'You'll tell me all that in two days' time,' she said, 'if you still think the same. At the moment, these sweet words only pain me.' And she moved away from him.

The carriages bringing the company Corinne had invited arrived at nightfall, at the time when the sea breeze rises and, freshening the atmosphere, allows man to pay attention to the natural scenery. The first stop on the walk was at Virgil's tomb. Corinne and her companions paused there before going through the Posilipo tunnel.* This tomb is in the most beautiful situation in the world; it looks out onto the Bay of Naples. This outlook is so calm and magnificent that one is tempted to think that it was Virgil himself who chose it. This simple verse from the *Georgics* could have been used as an epitaph:

> *Illo Virgilium me tempore dulcis alebat*
> *Parthenope . . .*†

---

† At that time, gentle Parthenope welcomed me.*

His ashes still rest there, and the memory of his name attracts the homage of the whole world to this spot. It is all that man, on this earth, can snatch from death.

Petrarch planted a laurel tree on this tomb, but Petrarch is no more and the laurel tree is dying. The crowds of foreigners who have come to honour Virgil's memory have written their names on the walls surrounding the urn. Those obscure names are irritating; they seem to be there just to disturb the peaceful idea of solitude which the place arouses. Petrarch alone was worthy of leaving a permanent mark of his visit to Virgil's tomb. You come down in silence from this funereal resting-place of fame; you recall the thoughts and images which the poet's talent has consecrated for ever. What an admirable dialogue with future generations, a dialogue perpetuated and renewed by the art of writing! What are you then, shades of death? A man's ideas, feelings, and language survive, so would it be possible that what he was should not survive? No, such a contradiction in nature is impossible.

'Oswald,' Corinne said to Lord Nelvil, 'the feelings you have just experienced are a bad preparation for a festive gathering, but,' she added with a kind of rapturous expression in her eyes, 'how many festivities have taken place not far from tombs!' 'What is the source of this secret sorrow that upsets you, my dear?' replied Oswald. 'Confide in me. I have owed you the happiest six months of my life. During this period, too, I have perhaps spread some balm over your existence. Oh! Who could be impious in the face of happiness? Who could deprive himself of the supreme pleasure of doing good to a soul such as yours? Alas! It is already a great deal to feel oneself necessary to the humblest of mortals, but to be necessary to Corinne, believe me, is too glorious, too delightful, to give up.' 'I believe your promises,' replied Corinne, 'but are there not moments when something violent and strange takes possession of one's heart and quickens its beats with a painful anxiety?'

They went through the Posilipo tunnel by torchlight. You need this light even at midday, for the path is hollowed out of the mountain for nearly a quarter of a league, and when you are in the middle, you can scarcely glimpse the light at the two ends. An extraordinary echo can be heard beneath this long vault; the horses' hoof-beats, their drivers' shouts, make a deafening noise which permits no coherent train of thought. Corinne's horses pulled her carriage with an astonishing speed, but still she was not satisfied with their pace and said to Lord Nelvil, 'Dear Oswald, how slowly they are moving! Tell them to hurry.' 'Why are you so impatient, Corinne?' replied Oswald. 'In the past, when we were together, you did not try to make the hours pass quickly, you enjoyed them.' 'At the moment,' said Corinne, 'everything must be decided. Everything must have its allotted span, and I feel the need of hastening everything, even if it were to be my death.'

On emerging from the tunnel, you experience a keen feeling of pleasure as you see the daylight and the landscape again. And what a landscape is presented to one's view! Often what the Italian country-side lacks is trees; in this spot, you can see an abundance of them. Here, moreover, the land is covered with so many flowers that it is the region where you can most readily do without the forests which are the greatest natural beauty of every other land. It is so hot in Naples that, during the day, you cannot walk about, even in the shade. But in the evening, this region of open countryside, surrounded by sea and sky, can be seen in its entirety, and from every direction you can breathe the cool atmosphere. The good visibility, the varied build-ings, the picturesque shapes of the mountains, are such outstanding characteristics of the Kingdom of Naples that its landscapes are a favourite subject for painters. In this region the scenery has a power and an originality that cannot be explained by any of the attractions that are sought elsewhere.

'I am taking you along the shores of Lake Averno, near the Phlegethon,'* said Corinne to her companions, 'and in front of you is the Cumaean Sibyl's temple. We are crossing the areas celebrated by the name of the delights of Baiae. But I do not suggest to you that we should stop there just now. We shall think about the historic and poetic memories surrounding us here when we reach a place where we shall be able to see them all at the same time.'

It was at Cape Miseno that Corinne had had the dances and music organized. Nothing was more picturesque than the display at this enter-tainment. All the sailors from Baiae were dressed in vivid, strongly contrasting colours. Some orientals from a Levantine vessel, then in the harbour, danced with peasant women from the nearby islands of Ischia and Procida, whose dress has retained a resemblance to Greek costume. Voices perfectly in tune could be heard in the distance, and the instruments answered each other behind the rocks, echoing and re-echoing as if the sounds were going to be lost in the sea. The air they breathed was delightful; it suffused the soul with a feeling of happiness that stimulated everyone present and even took hold of Corinne. She was asked to join in the peasant women's dance, and at first she gladly agreed. But she had no sooner started than the amusements she was taking part in were made hateful to her by the gloomiest feelings, and she went away quickly from the dancing and music to sit down at the very end of the cape by the sea. Oswald quickly followed her there, but as soon as he reached her, their companions joined him to beg Corinne to improvise in this beautiful place. She was so overwrought by then that she allowed herself to be led back to the elevated knoll where her lyre had been placed, without being able to think about what was expected of her.

CHAPTER IV

CORINNE, however, wanted Oswald to hear her once more with all the talent Heaven had given her, as on the day at the Capitol. If this talent were to be lost for ever, she wanted its last rays to shine for the man she loved, before they were extinguished. This wish enabled her to find the inspiration she needed in her heart's very distress. Her lyre was ready, and all her friends were impatient to hear her. Even the ordinary people who knew her by reputation, those ordinary people who, in the South, are, through their imaginations, good judges of poetry, silently surrounded the enclosure where Corinne's friends were gathered. Through their animated expressions all these Neapolitan faces expressed the keenest attention. On the horizon the moon was rising, but the sun's last rays still had a pale light. From the top of the little hill which juts out to sea and forms Cape Miseno, there is a perfect view of Vesuvius, the Bay of Naples, the islands scattered about in it, and the countryside extending from Naples to Gaeta. In short, it is the region in the world where volcanoes, history, and poetry have left most traces. So, by common accord, all Corinne's friends asked her to take *the memories aroused by these places* as the subject for the verses she was about to sing. She tuned her lyre and, in a faltering voice, began. The expression in her eyes was beautiful but those, like Oswald, who knew her could discern the anxiety in her heart. She tried to contain her distress, however, and, at least for a moment, to rise above her personal situation.

CORINNE'S IMPROVISATION
IN THE NAPLES COUNTRYSIDE

'Nature, poetry, and history are rivals in grandeur here. Here, at a glance, one can survey all times and all marvels.

'I glimpse Lake Averno, an extinct volcano, whose waves used to inspire terror in former times; the Acheron,* the Phlegethon, made to boil by a subterranean flame, are the rivers of the hell to which Aeneas made his way.

'Fire, that consuming life which creates and destroys the world, was all the more terrifying in that its laws were less well known. In the past, nature revealed its secrets only to poetry.

'The city of Cumae, the Sibyl's grotto, Apollo's temple, were on this hill. Here is the wood where the golden bough* was plucked. The land of the *Aeneid* surrounds you, and the fictions sanctified by genius have become memories, of which we still seek the traces.

'A Triton thrust into these waters the rash Trojan* who, with his songs, dared defy the gods of the sea. These hollow, resonant rocks are those that Virgil described. Imagination is faithful when it is all-powerful. Man's genius is creative when he feels nature, imitative when he thinks he is inventing it.

'In the midst of these terrible piles of rock, these ancient witnesses of creation, can be seen a new mountain, which a volcano brought into being. Here the earth is stormy like the sea and, like the sea, does not retreat peacefully to its boundaries. The heavy element, lifted up by the quaking abyss, hollows out valleys, raises up mountains, and its petrified waves bear witness to the tempests that tear its heart apart.

'If you strike this ground, the subterranean vault re-echoes. It is as if the inhabited world is now no more than a surface about to open. The Neapolitan countryside is the image of the human passions: sulphurous and fertile, its dangers and its pleasures seem to stem from these flaming volcanoes, which give the air so many charms and make the thunder rumble beneath our feet.

'Pliny studied nature, the better to admire Italy. He applauded his country as the most beautiful of lands, when he could no longer honour it on other grounds. Seeking knowledge as a warrior does conquests, he set off from this very promontory to observe Vesuvius through the flames, and its flames devoured him.*

'Oh, memory, noble power, thou reignest in these places! Strange destiny! From century to century man laments what he has lost. It is as if times gone by are all, in their turn, depositories of a happiness which is no more. And whilst thought takes pride in its progress, and leaps forward into the future, our feeling seems to regret a former homeland brought closer by the past.

'We envy the magnificence of the Romans, but did they not envy the virile simplicity of their ancestors? In the past they despised this luxuriant countryside, and its delights subdued only their enemies. Look at faraway Capua; it conquered the warrior* whose unyielding soul resisted Rome longer than anyone in the whole world.

'In their turn, the Romans inhabited these places. When the soul's strength served only the better to feel shame and grief, they grew soft with no regrets. At Baiae we saw them overcome the sea to make a shore for their palaces. They dug into mountains to wrest columns from them, and the masters of the world, slaves in their turn, subjugated nature to console themselves for being subjugated.

'Cicero lost his life near the promontory of Gaeta, which we can see before us. With no concern for posterity, the Triumvirate* robbed it of the ideas this great man might have conceived. The Triumvirate's crime still endures. It is still against us that they sinned grievously.

'Cicero succumbed beneath the tyrants' dagger. More unfortunate, Scipio was banished from his land when it was still free. He ended his days not far from this shore, and the ruins of his tomb are called *The Tower of the Fatherland*. What a touching allusion to the memory which filled his great soul!

'Marius took refuge in the Minturnae marshes, near Scipio's home. Thus, in all ages, nations have persecuted their great men. They are consoled, however, by their apotheoses, and heaven, where the Romans believed they still commanded, receives amongst its stars Romulus, Numa,* and Caesar. They are new stars, which, for our vision, combine rays of glory and celestial light.

'As if misfortunes were not enough, the traces of all crimes are here. See, at the end of the bay, the island of Capri, where Tiberius was disarmed by old age. There, that soul, at once cruel and sensual, violent and weary, became bored even with crime and wanted to immerse himself in the basest pleasures as if tyranny had not yet degraded him enough.

'Agrippina's tomb* is on these banks, opposite the island of Capri. It was built only after Nero's death. The murderer of his own mother proscribed even her ashes. For a long time he lived at Baiae, amongst the memories of his crime. What monsters chance has brought together before our eyes! Tiberius and Nero look upon each other.

'Almost from their birth, the islands brought out from the sea by the volcanoes were used in the commission of the ancient world's crimes. Relegated to these lonely rocks, in the midst of the waves, the unfortunates gazed from a distance at their native land; they tried to breathe its scents in the atmosphere, and sometimes, after a long exile, a sentence of death told them that their enemies, at least, had not forgotten them.

'Oh, land bathed in blood and tears, thou hast never ceased to produce fruit and flowers! Hast thou then no pity for man? And does his dust return to thy maternal bosom without making it tremble?'

At this point, Corinne paused for a few moments. All those gathered together there for the festivities cast branches of myrtle and laurel at her feet. The gentle, pure moonlight made her face more beautiful; the fresh sea wind blew her hair about in a picturesque manner, and nature seemed to enjoy adorning her. But Corinne was suddenly gripped by an irresistible emotion; she looked round at the enchanting place and the wonderful evening, at Oswald who was there but perhaps would not always be there, and tears flowed from her eyes. Even the common people, who had just applauded her so noisily, respected her emotion, and they all waited silently for her words to tell them of her feelings. For a time she played a prelude on her lyre, and no longer dividing her song into eight-line stanzas, in her poetry she gave herself up to an uninterrupted flow.

'Some memories of love, some women's names, also demand your tears. It was at Miseno, in the very place where we are, that Pompey's widow Cornelia* remained in noble mourning till her death. For a long time on its shores, Agrippina wept for Germanicus.* One day, the same assassin who robbed her of her husband deemed her worthy of following him. The island of Nisida witnessed the farewells of Brutus and Porcia.*

'Thus these women, beloved by heroes, saw their adored husbands perish. It was in vain that for a long time they followed in their steps.

The day came when they had to leave them. Porcia kills herself. Cornelia presses to her heart the sacred urn which no longer responds to her cries. For several years Agrippina vainly angers her husband's murderer. These unhappy creatures, wandering like shades on the devastated shores of the eternal river, long to land on the other bank. In their long solitude, they question the silence, and ask all nature, this starry sky as well as this deep sea, for a sound of a cherished voice, for an accent they will hear no more.

'Love, supreme power of the heart, mysterious passion, containing within itself poetry, heroism, and religion! What happens when destiny separates us from the man who has the secret of our soul and gave us the life of the heart, celestial life? What happens when absence or death isolates a woman on the earth? She languishes, she falls. How often the rocks surrounding us have given their cold support to these deserted widows, who once leaned on a lover's breast, on a hero's arm!

'Before you is Sorrento. There was the home of Tasso's sister when, as a pilgrim, he came to ask this humble loved one for a refuge* against the injustice of princes. His long suffering had almost made him lose his reason. All that was left to him was his genius. Only his knowledge of the divine remained; all the images of the earth were confused. Thus, frightened by the surrounding desert, talent searches all over the universe but finds nothing like itself. Nature responds to it no longer; ordinary people take for madness the malady of the soul which can no longer breathe enough air, enough emotion, enough hope, in this world.

'Fate,' continued Corinne with ever-increasing emotion, 'does not fate pursue exalted souls, poets whose imagination springs from the force of their love and suffering? They are those banished from another region; it was not to be that universal goodness should arrange everything for the small number of the elect or the proscribed. What did the ancients mean when they spoke of destiny with so much terror? What power has this destiny over ordinary, peaceful beings? They follow the seasons, they quietly follow the usual course of life. But the priestess who interpreted the oracles felt disturbed by a cruel power. I know not what involuntary power plunges the genius into misfortune. He hears the music of the spheres, which mortal ears are not made to grasp. He penetrates mysteries of feeling unknown to other men, and his soul conceals a God that it cannot contain!

'Sublime Creator of this beautiful countryside, protect us! Our enthusiastic outbursts have no power, our hopes are illusory. The passions control us with a tumultuous tyranny that leaves us with neither liberty nor peace. Perhaps our fate will be decided by what we do tomorrow; perhaps yesterday we said a word that nothing can redeem. When our minds rise to very noble thoughts, we feel a dizziness which confuses our vision of everything, as we do at the top of high buildings. But even when grief, terrible grief, is not lost in the clouds, it tears through them, it partly opens them. Oh, God, but what does it want to tell us?'

At these words Corinne's face became deathly pale. Her eyes closed and she would have fallen to the ground if Lord Nelvil, at that moment, had not been near her to support her.

CHAPTER V

CORINNE revived and the sight of Oswald, who looked touchingly concerned and anxious, restored her calm a little. The Neapolitans noticed the sombre tone of Corinne's poetry with surprise. They admired the harmonious beauty of her language. They would, however, have preferred her verses to be inspired by a less sad tendency. For they considered the arts and, amongst the arts, poetry only as a means of distraction from life's troubles and not a way of penetrating further into its terrible secrets. But the English who had heard Corinne were filled with admiration for her.

They were delighted to see melancholy feelings expressed in this way with Italian imagination. The beautiful Corinne, whose animated features and lively expression were destined to depict happiness, this daughter of the sun, beset by secret sorrows, was like those flowers which are still fresh and brilliant but which a black spot, caused by a fatal prick, threatens with an early end.

The whole company got into the boats to go back to Naples, and the warmth and calm which then prevailed made the pleasure of being at sea greatly appreciated. In a delightful poem,* Goethe has depicted the inclination one feels for water in hot weather. The nymph of the river vaunts to the fisherman the charm of its waves: she invites him to refresh himself in it and, gradually seduced, he finally plunges himself into it. The magical power of the waves in a way resembles the serpent's eye, which is both attractive and frightening. The wave which arises in the distance, gradually becoming larger as it hastens to reach the shore, seems to correspond to a secret desire of the heart, which starts quietly and becomes irresistible.

Corinne was calmer. The delightful, fine weather reassured her heart. She had gathered up the locks of her hair, the better to feel any breeze that might be around her. Her face was thus more charming than ever. The wind instruments that were following in another boat produced an enchanting effect. They were in harmony with the sea, the stars, and the intoxicating sweetness of an Italian evening. But they aroused a still more touching emotion; they were heaven's voice in the midst of nature. 'My dear,' said Oswald in a low voice, 'my dear love, I shall never forget this day. Could there ever be a happier one?' As he said these words, his eyes were filled with tears. One of Oswald's seductive charms was his easily aroused and yet restrained emotion, which often moistened his eyes with tears, in spite of himself. His eyes then had an irresistible expression. Sometimes, even in the midst of pleasant bantering, you could see that he was touched by a private emotion which, mingling with his cheerfulness, gave him a noble charm. 'Alas,' replied Corinne, 'no, I hope for no more days like this. At least, may it be blessed, as the last happy day of my life, if it is not, if it cannot be, the dawn of a lasting happiness.'

CHAPTER VI

THE weather began to change when they reached Naples. The sky was darkening, the approaching storm could be felt in the atmosphere, already stirring up the waves vigorously, as if the tempestuous sea responded from the depths of its waters to the tempestuous sky. Oswald was a few steps ahead of Corinne because he wanted to have torches brought so that he could take her to her home more safely. As he went along the quayside he saw a group of Lazzaroni who were shouting quite loudly: *Oh, the poor man! He won't be able to reach the shore; we must be patient; he'll perish.* 'What do you mean?' cried Lord Nelvil impetuously. 'Whom are you talking about?' *About a poor old man,* they replied, *who was bathing over there, not far from the pier. He's been caught by the storm and isn't strong enough to fight against the waves and get back to the shore.* Oswald's first impulse was to jump into the water. But thinking about the fright he would give Corinne when she came up to him, he offered all the money he had with him and promised twice the amount to the man who would jump into the water to pull out the old man. The Lazzaroni refused, saying: *We're too frightened. It's too dangerous. We can't.* At that moment the old man disappeared below the waves. Oswald hesitated no longer and dived into the sea, in spite of the billows which went over his head. He struggled against them successfully, however, reached the old man, who would have been gone a moment later, grasped hold of him, and brought him back to the shore. But the coldness of the water and Oswald's strenuous efforts against the stormy sea were such a strain on him that, just as he brought the old man to the shore, he collapsed, unconscious, and he was so pale in this condition that one was bound to think he was no longer alive.[28]

Just then Corinne came up, unable to guess what had happened. She noticed a great crowd gathered and, hearing people scream: *He's dead*, she was about to move on, giving in to the terror these words aroused, when she saw one of the Englishmen who accompanied her break hurriedly through the crowd. She took a few steps to follow him, and the first thing to strike her eyes was Oswald's jacket that he had left on the shore when he threw himself into the water. She grasped the jacket, convulsed with despair, thinking it was all that remained of Oswald and when she finally recognized him, although he seemed to breathe no more, she threw herself on his lifeless body with a kind of rapture. But ardently pressing him in her arms, she had the inexpressible happiness of still feeling the beats of Oswald's heart, for he was reviving, perhaps because Corinne was there. 'He is alive,' she cried. 'He is alive!' And at that moment she recovered a strength and courage barely possessed by those who were merely Oswald's friends. She called for all possible assistance. She herself was able to help. She supported the fainting Oswald's head. She covered it with her tears and, in spite of the cruellest emotion, she forgot nothing; she did not lose a moment and her attentions were not distracted by her distress. Oswald seemed a little better but he had not yet regained the use of his senses. Corinne had him brought to her lodging. She knelt beside him, surrounded him with scents which were bound to revive him, and spoke to him so tenderly and passionately that life was bound to return at the sound of her voice. Oswald heard her, reopened his eyes, and pressed her hand.

Can it be that to enjoy such a moment one must have felt hell's tortures? Poor human nature! Our only knowledge of the infinite is through pain, and in all the enjoyments of life nothing can compensate for the despair of seeing loved ones die.

'You cruel man!' exclaimed Corinne. 'You cruel man, what did you do?' 'Forgive me,' Oswald replied in a quavering voice, 'forgive me. At the moment when I thought I was about to die, believe me, my dear, my fears were for you.' What an admirable expression of shared love, of love at the happiest moment of mutual trust! Corinne, keenly moved by these delightful words, could not, till her last day, recall them without an emotion which, at least for a few moments, made her forgive everything.

CHAPTER VII

OSWALD'S second impulse was to put his hand on his chest to look for his father's portrait. It was still there, but the water had spoiled it so much that it was barely recognizable. Oswald, bitterly distressed by this loss, cried, 'Oh God! So you take away even his picture from me!' Corinne begged Lord Nelvil to allow her to restore the portrait. He agreed but without much hope. What was his surprise when, three days later, she brought it back, not only restored, but a still more striking likeness than before. 'Yes,' said Oswald, delighted, 'yes, you have guessed his features and his expression. It is a miracle from Heaven which marks you out to me as the companion of my lot, since it reveals to you the memory of the man who must for ever dispose of me. Corinne,' he continued, throwing himself at her feet, 'reign for ever over my life. There is the ring my father gave to his wife, the most holy, sacred ring, offered in the noblest good faith, accepted by the most faithful heart. I take it off my finger to put it on yours. From this moment I am no longer free. As long as you keep it, my dear, I am free no longer. I undertake this solemn engagement, before knowing who you are. It is your soul I believe in, for it is your soul that has told me everything. If they come from you, the events of your life must be noble, like your character. If they come from fate and you have been its victim, I thank Heaven that I have been entrusted with the task of making amends for them. So, tell me your secrets, my Corinne. You owe it to the man who made his promises before you confided in him.'

'Oswald,' replied Corinne, 'this touching feeling of yours is founded on an error, and I cannot accept the ring unless I correct it. You think an inspiration from the heart enabled me to guess your father's features, but I must inform you that I have actually seen him several times.' 'You have seen my father!' cried Lord Nelvil, 'but how? in what place? Is it possible, oh my God! Who then are you?' 'There is your ring,' said Corinne, stifling her emotion. 'I must give it back to you already.' 'No,' answered Oswald, after a moment's silence. 'I swear never to marry another woman, as long as you do not send me back this ring. But forgive me the agitation you have just aroused in my heart. Troubled thoughts come back to me. My anxiety is painful.' 'I see that,' replied Corinne, 'and I am going to shorten it. But your voice is no longer the same, and your language has changed. Perhaps when you have read my story, perhaps the horrible word "farewell" ...' 'Farewell!' cried Lord Nelvil. 'My dear love, it is only on my deathbed that I shall be able to say that to you. Do not fear before that moment.' Corinne left, and a few minutes later Theresina came into Oswald's room to give him her mistress's letter that you are about to read.

BOOK XIV
CORINNE'S STORY

CHAPTER I

'OSWALD, I am going to begin with the confession that is to decide my life. If, after reading it, you do not think it possible to forgive me, do not finish this letter and cast me far from you. But, if everything is not shattered between us when you know the name and the lot in life I gave up, what you learn from the following will perhaps serve to excuse me.

'Lord Edgermond was my father. I was born in Italy to his first wife, who was a Roman lady. Lucile Edgermond, who was chosen to be your wife, is my sister on my father's side. She is the daughter of my father's second marriage to an Englishwoman.

'Now hear my tale. I was brought up in Italy but lost my mother when I was only ten years old. As she lay dying, however, she had expressed a great desire that I should finish my education before going to England, so my father left me with an aunt of my mother's in Florence till I was fifteen. My talents, my tastes, even my character, were formed, when my aunt's death made my father decide to bring me back to his home. He lived in a little Northumberland town which, I think, can give no idea of England. But it was all I knew during the six years I spent there. From my childhood, my mother had talked to me only of the misfortune of no longer living in Italy, and my aunt had often told me that it was the fear of leaving her own country that had made my mother die of grief. My good aunt was convinced, too, that a Catholic was damned if she lived in a Protestant country, but although I did not share her fear, I was very frightened by the thought of going to England.

'I left Italy feeling inexpressibly sad. The woman who came for me did not know Italian. I still spoke a little, secretly, to my poor Theresina, who had agreed to accompany me, although she wept continuously as we left her native land. But I had to get used to not hearing the harmonious sounds which, even to foreigners, are so pleasing and whose charm for me was linked to all my childhood memories. As I travelled northwards I felt sad and gloomy without clearly understanding why. I had not seen my father for five years when I arrived at his house. I could barely recognize him. It seemed to me that his face had a more serious expression, but he received me affectionately and said repeatedly that I looked like my mother. My little sister, who was then three years old, was brought to me. She had the fairest complexion and the most silken, blond hair I had ever seen. I looked at her with amazement, for we have hardly any complexions like that in Italy. But from that moment, she appealed to me greatly. That very day I took some of her hair with which to make a bracelet and I have kept it ever since. Finally, my stepmother appeared, and the impression she made on me the first time I saw her was continually reinforced and renewed during the six years I spent with her.

'Lady Edgermond liked only the region where she was born, and my father, whom she dominated, had sacrificed residence in London or Edinburgh for her sake. She was a cold, dignified, taciturn woman, whose eyes softened when she looked at her daughter. But she had, besides, something so decided in her facial expression and in her conversation that it seemed impossible to make her listen to a new idea, or even a word to which her mind was not accustomed. She received me pleasantly, but I quickly saw that my whole bearing surprised her and that she was considering changing it if she could. Not a word was said during dinner, although several people from the neighbourhood had been invited. I was so bored by this silence that, in the middle of the meal, I tried to say a few words to an elderly man who was sitting beside me. I knew English quite well, for my father had taught it me from my babyhood, and, in the conversation, I quoted some very pure, discreet Italian verses commenting, however, on love. My stepmother, who knew a little Italian, looked at me, blushed, and, even earlier than usual, signed to the ladies to retire and prepare the tea, leaving the men alone at table during dessert. I did not understand this custom at all. In Italy it is very surprising, for these people cannot conceive of any pleasure in society without women. For a moment I thought my stepmother was so angry with me that she did not want to stay in the same room. I was reassured, however, because she signed to me to follow her and did not reproach me at all during the three hours we spent in the drawing room waiting for the men to join us.

'At supper my stepmother told me quite gently that it was not usual for young ladies to speak, and above all that it was never permissible for them to quote poetry in which the word 'love' was mentioned. "Miss Edgermond," she added, "you must try to forget everything connected with Italy; it is a country it would be better you had never known." I spent the night weeping. My heart was overwhelmed with sadness. In the morning I went for a walk; it was terribly foggy and I could not see the sun, which at least would have reminded me of my native land. I came upon my father, who approached me saying, "My dear child, it is not like Italy here. In our country women have no occupation but domestic duties. Your talents will relieve your boredom when you are alone. Perhaps you will have a husband who will enjoy them. But in a little town like this, everything that attracts attention arouses envy, and you would not find it at all possible to get married if people thought you had tastes foreign to our ways. Here the style of life must be subject to the old customs of a remote area. I spent twelve years in Italy with your mother, and the memory of it is very sweet to me. I was young then and I liked novelty. Now I have gone back into my shell and I am comfortable there. A regular life, even if it is a little monotonous, makes time pass without one's noticing it. But one must not struggle against the customs of the country where one is settled; one always suffers for it, for in a town as small as the one where we are, everything is known, everything is repeated. There is no place for emulation, but there is for jealousy. It is better to put up with a little boredom than always to encounter surprised and hostile faces which, every moment, would ask you to give an account of what you are doing."

'My dear Oswald, you cannot imagine the pain I felt while my father spoke in this way. I remembered him, charming and lively, as I had seen him in my childhood, and now I saw him bent beneath the leaden cloak in hell described by Dante, which mediocrity throws onto the shoulders of those who pass under its yoke. I saw everything slipping away from me, the love of nature, of the fine arts, of feeling; and my soul, having no external nourishment, tortured me like a useless flame consuming me. As I am naturally gentle, my stepmother had no reason to complain of me in my relationship with her. My father had still less reason, for I loved him dearly and it was in my conversations with him that I still found some pleasure. He was resigned but he knew he was, while most of our country squires, drinking, hunting, and sleeping, thought they were living the finest and most sensible life in the world.

'Their contentment worried me to such an extent that I wondered if it was not I whose way of thinking was crazy and if this material way of life, which avoids both pain and thought, feeling as well as daydreaming, was not much better than my way of life. But what use would this sad conviction have been to me? To be distressed about my gifts as a misfortune, while in Italy they were thought to be a bounty from heaven.

'Amongst the people we frequented, some did not lack intelligence. But they stifled it like an irritating light, and usually by the time they were about forty this slight mental activity had ossified like all the rest. Towards the end of autumn, my father often went hunting and sometimes we waited up for him till midnight. For most of the time while he was away, I stayed in my room to cultivate my talents, but this displeased my stepmother. "What is the use of all that?" she would say. "Will you be any the happier for it?" These words drove me to despair. "What is happiness?" I would say to myself. "Is it not the development of our talents? Is it not as bad to kill oneself mentally as physically? And if I have to stifle my mind and my soul, what is the use of preserving the miserable remainder of my life, which troubles me to no purpose?" But I took good care not to talk in this way to my stepmother. I tried it once or twice. She had replied that a woman was made to look after her husband's household and her children's health, that all other pretensions only did harm, and the best advice she had to give me was to hide them if I had them. This opinion, normal as it was, left me with absolutely no reply, for rivalry, enthusiasm, and all that stimulates the soul and genius have a peculiar need to be encouraged, and fade like flowers under a sad, icy sky.

'There is nothing so easy as assuming a very moral attitude, by condemning everything which is the mark of a lofty soul. Duty, man's most noble objective, can be distorted, like every other idea, and become an offensive weapon which narrow-minded and mediocre people, who are content to be so, use to impose silence on talent and rid themselves of enthusiasm and genius, indeed of all their enemies. To listen to them, one would say that duty lies in the sacrifice of all the exceptional abilities one has, and that intelligence is a failing one must expiate by leading the same life as those who lack it. But is it true that duty prescribes the same rule to every temperament? Are not great thoughts and generous feelings the debt owed this world by the beings able to discharge it? Ought not every woman, like every man, to make a way for herself according to her nature and talents? And must we imitate the instinct of bees, whose swarms follow each other without progress and all alike?

'No, Oswald, forgive Corinne's pride, but I thought I was made for another fate. I feel as submissive to what I love as these women surrounding me who did not allow their minds to have an opinion, or a desire to enter their hearts. If you wished to spend your days in the heart of Scotland, I would be happy to live and die there beside you, but far from abdicating my imagination I would use it, the better to enjoy nature. The greater the extent of the realm of my mind, the more I would find glory and happiness in declaring you its master.

'My stepmother was almost as much disconcerted by my ideas as by my actions. It was not enough for her that I should lead the same life as she did; I had, in addition, to do it from the same motives, for she wanted the abilities she did not have to be thought of only as a sickness. We lived quite near the sea, and the north wind could often be felt in our house. At night I heard it whistle through the long corridors of our home, and by day it encouraged our silence marvellously when we were gathered together. The weather was damp and cold, and I could hardly ever go out without a feeling of pain. There was something hostile in nature which made me miss bitterly its gentle benevolence in Italy.

'In winter we returned to town, if you can call a place a town where there is no theatre, no public building, no music, no pictures. It was a collection of gossip and irritations, both diverse and monotonous.

'Births, marriages, and deaths made up the whole story of our society, and these three events differed from each other less than elsewhere. Imagine what it was like for an Italian girl like me to sit round a tea-table for several hours a day after dinner with my stepmother's company. It consisted of the seven most solemn women of the district. Two of them were maiden ladies of fifty, shy as if they were fifteen, but much less cheerful than girls of that age. One woman would say to another: *My dear, do you think the water is boiling enough to put on the tea? My dear*, the other would reply, *I think it would be too soon, for the gentlemen are not yet ready to come. Will they stay at table a long time today?* the third would say. *What do you think, my dear? I do not know*, the fourth would reply. *I think the parliamentary elections are*

to take place next week and it is possible they will stay to talk about them.
No, the fifth would say. *I think rather they will talk about the fox hunt*
which they were so busy with last week, and which is to start again next
Monday. But I think dinner will soon be over. Oh! I doubt it, the sixth
would say with a sigh. And silence would fall again. I had been in
Italian convents; they seemed to me full of life in comparison with
this circle, and I did not know what was to become of me.

'Every quarter of an hour a voice would be heard asking the most
insipid question, to obtain the most non-committal answer, and the
boredom, momentarily lifted, fell back again with renewed weight on
these women you might have thought unhappy if habits acquired in
childhood had not taught them to put up with everything. At last,
the *gentlemen* came in, but this long awaited moment did not bring
a great change in the women's behaviour. The men continued their
conversation round the fireplace; the women remained at the back
of the room, distributing the tea cups. When the time for departure
came, they went away with their husbands, ready to begin again the
next day a life which differed from that of the previous day only by
the date on the calendar and the passage of the years, which finally
left their mark on these women's faces as if, during that time, they
had lived.

'I still cannot conceive how my talent was able to resist the deadly
cold surrounding me, for we must not hide the fact that there are
two sides to every way of seeing things. Enthusiasm can be praised
or blamed. Motion and rest, variety and monotony, are able to be
attacked and defended by different arguments. One can plead the cause
of life, but there is nevertheless quite a lot to be said on behalf of death
or what resembles it. So it is not true that what mediocre people say
can simply be despised. In spite of you, they get to the heart of your
thought. They wait for you at the times when your superiority has
caused you sorrows, to say, apparently quite calmly and reasonably,
Oh, well. Those words, however, are the hardest you can possibly hear,
for one can only put up with envy in countries where this very envy
is aroused by the admiration talents inspire. But what greater misfortune is there than to live where superiority would arouse jealousy
and no enthusiasm, in a place where one would be hated as a power,
though one were less powerful than an ordinary person? Such was my
situation in that cramped society. I was only an irritation to nearly everyone. I could not, as in London or Edinburgh, meet those superior

men who can appreciate and know everything. As they feel the need of the inexhaustible pleasures of wit and conversation, they would have found some charm in the conversation of a foreign girl, even though she would not conform wholly to the country's strict customs.

'Sometimes I spent whole days in my stepmother's social gatherings, without hearing a word which expressed a thought or a feeling. Even gestures were not allowed in speaking. On the young girls' faces there was the loveliest bloom and the most vivid colouring, but the most complete immobility. What a strange contrast between nature and society! All age-groups had similar pleasures. They drank tea, they played whist, and the women grew old always doing the same thing, always staying in the same place. Time certainly did not let them escape; it knew where to capture them.

'In the smallest Italian towns, there is a theatre, music, improvisers, much enthusiasm for poetry and the fine arts, beautiful sunshine; in short, there you feel alive. But I was forgetting these things completely in the district in which I was living, and it seems to me that I could have sent a delicately improved mechanical doll in my place. It would have fulfilled my function in society very well. As everywhere in England, there are different kinds of interests which honour humanity; men, in whatever seclusion they live, always have the opportunity to fill their leisure with a worthwhile occupation. But women's lives, in the isolated corner of the earth where I was living, were very dull. There were some who, by temperament and reflection, had developed their minds, and I had discovered a few expressions, a few glances, a few words said in an undertone, which were out of the usual line, but the petty opinions of this small place, all-powerful in its little circle, entirely stifled these seedlings. One would have seemed a troublemaker, a woman of doubtful virtue, if one had indulged in speaking or putting oneself forward in any way; but what was worse than any inconvenience, there was nothing to be gained from doing so.

'At first I tried to bring this slumbering society back to life. I suggested to them that we should read poetry or make music. On one occasion, the day was fixed for that, but suddenly one woman remembered that three weeks previously her aunt had invited her to supper; another recalled she was in mourning for an old cousin she had never seen and who had died more than three months before; lastly, another remembered she had domestic matters to see to. All this was very reasonable, but it was always the pleasures of the imagination and the mind that were sacrificed, and I heard it said so often: *that cannot be done*, that, amongst all the negatives, not to live would still have seemed to me the best of all.

'After struggling for a while, even I had given up my vain attempts. Not that my father forbade them; he had even asked my stepmother not to trouble me about the matter. But the insinuations, the stealthy glances while I was speaking, a thousand little hurts like the bonds in which the pygmies wrapped Gulliver, made all activity impossible, and I finished by behaving like the others with this difference, however, that in the depth of my heart, I was dying of boredom, impatience, and loathing. I had already spent four extremely tedious years in this way, but what distressed me even more, I felt my talent slipping away. In spite of myself, my mind was occupied with petty things, for in a society lacking all interest in science, literature, pictures, and music—in which, in short, no one is interested in the imagination—it is the little things, the minute criticisms, which of necessity form the subject of conversations. Moreover, minds which are not active or thoughtful have something narrow, touchy, and constrained about them which makes social relationships both painful and insipid.

'In such a life the only enjoyment is a methodical regularity, which suits those who want to wipe out all kinds of superiority, to reduce the world to their level. This uniformity, however, is a permanent sorrow for natures called to a destiny unique to them. The bitter, malevolent feeling I aroused, in spite of myself, combined with the oppressive feeling caused by the emptiness around me, to prevent me from breathing. It was in vain that I said to myself, that man is not fit to judge me, that woman is not capable of understanding me. The human face exercises a great power over the human heart, and when you read a secret disapproval on someone's face, it always upsets you, in spite of yourself. In short, the circle surrounding you always, in the end, hides the rest of the world from you. The smallest object placed before your eyes interferes with the sun. It is the same, too, with the society you live in. Neither Europe nor posterity could make you insensitive to the irritations of the neighbouring house, and the person who wants to be happy and develop his gifts must, above all, choose his immediate surroundings well.

CHAPTER II

'My only diversion was my little sister's education. My stepmother did not want her to learn music, but she had allowed me to teach her Italian and drawing, and I am sure she still remembers them both, for in fairness to her I must say that at that time she appeared very intelligent. Oswald, Oswald! If it is for your happiness I took such pains, I am still glad. I would be glad in my grave.

'I was nearly twenty years old; my father wanted to see me married, and it is here that my ill-fated lot begins to unfold. My father was your father's close friend and it was you, Oswald, that he thought of for my husband. If we had known each other then, and if you had loved me, the lot of both of us would have been unclouded. I had heard speak of you with such praise that, whether it was a presentiment or pride, I was extremely pleased by the expectation of marrying you. You were too young for me since I am eighteen months older than you, but people said your mind, your taste for study, was in advance of your age, and I imagined such a pleasant life spent with someone of a character such as yours was depicted that this hope completely wiped out my objections to the kind of lives led by women in England. I knew, moreover, that you wanted to settle in Edinburgh or London, and I was sure of finding the most distinguished company in each of these two cities. I told myself then, and I still believe, that all the unhappiness of my situation came from living in a little town, relegated to the depths of a northern county. Only big cities are suited to exceptional people when they want to live in society. As life there is varied, people like novelty. But in places where people have assumed fairly pleasant monotonous habits, they do not like to enjoy themselves on one occasion, only to realize that they are bored every day.

'I enjoy telling you repeatedly, Oswald, that although I had never seen you, I was really anxious as I waited for your father, who was due to spend a week with mine. There was so little justification for this feeling, however, that it must have been a premonition of my fate. When Lord Nelvil arrived, I wanted him to like me. Perhaps I wanted that too much, and to succeed I took a great deal more trouble than was required. I showed all my talents. I danced, I sang, I improvised for him, and my wit, restrained for a long time, was perhaps too lively as it broke its chains. Experience has calmed me down during the last seven years. I am less eager to show off; I am more used to myself; I am more able to wait; perhaps I have less confidence in other people's being well disposed towards me, but also less eagerness for their applause. Indeed it is possible that there was something unusual about me at that time. One is so ardent, so imprudent, in one's early youth! One rushes forward so eagerly into life! However superior our minds are, they never supplant time, and although with such a mind we can talk about men as if we knew them, we cannot act on our own observations. There is a restlessness in our thoughts which does not allow us to match our behaviour with our own reasoning.

'Without being quite sure, I think I appeared too lively to Lord Nelvil, for after spending a week with my father and being, more-over, very friendly to me, he left us and wrote to my father that, on reflection, he thought his son was too young for the proposed mar-riage. Oswald, what importance will you attach to this admission? I could conceal from you this incident in my life. I have not done so. But could you possibly condemn me for it? I have, I know, improved over the last seven years, and would your father have been unmoved by my affection and passion for you? Oswald, he loved you; we would have understood each other.

'My stepmother formed the plan of marrying me to the son of her older brother, who owned an estate in the neighbourhood. He was a man of thirty, rich, handsome, of distinguished birth and honour-able character. But he was so completely convinced of a husband's authority over his wife, and of the submissive domestic role of his wife, that a doubt on the matter would have upset him as if you had questioned honour or probity. Mr Maclinson (that was his name) was quite attracted to me, and what was said in town about my wit and unusual character did not worry him at all. His house was so orderly, everything was done so regularly, at the same time and in the same way, that it was impossible for anyone to change it. The two elderly aunts who kept house for him, the servants, even the horses, could not have done a single thing differently from the day before, and the furniture which for three generations had participated in this way of life would, I think, have moved itself if something new had appeared. Mr Maclinson was, therefore, right in having no fear of my arrival. The weight of habit was so heavy that the little liberty I would have been allowed might have amused him for a quarter of an hour each week, but would certainly have had no other result.

'He was a kind man, incapable of hurting anyone, but if I had told him of the countless sorrows which can torture an active, sensitive soul, he would have thought me a person with fanciful ideas and simply advised me to go riding on horseback and get some fresh air. He wanted to marry me precisely because he had no idea of the needs of the mind and the imagination and because he was attracted to me without understanding me. If he even had had an idea of what a superior woman was like, and her possible advantages and disadvantages, he would have been afraid of not being lovable enough in my eyes. But this kind of anxiety did not even enter his head. Imagine my aversion to such a marriage. I absolutely refused it. My father supported me. My stepmother, however, was deeply resentful. At heart she was a tyrannical woman, although often prevented by shyness from expressing her wishes. When you did not guess what she wanted, she would be annoyed; but when she had made the effort to express herself, the more it had cost her to break through her usual reserve, the less she would forgive you.

'The whole town blamed me most severely. Such a suitable marriage, such a solid fortune, such an admirable man, such a respected name, that was the general outcry! I tried to explain why such a suitable marriage did not suit me. I wasted my efforts. Sometimes I would make myself understood while I was speaking. As soon as I had gone, however, what I had said left no trace, for the usual ideas would return immediately to my listeners' heads and, with a new pleasure, they would welcome the old ideas I had momentarily removed.

'One day, when I had been even more outspoken than usual, a woman who, although conforming in every way to the common lifestyle, was much more intelligent than the others, took me aside and spoke to me. Her words impressed me deeply. "You are giving yourself a lot of trouble, my dear, for something that is impossible. You will not change the way things are. A little northern town, cut off from the rest of the world and with no appreciation of the arts or literature, cannot be other than it is. If you have to live here, accept it; go away, if you can. There are only these two decisions you can make." This reasoning was only too clear. I felt an esteem for this woman that I did not have for myself, for, with tastes like mine, she had been able to resign herself to the fate I could not endure. While liking poetry and intellectual pleasures, she judged much better than I did the force of circumstances and human obstinacy. I made a big effort to see her again, but in vain. Her mind escaped the circle, but her life was enclosed within it. I even think she was a little afraid of reawakening her natural superiority by our conversations. What would she have done with it?

CHAPTER III

'YET I would have spent all my life in this lamentable situation if I had not lost my father, but a sudden accident took him from me. In him I lost my protector and friend, the only one who understood me in that peopled wilderness, and such was my despair that I no longer had the strength to combat my feelings. I was twenty when he died and I had no other support, no other relation than my stepmother. Although we had been living under the same roof for five years, I was no closer to her than on the first day. She began to speak to me again about Mr Maclinson, and although she did not have the right to order me to marry him, he was the only man she invited to her house, and she told me quite plainly that she would encourage no other marriage. It was not that she had any particular affection for Mr Maclinson, although he was her close relative, but she thought my refusal was scornful of him. She made common cause with him, rather to defend mediocrity than out of family pride.

'Each day my situation became more unbearable. I was gripped by homesickness, the most disturbing sorrow that can take hold of the soul. For lively, sensitive natures, exile is sometimes a torture more cruel than death. The imagination takes a dislike to all its surroundings, the climate, the countryside, the language, the customs, life in general, life in its details. There is suffering in every moment, as in every circumstance, for our native land gives us a thousand daily pleasures that we ourselves are not aware of before we lose them.

> . . . La favella, i costumi,
> L'aria, i tronchí, il terren, le mura, il sassi!†*

---

† The language, the customs, the air, the trees, the earth, the walls, the stones!
METASTASIO

Not to see the places where you spent your childhood is in itself an acute sorrow. Memories of that age have a special charm, which makes the heart young again but yet sweetens the idea of death. The grave brought near to the cradle seems to cast the same shade over a whole life, while the years spent on foreign soil are like rootless branches. The previous generation has not known you from birth; for you it is not the generation of fathers and protectors. A thousand interests you share with your compatriots are incomprehensible to foreigners. You have to explain everything, comment on everything, say everything, instead of the instant communication, the outpouring of thoughts, which begins the moment you are reunited with compatriots. It was not without emotion that I could recall my country's kindly words. Sometimes, as I took a solitary walk, I would say *Cara, Carissima*, to imitate to myself the kindly welcome of Italian men and women, and I compared this welcome to the one I was receiving.

'Every day I would wander in the countryside where, usually, in the evening, in Italy, I would hear harmonious melodies perfectly sung, and where the crows' squawks rang out alone in the clouds. Fogs took the place of the beautiful sunshine and the soft air of my country. Fruit barely ripened; I saw no vines; the flowers grew languidly, few and far between. Like a black garment, fir trees covered the mountains the whole year round. One ancient building, one single picture, one beautiful picture, would have raised my spirits, but I would have sought it in vain for thirty miles around. Everything around me was drab and dismal, and what dwellings and inhabitants there were, were only of use in depriving solitude of the poetic horror which makes the heart tremble quite pleasantly. There was prosperity, a little trade, and some farming around us; in short, what was needed for people to say: *You ought to be content. You do not lack anything.* What a stupid opinion, based on the externals of life, while the whole centre of happiness and suffering is in the innermost and most hidden sanctuary of ourselves!

'At the age of twenty-one, I was naturally to gain possession of the inheritance which my mother and father had bequeathed to me. In my solitary daydreams I once had the idea that, since I was an orphan and had attained my majority, I could return to Italy to lead an independent life entirely devoted to the arts. At first, when this plan entered my mind, I was overcome with joy and I could not conceive of any possible objection. When my hopeful excitement had calmed down a little, however, I was afraid of this irreparable decision, and as I reflected on what everyone I knew would think of it, the plan which initially I had found so easy seemed to me quite impracticable. Nevertheless, the picture of my life surrounded by all the memories of the ancient world, by painting and music, had appeared to me in so much charming detail that I took a renewed dislike to my tedious life.

'My talent that I was afraid of losing had developed as a consequence of the thorough study I had made of English literature. The depth of thought and feeling which is characteristic of your poets had strengthened my mind and soul without my losing any of the lively imagination which seems to belong only to the inhabitants of our southern lands. I could therefore think that it was my destiny to have particular advantages because of the unusual circumstances of my dual education and, if I may put it that way, two different nationalities. I remembered the approval given by a few capable judges in Florence to my first attempts at poetry. I exulted in the new successes I might gain. In short, I had great hopes of myself. Is that not the first and noblest youthful illusion?

'I thought that on the day I no longer felt the withering breath of ill-intentioned mediocrity, I would gain possession of the universe. But when I had to make the decision to go, to escape secretly, I felt held back by public opinion, which had a much greater influence on me in England than in Italy; for although I did not like the small town where I was living, I respected the country as a whole. Had my stepmother agreed to take me to London or Edinburgh, if she had thought of marrying me to a man who was witty enough to appreciate my wit, I would never have given up my name or my way of life, even to go back to my former motherland. In short, however hard my stepmother's domination was for me, I would perhaps never have had the strength to change the situation, without numerous circumstances which combined to make my wavering mind reach a decision.

'With me I had the Italian maid you know, Theresina. She is from Tuscany, but although she has not been educated, she uses the noble, harmonious language which gives the least words of our lower classes so much charm. It was only with her that I spoke my own language, and this link made me fond of her. Often I saw she was sad and I did not dare ask her why, suspecting that, like me, she was missing her own country, and fearing that I would not be able to restrain my own feelings if they were aroused by someone else's. There are sorrows which are soothed by sharing them, but sorrows of the imagination are magnified when they are confided to another. They are magnified above all when you perceive a grief like your own in someone else. Then the pain you suffer seems invincible and you no longer try to fight against it. My poor Theresina fell seriously ill, and as I heard her moaning day and night, I resolved to ask her at last what was making her so unhappy. How surprised I was when I heard her tell me almost everything I had been feeling! She had not thought as deeply as I had about the cause of her sorrows. She complained more of the local situation, of the people in particular. But the bleak countryside, the dull town we were living in, the coldness of its inhabitants, their constrained ways, she felt all that but could not explain it and exclaimed continually, "Oh, my country, shall I never see you again?" But then she would add that she did not want to leave me, and with a bitterness which rent my heart she would weep because she could not combine her affection for me with enjoying Italy's sunny sky and the pleasure of hearing her native tongue.

'Nothing affected me more than the reflection of my own feelings in a very ordinary person, but one who had retained her Italian personality and tastes in all their native liveliness; so I promised her she would see Italy again. "With you," she replied. I said nothing. Then she tore her hair and swore she would never leave me, but, as she uttered these words, she seemed about to die before my eyes! At last, I let slip the words that I would go back too, and although I said them only to calm her, they became serious because of the inexpressible joy they aroused and the reliance she placed on them. Without saying anything about it, she struck up an acquaintance with some of the businessmen in the town and told me exactly when a ship was leaving for Genoa or Livorno from the neighbouring port. I would listen to her and say nothing. She would imitate my silence, but her eyes would fill with tears. Every day my health suffered more from the climate and from my repressed sorrows. My spirits needed activity and cheerfulness; I have often told you that grief would kill me. There is too much struggle within me against it; I must give in to it or die.

'So I returned frequently to the thought filling my mind since my father's death; but I was very fond of Lucile, who was then nine years old and whom I had cared for like a second mother since she was six. One day I had the thought that if I left secretly I would injure my reputation so much that my sister's name would suffer. This fear made

me give up my plan for a while. One evening, however, when I was
more affected than ever by my sorrows, as well as by my relationships both with my stepmother and with society, I found myself alone
at supper with Lady Edgermond. After an hour's silence, I suddenly
became so irritated by her imperturbable coldness that I began the
conversation by complaining of the life I was leading, more, at first,
to force her to speak than to lead her to any result which might concern me. As I became animated, however, I suddenly suggested that,
in a situation like mine, it would be possible to leave England for ever.
My stepmother was not put out by this and, with a sang-froid and
curtness I shall never forget all my life, she said: "You are twenty-
one years old, Miss Edgermond, so your inheritances from your mother
and from your father are yours. So you are your own mistress to do
as you please, but if you make a decision which dishonours you in
public opinion, you owe it to your family to change your name and
pass for dead." At these words, I got up impetuously and, without
replying, left the room.

    'This contemptuous hardness made me extremely indignant, and,
for a moment, a desire for vengeance quite foreign to my character
took possession of me. These feelings calmed down but the conviction that no one was interested in my happiness broke the links that
still bound me to the house where I had seen my father. To be sure,
I did not like Lady Edgermond, but I had not the indifference to
her that she had shown to me. I was touched by her love for her
daughter, and I thought I had aroused her interest by the care I gave
to her child, but perhaps, on the contrary, that very care had aroused
her jealousy; for the more she imposed every kind of sacrifice on herself, the more passionate she was in the only affection she had
allowed herself. Everything eager and fervent in the human heart, controlled by her reason in every other respect, was to be found in her
character where her daughter was concerned.

    'As my heart was still seething with the resentment aroused by my
conversation with Lady Edgermond, Theresina, in a state of great emotion, came and told me that a ship straight from Livorno had entered
the port only a few miles away, and on board were merchants she knew
who were the most honourable men in the world. "They are all Italian,"
she told me, weeping. "They speak only Italian. They will set sail again
in a week and are going directly to Italy; and if Madame had decided
. . ." "Go back with them, dear Theresina," I answered. "No,

Madame," she cried, "I would rather die here." And she left my room, where I remained, reflecting on my duty to my stepmother. It seemed clear to me that she no longer wanted me to stay with her. She did not like my influence on Lucile. She was afraid that my reputation of being an unusual person would one day be detrimental to her daughter's being settled in life. In short, she had revealed her innermost desire for me to pass for dead, and her bitter advice, which had upset me so much at first, on reflection seemed to me quite reasonable. "Yes, to be sure," I cried. "Let me pass for dead in this place, where my existence is no more than a restless sleep. I shall live again, with nature, with the sun, with the arts, and the cold letters which make up my name carved on an empty tomb will take my place in this lifeless town." This heartfelt enthusiasm for liberty did not, however, give me enough strength to make a firm decision yet. There are moments when one believes in the power of one's desires, and others when the customary order of things seems to win the day over all the feelings of the soul. I was in the state of indecision which can last for ever, since nothing outside myself required me to make up my mind, when, the Sunday after my conversation with my stepmother, towards evening, I heard Italian singers below my windows; they had come on the ship from Livorno and Theresina had induced them to give me a pleasant surprise. I cannot tell you the emotion I felt. A flood of tears covered my face and all my memories revived. Nothing brings back the past like music. It does more than bring back the past; when music evokes the past, it appears, clad in a mysterious and melancholy veil, like the ghosts of those who are dear to us. The musicians sang the delightful words which Monti wrote during his exile.

> Bella Italia, amate sponde,
> Pur vi torno à riveder.
> Tema in petto e si confonde
> L'alma oppressa dal piacer.[†]

'I was in a kind of rapture; for Italy I was feeling all that love makes you feel, desire, passion, regrets. I was no longer mistress of myself; all my heart was drawn towards my native land. I needed to see it, to breathe its air, to hear it; my every heartbeat was a summons to my beautiful dwelling place, to my smiling landscape! If life were

---

[†] Beautiful Italy, beloved shores, so I am going to see you once more. My soul trembles and gives way to this excess of pleasure.

offered to the dead in graves, they would not raise their covering stones with more impatience than I felt, to cast away all my shrouds and regain possession of my imagination, of my genius, of nature! In the enthusiasm evoked by the music, I was still far from making any decision, for my feelings were too confused to draw any firm conclusions from them; but just then my stepmother came in and asked me to put an end to this singing, because it was scandalous for music to be heard on a Sunday. I wanted to insist, saying the Italians were leaving the next day and it was six years since I had enjoyed a pleasure of this kind. My stepmother did not listen to me, telling me that, above all, one must respect the conventions of the country one was living in. She went to the window and ordered her servants to tell my compatriots to go. They went, singing a farewell that cut me to the heart from further and further away.

'My spirits could take no more. The ship was to leave the next day. Just in case and without telling me, Theresina had prepared everything for my departure. For the past week Lucile had been staying with one of her mother's relatives. My father's ashes were not buried in the country house where we were living. He had arranged for his tombstone to be erected at his Scottish estate. Finally, I left without telling my stepmother, leaving her a letter informing her of my decision. I left in one of those moments when you give in to fate, when everything seems better than servitude, distaste, and dullness, when thoughtless youth has faith in the future and sees it in the heavens like a brilliant star promising a happy lot.

CHAPTER IV

'MORE worrying thoughts took hold of me when I lost sight of the coast of England, but as I had not left any keen affection there, I was soon consoled by all Italy's charm when I reached Livorno. As I had promised my stepmother, I did not tell anyone my real name. I just took the name of Corinne, which I liked because of the story of a Greek woman, Pindar's friend* and a poetess.[29] As I had grown up, my appearance had changed so much that I was sure of not being recognized. I had lived a fairly secluded life in Florence and I counted on what in fact happened, which was that no one in Rome knew who I was. My stepmother wrote to me, saying she had spread the news that the doctors had prescribed a voyage to the South for the sake of my health and that I had died during the journey, but her letter contained no remarks beyond that. With scrupulous correctness she had all my considerable fortune sent on to me, but she did not write to me again. Five years have passed from that time till the moment when I saw you, five years during which I enjoyed considerable happiness. I came to Rome and settled there; my reputation grew. The arts and literature gave me even more personal pleasure than I obtained from success, and, till I met you, I did not know all the power that feeling can exercise. Sometimes my imagination increased or decreased my illusions without hurting me much; I had not yet been gripped by an affection which could dominate me. Admiration, respect, love, did not enlist all my heart's capabilities. Even when I was in love, I imagined more virtues and attractions than I encountered. In short, I remained in control of my own feelings instead of being entirely conquered by them.

'Do not ask me to tell you how two men, whose passion for me was only too obvious, filled my life in turn before I met you. You would have to do violence to my deep-seated conviction to persuade me now that anyone other than you could have been of interest to me, and it causes me as much regret as pain. I shall only tell you what you have already heard from my friends, that I so enjoyed my independent life that, after much indecision and painful scenes, I twice broke bonds which the need to love had made me form but which I could not bring myself to make irrevocable. A great German nobleman wanted, by marrying me, to take me to his own country, where his rank and inheritance required him to live. In Rome itself, an Italian prince offered a very brilliant life. The former aroused my love by inspiring my very great esteem but in time I realized that he had few mental resources. When we were alone together, I had to take a lot of trouble to sustain the conversation and to conceal his deficiencies from him. When I talked to him, I dared not show what I was capable of, for fear of making him ill at ease. I foresaw that his feeling for me would be bound to cool the day I stopped respecting his feelings, but it is difficult to retain enthusiasm for people whose feelings one is respecting. A woman's allowances for any kind of inferiority in a man always imply that she feels more pity than love for him, and the kind of calculation and reflection that these allowances require makes the heavenly nature of an involuntary feeling wither away. The Italian prince was charmingly and abundantly witty. He wanted to settle in

Rome, shared all my tastes, and liked my way of life. But, on one important occasion, I noticed that he lacked force of character, and in life's difficult situations I would have to support and strengthen him. Then everything was over for love, for women need support, and nothing cools their feelings more than the need to provide it. So I was twice disillusioned about my feelings, not because of misfortunes or faults, but my observant mind revealed to me what my imagination had hidden from me.

'I thought I was fated never to love with all the power of my heart. Sometimes I found this idea painful, more often I congratulated myself on being free. I was afraid of my capacity for suffering, of my passionate nature which threatens my happiness and my life. I always reassured myself by thinking it was difficult to captivate my judgement and I did not think anyone could ever live up to my conception of a man's mind and character. I hoped that I would always escape from the absolute power of being in love by noticing some failings in the man who might attract me. I did not know that there are failings in a man which can even increase love itself because of the unease it gives him. Oswald, the melancholy and indecision which deter you from doing anything, the severity of your opinions, disturb my peace of mind without cooling my feelings. I often think that these feelings will not make me happy, but then I pass judgement on myself, not on you.

'Now you know the story of my life. My flight from England, my change of name, my fickle heart, I have concealed nothing. You will probably think that my imagination has often led me astray, but if society did not fetter women with a thousand bonds from which men are free, what would there be in my life which would prevent me from loving? Have I ever deceived? Have I ever done harm? Has my heart ever been sullied by base concerns? Sincerity, kindness, self-respect, will God ask more of the orphan who found herself alone in the world? Happy are the women who, on taking their first steps in life, meet the man they are to love for ever! But do I deserve it less for knowing it too late?

'Yet, my Lord, I shall tell you, and you will believe my frank statement. If I could spend my life with you, without marrying you, I think that, in spite of the loss of a great happiness and of an honour, in my eyes the greatest of all, I would not wish to join my life to yours. Perhaps this marriage is a sacrifice for you; perhaps one day you will regret my beautiful sister Lucile, whom your father intended for you. She is twelve years younger than I and her name is as spotless as the first flower of spring. You would have to make my name, already presumed to be in the realm of the dead, come alive again in England. I know that Lucile has a pure, gentle soul. If I can judge by her childhood, she may be able to understand you, through loving you. Oswald, you are free. Your ring will be returned to you when you want it to be.

'You may want to know, before reaching a decision, what I shall suffer if you leave me. I do not know. Sometimes violent emotions which are stronger than my reason arise in my heart, and it would not be my fault if they made my life completely intolerable. It is also true that I have a great capacity for happiness. Sometimes within me I feel a rush of thoughts that stimulate the circulation of my blood. I am interested in everything, I take pleasure in talking. I take delight in other people's wit, in the interest they show in me, in the wonders of nature, and in works of art not done to death by affectation. But would it be in my power to live when I would no longer see you? It is for you to judge, Oswald, for you know me better than I know myself. I am not responsible for what I may feel. It is for him who thrusts the dagger in to know whether the blow he is inflicting is mortal. But even if it were, Oswald, I ought to forgive you.

'My happiness depends entirely on the feeling you have been showing me for the last six months. I would defy all your will-power and tact to deceive me about the smallest change in this feeling. In this respect, set aside all ideas of duty. I know of no promise or guarantee for love. Only divine power can revive a flower once the wind has made it wither. A tone of voice, a look from you, would suffice to tell me that your feelings are no longer the same, and I would detest everything you might offer me instead of your love, of that ray of light, of my celestial halo. So be free now, Oswald, free every day, still free even if you were my husband, for if you loved me no more, my death would free you from the indissoluble bonds which would tie you to me.

'As soon as you have read this letter, I want to see you again. My impatience will lead me to you and I shall know my fate the moment I catch sight of you; for misfortune travels fast and the heart, weak as it is, is bound not to mistake the fatal signs of an irrevocable destiny. Farewell.'

BOOK XV
THE FAREWELL TO ROME
AND THE JOURNEY TO VENICE

CHAPTER I

It was with deep emotion that Oswald had read Corinne's letter. He was troubled by a confusing mixture of different sorrows. At times he would be hurt by her picture of an English provincial town and say to himself in despair that such a woman could not be happy with domestic life; at times he would pity her suffering and could not help loving and admiring the frankness and simplicity of her account. He was jealous, too, of the loves she had experienced before knowing him, and the more he wanted to conceal his jealousy the more it tortured him. Above all, his father's role in her story upset him painfully, and he was in such a distressed state that he no longer knew what he was thinking or doing. At noon, he rushed out in the burning sun. At that time there is no one in the streets of Naples. Fear of the heat keeps all living creatures in the shade. He went towards Portici, walking aimlessly wherever chance took him, and his thoughts were both stimulated and troubled by the burning rays that fell on his head.

After waiting for several hours, however, Corinne could not resist the need to see Oswald. She went into his room and, not finding him at that moment, was seized with mortal terror. She saw her letter to Lord Nelvil on his table and, having no doubt that it was after reading it that he had gone away, she assumed he had gone for good and she would never see him again. She was then gripped by unbearable grief. She tried to wait, but every moment devastated her. She paced quickly up and down his room, and then stopped suddenly, in fear of missing the slightest sound that might signal his return. At last, resisting her anxiety no longer, she went downstairs to ask if they had seen Lord Nelvil pass by and in what direction he had gone. The innkeeper replied that Lord Nelvil had gone towards Portici, adding that he could certainly not have gone far, for just then exposure to the sun would be very dangerous. This fear combined with all the others, so that, although Corinne had no head covering to protect her from the burning heat of the day, she began to walk at random in the street. Naples's large white pavements, pavements made of lava and put there as if to multiply the effect of the heat and the light, were burning her feet and she was dazzled by the reflection of the sun's rays.

She had no plan to go as far as Portici, but she walked on and on, more and more quickly. Suffering and anxiety hastened her steps. There was no one to be seen on the main road. At that hour, even animals, afraid of nature, stay in hiding.

The atmosphere is filled with a horrible dust as soon as the least puff of wind or the lightest cart crosses the road. The meadows, covered with this dust, are no longer a reminder of either vegetation or life. Every now and then, Corinne felt about to fall. She did not come across a single tree to lean against and she was losing her reason in that blazing desert. She had only a few more steps to take to reach the King's palace, where she would have found shade under the porticoes and refreshing water. But her strength was failing. In vain she tried to walk; she could no longer see her way; a dizziness hid it from her and made her see a thousand lights, even more glaring than that of the day. But suddenly the lights gave way to a cloud which enveloped her with unrefreshing darkness. She was devoured by a burning thirst. She met a Lazzarone, the only human being who, at that moment, could brave the power of the climate, and she begged him to go and fetch her a little water; but when he saw, at that hour, a woman so outstanding in beauty and in fashionable clothes, he was sure she was mad and he ran away from her in terror.

Fortunately, at that moment, Oswald was coming back, and from a distance certain tones of Corinne's voice reached his ear. Beside himself, he ran to her and caught her in his arms as she fainted. He carried her beneath the portico of Portici palace and revived her with his affectionate care.

As soon as she recognized him, and still distraught, she said, 'You promised not to leave me without my agreement. I may now appear unworthy of your affection, but your promise, why do you despise it?' 'Corinne,' replied Oswald. 'Never did the thought of leaving you come near my heart. I wanted only to think about our fate, and collect my thoughts before seeing you again.' 'Well,' said Corinne, trying to appear calm. 'You have had the time during these mortal hours that nearly cost me my life. You have had the time. Speak, then, and

tell me what you have decided.' Oswald, frightened by the tone of
Corinne's voice which betrayed her inner turmoil, said, kneeling before
her: 'Corinne, your friend's heart has not altered. What then have I
learned which could disillusion me about you? But, listen to me.' And
as she was trembling more than ever, he repeated insistently: 'Listen
unafraid to the man who cannot live, knowing you are unhappy.' 'Oh,'
she cried, 'you are speaking of my happiness; it is no longer a question of yours. I do not reject your pity; just now I need it. But do
you think I want to live from your pity alone?' 'No, it is from my
love we shall both live,' said Oswald. 'I shall come back . . .' 'You will
come back,' interrupted Corinne. 'Oh! So you intend to go away? What
has happened? What has changed since yesterday? Unhappy woman
that I am!' 'My dear love, don't let your heart be upset like this,' replied
Oswald, 'and let me tell you, if I can, what I feel. It is less than you
fear, much less. But,' he said, making a big effort of self-control to
explain himself, 'I must know the reasons my father may have had
seven years ago to oppose our marriage. He never spoke to me about
it. I know nothing about the matter, but his closest friend, who still
lives in England, will know his reasons. If, as I think, they are all connected with unimportant matters, I shall take no account of them. I
shall forgive you for leaving your father's country, which is the same
as mine, my glorious native land. I shall hope love will bind you to
it again and you will prefer domestic happiness, and the sensitive
natural virtues, even to the brilliance of your genius. I shall hope for
everything, I shall do all I can. But if my father declared himself
against you, Corinne, I could never be the husband of another, but
I could never be your husband either.'

When he had spoken, a cold sweat broke out on Oswald's brow.
The effort he had made to speak in this way was so great that Corinne,
thinking only of the state she saw him in, could not answer him immediately. She took his hand, saying, 'So you are going away! So you
are going to England without me?' Oswald was silent. 'Cruel man!'
cried Corinne in despair. 'You make no answer; you do not contradict what I am saying. Oh, so it is true! Alas! Even as I was saying so, I still did not believe it.' 'Thanks to your care, I have regained
the life that I nearly lost,' replied Oswald. 'That life belongs to my
country in wartime. If I can marry you, we shall never leave each other
again and I shall restore to you your English name and your life in
England. If this most happy fate were denied me, I would return to

Italy when peace comes. I would remain at your side for a long time and the only change I would make in your situation would be to give you yet one more faithful friend.' 'Oh, you would make no change in my situation,' said Corinne, 'when you have become my only interest in the world, when I have drunk of that intoxicating cup which gives happiness or death! But at least, tell me—this departure, when will it take place? How many days remain to me?' 'My dear,' said Oswald, pressing her to his heart, 'I swear I shall not leave you in less than three months, and perhaps even then . . .' 'Three months,' cried Corinne, 'so I shall go on living all that time longer. It is a lot. I did not expect so much. Come, I feel better. Three months is a whole future,' she said, with a mixture of joy and sadness that deeply touched Oswald. Then, silently, they both climbed into the carriage which took them to Naples.

CHAPTER II

WHEN they reached Naples, they found Prince Castel-Forte, who was waiting for them at the inn. The rumour had spread that Lord Nelvil had married Corinne, and the news greatly saddened the Prince. He had come to ascertain for himself whether this was true, and to link himself still in some way to his friend's circle even though she would be for ever bound to another. Corinne's melancholy, the depressed state in which he saw her for the first time, made him keenly anxious, but he did not dare ask her any questions, as she seemed to avoid all talk of the matter. There are emotional conditions in which one is afraid to confide in anyone. A word spoken or heard would be enough to destroy the illusion which makes life endurable. Any kind of illusions about love have this peculiarity, that you spare your own feelings just as you would spare the feelings of a friend whom you would be afraid of upsetting if you told him the truth; without realizing it, you place your own pain under the protection of your own pity.

Corinne, who was the most unaffected person in the world and did not seek to make a display of her grief, tried the next day to appear cheerful and lively again. She even thought the best way to retain Oswald was to show herself lovable as she used to be. So, in a lively manner, she would begin an interesting subject of conversation, but then, suddenly, she would become distraught and her eyes would wander aimlessly. Although she had exceptional ability in using language, she would hesitate in her choice of words and she sometimes used an expression totally unconnected with what she meant to say. Then she would laugh at herself, but even while laughing her eyes would fill with tears. Oswald was desperately sad about the pain he was giving her. He wanted to talk to her alone, but she carefully avoided opportunities.

'What do you want me to tell you,' she asked one day, when he was insistent about speaking to her. 'I miss what I was; that is all. I used to take some pride in my talent. I used to like success and fame. My ambition used to be to win the applause even of those who were indifferent. But now I do not care about anything, and it is not happiness which has freed me from these empty pleasures, it is a complete loss of heart. I do not blame you; it comes from myself; perhaps I shall conquer it. In the depth of one's heart, there takes place so much that we can neither foresee nor control. But, to do you justice, Oswald, you suffer from my pain; I see that. I pity you too. Why should that feeling not suit both of us? Alas! it can be directed at everything that breathes without making many mistakes.'

So Oswald was not less unhappy than Corinne. He loved her ardently but her story had affected his way of thinking and hurt his feelings. He thought he could see clearly that his father had foreseen everything, had decided everything beforehand for him, and that he would be despising his father's warning if he made Corinne his wife. Yet he could not give up the idea and was beset again by the uncertainty he had hoped to end when he knew his friend's lot. She, for her part, had not wanted to be tied to Oswald by marriage, and if she had felt sure he would never leave her, she would have needed nothing more to be happy. But she knew him well enough to know that his idea of happiness lay only in domestic life, and if he was giving up the plan to marry her it could only be because he loved her less. Oswald's departure for England seemed to her an indication of death. She knew how much influence the manners and opinions of that country had over him. There was no point in his making the plan to spend his life with her in Italy. She had no doubt that when he was back in his native land, he would hate the idea of leaving it a second time. She knew, in fact, that all her power stemmed from her charm, and what power would this have in her absence? What are remembered images when one is surrounded on every side by the strength and reality of a social order which dominates all the more in that it is based on pure, noble ideas?

Tortured by these reflections, Corinne would have liked to exercise some control over her feeling for Oswald. She tried to talk to Prince Castel-Forte about the subjects that had always interested her, literature and the arts, but whenever Oswald came into the room, his dignified bearing, a melancholy glance he would cast at Corinne which seemed to say, *Why do you want to give me up?* would wreck all her plans. Twenty times Corinne intended to tell Lord Nelvil that his indecision hurt her and she had decided to go away. But she would see him, at times holding his head in his hands like a man overwhelmed by painful feelings, at times breathing with difficulty, or dreaming by the seashore, or, when musical sounds could be heard, raising his eyes to heaven. These simple reactions, whose magic only she could see, would bring a sudden reversal to all her efforts. The tone of voice, the facial expression, a certain gracefulness in every movement, reveal to love the innermost feelings of the heart; perhaps it was true that an apparently cold personality like Lord Nelvil's could be fathomed only by the woman who loved him. As impartiality sees only the superficial, it can judge only by what is obvious. In her silent meditations, Corinne tried what she had found successful in the past when she thought she was in love. She called to her aid her powers of observation, which shrewdly revealed the slightest weaknesses. She tried to arouse her imagination to portray Oswald in a less attractive light. But there was nothing about him that was not noble, touching, and straightforward; and how is one to destroy in one's own eyes the charm of a personality and mind so completely natural? Affectation alone can bring about this sudden enlightenment of the heart, amazed to have been in love.

Between Oswald and Corinne, moreover, there was an unusual, all-powerful fellow-feeling. Their tastes were not the same, their opinions rarely coincided, nevertheless in the bottom of their hearts there were similar mysteries, emotions derived from the same source, in short, an indefinable similarity which presupposed similar natures, although all the external conditions had moulded them differently. So Corinne realized—and was frightened at doing so—that, by observing Oswald again, by judging all the details of his personality, by fighting strongly against the impression he made on her, she had enhanced still further her feeling for him.

She invited Prince Castel-Forte to return to Rome with them, and Lord Nelvil felt that she wanted to avoid in this way being alone with him. He was sad about this but did not oppose the idea. He no longer knew if what he could do for Corinne would suffice for her happiness, and this thought made him nervous. Corinne, however, would have liked him to reject Prince Castel-Forte as a travelling companion, but she did not say so. Their situation was no longer as uncomplicated as it used to be. There was as yet no concealment between them but, nevertheless, Corinne made suggestions she would have liked Oswald to reject, and a strain had entered into an affection which, for six months, had given them almost unmixed happiness.

As they returned past Capua and Gaeta, and saw again the same places they had gone through with such pleasure shortly before, Corinne remembered them bitterly. The beautiful landscape, now vainly summoning her to happiness, added to her sadness. When the beautiful sky does not banish grief, its smiling aspect makes one suffer even more by contrast. They reached Terracina in the delightful cool of the evening, and the waves of the same sea were breaking against the same rock. After supper, Corinne disappeared. Not seeing her return, Oswald was anxious and went out. His heart, like Corinne's, guided him to the spot where they had rested on the way to Naples. From afar he caught sight of Corinne kneeling in front of the rock where they had sat down, and looking at the moon, he saw it was covered by a cloud, as it had been two months ago at the same time. At Oswald's approach, Corinne got up and said, pointing to the cloud, 'Was I right to believe the foreboding? So it is true there is some compassion in Heaven? It warned me of the future, and today, you see, it is in mourning for me.

'Do not forget, Oswald, to notice if this same cloud passes across the moon when I die.' 'Corinne! Corinne!' cried Lord Nelvil, 'have I deserved that you should make me die of grief? You can do so easily; I assure you. If you speak like this once more, you will see me fall lifeless at your feet. But what crime have I committed? Your way of thinking makes you independent of public opinion. You live in a country where that opinion is not at all strict, but even if it were, your genius makes you reign over it. In any event, I mean to spend my days at your side. That is what I mean to do. So what is the source of your grief? If I cannot be your husband without doing injury to a memory which reigns over my heart as much as you do, would you not love me enough to find happiness in my affection, in the devotion of my every moment?' 'Oswald,' said Corinne, 'if I thought we should never leave each other, I would want nothing more; but . . .' 'Do you not have the ring, the sacred pledge? . . .' 'I shall give it back to you,' she replied. 'No, never,' he said. 'Oh, I shall give it back to you,' she continued, 'when you want to take it back, and if you stop loving me, the ring itself will tell me. Does not an old belief tell us that diamonds are more faithful than men, and that they become dull when their giver betrays us?'[30] 'Corinne' said Oswald, 'you dare talk of betrayal! Your mind is wandering; you no longer know me.' 'Forgive me, Oswald, forgive me!' cried Corinne. 'But when love is deeply passionate, the heart is suddenly gifted with a miraculous instinct, and suffering becomes an oracle. What then is the meaning of this painful heaving of my breast? Oh, my dear, would that it caused no dread, would that it foretold only my death.'

After these words, Corinne went away hurriedly. She was afraid of having a long conversation with Oswald. She took no satisfaction in grief and she tried to destroy sad feelings; but when she had repelled them they only returned more violently. The next day, when they crossed the Pontine Marshes, Oswald's care for Corinne was even more affectionate than the first time. She accepted it gently and gratefully, but there was a look in her eyes which said: *Why do you not let me die?*

CHAPTER III

How deserted Rome seems when you come back from Naples! You enter by the Saint John Lateran gate; you go through long, empty streets. The noise of Naples, its population, the animation of its inhabitants, accustom you to a certain amount of activity which, at first, makes Rome seem strangely sad. After staying there a while, one likes it again. But when you are used to a busy social life, you always feel a little melancholy when you are left on your own, even if you are quite happy that way. In any case, the season of the year when Corinne and Oswald returned, at the end of July, is very dangerous. The bad air makes many districts uninhabitable and the infection often extends over the whole town. That year particularly people were more than usually anxious and a secret dread was stamped on every face.

When she arrived home, Corinne found a monk on her doorstep. He asked her for permission to bless her house to keep it free from infection. Corinne agreed and the priest went through all the rooms, scattering holy water and reciting Latin prayers. Lord Nelvil was slightly amused by the ceremony; Corinne was touched by it. 'I find an indefinable charm in everything religious, I would even say superstitious, if there is no hostility or intolerance in the superstition,' she said. 'Divine help is so necessary when thoughts and feelings are beyond the ordinary concerns of life. Above all, it is for exceptional minds that I think supernatural protection is required.' 'The need certainly exists,' replied Lord Nelvil, 'but is that the way to satisfy it?' 'I never refuse prayers linked to my own, whoever says them,' Corinne answered. 'You are right,' said Lord Nelvil, as he gave his purse for the poor to the old, timid priest, who went away blessing both of them.

As soon as Corinne's friends knew she had come home, they hurried to her house. Nobody was surprised that she had returned without being Lord Nelvil's wife. At least, no one asked for the reasons which might have prevented the marriage. The pleasure of seeing her again was so great that it banished every other thought. Corinne tried to behave as she used to, but she could not manage to do so. She went to gaze at the artistic masterpieces which used to give her such keen pleasure, but at the core of all her feelings there was grief. She sometimes went for a walk at the Villa Borghese, sometimes near Caecilia Metella's tomb,* but the sight of these places, formerly so loved, gave her pain. She no longer enjoyed the sweet daydreaming which, in arousing the feeling of the transience of all pleasures, makes them even more moving. One fixed, painful thought occupied her mind; nature, speaking only vaguely, does no good when we are dominated by a real anxiety.

There was, in short, an extremely painful constraint in the relationship between Corinne and Oswald. It was not yet unhappiness, for sometimes that, in the deep emotions it occasions, brings relief to the burdened heart and produces from the thunderstorm a flash of lightning which may illuminate everything. It was a reciprocal embarrassment, fruitless attempts to escape from the situation which depressed both of them and made them a little displeased with each other. Indeed, can one suffer without blaming the loved one? Would it not be enough for one look, one word, to erase everything? But the look, the word, does not come when it is expected, does not come when it is needed. In love, nothing is motivated. It is, as it were, a divine power which thinks and feels in us, without our being able to influence it.

Suddenly there developed in Rome an infectious illness of a kind that had not been seen for a long time. A young woman was attacked by it, and her family and friends, who had not wanted to leave her, perished along with her. The house next door to hers met the same fate. In the streets of Rome, at every hour, could be seen the white-robed, veiled brotherhood which accompanies the dead to the church. It is as if they are ghosts who carry the dead. These are put on a kind of stretcher with their faces uncovered. Only a yellow or pink satin cloth is thrown over their feet, and the children often amuse themselves by playing with the ice-cold hands of the departed. This sight, both terrible and familiar, is accompanied by the gloomy, monotonous muttering of a few psalms. It is an unmodulated music, in which the voice of the human soul can no longer be heard.

One evening, when Lord Nelvil and Corinne were alone together and Lord Nelvil was suffering greatly because of the pain and constraint he perceived Corinne was feeling, he heard under her windows the slow, lingering sounds which indicated a funeral ceremony. For a while he listened in silence, and then said to Corinne, 'Perhaps tomorrow I too shall be attacked by this illness against which there is no defence, and you will be sorry for not having said a few kind words to your friend on a day which could be the last of his life. Corinne, death threatens both of us nearly; are natural ills not enough then, that we must, in addition, tear out each other's hearts?' Corinne was instantly struck by the danger Oswald was incurring in the midst of the infection and she begged him to leave Rome. He absolutely refused. She then suggested they should go to Venice together; he was very happy to agree, since it was for Corinne he was afraid, as every day he saw the infection acquire new strength.

Their departure was fixed for next day but one. But on the morning of that day, Lord Nelvil had been detained by one of his English friends and so had not seen Corinne. She wrote to him, therefore, to say that important business had suddenly arisen, that it required her to go to Florence, and that in a fortnight she would join him in Venice. She asked him to go by Ancona, a town for which she gave him an apparently important errand. The letter's style was, moreover, sensitive and relaxed, and Oswald had not thought Corinne's language so tender and untroubled since Naples. So he believed the contents of the letter and got ready to go, when he felt he wanted to look at Corinne's house before leaving Rome. He went there, found it closed, and knocked at the door. The old woman in charge told him that all her mistress's servants had gone with her and, to all his questions, she would not answer another word. He went to Prince Castel-Forte's house, but the Prince knew nothing about Corinne and was extremely surprised that she had left without sending him a message. Finally, Lord Nelvil was consumed with anxiety and he had the idea of going to Tivoli to see Corinne's business adviser, who was settled there and must have received some order from her.

He mounted his horse and, his anxiety making him ride extremely quickly, he soon came to Corinne's house. All its doors were open; he went in, walked through some rooms without meeting anyone, and finally reached Corinne's room. In the prevailing darkness he saw her lying on her bed with only Theresina beside her. He uttered a cry when he recognized her, and this aroused Corinne. She saw him and, raising herself up, she said, 'I forbid you to come near me; I shall die if you come near me.' Oswald was gripped by a grim fear. He thought his friend was accusing him of some hidden crime that she believed she had suddenly discovered. He imagined that she hated and despised him for it and, falling on his knees, he expressed his fear with a despair and dejection which suddenly gave Corinne the idea of taking advantage of his mistake and she ordered him to leave her for ever as if he had been guilty.

Amazed and hurt, he was about to go and leave her, when Theresina exclaimed, 'Oh, my Lord, will you then leave my good mistress? She has sent everyone away and did not want even me to care for her, because she has the infectious illness!' At these words, which immediately enlightened Oswald about Corinne's touching ruse, he threw himself into her arms with a passion and affection which no other moment in his life had ever made him feel. In vain did Corinne push him away; in vain did she express all her indignation. After ordering Theresina with a sign to go away, Oswald pressed Corinne to his heart, covered her with his tears and kisses, and cried, 'Now, you will not die without me, and if the fatal poison flows in your veins, at least, thanks to Heaven, I have breathed it in on your heart.' 'What torture you condemn me to, dear, cruel Oswald!' said Corinne. 'Oh, God! Since he does not want to live without me, you will not allow this angel of light to perish! No, you will not allow it!' As she finished speaking, Corinne's strength deserted her. For a week she was in very great danger. In her delirium she kept saying again and again, *Keep Oswald away from me! Don't let him come near me! Don't tell him where I am!* And when she came to her senses again and recognized him, she said, 'Oswald, Oswald, you are there. So we shall be reunited in death as in life.' But when she saw how pale he was, a fatal terror gripped her and, in her anxiety, she summoned to Lord Nelvil's aid the doctors who, in not leaving her, had given proof of exceptional devotion.

Oswald held Corinne's burning hands continually in his own. He always emptied the cup of which she had drunk a half. Finally, he was so eager to share his friend's peril that even she had given up fighting his passionate devotion and, letting her head fall on Lord Nelvil's arm, she resigned herself to his wish. Is it not possible for two beings, who love each other enough to feel that they could not exist without each other, to attain to that noble and touching intimacy which puts everything in common, even death?[31] Fortunately Lord Nelvil did not catch the illness that he had nursed so well. Corinne recovered. But another trouble cut into her heart more deeply than ever. The generosity and love that her friend had shown towards her increased still further her affection for him.

CHAPTER IV

IT was agreed, then, that to get away from Rome's fatal air, Corinne and Lord Nelvil would go to Venice together. They had relapsed into their usual silence about their future plans. But they spoke about their feelings more affectionately than ever, and, as carefully as Lord Nelvil, Corinne avoided the subject of conversation which disturbed the delightful peace of their relationship. A day spent with him was so enjoyable; he seemed to take such pleasure in his friend's conversation; he followed all her movements, he studied her slightest desires with such constant, sustained interest, that it seemed impossible he could have had a different life and that he could give so much happiness without being happy himself. Corinne founded her security on the very happiness she was enjoying. After some months of such a state, one ends up by thinking that it is inseparable from one's existence and that is what life is like. Corinne's anxiety had been allayed once more, and once more her lack of foresight had come to her aid.

The day before leaving Rome, however, she felt very sad. This time, she both feared and wanted to leave for ever. The night before the day fixed for her departure, unable to sleep, she heard a group of Roman men and women pass beneath her windows; they were strolling and singing in the moonlight. She could not resist the desire to follow them and thus to walk through her beloved town once more. She got dressed, ordered her carriage and servants to follow her, and, covering herself with a veil so as not to be recognized, followed a little way behind this company which had stopped on the Sant'Angelo Bridge opposite Hadrian's tomb. It was as if, in this spot, the music expressed the vanity of this world's splendours. In the air one seemed to see Hadrian's great shade, surprised to find on earth no traces of his power but a tomb. The group continued on its way, still singing, in the silent night when fortunate people are asleep. This sweet, pure music seemed to make itself heard to console those who were suffering. Corinne followed it, still drawn by the irresistible charm of the melody, which does not permit any feeling of fatigue and makes one walk on the earth with wings.

The musicians stopped at the columns of Antoninus and Trajan. They then bowed to the obelisk at Saint John Lateran, and sang in front of each of these structures. The ideal language of music harmonized nobly with the ideal expression of the monuments. Enthusiasm reigned alone in the town while all commonplace interests slept. Finally, the group of singers went away, leaving Corinne alone by the Colosseum. She wanted to go inside, to bid farewell there to ancient Rome. You cannot know the feeling aroused by the Colosseum if you have seen it only by day. In the Italian sunshine there is a brilliance which gives everything a festive air, but the moon is the star of ruins. Sometimes, through the apertures in the amphitheatre which seems to rise up to the skies, a part of heaven's vault appears behind the building like a dark blue curtain. Plants, which cling to dilapidated walls and grow in lonely places, take on the colours of the night; the soul, finding itself alone with nature, shudders and is touched at the same time.

One side of the building is much more dilapidated than the other and so two contemporaries battle unequally against time. It lays the weaker low, the other goes on resisting but falls soon after. 'Solemn place,' cried Corinne, 'where, at this moment, no living being exists with me, where my voice alone responds to my voice, how are passions' storms not soothed by this calm of nature, which lets generations go by so quietly before her? Has the universe no other goal than man, and are all its marvels there only to be reflected in our souls? Oswald, Oswald, why love you then with such idolatry? Why give oneself up to these feelings of a day, a day in comparison with the infinite hopes which unite us with the divine? Oh God, if it is true, as I believe, that the more one is capable of reflection the more one admires you, make me find a refuge in thought against the heart's tortures. That noble friend, whose touching expression cannot be erased from my memory, is he not a transient creature like myself? But amongst these stars there is an eternal love, which alone can satisfy the immensity of our desires.' For a long time, Corinne remained deep in her meditation. At last she slowly wended her way home.

But before going home, she wanted to go to Saint Peter's to wait for the day there, to go up onto the dome and, from that height, to bid farewell to the city of Rome. As she drew near to Saint Peter's, her first thought was to imagine what that building would be like when, in its turn, it would become a ruin, an object of admiration for future centuries. She imagined its columns, at present standing upright, half lying on the ground, its portico broken, its vault opened up. But even then the Egyptian obelisk was bound still to dominate the new ruins; that people worked for terrestrial eternity. At last the dawn appeared, and from the top of Saint Peter's Corinne gazed at Rome, cast onto the barren countryside like an oasis in the Libyan deserts. Devastation surrounds it, but the multitude of steeples, cupolas, obelisks, and columns which dominate it, with Saint Peter's rising higher still, make it appear quite marvellously beautiful. This city has, as it were, a unique charm. One loves it, as if it were a living being; its buildings and ruins are friends to whom one bids farewell.

Corinne said a regretful farewell to the Colosseum, to the Pantheon, to the Castel Sant'Angelo, to all the places whose sight had so many times renewed the pleasures of her imagination. 'Farewell, land of memories,' she cried, 'farewell, abode where life depends neither on society nor events, where enthusiasm is revived by what one sees and by the intimate union of the soul with external objects. I am leaving, I am going to follow Oswald without even knowing what lot he intends for me, the man whom I prefer to the independent destiny which has given me such happy days! Perhaps I shall return here, but with a wounded heart and a withered soul; and you yourselves, fine

arts, ancient monuments, sun, whom I have invoked so many times
in the cloudy lands where I was exiled, you will be unable to do more
for me!'

Corinne shed tears as she uttered these farewells, but not for
a moment did she think of letting Oswald leave alone. The special
characteristic of decisions which stem from the heart is that you judge
them as you take them; you often blame them severely yourself, without, however, hesitating to take them. When passionate love makes
itself mistress of a superior mind, it separates reason and action completely, and to lead the one astray it has no need to disturb the other.

Corinne's hair and her veil, picturesquely disarranged by the wind,
gave her face such a remarkable expression that, when the common
people saw her leaving the church, they followed her to her carriage
and eagerly expressed their enthusiasm. Corinne sighed once more
on having to leave a people whose feelings are always intense and sometimes so kindly.

But still that was not everything. Corinne had to undergo the trial
of the farewells and regrets of her friends. They devised festivities to
retain her for a few more days. They composed verses so as to repeat
in a thousand ways that she ought not to leave them, and when finally
she left they all accompanied her on horseback for twenty miles from
Rome. She was deeply moved. Oswald lowered his eyes with embarrassment; he reproached himself for snatching her from so many pleasures, and yet he knew that it would have been even more cruel to
suggest to her that she should stay. He appeared selfish at taking
Corinne away from Rome like this, but in fact he was not, because
the fear of distressing her by leaving her alone affected him even more
than the happiness he enjoyed with her. He did not know what he
would do; he did not see further than Venice. He had written to one
of his father's friends in Scotland to find out if his regiment would
soon be employed on active service in the war and he was waiting for
the friend's reply. Sometimes Oswald planned to take Corinne with
him to England, but he felt immediately that if he took her there without her being married to him he would ruin her reputation for ever.
Another time, in order to sweeten the bitterness of the separation, he
wanted to marry her secretly before leaving, but the next moment he
rejected the idea. 'Are there secrets from the dead,' he said to himself, 'and what would I gain by making a mystery of a marriage which
is prevented only by the worship of a grave?' In short, he was very

unhappy. His soul, lacking strength in all matters of feeling, was cruelly torn by contrary affections. Corinne, like a resigned victim, left it to him. In spite of her sufferings she gloried in the very sacrifices she was making for him and the generous imprudence of her heart. But Oswald, responsible for the fate of another, assumed new commitments at every moment, without finding it possible to satisfy any of them; he could benefit neither from his love nor his conscience, since he felt them both only through their struggles.

As Corinne's friends took leave of her, they urged Lord Nelvil to take great care of her happiness. They congratulated him on being loved by the most outstanding of women, but the secret reproach which seemed to be contained in these felicitations was yet another source of distress for Oswald. Corinne felt this and cut short these manifestations of friendship, pleasant though they were. Yet when her friends turned round repeatedly to wave to her as they receded further and further, she made only this remark to Lord Nelvil, 'I have no other friend than you.' Oh, how, at that moment, he wanted to swear he would be her husband! He was about to do so, but after long suffering one is prevented by an unconquerable misgiving from yielding to one's initial impulses, and even when one's heart demands them, all irrevocable decisions make one tremble. Corinne thought she could glimpse what was happening in Oswald's soul and she quickly directed the conversation to the region they were travelling through together.

CHAPTER V

THEY were travelling at the beginning of September. In the plain the weather was superb, but when they began to climb the Apennines, it felt like winter. These high mountains often affect the climate, and mild air is rarely combined with the pleasure given by the picturesque appearance of high mountains. One evening, when Corinne and Lord Nelvil were both in their carriage, a terrible storm suddenly arose. Thick darkness surrounded them, and the horses, which in this region are so lively that they have to be harnessed by surprise, pulled them along with amazing speed. On being carried away together in this way, they both felt a sweet emotion. 'Oh,' cried Lord Nelvil, 'if only we were being taken far from everything I know on earth, if one could scale the mountains, leap into another life where we would find my father again. He would welcome us, he would bless us. Do you want that, my dear?' And he pressed her violently to his heart. Corinne, no less moved, said, 'Do what you like with me. Chain me like a slave to your fate. In former times, did not slaves have the talents which charmed their masters' lives? Well, I shall be the same for you. Oswald, you will respect the woman who devotes herself to your lot in this way, but though society may condemn her, you would never, in your eyes, want her to blush.' 'I ought, I want to do that,' cried Lord Nelvil. 'I must gain everything or sacrifice everything: I must either marry you or die of love at your feet, stifling the ecstasy you inspire. But I hope, yes, I shall be able to be united to you openly, to take pride in your love. Oh, I implore you, tell me, have I not lost some of your affection by the combats that tear me apart? Do you think you are loved less?' He spoke in such a passionate tone that, for a moment, Corinne recovered all her trust in him. They were both moved by the purest and sweetest feeling.

However, the horses stopped. Lord Nelvil got out of the carriage first. He felt the bitter, cold wind which he had not noticed in the carriage. He could have thought he had reached the English coast. The icy air he was breathing was no longer in harmony with beautiful Italy. Unlike that of the South, this did not urge forgetfulness of everything but love. Soon Oswald returned to his melancholy reflections, and Corinne, who knew the anxious, wayward nature of his imagination, guessed this only too easily.

The next day they reached Our Lady of Loreto, which is at the mountain top and from where one can see the Adriatic. While Lord Nelvil was busy giving orders about the journey, Corinne went to the church, where the image of the Virgin is enclosed in the middle of the choir, in a little square chapel covered with quite remarkable bas-reliefs. The marble paving round the sanctuary is hollowed out by the pilgrims who have gone round it on their knees. As Corinne gazed at these traces of prayer, she was touched and, falling on her knees on the same paving which had been pressed by so many unhappy people, she prayed ardently to the image of kindness, the symbol of celestial compassion. Oswald found Corinne prostrated in this place of worship, bathed in tears. He could not understand how someone so intellectually superior could follow popular practices in this way. She realized what he was thinking from his looks and said, 'Dear Oswald, does it not often happen that one dare not raise one's wishes as high as the Supreme Being? How can one confide all the heart's sorrows to him? Is it not then sweet to be able to think of a woman as the intercessor for weak human beings? She suffered on this earth because she lived. I was less embarrassed to pray to her for you. Direct prayer would have seemed too presumptuous.' 'I do not always offer a direct prayer either,' replied Oswald. 'I too have my intercessor; the guardian of children is their father, and since mine has been in heaven I have often been given extraordinary help in life, moments of calm for no reason, unexpected consolations. It is in this miraculous protection too that I place my hopes of emerging from my dilemma.' 'I understand you,' said Corinne. 'I think there is no one in the world who, in the depth of his heart, has not a strange and inexplicable idea about his own destiny. An improbable event one has always dreaded, but which nevertheless happens, the punishment for a fault, although it is impossible to grasp the connection which links our misfortunes to it, often strikes the imagination. Ever since childhood, I have always been afraid of living in England. Well, perhaps regret at not being able to live there will be the cause of my despair, and I feel that in this respect there is something insurmountable in my lot, an obstacle against which I struggle and destroy myself in vain. In his heart everyone has an idea of his life quite different from what it appears to be. We have a vague belief in a supernatural power, which acts unbeknown to us, and is concealed in the shape of external circumstances, while it alone is the sole cause of everything. Thoughtful souls, my friend, plunge themselves in the abyss and never find the bottom of it!' Whenever Oswald heard Corinne talk in this way, he was always amazed that she could have such passionate feelings and, at the same time, in judging them, rise above them. 'No,' he would often say to himself, 'no other companion on earth can satisfy the man who has enjoyed the conversation of such a woman.'

They reached Ancona at night-time, because Lord Nelvil was afraid of being recognized there. But in spite of all his precautions, he was recognized, and the next morning all the inhabitants surrounded the house where he was staying. Corinne was awoken by the cries of *Long live Lord Nelvil! Long live our benefactor!* which rang out outside her windows. Thrilled by these words, she got up hurriedly and went out to mingle with the crowd to hear it praise the man she loved. Informed that the people were calling for him loudly, Lord Nelvil at last had to appear. He thought Corinne was still asleep and was bound to be unaware of what was happening. How surprised he was to find her in the middle of the square, already known and dearly loved by the grateful throng, who begged her to act as intermediary. Corinne's imagination rather enjoyed all unusual situations, but this imagination was her attraction though sometimes her weakness. In the people's name she thanked Lord Nelvil with such charm and dignity that all the inhabitants of Ancona were delighted. She said *We* when speaking of them. *You saved us; we owe our lives to you*. And going forward to present to Lord Nelvil, in their name, the oak and laurel wreath they had woven for him, she was gripped by an indescribable emotion. She felt nervous as she came up to Oswald. At that moment all the people assembled, so excitable and enthusiastic in Italy, prostrated themselves before him, and Corinne involuntarily bent her knee as she presented the wreath. Unable to bear any longer the public scene and the homage rendered by the woman he loved, Lord Nelvil was so moved that he carried her off with him far from the crowd.

As she left, Corinne, bathed in tears, thanked all the good inhabitants of Ancona, who sent her their parting blessings, while Oswald, hidden at the back of the carriage, repeated continually, 'Corinne, at my knees! Corinne, on whose footprints I would like to prostrate myself! Have I deserved this outrage? Do you think I have the unworthy pride . . .?' 'No, indeed,' interrupted Corinne, 'but I was suddenly overcome by the feeling of respect a woman always has for the man she loves. To all appearances homage is paid to us women, but, naturally, it is in fact the woman who reveres deeply the man she has chosen as her protector.' 'Yes, I shall be your protector till the last day of my life,' cried Lord Nelvil. 'Heaven is my witness! So much feeling and so much genius will not take refuge in the shelter of my love in vain.' 'Alas!' replied Corinne. 'I need only your love, and what promise could guarantee me that? No matter; I feel you love me more than ever at present. Let us not disturb this renewal of your love.' 'This renewal!' interrupted Oswald. 'I do not retract that word,' said Corinne; 'but let us not discuss it,' she continued, gently signing to Lord Nelvil to say no more.

CHAPTER VI

FOR two days they followed the shores of the Adriatic, but on the Romagna side this sea does not produce the impression of an ocean, nor even of the Mediterranean. The road runs alongside its waters

and there are stretches of grass on its banks. This is not how we imagine the dreaded dominion of gales. At Rimini and Cesena we leave
the classic land of the events of Roman history, the last reminder giving rise to reflection being the Rubicon, crossed by Caesar when he
decided to make himself master of Rome. By a strange coincidence,
not far from the Rubicon one can see today the Republic of San
Marino, as if this last weak remnant of liberty had to survive beside
the place where the Republic of the world was destroyed. After Ancona,
you gradually approach a region which looks quite different from
the papal state. The Bologna province, Lombardy, the environs of
Ferrara and Rovigo are remarkable for their beauty and their crop.
There is no longer the poetic devastation that heralds the approach
to Rome and the terrible events that happened there. Then you leave

> The fir trees, summer's mourning, winter's finery[†]

the coniferous cypress,[‡] image of the obelisks, the mountains, and the
sea. Nature, like the traveller, gradually bids farewell to the sunshine
of the south. First of all, orange trees no longer grow out of doors;
they are replaced by olive trees, whose pale, light green seems to suit
the shrubberies where the shades live in the Elysian fields, and some
leagues further on, even the olive trees disappear.

As you go into the Bologna province, you can see a smiling plain
where the vines form garlands which link the elm trees together. The
whole countryside looks decked out as for a holiday. Corinne felt moved
by the contrast between her inner state and the resplendent brilliance
of the landscape that struck her eyes. 'Alas,' she said to Lord Nelvil
with a sigh. 'Ought nature to show so many happy sights like this
to friends who perhaps are going to separate?' 'No,' said Oswald.
'They will not separate. Each day I have less strength for that. Your
unchanging gentleness adds the attraction of habit to the passion you
inspire. I am happy with you as if you were not an extremely remarkable genius, or rather because you are one, for real superiority entails
perfect goodness. One is pleased with oneself, with nature, with other
people. What bitter feeling could one have?'

They reached Ferrara together, one of the saddest towns in Italy,
for it is both vast and empty. The few inhabitants to be found from

---

[†] A line of verse by M. de Sabran.*
[‡] . . . et coniferi cupressi.
                Virgil

time to time in the streets walk slowly as if they were sure of having time for everything. You cannot imagine how a very brilliant court existed in this same place, the one that was celebrated in verse by Ariosto and Tasso. Manuscripts written in their own hands and in that of the author of the *Pastor fido** are still on show there.

Ariosto was able to live peacefully surrounded by a court, but at Ferrara you can still see the house where they had the audacity to confine Tasso as a madman and it is not possible to read without emotion the host of letters in which this ill-fated man asks for the death which he was granted so long ago. Tasso had that special kind of talent which makes it so much to be dreaded by those who have it; his imagination turned against him. He knew the secrets of the heart so well, he had so many thoughts only because he had many sorrows. *He who has not suffered, what does he know?* said a prophet.*

In some respects, Corinne was like that. Her mind was more cheerful, her feelings more varied, but her imagination had the same need to be very carefully treated for, far from distracting her from her sorrows, it increased their power. Lord Nelvil was mistaken in thinking, as he often did, that Corinne's brilliant gifts could provide her with a source of happiness independent of her affections. When a genius is endowed with real sensitivity, her sorrows are multipled by those same gifts. She makes discoveries in her own pain, as in the rest of nature, and as the heart's unhappiness is inexhaustible, the more ideas she has, the more she feels it.

CHAPTER VII

YOU take a boat down the Brenta to reach Venice, and from both sides of the canal you can see the Venetians' palaces. They are large and a little dilapidated, like Italian magnificence. They are decorated in an unusual way which is not at all like classical taste. Venetian architecture shows the influence of trade with the Orient. It is a mixture of Moorish and Gothic taste, which arouses interest without pleasing the imagination. Poplar trees, regular like the architecture, line the canal nearly everywhere. The sky is a bright blue, which contrasts with the brilliant green of the countryside. This green is maintained by an excessive abundance of water. The sky and the land are thus of two such strongly contrasted colours that nature itself seems to be arranged with a kind of artificiality, and you do not find in it that vague mystery which makes you love the south of Italy. Venice's appearance is more surprising than pleasing. At first you think you are seeing a submerged town and you have to reflect before admiring the genius of mortal men who have conquered the waters to build this town. Naples is built by the sea in the shape of an amphitheatre, but as Venice is on completely flat land, the church towers look like the masts of a ship which would remain motionless in the middle of the waves. The imagination is filled with sadness on entering Venice. You take leave of vegetation; you do not see even a fly in this town; all animals are banished from it, and man alone is there to struggle against the sea.

There is a deep silence in this town, the streets of which are canals, and the noise of oars is the only interruption to this silence. It is not the country, because there is not a tree to be seen. It is not the town, because there is not the least bustle to be heard. It is not even a ship, because it does not progress. It is a dwelling that thunderstorms turn into a prison; for there are times when you cannot leave either the town or your own house. In Venice there are men of the people who have never gone from one district to another, who have never seen the Piazza San Marco, and for whom the sight of a horse or a tree would be a veritable wonder. Those black gondolas which glide on the canals are like coffins or cradles, like the last and first of man's abodes. In the evening you can see, passing by, only the reflection of the lanterns which light up the gondolas, for, at night, their black colour makes them difficult to distinguish. It is as if they were shadows gliding on the water, guided by a little star. In this place, everything is mysterious, the government, the customs, love. There are probably a lot of pleasures for the heart and mind when you manage to penetrate all these secrets, but strangers must find their first impression peculiarly sad.

Corinne, who believed in premonitions and whose disturbed imagination turned everything into omens, said to Lord Nelvil, 'What is the source of the deep melancholy that takes hold of me as I enter this town? Does it not prove that some great misfortune will befall me here?' As she uttered these words she heard three cannon-shots fired from one of the islands of the lagoon. Corinne started at this sound and asked her gondoliers the reason for it. *It is a nun who is taking the veil at one of the convents in the middle of the sea*, they replied. *The custom in our city is that, at the moment when women make the religious vows, they cast behind them the bouquet of flowers they were carrying during the ceremony. It is the sign of their renunciation of the world, and the cannon-shots you have just heard were proclaiming this moment as we came into Venice.* These words made Corinne shudder. Oswald felt her cold hands in his and her face became deathly pale. 'My dear,' he said, 'how do you get such a strong feeling because of the merest chance?' 'No,' said Corinne, 'it is not mere chance. Believe me, the flowers of life are cast behind me for ever.' 'When I love you more than ever,' interrupted Oswald, 'when all my soul is yours . . .' 'Elsewhere', continued Corinne, 'these thunderous sounds of war proclaim victory or death; here they serve to celebrate a girl's meek sacrifice. It is a harmless use of the terrible arms that destroy the world. It is solemn advice given by a resigned woman to women who still struggle against fate.'

CHAPTER VIII

THE power of the Venetian government during the last years of its existence consisted almost entirely in the dominance of habit and imagination. It had been terrible; it had become very gentle. It had been brave; it had become timid. Hatred against it was easily aroused because it had been feared. It was easily overturned because it was feared no longer. It was an aristocracy that eagerly sought popularity but sought it as despotism does, by amusing the people and not by enlightening it. It is, however, quite pleasant for a people to be amused, especially in lands where the tastes of the imagination are developed by the climate and the fine arts right down to the lowest social class. The people were not given coarse, soul-destroying pleasures, but music, pictures, improvisations, festivities, and the government looked after its subjects, as a sultan does with his harem. It only asked them, like women, not to meddle in politics, not to judge authority. But at this price, it promised them many entertainments and even a certain amount of glory. For the remains of Constantinople which enrich the churches, the flags of Cyprus and Crete which fly in the public square, the horses of Corinth, delight the eyes of the people. And the winged lion of San Marco seems to it the emblem of its glory.

As the form of government does not allow its subjects to be occupied with political matters, and as the city's situation makes agriculture, walking, and hunting impossible, entertainment remained the only interest for the Venetians; so this city was a city of pleasures.

The Venetian dialect is soft and light like a breath of pleasant air. It is difficult to conceive how people who resisted the League of Cambrai* spoke such a flexible language. This dialect is charming when devoted to gracefulness or humour, but when it is used for more serious purposes, when you hear verses on death recited in those delicate, almost childlike tones, you would think that the event, spoken of in this way, is only a poetic fiction.

In general, men in Venice have even more wit than those in other parts of Italy, because their government, such as it was, has more often given them opportunities to think. But their imaginations are not naturally as passionate as in the south of Italy, and through the habit of living in society, most women, though very pleasant, use a *sentimental* language which, while it in no way interferes with easygoing ways, only introduces affectation into love affairs. For all their faults, the great merit of Italian women is their lack of any trace of vanity. In Venice, where there is more social life than in any other Italian city, this merit is a little lost. This is because vanity is fostered, above all, by social life, in which people are applauded so quickly and so often that judgements are instantaneous and that, for success, *no allowance is made for time*, not even a minute. Nevertheless, in Venice were still to be found many traces of Italian originality and ease of manners. The greatest ladies received all their visitors in the cafés of the Piazza San Marco, and this strange confusion prevented the salons from becoming too serious an arena for the pretensions of self-esteem.

There still remained, too, popular ways and ancient practices. Now, these customs always imply respect for ancestors and a certain youthful spirit which does not weary of the past and the emotion it arouses. Moreover, the appearance of the town itself is unusually prone to arouse a host of memories and ideas. The Piazza San Marco is surrounded by blue tents where a crowd of Turks, Greeks, and Armenians take their ease. The church, with an exterior more like a mosque than a Christian place of worship, is at the far end. The place gives an idea of the indolent life of orientals, who spend their days in cafés, drinking sherbet and smoking perfumes. Sometimes in Venice you can see Turks and Armenians pass by, lying nonchalantly in open boats with pots of flowers at their feet.

The most aristocratic men and women never went out without wearing a black cloak. Often, too, gondolas, which are always black (for the egalitarian system in Venice applies mainly to externals), are propelled by boatmen dressed in white with pink sashes. There is something striking about the contrast. It is as if festive clothes had been left to the people while the important personages of the state are in perpetual mourning. In most European towns, writers' imaginations must take care to set aside what happens every day, because our customs, and even our luxury, are not poetic. But in Venice, nothing of this kind is commonplace. The canals and the boats form a picturesque scene out of the simplest events in life.

Along the Riva degli Schiavoni you usually come across puppet shows, mountebanks, and story-tellers who appeal to the people's imagination in all kinds of ways. The story-tellers, above all, are worth listening to. Usually it is passages from Tasso and Ariosto that they recite in prose to the great admiration of the audience. The listeners, arranged in a circle round the story-teller, are mostly half-clothed and sit quite still, so great is their attention. From time to time they are brought glasses of water, for which they pay as much as you would for wine elsewhere, and they are so spellbound that this simple refreshment is all they need for hours. The story-teller makes extremely excited gestures; he has a high-pitched voice, he gets angry, he gets enthusiastic, and yet you can see that fundamentally he is perfectly calm. You could say to him, as Sappho said to the Bacchante who was getting excited in cold blood: *Bacchante, you are not drunk, what do you want of me?* Nevertheless, the excited gesticulation of the inhabitants of the South does not seem affected. It is a strange habit, transmitted to them by the Romans, who also gesticulated a lot. It stems from their lively, brilliant, poetic temperament.

The imagination of a people captivated by pleasure was easily frightened by the prestige of power which surrounded the Venetian government. No soldier was ever seen in Venice, and when by chance, in a comedy, one was put on the stage with a drum, people rushed to the theatre. But an official of the state inquisition wearing a ducal emblem on his cap had only to appear to make thirty thousand men, assembled on a public holiday, come to order. It would be a fine thing if this simple power stemmed from respect for the law, but it was strengthened by terror of the secret measures used by the government to maintain order in the state. The prisons (an exceptional situation) were inside the Doge's palace itself. They were both above and below his apartments. *The Lion's mouth*, into which all denunciations were cast, was also in the palace occupied by the head of the government. The room where the state inquisitors sat was hung with black, and daylight came only from above. The trial was like a condemnation in advance. *The Bridge of Sighs*, as it was called, led from the Doge's palace to the prison for state criminals. You could hear cries of *Justice, help!* as you walked along the canal which flowed past these prisons, and those wailing, mingled voices could not be recognized. Finally, when a prisoner of state was condemned, a boat came to take him during the night. He went out by a little gate which opened out onto the canal. He was led some distance away from the town, and he was drowned in a part of the lagoons where fishing was prohibited—a horrible idea which perpetuates secrecy even after death and allows no hope to the unfortunate victim that his remains at least will inform his friends that he has suffered and is no longer alive.

At the time when Corinne and Lord Nelvil came to Venice, such executions had not taken place for more than a century, but the mystery that strikes the imagination still exists. Although Lord Nelvil was the last person to interfere in any way in the political affairs of a foreign country, he was nevertheless oppressed by such arbitrary verdicts from which there was no appeal and which hovered over every head in Venice.

CHAPTER IX

'You must not limit yourself to the painful impressions that these silent tools of power have made on you,' Corinne said to Lord Nelvil. 'You must also pay attention to the great virtues of the Senate, which made Venice a republic for noblemen and in former times inspired in them the energy and aristocratic grandeur which are the fruits of liberty, even though it is limited to a few. You will see them strict towards each other and, at least among themselves, establishing the virtues and rights which ought to belong to everyone. You will see them paternal towards their subjects as much as is possible when that class of men is considered only as regards their physical well-being. Finally you will find they are very proud of their native land, which belongs to them but which nevertheless they are able to endear even to the common people who are excluded from it in so many respects.'

Corinne and Oswald went together to see the room where the Great Council met in those days. Portraits of all the Doges are hung round it, but instead of the portrait of the Doge who was beheaded as a traitor* to his native land, they have painted a black curtain on which the day of his death and the nature of his punishment are recorded. The magnificent royal apparel of the Doges in the other pictures adds to the impression made by the terrible black curtain. In this room there is a picture of the Last Judgement and another of the occasion when Frederick Barbarossa,* the most powerful of emperors, humiliated himself before the Venetian Senate. It is a fine idea to combine in this way everything which must exalt the pride of a government on earth and make the same pride bow down before Heaven. Corinne and Lord Nelvil went to see the arsenal. In front of the arsenal door there are two statues of lions, made in Greece, then transported from the port of Athens to be the guardians of Venetian power, immobile guardians who defend only what is respected. The arsenal is filled with naval trophies. The famous ceremony of the Doge's marriage to the Adriatic Sea, indeed all the institutions of Venice, bear witness to the Venetians' gratitude to the sea. In this respect they have some links with the English, and Lord Nelvil felt keenly the interest which must have been aroused in him by these links.

Corinne took him to the top of the tower called the Campanile San Marco, which is a few steps away from the church. It is from there that you can see the whole city surrounded by the water, and the huge dyke which defends it against the sea. In the distance can be seen the coasts of Istria and Dalmatia. 'Beyond those clouds lies Greece,' said Corinne. 'Is not the mere thought of that moving? There, there are still men with lively imaginations and passionate characters, degraded by their condition but perhaps, like us, destined to revive one day the ashes of their ancestors. A country which has been alive is always something; at least the inhabitants blush for their present state, but in lands not consecrated by history, man does not even suspect that there is a fate other than the servile obscurity which his ancestors have handed down to him.

'The land of Dalmatia that you can see from here, and which was formerly inhabited by a very warlike people, still retains something wild about it. The Dalmatians know so little of what has happened for fifteen centuries that they still call all the Romans *the all-powerful*. It is true they show they have more up-to-date knowledge by naming you English *the warriors of the sea* because you have often landed at their ports. But they know nothing of the rest of the world,' continued

Corinne. 'I should like to see all the countries where there is some-thing unique about their manners, dress, and language. The civilized world is very monotonous and it does not take long to know it all. I have lived long enough for that already.' 'When one lives in your com-pany, can one ever come to the end of what makes one think and feel?' interrupted Lord Nelvil. 'May it be God's will that this attraction too is inexhaustible!' replied Corinne.

'But let us give another moment to Dalmatia,' continued Corinne. 'When we have come down from the eminence where we are, we shall not be able to see any longer even the vague outlines indicating that country, as indistinct from a distance as a recollection in human memory. The Dalmatians have their improvisers, so have savages. There were some in ancient Greece. There nearly always are some in peoples who have imagination and no social vanity. But natural wit turns into epigrams rather than into poetry in countries where the fear of being laughed at makes everyone hasten to be the first to grasp that weapon. The peoples who have remained nearer to nature have retained a respect for it which is of great use to the imagination. *Caves are sacred* say the Dalmatians. This is probably how they express a vague terror of earth's secrets. Their poetry is a little like Ossian's, although they live in the South. But there are only two very distinct ways of respond-ing to nature, to animate it as the ancients did, to perfect it in a thou-sand different ways, or, like the Scottish bards, to succumb to the mysterious fear, to the melancholy inspired by the uncertain and the unknown. Since I have known you, Oswald, I like the latter way. In the past I had enough hope and animation to like smiling pictures and enjoy nature without being afraid of destiny.' 'So it is I who have dried up that fine imagination to which I have owed the most intox-icating enjoyments of my life,' said Oswald. 'It is not you who are to blame,' replied Corinne, 'but a deep-seated passion. Talent needs an independence that true love never allows.' 'Oh, if that is the case,' cried Lord Nelvil, 'may your genius be silent, and your heart be all mine.' He was unable to utter these words without emotion, for in his thoughts they promised even more than he said. Corinne under-stood him and did not dare reply for fear of disturbing in any way the sweet emotion she felt.

She felt loved and, as she was used to living in a country where people sacrifice everything to feeling, she easily reassured herself and was convinced that Lord Nelvil would never be able to leave her. Both passionate and indolent, she imagined that it was enough to let a few days go by and the danger, which they no longer mentioned, would be over. In short, Corinne lived as most people do when the same misfortune threatens over a long period. They end up by thinking it will not happen, only because it has not yet happened.

The air in Venice, the life one leads there, is unusually suited to lulling the heart with hopes. The calm swaying of the boats inclines one to daydreaming and idleness. Sometimes you can hear a gondolier on the Rialto bridge beginning to sing a stanza of Tasso, while another gondolier at the other end of the canal replies with the following stanza. The very old melody of these stanzas is like a hymn, and at close range you are aware of its monotony. But in the open air, in the evening, when the notes linger over the canal like the reflections of the setting sun, and so Tasso's lines add the beauty of feeling to the combination of sight and sound, these songs are bound to inspire a gentle melancholy. Side by side, Corinne and Oswald spent long hours on the canals. Occasionally they said a word; more often, hand in hand, they gave themselves up in silence to the vague thoughts aroused by nature and love.

BOOK XVI
DEPARTURE AND ABSENCE

CHAPTER I

As soon as people heard of Corinne's arrival in Venice, everyone was very anxious to see her. When she went to a café in the Piazza San Marco, people crowded under the arcades round the square to catch sight of her for a moment, and all society very eagerly sought her out. In the past she used quite to like producing this dazzling effect everywhere she went, and she admitted unaffectedly that admiration was very attractive to her. Genius inspires the need for fame and, moreover, there is no good that is not desired by those to whom nature has given the means of obtaining it. Nevertheless, in her present situation, Corinne dreaded everything that was opposed to the habits of domestic life so dear to Lord Nelvil.

For her happiness, Corinne was wrong to become attached to a man who was bound to oppose the life that was natural to her, and repress rather than stimulate her talents. But it is easy to understand how a woman who has taken a great interest in literature and art can love in a man virtues and even tastes which differ from her own. We are so often weary of ourselves that we cannot be attracted by someone like ourselves. Community of feeling and opposite characters are required for love to arise both from fellow-feeling and diversity. Lord Nelvil possessed both these attractions to the highest degree. Corinne and he had similar ways of life, the same gentleness and ease in conversation, but he was none the less irritable and easily hurt and this never allowed his charming and obliging manners to be taken for granted. Although the depth and range of his ideas made him capable of everything, his political opinions and his military ideas made him more inclined to an active rather than to a literary career. He thought that actions are always more poetic than poetry itself. He belittled his intellectual success and on this matter spoke of himself with great indifference. To please him, Corinne tried to imitate him in this respect and began to despise her own conquests so as to be more like the modest, retiring women whose model was to be seen in Oswald's native land.

However, the homage rendered to Corinne in Venice made only a pleasing impression on Lord Nelvil. There was so much goodwill in the Venetians' welcome, they expressed their pleasure in Corinne's conversation so graciously and animatedly that Oswald keenly enjoyed being loved by a woman who was so seductively charming and universally admired. He was no longer jealous of Corinne's fame, as he was sure she preferred him to everything, and his love even seemed enhanced by what he heard people say about her. He even forgot England and took on something of the Italians' lack of concern about the future. Corinne noticed this change and her imprudent heart delighted in it, as if it had been able to last for ever.

Italian is the only European language whose different dialects have separate geniuses. One can compare verses or write books in each one of these dialects, which differ more or less from classical Italian. Nevertheless, among the different languages of the various Italian states, only Neapolitan, Sicilian, and Venetian have the honour of counting, and it is Venetian which is said to be the most original and charming of all. Corinne spoke it with sweetness and charm, and the way she sang some *barcaroles* of a light-hearted kind showed that she could act in comedy as well as in tragedy. She was urged to take a part in a light opera that was to be produced in society the following week. Since she had come to love Oswald, Corinne had not wanted to acquaint him with her talent in this sphere. She had not felt mentally free enough for such entertainment and sometimes she had even said to herself that such an abandonment to frivolity might bring misfortune. But this time, with unusual confidence, she agreed. Oswald encouraged her keenly to do so and it was agreed that she would act in *The Daughter of the Air*. That was the name of the play they chose.

Like most of Gozzi's plays, this one was made up of very original, spectacular, amusing scenes.[32] In these burlesque dramas, Truffaldino and Pantaloon* often appear beside the greatest kings on earth. The marvellous is treated humorously. But the comic is enhanced by that same marvellous which can never be in any way vulgar or base. The *Daughter of the Air* or *Semiramis in her Youth* is the coquette gifted by hell and heaven to conquer the world. Brought up in a cave like a savage, skilful as an enchantress, imperious as a queen, she combines natural liveliness with premeditated charm, warlike courage with feminine frivolity, and ambition with heedlessness. The part demands an imaginative and comic verve that can be given only by the inspiration of the moment. All society united to beg Corinne to take it on.

CHAPTER II

SOMETIMES destiny plays a strange, cruel game. It is as if it were a power which wants to arouse fear and rejects confident familiarity. Often when one is more hopeful than ever, and above all when one seems to trifle with fate and count on happiness, something fearful happens in the fabric of our life story, and the fatal sisters* come to weave their black thread into it and tangle up our handiwork.

It was on the seventeenth of November that Corinne woke up quite delighted to act in comedy that evening. To appear as a savage in the first act, she chose a very picturesque outfit. Her hair, which was supposed to be dishevelled, was, however, arranged with a care which showed a keen desire to be attractive, and her elegant, light, fantastic costume gave her noble face a look of coquetry and strangely charming cunning. She arrived at the mansion where the comedy was to be acted. Everybody was gathered there. Only Oswald had not yet arrived. Corinne delayed the performance as long as she could and began to be anxious about his absence. At last, as she was coming on stage, she caught sight of him in a very dark corner of the room. Well, she had at last caught sight of him, and as the very suffering caused by waiting redoubled her happiness she was inspired by cheerfulness, as at the Capitol she had been inspired by enthusiasm.

There was a mixture of song and speech, and the play was written in such a way that dialogue could be improvised. This gave Corinne a great advantage and made the scene more lively. When she sang, she made you appreciate the wit of the Italian *buffa* arias with a special elegance. Her gestures, accompanied by the music, were simultaneously comic and noble. She made people laugh without ceasing to be imposing, and by her role and talent dominated the actors and spectators, charmingly mocking both.

Oh, who would not have had pity on this performance if they had known that this confident happiness was going to attract a devastating blow and this triumphant joy would soon be replaced by the bitterest sorrows?

The spectators' applause was so repeated and sincere that their pleasure was felt by Corinne. She experienced the kind of emotion that is caused by entertainment when it conveys a keen feeling of life, when it inspires forgetfulness of fate and, for a moment, detaches the mind from every bond as from every cloud. Oswald had seen Corinne enact the greatest grief at a time when he deluded himself that he would make her happy. Now he saw her express unmixed happiness when he had just received news disastrous for them both. Several times he thought of snatching Corinne away from this rash gaiety; but he savoured a sad pleasure at seeing the brilliant expression of happiness on that lovely face for a few moments longer.

At the end of the play Corinne appeared elegantly dressed as an Amazon queen. She commanded men, and almost the elements, by that confidence in her charms that a beautiful woman can have when she is not sensitive, for being in love is enough to make one incapable of being entirely reassured by nature or fate. But the crowned coquette, the sovereign fairy, whose part Corinne was playing, combining quite marvellously anger with jocularity, indifference with the desire to please, and charm with despotism, seemed to reign over destiny as well as over hearts; and when she ascended the throne, she smiled at her subjects, ordering them with a gentle arrogance to obey her. All the spectators rose to applaud Corinne as the rightful queen. This was perhaps the moment in life when the fear of grief had been furthest from her, but suddenly she saw Oswald, who, unable to restrain himself any longer, was hiding his head in his hands to conceal his tears. She became anxious immediately and, though the curtain had not yet fallen, she came down from her already ill-fated throne and rushed into the neighbouring room.

Oswald followed her and, when she was near him and saw how pale he was, she was gripped by such fear that she had to lean against the wall to support herself. Trembling, she said to him, 'Oswald! Oh my God, what is the matter with you?' 'I must leave tonight for England,' he replied, without knowing what he was doing, for he ought not to have compromised his unhappy friend by giving her this news in such a way. She went up to him quite beside herself, saying, 'No, it is not possible for you to give me such sorrow. What have I done to deserve it? But you will take me with you?' 'Let us leave this terrible crowd, right away,' replied Oswald. 'Come with me, Corinne.' She followed him, no longer understanding what was being said to her, replying at random, stumbling, and with her face already so changed that everyone thought she had been stricken by some sudden malady.

CHAPTER III

As soon as they were in the gondola together, Corinne, in her frenzy of grief, said to Lord Nelvil, 'What you have just told me is a thousand times more cruel than death. Be generous. Throw me into these waters so that I can get rid of the feeling that is tearing me apart. Oswald, do so courageously. Less courage is needed for that than you have just shown.' 'If you say another word,' Oswald replied, 'I shall throw myself into the canal before your eyes. Listen to me. Let us wait till we are at your apartment; then you will make a decision about my fate and yours. In heaven's name, calm down.' There was so much unhappiness in the tone of Oswald's voice that Corinne became silent, but she trembled so violently that she could barely go up the staircase that led to her apartment. When she got there, she tore off her ornaments in terror. Lord Nelvil, seeing her in this state, the woman who had been so resplendent a few moments previously, threw himself into a chair, burst into tears, and cried, 'Am I a barbarian? Corinne, good God! Corinne, do you think I am?' 'No,' she said, 'no, I cannot think so. Do you not still have the look that made me happy, each day? Oswald, you, whose presence was like a ray of sunshine for me, can I be afraid of you? Can I be unable to raise my eyes to you? Can I stand here before you as before a murderer, Oswald, Oswald?' As she finished speaking, she fell, a suppliant, at his knees.

'What do I see?' he cried in a fury, raising her up. 'You want me to dishonour myself? Well, I shall. My regiment sets sail in a month. I have just had the news. I shall stay. Take care. I shall stay if you show me such grief, that grief which has complete power over me. But I shall not survive my shame.' 'I do not ask you to remain,' replied Corinne, 'but what harm do I cause you by following you?' 'My regiment is leaving for the West Indies, and officers are not allowed to take their wives with them.' 'At least, let me go with you as far as England.' 'The same letters that I have just received inform me that news of our liaison has spread in England, that the news-sheets have spoken of it, that people have begun to suspect who you are, and that your family, alerted by Lady Edgermond, has declared that it will never recognize you. Let me have time to bring your stepmother round and to force her to recognize her duty towards you. But if I arrive with you and am obliged to leave you before making her restore your name, I would expose you to all the severity of public opinion without being there to defend you.' 'So you deny me everything,' said Corinne, and as she finished speaking she fainted and bumped her head violently on the ground so that blood gushed forth. At this sight, Oswald uttered heart-rending screams. Theresina arrived, extremely upset, and revived her mistress. But when Corinne regained consciousness, she caught sight in a glass of her pale, distraught face and of her dishevelled, blood-stained hair. 'Oswald, Oswald,' she said. 'I was not like this when you saw me at the Capitol. On my brow I wore the crown of hope and fame. Now it is soiled with blood and dust, but you have no right to despise me for the state you have put me in. Others can, but you, you cannot. You must take pity on the love you have aroused in me; you must.'

'Stop,' cried Lord Nelvil. 'This is too much,' and signing to Theresina to go away, he took Corinne in his arms, saying, 'I have decided to remain. You will do as you like with me. I shall endure the fate Heaven destines for me, but I shall not desert you when you are so unhappy and I shall not take you to England before ensuring your lot. I shall not let you be exposed to the insults of a haughty woman. I shall stay, yes, I shall stay, for I cannot leave you.' These words revived Corinne but put her into a depressed state that was even worse than the despair she had just felt. She felt the necessity that weighed upon her and, with bowed head, for a long time remained silent. 'Speak, my love,' Oswald said. 'Let me hear the sound of your voice. That is all I have left to support me. I want to be guided by it.' 'No,' replied Corinne, 'no, you will go, you must.' And floods of tears showed her resignation. 'My love,' cried Lord Nelvil, 'I take as witness your father's portrait which is there before our eyes, and you know if the name of a father is sacred for me! I take it as a witness that my life is in your power, as long as it is required for your happiness. When I come back from the Indies, I shall see if I can give you back your native land and enable you to find again there the rank and life which are your due; but should I not succeed, I would come back to Italy to live and die at your feet.' 'Alas,' replied Corinne, 'and the dangers of war you are going to face . . .' 'Have no fear of them,' answered Oswald. 'I shall escape them; if, however, I were to die, I, the most obscure of men, my memory would remain in your heart. You will never, perhaps, hear my name mentioned without your eyes filling with tears; is that not so, Corinne? You will say: *I knew him; he loved me.*' 'Oh! Leave me, leave me,' she cried. 'You are deceived by my apparent calm. Tomorrow, when the sun returns and I say to myself, "I shall never see him again, I shall never see him again!" I may stop living, and that would be a stroke of luck!' 'Why, why, Corinne, are you afraid of not seeing me again? The solemn promise we have made to be united for ever, is it nothing to me? Can your heart doubt it?' cried Lord Nelvil. 'No, I respect you too much not to believe you,' said Corinne. 'It would cost me still more to give up my admiration for you than my love. I look on you as an angelic being, as the purest and noblest character who has appeared on earth. It is not only your charm that has captivated me; it is the thought that never before have so many virtues been combined in the same person; and your heavenly look has been given to you only to express them all. So it is far from me to have a single doubt about your promises. I would flee from the appearance of the human face; it would arouse more than terror if Lord Nelvil could deceive. But separation exposes one to so many hazards, but that terrible word *farewell* . . .' 'Never,' he interrupted, 'never, only on his deathbed will Oswald be able to bid you a last farewell.' And as he uttered these words, his emotion was so profound that Corinne, beginning to fear its effect on his health, tried to restrain herself, although she was the more to be pitied.

So they began to talk of the cruel departure, of the means of corresponding, and of the certainty of being reunited. A year was the limit fixed for Lord Nelvil's absence. Oswald was sure that the expedition should not take longer, but they still had a few hours left to them, and Corinne hoped she would have enough strength. Yet when Oswald told her that the gondola would come for him at three o'clock in the morning and when she saw on her clock that the moment was not very far away, all her limbs began to tremble. Indeed the approach of the scaffold would not have made her more fearful. At every moment Oswald, too, seemed to lose his resolve; Corinne had always seen him in control of himself, but her heart was torn by the sight of his anguish. Poor Corinne! She was comforting him, while she must have been a thousand times more unhappy than he was. 'Listen to me,' she said to Lord Nelvil. 'When you are in London, the frivolous men about town will tell you that promises of love do not bind a man's honour, that all Englishmen in the world have loved an Italian woman in the course of their travels and have forgotten her on their return, that a few months' happiness bind neither the woman who receives them nor the man who gives them, and that at your age your whole life cannot depend on the attraction you found for a time in the company of a foreign woman. They will appear to be right, according to society, but you, you who have known my heart whose master you have become, you who know how it loves you, would you find sophistry to excuse a mortal wound? And the frivolous, barbarous jokes of the fashionable men, will they stop your hand trembling as it plunges a dagger into my heart?' 'Oh, what are you saying?' cried Lord Nelvil. 'It is not only your grief that retains me; it is my own. Where shall I find a happiness like that I have enjoyed with you? Who in the universe would understand me as you have done? Love, Corinne, love, it is you alone who feel it, it is you alone who inspire it. That harmony of the soul, that mutual understanding of the mind and heart, with what woman other than you can it exist? Corinne, your friend is not a frivolous man, you know that; he is far from being that. He takes everything in life seriously. So is it only for you that he would be false to his own character?'

'No, no,' replied Corinne. 'You will not treat a sincere heart with contempt. And it is not you, Oswald, it is not you I would find unfeeling in my despair. But a redoubtable enemy near to you threatens me. It is the strict tyranny, the contemptuous mediocrity, of my stepmother. She will tell you everything that can discredit my past life. Spare me in advance the repetition of her pitiless remarks. The talents I may have are far from being an excuse in her eyes, and I know that for her they will be the greatest of my sins. She does not understand their attractions; she sees only their dangers. She finds useless, even blameworthy, everything that does not fit in with the destiny she planned for herself, and all the poetry of the heart seems to her an importunate caprice which claims the right to despise her reason. It is in the name of virtues which I respect as much as you do that she will condemn my character and my fate. Oswald, she will tell you I am unworthy of you.' 'And how shall I be able to listen to her?' interrupted Oswald. 'What virtues can one rate more highly than your generosity, your frankness, your kindness, your affection? Heavenly creature, may ordinary women be judged by the ordinary rules! But shame on him you would have loved, if he would not respect you as much as he adores you! Nothing in the universe equals your mind and heart. At the divine spring which is the source of feelings, everything is love and truth. Corinne, Corinne, oh, I cannot leave you! I feel my courage failing. If you do not support me, I shall not leave. And is it from you that I have to get the strength to give you pain?'

'Well,' said Corinne, 'I have a few more moments before commending my soul to God, so that he may give me the strength to hear the clock strike the hour fixed for your departure. We have loved each other, Oswald, with deep affection. I have confided in you the secrets of my life. The facts are nothing, but you know all the most intimate secrets of my being. I have not one idea which is not linked to you. If I write a few lines pouring out my soul, it is you alone who inspire me. It is to you I address all my thoughts, as my last breath will be for you. So where would my refuge be, if you deserted me? The fine arts portray your picture for me; music is your voice; heaven, your look. All the genius which, in the past, set my thoughts aflame is now nothing but love. Enthusiasm, reflection, understanding, I have nothing any more but what is in common with you.

'Almighty God who hears me!' she said, raising her eyes to Heaven. 'God who is not without pity for the sorrows of love, the noblest of all! When he stops loving me, take away my life, take away the pitiful remnant of existence which will be of no further use to me, except to suffer. He takes away with him the most generous and affectionate part of my nature. If he lets this fire I have placed in his heart be extinguished, my life, too, will be extinguished. Good God! You have not made me so that I can survive all noble feelings. And what would remain to me when I have ceased to esteem him? For he too must love me, he must. At the bottom of my heart I feel an affection which demands his. Oh, my God!' she cried once more, 'death or his love.' As she finished this prayer, she turned round towards Oswald, and found him prostrate before her in frightening convulsions. The excess of his emotions had surpassed his strength. He rejected Corinne's help, he wanted to die, and his reason seemed completely gone. Gently Corinne pressed his hands in hers, repeating to him all he had said himself. She assured him that she believed him, that she trusted in his return, and that she felt much more calm. These gentle words did Lord Nelvil some good. The nearer he felt the hour of separation had come, the more impossible he found it to make up his mind.

'Why should we not go to the Protestant church before my departure to make the vow of an eternal union?' he said to Corinne. At these words Corinne started, looked at Lord Nelvil, and her heart became extremely agitated. She remembered that when Oswald told her his story, he had said that a woman's grief had complete power over his behaviour, but he had added that his feelings cooled because of the very sacrifices that this grief aroused in him. All Corinne's strength of mind, all her pride, were revived at this thought, and after a few moments' silence, she replied, 'You must see your friends and your native land again before taking the decision to marry me. At this moment, my Lord, I would owe it to the emotion aroused by your departure. I do not want your decision to be influenced by that.' Oswald did not insist. 'At least,' he said, grasping Corinne's hand, 'I again make that vow; my faith is linked to the ring I gave you. As long as you retain it, no other woman will have rights over my lot. If you ever despise it, if you send it back to me . . .' 'Stop; stop expressing an anxiety you cannot feel. Oh, it is not I who will be the first to break the sacred union of our hearts. You know very well that it is not I, and I almost blush to assert again what is only too certain.'

However, time was marching on. Corinne turned pale at every sound, and Lord Nelvil was sunk in profound grief, no longer having the strength to utter a single word. At last, in the distance, the fatal light appeared, and soon afterwards the black boat stopped in front of the door. At the sight of it, Corinne screamed, drew back in terror, and fell into Oswald's arms, crying, 'There they are, there they are! Farewell, go, it is all over.' 'Oh, my God!' said Lord Nelvil, 'Oh, my father! Do you require this of me?' And pressing her to his heart, he covered her with his tears. 'Go,' she said, 'go, you must.' 'Call Theresina,' replied Oswald. 'I cannot leave you alone like this.' 'Alone, alas!' said Corinne. 'Am I not so till your return?' 'I cannot go out of this room,' said Lord Nelvil. 'No, I cannot.' And as he uttered these words his despair was such that his looks and his wishes called for death. 'Well,' said Corinne, '*I* shall give the sign; I shall go myself to open this door. But grant me a few moments.' 'Oh, yes,' cried Lord Nelvil, 'let us still stay together, let us stay. These cruel struggles are still better than not seeing you.'

Then, from Corinne's windows, the boatmen could be heard calling for Lord Nelvil's servants. They replied and one of them came and knocked at Corinne's door, announcing that *everything was ready*. 'Yes, everything is ready,' replied Corinne, and detaching herself from Oswald she went to pray, leaning her head against her father's portrait. At that moment her whole life must have appeared before her eyes. Her conscience exaggerated all her faults; she feared she did not deserve divine mercy, and yet she felt so unhappy that she had to believe in Heaven's pity. At last, lifting up her head, she held out her hand to Lord Nelvil, saying, 'Go; at the moment, I want you to, but perhaps in an instant I shall no longer be able to. Go, may God bless your steps, and may he protect me too, for I have sore need of his protection.' Oswald threw himself into her arms once more, and pressing her against his heart with a passion beyond words, trembling and pale like a man who goes to execution, he left the room. There, perhaps for the last time, he had loved, he had felt loved, in a way that destiny does not grant a second time.

When Oswald disappeared from Corinne's view, her heart began beating so violently that she could no longer breathe; her vision was so disturbed that the things she saw seemed to lose all reality and to wander, now near, now far from her eyes. She thought she felt the room sway as in an earthquake and she steadied herself to resist the motion. For a further quarter of an hour she heard the noise made by Oswald's servants as they completed the preparations for his departure. He was still there in the gondola; she could still see him again, but she was afraid of herself. And he, for his part, was lying almost unconscious in the gondola. At last he left, and at that moment Corinne rushed out of her room to call him back. Theresina stopped her. Then a terrible rainstorm began; a most violent wind could be heard, and the house where Corinne was staying shook almost like a ship in the middle of the sea. She felt very anxious about Oswald crossing the lagoons in that appalling weather and she went down to the water's edge with the intention of taking a boat, and following him at least until he reached solid ground. But the night was so dark that not a single boat was there. In a state of cruel anxiety, Corinne walked along the narrow pavements which separate the canal from the houses. The storm was becoming worse all the time, and every moment she was more afraid for Oswald. At random she called boatmen, who took her cries for the distress cries of the unfortunate people who were being drowned in the storm. No one dared go near the Grand Canal, however, so terrible were its violent waters.

In this state Corinne waited for the day. The weather calmed down, however, and the gondolier who had taken Oswald brought back the message from him that he had safely crossed the lagoons. This was almost like a moment of happiness again and it was only some hours later that the unfortunate Corinne felt again the void, the long hours, the sad days, and the anxious, all-consuming pain that henceforth was to possess her completely.

CHAPTER IV

FOR the first days of his journey, Oswald almost turned back twenty times to return to Corinne. But the reasons which were driving him on conquered this desire. To conquer love once is, in fact, a solemn step; the prestige of its omnipotence is at an end.

As he drew near to England, all the memories of his native land came back to Oswald. The year he had just spent in Italy had no connection with any other period of his life. It was like a brilliant apparition which had struck his imagination but had not been able to alter completely the opinions or tastes which had constituted his life till then. He found his former self again, and although the sorrow at being separated from Corinne prevented him from having any feeling of happiness, he nevertheless returned to a certain rigidity in his ideas that the intoxicating wave of the arts and Italy had washed away. As soon as he set foot in England, he was struck by the order and prosperity, by the wealth and industry, that greeted his eyes. The inclinations, habits, and tastes born with him were reawakened with more strength than ever. In this country where men have so much dignity and women so much modesty, where domestic happiness is linked to public happiness, Oswald thought of Italy to pity it. It seemed to him that in his native land human reason had left its noble imprint everywhere, while in Italy, in many respects, the institutions and social conditions only reflected confusion, weakness, and ignorance. The entrancing pictures, the poetic impressions, gave way in his heart to the deep feeling of liberty and morality. Although Corinne was still dear to him, he gently reproached her for being tired of living in a country that he found so noble and well ordered. In short, if he had gone from a land where imagination is worshipped to a barren or frivolous country, all his memories, all his soul, would have brought him back eagerly to Italy. But he was exchanging the vague desire of romantic happiness for pride in the true goods of life, independence, and security; he was returning to the life suited to men, action with a goal. Reverie is more for women, beings who are weak and resigned from birth. Men intend to get what they want, and the habit of courage, the feeling of strength, make them annoyed with their fate if they do not manage to guide it to their liking.

When he arrived in London, Oswald found his childhood friends again. He heard them speak the strong, concise language that seems to suggest far more feeling than it expresses. He saw again those serious faces which suddenly open up when deep affections conquer their usual reserve. He felt again the pleasure of making discoveries in hearts which gradually reveal themselves to observant eyes. In short, he felt he was in his native land, and those who have never left theirs do not know how many bonds make it dear to us. Yet Oswald did not separate the memory of Corinne from any of the impressions he was receiving, and as he felt more than ever that he belonged to England, he was very disinclined to leave it again, and all his thoughts brought him back to the resolution to marry Corinne and to settle in Scotland with her.

He was impatient to set sail so as to come back more quickly, when the order arrived to postpone the departure of the expedition of which his regiment formed a part. At the same time, however, it was announced that this delay might be ended, from one day to the next, and the situation was so uncertain that no officer could be free for a fortnight. This made Lord Nelvil very unhappy. He suffered cruelly at being separated from Corinne and at having neither the time nor the freedom necessary to form or follow any firm plan. He spent six weeks in London without going into society, entirely occupied by the moment when he would be able to see Corinne again, and suffering greatly from the time he was forced to spend far away from her. Finally he decided to use the waiting period to go to Northumberland to see Lady Edgermond and make her decide to recognize honestly that Corinne was Lord Edgermond's daughter and that the news of her death had been spread falsely. His friends showed him news-sheets in which very unfavourable insinuations had been made about Corinne's life, and he felt a burning desire to give her back both the rank and the esteem which were her due.

CHAPTER V

OSWALD left for Lady Edgermond's estate. He was moved at the thought of going to see the place where Corinne had spent so many years. He also felt some embarrassment at having to explain to Lady Edgermond his determination to give up her daughter. These different, mixed feelings upset him and made him thoughtful. As he got nearer to the north of England, the places he saw reminded him more and more of Scotland and of his father, who, never forgotten, entered even more deeply into his heart. When he reached Lady Edgermond's house, he was struck by the good taste of the layout of the garden and the house, and as the mistress of the establishment was not yet ready to receive him, he went for a stroll in the grounds. Through the foliage he saw, in the distance, a girl with a most elegant figure and with wonderfully beautiful fair hair barely contained under her hat. She was reading very attentively. Oswald recognized her as Lucile, despite not having seen her for three years, and in that period, having passed from childhood to being a young lady, she had become surprisingly more beautiful. He went up to her, bowed to her, and forgetting he was in England, he wanted to take her hand and kiss it respectfully according to Italian custom. The young lady took two steps backwards, blushed deeply, made a profound curtsey, and said, 'I shall tell my mother, Sir, that you want to see her,' and went away. Lord Nelvil was struck by her imposing, modest look and truly angelic face.

It was Lucile, who was just sixteen. Her features were remarkably delicate, her figure almost too slender, for a little weakness could be seen in her walk. Her complexion was wonderfully beautiful and paleness gave way to blushes in a moment. Her blue eyes were lowered so often that her expression lay mainly in that delicate complexion which, unknown to her, betrayed emotions which her deep reserve concealed in every other way. Since his travels in the South Oswald had forgotten the existence of such a face and such an expression. He was filled with a feeling of respect; he reproached himself keenly at having gone up to her with a kind of familiarity. When he saw that Lucile had entered the house, he went back there, meditating on the heavenly purity of a young girl who has never left her mother's side and whose only knowledge of life is filial affection.

Lady Edgermond was alone when she received Lord Nelvil. A few years previously, he had twice seen her with his father, but at that time he had not paid much attention to her. This time he looked at her closely, to compare her with the description that Corinne had given him. In many ways he found that description true, but it seemed to him that Lady Edgermond's eyes expressed greater sensitivity than Corinne had ascribed to her and he thought she was not as used as he was to reading reserved expressions. His first concern with Lady Edgermond was to persuade her to recognize Corinne by countermanding all the arrangements that had been made to make people believe she was dead. He began the conversation by speaking of Italy and the pleasure he had found there. 'It is an entertaining place for a man,' replied Lady Edgermond, 'but I should be very annoyed if a woman I was interested in could be happy there for long.' 'Nevertheless, I found there the most distinguished woman I have known in my life,' replied Lord Nelvil, already hurt by this insinuation. 'That is possible as far as the intellect is concerned,' answered Lady Edgermond, 'but an honest man looks for other virtues in his life's companion.' 'And he finds them too,' interrupted Oswald heatedly. He was about to continue and to express clearly what both he and Lady Edgermond had only suggested, but Lucile entered, came up to her mother, and spoke to her quietly. 'No, dear,' Lady Edgermond replied out loud. 'You cannot go to your cousin's today. You must dine here with Lord Nelvil.' At these words Lucile blushed even more deeply than in the garden and sat down beside her mother. Then she took some embroidery from the table and worked at it without ever raising her eyes or taking part in the conversation.

Lord Nelvil was almost annoyed at this behaviour, for probably Lucile was not unaware that there had been talk of their marriage. Although he was more and more impressed with Lucile's charming face, he recalled everything Corinne had said about the probable effect of the strict upbringing Lady Edgermond was giving her daughter. Usually in England, young girls have more freedom than married women, and reason as well as morality explains this custom. But Lady Edgermond departed from it, not for married women but for unmarried girls. She was of the opinion that, in all situations, the strictest reserve was appropriate for women. Lord Nelvil wanted to disclose his intentions about Corinne to Lady Edgermond as soon as he was alone with her again, but Lucile did not go away, and until dinnertime Lady Edgermond sustained the conversation about many subjects in a straightforward, clear, and rational way which aroused Lord Nelvil's respect. He would have liked to argue against opinions so fixed in every respect and often not in agreement with his own, but he felt that if he said a word to Lady Edgermond which did not fit in with her ideas, he would give her an opinion of him which nothing would erase, and so he hesitated to take this first, completely irrevocable step with someone who admitted of no nuances or exceptions and judged everything by general, unsentimental rules.

Dinner was announced. Lucile went up to her mother to give her her arm. Oswald noticed then that Lady Edgermond was walking with great difficulty. 'I have a very painful illness which may be fatal,' she said to Lord Nelvil. At these words Lucile turned pale. Lady Edgermond noticed this and continued gently. 'My daughter's care, however, has already saved my life once and perhaps will save it for a long time yet.' Lucile bowed her head to hide her emotion. When she lifted it again, her eyes were still wet with tears. But she had not even dared to take her mother's hand. Everything was in the depth of her heart and she had thought of others only to hide her feelings from them. Oswald, however, was deeply moved by her reserve and restraint, and his imagination, recently fired by eloquence and passion, enjoyed gazing at this picture of innocence; he thought he could see some indescribable cloud of modesty around Lucile which was extremely soothing.

Lucile wanted to spare her mother the slightest fatigue during dinner and served her everything with unremitting care. Lord Nelvil heard the sound of her voice only when she offered him the different dishes. These insignificant words were, however, spoken with charming sweetness and Lord Nelvil wondered how it was possible for the simplest movements and the most ordinary words to reveal a whole soul. 'You need either Corinne's genius, which surpasses everything the imagination can wish for, or mysterious veils of silence and modesty, which allow every man to infer whatever virtues and feelings he desires,' he said to himself. Lady Edgermond and her daughter rose from table and Lord Nelvil wanted to follow them. But Lady Edgermond kept so scrupulously the custom of leaving the table at dessert that she told him to remain at table until she and her daughter had made tea in the drawing room; Lord Nelvil joined them a quarter of an hour later. He could not spend a single moment alone with Lady Edgermond the whole evening, for Lucile did not leave her. He did not know what he ought to do and he was about to leave for the neighbouring town, thinking he would come back the next day to speak to Lady Edgermond, when she invited him to spend the night at the house. He accepted immediately without attaching any importance to it, and yet afterwards he regretted he had done so, because he thought he could notice in Lady Edgermond's look that she considered this consent a reason for believing he was still thinking of her daughter. It was an additional reason which made him decide to ask her straight away for an interview, which she set for the following morning.

Lady Edgermond had herself carried into the garden. Oswald offered to help her to take a few steps. Lady Edgermond looked at him steadily and then said, 'Yes, please.' Lucile gave him her mother's arm and, fearing her mother might hear her, whispered to him, 'My Lord, walk carefully.' Lord Nelvil started at these words, said in secret. Thus a sensitive word could have been addressed to him by that angelic face which did not seem made for earthly affections. It did not occur to Oswald that his emotion at that moment might have offended Corinne. It seemed to him it was merely a homage to Lucile's celestial purity. They returned in time for evening prayers, which Lady Edgermond held in her house every evening with all her assembled servants. They were gathered together in the great hall downstairs. Most of them were old and infirm. They had served Lady Edgermond's father and the father of her husband. Oswald was keenly moved at the sight, which reminded him of what he had often seen in his father's house. Everyone knelt down, except for Lady Edgermond, whose illness prevented her, but she put her hands together and lowered her eyes in a meditation worthy of respect.

Lucile was on her knees beside her mother and it was she who had the task of doing the reading. First of all, it was a chapter of the Gospels, and then a prayer adapted to domestic and rural life. This prayer was composed by Lady Edgermond, and in its language there was a kind of severity which contrasted with the sound of her daughter's gentle shy voice, but this very severity increased the effect of the last words which Lucile uttered in a quavering tone. After praying for the servants of the house, for relatives, for the King, for the country, came the words, 'Oh God, vouchsafe us the grace that the daughter of this house may live and die without her soul being stained by a single feeling in discordance with her duty, and may her mother, who is soon to return to you, obtain forgiveness for her own failings in the name of the virtues of her only child.'

Lucile repeated this prayer every day. But that evening, in Oswald's presence, she was more moved than usual, and tears fell from her eyes before she had finished reading and could cover her face with her hands to conceal her tears from every gaze. But Oswald had seen them flow, and pity mingled with respect filled his heart. He looked at the youthful appearance, so much like a child's, and at the expression still seeming to retain the recent memory of Heaven. Such a charming face, in the midst of these faces all depicting old age or

illness, seemed the image of divine pity. Lord Nelvil reflected on
the austere, secluded life Lucile had led, on her matchless beauty,
deprived in this way of all the pleasures as well as of all the homage
of society, and his soul was filled with the purest emotion. Lucile's
mother, too, deserved his respect and she obtained it. She was someone who was even more strict with herself than with others. The limitations of her mind were attributable to her extremely strict principles
rather than to a lack of natural intelligence. Within all the bonds she
had imposed on herself, within all her natural and acquired rigidity,
there was a passion for her daughter, all the deeper since the severity
of her character came from a repressed sensitivity, giving new strength
to the only affection she had not stifled.

At ten o'clock in the evening, the deepest silence reigned in the
house. Oswald could reflect at his ease on the day that had just passed.
He did not admit to himself that Lucile had made an impression on
his heart. Perhaps that was not even true as yet, but although Corinne
charmed the imagination in a thousand ways, there was nevertheless
a class of ideas, a musical note, if one may put it that way, which harmonized only with Lucile. The pictures of domestic happiness were
more easily linked to the Northumberland retreat than to Corinne's
triumphal chariot. In short, Oswald could not conceal from himself
that Lucile was the wife his father would have chosen for him. But
he loved Corinne; he was loved by her; he had sworn never to form
other ties, and that was enough to make him persist in his plan of
declaring to Lady Edgermond the next day that he wanted to marry
Corinne. He fell asleep thinking of Italy but nevertheless he dreamt
he saw Lucile passing lightly before him in the shape of an angel. He
woke up and wanted to put this dream aside, but the same dream came
back again and again, and the last time it appeared, the figure seemed
to fly away. He woke up again, regretting this time that he could not
retain the form that was disappearing from view. Then day began to
appear. Oswald went downstairs to go for a walk.

CHAPTER VI

THE sun had just risen and Lord Nelvil thought no one in the house
had yet woken up. He was mistaken. Lucile was already drawing on
the balcony. Her hair, which she had not yet tied back, was blowing
about in the wind. Like this, she resembled Lord Nelvil's dream, and

for a moment he was moved at seeing her, as if she were a supernatural apparition. But, soon afterwards, he was ashamed of being so moved by something so ordinary. For some time, he remained in front of the balcony. He bowed to Lucile, but he could not have been noticed, for she did not lift her eyes from her work. He continued his walk and then, more than ever, he would have liked to see Corinne so that she could dispel the vague feelings he could not explain to himself. Lucile attracted him as the mysterious and the unknown. He would have liked Corinne's genius to bring about the disappearance of the slight figure which took all shapes successively in his eyes.

He returned to the drawing room and there he found Lucile, who was putting the picture she had just drawn into a little brown frame opposite her mother's tea-table. Oswald saw the drawing. It was only a white rose on its stem, but perfectly and gracefully drawn. 'So you can paint,' Oswald said to Lucile. 'No, my Lord, I only know how to copy flowers, and even then only the easiest ones. There is no teacher here, and the little I have learned I owe to a sister who gave me lessons.' She sighed as she said these words. Lord Nelvil blushed deeply, saying, 'And this sister, what happened to her?' 'She is no more,' answered Lucile, 'but I shall always miss her.' Oswald realized that, like the rest of the world, Lucile had been deceived about her sister's fate, but the words, *I shall always miss her*, seemed to him to disclose an affectionate nature and this touched him. Lucile was about to withdraw, suddenly realizing she was alone with Lord Nelvil, when Lady Edgermond came in. With a glance that was both strict and surprised, she looked at her daughter and signed to her to leave the room. This glance told Oswald something he had not yet appreciated, namely that Lucile had done something quite unusual for her, in staying in the same room alone with him for a few minutes without her mother. He was as much moved by this as he would have been by a very obvious indication of interest from another woman.

Lady Edgermond sat down and dismissed her servants, who had supported her as far as her chair. She was pale and her lips were trembling as she offered Lord Nelvil a cup of tea. He noticed her agitation and this increased his own embarrassment. Yet, motivated by the desire to render service to the woman he loved, he began the conversation. 'My Lady,' he said to Lady Edgermond, 'in Italy, I saw a great deal of a woman of particular interest to you.' 'I do not think so, for no one in that country interests me,' replied Lady Edgermond curtly. 'Yet I would have thought your husband's daughter had claims to your affection,' continued Lord Nelvil. 'If my husband's daughter were someone negligent of her duties as of her reputation, I would certainly wish her no harm, but I should be very pleased never to hear of her,' replied Lady Edgermond. 'And if the daughter you have abandoned were the woman in the world most justly famous for her wonderful talents of every kind, would you still reject her?' asked Oswald, heatedly. 'Just as much,' answered Lady Edgermond. 'I have no esteem for talents which divert a woman from her real duties. There are actresses, musicians, and artists to entertain people. But for a woman of our rank, the only fitting lot is to devote herself to her husband and to bring up her children well.' 'What!' replied Lord Nelvil. 'Those talents which come from the soul, and which can occur only in the loftiest, the most sensitive character, those talents which are combined with the most touching goodness, the most generous heart, you would blame them because they extend the mind, because they give even to virtue a greater sway, a wider influence?' 'To virtue?' answered Lady Edgermond, smiling bitterly. 'I do not know what you understand by the word used in that way. The virtue of a woman who fled from her father's house, the virtue of a woman who settled in Italy, leading an extremely independent life, accepting homage from every one, to say the least, setting an example even more harmful to others than to herself, abdicating her rank, her family, even her father's name . . .' 'My Lady,' interrupted Oswald, 'it was a generous sacrifice she made to your wishes, to your daughter. She was afraid of harming you by keeping your name.' 'She was afraid,' exclaimed Lady Edgermond. 'So she felt she was dishonouring it.' 'You have gone too far,' interrupted Oswald violently. 'Corinne Edgermond will soon be Lady Nelvil, and then, my Lady, we shall see if you blush to recognize in her your husband's daughter! You apply ordinary rules to someone who is gifted as no woman has ever been, an angel of intelligence and goodness, a wonderful genius but nevertheless a sensitive and reserved nature, a sublime imagination, unlimited generosity, someone who might have done wrong because such remarkable superiority does not always fit in with ordinary life, but a woman with such a beautiful soul that she is above her faults, and one single deed or word erases them all. She honours the man she chooses as her protector more than the queen of the world would do in nominating her husband.' 'Perhaps, my Lord,' replied Lady Edgermond, making a great effort to control herself, 'you may blame my limited mind, but there is nothing in all you have just told me which is within my understanding. By morality I mean only the exact observation of the established rules. Beyond that, I perceive only a bad use of gifts which, at most, deserve pity.' 'The world would have been very dull, my Lady, if there had never been either genius or enthusiasm and if human nature had been made so regimented and monotonous,' replied Oswald. 'But without further continuing this useless argument, I have to ask you formally if you will recognize Miss Edgermond as your stepdaughter when she has become Lady Nelvil.' 'Less than ever,' answered Lady Edgermond, 'for I owe it to your father's memory to prevent, if I can, a most disastrous marriage.' 'What, my father!' said Oswald, always upset at hearing this name. 'Are you not aware,' Lady Edgermond continued, 'that he refused Miss Edgermond's hand for you before she had committed any fault, when, with his characteristic wisdom, he only foresaw what she would be one day?' 'What! You know . . .' 'Your father's letter to Lord Edgermond on the matter is in the hands of his old friend, Mr Dickson,' interrupted Lady Edgermond. 'When I heard of your relationship with Corinne in Italy, I sent it to him so that he would enable you to read it on your return. It was not fitting for me to take charge of it.'

For a few moments Oswald was silent. Then he replied, 'What I ask of you, my Lady, is what is right, what you owe to yourself. Contradict the tales you have authorized about your stepdaughter's death and recognize her honourably for what she is, for Lord Edgermond's daughter.' 'I do not want to add to the unhappiness of your life in any way,' replied Lady Edgermond, 'but if Corinne's present existence, her anonymous, independent existence, may be a reason for your not marrying her, may God and your father preserve me from removing that obstacle!' 'My Lady,' answered Lord Nelvil, 'Corinne's misfortune would be an additional bond between her and me.' 'Indeed!' replied Lady Edgermond, with an indignation she had never before expressed and which no doubt came from her disappointment at losing for her daughter a husband who suited her in many ways. 'Indeed,' she continued, 'make yourselves unhappy, then, both of you, for she will be, too. She hates this country. She is unable to fit in with our ways, with our strict life. She needs a theatre where she can display all those gifts you prize so highly and which make life so difficult. You will see her become bored in this country and want to go back to Italy. She will take you with her. You will leave your friends, your and your father's native land, for a foreign woman who, I admit, is pleasing, but who would forget you if you wanted her to, for there is nothing more fickle than these passionate imaginations. Deep grief is felt only by what you call ordinary women, that is to say, those who live only for their husbands and children.' Lady Edgermond, always used to self-control, had, perhaps, not once in her life let herself go to such an extent, and her nerves, already in a bad state, were so shaken that, as she finished speaking, she fainted. When Oswald saw her in this state, he rang vigorously for help.

Lucile arrived, very frightened, hastened to help her mother, and gave Oswald an anxious look which seemed to say: *Is it you who have harmed my mother?* Her look moved Lord Nelvil deeply. When Lady Edgermond had recovered, he tried to show her his concern, but she spurned him coldly and blushed to think that, in showing her emotion, she had perhaps lacked pride for her daughter and disclosed her wish to give her Lord Nelvil as a husband. She motioned to Lucile to go away, and said, 'In any case, my Lord, you must consider yourself free from any kind of commitment which might have existed between us. My daughter is so young that she cannot have been able to become attached to the plan that your father and I had formed. As this plan has changed, however, it is more fitting that you should not return to my house as long as my daughter is unmarried.' Oswald bowed to her, saying, 'I shall restrict myself, then, to writing to you to discuss the fate of someone whom I shall never desert.' 'That is for you to decide,' replied Lady Edgermond in a choked voice. Lord Nelvil left.

As he rode down the drive he saw Lucile's slim figure at a distance in the wood. He slowed his horse's pace to see her for longer and it seemed to him that Lucile, hiding behind the trees, was going in the same direction as he was. The main road passed in front of a lodge at the end of the grounds and Oswald noticed that Lucile went into it. Touched, he rode past the house, but could not see her. After passing it, he turned his head round several times and in another place, from which all the main road could be seen, he noticed a slight movement by one of the trees near the lodge. He stopped opposite the tree, but he could not perceive the smallest movement. Unsure whether his surmise was correct, he left. Then suddenly he retraced his steps with lightning speed, as if he had dropped something on the road.

He then saw Lucile by the roadside and he bowed to her respectfully. Lucile lowered her veil hurriedly and plunged into the wood, not thinking that to hide like this was to confess the motive bringing her there. The poor child had never in her life experienced any feeling so intense or arousing such a sense of guilt as that which led her to want to see Lord Nelvil go by. She did not even remotely think of simply greating him; instead she believed she had lost his esteem through his guessing her intention. Oswald understood all these impulses and felt pleasantly flattered by the innocent interest which was so shyly and sincerely expressed. 'No one could be more sincere than Corinne,' he thought, 'but no one knew herself and others better. Lucile has to be taught both the love she would feel and the love she would arouse. But can this attraction of one day last a lifetime? Since this attractive ignorance of one's own feelings does not last, however, and since in the end one must understand one's own heart and know what one feels, is not the frankness which survives this discovery worth still more than the frankness which precedes it?'

Thus his thoughts compared Corinne and Lucile. But this comparison was as yet only a simple intellectual diversion; at least he thought so, and he did not imagine that it could ever give him further food for thought.

CHAPTER VII

AFTER leaving Lady Edgermond's house, Oswald went to Scotland. The agitation aroused by Lucile's presence, the feeling he retained for Corinne, all that gave way to his emotion at the sight of the places where he had spent his life with his father. He blamed himself for the amusements he had indulged in over the past year. He was afraid of no longer being worthy to enter the house which he wished he had never left. Alas, after we have lost the person we have loved most in the world, how can we be satisfied with ourselves if we have not remained in the deepest seclusion? We have only to live in society to neglect in some way the worship of those who are no more. It is in vain that their memory remains in the depth of our hearts. We take part in the activities of the living, which set aside the idea of death as either painful or useless or even as only tiring. Indeed, if solitude does not prolong sorrow and meditation, life, such as it is, takes a fresh hold of the most affectionate souls and restores to them interests,

desires, and passions. This need for distractions is a pathetic require-
ment of human nature. Although Providence has willed man to be
like this so that, in the midst of these distractions, he can bear death
both for himself and others, we feel gripped by remorse at being capable of them, and it is as if a touching, resigned voice is saying to us:
You whom I loved, have you then forgotten me?

These feelings filled Oswald's mind as he returned to his home.
This time, when he came back, he did not feel the same despair as
the first time, but he had a deep feeling of sadness. He saw that time
had made everyone used to the loss of the man for whom he mourned.
The servants no longer felt they had to mention his father's name to
him, and everyone had returned to his usual occupations. Ranks had
been closed and the children's generation was replacing their fathers'.
Oswald went and shut himself in his father's room, where he still
found his cloak, his stick, and his chair, all in the same place. But
what had become of the voice that replied to his, and the father's heart
which beat faster when he saw his son again? Lord Nelvil remained
sunk in deep meditation. 'Oh human destiny,' he cried, his face bathed
in tears, 'what do you want of us? So much life in order to perish, so
many thoughts only for everything to come to an end! No, no, he can
hear me, my only friend. He is present in this very place, sees my
tears, and our immortal souls wait for each other. Oh father! Oh God!
Guide me in life. Those iron souls, which seem to contain in themselves the unchanging qualities of physical nature, they do not know
either indecision or repentance. But beings with imagination, sensitivity, and conscience, can they take one step without being afraid
of going astray? They look to duty as a guide, but duty itself is not
clear to them, unless God reveals it to our innermost hearts.'

In the evening, Oswald went for a walk along his father's favourite
path. He followed his image through the trees. Alas! Who, in his fervent prayers, has not sometimes hoped that a beloved shade would
appear, in short, that by dint of loving, a miracle would be vouch-
safed? Vain hope! Before the grave we shall know nothing. Greatest
of all uncertainties, you are of no interest to ordinary people. But the
more noble thoughts become, the more they are invincibly attracted
to the unfathomable abyss of meditation. While Oswald was totally
absorbed in them, he heard a carriage in the drive; an old man got
out and walked slowly towards him. Lord Nelvil was moved at the
sight of an old man at this hour and in this place. He recognized Mr

Dickson, his father's old friend, and he greeted him with an emotion he would never have felt for him at any other moment.

CHAPTER VIII

MR DICKSON was not at all the equal of Oswald's father. He had neither his mind nor his character. But he had been with him when he died, and, being born in the same year, it was as if he had remained behind for a few days to bring him news of this world. Oswald gave him his arm to help him climb the stairs. He felt some pleasure in taking this care of an old man whose age was the only resemblance to his father that he could find in Mr Dickson. The old man had seen Oswald's birth and was not slow to talk to him frankly about all his affairs. He strongly disapproved of his liaison with Corinne, but his weak arguments would have had much less ascendancy over Oswald's mind than Lady Edgermond's if Mr Dickson had not handed him the letter that his father, Lord Nelvil, had written to Lord Edgermond when he wanted to cancel the planned marriage between his son and Corinne, at that time Miss Edgermond. Here is the letter, written in 1791 during Oswald's first journey to France. He trembled as he read it.

Oswald's father's letter to Lord Edgermond

'Will you forgive me, my friend, if I suggest a change in the marriage plans between our two families? My son is eighteen months younger than your elder daughter. It would be better to give him Lucile, your younger daughter, who is twelve years younger than her sister. That alone would be sufficient reason, but as I knew Miss Edgermond's age when I asked you for her hand for Oswald, I would think I was betraying the trust of friendship if I did not tell you the reasons why I do not want this marriage to take place. We have been friends for twenty years; we can speak to each other frankly about our children, all the more so as they are young enough still to be able to be moulded by our advice. Your daughter is charming, but I think I see in her one of those beautiful Greek women who delighted and conquered the world. Do not take offence at the idea which this comparison may suggest. I am sure you have given your daughter, and she has found in her heart, only the purest principles and feelings, but she needs to please, to charm, to attract attention. She has far more gifts than vanity, but such exceptional talents are bound to arouse the desire to develop them, and I do not know what audience can satisfy the intellectual activity, the eager imagination, the ardent nature, which can be felt in all she says. She is bound to lead my son to leave England, for such a woman cannot be happy here, and Italy alone will suit her.

'She needs the independent life which is subject only to the imagination. Our country life, our domestic habits, are bound to be contrary to all her tastes. A man born in our fortunate native land must, above all, be English. He must fulfil his duties as a citizen, since he has the good fortune to be one, and in a country where political institutions give men honourable opportunities for action and public appearances, women must stay in the shade. How do you expect a person as exceptional as your daughter to be content with such a lot? Believe me, marry her in Italy; her religion, her tastes, and her talents call her there. If my son married Miss Edgermond, he would certainly love her greatly, for no one could be more attractive, and then, to please her, he would try to introduce foreign ways into his house. Soon he would lose the national spirit, the prejudices, if you like, which unite us and our nation; we are a group, a community, which is free but indissoluble, and can perish only with the last one of us. My son would soon be ill at ease in England when he saw that his wife would not be happy here. He has, I know, all the weakness resulting from sensitivity, and so he would settle in Italy, and if I were still alive, his expatriation would make me die of grief. It is not only because it would deprive me of my son, but also because it would deny him the honour of serving his country.

'What a fate for one of our mountain dwellers to lead an idle life in the heart of Italy's pleasures! A Scotsman to be his own wife's *cicisbeo*,* unless he is to be that of another man's wife! Useless to his family, whom he no longer leads and supports! Your daughter would exercise a great influence on Oswald, being the man I know him to be. So I am gratified that his present stay in France has kept from him the opportunity of seeing Miss Edgermond. I beg you then, my friend, that if I should die before my son marries, you should not give him the opportunity of knowing your elder daughter until your younger daughter is old enough to attract his attention. I believe our friendship is old enough and sacred enough to ask of you this sign of affection. If necessary, tell my son my wishes in this matter. I am sure he will respect them, and even more so if I am no longer alive.

'Please do all you can to promote the marriage between Oswald and Lucile. Although she is still very much a child, I have discerned the most touching modesty in her features, in the expression of her face, in the sound of her voice. She is the kind of truly English woman who will make my son happy. If I do not live long enough to witness this marriage, I shall rejoice in it in Heaven. When we are reunited there one day, my good friend, our blessing and our prayers will still protect our children.

'Ever yours,
'NELVIL'

When Oswald had read this letter, he remained in profound silence for a long time. That gave Mr Dickson an opportunity to continue his lengthy discourse without being interrupted. He admired the wisdom of his friend, who had made such a sound judgement about Miss Edgermond, although, he said, he was far from being able to imagine the blameworthy way she had since behaved. In the name of Oswald's father, Mr Dickson declared that such a marriage would be a mortal insult to his memory. From his father's friend Oswald learned that, during his disastrous stay in France, in 1792, a year after this letter had been written, his father had found solace only at Lady Edgermond's house, where he had spent a whole summer and had taken care of Lucile's education, and he was exceptionally fond of her. In short, clumsily but also unsparingly, Mr Dickson attacked Oswald's heart in the most sensitive places.

Thus it was that everything combined to destroy the absent Corinne's happiness. All she had to defend herself were her letters, which, from time to time, recalled her to Oswald's memory. She had to fight against natural circumstances, the influence of the native land, a father's memory, the conspiracy of friends in favour of easy decisions and the usual road in life. She had to fight, too, the burgeoning charm of a young girl who seemed so well in tune with the pure, calm hopes of domestic life.

BOOK XVII
CORINNE IN SCOTLAND

CHAPTER I

MEANWHILE Corinne had settled near Venice in a district on the shores of the Brenta. She wanted to stay in the area where she had seen Oswald for the last time; moreover, she thought that there she was nearer than in Rome to letters from England. Prince Castel-Forte had written to her, offering to come and see her, but she had declined. Their friendship deserved trust, but if he had tried to detach her from Oswald, if he had said the usual thing, namely that absence is bound to cool feeling, such thoughtless words would have been like a dagger blow for Corinne. She preferred, therefore, to see no one. But it is not easy to live alone with a passionate soul in an unhappy situation. Solitary occupations all require a calm mind, but when one is troubled by anxiety, a forced distraction, however intrusive it may be, is better than the same unremitting feeling. If one can surmise what leads to madness, it is surely when a single thought takes hold of the mind and no longer allows a succession of subjects to vary one's ideas. Moreover, Corinne had such a lively imagination that she wore herself out when her faculties no longer obtained food from outside.

What a life followed after the one she had recently been leading for nearly a year! Oswald had been with her almost the whole day; he followed all her movements; he listened eagerly to every one of her words; his mind stimulated Corinne's. The similarities and the differences between the two of them enlivened their conversation, and all the time Corinne could see his gentle, affectionate look which unceasingly paid attention to her. When she had the slightest anxiety, Oswald would take her hand and press it to his heart; then calm, and more than calm, a vague and delightful hope, would be reborn in Corinne's soul. Now, outside all was desert, and in the depth of her heart was only gloom. The only event, the only change in the variety of her life, was Oswald's letters and, during the winter, the irregularity of the post aroused in her a torturing expectancy; often, however, this expectancy was disappointed. Every morning she would go for a walk by the banks of the canal, whose waters are slowed down by the weight of large leaves called water lilies. She would wait for the black gondola which brought the letters from Venice. She had become able to make it out from far away and her heart would beat with frightening violence as soon as she caught sight of it. The courier would get out of the gondola and sometimes he would say: *Madame, there are no letters*. Then he would calmly go on dealing with the rest of his business, as if nothing were so simple as having no letters. Another time he would say: *Yes, Madame, there are some*. With trembling hands she would look through them all but Oswald's writing could not be seen. Then the rest of the day was terrible. She would not sleep all night, and the next day she felt the same anxiety which filled all her hours.

In the end, she blamed Lord Nelvil for her suffering. It seemed to her he could have written more often, and she reproached him. He justified himself, and his letters already became less affectionate, for instead of expressing his own anxieties he was concerned to dispel his beloved's.

These subtleties did not escape the sad Corinne, who, day and night, would study a sentence, a word of Oswald's letters, trying by constant re-reading to discover an answer to her fears, a new interpretation which could give her a few calm days.

This situation shattered her nerves and weakened the power of her mind. She became superstitious and busied herself with the continual predictions that one can make from every event, when always pursued by the same fear. One day a week she would go to Venice so that she could have her letters a few hours earlier that day. In this way she varied the torture of waiting for them. At the end of a few weeks, she had conceived a kind of horror at all the things she saw on her way there and back. All of them were like ghosts of her thoughts and would repeat them before her eyes with horrible features.

Once, when she went into Saint Mark's church, she recalled that, on arriving in Venice, the thought had occurred to her that, before he left, Lord Nelvil would take her there and make her his wife before Heaven. She then gave herself up to this illusion completely. She saw him enter under these porticoes, go up to the altar, and promise God to love Corinne for ever. She thought she knelt before Oswald and in this position received the nuptial crown. The organ which could be heard in the church, the torches which illuminated it, brought her vision to life, and, for a moment, instead of the cruel void of absence, she felt the loving emotion which fills the soul and makes the voice of the loved one audible in the depth of the heart. Suddenly a dismal murmur attracted Corinne's attention, and as she turned round she noticed a coffin being brought into the church. When she saw this, she stumbled, her vision was clouded, and from that moment her imagination convinced her that her feeling for Oswald would be the cause of her death.

CHAPTER II

WHEN he had read his father's letter, handed to him by Mr Dickson, for a long time Oswald was the most unhappy and undecided of men. To break Corinne's heart or fail in his duty to his father's memory was such a cruel dilemma that he prayed for death a thousand times in order to escape it. In the end he did again what he had done so many times; he postponed the moment of decision and said to himself that he would go to Italy to make Corinne herself judge of his torments and of the decision he ought to take. He thought his duty required him not to marry Corinne. He was free never to espouse Lucile. But in what way could he spend his life with his beloved? Ought he to sacrifice his country to her or bring her to England with no regard for her reputation or her fate? In this painful perplexity he would have gone to Venice if, from month to month, the rumour had not got abroad that his regiment was going to embark. He would have gone to tell Corinne what he could not yet bring himself to write to her.

The tone of his letters, however, had perforce changed. He did not want to write about what was going on in his heart, but he could not express himself so freely. He had resolved to hide from Corinne the obstacles he was encountering in the plan to have her recognized, because he was still hoping it would, in time, be successful, and he did not want to embitter her uselessly against her stepmother. Different kinds of reticence made his letters shorter. He filled them with irrelevant topics, saying nothing about his future plans. Indeed, someone other than Corinne would have certainly known what was going on in Oswald's heart, but passionate love makes one more understanding though, at the same time, more credulous. In this state it is as if you can look at things only in a supernatural way. You discover what is hidden and delude yourself about what is clear, for you are repelled by the thought that you suffer to such an extent without some extraordinary cause, and that such despair is produced by very ordinary situations.

Oswald was very unhappy because of both his personal situation and the pain he was bound to cause to the woman he loved. His letters expressed his irritation without giving its cause. In a strange way, he blamed Corinne for his distress, as if she had not been a thousand times more to be pitied than he was. In short, he made Corinne completely distraught. She was no longer in control of herself. Her mind became clouded, her nights were filled with the most disastrous visions. By day they did not disappear and the unhappy Corinne could not believe that the Oswald who wrote such harsh, anxious, and bitter letters was the one she had known so generous and so affectionate. She felt an irresistible desire to see him again and to speak to him. 'Let me hear him,' she cried, 'let him tell me that it is he who can so pitilessly thus rend the heart of the woman whose least pain used formerly to grieve him deeply. Let him tell me so and I shall submit myself to fate. But surely some infernal power must inspire such language. It is not Oswald; no, it is not Oswald who writes to me. Someone close to him has slandered me. Indeed there is some perfidy when there is so much unhappiness.'

One day Corinne made the decision to go to Scotland, if the overwhelming pain which compels a change of situation at any price can be called a decision. She did not dare write to anyone that she was leaving. She had not been able to make up her mind to tell even Theresina and she still deceived herself that her own reason would persuade her to stay. She only soothed her imagination by planning a journey, with a thought different from that of the day before, with a little hope for the future put in place of regrets. She was incapable of doing anything; reading had become impossible for her, music only made her quiver painfully, and natural scenery, which inclines one to reverie, only increased her suffering. This lively woman spent whole days motionless, or at least without any visible movement. The torments of her soul were only revealed by her deathly pallor. At every moment she would look at her watch, hoping that an hour had passed. She did not know, however, why she wanted the name of the hour to be changed, since it brought nothing new other than a sleepless night and a still more painful day.

One evening, when she thought she was ready to leave, a woman asked to see her. She received her because she was told that the woman seemed very eager in her desire. She saw a completely deformed person come into the room, her face disfigured by a frightful illness. She was dressed in black and covered with a veil to conceal, if possible, her appearance from those she approached. This woman, so ill-treated by nature, was given the task of collecting alms. Nobly and with a touching confidence, she asked for help for the poor. Corinne gave her a great deal of money, only making her promise to pray for her. The poor woman, who had become resigned to her fate, looked with surprise at this beautiful lady so full of strength and life, rich, young, and admired, but who seemed overwhelmed by unhappiness. 'My goodness, Madame!' she said, 'I wish you were as calm as I am.' What words from a woman in this state addressed to the most brilliant person in Italy, who was succumbing to despair!

Oh, the power of love is too great, too much for passionate souls! How happy are those who devote to God alone the deep feeling of love, for which the earth's inhabitants are unworthy! But the time for that had not yet come for Corinne. She still had to have illusions, she still wanted happiness. She prayed, but she was not yet resigned. Her rare talents, the fame she had acquired, still meant too much to her. It is only by detaching oneself from everything in this world that one can renounce what one loves. All the other sacrifices precede that one, and life can be a desert for a long time before the fire which has devastated it is extinguished.

Finally, in the midst of the doubts and struggles which constantly overturned and renewed Corinne's plan, she received a letter from Oswald. In it he announced that his regiment was to embark in six weeks and that he could not use this time to go to Venice because a colonel who went away at such a time would lose his reputation. There only remained time for Corinne to reach England before Lord Nelvil left Europe, perhaps for ever. This fear finally made Corinne decide to go. Corinne has to be pitied, for she was not unaware that her step was unwise. She judged herself more severely than anyone else did, but what woman would have the right to cast *the first stone** at the unfortunate who does not justify her error, who expects no pleasure from it but flees from one misfortune to another as if dreadful spectres pursued her from all directions?

Here are the last lines of her letter to Prince Castel-Forte: 'Farewell, my faithful protector, farewell, my Roman friends, farewell, all of you with whom I have spent such pleasant, carefree days. It is all over; destiny has struck me; I feel its fatal wound within me; I am still struggling, but I shall succumb. I must see him again. Believe me, I am not responsible for my own actions. Within my heart are storms which my will cannot control. But I am drawing near to the conclusion when all will be over for me. What is taking place now is the last chapter of my story; after that will come penitence and death. What strange confusion in the human heart! At this very moment when I behave like someone so passionately in love, in the distance I can see nevertheless the shadows of twilight; I think I hear a divine voice saying to me: *Unfortunate woman, still some turbulent days of love and then I await you in eternal rest*. O, God! Grant me Oswald's presence once more, one last time. The memory of his features has become, as it were, dimmed in my despair. But was there not something divine in his look? When he entered, did not a gleaming, pure atmosphere herald his coming? My friend, you saw him stand near me, surround me with attention, protect me by the respect aroused for his choice. Oh, how can I exist without him? Forgive my ingratitude. Ought I to thank in this way the faithful, noble affection you have always shown me? But I am no longer worthy of anything, and I would be thought crazy if I did not have the sad gift of observing my folly myself. So, farewell, farewell.'

CHAPTER III

How unhappy is the sensitive, refined woman who behaves very imprudently, who does it for a man who, she thinks, loves her less, and when she has only herself to support her in all she is doing! If she risked her reputation and peace of mind to render a great service to the man she loves, she would not need to arouse pity. It is so delightful to devote oneself. There are so many joys in the heart when one braves all dangers to save a life which is dear to us, to relieve the grief which is rending a heart beloved by our own. But to cross unknown lands alone, to arrive without being expected, to blush straight away in front of the loved one because of the very proof of love you give him, to risk everything because you want to, and not because another asks you to, what a painful feeling that is! What humiliation, yet worthy of pity! For all that stems from love deserves pity. How would it be if one compromised the lives of others in this way, if one failed in one's duties to sacred ties? But Corinne was free; she sacrificed only her reputation and her peace of mind. There was no reason, no prudence, in her behaviour, but nothing that could hurt any other fate than her own, and her fatal love ruined only herself.

When she reached England, Corinne learned from the news-sheets that the departure of Lord Nelvil's regiment was delayed still further. In London she saw only the banker to whom she was recommended under an assumed name. He took an interest in her straight away and hastened to render her all kinds of service, as did his wife and daughter. When she arrived she fell dangerously ill, and for a fortnight her new friends looked after her with the most affectionate kindness. She learned that Lord Nelvil was in Scotland but that in a few days he was to come to London, where his regiment then was. She did not know how to make up her mind to tell him she was in England. She had not written to him about her departure. She was so embarrassed about this that Oswald had not received any letters from her for a month. He began to be very worried by this and accused her of frivolity as if he had had the right to complain. When he reached London, he went straight away to his banker, where he hoped to find letters from Italy. He went out and, as he thought sadly about this silence, he met Mr Edgermond, whom he had seen in Rome and who asked him for news of Corinne. 'I haven't any,' replied Lord Nelvil crossly. 'I am not surprised,' said Mr Edgermond. 'These Italian women always forget foreigners as soon as they stop seeing them. There are a thousand examples of that, and one must not be upset about it. They would be too lovable if they combined constancy with so much imagination. Some advantage must remain to our women.' As he said this, he shook Lord Nelvil's hand and took leave of him to go back to the principality of Wales, where he usually lived. But in a few words he had filled Oswald's heart with sadness. 'I was wrong,' he said to himself, 'wrong to want her to miss me, since I cannot devote myself to her happiness. But to forget so quickly somebody one has loved is to sully the past at least as much as the future.'

As soon as Lord Nelvil had learned his father's wish, he had resolved not to marry Corinne. He had also decided not to see Lucile again. He was annoyed at the rather strong impression she had made on him and said to himself that, as he was condemned to hurt his beloved so much, he should at least retain in his heart the fidelity which no duty commanded him to sacrifice. He satisfied himself with writing to Lady Edgermond to renew his earnest request about Corinne's existence. But she steadily refused to reply to him about the matter, and from his conversations with Mr Dickson, Lady Edgermond's friend, Lord Nelvil learned that the only way of obtaining what he wanted from her was to marry her daughter. This was because she thought that Corinne could stand in the way of her daughter's marriage if she took her real name again and if her family recognized her. Corinne did not yet suspect the interest Lucile had aroused in Lord Nelvil. Till then fate had spared her that grief. Never had she been so deserving of him, however, as at the very moment when fate separated her from him. During her illness, amongst the unpretentious, honest business people at whose home she was, she had acquired a genuine taste for English ways and customs. The small number of people whom she saw in the family that had received her were in no way distinguished but had remarkable rationality and good judgement. They showed her an affection less demonstrative than what she was used to but which made itself known at every opportunity by new services. Lady Edgermond's strictness, the boredom of a little provincial town, had given her a cruel illusion about everything that was good and noble in the country she had renounced, but she linked herself to it again in a situation in which, for her happiness at least, it was perhaps no longer desirable that she should have this feeling.

CHAPTER IV

ONE evening the family who showed friendship and concern for Corinne in a thousand ways keenly urged her to come and see Mrs Siddons* in *Isabella, or the Fatal Marriage*, one of the English plays in which that actress shows a very outstanding talent. For a long time, Corinne refused to go, but remembering at last that Lord Nelvil had often compared her elocution with Mrs Siddons's, she was curious to hear her and went veiled to a little box, from which she could see everything without being seen. She did not know that the previous day Lord Nelvil had arrived in London, but she was afraid of being seen by an Englishman who had known her in Italy. The actress's noble demeanour and deep sensitivity so riveted Corinne's attention that during the first scenes she did not look away from the stage. English elocution is more suited than any other to move the heart when a fine talent makes one appreciate the force and originality of the words. It is less artificial, less conventional, than the French. It arouses feeling immediately. Genuine despair would be expressed like this. As the kind of play and the style of versification place dramatic art less far from real life, the effect produced is all the more heart-rending. You need to be all the more gifted to be a great actor in France, as there is very little freedom for individual style and the general rules are so important.[33] But in England you can risk everything if it is inspired by nature. Those long groans which are ridiculous when you just talk about them are thrilling when you hear them. Mrs Siddons, the actress with the noblest demeanour, loses none of her dignity when she prostrates herself on the ground. There is nothing that cannot be marvellous when a deep emotion inspires it, an emotion which stems from the innermost heart and dominates the person who feels it even more than the person who witnesses it. Each nation has a different way of performing tragedy, but the expression of grief can be understood from one end of the world to the other. From the savage to the king, there is something alike in all men when they are really unhappy.

In the interval between the fourth and fifth acts Corinne noticed that all eyes were turned towards one box, and in this box she saw Lady Edgermond and her daughter, for she had no doubt that it was Lucile, although in seven years she had become remarkably more beautiful. The death of a very rich relative of Lord Edgermond had obliged Lady Edgermond to come to London to attend to the business of the inheritance. Lucile had dressed more elegantly than usual to come to the theatre, and even in England, where the women are so beautiful, no one had seen such a remarkably beautiful girl. Corinne was painfully surprised when she saw her. It seemed impossible to her that Oswald could resist the attraction of such a face. Mentally she compared herself to Lucile, and she thought herself so inferior, she exaggerated to herself, if that were possible, the charm of youth, of that fair complexion, of that blond hair, of that innocent picture of the springtime of life; and so she felt almost humiliated to struggle, by means of talent and wit, in short, by acquired or at least perfected gifts, against these charms lavished by nature itself.

Suddenly, in the opposite box, she caught sight of Lord Nelvil, whose eyes were fixed on Lucile. What a moment for Corinne!

For the first time, she saw again the features which had filled her thoughts so much, the face which, at every moment, she sought in her memory and which had never left her. And it was when Lucile alone filled Oswald's thoughts. Of course he could not have suspected Corinne's presence, but if, by chance, his eyes had been turned towards her, the unfortunate woman would have drawn from this some omen of happiness. At last, Mrs Siddons reappeared and Lord Nelvil's eyes turned to the stage to look at her. Corinne then breathed more easily and persuaded herself that a simple impulse of curiosity had attracted Oswald's attention to Lucile. From moment to moment, the play became more moving and Lucile was bathed in tears; she tried to hide them by retiring to the back of her box. Then Oswald looked at her again with even more interest than the first time. Finally the terrible moment came when Isabella, escaping from the hands of the women who want to prevent her from killing herself, laughs at the futility of their efforts as she stabs herself with a dagger. This laugh of despair is the most difficult and remarkable effect that dramatic art can produce. It is more moving than tears; such bitter irony is the most heart-rending expression of unhappiness. How terrible is the suffering of the heart when it inspires such barbaric joy, when at the sight of its own blood it gives the fierce pleasure of a savage enemy who would have avenged himself!

Presumably Lucile was then so moved that her mother was alarmed, for she could be seen to turn round anxiously. Oswald got up as if he wanted to go towards her, but soon afterwards he sat down again. This second movement made Corinne a little happier, but she said to herself with a sigh, 'My sister Lucile, formerly so dear to me, is young and sensitive. Ought I to want to deprive her of something good, which she would be able to enjoy unhindered, without the man she would love making any sacrifice for her sake?' When the play was over, Corinne wanted to let everyone go out before leaving, for fear of being recognized, and she placed herself behind a little aperture in her box from where she could see what was happening in the corridor. When Lucile went out, the crowd collected to see her, and exclamations about her beautiful face could be heard on all sides. Lucile became more and more embarrassed. Lady Edgermond, crippled and ill, had difficulty in making her way through the crowd, in spite of her daughter's attentions and the consideration they were shown. They knew no one, however, and consequently no man dared approach them.

Seeing their difficulty, Lord Nelvil hastened to go up to them. He gave one arm to Lady Edgermond and the other to Lucile, who took it shyly, lowering her head and blushing excessively. In this manner they passed in front of Corinne. Oswald could have no idea that his poor friend was the witness of a sight that was so painful to her. He had, in fact, a slight touch of pride in escorting the most beautiful girl in England through the countless admirers who followed her steps.

CHAPTER V

CORINNE returned to her lodgings in a cruelly agitated state. She did not know what she would decide, how she would let Lord Nelvil know of her arrival, and what she would tell him to justify herself. Every moment she was losing her confidence in her friend's feelings, and it seemed to her sometimes that she was going to see a stranger. He was a stranger whom she loved passionately but who would no longer recognize her. She sent a message to Lord Nelvil the next evening and she learned that he was at Lady Edgermond's. The following day, she received the same reply but she was also told that Lady Edgermond was ill and would go back to her estate as soon as she was better. Corinne was waiting for this moment to let Lord Nelvil know she was in England, but every evening she would go out, walk past Lady Edgermond's house, and see Oswald's carriage at her door. An inexpressible pang burdened her heart and she would return to her own lodgings. The next day she would take the same walk to experience the same grief. Corinne was wrong, however, when she persuaded herself that Oswald went to Lady Edgermond's with the intention of marrying her daughter.

On the day they had gone to the theatre, as he was escorting her to her carriage Lady Edgermond had told Oswald that the legacy of Lord Edgermond's relative, who had died in India, affected Corinne as well as Lucile. She therefore asked him to come and see her, and to agree to let Corinne in Italy know what arrangements she wanted to make in the matter. Oswald promised to go and it seemed to him that, just then, Lucile's hand, which he was holding, had trembled. Corinne's silence could have made him think he was no longer loved and this young girl's emotion must have given him the idea that in

the depth of her heart she was interested in him. He did not, however, have any thought of failing in his promise to Corinne, and the
ring she had in her possession was a certain pledge that he would never
marry another without her consent. He went back the following day
to take care of Corinne's interests, but Lady Edgermond was so ill,
and her daughter was so worried at being alone like this in London
with no relative (since Mr Edgermond was not there), without even
knowing which doctor to call, that Oswald thought his duty to his
father's friend obliged him to devote his time to looking after her.

Lady Edgermond, who was by nature harsh and proud, seemed to
soften only towards Oswald. She allowed him to visit her every day,
although he did not say a word which might lead her to think he
intended to marry her daughter. Lucile's name and beauty made her
one of the most brilliant matches in England. Since her appearance
at the theatre, people knew she was in London and so her door was
besieged by visits from the greatest nobles in the land. Lady Edgermond steadily refused to receive anyone. She never went out and
received only Lord Nelvil. How could he not have been flattered by
such sensitive behaviour? This silent generosity, which relied on him
without making any demands or complaints, touched him keenly.
Nevertheless, each time he went to Lady Edgermond's house, he was
afraid that his presence would be interpreted as a pledge. He would
have stopped going there as soon as Corinne's interests had no longer
required him to, if Lady Edgermond had recovered her health. But
just as she was thought to be better, she fell ill again, more dangerously than the first time. If she had died just then, Lucile's only support in London would have been Oswald, since her mother had made
no contact with anyone.

Lucile had not allowed herself to say a single word which would
have made Lord Nelvil think she preferred him, but sometimes he
could suspect it by a slight, sudden change in the colour of her complexion, by too quick a lowering of her eyes, by quicker breathing.
In fact he studied the girl's heart with a curious affectionate interest,
but her complete reserve always left him in doubt and uncertainty
about the nature of her feelings. The highest point of passionate love
and the eloquence it inspires still do not satisfy the imagination. You
always want something more, and if you cannot get it you become
cold and weary. But the faint glimmer you can see through the clouds

holds curiosity in suspense for a long time and seems to promise new feelings and new discoveries in the future. This expectation, however, is not satisfied. In the end, when you know what is hidden by all the charm of silence and the unknown, the mystery, too, fades and you come back to regretting the lack of restraint and the animation of a lively personality. Alas! How can one prolong the enchantment of the heart, the delights of the soul, that confidence and doubt, happiness and unhappiness, dissipate equally in the end? So alien to our fate are heavenly joys! Sometimes they pass through our hearts only to remind us of our origin and our hope.

When Lady Edgermond was feeling better, she fixed her departure two days from then to go to Scotland, where she wanted to pay a visit to Lord Edgermond's estate, which was next to Lord Nelvil's. She expected him to suggest going with her since he had declared his plan of going back to Scotland before his regiment left. But he said nothing about it. At that moment Lucile looked at him, but he was still silent. She got up hurriedly and went to the window. A few moments later, Lord Nelvil made a pretext to go up to her and it seemed to him that her eyes were wet with tears. He was moved by this and sighed, and remembering again that he blamed his beloved for forgetting him, he wondered if this girl was not more capable of fidelity than Corinne.

Oswald tried to remedy the pain he had given Lucile. It is so enjoyable to bring happiness back to a still childlike face! Sorrow is not made for these countenances, where even reflection has not yet left a mark. Lord Nelvil's regiment was to be on parade the following morning in Hyde Park, so he asked Lady Edgermond if she wanted to go in a barouche with her daughter and if, after the review, she would allow him to ride on horseback with Lucile beside her carriage. Lucile had said once that she very much wanted to go horse-riding. She looked at her mother with an expression that was still very obedient but where one could see the desire for permission. Lady Edgermond thought for a few moments, then she held out to Lord Nelvil her feeble hand, which every day became more and more wasted, saying: 'If you ask, my Lord, I agree.' These words made such an impression on Oswald that he himself was going to give up his suggestion, but suddenly Lucile, more animated than before, took her mother's hand and kissed it to thank her. Lord Nelvil then had not the heart to deprive of a pleasure an innocent creature who led such a sad, lonely life.

CHAPTER VI

FOR a fortnight Corinne had felt cruelly anxious. Every morning she wavered about writing to Lord Nelvil to tell him where she was, and every evening she was inexpressibly grieved to know that he was at Lucile's. What she suffered in the evening made her more nervous for the next day. She blushed at the thought of telling the man who perhaps did not love her any more about the thoughtless step she had taken for him. 'Perhaps,' she said to herself, 'all the memories of Italy have been erased from his mind? Perhaps he no longer needs to find a superior mind and a passionate heart in women? What attracts him now is the remarkable beauty of a sixteen-year-old, the angelic expression of that age, the shy, virgin heart which devotes the first feelings she has ever experienced to the man of her choice.'

Corinne's imagination was so impressed by her sister's advantages that she was almost ashamed to fight against such charms. It seemed to her that even talent was a ruse, wit a tyranny, and passionate love a violence beside this unarmed innocence, and although Corinne was not yet twenty-eight, she already foresaw that period of life when, with so much pain, women mistrust their ability to be attractive. In short, jealousy and shy pride fought against each other in her soul. From day to day she put off the dreaded, longed for moment when she was to see Oswald again. She heard that his regiment was to march past, the next day, in Hyde Park and she resolved to go. She thought it possible that Lucile would be there and she trusted her own eyes to form an opinion about Oswald's feelings. At first she had the idea of dressing with carefully chosen elegance, and then appearing suddenly before him. As she began to dress, however, her black hair, her complexion, slightly tanned by the Italian sun, her prominent features (and as she looked at herself she could not judge their expression), made her doubt her attractions. She kept seeing in her mirror her sister's ethereal face, and throwing far from her all the jewels she had tried on, she put on a Venetian-style black dress, covered her face and figure with the cloak worn in that country, and, thus clad, plunged into the back of a carriage.

She had barely arrived at Hyde Park when she saw Oswald appear at the head of his regiment. In his uniform he had the most handsome and imposing appearance in the world. He guided his horse with perfect skill and elegance. The music that could be heard had something simultaneously proud and gentle about it, nobly commanding sacrifice of one's life. Crowds of men, elegantly and simply dressed, bore the stamp of male virtues on their faces, while beautiful, modest women bore that of the virtues of timidity. The soldiers of Oswald's regiment seemed to look at him with trust and devotion. They played the famous tune, *God save the King*, which touches all hearts so deeply in England. And Corinne cried, 'Oh! worthy country which was to have been my mother country, why did I leave you? What did personal fame matter in the midst of so many virtues, and what fame was worth that of being your dignified wife, Lord Nelvil?'

The gunfire that could be heard reminded Corinne of the dangers that Oswald was going to encounter. She looked at him for a long time without his being able to see her, and said to herself, her eyes full of tears: 'May he live, even if it will not be for me! Oh God, it is he that must be preserved!' Just then Lady Edgermond's carriage arrived. Lord Nelvil greeted her respectfully by lowering the point of his sword in front of her. The carriage went to and fro several times. Everyone who saw Lucile admired her. Oswald gazed at her with looks that pained Corinne's heart. The unfortunate woman knew those looks; they had once been directed towards her.

The horses Lord Nelvil had lent to Lucile galloped down the avenues of Hyde Park with dazzling speed, while, almost like a funeral procession, Corinne's carriage moved forward slowly behind the swift chargers with their tumultuous clatter. 'Oh!' thought Corinne. 'It was not like this, no, it was not like this that I went to the Capitol the first time I met him. He has hurled me from the triumphal chariot into the abyss of grief. I love him, and all life's joys have disappeared. I love him, and all nature's gifts are withered. Forgive him, God, when I am no more!' Oswald on horseback passed by Corinne's carriage. The Italian style of the black garment which enveloped her struck him strangely. He stopped, went round the carriage, retraced his steps to see it again, and tried to catch sight of the woman who was hidden there. Meanwhile Corinne's heart was beating with extreme violence. She feared only that she would faint and so would be discovered. She conquered her emotion, however, and Lord Nelvil abandoned the thought that had first occurred to him. So as not to attract Oswald's attention further, when the review ended Corinne got out of the carriage while he could not see her, and hid behind the trees and the crowd in such a way that she could not be seen. Oswald then went up to Lady Edgermond's barouche and, show-ing her a very gentle horse that his servants had brought, he asked permission for Lucile to ride it alongside her mother's carriage. Lady Edgermond agreed, asking him repeatedly to look after her daughter. Lord Nelvil had dismounted. Bareheaded, he was speaking at Lady Edgermond's carriage door with an expression on his face so respect-ful and, at the same time, so full of feeling that Corinne saw in it only too clearly an affection for the mother, stimulated by the attraction aroused by the daughter.

Lucile got out of the carriage. She had a riding habit which out-lined delightfully her elegant figure; on her head she had a black hat decorated with white feathers, and her beautiful blond hair, light as air, fell gracefully round her charming face. Oswald lowered his hand so that Lucile could put her foot on it to mount the horse. Lucile expected that one of her servants would render this service. She blushed to receive it from Lord Nelvil. He insisted; at last Lucile put a charm-ing foot on his hand and leapt onto the horse so lightly that all her movements gave the impression of one of those sylphs whom our imag-inations depict in such delicate colours. She set off at a gallop. Oswald followed and did not lose sight of her. Once the horse stumbled. Lord Nelvil stopped it instantly, examined the bridle and the bit with an affectionate concern. Another time he mistakenly thought the horse was bolting. He turned pale as death and, urging on his own horse with extraordinary eagerness, he reached Lucile's in a second, dis-mounted, and rushed in front of her. Lucile, unable to restrain her horse any more, trembled in her turn in case she knocked Oswald down. But with one hand he grasped the bridle, and with the other supported Lucile, who leaned upon him lightly as she jumped down.

What more was needed to convince Corinne of Oswald's feelings for Lucile? Did she not see all the marks of interest which formerly he had lavished on her? And even, to her eternal despair, did not she think she could see more shyness and reserve in Lord Nelvil's eyes than he had ever had at the time of his love for her? Twice she pulled the ring from her finger; she was ready to cut through the crowd to throw it at Oswald's feet, and the hope of dying instantly encouraged her in this resolution. But what kind of woman, even one born in the sunny South, can, without trembling, attract the attention of the crowd to her feelings? Soon Corinne shuddered at the thought of appear-ing before Lord Nelvil just then and left the crowd to go back to her carriage. As she was crossing a lonely path Oswald saw again from a distance the same black figure which had struck him before, and this time it produced a much keener impression on him. He attributed the emotion he felt, however, to remorse at having been on that day, for the first time, unfaithful in the depth of his heart to the image of Corinne. On returning home he immediately resolved to go back to Scotland, since his regiment was still not going to set sail for some time.

CHAPTER VII

CORINNE went back to her lodgings in a state of grief which shook her reason, and from that moment her health was permanently affected. She decided to write to Lord Nelvil to tell him both about her arrival in England and about all she had suffered since she had been there. At first she began the letter with the most bitter reproaches, and then she tore it up. 'What is the point of reproaches in love?' she cried. 'Would this feeling be the purest, the most intimate and generous of feelings if it were not in every way involuntary? What use would my complaints be? Another voice, another look, have the key to his heart. So has not everything been said?' She began her letter again, and this time she wanted to describe the monotony he might find in his marriage with Lucile. She tried to prove to him that without perfect harmony of heart and mind no happiness in love would last. And then she tore up that letter even more eagerly than the first one. 'If he does not know my worth,' she said, 'is it I who will tell him about it? Moreover, should I speak like that about my sister? Is it true that she is as inferior to me as I try to persuade myself? And even if she is, I have pressed her against my heart like a mother in her childhood, is it I who ought to say so? Oh, no! one must not want one's own happiness in this way, at any price. This life, during which one has so many desires, this life passes. And even a long time before death something gentle and meditative gradually detaches us from existence.'

She took up her pen once more and spoke only of her unhappiness, but in writing about it she felt such self-pity that she covered her paper with tears! 'No,' she said again. 'I must not send this letter. If he resists it, I shall hate him. If he gives in to it, I shall not know if he has not made a sacrifice, if he does not retain the memory of another. It is better to speak to him, and give him back this ring, the pledge of his promises. And she hurried to wrap it up in a letter in which she wrote only the words: *You are free.* And putting the letter in her bodice, she waited till evening was coming to go to Oswald's house. It seemed to her that in broad daylight she would have blushed in front of everyone who would have looked at her, and yet she wanted to go before the time when Lord Nelvil usually went to Lady Edgermond's. So she set off at six o'clock, but trembling like a condemned slave. One is so afraid of the beloved, once confidence is lost! Oh, the man who is passionately loved is, in our eyes, either the most reliable protector or the most dreaded master.

Corinne stopped her carriage in front of Oswald's door and, in a trembling voice, asked the man who opened the door if Lord Nelvil was at home. 'Half an hour ago, Madam, his Lordship set off for Scotland,' he replied. This news wrung Corinne's heart. She trembled at the thought of seeing Oswald; her heart was ahead of this inexpressible emotion. The effort had been made; she thought she was about to hear his voice and now she had to take a new decision to find him, to wait several more days, to stoop to yet another step. Nevertheless, Corinne wanted to see him again at any price. So the next day she set off for Edinburgh.

CHAPTER VIII

BEFORE leaving London, Lord Nelvil had gone back to his banker's, and when he learned there had been no letter from Corinne, he wondered bitterly if he should sacrifice certain, permanent domestic happiness for someone who perhaps no longer remembered him. He decided, however, to write to Italy again, as he had already done several times during the last six weeks, to ask Corinne the cause of her silence, and to declare yet again that as long as she had not returned his ring, he would never be the husband of another woman. He travelled with very painful feelings. He loved Lucile almost without knowing her, for he had not yet heard her utter twenty words. But he missed Corinne and was saddened by the circumstances which separated them. He was captivated in turn by the shy charm of the one and by the outstanding gracefulness, the sublime eloquence, of the other as he recalled them. If, at that moment, he had known that Corinne loved him more than ever, that she had left everything to follow him, he would never have seen Lucile again. But he thought he was forgotten, and meditating on Lucile's character and on Corinne's, he said to himself that a cold, reserved exterior often concealed the deepest feelings. He was mistaken. Passionate hearts reveal themselves in a thousand ways and what is always restrained is very weak.

A circumstance arose which further added to Lord Nelvil's interest in Lucile. On coming back to his estate, he passed so close to Lady Edgermond's that he went there out of curiosity. He had opened for him the room where Lucile usually worked. This room was filled with mementoes of the time Oswald's father had spent with Lucile while his son was in France. She had erected a marble pedestal at the very place where, a few months before his death, he gave her lessons. On the pedestal was engraved: *To the memory of my second father*. And a book was lying on the table. Oswald opened it. He recognized the collection of his father's thoughts and on the first page he found these words in his father's hand, *To her who consoled me for my sorrows, to the purest heart, to the angel who will be the glory and joy of her husband*. With what emotion Oswald read these lines in which the opinion of the man he revered was so clearly expressed! In his father's reticence Lord Nelvil thought he could see the most exceptional tact, the fear of forcing his choice by the idea of a duty. And he was struck by the words: *To her who consoled me for my sorrows!* 'So it was Lucile,' he cried, 'it was she who softened the pain I caused my father, and should I desert her when her mother is dying, when she will have no one but me to console her? Oh, Corinne, you are so brilliant, so sought after, do you need a faithful and devoted friend, as Lucile does?' But she was no longer brilliant, she was no longer sought after, that Corinne who was wandering alone from inn to inn, not even seeing the man for whom she had left everything, but not having the strength to go far away from him. In a little town halfway on the road to Edinburgh, she had fallen ill and, in spite of her efforts, had not been able to continue on her way. During her long, painful nights, she often thought that, if she died in this place, only Theresina would know her name and inscribe it on her tomb. What a change, what a fate, for a woman who could not take a step in Italy without a crowd of admirers pursuing her! At last, after a week of indescribable anguish, she resumed her sad journey, for, although the hope of seeing Oswald was its objective, so many painful feelings were mingled with this eager expectation that she felt only grievous anxiety. Before reaching Lord Nelvil's house, Corinne felt the desire to stop for a few hours at her father's estate, which was not far from Lord Nelvil's and where Lord Edgermond had asked to be buried. She had not been there since that time and on this estate she had spent only one month alone with her father. It was the happiest time of her stay in England. These memories made her feel the need of seeing her home again, and she did not think Lady Edgermond would be there yet.

A few miles from the house Corinne saw an overturned carriage on the main road. She stopped her own and saw emerge from the broken-down carriage an old man, very frightened by the fall. Corinne hastened to assist him and offered to take him herself to the neighbouring town. He accepted gratefully and said his name was Mr Dickson. Corinne recognized the name that she had often heard mentioned by Lord Nelvil. She directed the conversation in a way to make the good old man speak about the only subject in life which interested her. Mr Dickson was the most willing man in the world to talk, and he did not suspect that Corinne (whose name he did not know and whom he took for an Englishwoman) had any particular interest in the questions she was asking him. So he began to tell her all he knew in the greatest detail and as, touched by her care of him, he wanted to please Corinne, he was indiscreet in order to entertain her.

He told how he himself had informed Lord Nelvil that his father was opposed in advance to the marriage Oswald now wanted to make. Mr Dickson quoted an extract from the letter that he had delivered to Oswald, repeating several times the words which pierced Corinne's heart: *His father forbade him to marry that Italian woman; to defy his will would be an insult to his memory.*

Mr Dickson did not restrict himself only to these cruel words. In addition he asserted that Oswald loved Lucile and Lucile loved him, that Lady Edgermond keenly desired this marriage, but that an engagement made in Italy prevented Lord Nelvil from agreeing to it. 'What!' said Corinne to Mr Dickson, trying to restrain the terrible anxiety which was upsetting her. 'You think it is only because of the engagement he has entered into that Lord Nelvil will not marry Miss Lucile Edgermond?' 'I am quite sure of it,' replied Mr Dickson, delighted at being questioned again. 'Only three days ago I saw Lord Nelvil, and although he did not make explicit to me the nature of the ties he had formed in Italy, he told me in his own words which I conveyed to Lady Edgermond: *If I were free, I would marry Lucile.*'

'If he were free!' repeated Corinne. But at that moment her carriage stopped at the door of the inn to which she was taking Mr Dickson. He wanted to thank her and to ask where he could see her again. Corinne no longer heard him. She shook his hand without being able to reply and left him without saying a word. It was late. She still wanted, however, to go to the place where her father's ashes lay. Her troubled mind made this a sacred pilgrimage, more necessary than ever.

CHAPTER IX

FOR two days Lady Edgermond had been at her estate, and that very evening there was a great ball at her house. All her neighbours and tenants had asked her to bring them all together to celebrate her arrival. Lucile wanted it too, perhaps in the hope that Oswald would come. Indeed, he was there when Corinne arrived. She saw many carriages in the avenue and stopped hers some steps away. She got out and recognized the place where her father had shown the most affectionate feelings towards her. What a difference between those times, which she then thought unhappy, and her present situation! Thus it is that in life one is punished for imaginary pains by real sorrows, which teach one only too well to know true unhappiness.

Corinne enquired why the house was lit up and who were the people who were there just then. It happened by chance that Corinne's servant questioned one of them whom Lord Nelvil had taken into his service in England and who was there at that moment. Corinne heard his reply. *It is a ball*, he said, *that Lady Edgermond is giving today, and*, he added, *my master Lord Nelvil opened the ball with Miss Lucile Edgermond, the heiress of the house*. At these words Corinne trembled, but she did not alter her decision. A biting curiosity led her to draw near to the place where so many sorrows threatened her. She signed to her servants to leave her and she entered the grounds alone. They were open and at this hour the darkness allowed her to walk for a long time without being seen. It was ten o'clock and, since the beginning of the ball, Oswald had been dancing English country dances with Lucile. These dances are begun again five or six times in the evening, but the same man always dances with the same woman, and sometimes the greatest solemnity reigns in this festivity.

Lucile danced in a dignified but not very lively way. The feeling which filled her heart added to her natural gravity. As people were

curious to know if she was in love with Lord Nelvil, everyone looked
at her even more attentively than usual and that prevented her from
raising her eyes to Oswald. She was so shy that she neither saw nor
heard anything. At first Lord Nelvil was very touched by her reserve
and embarrassment, but as the situation did not change he began
to get a little tired of it and he compared this long line of men and
women, and this monotonous music, with the lively charm of Italian
tunes and dances. This thought plunged him into deep meditation,
and Corinne would have tasted a few more moments of happiness if
she had then been able to know Lord Nelvil's feelings. But the unfortunate woman who felt she was a stranger on her father's land, isolated near the man she had hoped to marry, wandered at random along
the dark avenues of an estate which formerly she had been able to
think of as her own. The ground gave way beneath her, and grievous
emotion alone was her one source of strength. Perhaps she thought
she would meet Oswald in the garden, but she herself did not know
what she wanted.

The house was placed on an eminence with a river flowing at the
bottom. On one of the banks were a great many trees, but on the other
were only arid rocks covered with heather. As Corinne walked on,
she found herself near the river. There she could hear both the festive music and the murmur of the water. From above, the lamplight
of the ball was reflected as far as the middle of the water, while only
the pale reflection of the moon lit up the deserted banks of the other
side. As in the tragedy of Hamlet, it was as if ghosts were wandering round the palace where festivities were taking place.

Corinne, unhappy, alone, and forsaken, had only one step to take
to plunge into eternal forgetfulness. 'Oh!' she cried. 'If, when he walks
on these banks tomorrow with his happy band of friends, his triumphant steps were to stumble against the remains of the woman whom
nevertheless he once loved, would he not have an emotion which would
avenge me, a pain which would match what I am suffering? No, no,
it is not vengeance I must seek in death, but rest.' She fell silent and
gazed again at the swiftly, steadily flowing river, at nature, so well
controlled when the human heart is all in turmoil. She recalled the
day when Lord Nelvil plunged into the sea to save an old man. 'How
kind he was then!' cried Corinne. 'Alas!' she said, weeping. 'Perhaps
he still is! Why blame him because I am suffering? Perhaps he does
not know, perhaps if he saw me . . .' And suddenly she decided to

ask for Lord Nelvil in the middle of the festivities, and to speak to him straight away. She went back up to the house with the kind of movement inspired by a newly made decision, a decision which follows long uncertainty. But as she came near she was seized by such a severe fit of trembling that she had to sit down on a stone bench in front of the windows. The crowd of rustics collected to see the dancing prevented her from being noticed.

At that moment Lord Nelvil came out onto the balcony. He breathed in the cool evening air. Some rose bushes there reminded him of Corinne's usual perfume and he was struck by the impression it made on him. This long, boring party wearied him. He remembered Corinne's good taste in the arrangement of a party, her understanding of everything connected with the arts, and he felt it was only in regular, domestic life that he liked to think of Lucile as his companion. Everything in the least connected with the imagination, with poetry, recalled to him the memory of Corinne, renewing his regrets. While he was in this frame of mind one of his friends came up to him and they talked together for a few moments. Corinne then heard Oswald's voice.

What inexpressible emotion to hear the voice of a loved one! It is a confused mixture of affection and fear, for there are feelings so strong that our poor, weak nature is even afraid to experience them.

One of Oswald's friends said to him, 'Don't you think this is a delightful ball?' 'Yes,' he replied, unthinkingly. 'Yes, indeed,' he repeated with a sigh. This sigh and the melancholy tone of his voice gave Corinne a keen feeling of happiness. She felt sure of regaining Oswald's heart, of making him appreciate her again; she got up hurriedly and went towards one of the house servants to bid him ask for Lord Nelvil. If she had followed this impulse, how very different her and Oswald's fate would have been!

At that moment Lucile came up to the window and, as she saw, through the darkness, a woman dressed in white, but not wearing a ball gown, go past in the garden, her curiosity was aroused. She looked out and, gazing intently, thought she could recognize her sister's features, but as she did not doubt that Corinne had been dead for seven years the fright she received from this sight made her fall down in a faint. Everybody ran to help her. Corinne could no longer find a servant to speak to and she retreated further down the path so as not to be noticed.

Lucile recovered her senses, but did not dare admit what had upset her. But as, since her childhood, her mother had strongly impressed on her mind all the ideas connected with piety, she convinced herself that her sister's likeness, walking towards their father's grave, had appeared to her in order to reproach her for forgetting his grave and holding a party in these precincts without first at least fulfilling a pious duty towards revered ashes. So, when Lucile was certain of not being noticed, she left the ball. Corinne was surprised at seeing her alone in the garden like this and imagined that Lord Nelvil would not be long in joining her; perhaps he had asked for a private conversation to obtain her permission to make his wishes known to her mother. That thought made her stand still. She soon noticed, however, that Lucile was turning her steps towards a thicket that she knew must be the place where her father's tomb had been erected. In her turn she blamed herself for not initially taking her sorrows and tears there. So she followed her sister at some distance, concealing herself with the help of the trees and the darkness. At last she could see from a distance the black sarcophagus erected on the place where Lord Edgermond's remains were buried. A deep emotion compelled her to stop and lean against a tree. Lucile also stopped and bowed respectfully at the sight of the tomb.

At that moment Corinne was about to reveal herself to her sister and in the name of their father to ask her to give her back both her name and her husband, but Lucile took a few hurried steps towards the monument and Corinne's courage failed her. In a woman's heart there is so much bashfulness combined with impulsive feelings that a trifle can hold her back or lead her on. Lucile knelt down in front of her father's tomb. She put back her fair hair, which was held by a garland of flowers, and, with an angelic look, raised her eyes to heaven to pray. Corinne was standing behind the trees and, without being discovered, she could easily see her sister, who was gently lit up by a moonbeam. Suddenly she felt gripped by a purely generous feeling of affection. She looked at the religious expression which was so pure, at the face which was so young that it still bore traces of childhood; she recalled the time when she had acted as a mother to Lucile. She thought about herself, reflecting that she was not far from thirty, the time when youth begins to decline, while her sister had a long, indefinite future before her, a future which was not marred by any memory, by any past life for which one had to answer to others or to

one's own conscience. 'If I disclose myself to Lucile,' she said to herself, 'if I speak to her, her soul, still calm, will soon be disturbed, perhaps peace will never return to it. I have already suffered so much;
I shall be able to suffer still more, but in one moment, innocent Lucile
will pass from calm to the most cruel agitation. And it is I who held
her in my arms, who sent her to sleep on my breast; it is I who would
thrust her into the world of sorrows!' Such were Corinne's thoughts.
Nevertheless, love fought a fierce struggle with this disinterested feeling, with the exaltation of the soul which led her to sacrifice herself.

    Then Lucile said out loud: 'Oh, father, pray for me.' Corinne heard
her and, also dropping to her knees, asked at the same time for the
paternal benediction for both the sisters. She shed tears which drew
from her heart feelings still more pure than love. Lucile, continuing
her prayer, uttered these words distinctly: 'Oh, my sister, intercede
for me in heaven. You loved me in my childhood, continue to protect me.' Oh how this prayer moved Corinne! Finally, Lucile said with
great fervour: 'Father, forgive me the moment of forgetfulness caused
by a feeling you yourself commanded. I am not guilty in loving the
man you intended for my husband, but complete your work and
make him choose me for the companion of his life. I can be happy
only with him, but never will he know that I love him. Never will
this trembling heart betray its secret. Oh, God! Oh, father! Comfort
your daughter and make her worthy of Oswald's esteem and affection.' 'Yes,' repeated Corinne in an undertone. 'Grant her prayer,
father, and grant your other child a gentle, quiet death.'

    As she finished this solemn prayer, the greatest effort within the
power of Corinne's heart, she drew from her bodice the letter containing the ring Oswald had given her and quickly went away. She
knew quite well that by sending that letter, and keeping Lord Nelvil
in ignorance of her presence in England, she was breaking their ties
and giving Oswald to Lucile. In front of this grave, however, as she
reflected on the obstacles which separated her from him, they had
seemed stronger than ever. She had recalled Mr Dickson's words,
his father forbade him to marry that Italian woman, and it seemed to
her that her father too was in agreement with Oswald's and that all
paternal authority condemned her love. Lucile's innocence, her youth,
her purity, exalted Corinne's imagination and, at least for a moment,
she was proud to sacrifice herself so that Oswald could be at peace
with his country, his family, and himself.

The music that could be heard as one drew near to the house sustained Corinne's courage. She noticed a poor, blind, old man who, seated at the foot of a tree, was listening to the noise of the ball. She went up to him and asked him to convey the letter she gave him to one of the servants of the house. In this way she did not run the risk of Lord Nelvil's discovering that a woman had brought it. Indeed, anyone who had seen Corinne handing over this letter would have realized that it held her life's destiny. The expression of her eyes, her trembling hand, her solemn, troubled voice, all indicated one of those terrible moments when fate takes possession of us, when an unhappy being acts only as the slave of pursuing doom.

Corinne watched from afar the old man, guided by a faithful dog. She saw him give her letter to one of Lord Nelvil's servants who happened just then to be taking other letters to the house. All the circumstances combined to leave no more hope. Corinne took a few more steps, turning round to look at the servant going towards the door, and when she could see him no longer, when she was on the main road, when she could no longer hear the music, and when even the lights of the house were no longer visible, a cold sweat dampened her brow, a death-like shivering gripped her. She wanted to walk on still further, but nature rebelled, and she fell senseless on the road.

BOOK XVIII
THE STAY IN FLORENCE

CHAPTER I

AFTER spending some time in Switzerland and becoming bored by natural scenery in the Alps, just as he had wearied of the arts in Rome, Count d'Erfeuil suddenly felt the desire to go to England, where, he had been assured, profundity of thought was to be found. So when he woke up one morning, he had convinced himself that that was what he needed. As this third attempt did not succeed more than the first two, his affection for Lord Nelvil suddenly revived. Again, one morning, he said to himself that happiness lay only in true friendship, and so he set off for Scotland. First of all he went to Lord Nelvil's house and found he was not at home. The Count was told that Oswald was at Lady Edgermond's house, so he mounted his horse again immediately and went to seek him out, so great did he think was his need to see Lord Nelvil again. As he was riding on very quickly, he caught sight of a woman lying motionless by the roadside. He stopped, dismounted, and hastened to help her. What was his surprise at recognizing Corinne, despite her deathly pallor! He was filled with deep pity. Helped by his servant he arranged a few branches as a stretcher and intended to take her in this way to Lady Edgermond's house. But Theresina, who had stayed in Corinne's carriage, was worried at not seeing her mistress come back. Just then she arrived and, thinking that only Lord Nelvil could have put Corinne in such a state, she decided that her mistress should be taken to the neighbouring town. Count d'Erfeuil followed Corinne and for a week, while the unfortunate woman was feverish and delirious, he did not leave her. So it was the frivolous man who looked after her, and the sensitive man who cut her to the heart.

The contrast struck Corinne when she regained consciousness and, deeply moved, she thanked Count d'Erfeuil. He replied and immediately tried to comfort her. He was more capable of noble actions than of serious words and Corinne was to find in him help rather than friendship. She tried to recover her intelligence, to recall what had happened. For a long time she found it difficult to remember what she had done and her reasons for doing it. Perhaps she was beginning to consider her sacrifice too great and was thinking of saying at least a last farewell to Lord Nelvil before leaving England; but the day after she regained consciousness she saw by chance in a news-sheet the following item.

'Lady Edgermond has just learned that her stepdaughter, who she thought had died in Italy, is still alive and enjoys a great literary reputation in Rome under the name of Corinne. Lady Edgermond is proud to recognize her and to share with her the inheritance of Lord Edgermond's brother, who has just died in the Indies.

'Next Sunday, Lord Nelvil is to marry Miss Lucile Edgermond, younger daughter of Lord Edgermond and only daughter of his widow, Lady Edgermond. The contract was signed yesterday.'

To her misfortune, Corinne did not lose the use of her senses as she read this news. A sudden revolution took place within her; all interest in life deserted her. She felt like someone condemned to death, but who does not yet know when her sentence will be carried out. From that moment, the resignation of despair was her only feeling.

Count d'Erfeuil went into her room. He found her even more pale than when she had fainted, and he asked after her anxiously. 'I am no worse. I should like to leave the day after tomorrow, which is Sunday,' she said gravely. 'I shall go to Plymouth and I shall set sail for Italy.' 'I shall go with you,' Count d'Erfeuil replied eagerly. 'I have nothing to keep me in England. I shall be delighted to make the journey with you.' 'You are kind, really kind,' replied Corinne. 'One must not judge by appearances . . .' She stopped, and then continued her reply: 'I accept your help as far as Plymouth, for I am not sure that I can find my own way there. But once I have embarked, the ship takes me and it does not matter what state I am in.' She signed to Count d'Erfeuil to leave her alone and wept for a long time, asking God to give her the strength to bear her grief. There was no longer anything left of the impulsive Corinne, the power of her strong vitality was exhausted and this destruction, which she did not herself appreciate, made her calm. Misfortune had conquered her. Sooner or later must not the most rebellious bend their heads under its yoke?

On Sunday, Corinne left Scotland with Count d'Erfeuil. 'It is today,' she said, getting up from her bed to go to her carriage, 'it is today!' Count d'Erfeuil wanted to question her but she did not reply and fell silent again. They went past a church and Corinne asked Count d'Erfeuil's permission to go in for a moment. She knelt down in front of the altar and, imagining she could see Oswald and Lucile there, she prayed for them. But the emotion she felt was so powerful that, as she wanted to get up, she stumbled and could not take a step without being supported by Theresina and Count d'Erfeuil, who came to meet her. People in the church got up to let her past and showed great pity for her. 'I must look very ill,' she said to Count d'Erfeuil. 'There are younger and more brilliant people than I who at this moment are leaving the church rejoicing.'

Count d'Erfeuil did not understand the last of Corinne's remarks. He was kind but could not be sensitive. So on the way, while being fond of Corinne, he was irritated by her sadness; he tried therefore to take her out of it, as if, in order to forget life's sorrows you only need to have the will. Sometimes he would say to her: *I told you so*. A strange way of comforting, a satisfaction vanity gives itself at the expense of grief!

Corinne made tremendous efforts to conceal her suffering, for in front of frivolous people one is ashamed of strong affections. A feeling of modesty is linked to what is not understood, to everything needing explanation, to these secrets of the heart of which you can be unburdened only if they are understood. Corinne, too, was annoyed with herself at not being grateful enough for Count d'Erfeuil's devoted attentions, but in his voice, in his tone, in his eyes, there was so much distraction, so great a need of enjoyment, that one was continually on the point of forgetting his generous deeds, as he forgot them himself. No doubt it is very noble not to attach much value to one's good deeds. But it could be that the indifference one shows for the good one has done, this indifference in itself so fine, might nevertheless, in some characters, stem from frivolity.

During her delirium, Corinne had betrayed nearly all her secrets, and Count d'Erfeuil had learned the rest from news-sheets. Several times he would have liked Corinne to talk to him about what he called *her affairs*, but those words were enough to freeze Corinne's confidence, and she begged him not to require her to mention Lord Nelvil's name. As she left Count d'Erfeuil, Corinne did not know how to express her gratitude, for she was both very pleased to be alone and sorry to leave a man who behaved so well towards her. She tried to thank him but he told her so naturally to say no more about it that she stopped. She bade him tell Lady Edgermond that she refused her uncle's inheritance entirely, and she begged him to carry out this task as if he had received the request from Italy, without informing her stepmother that she had come to England.

'And is Lord Nelvil to know?' Count d'Erfeuil then asked. These words made Corinne tremble. She was silent for a while and then replied, 'You can tell him soon, yes, soon. My friends from Rome will tell you when you can.' 'At least look after your health,' said Count d'Erfeuil. 'Do you know, I am anxious about you?' 'Really?' Corinne replied with a smile. 'But, indeed, I think you are right.' Count d'Erfeuil gave her his arm to go as far as her ship. As she was about to embark, she turned towards England, towards the land she was leaving for ever and where lived the only person she loved and the source of her grief. Her eyes filled with tears, the first that had escaped her in front of Count d'Erfeuil. 'Beautiful Corinne,' he said, 'forget an ungrateful man. Remember the friends who love you so dearly. And, believe me, think with pleasure of all the advantages you possess.' At these words, Corinne withdrew her hand from Count d'Erfeuil and took a few steps away from him. Then reproaching herself for having done so, she came back and gently said goodbye to him. Count d'Erfeuil did not realize what had taken place in Corinne's heart. He went into the barge with her, strongly recommended her to the captain, and with the kindest attention even looked after all the details which might make her voyage more pleasant. As he was returning on the barge, he waved to the ship with his handkerchief as long as he could. Corinne responded gratefully to Count d'Erfeuil, but, alas, was *he* there, the friend on whom she ought to rely?

Light-hearted feelings often last a long time. Nothing destroys them because nothing strengthens them. They follow circumstances, disappear, and come back with them, while deep affections are torn apart without returning and leave nothing in their place but a painful wound.

CHAPTER II

A FAVOURABLE wind brought Corinne to Livorno in less than a month. She was feverish nearly all that time. Her emotional pain together with illness made her extremely depressed; all her impressions were so confused that she could not remember them clearly. When she arrived, she wondered whether she should first go to Rome, but although her

best friends expected her there, an insurmountable repugnance prevented her from living in the places where she had known Oswald.
She recalled her own house, the door he used to open twice a day
when he came to see her, and the thought of being there without him
made her shiver. She decided, therefore, to go to Florence. As she
had the feeling that her life would not withstand her sufferings for
long, it suited her quite well to detach herself from life gradually, and
to start first by living alone, far from her friends, far from the city
that had seen her successes, far from the place where they would try
to revive her wit, where they would ask her to be what she was before,
while an unconquerable despair made every effort odious to her.

As she passed through the fertile region of Tuscany and drew near
to flower-scented Florence, in being in Italy again Corinne felt only
sadness. All the beauties of the countryside which had delighted her
at another time, filled her with melancholy. *How terrible is the despair
that is not calmed by that gentle air!* said Milton.* Religion or love is
essential to the appreciation of nature, and at that moment Corinne
had lost the greatest good on earth without having yet regained the
calm that religion alone can give to sensitive, unhappy hearts.

Tuscany is a well-cultivated, very smiling region, but it does not
strike the imagination like the environs of Rome. The Romans have
so effectively wiped out the primitive institutions of the people who
used to live in Tuscany that there remain almost no traces of the past
which arouse so much interest in Rome and Naples. But you can see
there another kind of historic beauties; they are the towns that bear
the stamp of the republican spirit of the Middle Ages. At Siena, the
public square where the people assembled, the balcony from which
its Mayor addressed them, strike the least thoughtful of travellers. You
feel that a democratic government has existed there.

It is a real pleasure to hear the Tuscans, even those of the lowest
social class, speak. Their extremely imaginative and elegant language
gives an idea of the pleasure that must have been experienced in the
city of Athens when ordinary people spoke Greek that was harmonious like continual music. It is a very strange feeling to think you are
in the midst of a nation whose every individual member appears to be
equally cultured and to belong to the upper class. At least that is the
illusion which, for a few moments, the purity of the language creates.

The appearance of Florence recalls its history before the Medici
were elevated to be its rulers. The palaces of the principal families

are built like fortresses from which they could be defended. At the outside you can still see the iron rings to which the standards of each party were to be attached. Everything was, indeed, arranged far more to maintain individual forces than to unite them all in the common interest. It is as if the town were built for civil war. On the law courts there are towers from which they could see the enemy approach and defend themselves against him. The hatred between families was so great that you can see palaces strangely constructed because their owners did not want to extend them over the land where enemy houses had been razed to the ground. Here the Pazzi have conspired against the Medici; there the Guelfs have murdered the Ghibellines.* Traces of struggle and rivalry are indeed everywhere. But at the present time everything has gone to sleep and the stones of the buildings alone retain some character. They no longer hate each other, because there is no longer anything to lay claim to, because a state devoid of both glory and power is no longer quarrelled over by its inhabitants. Nowadays the life people lead in Florence is outstandingly monotonous. Every afternoon people go for a walk on the banks of the Arno and in the evening they ask each other if they have been.

Corinne settled in a country house not far from the town. She sent word to Prince Castel-Forte that she wanted to stay there permanently. That was the only letter Corinne wrote, for she had conceived such a horror of all life's normal activities that the least decision to be taken, the smallest order to give, increased her pain twofold. She could spend her days only in complete inactivity. She would get up, go to bed, get up again, and open a book without being able to understand a line. She would often remain for hours on end at her window, then would walk quickly in her garden. Another time she would take a bunch of flowers and try to be distracted by its scent. The sense of existence pursued her like a relentless pain and she tried a thousand ways of calming the consuming power of thought, which no longer, as in the past, gave her a great variety of ideas, but only one idea, only one picture, armed with sharp points which rent her heart.

CHAPTER III

ONE day Corinne decided to go and visit the beautiful churches which ornament the town of Florence. She recalled that a few hours spent at Saint Peter's in Rome always calmed her soul and she hoped for the same help from the Florence churches. To go to the town she went through the lovely wood on the banks of the Arno. It was a delightful June evening; the air was scented by an inconceivable abundance of roses, and there was an expression of happiness on the faces of all the strollers. Corinne felt doubly sad when she saw herself excluded from the general happiness that Providence gives to most beings. She blessed it gently, however, for doing good to men. 'I am an exception to the general rule,' she said to herself. 'There is happiness for everyone, and this terrible ability to suffer which is killing me is a way of feeling peculiar to me. Oh God, why have you chosen me to bear this pain? May not I, like your divine son, also ask *that this cup should pass from me?*'*

The active, busy look of the town's inhabitants surprised Corinne. Since she no longer had any interest in life, she could not imagine what made people walk on, come back, and hurry. As she slowly dragged her feet over the broad stone pavements of Florence, she would forget the idea of arriving, no longer remembering where she had intended to go. She found herself, in the end, in front of the famous bronze doors made by Ghiberti* for the St John Baptistery, which is beside Florence Cathedral.

For some time she studied this immense work. In it bronze groups, in tiny proportions but quite clear, show a multitude of different facial expressions, each of which conveys one of the artist's thoughts, one of the ideas in his mind. 'What patience!' cried Corinne. 'What respect for posterity! And yet how few people study these doors carefully! The crowd goes through them, absent-mindedly, ignorantly, or disdainfully. Oh! how difficult it is for man to escape oblivion, and how powerful is death!'

It was in this cathedral that Giuliano de' Medici was assassinated. Not far away, in the church of San Lorenzo, you can see the marble, jewel-bedecked chapel where the Medici tombs are, as well as Michelangelo's statues of Giuliano and Lorenzo.* The statue of Lorenzo de' Medici, planning to avenge his brother, has earned it the honour of being called *Michelangelo's Thought*. At the foot of these statues are Dawn and Night. The awakening of the one and especially the sleep of the other have remarkable expressions. A poet wrote lines about the statue of Night; it ends with these words: *Although she sleeps, she is alive; waken her if you do not believe it; she will speak to you.*

Michelangelo, who cultivated literature, without which imagination of all kinds quickly withers, replied on behalf of Night:

> Grato m'è il sonno et più l'esser di sasso.
> Mentre che il danno e la vergogna dura,
> Non veder, non sentir m'è gran ventura.
> Però non mi destar, dch parla basso.[†]

Michelangelo is the only sculptor of modern times who has given the human face a personality which is unlike either the beauty of the ancients or the affectation of our day. You think you see in it the spirit of the Middle Ages, an energetic, gloomy soul, ceaseless activity, very pronounced features which bear the stamp of the passions but do not remind you of the ideal of beauty. Michelangelo is a genius of his own school, for he has imitated no one, not even the ancients.

His tomb is in the church of *Santa Croce*. He wanted it to be placed opposite a window from where the dome built by Filippo Brunelleschi* could be seen, and his ashes under the marble must be thrilled by the sight of that cupola, the model for Saint Peter's. The church of Santa Croce contains perhaps the most brilliant assembly of the dead in Europe. Corinne felt deeply moved as she walked between the two rows of tombs. Here is Galileo, persecuted by men for having discovered the secrets of the sky. Further on is Machiavelli, who revealed the art of crime, more as an observer than a criminal, but whose teachings are of more use to the oppressors than to the oppressed; Aretino,* the man who devoted his days to humour and whose only experience on earth of the serious was death; and Boccaccio, whose cheerful imagination was undeterred by the joint scourges of civil war and plague. Then there is a picture in honour of Dante, as if the Florentines, who let him die in the misery of exile, could still boast of his fame.[34] And several other honourable names can be seen here, names famous in their lifetime but who become less and less famous from generation to generation, until they are heard of no more.[35]

The sight of this church, ornamented by so many noble memories, reawakened Corinne's enthusiasm. The sight of the living had disheartened her; the silent presence of the dead revived, at least momentarily, the striving for fame which had gripped her in the past.

[†] Sleep is sweet to me, and sweeter for it to be in marble. As long as injustice and shame last, I am very happy not to see and not to hear. So do not wake me, please speak quietly.

She walked more resolutely inside the church and, as in former times, a few thoughts still passed through her mind. She saw young priests approaching under the arches; they were singing quietly and walking slowly round the choir. She asked one of them the meaning of this ceremony. *We are praying for our dead*, he replied. 'Yes, you are right to call them *your dead*,' thought Corinne. 'It is the only glory that is left to you. Oh, why has Oswald stifled those gifts I received from heaven and ought to use to arouse enthusiasm in hearts in harmony with mine? Oh, God,' she said as she knelt down, 'it is not out of vain pride that I beg you to restore to me the talents you had given me. No doubt those obscure saints who could live and die for you are the best of all. But there are different careers for mortal beings, and the talent which sings the praises of the generous virtues, the talent which devotes itself to everything noble, human, and true, might be received at least in the outer regions of heaven.' Corinne's eyes were lowered as she finished this prayer and she was struck by the inscription on a tombstone where she had knelt down: *Alone at my dawn, alone at my dusk, I am still alone here.*

'Oh,' cried Corinne, 'it is the reply to my prayer. What stimulus can there be when one is alone in the world? Who would share my successes if I should have any? Who is interested in my fate? What feeling would encourage me to exercise my mind? I needed his look for my reward.'

Another epitaph also arrested her attention. *Do not pity me*, said a man who died young. *How many sorrows this grave has spared me!* 'What detachment from life is inspired by those words,' said Corinne, weeping! 'Right in the midst of the town's bustle stands this church; it would teach the secret of everything if people were willing to learn. But they pass by without going in, and the wonderful illusion of forgetting makes the world go round.'

CHAPTER IV

THE impulse towards emulation that, for a few moments, had soothed Corinne led her the next day to revisit Florence's art gallery. She imagined she had regained her former love for the fine arts and had found some interest in her former occupations. The fine arts in Florence are still very republican. The statues and the pictures are readily displayed at all times. Well-informed men, paid by the government, are appointed as public officials to explain all these masterpieces. It is a remnant of the respect for talents of every kind which has always existed in Italy. This was particularly so in Florence when the Medici wanted to be forgiven for their power, by their intelligence, and for their control of events, by the free reign that they left at least to thought. The ordinary people in Florence are very attached to the arts and mingle this liking with religion, which is more usual in Tuscany than elsewhere in Italy. It is not infrequent for them to confuse mythical figures with Christian history. An ordinary Florentine would show foreigners a Minerva whom he would call Judith, an Apollo whom he would call David, and would affirm, as he explained a bas-relief portraying the capture of Troy, that Cassandra *was a good Christian*.

The Florence art gallery has an enormous collection. You could spend days there without managing to know it. Corinne looked at all the exhibits and felt sadly that she was distracted and indifferent. The statue of Niobe aroused her interest. She was struck by her calm and dignity despite extreme grief. In a similar situation, no doubt, a real mother's facial expression would be distraught. But the ideal of the arts retains beauty in despair. In works of genius, what is deeply moving is not misfortune itself but the power of the soul over this misfortune. Not far from the statue of Niobe is the dying Alexander's head. The two kinds of facial expression give much food for thought. In Alexander there is astonishment and indignation that he could not conquer nature. The anguish of maternal love is depicted in all Niobe's features. She clasps her daughter tightly to her breast with heart-rending anxiety. The grief expressed by this wonderful face bears the stamp of the fatalism which, in the ancients, was without resource in religious feeling. Niobe raises her eyes to heaven but without hope, for the gods themselves are her enemies.

When she returned home, Corinne tried to reflect on what she had just seen and wanted to compose verse as she used to in the past. But at every page insurmountable fits of absent-mindedness made her stop. How far she was then from her talent for improvisation! It cost her an effort to find each word, and often she wrote words with no meaning, words which frightened even herself when she began to re-read them, as if she saw feverish delirium written down. As she felt incapable of diverting her thoughts from her own situation, she depicted what she was suffering. But she no longer expressed the general ideas, the universal feelings, which appeal to the hearts of all humanity. It was the cry of pain, which in the end becomes monotonous, like the cry of night birds. The language was too passionate, too impulsive, with too few gradations of tone; it expressed unhappiness, but there was no longer any talent. Admittedly, to write well you need a genuine emotion, but it must not be destructive. Happiness is necessary for everything and the most melancholy poetry has to be inspired by a kind of vigour which assumes strength and intellectual pleasures. Genuine grief is by nature infertile. What it produces is only a gloomy restlessness—which continually brings one back to the same thoughts. It is like the knight who, pursued by a disastrous fate, vainly went round and about a thousand times and always found himself again in the same place.

Corinne's bad health also impeded her talent. In her papers were found some of the meditations you are going to read, which she wrote when she was making futile efforts to become capable again of sustained work.

CHAPTER V

Fragments of Corinne's thoughts

'MY talent no longer exists; I miss it. I should have liked my name to reach him with some renown. As he read something I had written, I should have liked him to feel that I had some community of feeling with him.

'I was wrong to hope that when he returned to his own country and habits, he would retain the ideas and feelings which alone could unite us. There is so much to be said against someone like me and there is only one answer to all that, my mind and heart. But what a reply for most men!

'Yet people are wrong to fear superiority of mind and heart. But that superiority is very moral, for understanding everything makes one very indulgent, and feeling deeply inspires great kindness.

'How can it be that two beings who have confided their most intimate thoughts to each other, who have talked about God, the immortality of the soul, and grief, suddenly become strangers to each other? Astonishing mystery of love! Wonderful or non-existent feeling! Religious as the martyrs were, or colder than the merest friendship! Does the most involuntary feeling in the world come from heaven or from the earthly passions? Must one submit to it or fight against it? Oh, what storms take place in the depths of the heart!

'Talent ought to be a resource. When Domenichino was locked up in a monastery, he painted superb pictures on his prison walls and left masterpieces as a record of his stay. But he suffered because of external circumstances. The trouble was not in his heart. When it is there, nothing is possible; the source of everything is dried up.

'Sometimes I examine myself as a stranger might, and I have pity on myself. I was witty, sincere, kind, generous, and sensitive. Why has all that gone so badly wrong? Is society really wicked? And do certain virtues remove our weapons instead of giving us strength?

'It is a pity. I was born with some talent. I shall die without people knowing anything about me, although I am famous. If I had been happy, if the fever of love had not consumed me, I would have studied human destiny from a great height; there I would have discovered unknown bonds between nature and heaven. But unhappiness holds me in its grip. How can I think freely when it makes itself felt every time I try to breathe?

'Why did he not try to bring happiness to the only woman whose secret thoughts he alone knew, a woman who spoke from the bottom of her heart only to him? Oh, I am different from those ordinary women who love indiscriminately. But the woman who needs to admire the man she loves, whose judgement is perceptive despite her passionate imagination, for her there is only one man in the world.

'I had learned about life by reading the poets. It is not like that. There is something barren about reality that it is useless to try to change.

'When I recall my successes, I have a feeling of irritation. Why tell me I was charming, if I was not to be loved? Why make me feel I could trust you, so that it was all the more terrible for me to be disillusioned? Will he find any woman with more intelligence, more feeling, and more affection than I have? No, he will find less and he will be satisfied. He will feel in harmony with society. What artificial pleasures and pains it gives!

'In the presence of the sun and the starry spheres, we need only to love each other and to feel worthy of each other. But society, society! How it makes the heart hard and the mind frivolous! How it makes you live for what people think of you! If men were to meet each other one day, each freed from the influence of all the others, what pure air would enter into the soul! How many new ideas, how many sincere feelings, would refresh it!

'Nature too is cruel. That face I had, it is going to fade. Then I would have the most loving affections in vain; lacklustre eyes would no longer reveal my soul, would no longer plead for me.

'There are sorrows within me that I shall never express, not even by writing. I have not the strength to write. Love alone can plumb these depths.

'How fortunate men are to go to war, to risk their lives, to give themselves up to the passion for honour and danger! But there is nothing outside themselves which relieves women. Their lives, unchanging in the presence of misfortune, are a very long torture.

'Sometimes, when I hear music, it reminds me of the talents I used to have, song, dance, and poetry. Then I have a desire to free myself from unhappiness, to be happy again. But suddenly a feeling within me makes me shudder. It is as if I were a ghost who still wants to remain on earth when the sun's rays, when the approach of the living, force her to disappear.

'I would like to be able to enjoy society's pleasures. In the past I used to love them, they used to do me good, reflection and solitude used to take me too far ahead. My talent used to be enhanced by the quick succession of my feelings. Now I have a fixed look in my eyes and my thoughts are unchanging. Gaiety, charm, imagination, what has become of you? Oh, if only for a moment, I should still like to savour hope! But it is all over, the desert is inexorable, the drop of water, like the river, has dried up, and one day's happiness is as difficult as a whole lifetime's destiny.

'I think he is guilty of behaving badly to me, but when I compare him to other men, how they seem to me affected, limited, worthless! But he, he is an angel, an angel armed with the flaming sword that has destroyed my lot. The man you love is the avenger of the sins you have committed on earth; divinity lends him its power.

'The first love is not the one which is indelible; it comes from the need to love. But when, after having known life and reached the full force of your judgement, you meet a mind and soul that you had sought in vain until then, imagination is subjugated by truth and you have good reason to be unhappy.

'On the contrary, most men will say, it is crazy to die for love, as if there were not a thousand other ways of living! All kinds of passion are ridiculous for those who do not experience them. Poetry, devotion, love, religion, have the same origin, and there are men in whose eyes these feelings are madness. If you like, everything is madness, apart from the care of your own life. Everywhere else there may be error and illusion.

'What above all makes me unhappy is that he alone understood me and perhaps some day he too will think that I alone could understand him. I am the easiest and the most difficult person in the world. All people of goodwill are agreeable to me as company for a few moments. But for a close relationship, for a genuine affection, Oswald was the only man in the world I could love. Imagination, intelligence, sensitivity, what a combination! Where is it to be found in the universe? And the cruel man had all these virtues, or at least all their charm!

'What would I have to say to others? To whom could I speak? What aim, what interest, remains to me? I am acquainted with the bitterest grief, with the most delightful feelings. What can I fear? What could I hope for? The pale future for me is only the ghost of the past.

'Why are happy situations fleeting? What is more fragile about them than about others? Is grief the natural order of things? For the body it is a spasm but for the soul it is a habitual state.

> Ah!! null' altro che pianto al mondo dura
> PETRARCH
>
> *Ah! in the world, only tears last!*

'Another life! Another life! There lies my hope! But such is the power of this life that in heaven we look for the same feelings which have filled our lives on earth. In the northern mythologies they depict the shades of huntsmen pursuing shades of stags in the clouds. But what right have we to say they are shades? Where is reality? Pain is the only certainty. Only pain keeps its promises without pity.

'I continually think about immortality, but no longer about that bestowed by men; those who, in Dante's words, *will call the present day ancient times* no longer interest me. I do not believe, however, in the annihilation of my heart. No, dear God, I do not believe that. That heart he did not want is for you, and you will deign to receive it after it has been disdained by a mortal man.

'I feel that I shall not live for long and this thought brings calm to my soul. In the state I am in, it is soothing to become weak; the feeling of pain is dulled.

'I do not know why, in the distress of grief, one is more able to be superstitious than devout. I make omens out of everything but I cannot be confident of anything. Oh, how agreeable is piety when one is happy! What gratitude to the Supreme Being must be felt by Oswald's wife!

'Grief undoubtedly improves the character. In our thoughts we always link our failings to our misfortunes and, at least in our own eyes, they seem to be obviously linked. But there is a limit to this beneficial effect.

'I need to reflect deeply before I can reach

> . . . Tranquillo varco
> A più tranquilla vita.
>
> *A tranquil passage towards a more tranquil life.*

'When I am extremely ill, calm will be bound to return to my heart. There is much innocence in the thoughts of the being who is going to die and I like the feelings aroused by this situation.

'Insoluble riddle of life, which no passion, no grief, no genius, can solve, will you be disclosed to prayer? Perhaps the simplest idea of all explains these mysteries! Have we perhaps come close to it a thousand times in our daydreams? But this last step is impossible, and our futile efforts of every kind weary the soul. It is high time for mine to take a rest.

> Fermossi al fin il cor che balzo tanto.[†]
> IPPOLITO PINDEMONTE'

CHAPTER VI

PRINCE CASTEL-FORTE left Rome to settle in Florence near Corinne. She greatly appreciated this proof of friendship, but she was a little ashamed of no longer being able to make her conversation as attractive as it used to be. She was absent-minded and silent. The deterioration in her health deprived her of the strength to overcome even for a moment the feelings that filled her heart. She still had the pleasure

---

[†] This heart which beat so fast has stopped at last.

in speaking inspired by benevolence but she was no longer stimulated by the wish to please. When love is unhappy, it makes all the other affections cold. We cannot explain to ourselves everything that is taking place in our hearts, but one loses in grief as much as one benefits from happiness. The enhanced vitality given by a feeling which makes us enjoy everything in nature involves all relationships in life and society, but life is so impoverished by the destruction of this immense hope that we become incapable of any spontaneous emotion. It is for that very reason that so many obligations compel women and, above all, men to respect and hear the love they arouse, for that passion can devastate for ever the mind as well as the heart.

Prince Castel-Forte tried to talk to Corinne about the subjects that used to interest her in the past. Sometimes it was several minutes before she answered him because she did not hear him immediately. Then the sound and the thought would reach her and she would say something devoid of the richness and animation that people used to admire in her way of speaking but which enabled the conversation to proceed for a few moments and allowed her to relapse into her meditations. Then she would make a new effort not to discourage Prince Castel-Forte's kindness, but often she mistook one word for another or would say the opposite of what she had just said. Then, smilingly, she would take pity on herself and beg her friend's pardon for the kind of silliness of which she was aware.

Prince Castel-Forte wanted to risk speaking to her about Oswald and it even seemed as if Corinne took a bitter pleasure in this conversation, but after it she suffered so much that her friend felt absolutely obliged not to allow himself to mention the subject. Prince Castel-Forte had a sensitive soul, but a man, above all a man who has been very greatly interested in a woman, however generous he may be, cannot console for the feeling she has for another. A little pride on his part, a little shyness in her, prevent trusting intimacy from being perfect. Besides, what would be the use of it? There is a remedy only for sorrows which would be cured by themselves.

Every day Corinne and Prince Castel-Forte would take a walk together along the banks of the Arno. He would talk on every subject of conversation with a mixture of friendliness and consideration. She would thank him by pressing his hand. Sometimes she would try to speak about the subjects which cling to the heart. Her eyes would fill with tears and her emotion would distress her. It was painful to see her pallor and her trembling, and her friend would very quickly try to distract her from these thoughts. Once she suddenly began to be witty with her usual charm. Prince Castel-Forte looked at her, surprised and pleased, but, bursting into tears, she immediately hurried away.

She returned for dinner and shook her friend's hand saying, 'Forgive me. I wanted to be agreeable to reward you for your kindness, but it is impossible for me. Be generous enough to put up with me as I am.' Prince Castel-Forte was made extremely anxious by the state of Corinne's health. No imminent danger threatened her yet, but she could not possibly live for long unless some happy circumstances renewed her strength. Meanwhile Prince Castel-Forte received a letter from Lord Nelvil, and although it did not change the situation, since it confirmed that he was married, the letter contained passages which would have deeply moved Corinne. For hours Prince Castel-Forte meditated whether or not he ought to show his friend this letter; it would affect her deeply, but when he saw how weak she was, he did not dare. While he was still turning the matter over in his mind, he received a second letter from Lord Nelvil and it too was filled with feelings that would have touched Corinne. However, it contained the news of his departure for America. Then Prince Castel-Forte definitely decided to say nothing. Perhaps he was wrong, for one of Corinne's most bitter sorrows was that Lord Nelvil did not write to her. She did not dare admit this to anyone, but although Oswald was separated from her for ever, she would have greatly valued a word of regret from him. What upset her most of all was the absolute silence which did not even give her the opportunity of mentioning his name or of hearing his name mentioned.

A sorrow that no one talks about to you, a sorrow which is not changed at all either by the days or the years and cannot be changed by any event or circumstance, is more painful than a variety of painful feelings. Prince Castel-Forte followed the usual maxim which advises one to do everything to bring about forgetfulness. But there is no forgetfulness for people with a powerful imagination and for them it is better to go on reviving the same memory, in fact, to weary the heart with tears, than to make it turn in on itself.

BOOK XIX
OSWALD'S RETURN TO ITALY

CHAPTER I

LET us now return to what happened in Scotland the day following that sad festivity at which Corinne made such a painful sacrifice. Lord Nelvil's servant gave him his letters at the ball. He went out to read them. He opened several that his London banker had sent him before realizing that one letter was to decide his fate; but when he saw Corinne's handwriting, when he saw the words, *you are free*, and recognized the ring, he felt both deeply grieved and extremely annoyed. For two months he had received no letters from Corinne and her silence had been broken by so few words and by such a decisive action! He had no doubt about her fickleness. He recalled everything Lady Edgermond could say about Corinne's fickleness and instability. He began to feel hostile towards her, for he still loved her enough to be unfair. He forgot that several months previously he had completely given up the idea of marrying Corinne and that he had been quite attracted to Lucile. He thought he was a sensitive man betrayed by a faithless woman. He felt upset, angry, and unhappy, but above all he had a feeling of pride which dominated all the others and aroused the desire to show himself superior to the woman who was deserting him. One must not have too much pride in love affairs. It hardly ever exists except when vanity is stronger than affection, and if Lord Nelvil had loved Corinne as he had in the days in Rome and Naples, resentment against the wrong which he believed she had done him still would not have alienated him from her.

Lady Edgermond noticed Lord Nelvil's disarray. She was an emotional woman beneath a cold exterior, and the fatal illness by which she felt threatened increased her passionate interest in her daughter. She knew that the poor child was in love with Lord Nelvil and trembled at having compromised her happiness by telling him of her daughter's feelings. So she did not lose sight of Oswald for a moment and had discerned the secrets of his heart with a shrewdness that people attribute to the feminine mind, but which stems entirely from the incessant attention aroused by a sincere feeling. As a pretext for an interview with Lord Nelvil the next day, she made use of Corinne's affairs, that is to say, her uncle's legacy which she wanted him to convey to her. In this interview Lady Edgermond quickly realized he was displeased with Corinne and, stimulating his resentment with the idea of a noble revenge, she suggested to him that she should recognize Corinne as her stepdaughter. Lord Nelvil was surprised at this sudden change in Lady Edgermond's intentions. But although the thought was never expressed in any way, he realized that this offer would be implemented only if he married Lucile, and in one of those moments of acting before one has had time to think, he asked her mother for Lucile's hand in marriage. Lady Edgermond was so delighted that she could barely restrain herself enough not to say yes too quickly. Consent was given and Lord Nelvil left the room bound by an engagement that he had had no idea of making when he went in.

While Lady Edgermond was preparing Lucile to receive him, he walked up and down the garden in great agitation. He told himself that he had been attracted by Lucile precisely because he knew her so little and that it was strange to base all one's life's happiness on the charm of a mystery which is bound to be uncovered. A feeling of affection for Corinne returned to him and he recalled the letters he had written to her and which expressed only too well his heart's conflicts. 'She was right to give me up,' he cried, 'and I did not have the spirit to make her happy, but it must have cost her more and that one line is so cold . . . But who knows if it was not watered with her tears?' And as he uttered these words, his own tears flowed in spite of himself. These meditations preoccupied him to such an extent that he wandered away from the house. Lady Edgermond's servants, whom she had sent to tell him he was expected, had to look for him for a long time. He was surprised himself at his lack of enthusiasm and hastened to return.

When he came into the room he saw Lucile on her knees with her head hidden in her mother's lap. In this pose she was touchingly charming. When she heard Lord Nelvil, she lifted up her face bathed in tears and said to him, as she held out her hand, 'Is it not true, my Lord, that you will not separate me from my mother?' This kindly way of giving her consent aroused Oswald's interest in her considerably. In his turn he knelt down and asked Lady Edgermond to allow Lucile to incline her face towards his. Thus did the innocent girl have the first feeling which made her emerge from childhood. A deep blush spread over her face. When he looked at her, Oswald felt what a pure and sacred bond he had just formed, and Lucile's beauty, however enchanting it was at that moment, made less impression on him than her angelic modesty.

The days preceding the Sunday that had been fixed for the ceremony were spent in the necessary arrangements for the wedding. During this time Lucile did not speak much more than usual, but what she said was dignified and to the point; Lord Nelvil liked and approved of every word she spoke. He felt, however, that there was something lacking in her. The conversation always consisted of a question and a reply. She did not commit herself; she did not elaborate; all was well. But there was not the animation, the inexhaustible vitality, which it is difficult to dispense with once one has enjoyed it. Then Lord Nelvil would remember Corinne, but as he heard nothing more of her, he hoped this memory would finally become a dream, merely an object of his vague regrets.

When Lucile learned from her mother that her sister was still alive and that she was in Italy, she had a very strong desire to ask Lord Nelvil about her, but Lady Edgermond had forbidden her to, and, as usual, Lucile had obeyed without asking the reason for this command. On the day of the wedding Lord Nelvil's feeling for Corinne returned to his heart more keenly than ever and he was frightened himself by the impression it made on him. But he prayed to his father. From the depth of his heart Oswald told his father that it was for him, to obtain his blessing in heaven, that he was doing his will on earth. Strengthened by these feelings, he arrived at Lady Edgermond's and reproached himself for the wrong he had done in his thoughts to Lucile. When he saw her, she was so charming that an angel who had come down to earth could not have chosen another figure to give mortals an idea of the celestial virtues. They walked to the altar. The mother was even more deeply moved than the daughter, for among her feelings was the fear which is always experienced when an important decision is made by anyone who knows life. Lucile felt only hope. In her, childhood was mingled with youth, and happiness with love. In coming back from the altar she leaned shyly on Oswald's arm; in this way she was assuring herself of her protector. Oswald looked at her affectionately. It was as if he felt that there was an enemy at the bottom of his heart, an enemy who was threatening Lucile's happiness, and that he was promising to defend her against it.

When Lady Edgermond had returned to the house, she said to her son-in-law, 'Now, my mind is at rest. I have entrusted Lucile's happiness to you. I have so little time left to live that I am comforted to feel I shall be replaced so well.' Lord Nelvil was very affected by these words and, moved as well as anxious, he reflected on the duties they imposed upon him. Few days had passed, and Lucile was barely beginning to raise her eyes shyly to her husband and to assume the confidence which could have enabled him to get to know her, when unfortunate events took place to disturb the marriage. Initially it had been begun under more favourable auspices.

CHAPTER II

MR DICKSON came to see the newly wedded couple and apologized for not having been at the wedding, telling how he had been ill for a long time through the shock caused by a violent fall. As they were talking about the fall, he said he had been helped by the most attractive woman in the world. At that moment Oswald was playing shuttlecock with Lucile. She was very graceful as she played this game. Oswald was looking at her and not listening to Mr Dickson when the latter shouted to him from one end of the room to the other, 'My Lord, the beautiful stranger has certainly heard a lot about you for she asked me many questions about your situation.' 'Whom are you talking about?' asked Lord Nelvil, continuing to play. 'About a charming woman,' replied Mr Dickson, 'although she already looked altered by suffering and could not speak about you without emotion.' This time the words attracted Lord Nelvil's attention and he came up to Mr Dickson as he asked him to repeat them. Lucile, who had taken no interest in what had been said, went to join her mother, who had sent for her. Oswald was alone with Mr Dickson and asked him who was the woman he had just been talking about. 'I know nothing about her,' he replied. 'Her pronunciation convinced me she was English. But among the women of our country, I have not often seen such an obliging person who could talk so readily. She looked after me, a poor old man, as if she had been my daughter, and the whole time I spent with her I was not aware of all the bruises I had received. But, my dear Oswald, I wonder if you have been as fickle in England as you were in Italy, for my charming benefactress turned pale and trembled when she mentioned your name.' 'Good God! whom are you talking about? An Englishwoman, you say?' 'Yes, certainly,' replied Mr Dickson. 'You know perfectly well that foreigners never pronounce our language without an accent.' 'And her face?' 'Oh, the most expressive I have ever seen, although she was painfully thin and pale.' Corinne, who was so sparkling, was not at all like this description, but might she not be ill? Must she not have suffered greatly if she had come to England, if she had not seen there the man she came to look for? These fears suddenly occurred to Oswald and he continued his questions in extreme anxiety. Mr Dickson kept on telling him that the unknown lady spoke with a charm and eloquence that he had never encountered in any other woman, that in her eyes there was an expression of heavenly kindness, but she seemed listless and sad. It was not Corinne's usual manner, but again might she not be changed by grief? 'What colour are her eyes and hair?' asked Lord Nelvil. 'The most beautiful black in the world.' Lord Nelvil turned pale. 'Does she speak in a lively manner?' 'No,' continued Mr Dickson. 'She said a few words from time to time, to question and answer me, but the few words she uttered were very charming.' He was about to go on when Lucile came back with Lady Edgermond. He said no more; Lord Nelvil stopped interrogating him but withdrew into deep thoughtfulness and went out for a walk until he could find Mr Dickson alone.

Lady Edgermond, struck by his sadness, sent Lucile away so that she could ask Mr Dickson if there had been something in their conversation which might have distressed her son-in-law. Naively he told her what he had said. Immediately Lady Edgermond guessed the truth and shuddered at the thought of the pain Oswald would feel if he knew with certainty that Corinne had come to look for him in Scotland. As she foresaw that he would certainly question Mr Dickson again, she told him what he ought to reply to avert Lord Nelvil's suspicions. In a second conversation, Mr Dickson did not increase Lord Nelvil's anxiety on the matter but he did not dissipate it, and Oswald's first idea was to ask his servant if all the letters he had handed to him during the last three weeks came from the post, and if he did not recall receiving some in another way. The servant gave assurances to the contrary, but as he was leaving the room he retraced his steps, saying to Lord Nelvil, *Yet I seem to remember that on the day of the ball a blind man gave me a letter for your Lordship, but it was probably to beg for help.* 'A blind man,' replied Oswald. 'No, I did not get a letter from him. Could you find him for me again?' 'Yes, very easily,' answered the servant. 'He lives in the village.' 'Go and fetch him,' said Lord Nelvil and, unable to wait patiently for the blind man's arrival, he went to meet him and came upon him at the end of the avenue.

'My good man,' he said, 'you were given a letter for me on the day of the ball at the castle. Who handed it to you?' 'My Lord can see that I am blind; how could I tell him?' 'Do you think it was a woman?' 'Yes, my Lord, for she had a very sweet voice, as far as I could tell, in spite of her tears, for I certainly heard her crying.' 'She was crying,' continued Oswald, 'and what did she say to you?' '*You will hand this letter to Oswald's servant, good old man.* Then, suddenly correcting herself, she added, *to Lord Nelvil.*' 'Oh, Corinne!' cried Oswald; and he had to lean on the old man, for he almost fainted. 'My Lord,' continued the blind old man, 'I was sitting at the foot of a tree when she gave me this errand. I wanted to do it immediately but as, at my age, I find it painful to get up, she deigned to help me herself, gave me more money than I had had for a long time, and I felt her hand tremble as she supported me, as yours is doing just now, my Lord.' 'That is enough,' said Lord Nelvil. 'Take this, good old man. I too am giving you money as she did. Pray for both of us.' And he went away.

From that moment, terrible distress gripped Lord Nelvil's heart. In vain he made enquiries in all directions, but could not imagine how it was possible for Corinne to arrive in Scotland without asking to see him. He worried in a thousand ways about the motives for her behaviour, and his distress was so great that, in spite of his efforts to hide it, it was impossible for Lady Edgermond not to be aware of it and even for Lucile not to notice how unhappy he was. His sadness sent her into a permanent thoughtfulness and their home was very silent. It was then that Lord Nelvil wrote the first letter to Prince Castel-Forte which the Prince thought he should not show to Corinne and which, because of the deep distress expressed in it, would certainly have moved her.

Count d'Erfeuil returned from Plymouth, where he had taken Corinne, before Prince Castel-Forte's reply to Lord Nelvil's letter arrived. He did not want to tell Lord Nelvil everything he knew about Corinne and yet he was vexed that no one was aware that he knew an important secret but was discreet enough to keep quiet. At first his hints had made no impact on Lord Nelvil, but they aroused his attention as soon as he thought they might have some connection with Corinne. He then keenly interrogated Count d'Erfeuil, who defended himself quite well as soon as he had managed to get himself questioned.

Nevertheless, in the end, Oswald dragged all Corinne's story from him, through Count d'Erfeuil's pleasure in telling everything he had done for her, the gratitude she had always shown him, and the terrible state of loneliness and grief in which he had found her. He told this tale, however, without noticing in the least the terrible effect it had on Lord Nelvil, with no other aim at the time than of being, as the English say, *the hero of his own story*. When Count d'Erfeuil had finished speaking, he was really upset by the pain he had caused. Till then Oswald had restrained himself, but he suddenly became crazy with grief. He accused himself of being the most uncivilized and faithless of men. He recalled Corinne's devoted affection, her resignation, and her generosity at the very moment when she thought he was most blameworthy, and he contrasted this with the harsh fickleness with which he had repaid her. He kept on repeating to himself that no one would ever love him as she had done and that somehow he would be punished for his cruelty to her. He wanted to set off for Italy, to see her, if only for a day, if only for an hour. But Rome and Florence were already occupied by the French,* his regiment was about to embark, and he could not go away without dishonour. He could not wound his wife's heart and repair wrongs by wrongs and grief by grief. In the end he rested his hope on the risks of war and this thought gave him back some tranquillity.

It was in this frame of mind that he wrote the second letter to Prince Castel-Forte, which the Prince again decided not to show to Corinne. The replies of Corinne's friend depicted her as being sad but resigned, and as he was proud and hurt on her behalf he minimized rather than exaggerated the unhappy state into which she had lapsed. Lord Nelvil thought, therefore, that he ought not to torture her with his regrets after having made her so unhappy through his love, and he set off for the Indies with feelings of grief and remorse which made his life intolerable.

CHAPTER III

Lucile was distressed by Oswald's departure, but the gloomy silence he had maintained with her during the last days of their life together had so increased her natural shyness that she could not bring herself to tell him she was pregnant. He only learned this when he was in the Indies, through a letter of Lady Edgermond's, from whom her daughter had concealed the fact till then. Lord Nelvil thought, therefore, that Lucile's farewells were very cold. He did not fully appreciate what her feelings were, and comparing her silent grief with Corinne's eloquent expressions of grief when they separated in Venice, he had no hesitation in thinking that Lucile loved him only a little. During his four years of absence, however, she did not enjoy one day's happiness. The birth of her daughter was barely able to distract her for a moment from the risks her husband was running. Another sorrow was added to this anxiety; she gradually discovered everything about Corinne and her relationship with Lord Nelvil.

Count d'Erfeuil, who spent almost a year in Scotland and often visited Lucile and her mother, was strongly convinced that he had not revealed the secret of Corinne's journey to England. He said so much, however, which touched on the matter and, when conversation languished, it was so difficult for him not to return to the subject which interested Lucile so keenly, that in the end she knew everything. Completely innocent as she was, she had enough skill to make Count d'Erfeuil talk, so little being needed for that.

Lady Edgermond, more preoccupied by her illness every day, had not suspected the effort her daughter had made to learn what was to give her so much pain, but when she saw her so sad, she found out from her the secret of her sorrows. Lady Edgermond expressed a very severe opinion on Corinne's journey to England. Lucile had a different feeling about it. She was in turn jealous of Corinne and displeased with Oswald for having been so cruel to a woman who loved him so much, and it seemed to her that, for her own happiness, she must fear a man who had thus sacrificed the happiness of another. She had always remained interested in her sister and grateful to her; and this increased further the pity she felt for her. And far from being flattered by the sacrifice Oswald had made for her, she was worried by the thought that he had chosen her only because her social position was better than Corinne's. She recalled his misgivings before the marriage, his sadness a few days after it, and she was continually reaffirming the cruel thought that her husband did not love her. In this frame of mind she might have been greatly helped by Lady Edgermond if she had calmed her down, but Lucile's mother was a lady without indulgence, who was concerned only with duty and the feelings it allows; everything which departed from this path was anathema to her. She did not think of winning someone back by being considerate but, on the contrary, thought that the only way to arouse remorse was to show resentment. She shared only too keenly Lucile's anxieties, was annoyed at the thought that such a charming girl was not appreciated by her husband, and, far from helping her by persuading her she was better loved than she thought, she confirmed her fear on the matter in order to give added stimulus to her pride. Lucile, gentler and more enlightened than her mother, did not follow strictly the advice Lady Edgermond gave her, but some traces still remained and her letters to Lord Nelvil were much less affectionate than her innermost feelings.

Meanwhile, Oswald distinguished himself in the war by outstandingly brave deeds. He exposed his life countless times, not only because of his passion for honour, but because of a desire for risk. It was noticed that danger was a pleasure for him, that he seemed more cheerful and happier on days of battle. His face turned red with joy when the clash of arms began, and it was only at that moment that a weight on his heart was lifted and let him breathe freely. He was adored by his soldiers, admired by his fellow officers, and he led a very active life which, although it did not make him happy, at least made him stop worrying about the past or the future. From his wife he received letters he thought were cold, but became used to them. He often remembered Corinne during the fine tropical nights when one has such great thoughts about nature and its author. But as the climate and the war were threatening his life every day and he was so close to death, he thought he was less guilty. You forgive your enemies when they are threatened with death; in a similar situation you feel indulgent towards yourself. Lord Nelvil thought only of Corinne's tears when she would learn that he was no more. He forgot those she had shed because of the wrong he had once done her.

Amongst the perils which make one think so often about the uncertainty of life, he thought much more about Corinne than about Lucile. They had talked together so much about death, they had so often discussed the most serious ideas, that he thought he was still talking to Corinne when he was thinking about the lofty ideas which are recalled by the regular sight of war and its dangers. It was she whom he was talking to when he was alone, although he ought to have thought she was angry with him. It seemed to him that they still understood each other, in spite of absence, even in spite of his infidelity, while the gentle Lucile, whom he did not think was annoyed with him, presented herself to his memory only as someone worthy to be protected but who must be spared all sad, deep reflections. Eventually, the troops commanded by Lord Nelvil were recalled to England. He returned. He already liked the peaceful atmosphere of the ship much less than the activity of war. For him physical action had replaced the pleasures of the imagination, which Corinne's conversation had made him appreciate. He had not yet tried to lead a quiet life far from her. He had been able to make himself so loved by his soldiers, and aroused in them so much enthusiastic affection, that during the voyage their admiration and devotion renewed for him yet again the interest of military life. This interest ended completely only when they disembarked.

CHAPTER IV

LORD NELVIL then left for Lady Edgermond's estate in Northumberland. He had to renew acquaintance with his family, whom he had been used to doing without for four years. With as much shyness as a guilty woman might feel, Lucile introduced his daughter to him. She was now more than three years old and looked like Corinne. During her pregnancy Lucile's thoughts had been greatly concerned with the memory of her sister, and Juliet (for that was the child's name) had Corinne's hair and eyes. Lord Nelvil noticed the resemblance and was disturbed by it. He took the child in his arms and pressed her affectionately to his heart. In this action Lucile saw only a memory of Corinne and from that moment her pleasure in Lord Nelvil's affection for Juliet was not unmixed.

Lucile had become even more beautiful; she was nearly twenty years old. Her beauty had assumed an imposing aspect and aroused a feeling of respect in Lord Nelvil. Lady Edgermond was no longer fit to leave her bed and her situation made her very bad-tempered and melancholy. Still, she was glad to see Lord Nelvil, for she was very worried by the fear of dying in his absence and thus leaving her daughter alone in the world. Lord Nelvil had become so used to an active life that it was very hard for him to stay almost the whole day in his mother-in-law's room; she no longer received anyone but her daughter and son-in-law. Lucile was still very much in love with Lord Nelvil but she had the sorrow of not thinking herself loved, and out of pride hid from him what she knew of his feelings for Corinne and the jealousy they caused her. This constraint added further to her habitual reserve and made her colder and more silent than she naturally would have been. When her husband wanted to give her some advice about the charm she could have added to conversation by showing more interest in it, she thought she could see a memory of Corinne in his advice and, instead of profiting from it, she was hurt. Lucile had a very gentle nature but her mother had given her definite ideas about everything, and when Lord Nelvil lauded the pleasures of the imagination and the attraction of the fine arts, she always saw memories of Italy in what he was saying and rather curtly clamped down on Lord Nelvil's enthusiasm because she thought Corinne was its sole cause. In another frame of mind, she would have thought carefully about her husband's words so as to study every way of pleasing him.

Lady Edgermond, whose failings were increased by illness, showed an increasing antipathy to everything which departed from the monotony and customary regularity of life. She saw harm in everything, and her imagination, irritated by suffering, was distressed both physically and mentally by every sound. She would have liked to reduce existence to the least possible effort, perhaps in order not to regret so keenly what she was about to leave, but as no one admits the personal motive for their opinions, she based hers on the general principles of an excessive morality. She was perpetually disillusioned about life, considering the least pleasures wrong, opposing duty to every use of time which might be slightly different from what had been done the day before. Although Lucile was obedient to her mother, she was nevertheless naturally more intelligent and less rigid, and would have joined her husband in gently opposing her mother's ever-increasing austerity and demands. But Lady Edgermond had convinced her that she was behaving in this way only to oppose Lord Nelvil's liking for life in Italy. 'We must never cease to fight,' she said, 'through the power of duty, against the possible return of this disastrous inclination.' Lord Nelvil, too, had certainly a great respect for duty but he thought of it in a wider context than did Lady Edgermond. He liked to go to its source; he thought it was perfectly in accordance with our genuine inclinations and did not require of us continual sacrifices and struggles. In short, it seemed to him that virtue, far from harassing life, contributed so much to lasting happiness that one could consider it as a kind of foreknowledge granted to man on this earth.

As Oswald developed his ideas, he sometimes indulged in the pleasure of using Corinne's expressions. He enjoyed hearing himself borrow her language. Lady Edgermond showed irritation as soon as he indulged in this way of thinking and speaking. Elderly people do not like new ideas. They like to convince themselves that the world has lost rather than gained once they are no longer young. In the more lively interest which Lord Nelvil put into his own language, Lucile, with the instinct of the heart, recognized the influence of his affection for Corinne. She lowered her eyes so as not to let her husband see what she was feeling, and he, not suspecting that she was informed of his relationship with Corinne, attributed his wife's immobile silence to the coldness of her nature while he spoke with warmth. As he did not know where to turn in order to find a mind which responded to his own, his regrets for the past were renewed within him more keenly than ever and he fell into a deep melancholy. He wrote to Prince Castel-Forte, asking for news of Corinne. His letter did not arrive because of the war. His health suffered greatly from the English climate; the doctors told him repeatedly that his chest would suffer again if he did not spend the winter in Italy. It was not possible to think of it, however, since peace had not been made between France and England. Once, in the presence of his mother-in-law and his wife, he spoke of the advice the doctors had given him and of the obstacle which stood in its way. 'When peace is made,' said Lady Edgermond, 'I do not think you will permit yourself to see Italy again.' 'If my Lord's health requires it,' interrupted Lucile, 'he would be very wise to go.' These words seemed very kind to Lord Nelvil and he was quick to express his gratitude to Lucile. This very gratitude hurt her, however, for she thought she could see in it his intention of preparing her for the journey.

Peace was made* in the spring and the Italian journey became possible. Every time Lord Nelvil let slip a few thoughts on the bad state of his health, Lucile was torn between her anxiety and her fear that Lord Nelvil wanted to hint that he ought to spend the winter in Italy. But while her affection would have inclined her to exaggerate her husband's illness, her jealousy, which stemmed from the same feeling, made her look for reasons to minimize the risk which the doctors said he ran by remaining in England. Lord Nelvil attributed her behaviour to indifference and selfishness, and each of them hurt the other, because they did not frankly confess their feelings.

Finally Lady Edgermond fell so dangerously ill that Lucile and Lord Nelvil had no other subject of conversation together than her illness. The poor lady lost the power of speech a month before she died. One could tell what she wanted to say only from her tears or her way of gripping one's hand. Sincerely moved, Oswald spent every night at her bedside and, as it was November, he did himself a lot of harm through the care he lavished on her. Lady Edgermond seemed pleased by her son-in-law's signs of affection. The failings in her character disappeared just when her terrible state would have made them more pardonable, so greatly are the soul's agitations soothed by the approach of death. Most failings stem only from this agitation.

On the night of her death she took Lucile's and Lord Nelvil's hands and, putting them in each other's, she pressed them both against her heart. Then she lifted her eyes to heaven and did not seem to regret her lack of the power of speech, which would have said nothing more than her look and her movement. A few minutes later she expired.

Lord Nelvil, who had exercised considerable self-control so as to be able to care for his mother-in-law, became dangerously ill, and the unfortunate Lucile, at a time of grievous sorrow, had to endure the most frightful anxiety. Apparently in his delirium Lord Nelvil uttered the names of Corinne and Italy several times. In his ramblings he often asked for *the southern sun, a warmer atmosphere*; when gripped by a fit of feverish shivering, he would say: *It is so cold in this northern climate that I shall never be able to get warm in it.* When he came to himself again, he was very astonished to learn that Lucile had arranged everything for the journey to Italy. He was surprised by this. She gave as her reason the doctors' advice. 'With your permission,' she added, 'my daughter and I will go with you: a child should not be parted from either her father or her mother.' 'Indeed,' replied Lord Nelvil, 'we must not be parted. But does this journey upset you? Say so, and I shall give it up.' 'No,' replied Lucile, 'it is not that which upsets me . . .' Lord Nelvil looked at her and took her hand. She was going to say more about her feelings, but the memory of her mother, who had advised her never to admit her jealousy to Lord Nelvil, suddenly stopped her and she continued, saying: 'You must believe me, my Lord; my main concern is the restoration of your health.' 'You have a sister in Italy,' continued Lord Nelvil. 'I know,' replied

Lucile. 'Have you any news of her?' 'No,' said Lord Nelvil. 'Since I left for America I know nothing at all of what has become of her.' 'Well, my Lord, we shall find out in Italy.' 'Are you still interested in her?' 'Yes, my Lord,' replied Lucile. 'I have never forgotten the affection she showed me in my childhood.' 'Yes, one must never forget anything,' said Lord Nelvil with a sigh. And both of them remained silent, and that was the end of the conversation.

Oswald was not going to Italy with the intention of renewing his ties with Corinne. He was too scrupulous even to entertain such a thought. But if he was not going to recover from the chest complaint hanging over him, he thought it would be a consolation to die in Italy and, by a final farewell, to obtain Corinne's forgiveness. He did not think Lucile could know the passion he had had for her sister; still less that, in his delirium, he had betrayed the regrets that still distressed him. He did not do justice to his wife's intelligence, because it was sterile and was used more to read the thoughts of others than to interest them by what she thought herself. So Oswald had become used to thinking of her as a beautiful, cold, young woman, who fulfilled her duties and loved him as much as she could love. But he was not aware of Lucile's sensitive nature; she took the utmost care to hide it. It was out of pride that in this situation she concealed what was distressing her; even if she were in a perfectly happy situation, she would still have reproached herself for showing that she felt deep affection, even for her husband. It seemed to her that modesty was hurt by the expression of all passionate feeling. But as she was capable of having such feelings, her upbringing, by imposing on her the law of restraint, had made her sad and silent. She had been thoroughly convinced that she must not reveal her feelings but she took no pleasure in saying anything else.

CHAPTER V

LORD NELVIL was afraid of the memories which France recalled to him. So he crossed it quickly for, on the journey, Lucile showed no wish or desire for anything; he alone decided everything. They arrived at the bottom of the mountains which separate Dauphiné from Savoy and climbed what is called *the stepladder* on foot. It is a road cut into the rock and its entrance is like that of a deep cave. It is dark the whole length of the way, even on the finest summer days.

It was then the beginning of December. There was no snow yet but autumn, the season of decay, was itself coming to an end and giving way to winter. The whole road was covered with dead leaves, brought there by the wind, for there were no trees on the rocky path, and near the remains of withered nature, no branches, the hope for the following year, could be seen. Lord Nelvil liked the sight of the mountains. In flat countries it seems that the earth has no other aim than to support and nourish man, but in picturesque regions we think we recognize the stamp of the Creator's genius and omnipotence. Man has become familiar with nature everywhere, however, and the roads he has opened up climb mountains and go down into ravines. No longer is anything inaccessible to him except the great mystery of himself.

In the Maurienne,* winter became more severe at every step. It was as if you were going towards the North when you drew near to Mont Cenis. Lucile, who had never travelled, was terrified by the icy roads which made the horses' steps uncertain. She hid her fears from Oswald but frequently reproached herself for having brought her little girl with her. She often wondered if the most perfect morality had motivated this decision and if her great affection for the child, and also the idea that Oswald loved her more because he always saw her with Juliet, had not made her oblivious of the perils of such a long journey. Lucile was a very timid person and she often wearied herself with scruples and inner questioning about her behaviour. The more virtuous you are, the more fastidious you become, and with that come anxieties of conscience. Lucile's only refuge from this trait was religious devotion, and long, silent prayers calmed her.

As they went on towards Mont Cenis, the whole of nature seemed to assume a more terrible aspect. Snow fell abundantly on the already snow-covered ground. It was as if they were going into the icy hell so well described by Dante. All the earth's features had only one monotonous appearance, from the depths of the precipices to the mountain tops; the same colour made all the varieties of vegetation disappear. The rivers still flowed at the foot of the mountains, but the pine trees, turned completely white, were reflected in the water like ghost trees. Oswald and Lucile looked silently at this scene. Speech seems alien to such frozen nature and you are silent before it. Then suddenly, on a vast plain of snow, they caught sight of a long procession of black-robed men who were carrying a coffin towards a church. These priests, the only living beings who appeared in this cold, deserted countryside, walked at a very slow pace, which would have been quickened by the severity of the weather if the thought of death had not stamped its solemnity on all their steps. The mourning of nature and of man, of vegetation and of life, those two colours, black and white, which alone struck the eye and made the one stand out against the other, filled their hearts with fear. Lucile said in a whisper, 'What a sad omen!' 'Lucile,' interrupted Oswald, 'believe me, it is not for you.' 'Alas!' he thought. 'It was not under such auspices that I travelled in Italy with Corinne. What has happened to her now? And do all these mournful things around me foretell what I am going to suffer?'

Lucile was shaken by the anxieties which the journey aroused in her. Oswald did not think of this kind of terror, which is very alien to a man, above all to a nature as intrepid as his. Lucile took for indifference what was entirely due to his being unaware of the possibility of fear in this situation. Everything combined, however, to increase Lucile's anxieties. The local peasantry find a kind of satisfaction in exaggerating the danger; it is their sort of imagination. They like the effect they produce in this way on people of another class, whom they compel to listen to them by frightening them. When you want to cross Mont Cenis in winter, the travellers and innkeepers give you up-to-date news about the passage over the *mount*, as they call it. It is as if they were speaking about a motionless monster, guardian of the valleys which lead to the promised land. They observe the weather to know if there is anything to dread, and when there are grounds to fear the wind called *the tempest*, strangers are strongly advised not to risk themselves on the mountain. This wind is heralded by a white cloud, which stretches like a shroud over the sky and not long afterwards darkens the whole horizon.

Without Lord Nelvil's knowledge, Lucile had secretly obtained as much information as possible. He had no idea of her terrors and gave himself up completely to the reflections aroused in him by the return to Italy. Lucile, who was made more anxious by the purpose of the journey even than by the journey itself, judged everything with an unfavourable prejudice and silently blamed Lord Nelvil for feeling so certain of her and her daughter's safety. On the morning of going over the Mont Cenis pass, several local people collected round Lucile and told her there was a threat of *the tempest*. Nevertheless the men who were to carry her and her daughter assured her there was nothing to fear. Lucile looked at Lord Nelvil; she saw that he did not worry about the fear the local people wanted to arouse in them, and, hurt yet again by his courage, she quickly announced that she wanted to set off. Oswald did not notice the feeling which had prompted this decision and rode on horseback behind the litter which carried his wife and daughter. They climbed up fairly easily but when they had reached halfway, on the plateau which separates the climb up from the descent, a terrible hurricane arose. Whirlwinds of snow blinded the guides, and several times Lucile lost sight of Oswald, whom the storm had, as it were, enveloped in its violent mists. The worthy friars who, on the summit of the Alps, devote themselves to the safety of travellers began to ring their alarm bells, and although this signal proclaimed the pity of the men who gave it, the sound had something gloomy in itself and the hurried clanging of the bells expressed fear still more than help.

Lucile hoped that Oswald would suggest stopping at the monastery and spending the night there, but as she did not want to tell him what she would like, he thought it would be better to hurry on and arrive before nightfall. Lucile's bearers asked her anxiously if they should begin the descent. 'Yes,' she replied, 'since my Lord has no objection to doing so.' Lucile was wrong not to express her fears, for her daughter was with her, but when you are in love and think you are not loved, you are hurt by everything, and every moment of your life is painful and almost humiliating. Oswald remained on horseback although it was the most dangerous way of descending, but he thought it was the surest way of not losing sight of his wife and daughter.

When, from the top of the mountain, Lucile saw the road down, a road so steep that you would take it for a precipice itself, were it not that the ravines beside it made you see the difference, she pressed her daughter to her heart with intense feeling. Oswald noticed this and, leaving his horse, he came himself to help the bearers support the litter. Oswald did everything so charmingly that when Lucile saw him attending her and Juliet with great zeal and concern, she felt her eyes fill with tears. But at that moment there arose such a terrible gust of wind that the bearers themselves fell to their knees, crying *Oh, God, help us!* Then Lucile summoned up all her courage and, sitting up on the litter, she handed Juliet to Lord Nelvil, saying, 'My dear, take your daughter.' Oswald grasped her, saying to Lucile, 'And you too, come, I shall be able to carry you both.' 'No,' answered Lucile, 'save only your daughter.' 'What do you mean, save?' repeated Lord Nelvil. 'Is there any question of danger?' And turning round to the bearers again he cried, 'Miserable creatures, why did you not tell me ...?' 'They warned me of it,' interrupted Lucile ... 'And you concealed it from me,' said Lord Nelvil. 'What have I done to deserve this cruel silence?' While saying these words, he wrapped his daughter in his coat and, extremely concerned, he looked down at the ground. But Heaven, Lucile's protector, sent a ray of light which pierced the clouds, calmed the wind, and revealed the fertile plains of Piedmont. In an hour, the whole procession arrived unscathed at Novalesa, the first town in Italy beyond Mont Cenis.

When she came into the inn, Lucile took her daughter in her arms, went up to her room, knelt down, and fervently thanked God. While she was praying, Oswald leaned against the mantelpiece, looking thoughtful, and when Lucile got up, he held out his hand to her, saying, 'Lucile, were you afraid then?' 'Yes, my dear,' she replied. 'Then why did you set out?' 'You seemed impatient to go.' 'Do you not know,' replied Lord Nelvil, 'that, more than anything, I fear for you either danger or death.' 'It is for Juliet they are to be feared,' said Lucile. She took her daughter on her knees, to warm her by the fire, and, with her hands, curled up the child's beautiful dark hair, which the snow and rain had flattened down on her forehead. At that moment, the mother and daughter were charming. Oswald looked at both of them affectionately. But, once again, silence interrupted a conversation which might have led to a happy explanation.

They arrived in Turin. That year the winter was very severe. The huge rooms in Italy are intended to receive the sun; they are like deserts in the cold weather. Men are very small beneath the great arches. In summer they are pleasing because they are cool, but in the middle of winter you can only feel the emptiness of the huge mansions whose owners seem like pygmies in the giants' dwelling.

People had just heard of Alfieri's death* and there was general mourning amongst all Italians who wanted to take pride in their native land. Lord Nelvil thought he could see indications of sadness everywhere, and he no longer had the feeling that Italy had aroused in him in the past. The absence of the woman he had so greatly loved took away the charm of nature and the arts in his eyes. At Turin, he asked for news of Corinne. He was told that she had published nothing for five years and lived in the deepest seclusion. He was assured, however, that she lived in Florence. He decided to go there, not in order to stay in that town and so to be false to the affection he owed Lucile, but at least to explain to Corinne, himself, how he had not known of her journey to Scotland.

As they passed through the Lombardy plains Oswald exclaimed, 'Oh! How beautiful it all was when the elms were covered with leaves and the green vines linked them together!' Lucile said to herself, 'It was beautiful when Corinne was with him.' The view of the countryside was obscured by a damp mist of the kind that often arises in these plains, crossed by a great number of rivers. In the inns, during the night they could hear the copious rain of the South, which falls like a deluge on the roofs. It makes its way into the houses, and the water follows you everywhere, with the speed of fire. In vain Lucile looked for Italy's attraction; it was as if everything was combining to conceal it with a dark veil from her sight and from Oswald's.

CHAPTER VI

SINCE Oswald had come to Italy, he had not uttered one word of Italian. It was as if the language pained him and he avoided hearing it as well as speaking it. In the evening of the day when he and Lady Nelvil arrived at the Milan inn, they heard a knock at the door and saw a Roman with a very dark face and pronounced features yet without any real character; he had a countenance made to show expression but lacking the soul which gives it. On this face there was a fixed charming smile and a look which wanted to be poetic. Right from the door, he began to improvise verses filled with praise of the mother, the child, and the husband, the kind of praise suitable for all mothers, all children, and all the husbands in the world. The whole subject was exaggerated, as if the words and truth had no connection between them. However, the Roman used the musical tones which are so attractive in Italian. He declaimed with a vigour which made the insignificance of what he said even more noticeable. Nothing could be more painful to Oswald than to hear, in this way, a beloved language, for the first time after a long interval, to recall his memories travestied like this, and to have a feeling of sadness renewed by something ridiculous. Lucile noticed the painful state of Oswald's feelings. She wanted to make the improviser stop, but it was impossible to persuade him to listen. He walked up and down the room with long strides; he continually exclaimed and gestured and was not in the least put out by the pain he was giving his listeners. He was like a mechanism which stops only after a set time. At last the time arrived and Lady Nelvil managed to dismiss him.

When he had gone, Oswald said, 'Poetic language is so easy to imitate in Italy, that it should be forbidden to all who are not fit to speak it.' 'That is true,' replied Lucile, perhaps a little too curtly. 'It is true that it must be unpleasant to be reminded of something you admire by what we have just heard.' These words hurt Lord Nelvil. 'Far from it,' he said. 'It seems to me that such a contrast makes the power of genius stand out. It was this same, miserably degraded, language which became heavenly poetry when Corinne, your sister, used it to express her thoughts,' he continued in an artificial tone. Lucile was almost shattered by these words. During the whole journey Oswald had not yet uttered Corinne's name, still less the words *your sister* which seemed to suggest a reproach. Tears were ready to choke her, and if she had given herself up to her emotion, this moment would perhaps have been the sweetest in her life. But she controlled herself and, as a result, the constraint between husband and wife became even more painful.

The next day the sun came out and, in spite of the preceding bad weather, it shone, brilliant and radiant, like an exile returning to his native land. Lucile and Lord Nelvil took advantage of it to go and see Milan Cathedral. It is the masterpiece of Gothic architecture in Italy, as Saint Peter's is of modern architecture. This church, built in the shape of a cross, is a beautiful representation of grief, rising over the rich, cheerful town of Milan. As you go up to the top of the tower, you are overwhelmed by the scrupulous work of every detail. The whole building in all its height is decorated with carvings sculpted, as it were, like a little ornament. What patience and time were needed to produce such a work! In the past, perseverance with the same goal was handed on from generation to generation, and humankind, stable in its ideas, erected monuments as unshakeable as itself. A Gothic church arouses very religious feelings. Horace Walpole* said that *The Popes assigned the wealth, acquired from the piety inspired by the Gothic cathedrals, to the building of modern places of worship*. The light filtering through the stained-glass windows, the remarkable forms of the architecture, in fact the whole appearance of the church, is a silent image of the mystery of the infinite, which we

feel within ourselves, never able to free ourselves from it nor understand it.

Lucile and Lord Nelvil left Milan on a day when the ground was
covered with snow, and nothing is more sad than snow in Italy. People
are not used to seeing nature disappear beneath a uniform frosty veil.
All Italians are as upset by bad weather as they are by a public disaster. Travelling with Lucile, Oswald had a kind of coquetry on Italy's
behalf which was not satisfied. Winter is disliked there more than anywhere else, because the imagination is unprepared for it. They went
through Piacenza, Parma, and Modena. Their churches and palaces
are too vast for the number and wealth of the inhabitants. It is as if
these towns were planned to receive great noblemen who are due to
arrive, but only some of their retinue have gone ahead.

The night before the morning when Lucile and Lord Nelvil proposed to cross the Taro, the river had overflowed its banks; it was as
if everything was to contribute to making this Italian journey miserable. The flooding of the rivers which come down from the Alps and
the Apennines is very frightening. From a distance you can hear them
growling like thunder, and their flow is so swift that the water and
the noise that heralds it arrive almost at the same time. It is hardly
possible to have a bridge over such rivers because they continually
change their beds and rise well above the level of the plain. Suddenly
Oswald and Lucile were halted at the bank of this river. The boats
had been carried away by the current and they had to wait till the
Italians, a people who never hurry, had brought them back to the new
bank formed by the torrent. Meanwhile, Lucile, deep in thought and
frozen, was pacing up and down. The fog was so thick that the river
could not be distinguished from the horizon, and the scene recalled
poetic descriptions of the Styx rather than the beneficent waters which
should delight the eyes of a population burned by the sun's rays. Lucile
feared the severe cold for her daughter and took her to a fisherman's
cottage, where the stove was lit in the middle of the room as in Russia.
'So where is your beautiful Italy?' asked Lucile, smiling at Lord Nelvil.
'I do not know when I shall find it again,' he replied sadly.

As you approach Parma and all the towns on this route, you can
glimpse from the distance the picturesque terraced roofs, which give
the Italian towns an oriental appearance. The churches and towers
stand out particularly in the middle of these plateaux, and when you
return to the North, the pointed roofs, made in this shape as a

protection against the snow, make a very unpleasant impression. Parma still preserves some masterpieces by Correggio. Lord Nelvil took Lucile to a church where you can see a fresco the artist painted called the *Madonna della Scala*.* It is covered with a curtain. When the curtain was drawn, Lucile lifted Juliet up in her arms so that she could see the picture better. At that moment, the attitude of the mother and child happened to be almost the same as the Virgin's and her son's. Lucile's face was so like the ideal of modesty and grace painted by Correggio that Oswald turned his gaze alternately from the picture towards Lucile and from Lucile towards the picture. She noticed this, lowered her eyes, and the resemblance became even more striking, for Correggio is perhaps the only painter who can give lowered eyes as penetrating an expression as if they were lifted towards heaven. The veil he casts over the eyes detracts nothing from their expression of feeling or thought, but gives them an additional charm, that of a heavenly mystery.

This Madonna is on the point of flaking away from the wall and you can see the almost trembling colour that could be knocked down by a puff of air. That gives the picture the melancholy charm of all transient things and you come back to it several times, as if to bid a final farewell to its beauty, which is about to disappear.

As they left the church, Oswald said to Lucile, 'In a short time that picture will cease to exist, but *I* shall always have its image before my eyes.' These kindly words touched Lucile. She pressed Oswald's hand, and was about to ask him if her heart could trust this expression of affection. But when what Oswald said seemed to her cold, her pride prevented her from complaining, and when an expression of affection made her happy, she was afraid of disturbing the moment of happiness by wanting to make it more lasting. In this way her heart and her mind always found reasons for saying nothing. She deluded herself into thinking that time, resignation, and gentleness would bring a happy day that would banish all her fears.

CHAPTER VII

LORD NELVIL's health improved in the Italian climate, but he was continually troubled by a cruel anxiety. He asked everywhere for news of Corinne and everywhere people replied, as they had done at Turin, that she was thought to be in Florence, but ever since she had been seeing nobody and writing nothing, they knew nothing about her. Oh, it was not in this way that Corinne's name was pronounced in the past, and could the man who had ruined her happiness and her brilliance forgive himself?

As you come near to Bologna, you are struck by two very high towers in the distance. One of them, particularly, is leaning in a way that looks frightening. In vain you know it is built like that, and like that it has seen the centuries go by. This view disturbs the imagination. Bologna is one of the towns where there is the greatest number of men learned in every branch of knowledge, but the common people make an unpleasant impression. Lucile was expecting the harmonious Italian language she had been promised, and the Bolognese dialect must have been a painful surprise to her. There is none harsher in the northern regions. Oswald and Lucile reached Bologna in the middle of the carnival. Night and day they could hear jubilant shouts exactly like shouts of anger. At night, people just like the Neapolitan Lazzaroni sleep under the many arcades which line the streets of Bologna. In winter, they carry little fires in pottery vases, eat in the street, and continually pursue foreigners with their begging. In vain Lucile hoped to hear the melodious voices which can be heard at night in Italian towns. In cold weather they are all silent, and in Bologna they are replaced by shouts which are frightening when you are not used to them. The common people's jargon seems hostile, because it sounds so harsh, but in some southern regions the habits of the populace are much more coarse than in the lands of the North. Sedentary life perfects the social order, but, by enabling people to live in the streets, the sun introduces something uncivilized into the habits of the common people.[36]

Oswald and Lady Nelvil could not take a step without being beset by a great number of beggars, who, in general, are the scourge of Italy. As they walked past the Bologna prisons, whose barred windows look out onto the streets, the prisoners indulged in most unpleasant jubilation; they shouted in thundering voices at the passers-by and asked for help with coarse jokes and raucous laughter. In short, everything gave the impression of a people without dignity. 'In England, our common people, its leaders' fellow-citizens, do not make a nuisance of themselves like this,' said Lucile. 'Can you like such a country, Oswald?' 'May God preserve me from ever giving up my native land, but when you have crossed the Apennines you will hear Tuscan spoken and you will see the real South,' replied Oswald. 'You will become acquainted with the witty, lively people of those regions and I think you will be less severe on Italy.'

The Italian people can be judged in quite different ways, according to circumstances. Sometimes the ill that is so often spoken of them fits what one sees; at other times it seems entirely unjust. In a country where most governments were without safeguards and the power of public opinion was almost as non-existent for the highest as for the lowest classes; in a country where religion is taken up more with ritual than with ethics, there is little good to say about the nation considered as a whole, but you come across many private virtues. So it is the luck of individual relationships which arouses satire or praise in travellers. The individual people you know decide the judgement you make of the nation, a judgement which cannot be based on anything fixed, either in the institutions, the way of life, or public attitudes.

Oswald and Lucile went together to see the beautiful collections of pictures in Bologna. When they were looking at them, Oswald stopped a long time in front of the Sibyl painted by Domenichino. Lucile noticed the interest this picture aroused in him and, seeing that he was lost in thought for a long time gazing at it, she finally dared to go up to him and ask him shyly if Domenichino's Sibyl appealed to him more than Correggio's Madonna. Oswald understood Lucile and was surprised at the full meaning of these words. For some time he looked at her without replying, and then said, 'The Sibyl no longer utters oracles; all her genius and talent are no more. But the angelic face painted by Correggio has lost none of its charming features, and the unhappy man who caused the one so much pain will never betray the other.' As he finished speaking, he went out in order to conceal his distress.

BOOK XX

CONCLUSION

CHAPTER I

AFTER what had happened in the Bologna art gallery, Oswald realized that Lucile knew more about his relationship with Corinne than he had thought. He had, at last, the thought that her cold silence was perhaps the result of some secret grief. This time, however, it was he who was afraid of the explanation that, till then, Lucile had dreaded. Now that the first words had been said, she would have disclosed everything if Lord Nelvil had so wished, but it was too painful for him to talk about Corinne just when he was going to see her again; he could not bear to commit himself by a promise to talk about a subject which still touched him nearly, to someone with whom he always felt ill at ease and whose character he only partly knew.

They crossed the Apennines and on the other side they found Italy's beautiful climate. The wind from the sea, so stifling in the summer, brought a gentle warmth at that time. The grass was green; autumn was barely over and already there were signs of spring. In the markets you could see all kinds of fruit, oranges, pomegranates. They began to hear the Tuscan language. In short, all his memories of beautiful Italy returned to Oswald, but unmixed with any hope. All his feelings were connected only with the past. The gentle southern breeze also affected Lucile's frame of mind. She would have been more confident, more lively, if Lord Nelvil had encouraged her; both equally constrained, however, by shyness, and uneasy about each other's attitude, they did not dare talk to each other about what was on their minds. In such circumstances Corinne would have discovered Oswald's secret very quickly and Lucile's as well. But they both had the same kind of reserve, and the more they were like each other in this respect, the more difficult it was for them to emerge from their constrained situation.

CHAPTER II

WHEN they arrived in Florence, Lord Nelvil wrote to Prince Castel-Forte, and a short while later the Prince came to visit him. Oswald was so moved at seeing him that it was a long time before he could speak. At last he asked him for news of Corinne. 'I have only sad news about her,' Prince Castel-Forte replied. 'She is in very poor health and gets weaker every day. She sees no one but me; she finds it very difficult to do anything. I think she is a little calmer, however, since we learned of your arrival in Italy. I cannot conceal from you that her emotion was so great when she heard the news that she had a renewed attack of the fever from which she had recovered. She did not tell me her intentions concerning you, for I very carefully refrain from mentioning your name.' 'Be so good, your Highness, as to show her the letter you received from me nearly five years ago,' Oswald replied. 'It contains all the details of the circumstances which prevented me from learning about her journey to England before I married Lucile. Ask her to receive me when she has read it. I need to speak to her to justify my behaviour, if that is possible. I must have her esteem, even though I may not lay claim to her concern.' 'I shall comply with your wishes, my Lord,' said Prince Castel-Forte. 'I would like you to do her some good.'

At that moment, Lady Nelvil came in. Oswald introduced Prince Castel-Forte to her. She received him rather coldly; he looked at her with great interest. Presumably he was struck by her beauty, for he sighed, thinking of Corinne. Then he left the room. Lord Nelvil followed him. 'Lady Nelvil is quite charming,' said Prince Castel-Forte. 'How delightfully youthful she is! My poor friend no longer has any of that sparkle. But, my Lord, you must not forget that she too had that shining look when you saw her for the first time.' 'No, I do not forget,' cried Lord Nelvil. 'No, I shall never forgive myself . . .' And he stopped without being able to finish what he wanted to say. The rest of the day he was gloomy and silent. Lucile did not try to cheer him and Lord Nelvil was hurt that she did not try. He said to himself, 'If Corinne had seen that I was sad, she would have comforted me.'

The next morning he was so troubled that he called on Prince Castel-Forte very early. 'Well,' he said. 'What was her reply?' 'She is not willing to see you,' Prince Castel-Forte replied. 'But for what reasons?' 'I went to see her yesterday and found her in a very pitiful state of distress. She was striding up and down although she was extremely weak. Sometimes her pallor changed to a violent blush which disappeared immediately. I told her you wished to see her. For a few moments she said nothing, but finally said these words which I shall repeat to you faithfully, since you insist. *He is a man who has hurt me too much. An enemy who threw me into prison, banished, and proscribed me would not have rent my heart to that extent. I suffered what no one has ever suffered, a combination of affection and annoyance which made my thoughts continuous torture. For Oswald, I felt as much admiration as love. He must remember I once told him it would cost me as much to cease admiring him as to cease loving him. He has sullied the object of my devotion. It does not matter whether or not he felt he had good reason to go back on his word. He is not the man I thought he was. What has he done for me? For nearly a year, he benefited from the feeling he inspired in me, but when he should have proved his love by one action, he ought to have defended me; did he do so? Can he lay claim to one sacrifice, to one generous impulse? He is happy now. He has all the advantages society values. I am dying. Let him leave me in peace.'*

'These are very hard words,' Oswald said. 'Suffering has made her bitter,' Prince Castel-Forte replied. 'I have often seen her in a gentler frame of mind. May I say she has often defended you against me.' 'So you think I am very guilty?' Lord Nelvil asked. 'May I say that I think you are,' said Prince Castel-Forte. 'The wrong you may do a woman may not hurt you in the eyes of the world. The fragile idols adored today may be smashed tomorrow without being defended by anyone, and it is for that very reason that, as far as they are concerned, I respect them more. Morality is upheld only by our own hearts. We suffer no inconvenience when we cause them pain, and yet the pain is terrible. A dagger blow is punished by the law but the rending of a sensitive heart is only the subject of a joke. So it would be better to allow yourself to strike with a dagger.' 'Believe me,' replied Lord Nelvil, 'I, too, have been very unhappy. It is my only justification, but in the past Corinne would have understood. It is possible that now it does not touch her at all. Nevertheless I want to write to her. I still believe that, in spite of all that separates us, she will listen to her friend's voice.' 'I shall give her your letter,' said Prince Castel-Forte, 'but, I beg you, spare her feelings. You do not know what you still mean to her. Five years only make a feeling deeper when there is nothing else to take the mind off it. Do you want to know in what state she is just now? A strange whim, that my entreaties have not been able to persuade her to give up, will give you an idea.'

As he finished speaking, Prince Castel-Forte opened his study door and Lord Nelvil followed him in. The first thing he saw was

Corinne's portrait. She was wearing the costume she had worn in the first act of *Romeo and Juliet*; that was the day when he felt his passion for her at its height. A happy, confident look enlivened her whole face. Memories of that festive period in its entirety were aroused in Lord Nelvil's mind, and as he was enjoying being lost in them, Prince Castel-Forte took him by the hand and opened a black curtain which covered another picture. He showed him Corinne as she had wanted to be painted in the present year; she was wearing a black dress; that was the attire she had worn all the time since her return from England. Suddenly Oswald remembered the impression made on him by a woman dressed like that, whom he had caught sight of in Hyde Park; but what struck him above all was the unimaginable change in Corinne's face. She was there, pale as death, her eyes half-closed; her long lashes concealed their expression and cast a shadow on her white face. At the bottom of the portrait was written this line from the *Pastor fido*:

> A pena si può dir: questa fu rosa.†

'Is she really like that now?' asked Lord Nelvil. 'Yes,' replied Prince Castel-Forte, 'and for the last fortnight she has been even worse.' At these words Lord Nelvil left the room like a madman. His distress was so great that it unsettled his mind.

CHAPTER III

WHEN he got back to his own lodging, he shut himself up in his room and stayed there the whole day. At dinner-time Lucile came and knocked quietly at his door. He opened it and said, 'My dear Lucile, allow me to remain alone today. Do not be annoyed with me.' Lucile turned round to Juliet, whom she was holding by the hand, kissed her, and went away without saying a word. Lord Nelvil shut his door again and went up to his table, where the letter he was writing to Corinne was lying. But he wept, saying to himself, 'Could I possibly make Lucile suffer too? What is the point of my life if I make everyone who loves me unhappy?'

---

† One can hardly say: she was a rose.

Lord Nelvil's letter to Corinne

'If you were not the most generous person in the world, what would I have to say to you? You may overwhelm me with reproaches, and what is still more terrible, rend my heart with your grief. Am I a monster, Corinne, since I have inflicted so much pain on what I loved? Oh, I am suffering so much that I cannot think I am an utter barbarian. You know that when I met you I was overwhelmed by the sorrow which will follow me to my grave. I did not hope for happiness. For a long time I struggled against the passion you aroused in me. In the end, when it conquered me, I always retained a feeling of sadness in my heart, the harbinger of an unhappy lot. At times I thought it was a boon from my father, who watched over my destiny from heaven and wanted someone to love me in this world, as he had loved me while he was alive. At times I thought I was disobeying his wishes by marrying a foreign woman and straying from the path marked out by my duty and position. On my return to England, when I learned that my father had already condemned my feeling for you, the latter feeling prevailed. If he had lived, I would have thought I had the right to fight against his authority on this point, but those who are no more can no longer hear us, and their powerless wishes affect us and are sacred to us.

'I was again surrounded by the customs and ties of my native land; I met your sister, whom my father had intended for me and who was so fitted to a plan for a calm, regular life. In my character, I have a weakness which gives me a dread of whatever makes life troublesome. My mind is attracted by new expectations, but I have suffered so much that my sick heart is afraid of everything that arouses very strong emotions or requires decisions which conflict with my memories and the feelings I have had from birth. Yet, Corinne, if I had known you were in England, I would never have been able to detach myself from you. Such a remarkable proof of affection might have carried away my wavering heart. Oh, what is the use of saying what I would have done? Would we have been happy? Am I capable of being so? Indecisive as I am, could I choose one lot, however fine it might be, without regretting another one?

'When you gave me back my freedom, I was annoyed with you. I accepted the opinion that ordinary men must adopt when they see you. I told myself that a person as superior as you would easily do without me. Corinne, I know I have rent your heart, but I thought I was sacrificing only myself. I thought I was more inconsolable than you, and that you would forget me, although I would always regret you. In short, I was a victim of circumstances, and I do not want to deny that Lucile is worthy of the feelings she arouses in me, and of much better still. But from the moment I learned of your journey to England and of the unhappiness I had caused you, my life was nothing but never-ending suffering. For four years, at the centre of the war, I sought out death, convinced that when you learned I was no more you would think I was justified. To hold against me, you certainly had a life of sorrow and pain and a deep-seated fidelity to an ungrateful man who did not deserve it. But bear in mind that human destiny is complicated by a thousand different ties which disturb the heart's constancy. Yet, if it be true that I have never been able to find or give happiness, if it be true that I have lived alone since I left you, that I never speak from the bottom of my heart, that the mother of my child, the woman whom I ought to love for so many reasons, remains a stranger to my secrets, as to my thoughts, if it be true that a permanent state of sadness has again thrust me into the illness from which your care, Corinne, rescued me in the past, if I have come to Italy, not to be cured,—do not think I love life—but to bid you farewell, will you refuse to see me once, only once? I hope you will see me because I think I would do you good. It is not my own suffering which influences me. What does it matter that I am very unhappy? What does it matter if a terrible burden weighs heavily on my heart, if I leave this country without having spoken to you, without my having obtained your forgiveness? I must be unhappy and I shall certainly be so. But it seems to me that if you could think of me as your friend, if you had seen how dear you are to me, if you had felt it by the look and tone of voice of that guilty Oswald, whose heart is more unchanged than his fate, your heart would be relieved.

'I respect my ties, I love your sister. But the human heart, strange and inconsequential as it is, can contain both that affection and the one I feel for you. I have nothing to say about myself which I can write; every explanation I have makes me blameworthy. If you could see me on my knees in front of you, through all my failings and all my duties, you would fathom what you still are for me, and such a conversation would leave you soothed. Alas, we are both in very poor health and I do not think heaven intends us to live for long. May the one who goes first feel regretted and loved by the friend left behind in this world! The innocent one alone should have that satisfaction, but may it also be granted to the guilty one!

'Corinne, my most perfect friend, you who can read the heart, who can imagine what I cannot express, listen to me as you used to listen to me. Let me see you. Allow my pale lips to press your enfeebled hands. Oh, it is not only I who have done this harm. It is the same feeling that has destroyed us both. It is fate which has struck two beings who loved each other. But it has destined one of them to commit a crime, and that one, Corinne, is, perhaps, not the least to be pitied!'

Corinne's reply

'If, to forgive you, I needed only to see you, I would not have refused for a moment. I do not know why I have no resentment against you, though the sorrow you have caused me makes me shudder with terror. I must still love you since I do not have any feeling of hatred against you. Religion alone would not suffice to disarm me in this way. I have had moments when my mind was deranged. At other times, and these were the most soothing, the pain burdening my heart made me think I would die before the day was done; at others I doubted everything, even virtue. For me, you were its image here below. To my thoughts, as to my feelings, I no longer had a guide, since the same blow struck my admiration and my love.

'What would have become of me without divine help? There is nothing in this world that was not poisoned by the memory of you. At the bottom of my heart, one single refuge remained; God received me into it. My physical strength goes on declining, but that is not the case with the passion which sustains me. To make oneself worthy of immortality is the only purpose of life; happiness, suffering, everything, is a means towards that end; this is what I am happy in believing. You have been chosen to uproot my life from this earth; I was clinging to it by too strong a bond.

'When I heard of your arrival in Italy, when I saw your writing again, when I knew you were on the other side of the river, I felt a terrible perturbation in my heart. I had to keep on reminding myself that my sister is your wife, so that I could struggle against what I was feeling. I will not conceal from you that to see you again would be a happiness, an indefinable emotion that my heart, again impassioned, preferred to centuries of calm. But Providence did not desert me in that peril. Are you not the husband of another woman? What then could I have to say to you? Was it permissible for me to die in your arms? And what would be left for my conscience if I made no sacrifice, if I still wanted one last day, one last hour? Perhaps now I shall appear before God more confidently, since I have been able to give up seeing you. This great resolution will calm my heart. Happiness, as I experienced it when you loved me, is not in accord with our nature: it excites, it disturbs, it passes so quickly! But a regular prayer, a religious meditation aiming at self-perfection, at deciding everything by a feeling of duty, is a pleasant state, and I cannot know what ravages the mere sound of your voice might produce in the calm life to which I have attained. You grieved me very much by telling me your health was affected. Oh, it is not I who look after it, but it is still I who suffer with you. May God bless your days, my Lord. Be happy, be happy out of pity. A secret communication with the divine seems to place within ourselves the being who confides and the voice which replies; out of two friends it makes one soul. Would you still seek what is called happiness? Oh, will you find anything better than my affection? Do you know that in the deserts of the New World I would have blessed my lot if you had allowed me to follow you? Do you know that I would have served you like a slave? Do you know that I would have prostrated myself before you as before an emissary from heaven if you had loved me faithfully? But what have you done with so much love? What have you done with that affection which is unique in this world, with an unhappiness equally unique? So lay no further claim to happiness. Do not hurt me by believing you can still achieve it. Pray as I do, pray, and may our thoughts come together in heaven!

'When I feel, however, that I am quite at the end of my days, perhaps I will put myself in some place to see you pass by. Why should I not? When my sight becomes dim, when I can see nothing of the outside world, your image will appear. If I had recently seen you again, would this illusion not be more vivid? In the ancient world, the gods were never present at the time of death. I shall keep you away from mine. But I should like to be able to recall a recent memory of your features in my expiring soul. Oswald, Oswald, what have I said? You see what I am like when I lose myself in remembering you.

'Why did not Lucile want to see me? She is your wife, but she is also my sister. I have kind, even generous, words to say to her. And your daughter, why has she not been brought to see me? I ought not to see you, but those around you are my family; am I rejected by it? Are you afraid that poor little Juliet will be saddened at the sight of me? It is true that I look like a ghost, but I would know how to smile for your child. Farewell, my Lord, farewell. Realize that I could call you my brother, because you are my sister's husband. Oh, at least you will wear mourning when I die; as a relative you will be present at my funeral. It is to Rome that my ashes will first be conveyed. Have my coffin carried by the route traversed in the past by my triumphal chariot, and take a rest in the exact place where you gave me back my laurel crown. No, Oswald, no, I am wrong. I do not want anything which would grieve you. I want only a tear and some glances towards heaven, where I shall await you.'

CHAPTER IV

SEVERAL days elapsed before Oswald's peace of mind could be restored after the heart-rending feeling aroused in him by Corinne's letter. He shunned Lucile's company; he spent whole hours by the bank of the river leading to Corinne's house and he was often tempted to throw himself into the water so that, at least when he was no more, he would be carried towards the dwelling which he had not been allowed to enter while he was alive. Corinne's letter told him she would like to have seen her sister, and although this desire surprised him, he wanted to satisfy it. But how should he broach the matter to Lucile? He was fully aware that she was hurt by his sadness. He would have liked her to question him, but he could not bring himself to speak first and Lucile always found a way of guiding the conversation to indifferent matters, of suggesting an excursion, in short of putting off a conversation which might have led to an explanation. Sometimes she would speak of her wish to leave Florence to go and see Rome and Naples. Lord Nelvil never contradicted her. He would only ask for several days' delay, and with a cold, dignified expression on her face, Lucile would then agree.

Oswald wanted Corinne to see his daughter at least, and he secretly told her nurse to take her to Corinne's dwelling. He went to meet the child as she was coming back and asked if she had enjoyed her visit. Juliet used an Italian phrase in reply, and her pronunciation, so like Corinne's, made Oswald start. 'Who taught you that, my child?' he asked. 'The lady I have just seen,' she replied. 'And how did she receive you?' 'She cried a lot when she saw me,' said Juliet. 'I do not know why. She kissed me and cried, and that upset her, for she looks very ill.' 'And did you like that lady, my dear?' continued Lord Nelvil. 'Very much,' replied Juliet. 'I want to go there every day. She promised to teach me everything she knows. She says she wants me to be like Corinne. What is Corinne, papa? The lady would not tell me.' Lord Nelvil made no further answer and went away to hide his emotion. He said that every day, when out for her walk, Juliet should be taken to Corinne's. But perhaps he wronged Lucile by making arrangements for his daughter in this way without her mother's consent. In a few days, however, the child made remarkable progress in every subject. Her Italian teacher was delighted with her pronunciation. Her music teachers admired her first efforts.

Nothing of all that had happened had hurt Lucile more than the influence over her daughter's education given to Corinne. Juliet had told her mother that Corinne, in her feeble, wasted state, gave herself very great trouble to teach the child all her talents, as a legacy she wanted to leave while still alive. Lucile would have been touched if she had not thought she saw in all these efforts a plan to detach Lord Nelvil from her. But she was torn between wanting, very naturally, to have sole responsibility for her daughter's education and reproaching herself for taking away from Juliet lessons which added so remarkably to her accomplishments. One day Lord Nelvil was passing through the room where Juliet was having a music lesson. She was holding a harp shaped like a lyre but proportionate to her size, in a way like Corinne's; her little arms and the look in her pretty eyes were a complete imitation of Corinne's. It was as if you saw a miniature of a beautiful picture, with the addition of a childhood charm which gives an innocent attraction to everything. On seeing this, Oswald was so moved that he could not utter a word, but, trembling, sat down. Then Juliet played a Scottish melody on her harp; it was a melody that Corinne had performed for Lord Nelvil at Tivoli, in front of a picture of Ossian. While Oswald listened, barely able to breathe, Lucile came up behind him, without his noticing her. When Juliet had finished, her father took her on his knees, saying, 'Did the lady who lives on the banks of the Arno teach you to play like that?' 'Yes,' replied Juliet, 'but in doing so, she suffered greatly. She often felt faint while she was teaching me. Several times I begged her to stop but she did not want to. She only made me promise to play that melody to you on a certain day every year; I think it was the seventeenth of November.' 'Oh, good God!' cried Lord Nelvil and, weeping profusely, he kissed his daughter.

Then Lucile revealed her presence. Taking her daughter by the hand, she said to her husband in English, 'My Lord, it is too much to want to turn my daughter's affection against me as well. In my unhappiness, I was owed that consolation.' As she finished speaking, she took Juliet away. In vain Lord Nelvil wanted to follow her; she would not allow him to. Only at dinner-time did he learn that she had been gone for some hours, alone, and had not said where she was going. He was in a state of mortal anxiety when he saw her coming back with a gentle, calm expression on her face, quite different from what he was expecting. He wanted, at last, to confide in her and, by being sincere, to gain her pardon. But she said, 'My Lord, this explanation is necessary for both of us, but permit its delay for a little while yet. You will soon learn the reasons for my request.'

During dinner, she made her conversation much more interesting than usual. Several days went by like this and, during them, Lucile appeared continually more pleasant and lively than usual. Lord Nelvil could not understand this change. Here is its explanation. Lucile had been very hurt by her daughter's visits to Corinne and by Lord Nelvil's apparent interest in the progress that Corinne's lessons had enabled the child to attain. Everything she had been concealing in her heart for such a long time had then escaped. As often happens with people who do something out of character, she suddenly made a very firm decision to go and see Corinne; she intended to ask her if she was determined always to upset her feelings for her husband. Lucile was speaking to herself forcefully till the moment she arrived at Corinne's door. But she was then overcome by such an attack of shyness that she would never have been able to make up her mind to go in if Corinne, who had caught sight of her from her window, had not sent Theresina to ask her to come into her apartment. Lucile went upstairs to Corinne's room, but when she saw her sister, all her annoyance vanished. On the contrary, she found herself deeply moved by the lamentable state of her sister's health, and, weeping, she kissed her.

Then the two sisters began to talk very frankly to each other. Corinne was the first to set an example of being frank, and it would have been impossible for Lucile not to follow it. Corinne exercised over her sister the ascendancy she had over everyone. With her it was not possible to go on pretending or being reticent. Corinne did not conceal from Lucile that she was sure she had not long to live; her pallor and weakness were only too much evidence for this. She broached the most sensitive subjects of conversation directly with Lucile. She spoke to her of her and Oswald's happiness. She mentioned everything Prince Castel-Forte had told her, and also that she had guessed there was constraint and coldness in their home. Then, using the ascendancy given her by both her intelligence and her threatened approaching end, she generously tried to make Lucile happier with Lord Nelvil. As she was intimately acquainted with Oswald's temperament, she explained to Lucile why he needed to find a type of behaviour, in some ways quite different from hers, in the woman he loved. He needed her spontaneous confidences because his natural reserve prevented him from asking for them; he needed her to show more interest because he was liable to be discouraged, and he needed cheerfulness precisely because he suffered from his own sadness. Corinne depicted herself in her brilliant days. She judged herself as she would have judged a stranger, clearly showing Lucile the attractiveness of someone who combined the most regular behaviour and the strictest morality with all the charm, all the spontaneity, and all the desire to please that the need to make up for wrongs sometimes inspires.

Corinne told Lucile that there were women loved not only in spite of their faults, but because of those same faults. The reason for this strange state of affairs is perhaps that these women would try to be more agreeable so as to be forgiven and, because they needed indulgence, did not impose restraints. 'So do not be proud of your perfection, Lucile. May your attraction lie in forgetting it and not using it to show your superiority. You must be both you and me at the same time. Let your virtues never allow you the slightest neglect of your accomplishments and do not let these same virtues give you a right to be proud and cold. If there were not good reason for this pride, perhaps it would hurt less, for the use of one's rights makes the heart colder than unjustified claims. Feeling delights most in giving what is not owed.'

Lucile thanked her sister affectionately for the kindness she showed her. 'If I were going to live, I should not be able to do it,' said Corinne, 'but since I must soon die, my only personal wish is that Oswald should find again in you and in his daughter some traces of my influence, and that at least he may never enjoy a feeling without recalling Corinne.'

Every day Lucile came back to see her sister and, with very pleasing modesty, examined herself. With an even more pleasing delicacy of feeling she strove to resemble the person whom Oswald had most loved. Every day Lord Nelvil's curiosity grew stronger as he noticed Lucile's new charms. He guessed very quickly that she had seen Corinne, but he could not persuade her to admit this. From her first conversation with Lucile, Corinne had insisted on secrecy about their meetings. She planned to see Oswald and Lucile together, once, but only, apparently, when she was sure she had no more than a few moments to live. She wanted to say and to experience everything at once, but she surrounded her plan with so much mystery that even Lucile did not know how she had decided to carry it out.

CHAPTER V

BELIEVING she was attacked by a fatal illness, Corinne wanted to bid Italy, and especially Lord Nelvil, a last farewell which would recall the time when her genius shone in all its glory. It was a weakness which we must forgive her. Love and fame had always been mingled in her mind, and until the moment when her heart made the sacrifice of all earthly affections, she wanted the ungrateful man who had deserted her to feel once more that he had given the death blow to the woman who, of all those of his time, knew best how to love. Corinne no longer had the strength to improvise, but in her solitude she still composed verses, and since Oswald's arrival she seemed to have taken a keener interest in this occupation. Perhaps, before dying, she wanted to remind him of her talent and her success, in short, of everything that she was losing because of unhappiness and love. So she chose a day to assemble in one of the Florence Academy rooms all who wanted to hear what she had written. She confided her plan to Lucile, asking her to bring her husband. 'In my present state, I can ask that of you.'

Oswald was gripped by a terrible anxiety when he learned of Corinne's resolution. Would she read her verses herself? What subject did she want to deal with? Indeed, the possibility of seeing her was enough to unsettle Oswald's soul completely. On the morning of the appointed day, winter, which makes itself felt so infrequently in Italy, momentarily showed itself as it does in northern climates. A horrible wind could be heard whistling through the houses. The rain beat violently against the window panes, and, unusually, though this happens in Italy more often than elsewhere, thunder could be heard in the middle of January, mingling a feeling of terror with the sadness of the bad weather. Oswald did not utter a single word, but all the sensations coming from external conditions seemed to increase the shudder in his soul.

He came into the hall with Lucile. A huge crowd had collected there. In a very dark corner at one end, a chair had been prepared, and Lord Nelvil heard people around him say that Corinne was to sit there because she was so ill that she would not be able to recite her verses herself. She was so changed that she was afraid to be seen and had chosen this way of seeing Oswald without being seen. As soon as she knew he was there, she went, veiled, towards the chair. She had to be supported to enable her to move forward. Her walk was unsteady. From time to time she paused to draw breath and it looked as if the short distance was a painful journey. Life's last steps are always slow and difficult like this. She sat down, looked round to find Oswald, caught sight of him, and, with a quite involuntary movement, she got up and stretched out her arms to him. A moment later, however, she fell back, turning away her face like Dido when she met Aeneas in another world, impervious to human passions. Prince Castel-Forte restrained Lord Nelvil, who, quite beside himself, wanted to throw himself at her feet. The Prince held Oswald back by appealing to the respect he owed Corinne in the presence of so many people.

A young girl, dressed in white and crowned with flowers, appeared on a kind of amphitheatre that had been prepared. It was she who was to sing Corinne's lines. There was a touching contrast between her face, so calm and sweet, a face not yet marked by life's troubles, and the words she was about to utter, but Corinne liked this very contrast. It spread a kind of serenity on the extremely gloomy thoughts of her dejected soul. Noble, sensitive music prepared the listeners for the impression they were about to receive. The unhappy Oswald could not take his eyes off Corinne, off that shadow, which seemed to him a cruel apparition in a night of delirium. Through his sobs, he heard the swan-song with which the woman he had so badly wronged still appealed to the depth of his heart.

CORINNE'S LAST SONG

'Fellow citizens, listen to my solemn greeting. Darkness already draws near to my vision, but is not the sky more beautiful at night? Thousands of stars adorn it. By day, it is but a desert. The eternal shadows reveal countless thoughts which gleaming prosperity made us forget. But the voice which could tell of them gradually grows faint. The soul withdraws into itself and seeks to gather up its last warmth.

'From my earliest youth, I promised to bring honour to the name of Roman which still thrills my heart. You have allowed me glory, oh, liberal nation, you who do not banish women from your temple, you who do not sacrifice immortal talents to passing jealousies, you who always applaud the soaring flight of genius, that victor with no vanquished, that conqueror with no spoils, who draws on eternity to enrich the scope of time.

'In the past, nature and life used to inspire in me so much confidence! I used to think that all misfortunes were the result of not thinking enough, of not feeling everything enough. I thought, too, that, on earth, one could already savour celestial bliss which is merely continuance of passion and fidelity in love.

'No, I do not repent of that noble rapture, of that uplifting passion. No, that is not what made me shed tears, which still water the dust that awaits me. If I had devoted my resounding lyre to sing the praises of the divine generosity revealed in the universe, I should have fulfilled my destiny, I should have been worthy of Heaven's bounty.

'Oh God, you do not reject the tribute of talent; the homage of poetry is religious, and the wings of thought serve to bring us closer to you.

'There is nothing narrow, nothing servile, nothing restricted, in religion. It is the immense, the infinite, the eternal. Genius is far from being likely to turn away from it. The imagination, right from its first flight, outstrips life's limits, and the sublime in every genre is a reflection of the divine.

'Oh, if I had loved only the divine, if I had raised my head to heaven when I would be shielded from passionate affections, I would not be prematurely destroyed; ghosts would not have taken the place of my brilliant fantasies. Unhappy woman! My genius, if it still survives, makes its presence felt only by the strength of my pain. It is in the shape of a hostile power that it can still be recognized.

'So, farewell, my country, so, farewell the country where I saw the light of day. Childhood memories, farewell. What have you to do with death? You, who found in my writings feelings which responded to those in your own soul, oh, friends, wherever you may be, farewell. It was not for an ignoble cause that Corinne suffered so much. At least she has not lost her right to be pitied.

'Beautiful Italy, you promise me all your charms in vain. What could you do for a deserted heart? Would you revive my desires to increase my pain? Would you remind me of happiness to make me rebel against my lot?

'I submit to it serenely. Oh, you who survive me, when spring comes, remember how I loved its beauty, how many times I sang the praises of its air and its perfumes. Remember my verses sometimes, for my soul is stamped on them. But deadly muses, love, and unhappiness have inspired my last songs.

'When Providence's intentions for us have been carried out, an inner music prepares us for the arrival of the angel of death. There is nothing frightening, nothing terrible, about him. His wings are white, though he goes surrounded by darkness. But before his arrival, a thousand omens herald his coming.

'If the wind sighs, you think you hear his voice. When daylight is fading, great shadows in the countryside seem like folds of his trailing gown. At midday, when those possessed of life see only a cloudless sky, perceive only a beautiful sun, he who is claimed by the angel of death sees a cloud in the distance, a cloud which, for his eyes, will soon cover all nature.

'Hope, youth, emotions of the heart, all is over with them. Far from me are bitter regrets. If I still can shed a few tears, if I still feel loved, it is because I am about to disappear. But if I were to regain a hold on life, it would soon turn all its daggers against me.

'And you, Rome, where my ashes will be conveyed, you who have seen so many die, if, with trembling step, I join your illustrious dead, forgive me for complaining. Perhaps noble, fruitful feelings and thoughts die with me, and of all the faculties of the heart I receive from nature, that of suffering is the only one I have fully put into practice.

'No matter, let us submit. The great mystery of death, whatever it may be, must grant peace. You assure me of that, silent tombs; you assure me of that, beneficent divinity! I had made a choice on earth and my heart no longer has a refuge. You decide for me; my fate will be the better for it.'

So ended Corinne's last song. The hall was filled with a sad, deep murmur of applause. Lord Nelvil, unable to withstand the violence of his emotion, lost consciousness entirely. Seeing him in this state,

Corinne wanted to go to him, but her strength failed her when she tried to get up. She was brought home and from that moment on there was no more hope of saving her.

She sent for a worthy priest whom she greatly trusted and had a long talk with him. Lucile went to see her. Oswald's grief had so greatly moved Lucile that she herself fell at her sister's feet to beg her to receive him. Corinne refused, although her refusal was not the result of any feeling of resentment. 'I forgive him for having rent my heart,' she said. 'Men do not realize what harm they do. Society persuades them that to fill a heart with happiness and then to put despair in its place is a game. But as I am on the point of death, God has granted me the favour of being restored to calm, and I feel that the sight of Oswald would fill my heart with feelings not in harmony with the agony of death. Only religion has secrets for this terrible passage. I forgive the man I loved so much,' she continued in a weakened voice. 'May he live happy with you. But when the time comes at which he, in his turn, is about to depart from this life, may he then remember poor Corinne. God willing, she will watch over him, for you do not stop loving when the feeling of love is strong enough to destroy life.'

Oswald was at the door, sometimes wanting to go in, in spite of Corinne's express prohibition, sometimes prostrate with grief. Lucile went from one to the other—an angel of peace between despair and the throes of death.

One evening they thought Corinne was better, and Lucile obtained Oswald's agreement to their going together to spend a little time with their daughter, whom they had not seen for three days. Meanwhile Corinne became worse and fulfilled all her religious obligations. It is asserted that she said to the venerable old man who received her solemn confession, 'Father, now you know my tragic fate, judge me. I have never taken revenge for the harm done to me. I have never been insensitive to any genuine sorrow. My sins are those of the passions, which in themselves would not have been blameworthy had they not been mingled with pride and human weakness. Father, you who have been tried by life longer than I, do you think God will pardon me?' 'Yes, my daughter, I hope so,' said the old man. 'Is your heart now entirely his?' 'I think so, Father,' she replied. 'Remove that portrait far from me (it was Oswald's) and on my heart place the picture of him who came down to earth, not for power, not for genius, but for the suffering and the dying; they had great need of him.' Corinne then noticed

Prince Castel-Forte, who was weeping at her bedside. 'My friend,' she said, holding out her hand to him. 'Only you are with me at this moment. I have lived for love, and but for you I would die alone.' At these words, her tears flowed. Then she spoke again. 'Besides, no help is possible at this moment. Our friends can follow us only to the threshold of life. The thoughts beginning there are so confused and deep, they cannot be confided.'

So that she might still see the sky, she had herself carried to a chair near the window. Then Lucile came back. The unhappy Oswald, no longer able to control himself, followed her and fell on his knees as he came near to Corinne. She wanted to speak to him, but was not strong enough. She raised her eyes to heaven and saw the moon covered with the same cloud as the one she had pointed out to Lord Nelvil when, on the way to Naples, they had stopped by the seashore. Then, with her dying hand, she pointed it out to him, and with her last breath that hand dropped down.

What happened to Oswald? He was so distraught that at first they feared for his reason and then for his life. He followed Corinne's funeral procession to Rome. For a long time he shut himself up at Tivoli without wanting his wife or daughter to go there with him. In the end, his affection and his duty brought him back to them. They went back to England together. Lord Nelvil was a model of the purest and most orderly domestic life. But did he forgive himself for his past behaviour? Was he consoled by society's approval? Was he content with the common lot after what he had lost? I do not know, and, on that matter, I want neither to blame nor to absolve him.

MME DE STAËL'S NOTES

[Translator's additions are enclosed in square brackets.]

1. Ancona is just about as destitute now, in this respect, as it was then.
2. This thought is taken from a letter about Rome by Mr von Humboldt, brother of the famous explorer and Prussian envoy to Rome. It would be hard to find anywhere a man whose conversation and writings indicate more knowledge and ideas.
3. We must exclude from this criticism of the Italian manner of recitation, first and foremost, the celebrated poet Monti, who speaks verse in the same way as he composes it. It is truly one of the greatest of dramatic pleasures that one can experience to hear him recite the episodes of Ugolino, Francesca da Rimini, the death of Clorinda, etc. [The first two are in Dante, the third in Tasso.]
4. It seems that Lord Nelvil was alluding to this beautiful couplet of Propertius:

> Ut caput in magnis ubi non est ponere signis;
> Ponitur hic imos ante corona pedes.

['As when it is not meet to touch the head of august statues, the crown is placed here before the feet below—'. *Ponere* in line 1 is a slip for *tangere*, no doubt from association with *ponitur* in line 2. Mme de Staël's own sentence on p. 34 shows that she was well aware of the correct reading.]
5. During the last war a Frenchman was in command of the Castel Sant' Angelo. The Neapolitan troops called on him to surrender, he replied that he would give himself up when the bronze angel sheathed his sword.
6. These facts are given in the *Histoire des républiques italiennes du moyen âge* by M. Sismondi of Geneva. This history will certainly be considered authoritative; for one sees, on reading it, that its author is a man of penetrating shrewdness, as conscientious as he is forceful in his manner of narration and portrayal.
7. Eine Welt zwar bist du, o Rom; doch ohne die Liebe
   Wäre die Welt nicht die Welt, wäre denn Rom auch nicht Rom.

   These two lines are from Goethe, the living German poet, philosopher, and man of letters, whose originality and imagination are most remarkable. [The inaccurate quotation in Mme de Staël's own text was presumably written from memory.]
8. It is said that this church of Saint Peter's is one of the main causes of the Reformation, because it cost the Popes so much money that they multiplied indulgences in order to build it.
9. Mineralogists maintain that these lions are not basalt, because the volcanic rock that is referred to under that name today could not have existed in Egypt; but since Pliny describes as basalt the Egyptian rock of which these

lions are formed, and since the art historian Winckelmann also retains this name, I thought I could use it in its original sense.

10.   Carpite nunc, tauri, de septem collibus herbas,
              Dum licet. Hic magnae jam locus urbis erit.

TIBULLUS

Hoc quodeunque vides, hospes, quam maxima Roma est,
Ante Phrygem Ænean collis et herba fuit, etc.

PROPERTIUS, lib. IV, el. I

11. Augustus died at Nola, as he was on the way to Brundisium to take the waters, which had been prescribed for him; but he was dying when he left Rome.

12.   Viximus insignes inter utramque facem.

PROPERTIUS

13. Pliny, *Historia naturalis*, lib. III. 'Tiberis . . . quamlibet magnorum navium ex Italo mari capax, rerum in toto orbe nascentium mercator placidissimus, pluribus probe solus quam ceteri in omnibus terris amnes, accolitur, aspiciturque villis. Nullique fluviorum minus licet, inclusis utrinque lateribus: nec tamen ipse pugnat, quanquam creber ac subitis incrementis, et nusquam magis aquis quam in ipsa urbe stagnantibus. Quin imo vates intelligitur potius ac monitor, auctu semper religiosus verius quam saevus.'

14. It was Madame Récamier's* dancing that gave me the idea of the dance I have tried to depict.

This lady, so renowned for her grace and beauty, gives an example of showing, in the midst of adversity, such touching resignation and total disregard of personal interest that her moral qualities seem to all eyes as remarkable as her charms.

15. Mr Roscoe, author of the History of the Medici, has published more recently in England a history of Leo X, which is a real masterpiece in this genre, and he there relates all the marks of esteem and admiration that the princes and people of Italy have given to distinguished men of letters; he also shows, impartially, that a large number of Popes have acted very liberally in this respect. [The two books, by William Roscoe, are *Life of Lorenzo de' Medici* (1796) and *The Life and Pontificate of Leo the Tenth* (1805).]

16. Cesarotti, Verri, and Bettinelli are three living authors who have put thought into Italian prose. One has to admit that it has not been used to that end for a long time.

17. Giovanni Pindemonte has recently published a set of plays whose subjects are taken from Italian history, and it is a very interesting and commendable enterprise. The name of Pindemonte is also renowned through Ippolito Pindemonte, the most charming and the most tender of Italian poets of the present time.

18. Alfieri's posthumous works have just been published and they include many biting passages; but we may infer, from a rather strange drama which he attempted on the tragedy of Abel, that he himself felt his plays were too

austere and thought that a production on the stage should concede more to the pleasures of the imagination.

19. I have taken the liberty of borrowing here some passages from the discourse 'On Death' to be found in M. Necker's *Treatise on Religious Ethics*. Another of his works, *The Importance of Religious Thought*, having had the most resounding success, is sometimes confused with this book, which appeared in the days when political events diverted attention from its purpose. But I make bold to say that the *Treatise on Religious Ethics* is my father's most eloquent work. No minister of state before him, I think, had written works for the Christian pulpit; and what must distinguish this kind of writing by a man who had so much to do with men is the knowledge of the human heart and the leniency induced by that knowledge. So it seems that in these two respects the *Treatise on Ethics* is completely original. Religious men, in general, do not live in the world; men of the world, for the most part, are not religious. Where, then, could one find such a degree of observation of life and the high-mindedness that is sifted from it? I shall say, with no fear that my opinion will be imputed to my feelings, that among religious writings this book is in the van for consoling a sensitive being and for engaging the interest of minds that reflect upon the great questions which our soul and our thought debate endlessly within ourselves.

20. In a journal called *Europe* there are some remarks full of depth and shrewdness on the subjects which are suitable for painting; I have drawn from them several of the thoughts just given in the text; their author is Mr Friedrich Schlegel. This writer is an inexhaustible source of wisdom, as are German thinkers in general.

21. The historical pictures that make up Corinne's art gallery are originals or copies of David's *Brutus*, Drouet's *Marius*, and Gérard's *Belisarius*. Among the other pictures cited, that of Dido is by Mr Rehberg, a German artist; that of Clorinda is in the Gallery of Florence; that of Macbeth is in the English collection of Shakespeare pictures [i.e. the Shakespeare Gallery in London, founded by John Boydell]; and that of Phaedra is by Guérin. Finally, the two landscapes on Cincinnatus and Ossian are in Rome; they are by an English artist, Mr Wallis. [But on the Ossian picture see explanatory note for *Cairbar's son* on p. 418 below.]

22. I asked a little Tuscan girl who was prettier, she or her sister. 'Ah!' she replied, '*il piu bel viso è il mio*, the prettiest face is mine.'

23. An Italian postilion, on seeing his horse die, prayed for it and cried out: '*O sant'Antonio, abbiate pietà dell'anima sua!* Oh, St Anthony, have pity on its soul!'

24. On the Roman carnival, you should read a charming description by Goethe, a picture as accurate as it is lively.

25. There is a charming description of the Lake of Albano in a collection of poems by Madame Bruun [Friederike Brun], née Munter, one of the most laudable women of her country [Denmark] for talent and imagination.

26. Discourse 'On the Duties of Children to their Fathers': *Treatise on Religious Ethics*. See note 19.

27. Discourse 'On Indulgence', in the *Treatise on Religious Ethics*. See note 19.
28. Mr Elliot, envoy of England, saved the life of an old man at Naples in the same way as Lord Nelvil. [He was Hugh Elliot (1752–1830), a diplomat who served as Britain's envoy plenipotentiary at Naples in the early years of the 19th century.]
29. The name of Corinne should not be confused with that of Corilla, an Italian improviser, of whom everyone has heard. [Corilla Olimpica (d. 1800); the name was a professional one adopted by Maddalena Morelli.] Corinna was a Greek woman famous for her lyric poetry; Pindar himself had been taught by her.
30. An old tradition backs up the imaginary supposition which persuades Corinne that diamonds give warning of betrayal. This tradition is recalled in some Spanish verses of a truly remarkable character. They are spoken, in a tragedy of Calderón's [*The Constant Prince*], by the Portuguese Prince Ferdinand to the King of Fez, who has taken him prisoner. This prince preferred to die in chains rather than give up to a Moorish king a Christian city which his brother, King Edward, was offering as a ransom. The Moorish king, angered by this refusal, had the most shameful treatment inflicted on the noble prince, who, to sway the king, reminds him that mercy and generosity are the true marks of supreme power. He cites everything regal in the universe: the lion, the dolphin, the eagle, among the living creatures; he also seeks among plants and stones the traits of natural goodness which are attributed to those that seem to dominate all the others; and that is when he says that a diamond, which can resist iron, shatters of its own accord and disintegrates into powder in order to warn its wearer of the betrayal which threatens him. We cannot know if this manner of considering the whole of nature as conforming to human feelings and destiny is inevitably true; but the fact remains that it pleases the imagination, and that poetry in general, and the Spanish poets in particular, draw great beauty from it.

    I know Calderón only from the German translation of August Wilhelm Schlegel. But everyone in Germany knows that this writer, one of the leading poets of his country, has found the means of conveying in his language, with the rarest perfection, the poetic beauty of the Spaniards, the English, the Italians, and the Portuguese. You can have a living impression of the original, whatever it may be, when you read it in a translation done like that.
31. M. Dubreuil, a very skilful French doctor, had a close friend, M. de Péméja, a man as distinguished as himself. M. Dubreuil fell ill of a contagious and fatal disease, and the interest he inspired filled his bedroom with visitors. M. Dubreuil called for M. de Péméja and said to him: 'Everyone must be sent away; you know well, my friend, that my disease is contagious; no one but you should be here.' What words! Happy the man who hears them! M. de Péméja died a fortnight after his friend.
32. Among the Italian writers of comedy who depict manners, account must be taken of a Roman nobleman, de Rossi [Giangherardo De Rossi (1754–1827], who shows in his plays an exceptional capacity for perceptive satire.

33. Talma, having spent several years of his life in London, knew how to combine, with his admirable talent, the character and the beauty of the dramatic art of both countries. [François-Joseph Talma (1763–1826) was a distinguished French actor-manager who developed realism both in production and in the delivery of speech.]

34. After Dante's death, the Florentines, ashamed of having let him perish far from his native abode, sent a deputation to the Pope, begging him to return to them Dante's remains, which had been buried in Ravenna. But the Pope refused, judging, reasonably enough, that the country which had given asylum to the exile had become his fatherland, and being unwilling to give up the glory attached to the possession of his grave. [Dante left his native Florence in 1301 and spent the rest of his life in exile, residing for his last three years in Ravenna, where he died in 1321. Ravenna at that period was under the rule of the Pope.]

35. Alfieri says he felt the love of glory for the first time while walking in the church of Santa Croce; and that is where he is buried. The epitaph which he composed in advance for his worthy friend the Countess of Albany and himself is the most touching and the simplest expression of a long and perfect friendship. [Alfieri (see explanatory note for p. 59) fell in love with the Countess of Albany, unhappily married to Bonnie Prince Charlie, and lived with her after she became legally separated from her husband. The epitaph is in Alfieri's posthumously published autobiography.]

36. An eclipse of the sun was once predicted at Bologna for two o'clock in the afternoon. The populace gathered in the public square to see it and, becoming impatient at its delay, they impetuously called for it as if it were an actor who had made them wait. Eventually it began, and since the cloudy weather prevented it from producing a grand effect, they began to hiss with a loud noise because the spectacle did not come up to their expectations.

EXPLANATORY NOTES

20 *column of Antoninus*: Antoninus Pius, Roman Emperor, AD 138–61.

21 *Petrarch and Tasso*: Francesco Petrarca (1304–74), Italian poet, famous for his sonnets. Torquato Tasso (1544–95); his most celebrated poem tells the story of the First Crusade and the capture of Jerusalem.

22 *Ariosto*: Lodovico Ariosto (1474–1533), epic poet, author of *Orlando furioso*.

23 *Domenichino's Sibyl*: Domenico Zampieri (1581–1641), Italian painter. Sibyl: name applied to a number of prophetic women; the most famous was the Cumaean Sibyl, said to have been consulted by Aeneas before he entered the underworld, and also to have sold books of prophecies to the Roman King Tarquinius Priscus. There are three paintings of the Sibyl by Domenichino; Mme de Staël saw two of them, one in Bologna, the other in the Palazzo Borghese, Rome (now in the Villa Borghese). At the end of Book XIX Oswald and his wife Lucile see the first of these paintings in Bologna and are both reminded of Corinne. That painting is either the one now in the Pinacoteca Palatina, Rome, or (perhaps more probably) a variant of it now in a private collection in Edinburgh.

24 *Sappho*: born *c*.600 BC, poetess of ancient Greece, renowned for her passionate love.

28 *Ausonia*: name of part of old Italy, often used by poets for all Italy.

30 *Laura*: the girl to whom Petrarch wrote his sonnets.

Know you the land where bloom the orange-trees: the opening line of a poem by Goethe.

32 *Leo X*: Pope, 1513–21.

32–3 *the lilies of the field . . . flowers*: cf. Matt. 6: 28–9.

37 *Niobe*: forced to watch the killing of her seven sons and seven daughters; symbol of maternal suffering. The statue of Niobe, probably a Roman copy of a Greek original, is in the Uffizi Gallery, Florence.

Laocoön: suffocated with his sons by serpents. The statue of Laocoön, a Greek original from Rhodes, is in the Vatican Museum.

Medici Venus: ancient Greek statue with expression of frightened modesty, housed in the Villa Medici, Rome, until 1678, thereafter in Florence.

the dying gladiator: also known as the 'dying Gaul', a marble copy of a bronze Greek original from Pergamum; in the Capitoline Museum, Rome.

40 *Armida*: one of the most seductive heroines in Tasso's poem *Jerusalem Delivered*.

45 *Aeolian harps*: an Aeolian harp consists of a sound-box with strings slackened so as to vibrate and resound when the wind blows. The name comes from the Greek god Aeolus, who controlled the winds by playing his harp.

52 *Pantheon*: a famous temple in Rome.

54 *Agrippa*: 63–12 BC, distinguished general and right-hand man of the Emperor Augustus.

55 *Saint John Lateran*: a church in Rome.

56 *Belisarius*: *c*.505–65, Byzantine general, the most illustrious military figure in the reign of the Emperor Justinian. Book VIII, ch. 4, of *Corinne* refers to a favourite theme of artists that Belisarius ended his days as a blind beggar, but this is simply a fiction which arose in the tenth century.

Crescentius: a Roman tribune, put to death in AD 998 by the Roman Emperor and German King Otto III, after trying to re-establish the Republic.

Arnault de Brescia: 1100–55, religious and political reformer who led an uprising against the Popes.

Nicolas Rienzi: Roman tribune, leader of a popular uprising in 1347, killed in a riot in 1354.

57 *Caligula*: Roman Emperor, AD 37–41, notorious for his cruelty.

Sixtus V: Pope, 1585–90.

58 *M. de Fontanes*: Louis, Marquis de Fontanes (1757–1821), poet and politician.

59 *Alfieri*: Vittorio Alfieri (1749–1803), writer of tragedies designed to instil hostility to tyrants. Madame de Staël's quotation of the Italian is a little inaccurate.

60 *Christina*: Queen of Sweden, 1632–54, when she abdicated and went to live an unconventional life in poverty in Rome.

the Stuarts: the 'Glorious Revolution' of 1688 ousted James II from the throne of Great Britain. His son James Stuart, the Old Pretender, and *his* son Charles Edward Stuart, the Young Pretender, spent their last years in Italy after the failure of the Jacobite Rebellions of 1715 and 1745.

Cadono le città . . . sdegni: a quotation (again slightly inaccurate) from Tasso's poem *Jerusalem Delivered*.

61 *Ossian*: Gaelic hero and bard of the third century AD, the central figure in James Macpherson's 'Poems of Ossian' (1760–3), a very popular work in its day.

Ovid's Metamorphoses: a long poem about mythical or imaginary transformations by the Roman poet Ovid (43 BC–AD 17).

62 *Scipio*: Scipio Africanus (236–*c*.185 BC), Roman general who defeated Hannibal of Carthage. When accused of accepting bribes, he called on the people to follow him to the Capitol to thank the gods for his victories.

Tarpeian Rock: Tarpeia was the daughter of the Roman commander of the Capitol, which she offered to betray to the Sabine enemy, who then crushed her to death. The Tarpeian Rock was the site where traitors were executed.

63 *Marius*: 157–86 BC, Roman general who defeated Jugurtha of Numidia and hostile tribes invading Italy from the north.

63 *Marcus Aurelius*: Roman Emperor, AD 161–80; famous for his *Meditations*.

Dioscuri: Castor and Pollux, traditionally held to be sons of Jupiter (the word comes from the Greek for 'sons of Zeus').

Jupiter Feretrius: name given to Jupiter as guardian of treaties.

Jupiter Capitolinus: statue of Jupiter on the Capitol.

Romulus' she-wolf: Romulus, legendary founder of Rome, was said to have been suckled by a she-wolf.

Mamertine prisons: ancient prison whose name was derived from a statue of Mars (Mamers).

Ancus Martius: fourth legendary King of Rome, reigned 640–616 BC.

Servius Tullius: sixth King of Rome, reigned 578–535 BC.

Jugurtha: *c.*160–104 BC, King of Numidia, who fought against Rome and died in prison.

Catiline: *c.*108–62 BC, Roman politician who conspired against the Senate.

Aurelian: Roman Emperor, AD 270–5.

Tibullus and Propertius: Tibullus (d. 19 BC) and Propertius (b. *c.*51 BC) were elegiac poets of the Augustan age.

64 *poet of Nero's day*: anonymous, quoted by Suetonius, *Life of Nero*, ch. 39.

65 *Septimius Severus*: Roman Emperor, AD 193–211.

Caracalla: succeeded his father as Emperor, AD 211–17.

65–6 *Faustina . . . Marcus Aurelius*: Faustina the Younger was the wife of the Emperor Marcus Aurelius; his alleged 'blind weakness' reflects a groundless tale that Faustina was disloyal and therefore unworthy of the love and honour that he bestowed on her.

66 *Pallas*: Greek name for the goddess of wisdom.

Curtius plunged: Lacus Curtius, the name of a pit or pond in the Roman Forum, was attributed by legend to a brave feat of a young man Marcus Curtius in 362 BC. Soothsayers declared that a chasm which had suddenly appeared in the Forum could be filled only by throwing in Rome's greatest treasure. Curtius, believing that the treasure must be a good citizen, leapt on horseback into the chasm, which duly closed up.

Trajan: Roman Emperor, AD 98–117.

Vespasian: Roman Emperor, AD 69–79.

67 *Sana vivaria, sandapilaria*: Latin terms applying to the two entrances; the first means 'for the hale survivors', the second 'for the corpse-bearers'.

69 *Hortensius*: Quintus Hortensius (114–50 BC), Roman orator, at first a rival of Cicero.

Gracchi: two brothers, Tiberius (killed 133 BC) and Gaius (killed 121 BC), Roman tribunes and orators who tried to control the greed of the Roman aristocracy.

Livia: wife of the Emperor Augustus.

69 *Veturia*: mother of Coriolanus.

Coriolanus: legendary hero, said to have withdrawn from Rome when charged with tyrannical conduct and opposing distribution of corn to the plebs. He then led an army against Rome but withdrew after entreaties from his wife and mother.

Janiculum: a prominent ridge on the west bank of the Tiber at Rome.

Porsena: King of the Etruscan town of Clusium, who led an army against Rome with the aim of restoring Tarquinius Superbus, the exiled last King of Rome.

Horatius Cocles: legendary hero, said to have kept Porsena's Etruscans at bay while his comrades broke down the bridge connecting Rome with the Janiculum.

70 *Vesta*: Roman goddess of the hearth and home.

act of filial piety: The legend of *caritas Romana*, a popular subject of later pictorial art, was first recorded by Valerius Maximus and Pliny the Elder (first century AD): a man imprisoned and left to die of starvation was kept alive by his daughter, who secretly fed him on the milk from her breast. The church of San Nicola in Carcere was thought to replace a temple built on the site of a debtors' prison to commemorate that act.

Cloelia: one of several hostages given to Porsena; she escaped by swimming across the Tiber to Rome.

Cacus' cave: the story of Cacus, who stole Hercules' oxen and hid them in a cave, is told in Book 8 of Virgil's *Aeneid*.

Maecenas: d. 8 BC, one of the chief friends and ministers of the Emperor Augustus; patron of the most eminent poets of his day.

Vidimus flavum Tiberim, etc.: quotation from an Ode of Horace.

71 *Farnese Hercules, Flora, and the Dirce group*: statues found in the Baths of Caracalla during excavations in 1546, kept for a time in the Palazzo Farnese, Rome, and then removed to the National Museum, Naples. The Hercules is by Glycon, Athenian sculptor of the first century BC; the Flora is a Roman copy of a Greek statue of Aphrodite of the fourth century BC; the Dirce group, also known as the Farnese Bull, by Apollonius and Tauriscus, two brothers (*c.*150 BC) of Tralles, Lydia, is a sculpture showing Dirce being bound to the horns of a bull by Zethus and Amphion as a punishment for her cruelty to their mother Antiope, whom she had replaced as the wife of King Lycus of Thebes.

Apollo Belvedere: Roman copy of a Greek statue, probably by Leochares (fourth century BC); a masterpiece of classical sculpture, housed in the Vatican.

Marcellus: Marcus Claudius Marcellus (42–23 BC), nephew and adopted son of the Emperor Augustus, who commemorated his early death by naming this theatre after him.

72 *Sallust*: Gaius Sallustius Crispus (probably 86–35 BC), military and political associate of Julius Caesar, but better known for his later activity as
historian of the conspiracy of Catiline and the war with Jugurtha.

Conti tower: originally a tall tower, not in fact dating from Nero's time
but built in the thirteenth century by Riccardo dei Conti; the upper part
was demolished by an earthquake in 1348.

Octavia: d. 11 BC, sister of Augustus and wife of Mark Antony, who treated
her very badly and divorced her, although she gave devoted service to him
and to the children of his other marriages as well as her own. The Porticus,
a large colonnaded structure enclosing two temples, was erected in her honour by Augustus.

Tullia: daughter of King Servius Tullius. Legend has it that she induced
her brother-in-law Lucius Tarquinius (later known as Superbus) to murder her husband and then her father in order that Lucius should become
king and she his queen. When shown the corpse of her father in the path
of her chariot, she drove on over him.

Agrippina in honour of Claudius: Julia Agrippina (AD 15–59), known as
Agrippina Minor, mother of the Emperor Nero by her first marriage; was
later married to her uncle Claudius (Emperor, AD 41–54), and persuaded
him to adopt Nero as his son and heir, a step which he then regretted and
in consequence, it is said, Agrippina poisoned him to ensure the succession for Nero.

74 *virgin water*: according to H. V. Morton, the reason for calling the Trevi
water 'virgin' is that it comes from the Acqua Vergine aqueduct, which
replaced the Roman Aqua Virgo, so named because the engineers were led
to the spring by a girl (*virgo* in Latin).

77 *Egeria*: Roman goddess of fountains, said to have been the adviser and
wife of Numa, legendary second King of Rome.

78 *the Cincinnati*: Cincinnatus was a hero of the old Roman Republic, who
left his farm when made consul and dictator to save Rome from enemies.
Having defeated them, he returned to his farm, where he cultivated the
land with his own hand.

Caecilia Metella: nothing is known of her other than the names of her father
and husband given on the epitaph of her magnificent tomb.

79 *Cornelia*: daughter of Publius Cornelius Scipio and Scribonia; wife of Paulus
Aemilius Lepidus (censor in 22 BC), who is best known from this poem
of Propertius.

80 *Vestals*: the sacred fire of the goddess Vesta was guarded by maidens
pledged to virginity.

Cestius' pyramid: Cestius was a rich praetor who was buried beneath it about
12 BC.

82 *Pliny*: the Elder (AD 23–79), author of an encyclopaedic work, *Historia
naturalis*, including an account of Rome and other cities.

82 *Bernini*: It seems most likely that the reference is to Gian Lorenzo Bernini (1598–1680), sculptor and architect, virtual creator of the Baroque style in sculpture and arguably the greatest sculptor of the seventeenth century. Rome contains many of his works, including the colonnade and the spectacular baldachin at Saint Peter's. He was known in France as *le Cavalier* and has that appellation, but without the initial capital, in the text of *Corinne*. But Mme de Staël goes on to write of his 'mannered style', which would seem to refer to his less famous father Pietro Bernini (1562–1629), a Mannerist sculptor who decorated several Roman churches for Pope Paul V. Perhaps she failed to distinguish the two men.

83 *the geese*: in 390 BC besieging Gauls captured most of the city of Rome, and the defending force withdrew to the Capitol. Tradition has it that the Gauls tried to scale the Capitol secretly at night but were foiled when the cackling of the sacred geese in the temple of Juno wakened Marcus Manlius, who repulsed the attack.

Cambyses: King of Persia, 529–522 BC; conquered Egypt (brutally, according to Herodotus) in 525.

a king pledged . . . his . . . son: Ramses II, King of Egypt, 1304–1237 BC. Mme de Staël is again drawing on Pliny (*Historia naturalis*, 36. 14). He says that 'Ramses, during whose reign Troy was taken', tied his son to the pinnacle of a massive obelisk at Heliopolis before its erection in order to make the workmen take the greatest care that it be not broken when hoisted up; and that Cambyses, having set the city on fire in war, quenched the flames when they reached the obelisk, showing the block of stone a respect that he had not shown for the city. However, the obelisk in the piazza of St John Lateran, brought to Rome after Pliny's time, was in fact erected at Karnak (later called Thebes) by Thutmose III (reigned 1504–1450 BC). It is not the oldest of the ancient obelisks still extant but it is the largest.

84 *Pausanias*: Greek traveller and geographer of the second century AD.

86 *Aesculapius*: god of the medical art.

91 *the dancing girls of Herculaneum*: a fine piece of bronze statuary excavated with several others at Herculaneum in the eighteenth century and now housed in the Naples Museum.

92 *cavaliere servente*: Italian for the constant escort of a married woman.

94 *La Rochefoucauld*: François, Duc de La Rochefoucauld (1613–80), author of *Réflexions ou sentences et maximes morales*.

95 *Belvidera . . . in Otway*: Thomas Otway (1652–85), English author of tragedies, of which *Venice Preserv'd* is one of the three best; Belvidera is the heroine in that play.

Thompson: James Thompson (1700–48), author of the poem *The Seasons*.

102 *Pergolesi*: Giovanni Battista Pergolesi (1710–36), composer of operas and sacred works; *Stabat Mater* was his last work, but his early death was due to ill health, not murder.

102 *Giorgione*: Venetian painter (*c.*1477–1510) of great influence, an initiator of the High Renaissance style of Venetian art.

109 *Guarini*: Giovanni Battista Guarini (1538–1612), pastoral poet, author of *Il pastor fido*.

Metastasio: adopted name of Pietro Trapassi (1698–1782), poet and librettist; his *melodrammi* attracted almost every composer of distinction to set some of them to music.

Chiabrera . . . Poliziano: Gabriello Chiabrera (1552–1638), notable especially for his lyric poetry. Alessandro Guidi (1650–1712), leader of a group that urged a return to simple classical forms of poetry. Vincenzo da Filicaia (1542–1707), noted for his patriotic sonnets. Giuseppe Parini (1729–99), satirical poet, author of *Il giorno*, mocking aristocrats. Jacopo Sannazzaro (1456–1530), author of *Arcadia*, a pastoral romance in prose and verse. Angelo Poliziano (1454–94) translated the *Iliad* and many other Greek works into Latin; author of *Orfeo* in Italian.

Cesarotti: Melchiore Cesarotti (1730–1808) translated the *Iliad* and Voltaire's tragedies as well as Ossian.

110 *Machiavelli . . . Bettinelli*: Niccolò Machiavelli (1469–1527), diplomat and political philosopher, author of *The Prince* and *Discourses on Livy*. Giovanni Boccaccio (1313–75), author of the *Decameron*, a collection of stylish amatory tales. Giovanni Vincenzo Gravina (1664–1718) and Gaetano Filangieri (1752–88), both jurists, authors of works of legal theory. Alessandro Verri (1741–1816), writer of romantic novels. Saverio Bettinelli (1718–1808), a Jesuit man of letters, best known for his polemical 'Letters of Virgil'.

111 *Bossuet . . . Louis XIV*: Jacques Bénigne Bossuet (1627–1704), distinguished preacher and historian. Jean de La Bruyère (1645–96), satiric moralist, author of *Les Caractères . . . de ce siècle*. Charles Louis de Secondat, Baron de Montesquieu (1638–1755), political philosopher and sociologist. Georges Louis Leclerc, Comte de Buffon (1707–88), natural scientist, author of *Histoire naturelle*. Louis XIV, King of France, 1643–1715.

Young: Edward Young (1683–1765), author of *The Complaint: or Night Thoughts*, a didactic poem on death.

Concetti: literary conceits.

Charles V: King of France, 1364–80, nicknamed 'the Wise'.

114 *Tartuffe and the Misanthrope*: two of the finest plays of Molière.

Maffei . . . Monti: Francesco Scipione Maffei (1675–1755), author of a tragedy, *Merope*, mentioned by Corinne a little later. Carlo Goldoni (1707–93), a prolific writer of comic drama, both in Italian and in French, founder of Italian realistic comedy, which virtually displaced the traditional *commedia dell'arte*. Vincenzo Monti (1754–1828), more of a poet than a dramatist but he did also write three tragedies.

115 *Gozzi*: Carlo Gozzi (1720–1806) defended the traditional *commedia dell'arte* against the innovative realistic drama of Goldoni, and wrote many *fiabe*, fantastic or 'fairy-tale' plays.

131 *Thomas Walpole*: of Stagbury, British diplomat; his remark, referring to the Marquise de Fleury, is reported in the posthumous *Mélanges* of Suzanne Necker, Mme de Staël's mother.

132 *corso*: the Via del Corso, described at the end of Book I as the main street of the modern city of Rome.

134–5 *the apostle*: St Paul; cf. 2 Tim. 1: 12.

141 *Apollo Musagetes*: Apollo as leader of the Muses, i.e. the god of music and poetry.

   Tiberius: Roman Emperor, AD 14–37, described here as 'master' of the animals and reptiles because he developed a reputation for cruelty.

142 *Canova*: Antonio Canova (1757–1822), foremost practitioner of neoclassical sculpture in Italy.

144 *Andrea Mantegna*: ?1431–1506, noted especially for his frescos.

   Perugino: Pietro di Cristoforo Vannucci (c.1450–1523), adopted the name of Perugino to show his connection with Perugia; best known for his frescos in the Sistine Chapel.

   the Bolsena Mass . . . Saint Cecilia: three paintings by Raphael. The first commemorates 'the miracle at Bolsena', where a sceptical priest, conducting a Mass in 1263, saw drops of blood appear on the Host and was thereby convinced of the truth of the doctrine of transubstantiation. The second is an allegory of philosophy, with Plato and Aristotle in a throng of philosophers and students. The third, depicting St Cecilia with a miniature organ and other musical instruments, helped to establish her as the patron saint of music.

146 *Philoctetes*: subject of a tragic drama by Sophocles. An essential part of the myth is that he was afflicted by a wound which would not heal.

148 *Zenobia*: claimed suzerainty over the Eastern Empire of Rome after having conquered Egypt and much of Asia Minor; defeated and captured by the Emperor Aurelian in AD 273, but allowed to live out her life in Rome. The friend whom she is (unreliably) said to have betrayed was the philosopher Longinus, who resided at her court and was put to death by Aurelian for having advised her to revolt against Rome.

   Brutus: Marcus Junius Brutus (c.85–42 BC), leading member of the conspiracy to kill Julius Caesar.

150 *Brutus*: Lucius Junius Brutus, held to be the founder of the Roman Republic (and elected as the first consul in 509 BC) because he led the revolt against the last king, Tarquinius Superbus; also said to have sentenced his two sons to death for having tried to restore the monarchy.

151 *Cimbrian*: in 88 BC Marius was taken prisoner at Minturnae and sentenced to death, but the Cimbrian soldier who entered his dark room to kill him

was terrified by being asked fiercely, 'Man, do you dare to murder Marius?' and threw down his sword.

151 *Albani*: Francesco Albani (1578–1660), noted for his paintings of sacred subjects.

153 *Meleager*: hunted and killed a fierce wild boar; is represented in paintings and sculpture as a handsome young man with a spear and a dog. Hippolytus, in ancient legend, preferred hunting to love; his love for Aricia is an invention of Racine.

154 *Salvator Rosa*: 1615–73, noted for his paintings of landscapes and battles.

Cairbar's son: Mme de Staël's note 21 explains that this last picture, by the English artist [George Augustus] Wallis, takes its subject from the Poems of Ossian. In the world of Ossian the souls of the dead cannot rest in peace until a bard has sung a eulogy at their grave. But Mme de Staël has confused two tales. In book II of the poem *Temora*, Ossian magnanimously promises to sing a eulogy over the grave of his enemy Cairbar; and in book III Connal sleeps for seven nights on the tomb of his father Duthcaron, waiting for a bard to come and sing the required eulogy. Wallis portrayed the second tale.

no more: in a pathetic song, 'Lochaber no more', by the Scottish poet Allan Ramsay.

157 *Saturnalia*: annual festival in ancient Rome, when slaves were treated as equal to their masters.

167 *Time sleeps . . . worlds*: from *Le Jugement dernier* (1773) by the French poet Nicolas J. L. Gilbert.

171 *Camaldulian fraternity*: a monastic order of hermits founded by St Romuald; the chief foundation was at Camaldoli in Tuscany.

174 *Miserere*: the Latin version of Psalm 51, set to music by Allegri.

Teste David cum Sibylla: 'David witnessing with the Sibyl'; a line from the medieval Latin hymn 'Dies irae'.

177 *She will be forgiven . . . much*: cf. Luke 7: 47.

179 *Let her be . . . long*: cf. Mark 14: 6–7 and John 12: 7–8.

When two or three . . . them: cf. Matt. 18: 20.

181 *A German philosopher*: Immanuel Kant (1724–1804), but he did not say, 'I know but two fine things (*belles choses*)'; that would hardly impress anyone. He said, 'Two things fill the mind with ever new and increasing admiration and awe' (*Critique of Practical Reason*, conclusion).

187 *Horatii . . . Curiatii*: according to tradition, Alba became subject to Rome as the result of a combat between three Roman brothers, the Horatii, and three Alban brothers, the Curiatii.

She did not let horses come near: Hippolytus was especially associated with horses; his name means 'loose horse', perhaps suggesting 'wild rider'; he was killed when his horses, frightened by a sea-monster, upset the chariot and dragged him along the ground.

188 *Circe*: a witch who turned Odysseus' companions into swine when a storm cast them upon the shore of her abode.

189 *E non udite . . . marino*: a quotation from Tasso, *Jerusalem Delivered*.

191 *Lazzaroni*: idle beggars; a derogatory name given to the beggars of Naples by the Spaniards.

193 *Galiani, Caraccioli*: Ferdinando Galiani (1726–87), diplomat and economist; Luigi Antonio Caraccioli (1721–1803), man of letters; both had been associated with Mme de Staël's father, Jacques Necker.

201 *Ne greggi . . . pastore*: a (slightly inaccurate) quotation from Tasso, *Jerusalem Delivered*.

212 *When war was declared*: in February 1793.

218 *the augurs*: official diviners, in ancient Rome, of the gods' approval or disapproval of a course of action. The meaning here is that popular ideas of right and wrong count for nothing with those who wield power.

230 *Posilipo tunnel*: constructed in the first century AD to pierce a ridge, Mons Pausilypus, behind Naples; called then *Crypta Neapolitana*, now *Grotta di Posilipo*.

Parthenope: ancient name for Naples. The verb *alebat* means 'nourished', not 'welcomed'.

232 *Phlegethon*: ancient myth represented Lake Avernus (its Latin name) as the entrance to the underworld and spoke of Phlegethon (Greek for 'blazing') as a river of fire in Hades.

234 *Acheron*: not another river of fire, as Corinne says, but a normal river of water.

the golden bough: required as a tribute to Proserpine, Queen of the underworld, if Aeneas, a living person, was to be allowed to enter it (Virgil, *Aeneid*, book 6).

the rash Trojan: Misenus, Aeneas' trumpeter, challenged the gods to compete with him in music-making and was drowned by an envious Triton.

flames devoured him: Pliny the Elder, observing Vesuvius in AD 79, was overcome by the fumes and died.

235 *the warrior*: Hannibal of Carthage, who spent the winter of 216–215 BC at Capua after his crushing defeat of the Roman army at Cannae. It was said in later ages that his own army became demoralized by the wealth and luxury of Capua.

the Triumvirate: Octavian, Antony, and Lepidus: Cicero had approved of the assassination of Julius Caesar and had supported the Republican opponents of the Triumvirate.

Numa: legendary second King of Rome, successor of Romulus; revered for his wisdom and piety.

236 *Agrippina's tomb*: Agrippina Minor (see note for p. 72); she was murdered at Baiae, not by Nero himself but on his instructions.

236 *Pompey's widow Cornelia*: Pompey (Gnaeus Pompeius Magnus, 108–46 BC) became leader of the opponents of Julius Caesar in the Civil War, was defeated by Caesar at the battle of Pharsalus, and was stabbed to death after fleeing to Egypt. His wife Cornelia was with him and saw him murdered.

Agrippina wept for Germanicus: Vipsania Agrippina (*c.*14 BC–AD 33), known as Agrippina Major, was the mother of Agrippina Minor, annotated above. She married Germanicus Julius Caesar (15 BC–AD 19), adopted son of the Emperor Tiberius. She was with her husband when he died in Syria, allegedly by poisoning, and she suspected Tiberius of causing it. Her subsequent relations with Tiberius in Rome were consistently bad and in AD 29 she was banished to Pandateria, where she eventually died, probably by voluntary starvation.

Brutus and Porcia: Marcus Junius Brutus, one of Caesar's assassins (see note for p. 148 above), committed suicide in 42 BC after his defeat at Philippi by Antony and Octavian. His wife Porcia shared the moral earnestness of her husband and her father Cato; she too committed suicide, probably in 43 BC, but one tradition says she did so in 42 BC on learning of the death of Brutus.

237 *a refuge*: in 1577, when Tasso had a neurotic fear that he might be murdered by his patron, the Duke of Ferrara.

238 *a delightful poem*: 'Der Fischer'.

254 *La favella . . . sassi*: a truncated quotation from Metastasio's drama *Themistocles*; there are a couple of slips in Mme de Staël's reproduction of the Italian.

260 *Pindar's friend*: Pindar (518–438 BC) was the greatest of Greek lyric poets. Corinna, of whose poetry only a few fragments survive, is said to have been an older contemporary of Pindar, and (though the evidence for this is unreliable) to have given him guidance in the writing of poetry and to have defeated him in public competitions.

272 *Caecilia Metella's tomb*: see note for p. 78.

283 *M. de Sabran*: Elzéar-Louis-Marie, Comte de Sabran (1774–1846), poet, close friend and political associate of Mme de Staël.

284 *author of the Pastor fido*: Guarini; see note for p. 109 above.

said a prophet: the thought is Greek rather than biblical, prominent in Greek tragic drama and generally familiar in a crisp aphorism *pathein mathein* (to suffer is to learn). Mme de Staël's vague reference to 'a prophet' suggests that she had forgotten the provenance of a quotation she had read.

287 *League of Cambrai*: an alliance of the Pope, the Holy Roman Emperor, and the Kings of France and Aragon, formed in 1508 with the intention of conquering the Republic of Venice and seizing its territorial possessions.

290 *the Doge . . . beheaded as a traitor*: Marino Faliero, in 1355.

Frederick Barbarossa: Holy Roman Emperor, 1155–90; after earlier hostility, he acknowledged Alexander III as Pope at St Mark's, Venice, in 1177.

294 *Truffaldino and Pantaloon*: stock characters of the *commedia dell'arte*.

295 *the fatal sisters*: the three Fates (*Moirae*) of Greek mythology, daughters of Zeus and Themis, who spin and weave the thread of a person's life at birth.

318 *cicisbeo*: a term formerly used in Italy for the *cavaliere servente* (see note for p. 92) of a married woman.

324 *cast the first stone*: John 8: 7.

327 *Mrs Siddons*: Sarah Siddons, *née* Kemble (1735–1831), often called the greatest of English tragic actresses. Her performance in 1782 as Isabella, in David Garrick's revision of a play by Thomas Southerne, was a phenomenal success.

350 *Milton*: Mme de Staël is perhaps misremembering *Paradise Lost*, iv. 153–6:

> And of pure now purer aire
> Meets his approach, and to the heart inspires
> Vernal delight and joy, able to drive
> All sadness but despair.

351 *Guelfs . . . Ghibellines*: opposed political factions in Italy during the thirteenth and fourteenth centuries. The Guelfs supported the papacy while the Ghibellines supported the German ('Holy Roman') emperors.

352 *this cup*: Matt. 26: 39.

Ghiberti: Lorenzo Ghiberti (1378–1455), sculptor and goldsmith; these bronze doors are his finest achievement.

Giuliano and Lorenzo: Lorenzo de' Medici (1449–92), known as 'the Magnificent', and his brother Giuliano (1453–78) were attacked by Pazzi conspirators in Florence Cathedral on 26 April 1478. Giuliano was killed; Lorenzo escaped and exacted a fierce vengeance. But Mme de Staël is mistaken in thinking that they are represented by the Michelangelo statues in one of the Medici chapels; the subjects of these statues are in fact Giuliano, Duke of Nemours (1479–1510), a son of Lorenzo the Magnificent, and Lorenzo, Duke of Urbino (1492–1519), a grandson of Lorenzo the Magnificent. Each of the statues has a *pair* of allegorical figures at its foot, Day and Night for Giuliano, Dawn and Dusk for Lorenzo. The chapel containing these statues is not the same as 'the marble, jewel-bedecked chapel' (which houses the tombs of six Grand Dukes of Tuscany).

353 *Filippo Brunelleschi*: (1377–1446), architect and engineer, whose technical inventions enabled him to construct the dome of Florence Cathedral without exterior buttresses or skeletal framework.

Aretino: the tomb is not that of Pietro Aretino (1492–1556), a celebrated satirist, who lived in Rome and then Venice, but of Leonardo Bruni (1370–1444), who became chancellor to the Republic of Florence. He is generally known as Leonardo Aretino because, like Pietro, he was born in Arezzo. But since he was a diligent classical scholar who also wrote a rather dull history of Florence, he does not fit Mme de Staël's description. She evidently confused him with the better-known satirist. Ugo Foscolo, Romantic poet and novelist, never forgave her this error.

369 *occupied by the French*: Rome in 1798, Florence in 1799.

374 *Peace was made*: by the Treaty of Amiens in March 1802.

377 *the Maurienne*: a high Alpine valley in south-east France.

380 *Alfieri's death*: on 8 October 1803. See explanatory note for p. 59 and Mme de Staël's note 35.

382 *Horace Walpole*: 1717–97, 4th Earl of Orford. His letters, intended for publication, are noted for their wit.

384 *Madonna della Scala*: so called because it used to be in the Oratory della Scala at Parma; it is now in the city's art gallery. Correggio (Antonio Allegri (1494–1534), known as Correggio from the name of his birthplace) devoted most of his paintings to religious subjects.

406 *Madame Récamier*: Jeanne Françoise Julie Adelaide Récamier (1777–1849), noted for the charm and wit with which she conducted a salon that attracted most of the important literary and political figures of Paris; she was a close friend of Mme de Staël and of Chateaubriand.

Six French Poets of the Nineteenth Century

HONORÉ DE BALZAC   **Cousin Bette**
Eugénie Grandet
Père Goriot

CHARLES BAUDELAIRE   **The Flowers of Evil**
The Prose Poems and **Fanfarlo**

BENJAMIN CONSTANT   **Adolphe**

DENIS DIDEROT   **Jacques the Fatalist**
The Nun

ALEXANDRE DUMAS (PÈRE)   **The Black Tulip**
The Count of Monte Cristo
Louise de la Vallière
The Man in the Iron Mask
La Reine Margot
The Three Musketeers
Twenty Years After
The Vicomte de Bragelonne

ALEXANDRE DUMAS (FILS)   **La Dame aux Camélias**

GUSTAVE FLAUBERT   **Madame Bovary**
A Sentimental Education
Three Tales

VICTOR HUGO   **The Essential Victor Hugo**
Notre-Dame de Paris

J.-K. HUYSMANS   **Against Nature**

PIERRE CHODERLOS   **Les Liaisons dangereuses**
DE LACLOS

MME DE LAFAYETTE   **The Princesse de Clèves**

GUILLAUME DU LORRIS   **The Romance of the Rose**
and JEAN DE MEUN

A SELECTION OF OXFORD WORLD'S CLASSICS

ÉMILE ZOLA
L'Assommoir
The Attack on the Mill
La Bête humaine
La Débâcle
Germinal
The Kill
The Ladies' Paradise
The Masterpiece
Nana
Pot Luck
Thérèse Raquin

JANE AUSTEN	**Emma**
	Mansfield Park
	Persuasion
	Pride and Prejudice
	Sense and Sensibility
MRS BEETON	**Book of Household Management**
LADY ELIZABETH BRADDON	**Lady Audley's Secret**
ANNE BRONTË	**The Tenant of Wildfell Hall**
CHARLOTTE BRONTË	**Jane Eyre**
	Shirley
	Villette
EMILY BRONTË	**Wuthering Heights**
SAMUEL TAYLOR COLERIDGE	**The Major Works**
WILKIE COLLINS	**The Moonstone**
	No Name
	The Woman in White
CHARLES DARWIN	**The Origin of Species**
CHARLES DICKENS	**The Adventures of Oliver Twist**
	Bleak House
	David Copperfield
	Great Expectations
	Nicholas Nickleby
	The Old Curiosity Shop
	Our Mutual Friend
	The Pickwick Papers
	A Tale of Two Cities
GEORGE DU MAURIER	**Trilby**
MARIA EDGEWORTH	**Castle Rackrent**

	Women's Writing 1778–1838
WILLIAM BECKFORD	Vathek
JAMES BOSWELL	Life of Johnson
FRANCES BURNEY	Camilla
	Cecilia
	Evelina
	The Wanderer
LORD CHESTERFIELD	Lord Chesterfield's Letters
JOHN CLELAND	Memoirs of a Woman of Pleasure
DANIEL DEFOE	A Journal of the Plague Year
	Moll Flanders
	Robinson Crusoe
	Roxana
HENRY FIELDING	Joseph Andrews and Shamela
	A Journey from This World to the Next and The Journal of a Voyage to Lisbon
	Tom Jones
WILLIAM GODWIN	Caleb Williams
OLIVER GOLDSMITH	The Vicar of Wakefield
MARY HAYS	Memoirs of Emma Courtney
ELIZABETH HAYWOOD	The History of Miss Betsy Thoughtless
ELIZABETH INCHBALD	A Simple Story
SAMUEL JOHNSON	The History of Rasselas
	The Major Works
CHARLOTTE LENNOX	The Female Quixote
MATTHEW LEWIS	Journal of a West India Proprietor
	The Monk
HENRY MACKENZIE	The Man of Feeling
ALEXANDER POPE	Selected Poetry

ANN RADCLIFFE	**The Italian**
	The Mysteries of Udolpho
	The Romance of the Forest
	A Sicilian Romance
SAMUEL RICHARDSON	**Pamela**
FRANCES SHERIDAN	**Memoirs of Miss Sidney Bidulph**
RICHARD BRINSLEY SHERIDAN	**The School for Scandal and Other Plays**
TOBIAS SMOLLETT	**The Adventures of Roderick Random**
	The Expedition of Humphry Clinker
	Travels through France and Italy
LAURENCE STERNE	**The Life and Opinions of Tristram Shandy, Gentleman**
	A Sentimental Journey
JONATHAN SWIFT	**Gulliver's Travels**
	A Tale of a Tub and Other Works
HORACE WALPOLE	**The Castle of Otranto**
MARY WOLLSTONECRAFT	**Mary and The Wrongs of Woman**
	A Vindication of the Rights of Woman

The Oxford World's Classics Website

www.worldsclassics.co.uk

- Information about new titles
- Explore the full range of Oxford World's Classics
- Links to other literary sites and the main OUP webpage
- Imaginative competitions, with bookish prizes
- Peruse the Oxford World's Classics Magazine
- Articles by editors
- Extracts from Introductions
- A forum for discussion and feedback on the series
- Special information for teachers and lecturers

www.worldsclassics.co.uk

American Literature

British and Irish Literature

Children's Literature

Classics and Ancient Literature

Colonial Literature

Eastern Literature

European Literature

History

Medieval Literature

Oxford English Drama

Poetry

Philosophy

Politics

Religion

The Oxford Shakespeare

A complete list of Oxford Paperbacks, including Oxford World's Classics, Oxford Shakespeare, Oxford Drama, and Oxford Paperback Reference, is available in the UK from the Academic Division Publicity Department, Oxford University Press, Great Clarendon Street, Oxford OX2 6DP.

In the USA, complete lists are available from the Paperbacks Marketing Manager, Oxford University Press, 198 Madison Avenue, New York, NY 10016.

Oxford Paperbacks are available from all good bookshops. In case of difficulty, customers in the UK can order direct from Oxford University Press Bookshop, Freepost, 116 High Street, Oxford OX1 4BR, enclosing full payment. Please add 10 per cent of published price for postage and packing.